D1316335

Heather Graham describes her life as "busy, wild and full of fun." A master storyteller with over ten million copies of her books in print around the world, Heather says her first career choice was not writing but acting on the Shakespearean stage. Happily for her fans, fate intervened, and now she is a *New York Times* bestselling author. Married to her high school sweetheart, this mother of five spends her days picking up the kids from school, attending Little League games and taking care of two cats. Although Heather and her family enjoy traveling, southern Florida—where she loves the sun and water—is home.

Patricia Potter has become one of the most highly praised writers of historical romance since her impressive debut in 1988, when she won the Georgia Romance Writers of America's Maggie Award and a Reviewer's Choice Award from *Romantic Times Magazine* for her first novel. Among her other achievements, she has been a Romance Writers of America RITA finalist three times and has received a total of three Maggie Awards. Prior to writing full-time, she worked as a newspaper reporter in Atlanta. She has served as president of Georgia Romance Writers and as a member of the national board of Romance Writers of America.

Merline Lovelace served tours in Taiwan and Vietnam during her twenty-three-year career in the United States Air Force. She achieved the rank of colonel and also served at the Pentagon with the Joint Chiefs of Staff and on the staff of a presidential appointee. When she hung up her uniform in September 1991, she combined her love of romance with her flair for storytelling, and has based many of her tales on her experiences in the service. She now has thirty published novels to her credit, many of which have ranked on the *USA Today* and Waldenbooks bestseller lists. More than four million copies of her books are in print in more than two dozen countries.

HEATHER GRAHAM

PATRICIA POTTER

MERLINE LOVELACE

Daughters of Destiny

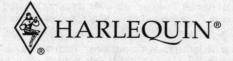 HARLEQUIN®

TORONTO • NEW YORK • LONDON
AMSTERDAM • PARIS • SYDNEY • HAMBURG
STOCKHOLM • ATHENS • TOKYO • MILAN • MADRID
PRAGUE • WARSAW • BUDAPEST • AUCKLAND

HARLEQUIN BOOKS
225 Duncan Mill Road, Don Mills,
Ontario, Canada M3B 3K9

ISBN 0-373-83481-0

DAUGHTERS OF DESTINY

Visit us at www.eHarlequin.com

Printed in U.S.A.

CONTENTS

Rides a Hero
Heather Graham

Prologue

May 30th, 1865
Kentucky
The Road Home

"It's him, I tell you. It's Captain Slater! Captain Malachi Slater!" The young man seated on the wagon that blocked the road could hardly control his excitement. "We done got him, Bill," he cried.

Startled, Malachi pulled back on the reins of the bay mare that had taken him through numerous battles, and stared ahead. Two young Union sentries were guarding the road that eventually led to his own home. The sight of the sentries here in Kentucky didn't surprise him. The war was over. The Yankees had won. Yanks were everywhere now, and that was the way it was.

At least he no longer had to be wary. His fighting days were over. He was going home. His unit had surrendered, and he had put his own signature on the paper, swearing an oath of allegiance to the Yankee flag. He should have been bitter, but right now he was just tired. He had seen the death toll, and he was just damned glad that it was all over.

So he didn't need to fear hostility from the sentries. And hell, seeing them, he couldn't feel much fear. The Yanks, it seemed, had been dipping into the bottom of the barrel as the war ended, almost as much as the Confederates had. These boys were teenagers, green-gilled, and he was certain that neither of them had ever shaved.

Except there was something...something about the way they said his name.

"Captain Slater, you just hold on there," the first boy said nervously.

They shouldn't have known his name. His rank, of course, was apparent from the worn gold braid on the shoulders of his gray wool cavalry greatcoat. But his name...

"You're under arrest," the second boy—the one called Billy—began, and then his mouth started to work hard as if he couldn't seem to remember the right words to say.

"Under arrest?" Malachi roared out in his best voice of command. "What in hell for? The war is over, boys. Haven't they told you yet?"

"You're a murderin' outlaw, Captain Slater!" the first boy said. Malachi frowned and the boy quickly added, "Sir!"

"Outlaw, murderer? I know that you don't give the Rebels much credit, but our cavalry fought as soldiers, same as yours."

"Captain, the poster that's out on you has nothing to do with the cavalry!" Billy said. "And that's a fact. You're wanted for murder in Kansas—"

"I've never been in Kansas!"

"It says right on the poster that you and your brothers are part of the Slater gang, and that you rode into Kansas and murdered private citizens. Yes, sir, you are under arrest!"

Kansas?

Hell.

He'd not been in Kansas for years. But his brother Cole had been in Kansas, and he had waged a single-handed battle against the cutthroat who had murdered his first wife.

Malachi hadn't been anywhere near Kansas during that time, but that was only part of what was taking him aback. Cole was no murderer either. Someone must be out for them.

The Slater gang indeed! That must mean that someone wanted his younger brother, Jamie, dead, too.

The Union boys were trying to ready their breech-loading rifles. They were both so nervous they couldn't seem to rip open their powder bags, not even with their teeth.

Malachi's cavalry saber was at his side and he had a Colt stuffed into the holster beneath his greatcoat. He had enough time to fill them both full of holes. "Listen to me, fellows. I am not going to let you put me under arrest," he said.

The boys looked green. They glanced his way, but they kept trying to get to their powder. When they did get to it, they spilled most of it trying to get it into the well of the gun. They glanced at him again with terror, but they still moved to their pouches for balls, and tried to ram them down according to proper military procedure.

"Confound it," Malachi said irritably. "Do your mothers know where you are?"

The boys looked up again. "Hank, you got him?"

"Hell, no, Billy, I ain't ready. I thought you were ready."

Malachi sighed deeply. "Boys, for the love of God, I don't want your deaths on my conscience—"

"There's a big, big bounty out on you, Captain Slater! A Mr. Hayden Fitz in Kansas is fierce and furious. Says if'n somebody don't shoot you and your brothers, he's going to see you all come to justice and hang by the neck until dead."

"Oh, hell!" Malachi swore savagely. "Damn it!" He dismounted, sweeping his hat from his head and slamming it against his thigh as he paced back and forth before the two. "It's over! The war is over! I fought off the Kansas jayhawkers before the war, and then I fought all those damn years in the war, and I am tired! I am so damned sick and tired of killing people. I can barely stand it! The bounty isn't worth it, boys! Don't you understand? I don't want to kill you."

They didn't understand. He stopped and looked at them, and they might be still green, but they'd gotten their muskets loaded. Billy started to aim his.

Malachi didn't wait any longer. With a savage oath escaping him, he charged the boy, pulling out his saber.

But he was sick and tired of killing. As he leaped atop the wagon where the boys sat, he could have skewered them through, both of them. But he didn't. For some damned reason, he wanted them to grow old enough to have the wisdom not to pull such a stunt again.

He sliced his saber against the boy's musket and sent it flying.

"Run, Bill, run!" Hank suggested wisely.

But Hank was holding tight to his own rifle. Malachi swore at him and leaped from the wagon and hurried for the bay mare. He leaped on the horse and just barely nudged her. Like a true warrior, she soared forward like the wind, straight for the wagon.

She carried him up and up and they were sailing. But just as they were over the top of the wagon, a burst of pain exploded in his thigh.

Hank had apparently managed to shoot his rifle. Amazingly enough, he had struck his target.

Malachi didn't dare stop. He kept the bay racing, veering into the woods. She was a good old horse, a fine companion, and she had been with him through many a battle. When pain and exhaustion claimed him and he slunk low against her, she kept going, as if she, too, knew the road home, the long, long road home.

Finally the bay stopped before a stream. For a long moment, Malachi clung to her, then he fell and rolled until he could reach the water. He drank deeply before falling back. His leg was burning; his whole body was burning. Surely it wasn't such a deep wound. He needed to keep moving. He had to get to Cole as quickly as possible.

But it wasn't going to be that night. Despite the strength of his will, his eyes closed.

It seemed to him that a fog swirled up from the stream. Pain no longer tormented him, nor hunger, nor exhaustion.

The stream was inviting. He stood and shed his worn uniform. Balancing his way out on the rocks, he dived in. The water was cool and beautiful, the day warm with a radiant sun, and birds were singing. There was no smell of burned powder near him, no screams of the dead or dying; he was far, far from the anguish of the war.

He swam through the coolness, and when he surfaced, he saw her.

An angel.

She was standing on the shore, surrounded by the mist, her hair streaming gold and red, sweeping down and around her back. She was a goddess, Aphrodite emerging from the sparkling beauty of the stream. She was naked and lithe and beautiful, with sultry sky-blue eyes and ink-dark lashes, ivory cheeks, and lush, rose-colored lips.

She beckoned to him.

And he came.

Looking at her, he knew that he must have her. Naked, he tried to hurry, thrashing through the water. He had to touch her. To feel the fullness of her breast beneath his hands, caress her with his whisper and his kiss. But even in the strange seduction of the dream, he knew she was familiar. She was his Circe, calling him with magical promises of unimaginable pleasure, but he also knew her.

Nearer, he drew nearer to her, nearer and nearer...

He started to cough. His eyes flew open.

The only Circe that awaited him was the faithful bay mare, snorting now upon his soaking cheek. Malachi staggered to his feet and looked from his sodden clothing to the stream. He had fallen in, he realized, and nearly drowned.

He had been saved by a dream. The dream of a lush and beautiful woman with golden hair that streamed down her back, and eyes to match a summer's day.

He touched his cheek. At least the stream had cut his fever. He could ride again.

He should find attention for his leg, he thought. But he

couldn't spare the time. He had to reach Missouri. He had to warn Cole.

"Come on, Helena," he told the mare, securing the reins and leaping upon her back. "We need to head on west. Home. Only we haven't got a home anymore. Can you believe that? All these damned years, and we still aren't at peace yet. And I get shot by a kid who still has to have his mother tell him to scrub behind the ears. And I dream about beautiful blond temptresses." He shook his head, and Helena whinnied, as if she doubted the sanity of her rider.

Maybe he wasn't sane anymore.

He grinned as he kept riding through the night. It had been a funny dream. Curious how his Circe had seemed so familiar. His sister-in-law, Kristin, was a beautiful blond, but it hadn't been Kristin...

Malachi was so startled that he drew in sharply on his reins and the bay spun around.

"Sorry, old girl, sorry!" Malachi told the horse. Then he went thoughtfully silent, and finally laughed out loud.

It hadn't been his sister-in-law in the dream, but it had been Shannon, Kristin's little sister. Kristin's obnoxious little sister! Willful, spoiled, determined, proud...obnoxious! He'd itched to take a switch to her from the moment they had first met.

But it had been Shannon in the dream. Shannon's eyes had beckoned him, sultry and sweet. Shannon's hair had streamed in a burst of sun and fire around the slender beauty of her form. Shannon's lips had formed to issue whispers of passion.

And he had thought when the dream ended that he had lost his temptress! he told himself dryly.

Well, he had not. He was riding toward the spitfire now, and he could almost guarantee that their meeting would not be sweet, nor would she beckon to him, or welcome him.

If he knew Shannon, she wouldn't be waiting with open arms.

She'd be waiting with a loaded Colt.

"Doesn't matter much, Helena," he told his horse. "Damn it!" he swore out loud to the heavens. "When will this war be over for me?"

There was no answer. He kept riding through the night.

Chapter One

June 3rd, 1865
The Border Country, Missouri
The McCahy Ranch

Someone was out there.

Someone who shouldn't have been out there.

Shannon McCahy knew it; she could feel it in her bones.

Even though the sunset was so deceptively peaceful!

It was peaceful, beautiful, quiet. Radiant colors soared across the sky, and sweetly kissed the earth. There was a silence and a stillness all around. A soft breeze just barely stirred, damp and sweet against the skin. The war was over, or so they said.

The night whispered tenderly of peace.

Peace...

She longed for peace. Just ten minutes ago she had come outside to watch the night, to try to feel the peace. Standing on the wide veranda, leaning idly against a pillar, Shannon had looked out over the landscape and had reflected on the beauty of the night.

The barn and stables stood silhouetted against the pink-streaked sky. A mare and her foal grazed idly in the paddock. The hills rolled away in the distance and it seemed that all the earth was alive with the verdance and richness of the spring.

Even Shannon had seemed a part of the ethereal beauty of

the night. Elegant and lovely, her thick hair twisted into a knot at her nape, little tendrils escaping in wisps about her face. Tall and slim, and yet with curved and feminine proportions, she wore a luxurious velvet evening gown with a delicate ivory lace collar that fell over the artfully low-cut bodice.

She was dressed for dinner, though it seemed so very peculiar that they still dressed every evening. As if their pa was still with them, as if the world remained the same. They dressed for dinner, and they sipped wine with their meat— when they had wine, and when they had meat—and when their meal was over, they retired to the music parlor, and Kristin played and Shannon would sing. They clung so fiercely to the little pleasures of life!

There hadn't been much pleasure in years. Shannon McCahy had grown up in the shadow of war. Long before the shots fired at Fort Sumter signaled the start of the Civil War in April 1861, Missouri and Kansas had begun their battling. Jayhawkers had swooped in from Kansas to harass and murder slave owners and Southern sympathizers, and in retaliation, the South had thrown back the bushwhackers, undisciplined troops who had plundered and killed in Kansas. Shannon McCahy had been only a child when John Brown had first come to Missouri, but she remembered him clearly. He had been a religious man, but also a fanatic, ready to murder for his religion. She had still been a child when he had been hanged for his infamous raid on the arsenal at Harper's Ferry.

So she really couldn't remember a time of real peace.

But at least the thunder now no longer tore at the earth. Rifles and pistols no longer flared, nor did swords clash in fury. The passion of the fight was over. It had died in glorious agony and anguish, and now every mother, sister, lover and wife across the nation waited...

But Shannon McCahy hadn't come outside to await a lover, for she had the questionable luxury of knowing that her fiancé lay dead. She even knew where he was buried. She had watched the earth fall, clump by clump, upon his coffin, and each soft thud had taken a bit more of her heart.

The war had robbed her blind. Her father had been brutally murdered in front of her by bushwhackers, a splinter group of Quantrill's infamous Raiders. And in the summer of 1862 Zeke Moreau and his bushwhackers had returned to the McCahy ranch to take her sister, Kristin. But that had also been the day that Cole Slater had walked into their lives, his guns blazing. He had saved them from being murdered and eventually married Kristin. After that his name kept them safe from the bushwhackers, but the war had still gone on. And ironically, she and Kristin had then been arrested by the Yankees for giving aid and succor to Cole, just because once upon a time Cole had briefly ridden with Quantrill.

But Shannon had fallen in love with the Yankee officer who had pulled her from the wreckage of their prison when the faulty old building had literally fallen to pieces. For a brief time, she had believed in happiness.

Until Robert Ellsworth had been slain by the bushwhackers.

In the end, Zeke Moreau and his bushwhackers had come back to the ranch one last time. Cole had ridden in with his brothers and their Confederate cavalry company, and Shannon's brother, Matthew, had brought his Union compatriots. For one sweet moment, there had been no North, and no South, just a fierce and valiant stand against injustice.

But the war was over now.

No…never. Never in her heart, she thought. Then she stiffened, suddenly alert and wary.

There was a movement out by the stables. She blinked and stared again, and felt a quickening in her stomach, a streak of cold along her spine.

Now she was sure.

Someone was out there.

Someone who shouldn't have been out there.

Someone furtive, stealthy, sneaking around the stables.

"Cole? Kristin?" she whispered. She cleared her throat and called their names again a little louder.

Where were her brother-in-law and sister? They should have been in the house, but no one was answering her. She bit into her lower lip, wondering what she should do. There was a pair of Colt six-shooters over the cabinet just inside the hallway; Cole had set them up the very night they heard the war was over.

After that last fight, Malachi and Jamie Slater had ridden back to the war, not knowing that it was already over. Matthew McCahy had known it was over before he left, for he had stayed until his injury had healed, but then he had left also, to return to his Union Army unit. The war might be over, but he knew that peace was yet to be assured. The aftermath of the war would follow them.

And Cole Slater knew that he would eventually have to flee Missouri. He *had* ridden with Quantrill, although only briefly, and certain Yanks with power might consider him ripe for hanging. But Cole intended to wait for Matthew to return home before leaving the ranch. It wouldn't be safe to leave Kristin and Shannon alone. He had friends who would warn him if danger threatened.

Meanwhile, Cole had hung the Colts and had given Shannon some stern advice. "Most of the men coming home will be good ones," he had told her, hammering nails into the wall. "Yep, lots of good men, both blue and gray. Those who have fought with heart and soul for their ideals. And all that those men want to do now is come home. They want to pick up their plows again, open their shops again, start up their businesses once more. They want to hold their wives, and kiss their children, and lick their wounds and try to find a future. They'll come through here. They'll want water, and they'll want meals. And we'll help them when we can, both Union and Confederate."

"So what are the guns for?" Shannon asked, not even

wanting to think of helping Confederates, men like the bush-whackers who had killed Robert.

"Because there are men whom the war has maimed, Shannon. Not in body but in mind. Dangerous men. Deserters and vultures. And I can assure you that as many of that type fought for the Union as for the Confederacy. Mind your step, Shannon. You know how to use these guns. Use them well. If anyone threatens you at all, be ready to defend yourself."

"Yes. I will. I can shoot."

"The bad guys, Shannon. Not just some poor farmer in a gray uniform."

"Cole, I have fed and cared for the Rebels passing this way."

"Yes, you have. But not with a great deal of pleasure."

"You make me sound cruel and unreasonable—"

She saw a strange light of pity in his eyes as he answered. "I don't think that, Shannon. The war has done things to all of us."

But he shook his head as he walked away, and she could tell that he really did think she was heartless. He knew that she could never forgive what had happened, even now that the South had been broken. She would never, never forget Robert Ellsworth, his gentle love, his simple honor. Nor could she ever forget his death. She had seen him buried. He had never been laid out in a proper wake, for there had not been enough of him left for the undertaker to prepare. The brutality had made her hard, and very cold.

Cole was wrong, though, if he thought she could no longer feel. She could still feel way too much, it seemed at times. But it was so much easier to be cold, and it was easier to hate. Cole was wrong if he thought she would kill just any Rebel soldier, but she could very easily gun down the men who had so callously gone out and brutally slaughtered Robert and his men. She thought she could have faced it if Robert had died in battle, but what the bushwhackers had done to him had been worse than murder.

Cole was disappearing around the corner, and she longed to call out to him. She did love him, even if he was a Rebel. He had saved Kristin and Shannon from certain rape and probable death, and he was as dear to her as her blood brother, Matthew. But she didn't call out. It wasn't something she could explain.

Cole's first wife had been killed by Kansas jayhawkers, yet now he seemed to have come to terms with life. Maybe Kristin had taught him forgiveness. But Shannon didn't know how to forgive, and it wasn't something she thought she could learn. She just knew that she still lived with the anguish of the past, and she could not put it behind her.

For Cole's sake, though, she would bite her lip and hand out water to the Rebs heading home. This was Missouri; most of the state was Confederate. She might have been a Rebel herself, since the ranch stood on the border between Kansas and Missouri, and the McCahys actually had leaned toward the South at first. But then Pa had been murdered. Matthew had joined up with the Union Army, and everything that followed after that had conspired to make Shannon an avowed Yankee, through and through.

But that didn't matter now.

Over the past days they had been handing out water and meals to boys in blue and to boys in gray. She reminded herself that Matthew was still out there somewhere. Maybe some Reb girl was giving him a cup of water or a piece of bread.

Shannon had handed out water and hot soup without a word. She had bandaged up Rebs, just as she had done on the day when the two cavalry units—Matthew's Federals and the Slaters' Confederates—had joined forces and beaten Zeke Moreau's marauders. For Matthew's sake, she cared for the weary soldiers who passed the house. Somewhere out there, he would be wandering the countryside. And Cole's brothers, too. Perhaps some young woman was being kind to them.

Shannon hoped that someone would deal gently with Jamie.

But if Malachi passed by some strange farmhouse, well, then, she hoped they gave him salt water!

Both Cole's brothers were Rebels. Jamie she could tolerate. Malachi, she could not.

From the time they had first met, he had treated her like a bothersome child. She didn't know quite what it was that lurked between them, she only knew that it was heated and total and combustible. Every time they met, sparks flew and fury exploded.

She tried. She tried very hard not to let him creep beneath her skin. She was a lady. She had great pride, and tremendous dignity. But Malachi had the ability to strip her quickly of both. She would be pleased with her composure and the calmness of her temper, but then he would say just one word and she would lose all poise and restraint and long to douse him with a pail of water. And when she lost her temper at his needling, he would taunt her all over again, pleased that he had proven her to be a child, and a brat at that.

Not so much now, she assured herself. And it was true. She had grown colder since Robert Ellsworth had died. No one could draw much of a reaction from her anymore.

She thought Jamie might return soon. But Malachi wouldn't.

Malachi had probably thought to join up with General Edmund Kirby-Smith and fight to the bitter finish. But even Kirby-Smith had surrendered now. Maybe Malachi would head for Mexico, or for Central or South America. Good riddance to him. It was difficult to forget the last time they had met. It had been on the day when all hell had broken loose, when Moreau's band had been broken. Even then, in the midst of chaos, Malachi had managed to annoy her. In the thick of it all, he had ordered her around and they had very nearly come to blows. Well, she *had* slapped him, but Kristin and Cole had been there, and Malachi had been forced to calm his temper. Shannon hoped the Federals had picked him up and placed him in a prison camp. It would be good for him to cool his heels for a while. He was going to have to accept the truth.

The Confederacy was bested and broken, and the Glorious Cause was lost.

It was over.

But not yet ended. Some drifter was crawling around in the stables.

Shannon didn't stop to think a moment longer. She stepped back through the doorway to the entry hall and plucked one of the Colts from its crossed position. She reached into the top drawer of the secretary beneath it for the shells and quickly loaded the gun.

"Kristin! Cole! Samson, Delilah, someone!" she called out.

But the house was silent. Where were they all? She didn't know. She was on her own.

Shannon slipped back onto the porch.

The colors of the night were growing darker, deeper and richer. The sky seemed to have turned a deep purple; the land itself seemed to be blue. The outline of the stables stood black against the horizon, and the two loft windows looked like dusky, evil orbs, staring at her menacingly.

Her heart was beating hard, she realized. The coldness remained near her spine.

She should not be afraid. She had been under attack in one form or another several times now. She should have learned courage.

She was still frightened.

But not frightened enough that she would sit like a wounded lamb and wait to be assaulted, she assured herself. No, she would turn the tables. No honest man skulked and loitered in stables. No sincere fellow, Reb or Yank, hid, waiting for the coming of darkness.

She raced from the porch to the paddock, then paused, breathing fast. She listened intently, and heard nothing, but still, she knew. Someone was there. She could feel it in the air now. She could sense the danger.

She leaned against the paddock fence. She was good with a Colt. Damned, deadly good. Cole claimed that she could hit the eye of a fly from a distance of a hundred feet, and that wasn't far from the truth. As long as she held the weapon, she would be safe.

Don't ever tarry, Cole had warned her once. Make your decisions quickly. And if you decided to shoot, shoot to kill.

It shouldn't be too hard, she thought. She had lived through so many years of hell; she had grown up under the fire. In the world she knew, it was kill or be killed, hurt or tortured. She could manage any situation. She always had.

Shannon drew in a deep breath and pushed away from the paddock fence. Where was Cole? He had been born with a sixth sense. He should have known that there was trouble by now, yet he wasn't here. She couldn't depend on Cole. She had to depend on herself.

Shannon raced for the door to the stables. It stood as dark as the windows in the coming night, gaping open like a dark pit.

And she could feel the evil lurking and waiting inside.

She gritted her teeth and carefully flattened herself against the paneling by the stable door, then swiftly, flush against it, she stole inside.

The darkness was complete. For several long moments she stood where she was, her heart thundering, her fingers like steel around the Colt, her breath coming too fast and seeming to rasp more loudly than a twister. He would hear her, she thought. He would hear her, and find her.

She forced herself to be calm; she was not as loud as she thought. But she had to adapt to the darkness, or she would accomplish nothing.

One horse whinnied and a second one snorted. She tried to envision the place with light. The stalls were large and well constructed; there were fifteen of them across from her, but only nine of the horses would be in their stalls, for the men were still out on the range after the cattle. The tack room was to her immediate right, and to her left was a pile of fresh hay and the grain bags. There was more hay up in the loft above her head.

She caught her breath suddenly, barely daring to breathe.

That's where he was—in the loft.

She wasn't in a very good position if the intruder lurked right over her head.

She cocked her Colt and sank low to the floor, then began inching toward the bales of hay. They could provide her with some cover, and make her position a mystery in this stygian darkness, too.

But even as she moved, she heard the soft, careful shuffling above her. A board creaked, and then the building was still again.

Shannon waited.

There was no further movement. Time seemed to tick on endlessly.

All of a sudden she realized what she had to do. Move the ladder.

She ran for it with an impetuous burst of speed, determined to capture the intruder atop the loft.

"Hold!" a voice commanded.

She ignored it and continued racing for the ladder, then wrenched it away from the opening. It rattled to the ground, leaving no means of escape from the loft above.

A shot rang out. It whizzed high over her head and was imbedded into the wall far behind her. Was it a warning shot? Or did the man in the loft have extremely bad aim?

She shot back, aiming for the voice. She heard a low rasp of swearing, and knew then where her target was.

If you shoot, she had been warned, shoot to kill.

She had seen blood and death in wanton numbers...

And still she hesitated. The man was trapped in the loft. What could he do?

Even as she asked the question of herself in silence, the answer came to her, and in a most unexpected manner.

He leaped from the loft like a phantom in the night and landed softly in the hay.

Shannon screamed, whirling around and lifting her Colt, aiming toward the bales of hay. She could not see him. He had landed hard, but he had rolled in a flash, and now he hid behind the many bales.

She took aim and fired at the first bale. The shot exploded, loud and crystal clear, in the night.

Why had nobody come from the house? Surely they had heard the shots. But perhaps the noise was muffled by the barn walls and the hay.

And neither could she seem to hear anything from the house or from beyond the stables. She was pitched into a desperate world where she was on her own.

No noise had come from the intruder. No thud, no cry, no gasp of fear or anger or dismay. There was nothing at all.

Had she killed the man?

Shannon stepped forward, moving as silently as she could upon the earthen floor. She moved slowly, pausing with each step. She must have killed him. She heard nothing, nothing at all.

She took another step toward the hay, peering around the side of the tied bale. There was nothing there. She thought she heard something from the stalls. She swung around and realized that it was only the horses moving restlessly.

Then she sensed a movement in the corner. But that was impossible. No one could have gotten by her, not even in the darkness...

It was a mouse in the corner. A mouse, and nothing more. She had shot and probably killed the intruder, and he lay there, somewhere in the hay.

Shannon moistened her lips and tried to still the fear that swept along her spine. She still sensed danger. He wasn't dead. He was hiding, lurking in the darkness. She wanted to shriek and scream and turn and flee in terror. She didn't dare. She had to find him before he found her.

She turned once again and hurried to the next stack of hay, piled higher than the first. She looked to the rear and each side of it...and then a rustle came from just above her head.

She inhaled and jerked back, looking up, trying to aim her Colt. It was too late.

He leaped upon her.

They fell to the ground together. Shannon's Colt went flying through the darkness. He fell hard upon her and she was assailed with the scent of leather and fine pipe tobacco. His hard-muscled arms held her and a wire taut body covered her. A scream bubbled and rose within her.

His hand clapped hard over her mouth.

"Stop," he hissed.

She interrupted him with a savage kick.

He swore in the night, but his hold went slack.

She shoved against him with all her might, and found her escape. She leaped to her feet and dashed toward the door, inhaling for a loud, desperate scream.

"No!" The voice thundered behind her. He caught her by an elbow, wrenching her around. Her scream died in her throat as they crashed to the ground again. This time, he held her with force. He thrust his frock coat back and straddled her prone and dazed form. Shannon lashed out madly with her fists, thudding them furiously against his chest.

"Stop it, Shannon!"

His use of her name did not register in the raw panic that had seized her. She had not come this far to be raped and murdered in her own stables. She gasped for breath to scream again and raked out with her nails, seeking his eyes.

"Stop it!" He caught her wrists and pulled them high above her head. She started to scream, and he secured her with one hand, clamping the other hard over her mouth. She bit him. He swore in a white rage, but did nothing more than grip her jaw so hard between his thumb and forefinger that she could scream no more for the pain that it caused her.

"For the love of God, will you stop it, brat!"

She froze. She wondered how it was that she had not recognized his voice until he used that particular term.

Malachi!

Malachi Slater had come home.

Chapter Two

She stopped struggling and looked up at him. The moon must have come out, for some light was now filtering into the stable. He leaned very close against her, and she began to make out his features.

They were handsome features. She would grant Malachi that much. He was a striking man. His forehead was high and broad, his eyes were large, cobalt blue, sometimes nearly as black as the darkness that now surrounded them. His mouth was full and well defined, his jaw square beneath the gold and red sweep of his mustache and beard, and his nose and cheekbones chiseled in strong, masculine lines. He was a tall man, made lean by the war, and made hard by it, too.

With his face so close to hers, she realized that his beard was not so neatly clipped as it had always been before. There were shadows beneath his eyes. The rough wool of his Confederate uniform was tattered and torn in many places, and the gold braid, the insignia of his rank in the cavalry, was nearly worn away.

She should have known him much sooner. They had tangled often enough. She knew the strength of his arms and the deep tenor of his voice, and the bullheaded determination of his anger. She should have known him.

But he was different tonight. He was still Malachi, but more fierce than ever. Tonight, he seemed brutal. Tension lived and breathed and seethed all around him.

"You gonna be quiet now, brat?" he asked her harshly.

Shannon gritted her teeth. She could not begin to answer him. The gall of the bastard! He had known that it was her. He must have known that it was her from the moment she had entered the stables, and he had knocked her down and dragged her around—twice!—and had no apology for it.

She squirmed hard against him, fighting his hold. His hand pressed more tightly upon her, his breath warmed her cheeks, and she felt a new wave of his ruthless determination.

"Well?" he repeated. His teeth flashed white in the darkness as he smiled with a bitter amusement. "Shannon, are you going to be quiet now?"

He lifted his hand from her mouth. Her lips felt bruised and swollen from his casual disregard.

"Quiet!" she said, and her tone was soft at first, deceptively soft. She knew she should use some restraint. At the best of times, he had little patience with her.

Well, she had no patience with him. Her temper ignited like a fuse. "Quiet?" Her voice rose, and then it exploded. "Quiet? You scurvy, flea-ridden son of a jackass! What the hell do you think you're doing? Get off me!"

His lips tightened grimly and his thighs constricted around her hips.

"Miss McCahy, I'll be happy to do so. Just as soon as you shut that lovely little mouth of yours."

"Get off!" she whispered furiously.

"Shh!"

He was too close to her. His eyes were like pits of blue fire boring into hers, and she was acutely aware of him as a man. He leaned so close that his beard brushed her face. His thighs were hot and tight around her, and his arms, stretched taut across her as he maintained a wary grip upon her wrists, were as warm and threatening as molten steel.

"Malachi—"

"Shannon, I am waiting."

She closed her eyes and ground her teeth. She waited, feeling her heart pound, feeling the seconds pass. Then she smiled with savage sarcasm, but remained silent.

Slowly, he eased his hold. He released her wrists and sat up. He still straddled her hips, but he was no longer pinning her with his touch. Shannon tried counting to keep her smile in place. She longed to explode and shove him far, far away from her.

And still he kneeled there. He crossed his arms over his chest, and watched her through narrowed eyes.

She waited. She could stand it no longer.

"I have been quiet! Now get the hell off me!"

In a flash, his hand landed on her mouth, and he was near her again, so near that this time the warm whisper of his breath touched her cheek, and sent hot, rippling sensations seeping throughout the very length of her. He was tense, so tense that she wondered if she really knew the man at all, and she was suddenly afraid.

"I have been fighting blue bellies a long, long time, and you are the worst of them. Now, I am not going to wind up in prison or swinging from a rope at the end of this because of you. I do swear it. Shut up, Shannon—"

"Don't you threaten me!"

"Threaten! I'll act, and you know it!"

She didn't realize until it pulled and hurt that he had a grip upon her hair. She clenched her teeth, swallowed and tried to nod. Even for Malachi, this was strange behavior.

It was the war, she decided; he had finally gone insane.

"I'll be quiet!" she mouthed.

"Do so, Shannon, I'm warning you."

She nodded again.

He seemed to realize that he was hurting her. He stared at his hand where he gripped her hair, and he dropped it as if it were a golden fire that truly burned. He sat back again, then watched her.

"No sudden movement, no screams."

"No sudden movement," she repeated in a solemn promise. "No screams."

Seeming satisfied at last, he rose, finding his plumed cavalry hat on the floor nearby and dusting it off upon his thigh. He swept it low before her, and Shannon curiously caught her breath.

He was a charismatic man, a tall and arresting one. She knew he rode with elegance and finesse, as if he had been born to it. It sometimes seemed that he embodied some spirit of chivalry, something of a certain gallantry that had belonged to a sector of the deceased, prewar South. He had grace, and he had courage, she did not deny him those. He would never think of personal safety if something threatened someone he loved. He was loyal and devoted to his brother, and to her sister, Kristin.

He also seemed to have gone quite mad, and she needed desperately to escape him at the first opportunity. She didn't know whether to be terrified or furious.

"Miss McCahy," he murmured, reaching for her hand. "Please accept my hand. I admit, my manners were poor..."

It was too much. He had wrestled her to the ground twice, threatened her, bullied her and acted as if he belonged in an asylum. Now he was acting like the last of the cavaliers. She wanted no part of him; she had to escape.

She stared at his hand, creeping away on her elbows and haunches. "You must be completely out of your mind," she told him flatly. Then she leaped to her feet and spun around to run.

"Damn you!"

The oath left him in a fury. This time, when he caught her and dragged her back, he did not throw her to the floor. He curved one hand over her mouth and brought her flush against his chest with the other, his fingers taut beneath her breast. He whispered against her ear.

"Shannon, I am tired, I am bone tired. It has been my belief since I first had the pleasure of your acquaintance that a switch in the barnyard would have done you a world of good. Now, I am going to ask you one more time to behave, and then I am going to take action against you, as I see fit.''

Rage and humiliation boiled inside her. ''Malachi Slater, don't you ever talk to me like that, ever!''

''Don't push it.''

She brought her heel against his leg with a vengeance. It wouldn't do much damage against his boot, she thought regretfully, but it did incite him further.

She gasped as he swung her around to face him, locking her against his body, his arms around her, her fingers laced tightly through his and held taut at the small of her back, as if they were involved in a close and desperate waltz. She opened her mouth to protest, but something in his eyes silenced her, and she stared at him in stony silence instead.

So much for dignity. So much for pride. She did manage to lift her chin.

''Shannon, behave,'' he said, then paused, watching her. Then he said with a trace of amazement, ''You really meant to kill me!''

She inhaled, and exhaled, and tried to count. She tried to stop the trembling in her body, and the thunder in her heart. She was going to speak softly, and with bold, sheer reason. She could not stand being this close to him. She despised her vulnerability, and she hated the shivers that seized her and the way her blood seemed to heat and steam and sizzle throughout her. She hated the hardness of his body, like warm, living rock that she could lean against, when he was every inch the enemy.

''You would have!'' he repeated. ''You would have shot me. I wonder, did you or did you not know who I was?''

''Malachi, I'd love to shoot you. In both kneecaps, then right between the eyes. But you are Cole's brother, and because of that fact alone, I would never seek to take your miserable life. Besides, you lost, Malachi. I won.'' She paused, savoring the words. "The war, Malachi. I am the victor, and you, sir, are the loser."

He grinned, slowly, and shook his head. He leaned closer so that his eyes streaked blue fire straight into hers. His lips were almost against hers, the hair of his mustache teased her flesh, and she felt his words with every nerve of her body. "Never, Shannon. You'll never, never be the victor over me."

"You've already lost."

"We've yet to play the game."

"Malachi, you're hurting me!"

"You were trying to kill me."

"I was not! Every deserter and drunk and cutthroat and thief across the country thinks that this is playtime. I didn't know who you were! It's your fault. You should have come straight to the house. You shouldn't have been skulking around in the stables. I wouldn't have come out here if—" She broke off, frowning. "You Reb bastard!" she hissed. "You knew that it was me! You knew that it was me, but you jumped me anyway."

"You were wandering around with a Colt. I know what you are capable of doing with one, Miss McCahy."

"You could have called out—"

"Hell, ma'am, now how did I know that you wouldn't have been damned pleased to use the thing against me, and with such a good excuse."

She smiled, savagely gritting her teeth, trying to elude his hold. He would not release her. "Pity I don't have it now. I could be tempted."

"But you don't have it, do you? My point exactly."

"Malachi Slater—"

"Stop, Shannon. I told you. I'm exhausted. I'm bleeding and starving and exhausted and—"

"Bleeding?" Shannon interrupted, and then she wondered irritably why she cared. "Why didn't you come straight to the house?"

He twisted his jaw, watching her suspiciously. "I thought there might be a Yank patrol there."

"You saw that it was me—"

"Yes. But I didn't quite take the chance that you wouldn't just be thrilled to tears, little darlin', to turn me over to a patrol."

"Why, Captain Slater, you sound as if you believe I hate you."

"Miss McCahy, I am just fully aware that the sisterly love you offer to my brother does not extend to me. So you see, Shannon, at first I had to take care that you did not shoot me with pleasure, then I had to assure myself that you did not have a pack of blue-belly friends awaiting me in the house."

"My brother is a blue belly, you will recall," Shannon told him acidly.

"I said a patrol, and that's what I meant."

"A Yank patrol?" Startled, Shannon quit struggling and spoke curiously. "Why? Matthew isn't even back yet. Why would there be a Yank patrol at the house?"

He stiffened, his hold easing on her a bit. "You mean...you haven't heard?"

"Heard what?"

He stared at her for a moment longer and pulled her even closer.

"Swear to me, Shannon, that you're on the level. That you're not going to scream, or run, or try to shoot me again."

"If I had meant to shoot you, Malachi Slater, believe me, you'd be dead right now."

"Shannon, I'm going to let you go. If you scream or move or cause me another problem, I promise, you will live to regret it with all of your sweet heart. Do you understand?"

"There is no bloody patrol at the house!" she told him. Then she lowered her eyes and sighed. "I swear it, Malachi. You're safe for the moment."

Then she gasped, suddenly realizing that Cole's behavior had been a bit strange that afternoon. A friend of his had stopped by, and after that Cole had mentioned very casually that he might have to leave for a day or two to find a hiding place. Just in case, he had assured them. Just in case of trouble. Had Cole known something? It was his nature to be quiet and not alarmist. And he would have played any danger down for fear that Kristin would insist on accompanying him. He would just slip away, and then hurry back once he knew he could keep her safe…

"What?" Malachi demanded sharply.

"There's no patrol. It's just that…an old friend of Cole's stopped by today. And then Cole began to act strangely. Perhaps he does know something he's not telling us." Her heart felt as if it were sinking. Perhaps Cole was already gone. He could have slipped away already, looking for a place to take them. He had wanted to head to Texas before, but he wouldn't leave them for that length of time, Shannon knew. If he had gone off, it would be just for a few days, to find a hiding place deeper into Missouri.

Malachi tilted his head, watching her curiously, but he seemed to believe her. He released her and turned aside. With an uncanny agility in the darkness, he went to the door and found the lantern that hung there and lit it, bringing the flame down low.

And Shannon saw that Malachi was in worse shape than she had at first imagined.

His coat was indeed tattered, his braid frayed. He was very lean, and his handsome features were taut with fatigue. A deep crimson bloodstain marred his trousers high on the inner left thigh.

"You've been hit!" she cried, alarmed. "Oh, my God, I did hit you in the hay—"

He shook his head impatiently, sinking down upon one of the bales of hay. "You didn't hit me. A Union sentry hit me when I passed through Kentucky." He paused, and a gray cloud of memory touched his eyes as he stared into the shadows at nothing. "I could have taken them down," he mused, "but it didn't seem to make any sense. I thought that I could outrun them. They were just kids. They couldn't have been more than seventeen. More killing just didn't seem to make much sense."

None of it was making sense. He must have been in terrible pain, and yet he made his spectacular leap from the loft despite his injury. He must have been desperate indeed.

Curious, Shannon moved carefully over to him. "Malachi, the war is over. Why were they—"

"You really don't know?"

"Know what?" she demanded, exasperated.

"It isn't over. It isn't over at all." He hesitated. "Cole went into Kansas, you know. He killed the man who killed his wife."

Shannon nodded. "I know," she said stiffly. Malachi kept staring at her. "So?" she asked. "Cole knows that he's going to have to leave Missouri for a while. When Matthew comes home, Cole and Kristin will head for Texas."

Malachi leaned against the hay. He winced, and she thought that his leg must be hurting him very badly for him to display even a hint of pain. "Cole can't wait for Matthew to come home. He hasn't got the time. They've got wanted posters up on him. You see, the man he killed has a brother. And the brother seems to own half the property in Kansas. He virtually controls his part of the state. Anyway, he's calling Cole a murderer. He wants him brought in, dead or alive. And he's got enough influence—and money—to see that things are done his way."

Shannon felt weak. She wasn't terribly sure that she could stand. She staggered. She couldn't believe it. Cole had fought long and hard for a chance. He had battled a million demons, and now he had found his peace. He had Kristin and the baby, and with them the promise that there could be a normal life.

And now he was branded outlaw—and murderer.

"He's going to have to head out and hide, Shannon, right

away,'' Malachi said softly. ''They'll know to come for him here.''

She nodded, thinking that this was what Cole had heard earlier. He had quite possibly left already. But in a second, she was going to go back to the house to check. She would at least have to tell Kristin that the world of peace and happiness that she had just discovered was being blown to bits by the thunder of revenge.

''Why—why were they shooting at you? You weren't in Kansas with Cole,'' Shannon said.

Malachi grinned, a lopsided, caustic grin. ''Why, darlin', I'm the man's brother. A Slater. According to the powers that be, I ran with Quantrill, and I butchered half the population of Kansas.''

''But you were never with Quantrill. You were always regular cavalry,'' Shannon said.

''Thanks for the vote of confidence. I didn't think that you would rush to my defense.''

''I wouldn't,'' Shannon said coolly. ''Facts are facts.''

Malachi shrugged, leaning wearily back again. ''Well, it doesn't matter much anyway. You go on up to the house and get Cole. We'll ride out tonight. You seen Jamie?''

Shannon was sorry to have to shake her head. She liked Jamie. He was always calm and quiet. The peacemaker of the three brothers, she thought. The Slaters were close; she could understand that. She and Kristin were close. Too many times, Kristin had been all that she had had left.

Too many times…

In the days after Robert had died, she had wanted to die herself. She had lain there without eating, without speaking, without the will to move. Kristin had been there. Kristin had given her the desire to survive again.

She lowered her head, almost smiling. Malachi had even helped her then. It had been unwitting, of course. He had never allowed her the peace of silence, or the chance to dwell in self-pity. Since she'd met him he'd been demanding, a true thorn in her side. But his very arrogance and his endless determination to treat her like a wayward child had brought out her fury, and with that her passion to live.

"I'm sorry. I haven't seen Jamie," she told him softly.

"Well," Malachi said softly to the lamp. "Jamie is no fool. He'll lay low. He'll find us."

His words were a lie, Shannon thought. He was worried sick. She didn't say so, though, for there was nothing that either of them could do.

"You were in the same company," she said. "Why aren't you together?"

"Jamie set out a day or two before I did. He wanted to stop by to see some old friends who had lost a son." He gritted his teeth. "We've got to run. He'll know how to lie low."

"You're not running anywhere, not the way that you are," Shannon told him. She couldn't bear seeing the blood on his leg. She didn't know why. Most of the time she thought that not even the Comanches could think up a cruel enough death for Malachi. But tonight the sight of his blood disturbed her.

"What do you mean?" he asked her warily.

"Your leg."

"I can find a doc south of here to take out the ball—"

"The ball is still in it?" Shannon said.

He stiffened as he held his breath for several seconds, watching her. "Yeah, the ball is still in it."

Shannon whirled around and headed for the tack room. They kept some rudimentary surgical supplies there; it was a necessary precaution on a cattle ranch.

"Shannon!" he called to her. "What do you think you're doing?"

"I'll be right back."

She found the surgical box in the lower left hand drawer of the desk. She paused. They had no morphine; nothing for pain. Nobody did, not in Missouri. Not in most of the South.

She pulled open the next drawer and found a bottle of Kentucky whiskey. It would have to do.

Then, as she came out of the tack room, she paused, wondering why she was thinking of doing this for Malachi Slater.

Maybe she didn't hate him so much.

No...she hated him. He was Cole's brother, and if his leg wasn't fixed up, he might slow Cole down. That was it, surely.

She swept back to his side and kneeled down. She opened up the box and found a pair of scissors. She needed to slit his pants and find the extent of the wound.

"What do you think you're doing?" he asked her harshly.

"I'm going to cut your pants."

"If you think that I'm going to let you anywhere close—"

"The wound is in your thigh, you fool. Here." She handed him the whiskey. "Drink some of this."

He didn't hesitate to swallow a good shot of the whiskey. He closed his eyes, wincing when he was done. "That was good. It was an inestimable piece of kindness from a Yank to a Reb. Now forget it, I'll find—"

"Sit still, Malachi, and quit whining."

"I'll be damned if I'm whining. Shannon! Shannon, stop!"

He clenched his teeth, but when he went to grip her wrists, he was too late. He hesitated. She already had the shears snipping at his pants, and to make a move might have been dangerous. He inhaled sharply.

She paused and met his eyes. She smiled sweetly. "Sit back now, Captain Slater. Relax."

"You move carefully there, Miss McCahy, or I swear, I'll make you sorry this very night!"

"Why, Captain Slater, I would take great care with those silly threats of yours at this particular moment."

He caught her arm and her eyes once again. "Shannon, I don't make silly threats. Just promises."

"You aren't in any position to make...promises, not at this moment, captain."

"Shannon—"

"Trust me, Malachi."

"The way I would a black widow, Shannon."

She smiled and stared at his fingers, which were still locked around her arm. She looked at him again. His eyes remained clear and deep and blue upon hers. Slowly, he eased his fingers, releasing her.

She felt him inhale as she carefully snipped at the bloodstained wool. Seconds later, she pulled the material away from the wound. She could see the ball. It was sunk in just far enough that a man wouldn't be able to remove it himself. One swift slice with a scalpel and a quick foray with the forceps and it would be gone. Then she could douse it with some of the liquor and bind it, and his chances of a clean recovery would be very good indeed.

"Take another swig of the whiskey," she told him, staring at the wound because she didn't dare look into his eyes. "I'll just get the scalpel—"

His hand landed hard upon her wrist, and her eyes were drawn to his. "I don't trust you with a scalpel, Shannon."

She smiled sweetly. "You have to trust me. You have no choice."

"You bring it too close to any part of my anatomy that I consider near and dear, and you will regret it until your dying day."

"Alas, the ladies would be heartbroken!" she taunted in turn. "I will take the gravest care."

He released her wrist, but continued to watch her. There was a warning sizzle in his eyes that brought tremors to her heart. She had to steady her hands. "What the hell," she muttered. "Mr. Ego Reb. Were I to wound anything near and dear there's a likelihood that nobody would even notice."

It was a good thing that the knife had yet to touch his flesh. He caught her wrist again, pinning it, drawing her eyes to his once more. "Sometime, darlin', I just might let you find out."

She jerked away. "Darlin', don't even dream of it. Not in your wildest thoughts."

"Couldn't handle it, huh?"

"I'll handle it right now, if you're not careful, Captain Slater."

"Is that a promise, Miss McCahy?"

"No, a threat."

"Your hands better move with the skill of an angel, got that, Miss McCahy?"

His grip on her wrist was tight. But it wasn't the pain that gave her pause. It was his agony, for all that he concealed it so well.

She nodded. "Give me the bottle."

"What for?"

"To clean the scalpel." She doused the small sharp knife with the alcohol, and then he took the bottle back from her. He swallowed heartily. "Ready?" Shannon asked him.

"You are eager to take a blade against me," he said.

"Right."

"I can't wait to take one against you." His speech was slurred just a bit. When she glanced his way, she saw his grin, lopsided, heartstopping. She closed her eyes tightly against it, against the searing cobalt of his eyes, and the charisma of that smile. He was making her tremble tonight, and she couldn't falter.

She brought the scalpel against his flesh, holding his thigh to keep it steady. He didn't start or move at the swift penetration of the knife, but she felt his muscles jump and contract, and the power was startling.

He didn't make a sound. He just closed his eyes and clamped down on his jaw, and for a moment she wondered if he was conscious, and then she hoped that he was not. She quickly finished her cut, and brought the small forceps out. She had cut well. She quickly secured the ball and dug it from his flesh, then liberally poured whiskey over the wound and began to bind it with linen bandages. There weren't enough to finish the job. She glanced at his face, then lifted her skirt and tore her petticoat.

One of his eyes opened and he looked at her. "Thanks, darlin'." He wasn't unconscious.

"I don't want you getting Cole killed," she said flatly. She came up on her knees, and wrapped the linen around his thigh, moving higher and higher. Both his eyes were open now. She wished that her elegant bodice weren't cut quite so low. He was staring straight at her cleavage, and he was making no gentlemanly move to look away.

"Quit that," she ordered him.

"Why?"

"You're supposed to be a Southern gentleman," she reminded him.

He smiled, but the smile held pain. "The South is dead, haven't you heard? And so are Southern gentlemen. And you be careful right now, Miss McCahy. You're moving real, real close."

She was. She pulled her fingers back as if she had been burned.

"You did a good job," he told her, tying off the bandage.

"Because everything is intact?" she said caustically.

"I do appreciate that. But then, you wouldn't have dared do me injury, I'm certain."

"Don't be so certain."

A soft, husky chuckle escaped him. "Some day, I promise, I'll make it all worth your while."

"What does that mean?"

"Why, we'll have to wait and see, won't we?"

"Don't hold your breath, Captain Slater. And besides—" she widened her eyes with a feigned and sizzling innocence "—I'm just a child, remember? The McCahy brat."

She started to turn away. He caught her arm and pulled her back. She almost protested, but he moved with a curious gentleness, lifting a fallen tendril of hair, smoothing it. And his eyes moved over her again, over the rise of her breasts beneath the lace of her bodice, to her flushed cheeks, to the curve of her form where she knelt by his feet.

"Well, brat, it was a long war. I think that, maybe, you've begun to grow up."

"I had no choice," she said, and she was suddenly afraid that she would start to cry. She gritted her teeth and swallowed the tears harshly. She felt his eyes upon her, reading her thoughts and her mind and her heart.

"I was very sorry about your Captain Ellsworth, Shannon," he said. "I know what it did to you. But be careful. If you're not, you'll have scars on your soul, like Cole did when the jayhawkers killed his wife."

"Malachi, don't—"

"All right, Miss McCahy, I won't talk about sacred territory." He smiled, a devilish smile, taunting her, leading her away from the memory of pain. "You are maturing, and nicely. Thank you, Shannon." He paused, his eyes searching her, his smile deepening with a sensual curve to his lips. She thought that he was going to say something else, but he repeated himself. "Thank you, you did a good job. Your touch was gentle, nearly tender."

"I told you—"

His knuckles brushed her cheek. "Definitely growing up," he murmured softly.

She didn't know what to say. It should have been something scathing, yet she didn't feel that way at all, not at that moment. She just felt, curiously, as if she wanted to be held. As if she wanted to burst into tears and be assured that yes, indeed, the war was over, and peace had come. She wanted to feel his arms around her, the heat of his whisper as he caressed her tenderly and assured her that all was well.

But she had no chance to respond at all.

For at that moment, the quiet of the night beyond the stables was shattered. The thunder of hoofbeats sounded just outside, loud, staccato, a drumroll that promised some new portent of danger. Even through the closed door, she could feel the beat she knew well.

Shannon rose quickly, the blood draining from her face.

"Riders, Malachi! Riders coming to the house!"

As if in answer to her worried exclamation, she heard a faint scream of horror from the house. Shannon ran to the door, wrenching it open. The scream came again. Shrill now, then higher and higher.

"Kristin!" Shannon cried. "It's—it's Kristin! Oh, my God, it's Kristin!"

"Wait!" Malachi called.

Shannon barely heard him. Horses had come galloping down upon the ranch again. Numerous horses. The sound of those hoofbeats told her that the uneasy peace that had so briefly settled over the ranch would now be shattered once again.

She started to run.

"Shannon!" Malachi thundered.

She ignored him, unaware that he was behind her, swearing, raging that she should stop.

"Damned fool brat!" he called. "Wait!"

She didn't wait. She burst into the night, staring at the house. In the glow of the light from the house she could see twenty or so horses ranged before the porch. Most of them still carried their riders. Only a few of the men had dismounted.

"No!" Shannon breathed, but even as she ran, she saw her sister. A tall husky man with unruly dark whiskers was coming out of the house with Kristin tossed over his shoulder.

Kristin was dressed for dinner, too, in a soft blue brocade that matched the color of her eyes. Her hair had been pinned in a neat coil, but now it streamed down the giant's back, like a lost ray of sunshine.

Stunned, Shannon stopped and stared in horror.

"I've got her!" the man said sharply. "Let's get the hell out of here!"

"What about Slater?" someone asked.

Shannon couldn't hear the reply, but her heart seemed to freeze over. If Cole wasn't gone, then he was dead. If there was a single breath left in his body, the burly man wouldn't have his hands on Kristin.

Kristin was screaming and fighting furiously as the man walked hurriedly to his horse. Kristin bit him, hard.

He slapped her in return, harder. Swearing. Then he tossed a dazed Kristin onto his horse, and mounted behind her.

"No!" Shannon shrieked, and she started to run in a panic toward the house once again. She leaped one of the paddock fences in a shortcut to the house. She had to stop them. She had to save her sister.

Her feet flew over the Missouri dust, and her heart thundered. She had no thought but to reach the man before he could ride away with her sister. In terror, she thought only to throw herself at the man in a whirlwind of fury.

Suddenly, she was, in truth, flying. Hurtling through the air by the force of some rock-hard power behind her, and falling facedown into the red dust at her feet. Stunned, she inhaled, and dirt filled her lungs. Dizzy and gasping, she fought against the force now crawling over her, holding her tight. Panic seized her. It was one of the men, one of them...

"Stop it, Shannon!"

No! It was Malachi again. Damn Malachi. He was holding her down, holding her prisoner, when the men were about to ride away, ride away with Kristin...

"Let me go, you fool!"

He was lying over her, the length of his body flat on hers, hard and heavy. His chest lay on her back, and his hands were flat upon hers, pinning them down. She could barely raise her head to see.

She could only feel the tension and heat of his whisper as he leaned low against her in warning.

"You fool! You're not—"

"Damn you! Get off of me! He has my sister!" She couldn't even begin to fight; she couldn't twist away from him.

"Shannon! He has twenty armed men! And you're running after him without so much as a big stick!"

"He has—"

"Shut up!" One of his hands eased from hers, but only to clamp over her mouth. He kept them down, almost flat upon the earth. A trough lay before them. It hid them from view, Shannon realized, while they could still see the men and the house two hundred yards away.

"He has Kristin!" Malachi agreed. "And if you go any closer, he's going to have you, too! And if you don't shut up, he'll be after the two of us. We could try shooting down twenty men between us without killing your sister in the fire, but we'd still need our weapons—those wood and steel things back in the hay—to do it with!"

She went still, ceasing to struggle against him.

"My only hope is to follow them. Carefully," he said hoarsely. He eased his hand from her mouth. He did not lift his weight from hers, but pinned her there with him with a sure pressure.

She hated him for it.

But he was right. She had no weapon. She had panicked, and she had run off with nothing, and she could do nothing to help Kristin.

She would only be abducted, too.

"No!" she whispered bleakly, for the horses were moving. The men were all mounted, and the horses were beginning to move away.

With the same speed and thunder, they were racing away, into the night.

And red Missouri dust rose in an eerie fog against the darkness of the night...

And slowly, slowly settled.

Chapter Three

When the horses were gone, Malachi quickly stood and reached down for Shannon. She would have ignored his hand and risen on her own, but he didn't give her a chance. All the while, he kept his eyes fixed on the house. As soon as she was standing, he dropped her hands to start limping for the porch. He climbed over the paddock fence.

"Where are you going?" Shannon demanded, following him.

He didn't seem to hear her. He kept walking.

"Malachi!" Shannon snapped. He stopped and looked back at her as if she was a momentary distraction—like a buzzing fly. "Malachi! We have to get guns and horses; we have to ride after them. You're wasting time! Where are you going!"

"I'm going to the house," he said flatly. "Excuse me." He started walking again.

She ran after him and caught his elbow, wrenching him around to face her. Stunned, frightened and furious, she accosted him. "What? You're going to the house. Just like that. Sure, we've got all the time in the world! Let's take a rest. Can I get you dinner, maybe? A drink? A cool mint julep, or something stronger? What the hell is the matter with you? Those men are riding away with my sister!"

"I know that, Shannon. I—"

"You son of a bitch! You Rebel...coward! Good God, I wish to hell that you were Cole! He rode in here all alone and cleaned up a small army on his own! You didn't even fire a shot. You yellow-bellied piece of white trash—"

"That's it!" He stepped back, and his arm snaked out. He caught her wrist and held her in a bruising grip, speaking with biting rage. "I'm damned sorry that Cole isn't here, Miss McCahy. And I'm damned sorry that I didn't have the time to dig through the hay to find my gun or your gun or even my saber. If I had had my gun, I probably could have killed a few of them before they gunned me down. So I'm real, real sorry that I don't feel like dying like a fool just to appease your definition of courage. And, Miss McCahy—" he paused for a breath "—as for Cole, I really, honest to God can't tell you just how much I'd like to see his face. And that, to tell the truth, is what I'm trying to do right now. Those men are riding away with your sister. Well, my brother was in that house, and I—"

He paused again, inhaling deeply. Shannon had gone very pale and very still. She had forgotten Cole in her fear for Kristin. Malachi had not.

He dropped her arm, pushing her from him. "I want to find out if Cole is alive or dead," he said flatly, and he spun on his heels.

It took Shannon a few seconds to follow him, and when she did so, she did in silence. Dread filled her heart. She hoped Cole had left already. But the second that she learned something about her brother-in-law she would be gone. Maybe Malachi could let those men ride away with Kristin—she could not.

He heard her following behind. He spoke without turning around. "I am going after Kristin. If you don't mind, I will arm myself first."

"As soon as we…as soon as we find Cole," Shannon said. "I'll get everything we need. We can leave—"

"*We* aren't leaving. I'm leaving."

"I'm coming with you."

"You're not coming with me."

"I am coming—"

"You're not!"

Shannon opened her mouth to continue the argument, but she didn't get the chance. The porch door swung open again as Delilah came running out. Tall, black and beautiful, with the aristocratic features of an African princess, she was more family than servant, and no proclamation had made her free. Gabriel McCahy had released both her and her husband, Samson, years before the war had ever begun.

Now her features were wretchedly torn with anguish.

"Shannon!" she cried, throwing out her arms. Shannon raced to Delilah, accepting her embrace, holding her fiercely in return. Delilah spoke again, softly, quickly. "Shannon, child, I was so afraid for you! They dragged Kristin from here so quick—"

"Delilah," Malachi said harshly, interrupting her. His voice was thick. "Where is my brother? What happened? Cole would never—Cole would never have allowed Kristin to be dragged from his side."

Delilah shook her head, trying to get a grip on her emotions. "No, sir, Captain Slater," she said softly, "Cole Slater never would have done that. He—"

"He's dead," Malachi said, swallowing sickly.

"No! No, he isn't dead!" Delilah said with haste.

Relief flooded through Shannon. She couldn't stand any longer. She staggered to the porch and sank down on the lowest step. "Where *is* Cole, Delilah?"

"He rode out before—"

"When?" Shannon cried. "I didn't see him go!"

"Let's come inside. You both look as if you could use a little libation," Delilah said.

Shannon shook her head and stood with an effort. "I'm going after Kristin—"

"You're not going after anyone," Malachi said. "I'm going, and I'll do so as soon as I'm ready."

"Don't tell me what I can and can't do, Malachi Slater!"

He walked over to her, his eyes narrowed, his irritation as apparent as his limp. "Shannon McCahy, you are a willful little fool, and you will get us both killed, as well as your sister. I will tell you what to do, and if you don't listen to me, I'll lock you in your room. No, that wouldn't do, knowing you, you'd come right through the window. I'll tie you to your bed. Are we understood?"

She wasn't going to get into another test of strength with Malachi, not at that moment.

Nor was she about to listen to him.

But she inhaled and raised her chin with what she hoped was a chilling dignity. She walked up the steps to the porch and paused before the door. "Yes, let's do go in. I'll get Malachi some of Cole's breeches, and we'll all have a shot of whiskey. Delilah, you can tell us what happened. We do need to move quickly. Malachi needs to get going."

She smiled at him sweetly. She saw his lashes fall as his eyes narrowed, and she saw the cynical curl of his lips beneath his mustache. He didn't trust her. Not a bit. It didn't matter.

She entered the house with a serene calm, walking quickly through the Victorian parlor toward the office. It had been her pa's office; recently, she had begun to think of it as Cole's office. One day, she hoped, Matthew would reclaim it. The country would rebuild after the war, and Matthew's children would come and crawl on his lap while he went over accounts or the payroll.

Delilah and Malachi followed her. She opened the bottom drawer of the desk and drew out a bottle of Kentucky bourbon. With steady hands she found the shot glasses on the bookcase and poured out three servings, then handed one to Delilah and one to Malachi. She took her father's place behind the desk. "All right, Delilah, what happened?"

Malachi was watching her. He perched on the edge of the desk, waiting.

Delilah didn't sit. She swallowed the bourbon neat, and paced the floor.

"Cole left here about an hour ago. He came to speak with Samson and me, explaining that he thought things were going to get hotter a lot sooner than he expected. Some guy called Fitz wanted revenge. Cole didn't think that this Fitz would want to hurt the McCahys—but he knew that Fitz wanted all the Slaters, and just to be safe, he wanted to move Kristin and the baby right away. He didn't want to say anything to Kristin until he had a place to take her and little Gabe, and, well, you know your sister, Shannon, she wouldn't have let him get away. She'd have risked anything, herself and even little Gabe, I think. He meant to come back within a day or two. He didn't want her risking that child or herself." She paused.

"Go on, Delilah," Malachi prodded her. He leaned over the desk and opened the top drawer, reaching for a cigar. "Excuse me," he said to Shannon, smiling politely. She didn't care for the slant of his smile, nor for the touch of blue fire that sparkled in his eyes.

He was, indeed, watching her. And he wasn't about to trust her.

"I gave Cole some food. He gave me a kiss on the cheek, and said that he'd be back, and that everything would be fine. He also said that I shouldn't be surprised to see you coming here mighty soon, Captain Malachi, and that Jamie might be on his way, too. And he left a letter to Kristin on his desk. I brought it up to Kristin right away. She had guessed that he was gone. She ripped the letter open and read it quick, and then she let it drop to the floor. She just sat there, staring at me with her pretty face white as a sheet."

Delilah sighed, slumping down into the leather-covered sofa before the desk. "Then finally she started to cry. 'I knew that he'd have to run, but we meant to run together. He must be desperate, to have gone without me, without the baby! He knew, he knew...that I would follow him anywhere. But he was afraid that they might hurt me or the baby to get to him. Oh, Delilah!' she cried. She cried out my name, just like that.

It hurt so bad to hear. I told her that he'd be back for her, just as soon as he could find a place..."

Shannon nodded. So she had been right. Cole had been gone all along. Cole would have heard Malachi in the barn. He would have heard the shots. He would have come to her. Not that it mattered now.

Delilah paused, shaking her head, staring blankly at the desk before her. "Then the horses came."

"And the Red Legs took Kristin?"

"They swept right in here. But Kristin was so glad to tell them that they were too late. Cole was gone, long gone. Then that bearlike bastard brought his knife so tight against her throat that he drew blood. Thank God he didn't seem to know anything about the baby."

"The baby!" Shannon and Malachi cried in unison, jumping up in alarm.

Delilah smiled. If there was one thing in the world that Malachi and Shannon could agree upon, it was their nephew, Gabriel. They both doted on him, and their alarm was clearly written upon their faces. "Gabe is just fine. He's upstairs sleeping with my boy in my room. They fell asleep on the bed together, and so I left them there. I don't think those men even know that he exists." She stared straight at Shannon. "They know about you, though, missy. They were going to look for you, tear the place apart for you, but the dark-haired fellow with the beard said that they should hurry, they had Kristin Slater, they didn't need anyone else."

Shannon inhaled and exhaled slowly. She looked down at her hands. Maybe she had been lucky. If she hadn't been out at the stables with Malachi, she might have been taken, too.

Or she might be dead now, because she would have tried to fight them. She might have shot some of them down, but there had been an awful lot of them. Red Legs...

She jumped to her feet, staring at Malachi in renewed horror. "Red Legs! They were Red Legs!"

Malachi shrugged. "The Red Leg units are all part of the

army now, Shannon. Lane and Jennison were stripped of their commands long ago.''

His words didn't help her much. Shannon had learned to hate the Southern bushwhackers, but she'd always had the good sense to despise the jayhawkers as they had butchered and plundered and murdered and robbed and raped and savaged the people and the land with every bit as much—if not more—ruthless energy than the bushwhackers.

The Red Legs, as the men were called, were infamous for their brutality. She had seen the uniforms worn by the men in front of the house. But in the darkness, she had not realized who they were. But Malachi had seen them clearly, and he had known right away. He had good reason to know them. A unit of Red Legs had killed his sister-in-law, Cole's first wife.

''We have to get Kristin back,'' she said.

Malachi rose, too. ''I will get Kristin back, I promise you.''

''Malachi—''

''Shannon, damn it, you cannot come.''

''I'm an ace shot, and you know it.''

''And you also panicked just a little while ago. You started racing after them with your mouth wide open and your hands bare. Shannon, the only way I'm going to get Kristin away from those men is to sneak her out of their camp. I can't go in with guns blazing—they will kill her if I even try it.''

''Malachi, please just let me—''

''No.''

''You don't even know what I'm going to say!''

''Shannon, you listen. Stay here. Take care of Gabe. Wait, maybe Cole will come back, or will try to get a message through to you, or maybe Matthew will come home. Who knows, Matthew just may have some influence with these people. He fought long and hard in the Yank army. If he can get to the right authorities, maybe he can get Kristin back through legitimate means.''

She gritted her teeth, staring at him. ''Meanwhile they could kill, torture, rape or maim my sister.''

He sighed, hands on his hips, and gritted his teeth in turn. "Shannon, you may not come with me."

She lowered her head quickly, trying not to let him see her eyes. She was going about this all wrong. She knew Malachi. He was as stubborn as a worn-out mule. He wasn't going to say yes, and she was an idiot to argue it out.

She should let him leave and then follow his trail. He didn't ever have to know that she was near him. And if he didn't manage to get Kristin away from the band of Red Legs, she'd find a way herself.

"Well," she said, "let me go and get you a pair of Cole's breeches."

"Never mind," he told her. "I know where the room is." He turned on his heel and started out of the room.

"Captain Malachi, you'd better have some supper in you before you leave," Delilah said. "You wash up and dress and come on down, and eat something first. And I'll pack you up a little something for your saddlebag."

"Thanks, Delilah."

"He needs to hurry, Delilah," Shannon said sweetly.

Malachi's eyes met hers across the room, sharp and icy and blue, and he smiled. That chivalrous slant of a grin across his features might have been heart-stopping, she thought, if he had just been some other man.

"Oh, I think I have time to grab a bite," he said.

"Certainly. We wouldn't want you to go off hungry."

"I'm sure that you wouldn't."

He kept staring at her, so she kept smiling pleasantly. "You go on then, Malachi. I'll help Delilah see to some dinner."

"Fine," he said. "Thanks." He tipped his hat to her. The brim fell over his eyes, and she wondered once again what he was thinking. But he was quickly gone. She listened to the sound of his boots hitting the parlor floor, then moving up the stairway.

Delilah stood up quickly, eyeing Shannon warily. "What you got on your mind, missy?"

"Nothing that you need to worry about, Delilah."

"Oh, I'm worried," Delilah assured her. "I'm plenty worried." She rolled her eyes Shannon's way.

Shannon ignored her. "Let's go see to something to eat," she said hastily.

Delilah sniffed. "There's plenty to eat out there. Cold roast, cold potatoes and cold turnip greens. Not very nice anymore, but there's plenty. I'll set a plate over the fire. You come pack up some food for Captain Malachi."

Shannon followed Delilah from the office through the elegant little parlor and past the entry to the stairway. She paused, looking up the steps. Malachi would be changing. Then he would eat and leave. She would have to follow quickly. She wouldn't have time to change her clothing. She'd have to roll up a pair of trousers and a cotton shirt, grab a hat and be on her way.

"Shannon?" Delilah looked at her from the doorway to the dining room. "You comin'?"

"I'm right behind you, Delilah," she said, and meekly walked through the dining room to the kitchen. "Is the smoked meat in the pantry?"

"Yes'm, it is," Delilah said, slicing roast beef on the counter and watching Shannon from the corner of her eye. Shannon ignored her and pulled two clean cloths from the linen drawer. She found strips of smoked beef and pork and began to wrap them carefully. Delilah had just baked bread, so there were fresh loaves to pack, too. She turned around just as she was finishing. Delilah was leaning against the door frame, watching her.

"And what are you doing?"

"Packing food."

"I can see that. You're packing up two bundles."

"Malachi is a very hungry person."

"Um. And you're going to give him both of those bundles, right?"

Shannon exhaled slowly. "Delilah—"

"Don't you wheedle me, Shannon. You've been wheedling me since you came up to my knees. You're grown now. I know what you're going to do."

"Delilah, I have to go after Kristin—"

"Malachi will go after Kristin."

"And what if he fails?"

"You think that it will help Kristin if they take you captive, too?"

"Delilah—"

Delilah threw up her hands. "Shannon McCahy, I can't stop you. You're a grown woman now."

"Thank you, Delilah."

"Anyway," Delilah said with a sly smirk, "I don't need to stop you."

"Oh?"

"No, missy, I sure don't. I don't need to at all."

"And why is that?"

"Why, darlin', he's gonna stop you, that's why."

"Don't you dare say anything to him, Delilah."

"I won't. I promise you that I won't. And I can tell you this, it ain't gonna matter none!"

Without waiting for a reply, Delilah turned her back on Shannon, and went to work making up a plate for Malachi, humming as she did so.

Shannon wrinkled her nose at Delilah's back. She knew darned well that Delilah couldn't see, but she might have done so, her next words came so quickly.

"You've got hay in your hair, Shannon McCahy. Lots of it. And hay stuffed right into your cleavage, young woman. You might want to do something about that before dinner."

Instinctively, Shannon brought her hand to her hair, and she did, indeed, pluck a piece of hay from it.

"I thought you weren't terribly partial to Captain Malachi?" Delilah said sweetly.

Shannon found the hay sticking from her bodice. She

plucked that out, too, spinning on her heels and walking toward the door. "I'm not, Delilah. I'm definitely not."

"Hm."

She didn't have to defend herself to Delilah. She didn't have to defend herself to anyone.

Then why was she doing so?

"We had an accidental meeting in the stables, and that is all, Delilah. You were right—I'm not at all partial to Captain Slater."

Lifting her chin, she swept out of the kitchen. She paused, biting her lower lip as she heard Delilah's laughter following her. She shook her head and pushed away from the door. She needed to hurry.

She went up the stairs to her room. Beneath her bed she found a set of leather saddlebags. Dragging them out, she quickly stuffed one side with clean undergarments, a shirt and sturdy cotton breeches. The other side she would save for food and ammunition. She made a mental note to bring plenty of the latter, then shoved the saddlebags under the bed.

She stood quickly and hurried to her washstand, pouring clean water into the bowl. She washed her face and hands and realized that she was trembling. She dried off quickly, then moved to the mirror to repair her fallen and tumbling hair. Swearing softly, she discovered more hay. She brushed it out quickly and redid her hair in a neat golden knot at the nape of her neck.

When she was done, she stepped back. Subdued? Serene? She wondered. That was the effect she wanted. It wasn't to be. Her cheeks were very red with color, her eyes were a deep and sparkling blue, and despite herself, she felt that she looked as guilty as hell.

"I'm not guilty of anything!" she reminded herself out loud. "They've taken my sister..."

That thought was sobering. Where was Kristin now? Had they stopped to rest yet? They were heading for Kansas, she was certain. Surely they would keep her safe—until they had

Cole. And Cole was no fool. When he heard that they had Kristin, he would take care, of course he would...

Her eyes gazed back at her, very wide and misty now. She blinked and stiffened. She needed to find strength. She couldn't possibly sit around and wait. She had to do something to bring Kristin home again.

There...not too bad. She folded her hands before her, and a mature young woman with wise blue eyes and a slender face and soft wisps of blond hair curling around her face gazed back at her. A serene young woman, soft and feminine—with no more hay protruding from the bodice of her elegant dinner gown. She was ready.

Shannon started to run swiftly down the stairs, then she realized that Malachi was standing at the foot of them, waiting for her. She quickly slowed her pace, and her lashes swept low over her eyes as she tried to gaze at him covertly. He had that twisted grin of his again, that cocky, knowing grin.

"Miss McCahy, I was waiting to see if you were joining me for supper. We're all set, and all alone, so it seems. Delilah has gone out back to wait for Samson."

She had come to the foot of the stairs. He was very close, watching her face. She swept by him. "Of course, Malachi."

He followed behind her and pulled out her chair. Delilah had already set their dishes on the table. When Shannon sat, Malachi pushed her chair in to the table. He hovered behind her. She wished that he would sit.

He did not. He reached over her, pouring her a glass of burgundy. She look up at him.

"What is dinner without a fine red wine?" he said lightly. Then he gazed at the bottle, and she saw his handsome features grow taut. "I haven't had any in quite some time," he murmured.

Shannon quickly looked away, feeling that she intruded on some intimate emotion. He did not seem to remember that she was there, but if he had, she thought he would not want her watching.

He poured his wine and sat across from her. He sipped it and complimented the fine bouquet. He cut off a large bite of roast beef, and chewed it hungrily and cut another.

"You're not eating," he told Shannon.

"And you're eating too slowly," she muttered.

He looked up, startled, and smiled. "Shannon, I will catch up with them. I'm probably going to have to follow them for several days to learn their ways and find the best time to sneak in among them. Don't begrudge me one hot meal. I haven't had one in ages."

She felt a twinge of guilt. She knew that the Rebel soldiers had been down to bare rations at the end of the war, moldy hardtack and whatever they could find on the land. She lifted her wineglass to him. "Enjoy," she said softly.

Malachi paused in the midst of chewing, lifting his glass to hers, suddenly mesmerized by the girl before him.

Woman. It had been a long war, and she had grown up during the painful duration of it.

And in the soft candlelight, she was suddenly every bit the glorious image he had seen in his dream. Her lips were softly curled, her cheeks were flushed, her eyes were a crystal and beautiful blue, soft and inviting. Golden strands of hair escaped the knot at her nape and curled against the porcelain clarity and softness of her cheeks, down the length of her slender neck and over her shoulders. Her breasts pushed against the low bodice of her elegant gown. She might have been a study of wisdom and innocence, for her smile was soft and young, but her eyes seemed ancient.

Malachi swallowed a sip of wine. She was still smiling. The little wretch. She was up to something. She planned on following him.

He raised his glass in return. "To you, Shannon."

"Why, thank you, sir."

Just as gracious as a Southern belle. He was definitely in trouble if Shannon was being charming.

"You're welcome." His eyes were warm as he gazed at

her. He lowered his head, hiding a smile, then he allowed his hand to fall upon hers. She almost jumped a mile.

"Did I thank you for treating my leg?"

"It was my pleasure."

"Oh, I'm sure it was."

Shannon didn't know quite what he meant by that, but she was determined not to argue.

It might be nice not to do so, she thought suddenly.

He was such a striking man. He had washed quickly, and his hair was slightly damp, and he had trimmed his mustache and beard. He had donned a pair of Cole's gray trousers, and a clean cotton shirt, which lay open in a V at the neck, displaying a hint of the bronze flesh of his chest, and the profusion of red-gold hair that grew there. He was achingly masculine in the muted glow of the candles, and she was stunned that his wry smile could bring about a curious beating in her heart.

She had not thought of any man as really attractive...

As sexually attractive...

Not since Robert had died. Then she had dreamed.

For so long those dreams had seemed like dust in the tempest of the wind. She could barely remember Robert's kisses now, or the excitement they had elicited within her. She could scarcely recall the lovely satin and lace gown that Kristin had made for her. Kristin had laughed with mischievous pleasure, assuring her that it would be the perfect gown for her wedding night...

She had ripped the gown to shreds.

When Robert had died, she had ceased to lie awake at night and ponder the things between a man and a woman. The soft, exciting stirrings within her had died.

She had thought that they had died.

But with Malachi's hand so softly atop hers, his eyes with their devil's sparkle so close, his knee brushing hers, she was suddenly feeling them again.

Her cheeks flamed crimson, and she jerked her hand from

beneath his, nearly knocking over her wineglass. He cocked an eyebrow at her, and it seemed to her that he was still secretively smiling.

"Something wrong, darlin'?"

"I'm not your *darlin'*."

"Excuse me. Is something wrong, Miss McCahy?"

Wrong? It was horrid. And on a night when Kristin had been so savagely taken...

Kristin, remember Kristin, she told herself. That was why she was here, trying to be charming.

"No," she said quickly. "No, nothing's wrong. I'm just so tired. I mean, it's been such a long day. No, no, nothing is wrong at all. What am I saying? Everything is wrong!"

"Hey!" He leaned across the table and caught her chin with his forefinger. She sensed a tremendous warmth within him that she had never seen before, and it touched her, and embraced her. She didn't pull away when he held her, or when he sought out her eyes.

"I will find her, Shannon. I will find her. They—they aren't going to hurt her—"

"They are a Red Legs unit."

"They aren't going to hurt her. Fitz wants her alive. Why do you think they took Kristin?"

"Because they want Cole."

"Right. So they won't hurt her, or else they won't have her to use against my brother. It's going to be all right."

Shannon nodded. He released her, but his eyes stayed on her with a curious speculation, and it seemed that he had to force himself to return his attention to his meal.

And she had to force herself to forget his haunting touch.

"Is—is everything good?" she asked him.

"Delicious," he said briefly.

"I do hope so. More wine?"

"Thank you, Miss McCahy."

"My pleasure."

He sat back, sipping the wine that she had poured. He lifted his glass, and the speculation remained in his eyes. "No, my pleasure, Miss McCahy." He sighed, finished the wine, set his glass down and rose. She jumped up along with him.

"You're going now?"

"I'm going now."

"I'll get your food. And your coat and cavalry jacket." She paused. "You probably shouldn't ride into Kansas with that jacket. Do you want another one?"

He took his jacket and coat from her. "Why, haven't you heard, Miss McCahy? The war is over. Or so they say."

"Or so they say," Shannon echoed.

He grinned. He touched her cheek, and she quickly turned away. "I'll get your food."

"Thanks," he drawled, but when she started to walk away, he caught her hand and pulled her back.

He had put his plumed hat atop his head, and his Confederate greatcoat lay over his shoulders. His eyes were heavy-lidded and sparkled with a lazy sensuality and humor.

"It was a nice dinner, Miss McCahy. You were a beautiful companion. I enjoyed it. Whatever comes, I want you to know that. I enjoyed it."

It was very peculiar talk, coming from Malachi. She nodded nervously and pulled away from him. "I'll...I'll just get your food."

"I'll meet you out front. I want to take a last peek at Gabe, and tell Delilah goodbye."

"Fine."

She fled to the kitchen. She hurriedly secured his bundle of food, adding a bottle of her father's old Irish whiskey from the cupboard. Then she went outside and nervously waited.

Soon he passed by her on the porch. "Just need to get the bay," he told her.

"Of course."

She watched him walk to the stable, a tall figure, dominating the night, with his greatcoat falling from his shoulders and his plumed hat touching the sky.

He was swallowed up by the darkness.

Moments later he reappeared, a masterful horseman, cantering toward her on the bay.

He reined in before he reached the porch and waited as she approached him with the bundle of food and the liquor.

"Is your leg all right?" she asked him with a little pang of guilt. He should have had some rest, but he seemed to be doing well with the wound. As long as infection didn't set in, he should be fine.

But it was true that he should have rested.

"The leg feels good, thanks." He buckled the food into his saddlebag. The bay mare shuffled nervously, wanting to be gone.

Shannon stepped back. Malachi nodded to her, lifting the reins. "Take care of Gabe. I'll be back with Kristin as soon as I can. I hope Cole will hear of this and come back, but we can't rely on that. Be ready. We'll have to take her somewhere. She'll have to hide now, too, or they'll come after her again."

Shannon nodded. "I'll be ready."

"I'll bet you will. Goodbye."

She lifted a hand and waved. He saluted, swung the bay around and rode into the night.

Shannon could barely stand still. The second he was out of sight, she swung around and raced up the steps. She burst into the house and ran up the stairway. She didn't pause to change, but wrenched her saddlebags from beneath the bed and tore down the stairs again and into the kitchen.

Delilah was there. Shannon ignored her as she packed her own food, then she hurried over and hugged Delilah fiercely. "Take good care of Gabe, Delilah."

"Shannon, Shannon, you shouldn't be going! I thought that he would know, I thought that he would stop you—"

"No one can stop me, Delilah. You know that. Please, please, promise to take good care of the baby!"

"You know that I will, missy, you don't need to say a word."

"I know that. Oh, Delilah, you and Samson were God sent! I don't know what we'd ever have done without you."

"You might not be able to run off like this."

"Delilah, she's my sister. I have to go for her."

Shannon kissed Delilah quickly on the cheek, swept up her bags and left the kitchen.

In the hallway she plucked the second Colt from the wall and stuffed her bag full of ammunition. Delilah hovered behind her.

"Shannon, you take care, young lady. Don't go off impetuously and get yourself in trouble, you hear?"

Shannon nodded and threw the door open. She started to hurry out, and she hurried straight into Malachi's waiting arms.

"Malachi!"

"Shannon!"

He set her back on her feet, a broad, smiling barrier in the doorway. He took her saddlebags from her hands. "Going somewhere tonight, Miss McCahy?"

"Yes!"

She tried to snatch the bags from him. His smile faded from his face, and he tossed the saddlebags on the floor of the porch. The sound reverberated, but neither of them heard it. Their eyes were locked.

"Malachi Slater—"

"You aren't coming, Shannon."

"Damn you, you can't—"

"I am sorry, Miss McCahy, but what I can't do is let you get yourself killed."

"Malachi—" She cried out in soft and wary warning. He stepped forward anyway and dipped low, catching her in the midriff and throwing her over his shoulder.

"Put me down, you damn Reb!" she ordered him. He just

kept walking. She pummeled his back. "Malachi, Slater, you—"

"Shut up, Shannon."

"Scurvy bastard—"

His hand landed firmly upon her derriere. "This is such a delectable position!" He laughed, his footsteps falling upon the stairs.

She burst out with every oath she knew, beating savagely against his shoulders. He didn't seem to feel a thing, protected as he was by the heavy padding of his greatcoat.

Despite her wild fight, they came quickly to the second floor. His long strides brought them down the corridor to her room. He pushed the door open, and a second later tossed her hard upon her bed. Her skirts and petticoats flew around her, and she scrambled first for some dignity, pressing them down.

"Temper, temper, Shannon," he murmured.

"Temper!" She jumped to her knees, facing him. He arched a brow but didn't take a single step back. He seemed to be waiting for her next move, just waiting.

Shannon smiled and sank down on her pillows, comfortably crossing her arms over her chest. "Go ahead. Lock me in."

"I intend to."

"Aren't you forgetting?" she said sweetly. "This is so very foolish. The second that you're really gone, I will crawl right through that window. Now, it would just make so much more sense if you would be a reasonable man and—what are you doing?"

Shannon sat up, tensing, for he had turned away from her and was prowling through her drawers.

"Malachi?" She rose to her knees again, then leaped from the bed, accosting him. She pulled his hand out of her top drawer. A pair of her knit hose dangled from his hands.

"You're letting me come?" she said curiously. Then she realized from the grim determination on his features that he had no intention of letting her come. She still wasn't sure just what he meant to do.

Then he reached for her, sweeping her off her feet and plopping her down on her bed once again.

"Malachi, no!"

"Shannon, darlin', I'm sorry, yes!"

She let out a spate of oaths again, struggling fiercely against him. She didn't have much chance. He quickly had a grip on her wrists. No matter how she swore and raged and resisted, he tied them to the bedposts with her own knit stockings.

"I'll get you for this, Malachi Slater!"

"Maybe you will."

"I hope that your leg rots and falls off. Then I hope that the infection spreads, and that everything else rots and falls off."

Leaning over her, securing the last of the knots, he smiled. "Shannon, I don't think that was a very ladylike comment."

She narrowed her eyes. "This is no gentlemanly thing to do."

When he was done, he sat back, satisfied. She stared at him in trembling fury. A frightening and infuriating vulnerability drove her to try to kick him. He laughed and inched forward. He touched her cheek gently, almost tenderly.

"You're not coming, Shannon. I tried to warn you."

"Don't you dare touch me. Let me loose."

"You look lovely in bed."

"Get off my bed!"

"All that passion! It's quite—stirring, by God, Shannon, it is. I hope it remains if I'm ever tempted to take you into my bed."

"Malachi Slater, I promise you," Shannon grated out, straining at the bonds that tied her wrists and staring at him with rage and tears clouding her eyes, "the only way you'd ever get me into your bed would be to knock me out cold and then tie me to it!" She jerked hard upon her wrist.

He laughed, rose and bowed to her deeply, sweeping down his plumed hat. Then he came very close, and suddenly teased her forehead with the briefest touch. It might have been a kiss.

"Miss McCahy, I promise you. If I ever decide to bring you to bed, no ties or binds will be needed."

She gritted her teeth. "Get out!"

He swept his hat atop his head and offered her his slanted, rueful smile.

"Take care, Shannon. Who knows? Maybe the possibilities are worth exploring." He paused for a second. "And I promise you, darlin', that I will not let anything rot and fall off."

With that, he turned and left her.

Chapter Four

"You can't just leave me tied like this!" Shannon called in amazement to him as the door closed in his wake. She bit lightly into her lower lip. "*I* could rot and fall off and die!"

She heard the husky sound of his easy laughter—and the twist of the key in the door. "Delilah will be up in a few hours. You won't die, Shannon." He seemed to hesitate. "And you might well do so if you were to come with me. Delilah isn't going to let you go until my trail is as cold as ice, so just behave."

"Malachi!"

It was too late. He had gone. She could hear his footsteps as he pounded down the stairs.

With a cry of pure exasperation, Shannon jerked hard upon her wrists, then slammed her head against her pillow. Tears formed in her eyes.

How could she have been so incredibly stupid?

She tried to breathe deeply, to regain a sense of control. She stared at her left wrist, then tried to free it. He was good with knots, she determined. The ties did not hurt her, but they seemed impossible to loosen.

She fell back in exasperation.

There had to be some way out of it. There had to be.

She stared at the ceiling for several long minutes. The best she could come up with was a fairly dirty trick, but she had to try it.

She waited. This time, she wanted to make sure that he was gone. She waited longer.

Then she screamed, high-pitched, long and hard and with a note of pure terror.

Within seconds, Delilah burst in upon her, her dark skin gray with fear. "Shannon! What is it?"

"Beyond my window! Right outside! There's someone here, oh, I know it, Delilah!"

Shannon lowered her lashes quickly. She wondered if God would ever forgive her for the awful scare she was giving Delilah, then she figured that most men and women who had survived the war had a few sins on their consciences—God was just going to have to sort them all out. He would understand, after all they had been through, that she had to go after her sister herself, come what may.

"Outside, now?" Delilah whispered.

"Let me up before someone gets in!" Shannon urged her. She was whispering, too, and she didn't know why. It didn't make much sense, not after her blood-curdling scream.

Delilah hurried over to the bed, clicking her tongue as she worked on Shannon's left-hand knot. "Lord, child, but that man can tie a good knot!"

"Get a knife. There's a little letter opener in my top drawer. It's probably sharp enough."

Delilah nodded, hurrying. She came back and started sawing away at the stocking. "Yes, he sure can tie a knot!" she murmured once again.

"I know," Shannon said bleakly. Then she looked up, and her eyes met Delilah's.

Delilah jumped back, dropping the letter opener and shaking her finger at Shannon. "Why, you young devil! This whole thing was a ploy!"

Delilah had nearly severed the knot. Shannon yanked hard and managed to split the rest of the fibers. The letter opener was within her reach on the bed. She grabbed it before Delilah could reach it, and quickly severed the second bind.

Then she was free.

"Shannon McCahy—"

"I love you, Delilah," Shannon said, quickly hugging her and giving her a kiss on the cheek. "Take care of Gabe."

"Shannon, don't you go getting yourself killed! Your death will be on my conscience! Oh, Lord, but your poor pa must be rolling over in his grave!"

"Pa would understand," Shannon said, then she hurried from the room. She had lost a lot of time. Malachi would ride hard at night. It wouldn't be easy to catch up with him. Not that she wanted to meet up with him tonight. She just wanted to find him so that she could follow along behind him.

She hurried down the stairs. Delilah had picked up her saddlebags from the porch and dragged them into the hallway. Shannon knelt and checked her belongings. She reached into the top drawer beneath the empty Colt brackets and found matches and added them to her bags.

Delilah had followed her downstairs. Once again, Shannon hugged her.

"Come home soon," Delilah said.

"If Matthew comes, you tell him what happened. Maybe, maybe Matt can do something if the rest of us fail."

"Shannon—"

"We're not going to fail." She gave Delilah a brief, hard hug and hurried out of the house.

Entering the stables seemed strange, even just seeing the hay bales where she had fallen beneath Malachi.

She was startled to discover that she had paused and imagined the two of them as they had been that night, so very close in the hay. A curious heat swept over her, because she was remembering him as a man. The touch of his hands, the curve of his smile. The masculine scent of him. The husky tones of his voice.

She pressed her hands against her cheeks with shame. She wasn't in love with Malachi Slater. She didn't even like him. She had hated him for years.

But that wasn't what disturbed her. What disturbed her was a sense of disloyalty. She had been in love. Deeply in love. So in love that when she had heard of Robert's death, she had wanted to die herself. She had ceased to care about the war; she had ceased to care about the very world.

And now her cheeks were heating because Malachi Slater had spent the night touching her...

In anger, she reminded herself.

But with laughter, too, and with a new tension. And he had teased and taunted her.

And promised her things.

He had whispered against her flesh, and his words had often been husky and warm. She had never denied him his dashing charm or, in her heart, his bold masculinity.

She had just never realized how deeply it could touch her as a woman.

Her breath seemed to catch in her throat and she emitted a soft sound of annoyance with herself. He was a Rebel, and he was Malachi, and she would never forgive him for being either. She needed him tonight. And she would find him.

She quickly assessed the horses in the stables. She chose not to take Arabesque, her own mare, for the horse was a dapple gray, a color that glowed in the moonlight. She patted the mare quickly. "Not this time, sweetheart. I need someone dark as the night, and fleet as a bullet. Hmm..."

She had to hurry.

Without wasting further time, she decided on Chapperel, a swift and beautiful animal, part Arabian, part racer, nearly seventeen hands high and able to run like lightning.

He was also as black as jet, as black as the night.

"Come on, boy, we're going for a ride," she told the gelding, as she quickly saddled and bridled him and led him from the stables.

She looked at the sky. There was barely a sliver of a moon, but the stars were bright. Still, the trail would be very dark. It would be almost impossible for her to track Malachi.

But maybe it wouldn't be so hard to track the twenty horses that had raced before him. They had headed west—that much she knew for a fact.

And they would be staying off the main roads, she thought.

The Red Legs who had taken Kristin might still be a part of the Union army, and then again, they might not. No Union commander in his right mind was going to sanction the kidnapping of young women. No, these people had to be outlaws...

And they wouldn't be taking the main roads. They would be heading west by the smaller trails, and that was what she would do, too.

How much of a lead did Malachi have on her? An hour at most.

Shannon nudged the gelding, and he broke instantly into a smooth and swift canter.

And seconds later, he was galloping. The night wind cooled Shannon's face and touched her with the sweet fragrance of the earth. The darkness swept around her as she crossed the ranch and then the open plain.

Then it was time to choose a trail. She ignored the main road where the wagons headed west and where, over the past years, armies had marched by with their cannons and caissons. There was a smaller trail, rough and ragged and barely discernible, through the trees.

She reined in and dismounted and moved close to the ground, picking up a clump of earth. There were hoof marks all around.

She rose and felt a newly broken branch.

This was the trail she would take.

Malachi knew Missouri like the back of his hand.

He knew the cities, and he knew the Indian territories, and the farmlands and ranches. He could slip through Kentucky and Arkansas and even parts of Texas with his eyes nearly closed.

But these boys were moving west into Kansas. In another hour, they'd be over the border.

And he was an ex-Confederate cavalry captain, still wearing his uniform jacket.

He should have changed it. He should have accepted Shannon's offer of a civilian jacket, but somehow, he had been loathe to part with the uniform. He'd been wearing it for too many years. He'd ridden with too many good men, and he'd seen too many of them shot down in the prime of life, to forget the war. It was over. That was what they said. Abraham Lincoln had said that they must bind the wounds. "With malice towards none, with justice for all."

But then Old Abe had been gunned down, too, and in the blink of an eye, the South had begun to see what was going to be.

She was broken; she was laid to waste. Northern opportunists and plain old crooks swept down upon the fine manors and mansions, and liquor-selling con men were stirring up the ex-slaves to wage a new kind of war against their former masters. Homes and farms were being seized; men and women and children were starving in much of the devastated South.

No...

He probably shouldn't be heading into Kansas in a Confederate jacket. It was just damned hard to take it off. They didn't have a whole lot left. Just pride.

He had fought in the regular cavalry. Fought hard, and fought brilliantly. They had often hung on against impossible odds. They had a right to be proud, even in defeat.

And maybe, even in Kansas, he might have been able to ride through in his uniform if he wasn't who he was. If there hadn't been wanted posters out on him. But if he found himself picked up by the law because of his pride, he wouldn't be able to do Kristin any good, he would probably be hanged, and his pride would definitely be worthless stuff.

Tomorrow, he would pick up some clothes someplace. He'd

be much better off traveling as a simple rancher. Displaced, maybe. An ex-Reb. He wouldn't be so damned obvious.

Not that he meant to be in Kansas long. He would get Kristin and get out. There would be plenty of places, deep in Missouri, to hide out until he found Cole and Jamie and decided what to do.

A swift gray shadow seemed to fall over his heart.

They would probably have to leave the country. Head down to Mexico, or over to Europe. The thought infuriated him. The injustice of it was absurd, but no one was going to give any of the Slater brothers a chance to explain. That son of a bitch Fitz had branded them, and because they were Rebs, the brand was going to stick.

Malachi reined in suddenly. In the distance, far ahead, he could see the soft glow of a new fire.

The Red Legs had stopped to make camp for the night.

He nudged the bay mare forward once again. He had been riding hard for hours, and it was nearly midnight, but they still had a certain distance on him.

Carefully, warily, Malachi closed that distance.

When the crackling fires were still far ahead of him, he dismounted from the bay. He whispered to the horse and dropped the reins, then started forward on foot.

The Red Legs had stopped in a large copse right beside a slim stream. Coming up behind them through the trees, Malachi found a close position guarded by a large rock and hunkered down to watch.

There were at least twenty men. They were busy cooking up beans and a couple of jackrabbits on two separate spits. A number of the men had lain down against their saddles before the fire, but a number of them were on guard, too. Three men were watching the horses, tethered to the left of the stream. As he looked across the clearing, Malachi could see two of them against the trees.

They were armed with the new Spencer repeating rifles. They would be no easy prey.

Looking around again, he saw the worst of it.

Kristin was tied to a tree near the brook. Her beautiful blond hair tumbled around her face, but her skin was white and her eyes were closed. She was exhausted, and desolate...

And guarded by two men.

Even as Malachi watched, the situation changed. The tall, burly man who had taken her from the house was walking her way. He bent beside her. Her eyes flew open and she stared at him with stark hatred. The man laughed.

"Sweet thing, I just thought that you might be hungry."

"Hungry for the likes of you, eh, Bear?" shouted a tall, lean dirty blond with a scruffy mustache. He stood up and sauntered toward the tree. He leaned down by Kristin, too. "Sweet, sweet thing. My, my, why don't you come on over and have dinner with me? Roger Holstein, ma'am—"

Kristin spit at him. A roar of laughter went up, and the young man's face darkened with fury. He lunged for her.

The man he'd called Bear pulled him back. "You keep your hands off her."

"Why? We weren't even supposed to bring her back. We were supposed to find Cole Slater. So you tell me why I can't have the woman."

Another man by the fire stood up. "Why should you have her, Holstein? What's the matter with the rest of us?"

"No one's gonna have her, and that's the way I say it is!" Bear bellowed, and Malachi slumped against the rock, relieved. Bear took a step toward Roger Holstein, shaking his fist. "You listen, and you listen good. The woman is mine. I took her. And I'm still the law in this unit—"

"Hell!" Roger Holstein muttered. "We ain't no unit anymore. The war is over."

"We're a unit. We're a unit because we belong to Fitz, just like we always have. And I was there that day Cole Slater shot down Henry and half a troop. He ain't no fool. If he hears that she's already been abused by you pack of trash, he'll take his time. He'll come after us slow and careful. And he won't be alone. He's got a pair of brothers who can pick the eyes out of hummingbirds in the next damn state with their Colts.'' Bear hesitated, looking at Kristin. ''We don't hurt the woman.''

''Hell, Bear, I wasn't going to hurt her!'' Roger complained. ''I was gonna make her have a hell of a good time!''

''You don't touch her. Fitz decides what to do with her. By my mind, leaving the lady her tender flesh and sweet chastity will come in real handy as bargaining power.''

For a moment, Malachi thought that fighting was going to break out right then. He prayed silently that it would not; he would never be able to slip away with Kristin if it did.

He didn't think that his prayers would be answered. The tension among the men was as thick as flies on a steer carcass. It escalated until every man in the place was silent, until only the sound of the crackling fires could be heard.

Then Roger Holstein backed down.

''Have it your way, Bear. We'll see. When we get back to Fitz, we'll see.''

''Damned right, we will,'' Bear agreed.

Malachi looked at Kristin. Her eyes were closed again. She was silent and probably grateful that the situation had calmed.

Thank God it was Kristin there and not Shannon. Shannon was incapable of keeping silent. She would be raging and fighting and biting and kicking and creating complete disaster.

Malachi sank against the rock, closing his eyes, exhaling slowly. He wondered what had made him think of Shannon.

The whole damned night had been filled with Shannon, he reminded himself wryly. But she was safe. Delilah would just be releasing her sometime around now. And she would know that there would be no way in hell to follow a trail that cold.

Thank God it wasn't Shannon? he queried himself. Hmph! If it had been Shannon, he wouldn't be here now. He wouldn't be sneaking into Kansas in his Confederate uniform. He'd be headed south. If it had been Shannon kidnapped, he would have pitied the damned Red Legs.

No, she surely hadn't been a Circe this evening. She had been a complete spitfire, stubborn, willful and...

Beautiful.

Just like the woman in his dream, the sweet vision who had brought him from the brink of death. She was beautiful, perhaps even more beautiful than Kristin, for she was a searing flame, with a life so vibrant that her golden hair was touched by the fire, as were her eyes, brilliant, sparkling, searing. Her voice was like a lark's, sweet and pure...even when she yelled.

Actually, he wasn't thinking about her eyes.

He was thinking about her hands, and the tenderness in her fingers when she had cleansed and bound his wound.

No...

He wasn't even thinking about that.

He was thinking about the provocative swell of her breasts when she leaned over him, when she brushed against him. He was thinking of the lithe and shapely heat of her body, the slimness of her waist, the softness of her flesh, the full sensuality of her lips.

Shannon had grown up.

He slunk down into the rock, pulling his hat low over his forehead. She was still Shannon McCahy. The little brat who had been on his tail since he had first walked onto the McCahy ranch. She had fired at him that very first time, and she was firing at him still.

He smiled and leaned back.

He had kissed her once. To shut her up. They were all playing innocent when a Yank officer had come by the ranch, and Shannon, bless her sweet, sweet hide, would have gladly handed him right over.

And so he had kissed her.

It did seem to be the only way to shut her up.

But the kiss had been sweet. Her passion then had been that of anger, but passion nevertheless, and it had feathered against his senses until he had realized who she was, and what he was doing.

But now, tonight, he remembered that kiss.

He opened his eyes and clamped his teeth together. He knotted his fingers into fists and then slowly released them, suddenly aware that he wanted her. That he desired her, hotly, hungrily and completely.

Wanting a woman wasn't so strange, he reminded himself. Over the years, he had wanted a number of women, and, during the war, when lovers were quickly won and lovers quickly lost, many young women, like many men, were quick to seek the solace of the moment. The women he had wanted he had often had. The widow in Arkansas, the desolate, lonely farm woman in Kentucky, the dance-hall girl in Mississippi.

Once, it seemed like a long, long time ago now, there had been a girl he had loved. Ariel Denison. Ariel... He had even loved the sound of her name. They had been very young. The sight of him could bring a flush to her cheeks, and the warmth of her dark eyes upon him alone could bring forth all the ardor in his heart and soul. Her father had approved, and they were to have been married in June. They spent what May days they could together, hand in hand, racing down to the stream, daring to swim together, daring to come to the shore and lie naked in the sweet grasses, making love. He'd never known anything so deep, or so wonderful...

But by June, she was gone. A cholera epidemic swept through the countryside, and Ariel, smiling to the last, had died in his arms, whispering her last words of love with the last of her breaths. He had not cared then if he contracted the disease. He hadn't cared at all, but he had lived. Since then, he hadn't fallen in love again. He had given his passion to his land; his loyalty had been to his family and, once the war came, to the Confederacy.

He didn't remember much about love...

But no man lived long without desire. He was used to that.

So it was strange to discover with what depth and fervor he desired Shannon.

The brat. His foremost enemy. The ardent, fanatical Unionist. The bane of his every trip to the ranch. Shannon...

"Hey!" came a sudden, loud shout. "Did you hear that?"

Malachi turned around, looking over the rock toward the camp. The guards by the horses were moving. Half the men had begun to settle down for the evening.

Now they were waking up.

Bear strode toward the guards. "What? What is it? I don't hear anything."

"There's something there. Something out in the bushes."

They had seen him. They had heard him, Malachi thought.

But they hadn't. The guard was pointing in the other direction.

"You scared of a bobcat or a weasel?" Bear sneered.

"It weren't no weasel!" the guard protested.

Bear paused, then shrugged. He looked at two of the men. "You, Wills, and you, Hartman, go take a look around. The rest of you, keep your eyes open."

Hell! Malachi thought. If they went snooping around too far, they would find the bay. He cursed whatever creature had been sneaking around the camp. If it was a weasel, he hoped some poor bastard ate the creature.

He sank against his rock. They weren't going to look for him there, not right beneath their noses. He was going to have to sit tight and wait. If they would just settle down for the night, even with the guards on duty, he would be able to reach Kristin. Once the camp was quiet, he would be able to circle around and come at her from the stream. He would have to kill the guards by the horses; he wouldn't have any choice.

Malachi frowned suddenly, feeling the earth beneath his hands. He lay against the ground and listened to the tremors of the earth.

Someone else was out riding that night. Not too far distant, a group of horsemen was coming toward them.

A Union patrol?

He thought they were still in Missouri, but they might have crossed over the border. They had really headed south as much as they had headed west. Not that it mattered much. Union patrols were everywhere.

But it could also be a Southern outfit, heading home.

Maybe it didn't matter. Maybe it did.

He tensed, waiting.

Then a shrill and furious scream caught his attention. He swung around, looking into the center of the Red Legs camp.

"Son of a bitch!" he swore beneath his breath, staring. "If they leave behind just a piece of her, I'm going to skin her alive!"

Shannon had just been thrown into the center of the camp. Hartman and Wills had brought her, and with laughter and gusto cast her with force into the den of rogues.

Wills was limping, swearing away.

"She shot off my toe!" he howled.

"Thank God she can't aim," Roger said, chortling.

"I did aim, you stupid ass," Shannon said with venom. "If I'd have wished it, I'd have shot out your heart."

Wills went silent; even Roger went silent. There was a chill around them all, as if they knew her words to be the truth.

"Get down there, witch!" Wills swore savagely. He shoved her down, hard.

She landed on her knees. She had changed clothing, and wore tight black trousers, a gingham tailored shirt and a pair of sturdy brown boots. She'd worn a hat, a broad-brimmed hat, but now it lay several feet from her in the dust. Her hair had been pinned, but the pins were strewn around her, and her hair was falling, like a golden sunrise, in delicate rays down her back.

Malachi bit hard into his lip as she raised her chin to face Bear, all her heat and fury and passion alive in her eyes. She shouldn't have changed. The perfection of her form was even more apparent in the tight breeches and man's shirt, and he was not the only one to notice. The Red Legs were all rising, one by one, creating a circle around her.

"My, my, my," Roger Holstein drawled. He moved his tongue over his lips. "What have we here?" He stepped out of the circle, coming toward her. Shannon struggled quickly to her feet. Malachi tensed, watching the sizzle in her eyes.

"Don't be stupid, Shannon!" he muttered to himself. "Be quiet, be good, let them tie you up and I can get you out... don't be stupid!"

But she was going to be stupid. Roger reached for her, and Shannon moved like lightning, sinking her teeth into his hand. He screamed with pain, then caught her with his backhand, sending her spiraling into the dirt. "Bitch!" he roared.

The men laughed like hyenas. "Least she didn't shoot you, Roge!" Wills said.

Roger came forward again, sucking at his sore hand.

"Get away from her," Bear ordered, coming into the center of the ring.

"Oh, no, you don't," Roger said with hostility. "That one is for Fitz. Fine. This one is mine."

"I'll die first, I swear it!" Shannon hissed from the ground. She seemed to sense that her only hope was Bear. Holding her cheek, she rose and raced behind him. "I'll kill you—"

"Yeah, watch it, man, the little lady will bite you to death!" someone jeered.

"Get out of my way, Bear!" Roger howled. "She's mine!"

"No!"

"You've got Slater's wife—"

"This is his sister-in-law, you idiot."

Roger paused to look from one woman to the other. It was impossible to miss the resemblance. "So they're sisters. So what of it?"

Kristin called out then. "You touch her, and I'll kill myself, you bastard! Then you'll have nothing, nothing at all—"

"Kristin!"

Shannon burst through the throng of men, racing for her

sister. Bear caught her just before she could get to Kristin's side. He swept her up by the waist, laughing. "Little darlin'!" he exclaimed. "If you go to anybody, sweet pea, you go to old papa bear!"

He reached up with one of his great hands and clutched the front of her shirt, tearing. Shannon screamed and savagely swung a kick his way.

She did know how to aim.

With a tremendous groan, Bear dropped her and doubled over. Shannon pulled his gun from his holster and swung around, facing the men, who were all on their feet.

"Don't take a chance," she warned them, backing carefully toward Kristin. "I know what I'm doing with this thing."

"You can't kill us all," Roger told her, but he didn't take another step her way.

"I can castrate at least six of you," Shannon promised, and at least six of the men took a step backward.

"Now, all that I want is my sister," Shannon began. She kept talking, but Malachi no longer heard her words because there was movement behind her. One of the guards watching the horses had drawn his knife and was sneaking up behind her.

"Damn!" Malachi mouthed. He couldn't shoot at the man; Shannon was in the way. If she would move...just a hair.

She didn't. The guard came up behind her and slipped the knife around her quickly, right at her throat, against her jugular.

"Castrate us!" Roger chortled as she dropped the gun. "Why, honey, we're all going to make you glad that you didn't—"

The man with the knife moved. Just enough.

Damn her, damn her, damn her, Malachi thought. They were probably all dead now. But he couldn't wait any longer.

He rose and he fired. He got the guard right between the eyes. The man fell.

Shannon reached down for the gun she had dropped. Confusion reigned as men rushed toward her, as men looked around, anxious to discover who had fired the shot.

Malachi kept shooting. He didn't have any choice. He tried to aim and focus and to keep a good eye on Shannon, too. Men fell, and men screamed, and dust flew. But there were too many of them, just too many of them.

Shannon had been holding her own. But in the midst of the melee, Bear stumbled to his feet. He staggered toward Shannon from the rear while another man approached her from the front. She aimed forward...

And Bear took a firm swipe against her arm, sending the gun flying. She turned to fight, and he punched her hard in the mouth. Her eyes closed and she slumped to the ground.

"Get him! Get that varmint in the woods!" Bear ordered.

"Varmint?" Malachi stood up, staring at Bear. "Excuse me, you jayhawking jackals. Captain Malachi Slater, late of Hunt's magnificent cavalry, and still, my friends, a Southern gentleman. Shall we?"

"It's a damned Reb!" one of the guards shouted.

"It's more than that. It's a damned Reb Slater!" Bear roared. "Kill him!"

Well, this is it, Malachi thought. Shannon had wanted him to die for honor, and he would just have to go down that way. He stood, firing again and again as the Red Legs raced toward him, trying to fire, but failing. He ran out of bullets as a pair of them charged over the rocks, but he had his saber with him, and he drew that. He charged in turn, and managed to kill the first two men, but more of them were coming for him, more and more...

He was engaged with one fighter when he noticed a carbine aimed his way. He wasn't even going to have time to ask forgiveness of his sins, he thought. No time to mourn...

A blast sounded.

It was the Yank holding the carbine who fell, and not Malachi. Amazed, he looked around.

Hoofbeats! He had heard the hoofbeats! And now the riders were upon them.

"It's a pack of Red Legs!" shouted a man leaping into the scene on a dapple gray stallion. "Red Legs! Bloody, bleeding, murderin', connivin' Red Legs!"

"Reg Legs!" came another shout.

And they all let out with a sound near and dear to Malachi at that moment.

A Rebel cry went up. Savage, sweet, beautiful to his ears.

He watched as the six horsemen charged the scene. They were in plumed hats and railroad coats, no uniforms, and yet he thought he knew who they were. He was sure that he recognized the young man on the dapple gray mare.

He did. These boys had been with Quantrill. He knew two of them. Frank and Jesse James. Jesse had been a bare kid when he had tasted his first blood, but then lots of boys had become men quickly in the war.

Now this little group was probably headed home, toward southern Missouri. They still seemed young. Even with the war over. But then, Quantrill had depended on young blood, youthful, eager, savage raiders.

Quantrill was dead now. Bloody Bill Anderson was dead, and Little Archie Clement was dead. Archie who had loved to scalp his enemies. Archie had been with the bushwhackers who had so savagely mowed down the contingent of Union officers sent to catch them, the contingent that had included Shannon's fiancé...

Well, Malachi didn't think much of bushwhackers, but these boys had come just in time. Maybe Shannon would accept rescue. Maybe she would keep her mouth closed. But he had to get to her.

He could barely see through the tangle of fighting men and horses, bushwhackers and jayhawkers. He rose, staring over the wavering light of the fires.

He heard a high-pitched scream, and his heart thudded painfully.

He looked between a pair of horses as they danced, a deadly dance for their riders. In the gap he could see Bear. The man was cutting Kristin loose from the tree and throwing her over his shoulder.

Roger Holstein broke away from the battle and joined Bear. Wills, with his bloody toe, ran after them, too.

"Damn it, no!" Malachi swore. Where was Shannon? He couldn't see her. Did the bushwhackers have her, too?

No, they didn't, not that group, anyway. Bear and Holstein and Wills had mounted and pulled away. They were heading fast for the trail, heading west.

"Damn it, no!" Malachi raged again, pushing his way through the warring bushwhackers and jayhawkers, racing toward the Union horses. Bear was gone with Kristin, long gone before he could reach them.

"Malachi!"

It was Shannon. He whirled around in time to see one of the James brothers racing along beside her and sweeping her up onto his mount.

"Hey, you got yourself a girl, Frank!" One of the other riders laughed.

"Not just a girl, Jessie! D'you know who this is?"

"Who?"

"That Yankee-lovin' McCahy brat! Had herself hitched up to one for a while, before we did him in—ouch!" he screamed, looking down at the girl thrown over his saddle, then up at his brother again. "She bites."

"Yellow-bellied bushwhackers!" Shannon screamed. But Malachi sensed something different in her screams, in the sound of her voice.

He heard the pain.

She knew now that these men had been there the day when Robert Ellsworth had been killed, and she would never ask for their mercy.

"Shannon!" he thundered her name over the clash of steel and the explosion of gunfire.

"Let's go!" Frank shouted. He fired a number of shots into the air.

Malachi had swung around, racing toward Frank, when one of the Red Legs jumped in front of him, his sword drawn.

He didn't have time for a fight!

The mounted bushwhackers were gathering together. They had come, they had done their damage. Now they were riding away.

The Red Legs with the sword lunged toward Malachi.

"Ah, hell!" Malachi swore, engaging in the battle. The fellow wasn't a bad swordsman. In fact, he did damned well.

He grinned at Malachi as their swords locked at the hilt. "West Point, class of '58."

"Good for you, ya bloody Yank!" Malachi retorted. He pulled away, parrying a sudden thrust, ducking another.

The riders were pounding farther and farther away, into the night.

"You're good, Reb!" his opponent called.

"Thanks, and you're in my way, Yank," Malachi replied.

"In your way? Why, you're almost dead, man!"

"No, sir, you are almost dead."

Always fight with a cool head...

It had been one of the first rules that Malachi had ever learned. His comment had provoked his opponent. It was the advantage he needed.

The Red Legs lifted his sword high for a smashing blow. Malachi thrust straight, catching the man quickly and cleanly through the heart.

He fell without a whimper.

Malachi pulled his sword clean and leaped away from his fallen foe, swinging to counter any new attack.

But he was alone.

Alone with a sea of corpses.

At least twelve of the Red Legs lay dead, strewn here and there over their camp bags, over their saddles, over their weapons; some shot and some thrust through by swords. Only one of the raiders lay on the ground. A very young boy with a clear complexion.

He groaned. Malachi stooped beside him, carefully turning him over. Blood stained his shirt. Malachi opened it quickly. There was no way the boy could live. He'd been riddled with shot in the chest. Malachi pressed the tail ends of the shirt hard against him, trying to staunch the flow of blood. The boy opened his eyes.

"I'm going to die, captain, ain't I?"

He might have said something else, but the boy already knew. Malachi nodded. "The pain will be gone, boy."

"I can't die. I got tobacco in my pocket. Ma would just kill me. That's a laugh, ain't it? But she'd be awful, awful disappointed in me."

"I'll get that tobacco out, boy," Malachi said.

The youth's eyes had already closed again. Malachi thought that the boy had heard him, though. It seemed that his lip curled into a grateful smile just as the life left his eyes.

Malachi eased the boy to the ground. Someone would come, and someone would find him.

This was border country still. He might be sent to his home.

Malachi dug the tobacco out of the boy's pocket and tossed it over one of the older Red Legs. "Your ma won't find no tobacco, boy," he said softly. Then he stood and he looked around at the sea of dead again.

The clearing was absurdly silent and peaceful now. Its inhabitants all lay quiet, tumbled atop one another as if they rested in a strange and curious sleep. He walked among them quickly, cursing to himself, but he couldn't just leave a man if he was wounded, whether he was a Reb or a Yank.

He needn't have worried. Every one of the Red Legs in the clearing was dead. Dead, and growing cold.

Malachi stepped from the clearing and looked down the road. He stared up at the night sky. The silence was all around him. The sound of horses' hooves had died away in the distance.

"Damn!" he swore.

The Red Legs had taken Kristin in one direction.

The raiders had taken Shannon the opposite way.

Which the hell did he follow?

He didn't take long to decide. He would get Shannon first. He could bargain with the James boys, he was sure. If Shannon could keep quiet for about two seconds he could get her back quickly. He would go after Shannon first.

Though for the life of him, he wasn't at all sure why.

Chapter Five

Shannon could not remember a more miserable night in her life.

The raider party traveled through what remained of it. Somewhere, at the beginning, she had said something that the men really hadn't liked—though she couldn't see where they would like anything that she had to say to them—and she had been bound hand and foot and gagged and tossed over the haunches of the horse.

Then they had begun to ride, in earnest.

They knew their territory. They followed no specific route. They traveled over plains and through tangles of bracken and brush.

They talked about going home, and they talked about the friend they had left behind.

"Willie was dead, shot in the chest, there wasn't nothing that we could do. He went down fighting."

"Yeah, he went down fighting. Well, the war's over. Someone ought to find him and give his body to his ma."

"Yeah, someone ought to find him."

"God help him."

"God help us all."

For a while, Shannon listened to their words, but she couldn't believe that they would try to invoke God's aid, and then, as they kept on quietly conversing, she began to weave in and out of reality. She couldn't understand them anymore.

She knew who they were. The remnants of Quantrill's Raiders. They had ridden with Quantrill. They had ridden with Bloody Bill Anderson, and with little Archie Clement.

They might well have been with the raiders on a bloody awful day outside Centralia when the bushwhackers had massacred the small contingent of green recruits sent after them. When they had dismembered the corpses and the dying, scalped them and sliced off ears and noses and privates to be stuffed down their throats...

It was how Captain Robert Ellsworth had died. And as she lay trussed and tossed over the haunches of the horse, it made her feel faint, and it made her feel ill.

The night went on and on.

Then Shannon realized that it wasn't night anymore, it was day. They had traveled miles and miles without rest, or if they had paused to rest, she had been unconscious when they had done so.

It was no longer night. It was day. The sun streamed overhead, and the songs of larks could be heard on the air. Somewhere nearby, a brook bubbled and played.

They had come so far. So very far. She wondered bleakly where Kristin was. She had been so certain that when the Red Legs had settled down and slept, she would have been able to slip in and free her sister.

But then the men had come for her.

And now Kristin was being taken one way, and she was being taken another.

And where was Malachi? He had been there. She had seen him firing and fighting, and then he had disappeared. And then she had seen him again just when she had been swept up into the arms of the bushwhacker.

He had probably followed Kristin, she thought. He had gone for his brother's wife. And she was glad of it, Shannon thought. She was so glad of it, because the men might well hurt Kristin...

What were these men going to do with her?

The gag choked her, making her feel ill all over again. They knew her. They knew that she was old McCahy's daughter, and that her sympathy had been with the North. They surely knew that she was Cole Slater's sister-in-law, but that probably wouldn't count for much. She had been engaged to marry a Union officer, she was the sister of a Union officer, and they knew that she hated them with every breath in her body.

What would they do to her?

And what could be worse than this torture she had already endured, hanging hour after hour over the horse this way, her face slamming against the sweaty flesh and hair and flanks of the animal? She ached in every muscle of her body. It would never, never end.

Then suddenly, at last, they stopped.

Hands wound around her waist, pulling her from the horse. Had she been able to, she would have screamed at the sudden agony of the movement; it felt as if her arms were breaking.

"There you go, Yank," the man said, setting her down beneath a tree. The others were dismounting. They formed a semicircle around her, all of them staring at her.

"What are we going to do with her, Frank?"

The man who asked the question stepped forward. His name was Jesse, Shannon knew that much. And he was Frank's brother. The two of them had spoken occasionally during the endless ride.

Neither of them was much older than she, but they both carried a curious coldness in their eyes. Perhaps they had ceased to feel; perhaps they had even lost a sense of humanity in all the violence of their particular war. She didn't know. And at that moment, she was so worn and exhausted, she wasn't even sure that she cared.

"I wonder what the Red Legs wanted with her," Jesse mused.

"Same thing any man would want with her, I reckon," someone spoke up from the rear. Shannon blinked, trying to see him. He was tall and dark-haired with a pencil-slim mus-

tache, and he smiled at her in such a way that she felt entirely
naked.

She closed her eyes. At that particular moment, she just
wanted to die. Bushwhackers. The same men who had brutalized Robert might be about to touch her. Death would be
infinitely better.

"Better loosen up that gag," the one named Jesse said.
"We're losing her, I think. She's going to pass out on us."

Frank stepped forward, slipping the gag from her mouth.
Shannon fought a sudden wave of nausea. He leaned over her
and slit the ropes tying her wrists and ankles. Her blood started
to flow again, but she could still barely move. She rubbed her
wrists, backing against the tree, staring at the lot of them.
There were five of them left. Jesse and Frank, Jesse with a
round young face and dark, attractive eyes, Frank taller and
leaner, older. There was the dark-haired man who taunted, and
two smaller, light-haired men. Maybe they were brothers, too,
she didn't know.

"What's your name?" Jesse asked.

She stared at him in furious silence. They seemed to know
everything else. They ought to know her name.

"Shannon. Shannon McCahy," the tall, dark-haired one
said. "She was picked up with her sister when the Federals
decided to put all the families away. She was there when the
house fell apart, when Bill's sister and those other girls were
killed and wounded."

"Then she's a Southerner—" Jesse began.

Frank snorted and spit on the ground. "She ain't no Southerner, Jesse. You heard her. She's Yank through and through.
Just like her blue-belly pa with the yellow streak down his
back—"

Movement came back to her. She felt no pain. Like a bolt
of lightning, Shannon flew at the man in a rage. She did so
with such force that he went flying to the ground. "You murderers!" she hissed. "You hideous rodents...murderers!"
Pummeling the startled man who couldn't seem to fight her

fury, Shannon then saw the gun in his belt. She grabbed it and aimed it straight at his nose. The others had been about to seize her. She swung around with Frank's Colt, aiming it right at Jesse. He lifted his hands and backed away.

"We didn't kill your pa, little girl," Jesse said softly. "We weren't there. Zeke Moreau had his own splinter group. You know that."

She gritted her teeth, thinking about Robert, trembling inwardly at the depth of the hate that seared her. She could have pulled the trigger. She would have happily maimed or wounded or killed any one of them. When she thought about Centralia...

Jesse knelt in front of her, speaking earnestly. "You're just seeing one side of it, you know. One side. They came in—the jayhawkers, the Red Legs—they came in and ripped us all up really bad, too, you know. We all got farms burned down or kin slain. It always did work two ways—"

"Two ways!" Shannon exclaimed. "Two ways!" She was choking. "I never heard of anything as bad as Centralia. Ever. In the town, unarmed men were stripped and shot down. And outside the town, the things you people did to the Union men shouldn't have been done to the lowest of creatures, much less human beings—"

"You obviously haven't seen much of the handiwork done by your friends, the Red Legs," the tall, dark man said dryly.

"You ain't gonna change her mind," Frank said from the ground.

The dark-haired man moved closer, a wary eye on the Colt. "My name is Justin Waller, Miss McCahy. And I was there, at Centralia—"

"Bastard!" Shannon hissed.

"Justin—" Jesse warned sharply, but Shannon already had the gun aimed straight between Justin Waller's eyes. She pulled the trigger.

And she heard the click of an empty chamber.

"Son of a bitch!" Justin swore. He reached for Shannon.

She couldn't escape him quickly enough and he dragged her to her feet. She screamed as he twisted her arm hard behind her back.

"Justin—" Jesse began.

"That bitch meant to kill me!"

"Don't hurt her. We don't know what we're doing with her yet."

"I know what I'm gonna do with her," Justin growled savagely. His free hand played over her throat and the rise of her breasts, which had been left bare when the Red Legs had ripped her shirt. The little pink flowers and white linen of her corset were absurdly delicate against the tattered fragments of the man's ranch shirt.

Shannon recoiled, kicking out desperately. Justin pulled harder upon her arm and she choked back another scream of pain. He pressed her to her knees. "Get me some rope, Jesse. I'm too damned tired to truly enjoy what I intend to do with this little beauty. And she can't be trusted an inch."

Jesse lifted a length of rope from his saddle pommel, but he stared at Justin contemplatively as he walked toward him. "We ain't decided about her yet, Justin."

"We ain't decided what?" Justin had his knee in Shannon's back as he looped the rope around her wrists.

She gritted her teeth against the pain.

"She's kin to Cole Slater," Jesse said softly. "And I never did cotton to the idea of rape and murder, Justin."

"You rode with Quantrill."

"Quantrill didn't murder women."

"All right, Jesse. All right. I ain't gonna murder her."

"You're right, you ain't. I'm in control here."

"War's over, Jesse."

"I'm still in control here, you understand that."

Justin jerked hard on the rope, then shoved Shannon flat on the ground. She tasted dirt as he grasped her ankles and began looping a knot around them.

"Maybe we oughta just let her go," one of the light-haired

men said. "Hell, Justin, we ain't supposed to rape our own kind—"

"She ain't our own kind. And if we just let her go, she'll have the law down on us so fast our heads will spin. That is, if she doesn't get hold of another gun. She shot at me, you fools. She meant to kill me. And you all say what you want, she's going to pay for that."

He jerked hard on the last of his knots. He reached for Shannon's shoulders and dragged her face up close to his. "Bitch, when I wake up, we're going to have some real, real fun."

Shannon spit at him.

Swearing, he wiped his face and tossed her down hard beneath the tree. He stared at the four others, who were looking his way. "And you all can watch, join in or turn the other way, I just don't give a damn."

Shannon watched Jesse James set his jaw hard. "I'm in control here, Justin. We agreed. Don't you forget that."

Justin ignored Jesse and went to his horse. He loosened his saddle and pulled it off and threw it beneath the tree next to Shannon. He fumbled through his saddlebags for a canteen. Looking furiously at the other men, he walked down a grassy slope to the fresh-running spring water of a stream.

"Water," Frank James muttered, following Justin.

Jesse remained, staring at Shannon. She didn't know what he was thinking. "Lots of people lost in this war," he told her quietly. "Hell, ma'am, I do not like half the things I learned to do, but I doubt that I'll ever forget them. We all want to remember the weddings and the christenings and the flowers in the fields on a Sunday. Hell, I never really wanted to get so damned good at killing. I just did." He paused. "You shouldn'ta shot at Justin. It was a mistake."

"He's an animal. He was there—at Centralia. You heard him."

"You still shouldn't have tried to kill him. You got his temper up way high."

He turned away from her. Justin was back, drinking water from his canteen. It spilled over his face and trickled down his jaw. It reminded Shannon just how desperately thirsty she was. He stared at her, and she saw he knew of her thirst. He smiled and drank more deeply.

She wasn't going to beg. Not of a man like that.

Frank James was back by then, too. He was drinking from a wooden Confederate-issue canteen with his initials engraved into the wood. He looked at her, then knelt by her, lifting her head.

"Don't give her no water!" Justin said irritably. "I'll give it to her." He smiled, nudging at Shannon's rump with an evil leer. "If she's good, if she's real good, she'll get some water. You'll see, my friends. Old Justin knows how to take a Yankee shrew."

Frank ignored him, lifting Shannon's head, allowing a trickle of water to cool her face and seep into her mouth. She drank it thirstily.

"Frank!" Justin swore.

Frank told Justin what he should do with himself, and Justin jumped to his feet. Shannon watched the two men with interest, her heart thundering. If they would just rip each other to shreds...

Jesse, who was now leaning against the tree, paring off a bite of dried beef from a strip he'd taken from his saddlebags, spoke sarcastically. "That's good, you two. Real good. Kill each other. She's enjoying every minute of it."

Both men stopped. They stared at her.

"Let's all get some sleep," Jesse said. "You want her that bad, Justin, the girl's yours. But don't kill her. I ain't no murderer of women and children, and I ain't ever gonna be."

He stretched out on the ground, leaning his head upon his saddle. Frank swore and chose another tree.

The two light-haired men found their own shade, and Justin smiled as he settled down beside Shannon. She stared at him, her face against the earth, hating him. He laughed and reached out, slipping his arm around her, twisting her over and pulling her close against him. She squirmed and struggled, choking on the tears that threatened to stream down her face. "Bastard, I swear I'd just as soon die!" she hissed vehemently.

Justin laughed at her futile efforts. Tied hand and foot as she was, she wasn't going to do anything.

His hand hooked beneath her breasts as he pulled her against his chest and the curve of his body. His fingers played over her breasts and rested there. He whispered against her ear. "Just a few hours of sleep, honey. I apologize for being so exhausted. But just a little bit of sleep...I wouldn't want to disappoint you. I want to hear you scream and scream and scream..." Laughing again, he leaned his head back against his saddle, seeking sleep.

Shannon closed her eyes and set her teeth. She gave him time to fall asleep, then tried to edge away from him.

His hand tightened around her like a clamp. "Not on your life, my golden Yank. Not on your life." His fingers moved through her hair. Shannon held her breath, praying that he would stop.

He did. He dug into his saddlebags for another length of rope and grimly tied her wrists to his own. Shannon watched him in bitter silence. When he was done, he smiled and touched her cheek. "You're a beautiful Yank-lover, you know that?"

She ignored him. He lay down to sleep again, chuckling.

Shannon lay awake in misery until absolute exhaustion overwhelmed her. Despite her hunger and thirst and discomfort, she closed her eyes, and sleep claimed her.

To the best of Malachi's knowledge, there was no one on the lookout for the James boys.

But they were riding as if their lives depended on getting into the heart of Missouri just as fast as possible.

And they were hard to track. By the time he'd reached his

bay and found Shannon's big black gelding, the raiders were already well ahead of him.

And they knew where they were going. Thank God they had turned southward, deeper into Missouri. It was land he knew. If he hadn't been accustomed to the terrain, he'd never have managed to follow them. They cut a course right through forest lands, knowing unerringly where they could take short-cuts and pick up roads again and disappear back into the forests again.

By midmorning he realized that they were following the course of a small stream. Malachi stuck with it.

He was exhausted. His leg was aching, and he was afraid that the fever might be searing through him again. An hour's worth of sleep just might make it a bit better...

But he didn't dare take an hour. He knew Frank and Jesse James only slightly. He'd met them once in the short time that Cole had ridden with Quantrill, and he'd found them to be reckless, sometimes ruthless kids. He thought it might be the Younger brothers traveling with them, another set of reckless youths.

He didn't think that the James boys were especially cruel or brutal. They were still sane, at least, he thought. Like the Younger brothers. They were probably still sane, if nothing else.

But the other man...

His name was Justin. Malachi knew who he was. Cole had seen him in action early on in the war, and the malice with which the man killed and the pleasure he took from his brutal actions had turned Cole away from Quantrill's gang completely.

But to the most decent bushwhacker out there, Shannon would be quite a tonic to swallow. And she wouldn't keep quiet. She wouldn't be able to do so. He had already heard her ranting and raving.

He didn't have time to rest, not for ten damn minutes.

He paused only to give the horses water, and to douse himself with it, and drink deeply. He chewed on the dried meat he had brought, and swallowed some of the liquor Shannon had packed him. It was good, and it helped to keep the pain in his leg at bay.

It was almost night again when he came upon them at last.

He was still a little distance away when he saw the horses grouped in the trees. There were no cooking fires laid out in the camp; in fact, it was barely a camp at all. The bushwhackers had merely stopped along the road.

Malachi was pretty sure that he'd be able to reason with the men; hell, at least they had obstensibly fought on the same side. But the war had taught him to take nothing for granted, so he dismounted from the bay and tethered her with the black gelding some distance down the stream from the raiders. Then he approached them again in silence, coming close enough this time to see the layout in the camp.

They must have been sure of themselves; very sure. No one was left on guard. Each and every one of the bushwhackers was curled up, sound asleep.

Or maybe they weren't so sound asleep. Men like that learned to sleep differently, with one eye open. If a fly buzzed through that camp, the men would probably be aware of it. He'd be a fool to go sneaking in, no matter how silently he could manage it.

And as he had suspected, Shannon was in trouble.

The Younger brothers were stretched out in front of an oak; the others were all laid out beneath other trees, thirty yards apart, and perhaps fifty yards up the grassy slope from the stream.

Shannon was bound hand and foot, and tied to Justin.

He swore inwardly, thinking she must have fought them tooth and nail, because she seemed to have lost Jesse's protection. Jesse, like many other bushwhackers, despite their savagery, still put Southern womanhood on a pedestal. If she had just kept her mouth closed and acted out the part of the Southern belle...

But she hadn't.

Sweat broke out on Malachi's forehead and his hands went clammy as he watched her. She was pale and smudged with dirt, but even so, her features retained their angelic beauty, and her tangled hair swept around her face like a glorious halo. Where the sun fell upon it her hair glowed like golden fire.

She was tied to Justin—but at least she was decently clad. She seemed to sleep the sleep of the dead, but even in that sleep, it seemed she strained with all her heart against the man holding her prisoner.

He hadn't touched her yet. Justin hadn't touched her, Malachi assured himself. But he meant to do so.

At the periphery of the circle, Malachi inhaled and exhaled deeply, deciding what plan of action to take. He could try shooting them all, but the bushwhackers were damned good shots, and if he didn't kill Justin right away, he was certain that Justin would kill Shannon for the pure pleasure of it.

No. This wasn't the time to go in blazing away. He needed to play diplomat.

He stood at the periphery of the camp, his saber and his pistols at his side, but his arms relaxed. "Jesse. Jesse James!" he called out sharply.

They moved as one. As soon as he called out, the five of them were awake, staring at him down the length of their Colts and revolvers.

He lifted his hands. He saw five pairs of eyes look over his gray uniform jacket.

By the tree, Jesse stood.

"Malachi!" Shannon called out. "Malachi!" She struggled to rise. Justin jerked on the rope and clamped his hand hard over her mouth.

Malachi nodded toward Justin, trying to burn a message into Shannon's fool head with the strength of his eyes.

"Hey! It's the fool Reb who was taking on the whole of that Red Legs camp by himself!" One of the Younger brothers called out.

"Malachi. Malachi Slater," Jesse said. He walked forward, wary still, but a smile on his face. "You're Cole Slater's brother, right? Hey, they got a whole pack of wanted posters out on you, did you know that?"

"Yeah, I know it. But thanks for the warning."

"What are you doing here about? Heading south? It might be best if you were to take a hike into Mexico."

"Well," Malachi said, "I can't rightly do that yet, you know. I got to tie up with my brothers somewhere. And the Red Legs have got Cole's wife. That's what was going on when you fellows showed up there today. Those men report to a man named Hayden Fitz, and he wants my brother dead. We Slaters stick together; I can't leave yet."

One of the Younger brothers stood up. "Hey, Captain Slater. I seen Jamie. About two weeks ago. He knows about the posters, and he's making his way south. Thought you ought to know."

"Thanks. Thanks a lot. That's real good to hear."

Malachi smiled at the Younger brothers, then turned his eyes on Justin. He strode across the clearing between the trees and lowered himself down on the balls of his feet, staring straight into Justin's eyes.

"I've come for her."

"Well, now, Captain Slater, I'm rightly sorry. She's mine."

Shannon bit his hand. Justin let out a yelp, freeing her mouth, bringing his sore palm to his own mouth.

"Malachi—"

"Shut up, Shannon."

"Malachi—"

"Shut up, Shannon," he said again, smiling with clenched teeth. He stunned her by sending her a smart slap right across the face. She gasped. Tears that she would never shed brightened the blue beauty of her eyes.

"Justin, I don't prowl the countryside for just any woman. This one is mine. We're engaged to be married."

Shannon gasped, and Malachi glared at her.

Justin laughed crudely. "That won't wash, captain. That won't wash one little bit. I know all about this feisty little Yank lover. She hates Rebs. I don't think she even knows the difference between the bushwhackers and the regular army, captain. She just hates Rebs. I thought that I should give her a good taste of Johnny Reb, how about that, captain?"

There was no respect in his tone. There was an underlying hint of violence.

"She'll get a good taste of Reb. She's my fiancée, and I want her back now."

Malachi leaned across Justin with his knife and quickly slit the ropes holding Shannon down. She leaped to her feet, rubbing her wrists, and ran behind him. Malachi stood quickly as Justin leaped to his feet. The men stared at one another.

Malachi reached his hand behind him. "Come here, Shannon. Shannon—darlin'!—get your sweet...soul over here, ya hear?"

He grabbed her hand and jerked her up beside him. "Tell them, darlin'."

"What?" she whispered desperately.

"Tell them that you don't hate all Rebs."

She was silent. He sensed the turmoil in her, even as he breathed in the soft sweet scent of her perfume, still clinging to her despite the dirt that smudged her face.

He was ready to strangle her himself.

"Tell them!"

"I—" She was choking on the words, really choking on them. "I—I don't hate all Rebs."

"She ain't your fiancée!" Frank James said.

"She is!" Malachi insisted, his frustration growing. He swung Shannon around, none too gently, and brought her into his arms. "Darlin'!" he exclaimed, and he pulled her close. He stared into her sky-blue eyes, his own on fire.

Her eyes widened; it seemed that at last that she had discovered her own predicament, and realized that her freedom might well hinge on her ability to act.

"Yes! Yes!" She threw her arms around him. Her breasts pressed hard against his chest and her fingers played with the hair at his nape.

And her lips came full and soft and crushing against his.

There was a curious audience before them, and their very lives were hanging in the balance.

And at that instance, it didn't seem to matter.

He locked his arms around her, setting his hands upon the small of her back and bringing the whole of her body hard against his. His lips parted over hers, and in the breath of a second, he found himself the aggressor, heedless of the men watching. He thrust his tongue deep into the sweet crevice of her mouth, feeling the warmth and fever of her reach out and invade him. He held her tighter and tighter, and raped her mouth with the sheer demand of his own. The tension of it seared into the fullness of his body. Then she brought her hands between them, pressing hard against his chest, and he finally lifted his lips from hers, and stared into her wide, startled and glimmering eyes.

Glimmering...with fury, he thought. He only prayed that she had the sense to keep silent until they were away.

If they did get away.

One of the Younger brothers laughed. "Hot damn, but I believe him. That was one of the most sultry kisses I've ever seen. Set me burning for a bit o' lovin', that's for sure."

Shannon's lashes fell over her eyes. Malachi heard her teeth grate together as he swept her around him. "Jesse, she's mine. And I'm taking her."

"You got my go ahead," Jesse said. "Frank?"

Frank shrugged. "The man is still wearing a gray uniform, and he says that the girl is his. Guess it must be so."

There was a sound like a growl from Justin. "Well, captain, I don't say that it's so. The girl tried to kill me. I got a score to settle with her."

"She tried to kill you?" Malachi repeated, playing for time.

He didn't doubt one bit that Shannon had tried to kill any of them.

"That's right," Jesse said, sighing. "Why, Justin would be dead right now if Frank's gun hadn't been empty."

Malachi smiled, arching a brow. "What was she doing with Frank's gun?" he asked politely.

Every one of the bushwhackers flushed, except Justin, and he kept staring at Malachi with hatred in his eyes.

"I untied her," Frank James muttered. "I felt sorry for her, gagged and tied. She jumped me."

"She jumped you?"

"Captain, if you know that woman so well, you know that she's a damned hellcat, a bloody little spitfire." He swore again. "She's more dangerous than the whole lot of us."

Malachi lowered his head, adjusting the brim of his hat to hide the smile that teased at his lips. They weren't in the clear yet.

He looked up again, gravely, at Jesse. "Not much harm done, was there? I mean, the gun was empty. Justin looks alive and well and healthy to me."

"You ain't takin' her, Slater," Justin said.

Malachi inhaled deeply. "I am taking her, Justin."

"Maybe she ought to apologize to Justin," Jesse suggested. "Maybe that will smooth things over a bit."

"Oh, yeah," Justin said, tightening his lips, and leaning back with a certain pleasure. "Sure. Let's see this. You get her to apologize, captain."

"Shannon, apologize to the man."

She had been silent for several minutes, a long time for Shannon. She had stood behind him and at his side, quiet and meek. He gripped her fingers, drawing her in front of him. He hissed against her ear. "Shannon! Apologize."

"I will not!" she exploded. "He is a bloody, vicious, sadistic murder—"

Malachi's hand clamped over her mouth. Justin stood in a

silent fury. Frank James laughed, and Jesse didn't make a move or say a word at all.

"Your woman don't obey you real well, Captain Slater," Frank observed.

Malachi swept his arm around her, jerking her beneath his chin, laying his fingers taut over her rib cage and squeezing hard. "She's gonna obey me just fine." He lowered his voice, whispering against her earlobe. "'Cause if she doesn't obey me damned fast, I'm going to leave. I'm going to tell Justin to go ahead and enjoy himself to his heart's content—"

"He is a cold-blooded murderer!" Shannon whispered back. He sensed the tears in her voice, but he couldn't afford to care.

"Apologize!" he told her.

She inhaled deeply. He felt the hatred and the fury that swept from her in great waves, and he wondered if he would always be included in that pool of bitter hatred and rage. "I'm sorry that I tried to kill you," she spit out to Justin. She lowered her head. "And I'm sorry that I failed!" she whispered miserably.

Malachi tightened his hold upon her so that she gasped, but as he looked around, he realized, thankfully, that he was the only one who had heard her last words.

He smiled. "All right?"

He didn't want to give them all time to think. "Thanks, boys. I never would have made it against the Red Legs without your help. Be seeing you."

He adjusted his hat and shoved Shannon around, daring to bare his back to the raiders. They wouldn't shoot a Confederate officer in the back.

Even bushwhackers had a certain code of ethics.

He walked several feet, hurrying Shannon ahead of him.

"Slater!"

He stopped, pushing her forward, turning around.

Justin was walking toward him. "Captain Slater, they're letting you take the woman. I'm not."

Malachi stiffened. He stared at Justin. It was a direct challenge, and there was no way out of it.

"No, Malachi!" Shannon cried, racing to him. He shoved her back again, not daring to take his eyes off Justin.

"Then I guess it's between you and me," he said softly.

"That's right, captain. That's what it boils down to."

"Swords or pistols?"

"Draw when you're ready, captain—" Justin began, but he never finished. His eyes suddenly rolled up in his head and he fell to the ground with a curious, silent grace.

Jesse was standing there. He had just clobbered Justin with the butt of a Spencer repeater. He smiled at Malachi.

"I don't know what would have happened, captain, but you've got a powerful reputation as a crack shot. Of course, Justin is pretty damned good himself. One of you would have died. And I'm just sick of the bloodshed, you know. I figure the Yanks killed enough of us that we don't need to run around killin' one another, not now, not when we're all trying to get home for a spell. So you take your little hellcat and you go on, Captain Slater. Head for Mexico, as fast as you can. The best of luck to you, captain."

Malachi turned from the man on the ground to Jesse. He nodded slowly. Then he turned around. Shannon was still standing there, and he grasped her elbow firmly and pulled her along with him. "Come on!" he whispered to her when she seemed to be balking.

Jesse was still watching them. Malachi put his arm around Shannon's shoulder and pulled her close against him. She looked back once and didn't seem to want to protest, not one bit.

He hurried them down the slope to the embankment of the spring, then rushed along the embankment.

Darkness was coming once again. He wanted to sleep...badly. But he wanted to put some mean distance between them and Justin before he paused to sleep.

He didn't need to urge Shannon along. As soon as they had

left the raiders behind, she broke away from him and started to run. Her hair streamed behind her, and in the darkening twilight, he heard the soft, sobbing gasps of her breath as she hurried.

Groaning, he ran after her.

She meant to put distance between herself and the raiders, too. She ran so hard and so fast that she was quickly past the spot where he had tethered their horses.

"Shannon!"

He hurried after her. It was almost as if she hadn't heard him. She was probably furious, he thought wearily. She was angry because he had made her apologize. Because he had kissed her.

He had more than kissed her. He had kissed her and touched with an invasion so deep that the intimacy invoked could never be forgotten.

Nor, for her part, he was certain, forgiven.

"Shannon!"

Cursing the pain in his leg, he ran after her with greater speed. At last he caught up with her. She stumbled and fell, rolling down the grassy slope until she was nearly in the water. Malachi followed, dropping down beside her. Her eyes were huge and luminous and moist, a beautiful, glittering blue, still wet with tears. She stared at the sky unblinkingly while he knelt by her.

"Shannon! Damn it, I'm sorry. You fool! You damned bloody little fool. Didn't you understand? I had to get you out of there. Justin is a murdering sadist, and that's exactly why you don't mess with a man like him." He sighed. "All right, hellcat. Stay angry. Tear me up again whenever you get the chance. But for now, we've got to get on the road. We need to ride—"

"Malachi!"

She shot up suddenly and ran straight into his arms. She laid her cheek against his chest, and he felt the terrible beating of her heart and the shivering that seized the whole of her body. The soft cream mounds of her breasts rose above the pink-flowered white cups of her corset, brushing against the rough material of his wool greatcoat. Her hands seemed frail and delicate where they fell against him.

"Oh, Malachi!"

And she burst into tears.

He put his arms around her and he kissed the top of her head. He held her tight against him.

Hellcat. It was an apt name for her, but his little hellcat had broken. The war had made her build an impenetrable shield around herself. She was strong as steel and tough as nails, and no one, no one commanded Shannon McCahy.

But now...

Her shield had shattered and broken, and he wasn't sure that he could stand up to the soft and delicate beauty beneath it.

"It's all right. It's over. It's—"

"Malachi, thank you. Oh, my God, you came for me. You—you took me from him. Thank you!"

He curved his hand around her cheek, and he smoothed the tears from her face with his thumb. She stared at him, and her eyes were earnest and glorious, her hair a shroud of gold, cloaking her half-bared shoulders and breasts.

He swallowed hard and managed to stand. He reached down for her, lifting her high into his arms. "We have to ride," he told her.

She nodded trustingly. Her head fell against him. His boots sloshed through the stream as he walked toward the horses.

Chapter Six

When she was set on the black gelding, Shannon seemed well and eager to ride. Malachi was glad of it. He didn't know how long he could stay awake himself, but as long as they could, they would ride.

They crossed the stream, then followed along it. No words passed between them. When Malachi looked back in the darkness, he saw her slumped low in the saddle, but she didn't complain or suggest they stop. He had given her his greatcoat; her shirt was nothing but tatters now, and he didn't want to take the time to dig through his belongings for a new shirt for her. He wanted to move.

It was too late to steal Kristin back before the Red Legs left Missouri. They would have to travel deep into Kansas. The only benefit to that situation was that it was unlikely Justin would follow him into Kansas. There might be a bounty out on Malachi, but at least he had been regular army, not a bushwhacker. A man recognized as a bushwhacker in Kansas might not stand much of a chance.

"Shannon?"

"Yes," she called softly.

"You all right back there?"

"Yes."

"We'll go another hour."

"Fine."

They plodded onward. Where the stream forked, he took

the westward trail, telling her to walk the black gelding behind his bay mare in the rocky, shallow water. That way there would be no footprints for the bushwhackers to follow.

With the first light, he reined in. There was a perfect little copse beside the water. It was sheltered by magnificent oaks, and grass grew there like a blanket. On one side of the stream, the water deepened in a small natural pond. It was just like the swimming hole back home where he and Cole and Jamie had roughhoused after working hours, and where the neighborhood girls had come to watch and giggle from the trees, and where, sometimes, the young ladies had boldly determined to join them. He smiled, thinking about those days. They had been so long ago.

Malachi realized that Shannon had reined up behind him. "This is it," he said softly. "We'll rest here."

Nodding, she moved to dismount and missed her footing. She fell flat into the water on her rear and lay sprawled, apparently too tired to move.

Malachi dismounted and hunkered down in front of her, smiling. "Hey. Come on out of the water."

She nodded, barely. Her eyes fell on his, dazed.

He flicked water on her face and saw the surprise and then the anger spark her eyes. "You do need a bath," he told her. Dirt still smudged her face. "Badly. But this doesn't seem to be the right time. Come on, I'll help you out."

His greatcoat had fallen open, exposing the lace and flowers of her corset. When he went to take her hand, his fingers brushed over the lace, and over the firm satiny flush that rose above the border. Warmth sizzled straight to his loins, and he paused, stunned by the strength of the feeling. He shook his head, irritated with himself, and grabbed her hands. "Up, Shannon, damn it, get up."

Sensing the sudden anger in him, she staggered to her feet, using his hand for support.

"You're soaked. Let's get up on the bank."

Thank God he was exhausted, he told himself. Really so

exhausted that he couldn't even think about what the sight of her did...

She sighed softly as they cleared the water, throwing his coat from her shoulders and sinking down to remove her boots. Her hair, touched by the pale, new light of the coming morning, glowed with a fiery radiance and teased the flesh of her shoulders and breasts. He didn't touch her at all, but the warmth sizzled through him again, making his heart pump too fast and his tired body come alive.

Maybe it was impossible to be too exhausted.

He gritted his teeth and swore.

She paused in surprise. "Malachi, what's wrong?"

When had she learned to make those blue eyes so innocent and so damned sultry all in one? And her hair, just falling over one eye now...

"What's wrong?" he yelled at her. "All I was trying to do was get Kristin back from the Red Legs, and instead I'm running over half of Missouri to get you back from a pack of bushwhackers. And did you try to use one ounce of sense in the hands of death? No, Shannon, you just provoke them further, and almost get us both killed."

She jumped to her feet. She was trembling, he saw.

"You don't understand. You don't understand and you can't understand. You weren't there when my pa was killed, and you didn't get to hear, in rumor and in truth, day after day after day, what was done to the men outside Centralia. You don't—"

"Shannon, I fought in the war. I know all about dying."

"It wasn't the dying!" Tears glittered brightly in her eyes, but she wouldn't shed them, she wouldn't break down again, and he knew it. "It wasn't the dying. It was the way that they died. He admitted it; that bastard admitted that he had been there, outside Centralia. He might have been the one who—who...Malachi, they had to pick up his pieces! They had to pick up Robert's pieces. I loved him, I loved him so much."

Her face was smudged but her chin was high, and her eyes

were even more beautiful fevered with emotion. He felt her pain, and he wished heartily that he had never spoken to her. She still didn't understand. Justin just might want to do the same damned thing to her, if he could get his hands on her again. She'd fought Justin anyway. Or maybe she had understood, and hadn't cared.

She stared at him, her head high, her hands on her hips, her passion like an aura around her. "I loved him, and that bastard helped dismember him!"

"It can't matter!" Malachi told her curtly. "You can't allow it to matter right now!"

"You don't understand—"

"Maybe I don't understand, but you're not going to explain anything to me. No Yank is ever going to explain the horror of this war to a Confederate. We lost, remember? Oh, yes, of course, you're the one who likes to remind me of that fact."

"Maybe you do understand dying and killing. Maybe you just don't understand what love is."

"Shannon, you're a fool, and my life is none of your damned business."

"Malachi, damn you—"

"I don't want to listen right now, Shannon. I'm tired. I have to have some sleep," he said wearily. He didn't want to fight with her. He just didn't want to look at her anymore. He didn't want to see all the fire and excitement and beauty...and the pain and misery that haunted her.

He didn't want to desire her.

But he did.

He turned away from her, heading for the horses. For a moment he thought that she was going to run after him and continue the fight. But she didn't. She stayed still for several long minutes, tense, staring after him. Then she walked down to the water. He tried to ignore her as he unsaddled the horses and rolled out his bedroll and blanket beneath the largest oak. He hesitated, looked at her bedroll, rolled behind the seat of her saddle. He unrolled it, too, beside his own. He didn't want her too far away. He knew that he would awaken if footsteps came anywhere near them, but he was still wary of sleeping. Justin struck him as the type of man who worked hard toward vengeance.

He could hear her, drinking thirstily, splashing water, washing her face. Scrubbing her face and her hands again and again.

He threw himself down on the bedroll, using his saddle as a pillow and turning so he could keep an eye on her. Day was coming fast now. Sunlight played through the leaves and branches, caressing her hair and shoulders and arms. It rippled against the water in a magical dazzle.

"What are you doing?" he demanded.

"Scrubbing. Scrubbing away that awful bushwhacker!" she retorted.

"You can throw your whole body in later and scrub to your heart's content!" he called to her irritably. "Get out now. Let's get some sleep."

She turned around and saw him stretched out, then opened her mouth as if she was about to argue with him.

Maybe she was just tired. Maybe, just maybe, she was still a little bit grateful. Whatever, she closed her mouth and walked toward him.

She hesitated by her bedroll, looking at him. Strands of damp hair curled around her face, and its planes were delineated, soft and beautiful. Water beads hovered over her breasts.

He groaned inwardly and tipped his hat over his face. "Good night, Shannon."

"Perhaps I should move this." She indicated her bedroll.

"Lie down."

"I've never had to sleep this close to a Reb before."

"You slept with Justin just about on top of you yesterday."

She smiled with sweet sarcasm and widened her eyes. "I've never willingly slept this close to a Reb before."

"Willing or other, lie down, brat!"

He watched her mouth twist. He was too damned tired to argue, and if he touched her at that moment, he wasn't at all sure what it would lead to. "Please! For the love of God, lie down, Shannon."

She didn't say a word until she had settled down beside him, but then heard a tentative whisper. "Malachi?"

He groaned. "What?"

"What…what are we going to do now?"

He hesitated. "I should spank you, brat," he said softly. "And send you home."

"You—you can't send me home. You know that." There was just the touch of a plea in her voice, and the softest note of tears. "You can't send me back."

"That's right," he muttered dryly. "Justin is out there somewhere, waiting for you. Maybe I should let him have you. The two of you could keep on fighting the war, from here until doomsday."

"Malachi—"

"I'm not sending you back, Shannon. You're right about that; I can't."

"Then—"

"We're going to go onward for Kristin."

"But how will we find her? We'll never pick up the trail again. There's only a few of them left now, but they're so long gone that it would be impossible to find them."

"We don't need to find them."

"But—"

"Shannon, I know where they're taking her. They're taking her to Fitz. And I know how to find the town. We all know something about it, Cole, Jamie and I." He hesitated. "You forget, we've had dealings with the Red Legs before." He was silent for a moment, thinking back to when Cole's place had been burned down and his beautiful young wife killed. Malachi's jaw tightened. "I'm not sure if we can head them off quickly enough, or if we'll have to—figure out something else. We'll find her. We'll reach her."

"Do you think—do you think that she'll be all right?"

He lifted his hat and rolled toward her. She was staring at him so earnestly. Her eyes seemed old, so very wise and world-weary, and their tiredness added a curious new beauty and sensuality to her features.

He propped himself up on one elbow, watching her across the distance of the mere two feet that separated them.

"Shannon, they're going to take good care of Kristin. She is all that they have to use against Cole. Now, please, go to sleep." He lay back down, slanting his hat over his face.

"Malachi?" she whispered.

"What?" he asked irritably.

"Thank you—really."

Her voice was so soft. Like a feather dusting sweetly over his flesh. His muscles tightened and constricted and ached and burned, and he felt himself rising hard and hot.

"Shannon, go to sleep," he groaned.

"Malachi—"

"Shannon, go to sleep!"

She was silent. So silent then. She didn't try to speak again.

It was going to be all right. She was going to go to sleep; he was going to go to sleep. When he woke up, he wouldn't be so damned tired. He'd have so much more control over his emotions and needs.

A sound suddenly broke the silence of the morning.

He threw his hat off, leaping to his feet. She stared at him, startled.

She sat on her bedroll, cross-legged like an Indian, chewing on a piece of smoked meat. She had bread and cheese spread out before her, too, just like a damned picnic.

"What the hell are you doing?" he demanded.

"Eating!"

"Now?"

"Malachi, I haven't eaten in ages! It's been almost two full days."

His temper ebbed. He hadn't thought to stop for food last night, and she hadn't said anything, either.

"Just hurry it up, will you, please?"

"Of course," she said indignantly. She stared at him with reproach. He threw up his hands, issued a curt oath and plopped back down on the ground.

He just had to have some sleep.

He didn't sleep. He listened as she finished with the food and carefully wrapped it up to pack in her saddlebags. He listened as she stretched out on the ground, pulling her blanket tight around her shoulders.

Then he just listened to the sound of her breathing. He could have sworn that he could even hear the rhythmic thumping of her heart.

When he closed his eyes, he could see her. Could even see the pink satin flowers sewn into the lace of her corset. He could see her flesh, silky soft and smooth, and he could see the length of her, and the beautiful blue sizzle of her eyes...

He didn't even like her, he reminded himself.

But then again, maybe he didn't dislike her quite so much, either.

Somewhere in time, he did sleep.

He slept well, and he slept deeply. Warmth invaded him. He felt more than the hard ground beneath him, more than the coldness of the earth.

He felt flesh.

He awoke with a start.

He had rolled, or she had rolled, and now she lay curled against his chest. His chin nuzzled her hair; his arm lay draped around her. He was sleeping on her hair, entangled within it. Her features in repose were stunning, a study in classical beauty. Her cheekbones were high and her lips were full and red and parted slightly as she breathed softly in and out. Her lashes lay like dusky shadows over her flesh, enticing, provocative. The scent of her filled him deliciously. His arm was over her breast, the fullness of one round mound...

He jerked away from her, gritting his teeth. He should wake her up. He should shove her from him, as hard as he could.

He bit hard into his lip, then carefully eased her from him. She didn't whimper or protest. It he hadn't felt her breathing, he might have been afraid that she had died, her sleep was so deep and complete.

He sat up and pulled off his boots and socks and walked down to the water. It was cool and good, and just what he needed. He shucked his shirt, and let the water ripple over his shoulders and back. He came back to his bedroll stripped down to his breeches.

He sighed and laid back. He looked up at the sky. It was midafternoon now. They should ride again by night.

Damn her. He was the one who needed sleep so badly.

He closed his eyes. They flew open almost instantly.

She had rolled beside him again.

He looked at her and then sighed, giving up. He slipped his arm around her and held her close to the warmth of his body. He didn't listen to her heart but he felt it, beating sweetly.

It was so much worse now. He felt her with his naked flesh, and it was good to hold her as a woman. Too good. But he didn't release her. He held her and swallowed back his darker thoughts.

Knowing Shannon, he thought wryly, she would rise in a fury, accusing him of all manner of things. She would probably never believe that she had come to him in her sleep.

Come to him for the simple warmth and caring that she could not seek when she was awake.

We all need to be held, Malachi thought.

He sighed, shuddering against the fragrance of her hair. He would sleep again, he would sleep again. And she would never know just how fully he had played the gentleman, the cavalier...

He would never get back to sleep.

But finally, he did. Perhaps the very rhythm of her breath

and heartbeat finally lulled him to sleep. Perhaps abject exhaustion finally seized him.

When he slept, he dreamed again.

He was remembering, he realized. Remembering the day when he had been shot. To the day when he had fallen into the brook.

He was seeing things. Illusions. Soft sunlight playing down from the sky, glittering upon the warm, rich earth. Sunlight touching the earth…and touching upon the woman.

She had risen from the center of the brook like a phoenix reborn from the crystal-clear depths. She seemed to move with magic, bursting with gentle beauty from the depths. Her arms, long and graceful, broke the water first, then her head, with her hair streaming wet and slick, and then her shoulders and her breasts with tendrils of her hair plastered around them. And she continued to rise, rise and rise, until the full flare of her hips and the shapely length of her legs arose.

Venus…arising from her bath.

She was perfection, her breasts lush and ripe and full and firm and achingly beautiful with their rouge-tipped, pebbled peaks. Her waist was supple and slim, her hips…

She was illusion, illusion moving in slow motion. She was the product of a dream, of too many sleepless nights. Maybe she was a spirit of twilight, a creation of sunset. She blended with the colors of the sky, gold and red and soft magenta.

She dipped down again, cupping her hands, dashing the water up within them. She straightened, tossing it upon her face, and the little droplets fell and streamed from her hands like a cascade of diamonds.

He wasn't dreaming.

He was wide awake, he realized. Wide awake and staring at the stream. Obviously, she had thought he would stay asleep.

He rose and walked down to the water.

She paused, seeing him.

Their eyes met across the water, across the sky touched by sunset in gold and magenta and red.

She froze, as if some spell had been cast upon her there. She didn't drop down to the water, nor did she cover herself with her hands. She simply stared at him, her lips slightly parted, some words, perhaps, frozen upon them. She just watched him.

She just watched him.

And he didn't pause or hesitate.

He walked straight over to her. And when he reached her, he put his arms around her, lifted her chin and studied her face and her lips and her eyes, his fingers moving over the ivory softness of her face.

Then he lowered his head slowly over hers, capturing her lips with his own.

And still, she didn't move...

His arms tightened around her. He ran his fingers gently down her cheek to her throat, and he sent his tongue deeply into her mouth, stroking the insides. Desire burst upon him like the crystal shards of sunlight that sprinkled diamondlike upon the water. There would be no turning back for him now. Not now...

He moved his hand over her breast, massaging the fullness, teasing the nipple between his thumb and forefinger and encompassing the fullness of the weight again.

Her lips broke from his. A startled gasp escaped from her, but she didn't fight him. She slipped her arms around him, clinging close to him. Her lips settled upon his shoulder, and her fingers splayed across his back. He continued to play with her breast and she cast her head back as he pressed his lips against her throat, again and again and again. Then he moved downward, and lifted her breast to take it into his mouth, sucking upon the nipple and spiraling his tongue around the aureole.

She cried out, holding his shoulders. He rose to take her lips again, seizing them with hunger, plundering them apart, and seeking her mouth with a fire of passion. She pressed against him, trying to free herself. Her lips rose from his.

"We shouldn't..."

"For God's sake, don't tell me that now!" he said hoarsely, and his mouth closed over hers again, and this time, she made no protest at all. Her arms curled around his neck. He kissed her until he felt her tremble with the same deep desire that burned within him. Until he thought that she would fall.

Then he moved back, and drank in the sight of her again. He reached out and placed his hands around the enchanting fullness of both her breasts, awed by the sensual beauty of their deep-rose pebbled peaks. He touched her breasts, moving his fingers lightly over them, then possessing them with the fullness of his touch.

He stepped even closer, and swept her into his arms.

Splashing through the water, he carried her toward the grassy bank. Her eyes were closed. He knew he should have wondered if she dreamed of another man. He should have wondered if she had any experience with what she was doing, but he didn't wonder about anything at all. Holding her, carrying her to the shore, seemed to be the most natural thing to do, and he would not have ceased with his intent had lightning come from the sky to strike him down.

He laid her upon the soft grass embankment. Her eyes remained closed as the last rays of sunlight played over the beauty of her body again. He fell down beside her, and when the light shadowed magenta upon her, he kissed her, and then where the rays fell golden, he kissed her, too. The beautiful colors and musky light were broken by the dappling patterns of the oak leaves, waving above them in the softness of the breeze.

Holding his weight above her, he kissed her lips gently, then moved down between the valley of her breasts. He ran his hand over the lush curve of her flank as his tongue laved her flesh. She tasted of the water, and of the deep, rich colors of the sun.

Malachi stood, looking down at her, feeling the pulse that lived inside of him, increasing erratically with each touch against her. He stripped away his breeches, watching her still, watching the play of the sunset over her supple form. The world receded; the echoes of gunfire could not touch him here. There was nothing but the glorious, magenta sunset, and the girl, as golden and beautiful as the wavering rays of the falling sun, as naked and primitive as the simple earth where they lay.

He lay down beside her again, half covering her with the blanket of his naked flesh. Her eyes remained closed, and she was nearly motionless. He kissed her temple, whispered against her earlobe, trailed his lips down the snowy length of her throat and over the slender line of her collarbone. His hands teased her breasts again, and she arched against him, a curious cry coming from deep within her throat. He watched with fascination, seeking to judge the responses of her body. The shaft of his desire lay naked against her thigh, warmed there by her flesh and grazed by the evening air, so that the burning ache to have her beneath him soared high and fevered, and still he held himself in check.

He wondered if she even remembered who he was. He wanted her to open her eyes. To see his face, to know his name.

He moved his hands to lazily draw circles along her inner thigh, rising higher and higher. He buried his face against her throat and between her breasts, and feathered her flesh with the soft hairs of his beard. She whimpered slightly and began to undulate against him.

With bold and deliberate purpose, he parted her thighs. A certain resistance met him at first, but he caught her lips again, and his kiss seared and invaded and seduced. He wanted to slide down between them, but he kept his eyes hard upon hers instead. He stroked surely along her thigh until he came to the juncture of it, and swiftly, surely penetrated her with an intimate touch.

Her eyes flew open at last and met his. Wide and blue and beautiful and dazed. He knew how to make love, and his stroke moved with tender, sensual finesse.

"No..." she murmured softly, color flooding her cheeks.

He leaned close against her, speaking a breath away from her lips and keeping her eyes locked with his.

"Whisper my name, Shannon."

"No..." she murmured, and he knew that she didn't protest what they did, but only that he forced her to see the reality of it.

That he forced her to look his way, and say his name.

He found the most erotic places of her body and teased her, then plundered ruthlessly within her once again. She cried out, trying to twist from him, trying to elude his eyes. He shifted, burying his weight deep inside her, and holding himself just slightly away from her. She moved, she moved so sweetly against him even as she denied him.

"Put your arms around me, Shannon, tightly around me!" he urged her, and she did so. It was easy for her to cling tightly against him. Her fingers moved over his shoulders, over his back. Tentative, hesitant, seeking to hold him close as he held her, and seeking to give him a certain pleasure.

"Whisper my name, Shannon," he insisted. He hovered over her, teasing her with the fire of his own body. "Say my name. Open your eyes, and say my name."

Her eyes flew open again. There was a shimmer of fury deep within them. "Malachi!" she whispered tensely.

"Now..." He lowered his head to hers once again, and a ruthless grin touched his features. "Tell me what you want me to do."

She stared at him in astonishment, and a flush as crimson as the sunset touched her cheeks and seeped over her breasts. He couldn't bear it much longer. He had to have her soon. But they had always waged war between them, and this one, at least, he would not lose.

"Tell me what you want."

"No..."

"It's easy." She started to press against his shoulders. He caught her hands, and he laced his fingers with hers, and he drew them high over her head. "Say that you want me. I want you, Malachi." He kissed her. He slid his tongue into her mouth and withdrew it and then raked it along her lips. He drew her hands down and held her firm as he moved low against her, lazily taking her breast in his mouth again, slinking lower and lower against her. She escaped his grasp, and her nails raked into his shoulders. He heard her gasp and felt her fingers on his head when his kiss teased her belly.

She was alive with passion. Her head tossed and her hips moved, and she whispered something, moistening her lips. Her eyes were closed again, and her face lay to the side. They were both entangled in her hair.

"I can't hear you, Shannon."

"I—I want you."

"I want you, Malachi."

"I want you...Malachi."

Her voice was breathy, barely a whisper. It was all that he wanted, all that he needed. She moved against him with grace and exquisite sensuality, and a burst of triumph and fever took hold of him as he shifted, touching her, thrusting deep, deep inside her.

She stiffened, and screamed, and he realized then that he had believed her experienced because he had wanted to believe it. He had been deceived, but only because he hadn't wanted to think...

But he felt. He felt the tear within her body, and the constriction of pain, and the trembling that filled her. He started to jerk from her, but her hands pulled him back.

Her eyes were open now. Tears touched them, but they met his with a curious honesty. "No, no—I said that I wanted you. I said I want you...Malachi."

"Damn it, you didn't tell me that you were a—"

"You didn't ask," she reminded him softly. "Please..."

Her voice trailed away. He realized that it was too late to undo any harm, and yet perhaps not too late to recapture the magic.

He began to move very carefully. Slowly he entered fully within her, and just as slowly he withdrew. Then he plunged again, slowly...slowly.

Minutes later she cried out, straining high against him.

Innately, she seemed to know the craft of womanly art. Supplely, exquisitely, she moved beneath him. He matched his rhythm to hers, to the soft magic of the evening. The breeze rustled the leaves and silently caressed them. Birds cried out, and the water rippled and dazzled still. Malachi cried out hoarsely, giving himself free rein at long last, burying himself again and again with speed and fever within the moist and welcoming nest of her body.

The pressure built in him explosively, and still he held himself in a certain control, whispering to her, touching her bare flesh with kisses, urging her ever onward.

She cried out, straining hard against him, collapsing.

He allowed his own climax to come, and when it seized him it was sweet and violent; he shuddered as wave after little wave of pleasure shook him, and rippled anew. When he had finished at last he gazed down at her.

Her eyes were closed again, her lips were parted, and her breath still came swiftly...and he felt the little tremors that touched her. She seemed white, very pale.

"Shannon?" He stroked her hair, smoothing damp tendrils from her face. She moved, trying to free herself from the burden of his body. He shifted his weight, and she curled against him.

"Shannon—"

"Don't. Please, don't...not yet," she whispered.

While the twilight darkened, he held her, staring at the trees and watching the silhouette of the leaves against the sky until it was too dark to see them.

Then suddenly, in silence, she pushed away from him. She

rose, and her hair fell over her eyes, obscuring them. She walked quickly to the water, and did not pause at the edge, but hurried to where it was deep, and ducked beneath it. Malachi watched her pensively, thinking that the action wasn't much different than the one she had taken that morning when she washed her hands and face as if to wash away the scent and memory of Justin.

He rose and followed her into the water. "Shannon!" She ignored him, and he caught her arm, turning her around. She jerked away from him.

"Shannon, what are you doing now?"

"Nothing."

"Then why won't you talk to me?"

"I don't want to talk."

"Shannon, what just happened—"

"Shouldn't have happened. It shouldn't have happened!" she repeated fiercely. She sat in the water, pursing her lips, scrubbing her thighs and behaving now as chastely as a nun. She sank even lower into the water until the surface rippled against her breasts, and for some reason, the sight irritated him more than her perverse denial.

"Shannon—"

"Malachi, damn you! Could you at least have the decency to leave me alone now?"

"Could I have the decency?" He caught her elbow, pulling her to her feet. He was furious and she was distant. And yet, something was irrevocably and forever changed between them. It seemed natural now to hold her this way, to have her against him sleek and bare and intimate. She couldn't make love the way that she had and pretend that the moments hadn't existed.

"Decency?" he asked sarcastically. "Oh, I see. It was all my fault—"

"I didn't say that."

"It's what you mean."

"Well, you're just one hell of a Southern gentleman! You

know something? That's what Kristin always called you. You were the perfect Southern knight, the hero, the magnificent cavalier! Riding to a lady in distress! Well, she's wrong; you're no gentleman. You may have seen me bathing, but you might have turned your back.''

"Oh? And you, I suppose, were the perfect lady? Naked as a jay and strutting like a dance-hall girl out there—''

"You could have turned around. I thought that you were a gentleman!''

"Don't ever think, Shannon. Every time you do, someone gets into trouble. And don't you ever deny me, or—''

"Malachi, it was your fault.''

"My fault. Right. I didn't exactly drag you screaming from the water.''

She lowered her head.

He caught her chin, lifting it. "You just wanted to indulge in a little fantasy. You never made it into bed with the Yank when he was alive, so now you're willing to take on a Rebel captain just to see what it might have been like—''

She struck out at him like lightning, slapping his cheek with a stinging blow, then ducked, afraid that he would extract retribution. Every time she had touched Malachi in anger before, he had repaid her in some way.

But that night, he did not. He touched his cheek, then spun around. "You're right, Shannon. It never should have happened.''

He sloshed through the water to the shore and, ignoring her completely, dressed at his leisure. He heard her, though. He would always hear her, he realized. Hear her, and imagine her. Her eyes like the sky. Her grace and energy, her supple beauty. He would hear her, and imagine her, clothed and... unclothed.

He heard her coming to the shore, and imagined her slipping into her thin cotton pantalets and beautiful corset with the pink roses sewn into the lace. He sneaked a glance, and saw she had plunged into her jeans, and now sat on her bedroll pulling on her boots.

He dug into his saddlebags and found a clean checked cotton shirt. He tossed it to her.

"Thank you. I don't—"

"Put it on. If you ride around in that corset thing, every man jack we run into will fall under the illusion that you're ready and willing, too."

She slid the sleeves of the shirt over her arms and began to work on the buttons. Her head was high. "I wasn't going to refuse the shirt, Captain Slater. I was going to suggest that you should wear something similar. That Confederate coat of yours is pretty distinctive."

Malachi didn't reply. He turned around to pack up his bedroll, setting his greatcoat and jacket in with his blanket. His trousers were gray, but his shirt was plain blue cotton.

He couldn't quite part with his hat yet, so he set it atop his head, and stared at Shannon, waiting. When she had buttoned her shirt, she dug into her bag for a comb. She started trying to untangle the long strands of her hair.

Malachi saddled the horses, and she was still struggling. He walked over to her impatiently, snatching the comb from her fingers. "Get down on your knees," he told her gruffly.

"I won't—"

"It's the only way that I can handle this mane!"

She complied in silence. He quickly found the tangles, and eased them out. When he was done, he thrust the comb back to her. "May we go now, Miss McCahy?"

She nodded, lowering her head. They mounted and started out.

Malachi rode ahead of her, silent as death, wrapped up with his own demons. He felt as if they had been on the road for hours when she finally tried to catch up with him, calling to him softly.

"Malachi?"

"What?"

"I—I want to explain."

"Explain what?"

"What I said. I didn't mean to deny—"

"That's good. Because I won't let you deny the truth."

"That's not what I meant. I want to explain—"

She was still behind him. He couldn't see her face, and he was glad. It was easier to be cynical and cool that way. "Shannon," he said, with a grate to his voice, "you don't have to explain anything."

"But you don't understand—"

"Yes, I know. I never do."

"Malachi, before the war, I was always a lady—"

"Shannon, before, during and after the war, you always were a hellion."

"Malachi, damn you! I just meant that...I never would have done...what I did. I shouldn't have..."

He hesitated, listening to her fumbling for words. He could sense tears in her voice again, and though he ached for her, he was bitter, too. He didn't like playing substitute for a ghost. He might have forced her to admit that she had desired him, but the thought of her Yankee fiancé enraged him.

The ghost had never had what he had had, he reminded himself. He cooled slightly. "The war has changed lots of people," he said softly to her. "And you *are* a lady, brat. Still, I'm sorry."

"I don't want you to be sorry, Malachi. I just—it shouldn't have happened. Not now. Not between us."

"A Yank and a Reb. It would never do," he said bitterly.

She cantered up beside him, veering into his horse so that he was forced to look at her. She was soft and feminine now, her beautiful features and golden hair just brushed and kissed by the pale dusky moonlight.

"Malachi, please, I didn't mean that."

"I hope you meant something," he told her earnestly. "Shannon, you changed yourself tonight. Forever. You cast away something that some men deem very precious. You can't just pretend this didn't happen.''

Even in the dim light he saw her flush. She lowered her face. ''I know that. But that's not at all what I meant. What I meant is that…'' She hesitated.

''Shannon, I did not drag you down, I did not force you into my arms. I seduced, maybe, but not without your ready cooperation.''

He thought she might hit him. She didn't move. Only the breeze stirred her hair. They had both stopped, he realized.

She looked up at him, smiling painfully. Tears glazed her eyes. ''I did want you, Malachi. I shouldn't have. I knew it was you, and I wanted you…and I shouldn't have. Because I did love Robert, with all of my heart. And it hasn't even been a year. I…'' She shook her head. ''I…I'm the one who is sorry.''

She moved ahead of him. He suddenly felt exhausted, tired and torn to shreds.

He had never imagined, never, through hellfire, war and his meager taste of peace, that Shannon McCahy could come to brew this tempest in him. Anger, yes, she had always elicited his anger…

But maybe, just maybe, she had always aroused this fever in his loins, too. And maybe he was just beginning to see it now.

She was searing swiftly into his heart, too.

Maybe they could be friends. Maybe every war deserved a truce now and then.

''Shannon.''

She reined in and looked to him.

''Let's camp here and get some sleep. We'll move more westerly tomorrow night, away from the water, so let's take advantage of it now.''

He thought she raised her eyebrows, and he remembered clearly just what advantages the water had given them. ''To drink and bathe,'' he told her dryly.

She nodded and dismounted, removing her saddle. He would have helped her, but she had grown up on a ranch and knew what she was doing, so he decided to leave her alone. They both needed some privacy right now.

He unsaddled his horse, set her to graze, and hesitated. At last he decided it was safe, and he moved close to the water to build a small fire. Shannon watched him as the flames caught. He looked at her. "I need some small rocks. I've got a pan; we'll have coffee." And brandy, he added to himself. Lots of it.

He was the one who needed to keep away from her. This was going to be hard, damned hard now. He couldn't look at her, have her near, and not imagine her in his arms again. Maybe if she hadn't known how to move and arch and undulate and please a man, all by instinct...

She came back with the rocks, and he arranged them around his fire and set the pan so that the water would boil without putting out the flame. He stared at the water while she undid the bedrolls, setting them up for the remainder of the night.

The coffee was soon done; Shannon laid out bread and cheese and smoked meat. They barely spoke to one another as they ate, and when they were done, silence fell around them again.

"Why don't you go to bed," he told her.

She nodded. "Yes. I guess that I will." She rose and started for their bedrolls, then paused, looking at him.

She seemed angelic then. Soft and slim and wistfully and painfully feminine. She smiled at him awkwardly. "Malachi?"

"What?"

"Does it matter to you?"

"Does what matter to me?"

"A—er—a woman's..."

"Virginity?" He offered.

She flushed, and shook her head. "Never mind—"

"Shannon—"

"Never mind. Forget it. Sometimes I forget consequences and…"

He took a long sip of coffee, watching her over the rim of his cup. "Have you forgotten them this time?"

"What?" she murmured. It was her turn to be confused.

He stood and walked over to her. Malachi was irritated by the touch of malicious mischief in his own heart. He would set her to thinking and worrying for days, he thought.

But then he had spent these last hours in a type of hell, and he would surely spend all their moments together in torment from this day forth.

"Consequences. Procreation. Infants. Sweet little people growing inside a woman's body…"

Her eyes widened. She hadn't thought about it at all, he saw, and he was right—now she would worry for days.

He kissed her on the forehead. "Good night."

She was still standing there when he walked back to the fire.

Chapter Seven

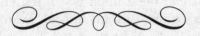

"What do you think?" Shannon murmured. It was late the next afternoon, and they had spent the day riding westward, avoiding the major roads, and had slipped quietly through the countryside.

"I think it's Kansas," Malachi replied flatly, turning toward her.

They sat on their horses looking down a cliff to a small, dusty town. On the distant rolling plains they could see farmhouses and ranches. Before them they could see a livery and a barbershop and a saloon. A sign stretching across the top of a long building advertised Mr. Haywood's Dry Goods and Mercantile, and next to it was a smaller sign, advertising Mrs. Haywood's Haywood Inn, Rooms to Let by the Day, Month, Year.

"Haywood, Kansas," Shannon murmured. She could still feel Malachi looking at her, and she couldn't bring herself to look his way. She'd had trouble looking at him ever since...

She couldn't believe what she had done. She hadn't had a single drop of liquor inside her. She hadn't been dragged, forced or coerced. She had done it all of her own free will, and if it were possible to live a thousand years, she would never be able to forget it. Or Malachi...

She could not look at him anymore and not remember everything. When his eyes touched her now she started to tremble deep inside. When she watched his hands resting on the reins, she remembered them against her body. The low male tenor of his voice moved against her now as if it touched her every time, as if it stroked the length of her back, just brushing over her flesh. And too often, way too often, she would grow hot and shivery all at once, and at the very core of her, and she would be ashamed to remember the feeling of unbelievable ecstasy that had burst upon her at the end.

She had never denied him his appeal, even in her moments of most vehement hatred. Even as the war had waged on and on, even as he dismissed her again and again as a child. And now she knew even more about him that she could not deny. That he was wonderfully muscled and sleek and bronze. His back was riddled with scars, and she knew that they were the result of cavalry battles, that he had been nicked time and again, and that he fought on, because a man just didn't walk away from a war, or from his duty as he saw it.

She knew that his chest was tufted with short red and gold hair, and that the hair narrowed enticingly at his hips, and that it flared out again to frame a demanding...masculinity.

He was an attractive man.

But she should have never been attracted, and each time she thought of her own behavior, it hurt. She knew that he thought that she had wanted to see him as a substitute for Robert. But he hadn't allowed it, and by then...she hadn't cared. She could make excuses. Maybe she had been striking out against the loss. Maybe she had just felt the need to be held.

No, the need to be loved.

But there really was no excuse. They hadn't even been friends. Passionate enemies, at best. What he must really be thinking of her, deep down inside, she couldn't even imagine...

And then she suddenly knew what her greatest fear was— that it had been a swift, casual fling for him, when for her it was a nightmare that changed her entire life and left her wondering if she had any morality whatsoever. And of all men to humiliate her so, it just had to be Malachi...

She had to be mature about it. She had to learn to forget it, and she had to learn to...quit worrying. Malachi had brought up a consequence that hadn't even passed through her mind. She'd never been that innocent, not on the ranch. She always knew what men and women did to create sons and daughters. It was just that she couldn't afford to think about it. She had to put it behind her now as well. Kristin was out there, somewhere. And Shannon did need Malachi's help. She didn't know the first thing about Kansas, or the awful man, Fitz. She needed Malachi.

"We need to go down," he said slowly, reluctantly. "We need to buy some food, if there's any to be had. And I'd give a hell of a lot to see a newspaper and try to find out what's been going on in the world."

"I'll go—" Shannon began.

"Don't be a fool," he told her impatiently. "I can't let you go down alone."

"I would be perfectly safe, and you wouldn't be."

"No one is safe anywhere around here. It wasn't safe before the war, and it surely isn't safe now."

"But I'm a Yank, remember?"

"Yeah, but they may not see it like that. To some, anyone from Missouri is a bushwhacker. Anyone at all."

"So what do you suggest?"

He gazed at her, lifting a brow. "Why, we pretend like hell, Miss McCahy, what else. We go in together—man and wife. Our place has been burned out. We're looking to keep on moving westward. Don't mess up, you hear?"

She eyed his hat pointedly. "You're riding in with a lantern of truth atop your head, captain," she said sweetly.

He swept the hat from his head and looked at it for a long moment, then dismounted and walked toward some bushes. He set the hat carefully in the midst of them.

"Is this a funeral?" Shannon asked sarcastically. "Maybe

we should run down and bring the preacher out to mutter a few last words.''

His face was savage when his eyes lit on hers. She swallowed, wishing that she hadn't spoken. He didn't reply. He walked around and mounted the bay again and reached out for her horse's reins, holding the horse there before him. ''Follow my lead, Shannon. I don't mind dyin' for Kristin, and I don't even mind dying for you—when it can't be helped. I will be bloody damned, though, if I'll die just because you can't keep a civil tongue in your body.''

His words fell into silence. Shannon stared at him without a word for what seemed like an endless time. She had only been teasing him. She hadn't realized how her words might wound, and she didn't know how to explain that or apologize.

''What about your saddle?'' she asked him coldly. ''Are there any Confederate markings on it, or on any of the other trappings on your horse?''

''My saddle came off a dead Ohioan's plow horse,'' he said. ''And the bridle is from your ranch. No markings at all.''

''Shall we go then?'' she said tautly.

He released her horse's reins and they started down the slope. ''We're going to buy some supplies and get some information,'' he told her. ''You keep careful.''

''Me?'' she inquired sweetly. ''You should be grateful to have me along, Malachi Slater. They aren't going to take your Confederate currency here. I've got Yankee dollars.''

He turned to stare at her. ''You keep your Yankee dollars, Shannon.''

''Oh?''

''I've got gold, Miss McCahy. Last I heard, they're still taking that stuff everywhere. Come on now, I want you close.''

He continued down the slope. Their horses broke into smooth canters as they crossed the empty plain and entered the town by the single road that cut through the line of buildings. Malachi reined in, nodding to Shannon to do the same.

They dismounted in front of the mercantile and tethered their horses on the wood rail that ran the length of the place, then started up the two dusty steps to the open doorway.

There was a portly, balding man behind a counter that stretched in front of a wall with rows and rows of just about everything. There were rolls of fabric, mostly cottons and linens, but there were brocades and silks and satins, too, and smaller rolls of elegant laces. There were sacks of flour and coffee and tea and sugar, and there were sewing goods and farm supplies, leather items, blankets, sheets, canteens. The whole store was composed of shelving, and Shannon saw jars of jams and preserves, pickled vegetables and smoked and dried meats. As small as this town was, it seemed to be a prosperous place.

"Howdy," the portly man said to the two of them.

Malachi grinned broadly, walking up to the man. "Howdy, sir."

"What can I do for you, young man?"

"Well, the wife and I are heading out west. We just need ourselves some food supplies."

"We can take care of that, Mr.—"

"Uh, Sloan," Malachi said.

"Gabriel," Shannon said quickly at the same time.

Malachi frowned at her, his jaw locking. The balding man looked from one of them to the other. "It's Sloan Gabriel, sir," Malachi said. He jerked Shannon over to his side. "And this is my wife, Sara."

The man looked from Malachi to Shannon. Shannon smiled and escaped Malachi's punishing grip, wandering away to look over the merchandise in the store. "Nice to meet you, Mrs. Gabriel."

"Likewise, I'm sure," she murmured demurely.

The man leaned toward Malachi. "My wife's got herself a little tea parlor next door, young man. Maybe the lady would like a cup?" He winked. "And you could take a walk on over to the saloon and have yourself a pint or two."

"That sounds mighty nice," Malachi told him. A saloon was always the best place to hear whatever news was passing around. He looked at Shannon.

"Sweetheart." She was looking at a roll of calico and didn't pay him the slightest heed. He walked over to her, catching her hands and spinning her around and into his arms. "Darlin'! That nice man, Mr.—"

"Haywood," the balding man supplied.

"That nice Mr. Haywood says his wife has a little tea shop next door. Wouldn't you like to have a cup of tea, complete with milk and sugar? It's been a long, hard road."

She smiled sweetly. "Are you going to have a cup of tea, darlin'?" she asked him. She came up on her toes, slipping her arms around his neck.

"I had reckoned that I might have a beer across the way," he told her, his jaw twisting. Her smile had been dazzling, and her eyes were absurdly large and innocent. Her body was pressed tight to his and he could feel all the curves and soft slopes that he had recently come to know so well.

His eyes narrowed. "Careful!" he mouthed. She couldn't be that innocent. She had to know what she was doing to him.

"Why, darlin'," she drawled sweetly. "I don't mind. I'll come over to the saloon with you." She wrinkled her nose up prettily. "I don't rightly care for that nasty old beer, but—"

He untangled her arms from around his neck. "Sweetheart," he said firmly, "you go on and have tea. It might be a rough place. There might be some...talk...I don't want you to hear."

"If you're there, my love, I'm sure that I'll be safe."

"You'll be much safer, sweetheart, having tea."

"But I don't mind hearing talk, beloved."

He was losing control. There was a definite note of irritation in his voice. "Honey love, sometimes a man just don't talk as freely when there's a lady present. You'll have tea."

"But, darlin', I—"

He didn't let her finish. He could hear Mr. Haywood snickering behind him, and he'd had about enough. She was the one pressing it. He pulled her even closer and slammed his lips down hard upon hers in a bruising, punishing kiss. He held her so tightly that she could barely breathe, and that was what he had intended. When he released her, she was silent, gasping for breath. He spun her around so that his back was toward Mr. Haywood and he whispered with vehemence. "Go over and have tea. Now. You ruin this—"

"But I want to hear, too—"

"Go. Now. Smile, kiss me sweetly, and damn you, go have a cup of tea. I mean it, Shannon."

He could hear her teeth grinding, but she went still. Malachi spun around. "Next door, you say, Mr. Haywood?"

"Sure thing. The little lady can go right through this door here."

Shannon didn't see a door. Then she realized that even the door was lined with shelves that were filled with merchandise.

"See you soon, sweetheart." Malachi pulled her into his arms, kissing her on the forehead. She longed to slap him, hard. She smiled instead, and threw her arms around him again, rising up on her toes, and quickly threading her fingers through the hair at his nape. She kissed him...

She kissed him with purpose...and with menace, pressing her lips fully against his, and teasing his lip with the thrust of her tongue. Startled, he gave way. She pressed her tongue fully into his mouth, slowly, provocatively, filling it.

Then she withdrew, dropping back on her heels with her body tight to his, rubbing him with the length of it. She saw a dark sizzle in his eyes, but ignored it despite her own breathlessness. She turned to Mr. Haywood and smiled brightly. "Newlyweds, you know!" she explained, flushing and batting her lashes. "I can't bear to see him go, even for a second. It's just been so hard, what with the war and all. The cows scattered, then the fields were trampled, and then the whole ranch was burned down one day. But now we're finally together, heading west, and it is just so hard to let my darlin' out of my sight..."

Both men were silent. Malachi was as stiff as a poker, not saying a word. But when she looked at him, his eyes were narrowed. Real narrow. The way he looked at her caused her heart to jump and shiver, and she decided then to make a hasty retreat. She offered Mr. Haywood another smile and quickly passed through the shelved door that he held open for her.

She found herself in a large parlor. For a moment, it reminded her so much of her home that she inhaled quickly, feeling a little dizzy. It was lovely. A piano stood on a braided rug before a polished wood staircase. Beautiful Victorian chairs sat all around the piano in pleasant angles, a grouping of three here, two there. There was a grouping around the fireplace, and there were lovely little marble-topped tables all around.

"Hello?"

A short, buxom woman with small brown eyes, iron-gray hair and warm, rosy cheeks came through a doorway, wiping her hands on a towel. She smiled at Shannon, then eyed her outfit.

She didn't fit in the beautiful little parlor, Shannon realized. Not in her dusty breeches and checked shirt.

But the woman didn't hesitate long. It was ranch country, farm country, and Shannon's outfit was not completely alien here.

"Hello, miss..."

"Uh—Gabriel," Shannon said quickly. "Sh—Sara Gabriel, Mrs. Haywood. Your husband sent me over."

"Oh, how lovely. Well, do sit down. I'll bring you in some of our finest, young lady." She extended her arm around the parlor. "As you can see, we're not terribly busy at the moment."

Shannon nodded, wondering if they were ever busy. It seemed to be such a small town to support the shop and boardinghouse.

"Sit, sit!"

She shooed Shannon into one of the chairs by the fireplace and disappeared. Shannon barely had a chance to get her breath and look around before Mrs. Haywood was back, carrying a large silver tray. She set it down on one of the marble-topped tables. She poured tea from a pot through a strainer and looked at Shannon. "Sugar, cream?"

"Yes, please," Shannon said.

As Mrs. Haywood continued fixing the tea, Shannon looked over the curve of her chair toward the street. Malachi was just going into the saloon, pushing his way through a set of swinging doors.

"Is that your husband, dear?" asked Mrs. Haywood, following Shannon's eyes.

"Yes," said Shannon, a little grimly.

"Now, now, don't worry about him, Mrs. Gabriel," Mrs. Haywood advised her. She sighed with an expansive smile and patted Shannon's knee. "You're such a pretty young thing, you needn't worry a bit. Newlyweds, eh?"

"Er, yes ma'am. How did you know?" Shannon said.

"The war, my girl, the war. Young ladies here and there are snatching up their fellers the second the boys come home. Too many young men dead. Too many young women left without husbands or intendeds. Those who can are marrying quick. Did your husband fight in the war, Mrs. Gabriel?"

"Yes—yes, he did," Shannon said quickly. She prayed that Mrs. Haywood wouldn't ask her any more questions.

She didn't. She pointed to the pastries on the plate. "Meat pies and cinnamon swirls and raisin muffins. And I'm the best cook this side of the Mississippi, I promise you. Help yourself, young lady."

Shannon hadn't known how hungry she was until she bit into the first pie. It was still warm from the oven, and the pastry was fluffy and light and delicious, and the meat was tender and seemed to melt in her mouth. She hadn't had anything nearly so good in ages, and it felt as if she and Malachi had been on the road forever, despite the fact that this would only be their fourth night away. Everything about the parlor felt good, from the elegance of the chairs to the fine food and sweet tea. It was nice to stop, even if Malachi had been his usual dictatorial self when he had refused to let her go to the saloon.

Mrs. Haywood kept talking as Shannon ate. She explained that Haywood was kept busy by the traffic that went through. There were roads all around the town. Some of them went south, Texas way, and some of them went to Missouri, and some of them headed toward the north, while an awful lot of them headed out west. "People are headin' for California, right and left, already. Almost as much as back in '49. The war...it left so many without a home, or without a home they could call their own anymore."

Shannon nodded vaguely. She found herself looking over the rear of the chair, out the curtained windows and across the street to the saloon. Heat suffused through her as she thought of the way she had kissed Malachi in the store, and she wondered why she had done so. If she were playing a game, it was a dangerous one. If she was hoping to taunt him or hurt him, she was risking herself by doing it. She didn't know what had seized her; she didn't seem to know herself at all any more.

Nor did she understand why she was so anxious over the length of time he was staying at the saloon. What was he doing over there?

Drinking it up with the whores, no doubt, she thought, and a flush of anger filled her. She didn't care; it was none of her business.

But she did care. It made no sense. She did care. Maybe it was the idea that he could move on from her to a whore so quickly. Maybe it left her with doubts about her abilities.

She almost bit through her cup with that thought, and she reminded herself fiercely that she really loathed Malachi, loathed him with all her heart, and she had never set out to please him, she had never set out to be with him at all. And she didn't want to be with him now; it was a matter of necessity.

Maybe he wasn't being entertained by a woman at all. Maybe he was in trouble, Shannon thought.

"You two staying the night?" Mrs. Haywood asked her.

"Uh—no, I don't think so," Shannon said. "Ma—my husband, Sloan, wants to keep moving. He says the sooner we get where we're going, the sooner we'll get settled down."

"But a little rest never did nobody any harm, either," Mrs. Haywood said. "Pity, I've got the coziest little room upstairs. Pretty lace curtains, a big wool comforter, a fireplace and—" she winked, leaning toward Shannon "—I got the most unbelievable hip bath you ever seen up there. It's a two seater, wood and copper, just right for a young mister and his new missus."

Shannon nodded, her face growing red despite herself. "I'm sure it's very, very nice, Mrs. Haywood—"

Mrs. Haywood jumped up, grabbing her hand. "Do come on. Your young man seems to be enjoying himself. You come on up here, and I'll show you my honeymooners' retreat!"

Shannon didn't have much choice. She stared across the roadway one more time, wishing she could give Malachi a good punch right in the gut. What did he think he was doing? Was he enjoying himself at her expense, or...

Was he in trouble?

She wished she knew.

It was a typical saloon, the type that had been cropping up in Kansas ever since the white man had first started to claim the land. Two men served behind the bar, and a beautiful brunette with a feathered hat and shoulderless gown played tunes at the piano. There were two lone drinkers at round tables, and a poker game going on in the rear of the room. Three of the players were ranchers; they had come with their dusty hats and kerchiefs and chaps and spurs, and they were swigging on whiskey bottles. A fourth man seemed to be a clerk or a banker. He was wearing a neat pin-striped suit with a crooked tie and white shirt.

The other two had a somewhat professional air about them. Both wore vested suits and tall hats. One was lean with a thin curling mustache, and the other was heavier set with small, very dark and very alert eyes.

Malachi wandered over to the bar, and one of the barkeeps hurried to serve him. "Beer," Malachi said briefly, throwing a coin on the bar. The man smiled and drew a foaming brew from the tap. Malachi nodded his thanks.

"Passing through?" the barkeep asked.

Malachi nodded again. From the corner of his eye, he saw that the gamblers were being served by a tall, buxom redhead. The sight of the woman gave him a start, and he almost forgot to answer the barkeep. "The wife and I are heading out for California. Seems the only thing to do now." He remembered Shannon's words and added, "We were burned out. End of the war, you know. Seems to make sense to up and start all over."

"Yep, seems to make sense. Lots of people heading west these days. You staying in town long?"

"Nope. Just came in to wet my whistle."

The barkeep smiled. "And your wife is over at Mrs. Haywood's having tea."

"Yeah, how'd you know?"

"Cause this is Haywood's saloon. His town, really. He entertains the lady folks on that side of the street, and the men on this side. Darned good scam, ain't it, Mr.—"

"Gabriel. Sloan Gabriel."

"Matey. Matey MacGregor. It all seems to come out clean in the wash here. The Haywoods are right nice folks themselves, and that seems to make it all right."

Malachi grimaced. "Yeah, maybe it does." He turned around, leaning against the bar, watching the tall red-haired woman again. He swore inwardly. It was Iris Andre from Springfield, and he did know her.

He thought he should turn around and hurry out of the saloon, but just at that moment, the woman looked up and saw him. Surprise and pleasure appeared on her attractive features, and she straightened, ignoring the poker players, and hurried toward him. She was going to call out his name, he knew it.

"Iris! I'll be damned!" He went to her quickly, hugging her and squeezing the air from her before she could speak. He picked her up to swing her around, whispering in her ear, "Sloan. Sloan Gabriel. Please."

She nodded swiftly—Iris always had been a bright woman. She meant to have her own business one day, and Malachi was sure that when she did, it would be a financial success.

"Sloan!" she said enthusiastically.

"You two know each other, Iris?" the barkeep called.

"Sure do, Matey. We're friends from way back. Sloan, grab your beer and come over here to a table for a moment."

He'd always liked Iris. She might be a whore, but she was a whore with class. He didn't miss a beat. She was almost as tall as he was, and though she wasn't beautiful, she was attractive with her strong features, blazing red hair, green eyes and regal height.

"Come on!" she urged him, pulling him farther and farther into the back. She sat him down at one of the small tables, far away from the others, far away from probing eyes. "Malachi! What the hell fool thing are you doing in Kansas? Wait a minute, don't answer that. Buy me a drink so this will look like business. Matey!" she called out. "We'll take a bottle of whiskey over here. The good stuff."

"Coming right up."

Iris dangled her fingers sensually over the back of Malachi's hand while they waited for Matey to come over with the whiskey. When he was gone, Iris lowered her head close to Malachi's. "Malachi! They've got wanted posters up all over the country! They say you were in on a raid with your brothers, that you went into Kansas and shot some guy named Henry Fitz, and that you're wanted on all kinds of other bushwhacking activities, too. I heard about what Fitz did to your brother, so I wasn't too surprised—''

''Iris, I wasn't with Cole, not that I wouldn't have gone with him if I could. But the war was ending right then. I had a whole contingent of men under me, and I couldn't just go running off to Kansas. Cole was a scout. I was regular cavalry. I went where I was ordered to go.''

''Malachi.'' She moved even closer to him. ''I know that none of you has done anything to be hanged for, but you don't know Hayden Fitz.''

''And you do?''

Iris nodded. ''Never met a meaner son of a bitch in my entire life. There's something evil about him. He likes bloodletting, and he likes to watch men die. He's worth money, too, Malachi. Big money. He invested with arms manufacturers during the war and made himself even richer. He owns Sparks—''

''Sparks?''

''The town where he lives. I mean, he owns it.'' She smiled, waving a hand around. ''All right, so the Haywoods own Haywood. But this is a two-bit rest stop, Malachi. Sparks is big. The stagecoach goes through. It's always filled with Conestogas. There's a jail and a circuit court, and if he manages to get you into that jail, he'll hang you, too. You fool! You gotta get out of Kansas.''

Malachi shook his head. ''I can't. Hayden Fitz sent men to my sister-in-law's place. Cole wasn't there, so they carried her away. I've got to find her.''

Iris sat back. ''At least you got rid of your Reb uniform,'' she said softly. ''You don't look like the poster so much anymore.''

''I still have the uniform,'' he said, pouring out shots of the whiskey. ''It's stuffed in my saddlebags. And my hat—well,

I left it out in some bushes. It was kind of hard to part with, you know?"

She nodded. "Old times," she murmured, then she looked at him. "Oh, Malachi!"

"What, Iris?"

"Malachi, I did hear something about Fitz holding a woman. Just the other day, some of the boys were talking about Fitz having a blond woman in his jail. Said she was part of a conspiracy to murder Union soldiers."

His heart sank, but it was what he had been expecting to hear. The Red Legs would have carried Kristin straight to Fitz. And Fitz surely knew that he was holding the key to Cole's whereabouts.

"You think he'll—hurt her?" Malachi asked.

She shook her head strenuously. "I—uh—I don't think so. He could kill her, Malachi, if he does anything. But hurt her? Not if he's using her for bait."

"You hear anything about my brothers?" he asked her.

She shook her head. "Not a word. Sorry, Malachi." She was silent for a minute. "But I can help you."

"What?"

"Like I said," she told him dryly, "I know Hayden Fitz. I know his sheriff, Tom Parkins, real well. The town ain't twenty miles from here, Malachi. I can take a trip over and bring you back some information."

"Iris, that's good of you. That's real good, but I can't stay here—"

"You can stay here if you can stay anyplace on God's good earth. I tell you, Malachi, for Yanks, these are real good people here. Stay. Just give me one or two days. I can ride over tomorrow, spend some time and ride back.

"I can't have you do that—"

"I do it now and then anyway, Malachi."

He hesitated. If anything happened to Iris, he would never forgive himself. But if she could help him free Kristin and he didn't let her, he'd never forgive himself, either.

"Iris, I can't believe I'm saying this, but all right. You think I'm really safe here?"

"As safe as you're going to be."

He exhaled slowly.

"I won't let nothing happen to me, Malachi, I swear it," she insisted. "It's all right. It really is."

He still hesitated, then he sighed. "All right. It's good to see you, Iris. So good. You stayin' on here?"

"Don't look at me like that—I'll feel like I want to stand up and sing 'Dixie,' and that just ain't no good anymore. No. I'm going to California. The war is too close here, Malachi. I want to leave it behind. My father fought with Grant, and he's dead. My brother was with General E. Kirby-Smith down south, and now he's dead, too. I want out of this hatred, Malachi. It ain't going to end here. Not in my lifetime."

He laced his fingers through hers and squeezed them. They were very close and intimate, two friends who had run the same gamut.

That's how they were sitting when the saloon doors burst open and Shannon came into the room.

She had a Colt shoved into her belt, and she looked around the saloon carefully, looking for any danger. He saw from the position of her hand that she could have grabbed the gun in a split second, and fired, with great accuracy, in less time than that.

Her eyes fell on his.

"Ma—Sloan!" she said, startled. Her eyes took in the two glasses, the whiskey bottle and his hand, his fingers interweaved with Iris's on the table. She took in Iris, from the little flare of her hat to her black petticoats peaking out from beneath her crimson gown. She looked from the poker players to the bar, where Matey was staring at her expectantly.

Her eyes narrowed, dark lashes falling over her brilliant blue eyes. Her hair was loose and beautiful, spilling all around her shoulders. It was one of those occasions when her masculine apparel made her look all the more feminine, for her slender legs seemed very long, and her derriere was defined by her trousers just as her breasts were full and defined by her cotton shirt.

She was furious. Malachi wondered why. Just because he had left her for so long, hadn't allowed her to take an equal part in this venture? Or was there, maybe, just maybe, more to it than that?

Thinking about it made a pulse beat hard against his throat. He wanted to be with her somewhere alone, then, at that moment.

He swallowed down his desire and fought the tension. She was striding his way. They were going to do battle again. Her claws were bared; he could almost see them. He nearly smiled. A woman didn't get that way unless she was jealous. At least a little bit jealous.

"Darlin', I'm so very sorry to interrupt," she drawled. Her voice dripped with honey. She smiled sweetly at Iris. Then she knelt close to Malachi. "You son of a bitch! You left me over there scared to death...never mind. Bastard! Well, darlin', at least the whole town will be expecting a marital dispute. I'm checking into Mrs. Haywood's. I assume you have other arrangements." She stood. "Nice to meet you, Miss—" she said to Iris.

"Iris, honey. Iris Andre. And you're...?"

"I'm—" Shannon paused and shot her very sweet and dazzling smile at Iris once again. "I'm Mrs. Sloan Gabriel," she said, and she picked up Iris's shot glass and tossed the whiskey into her face.

Matey inhaled in a massive gasp; even the poker players went dead silent.

Malachi leaped to his feet, reaching for Shannon. Iris was on her feet, too. Malachi knew Iris, and Iris didn't take that kind of thing from anybody. He jerked Shannon around behind him. "Iris, I do apologize for my wife's manners—"

"Don't you dare apologize for me to any who—"

He spun around, clamping his hand hard over Shannon's

mouth. "Iris, I apologize with all my heart." He jerked Shannon's wrist and twisted her arm around so that she couldn't possibly fight him without feeling excruciating pain. "Darlin', please, Iris is an old friend, and we just have a few things to say to one another." He dropped his voice and whispered against her ear. "Darlin', you are acting like a brat, and I promise you, if you don't act grown-up real quick here, I'm going to peel those breeches and tan your hide, just to prove that the man wears the real pants in this family. I'll do it, Shannon, because I'll have to." He hesitated. "She knows something about Kristin. She can help us, Shannon!"

He released her, very slowly. He waited expectantly, ready to snatch her back into his arms if need be.

For once in her life, she seemed to have believed his threat. Perhaps she was so concerned that she would grab at any scrap of information about her sister. She faced Iris.

"Miss Andre, it was a pleasure," she said. Her voice was the softest drawl, her manner that of a charming, well-mannered belle. She swept from the saloon like a queen.

A cheer went up from the poker crowd. One of the ranchers stood. "Mister, I sure salute you! That's one heck of a spirited filly, beautiful to boot, and you handled her like a man!"

"Buy him a drink!" the heavyset professional gambler called. "If I'd been able to manage my wife like that, I might be a rich man by now!"

Malachi laughed, sitting down and waving a hand in the air. "She's going to be mighty mad later, gents. We'll see how I handle her then." He looked at Iris. She sat beside him. He gave her his kerchief to wipe the whiskey from her face. She seemed more confused than angry.

"Malachi, that really was your wife?"

He shook his head. "Iris, she is my sister-in-law's sister. She wants Kristin back. I couldn't seem to stop her from coming with me, and that's another long story, too."

Iris sat back, smiling. Malachi poured her more whiskey, and she swallowed it.

"Thanks for not ripping her hair out."

"Don't kid yourself, Malachi. I saw that Colt in her pants. I'm willing to bet she knows how to use it."

"Like a pro—except that she has a bad time aiming at people."

Iris was smiling at him with a peculiar little grin. "She might not make you such a bad wife after all, my friend."

Malachi frowned. "Iris—"

"She's got spirit, and she's got courage. A little raw around the edges, as if she's got some scars on her. But we've all got scars. I can't see you with a namby-pamby woman, and she ain't that."

"No, she isn't that. She's a pain in the damned—"

"Butt!" Iris broke in, laughing. "Yes sir, she's that. But I can see something in your eyes there, Malachi. She ain't going to be checking into Mrs. Haywood's place alone, is she?"

Malachi smiled, idly twirling his whiskey around in his glass. Miss McCahy had seen fit to comment upon his actions and whereabouts.

He was damned ready to comment upon hers.

"I think I should give her time to check in and settle down and get real, real comfortable. What do you think?"

Iris laughed at the sizzle in his eyes.

She wished that it was her. But it wasn't. He was more like a married man than he knew. The beautiful little blonde with the delicate features and the tough-as-nails stature had those golden tendrils of hers wrapped tightly around him.

Still, Mrs. Sloan Gabriel's manners did need a little improvement.

"Let her get real, real comfortable," Iris advised him sagely. "A game of poker might be right in line here. Come on over, I'll introduce you to the boys."

"All right. I'm glad to meet the boys."

The heavyset gambler was Nat Green. The slimmer man with him was Idaho Joe, and the ranchers were Billy and Jay Fulton, Carl Hicks and Jeremiah Henderson. It was a good game. Iris held onto his shoulders, laughing, while he played. She brought him drinks.

Around supper time, she disappeared and came back with big plates of steak and potatoes and green beans.

He lost at cards—a little bit—and the meal cost him almost as much as the liquor, but he didn't care much. He had a good time.

And through all of it, he anticipated his arrival at Mrs. Haywood's Inn, Rooms by the Day, Month or Year.

He was just dying to see his darlin' wife.

Just dyin' to see her.

Chapter Eight

He knew that the door would be locked.

He even suspected that Shannon might have gone to Mrs. Haywood with quite a sob story about being ignored so that her husband could play around with another woman.

Shannon was a good little actress. He was learning that quickly.

And he was learning, too, that things had changed between them, irrevocably. Maybe they would always be at battle, but the battlegrounds were subtly changing. He might still spend ninety percent of his time thinking Mr. McCahy should have dragged his daughter into the woodshed a number of times at a far younger age, but he couldn't deny what she had done to him. Exactly what that was, he wasn't sure yet. And he didn't want to think about it; he didn't want to analyze it. He fixed it in his mind that Shannon had started this one. Either down in the store when she had kissed him with that pagan promise, or when she had come striding across to the saloon to douse Iris in whiskey. This one, she had begun.

But he was going to finish it.

He had his own fair share of acting ability.

"Mr. Gabriel!" Mrs. Haywood said with censure when Malachi came to ask for a key to the room. "Now, I know, sir, that a man has got to have a few simple pleasures of his own. And a saloon's a good place for a man to have whiskey and a cigar—keeps the scent out of his own parlor, you know.

But when it comes to other things...when he leaves a beautiful little bride..." She shook her head in reproach.

"Iris is just an old friend, ma'am." Mr. Haywood was in the kitchen, eating his supper. Malachi raised his voice a hair, determined to work on them both. "I don't know what my wife told you, Mrs. Haywood, but there was nothing going on. I had a few drinks, and I lost a few hands of poker. Ma'am, you got to understand. If a man lets his wife make a fool of him like that, well, then, he just ain't a man anymore."

"That's right, Martha." Mr. Haywood dropped his napkin on the butcher-block kitchen dining table and strode to the door. "Martha, if the man wants a key to his own room, we'd best give it to him. She's his wife, and that's that."

Mrs. Haywood was still uncertain. "Mr. Gabriel, I probably ain't got no right to keep man and wife apart, but—"

"I'm going to try to make her understand, Mrs. Haywood. Honest, I am."

"You give him the key, Martha," Mr. Haywood said.

"You're right, Papa, I suppose. Oh, Mr. Gabriel, I was just giving my husband a piece of apple pie. Won't you have some?"

"Why, that's mighty kind of you. Thank you, ma'am."

He had the key, and he had a cup of good strong coffee and some of the best apple pie he'd tasted in his entire life. And it was the middle of summer.

"I jar and preserve all my own fruits," Mrs. Haywood told him proudly.

"Well, it's the finest eating I've done, ma'am, since way before the war."

As Mrs. Haywood blushed, the door to the parlor opened. A pretty young girl in a maid's cap and smooth white apron walked in. She bobbed a nervous little curtsy to Malachi and looked at the Haywoods. "Mrs. Gabriel is all set for the night, Mrs. Haywood. She had me fetch her some of the lavender soap, and asked if we'd be so good as to put the price on the bill. She thanks you kindly for the use of the tub."

His heart started ticking a staccato beat. If he'd gone by instinct, he would have knocked the table over, brushed the maid aside, burst through the door and raced up the stairs.

Primitive, he warned himself reproachfully.

That wasn't what he wanted. Slow torture was what he had in mind.

He sipped his coffee like a gentleman. "My wife's in the bath?" he inquired innocently.

"Oh, why, yes, Mr. Gabriel," Mrs. Haywood said. "Don't worry, young man, you're welcome to stay here in the kitchen if you're worrying about disturbing her."

"Why, ma'am, I was thinking that I might steal a little of her water, and save someone having to haul more up the stairs." He spoke sincerely, rising.

"That's thoughtful of you, Mr. Gabriel," Mrs. Haywood said. Around her ample figure, Mr. Haywood looked up at Malachi with his brow arched and a skeptical smile slipping onto his lips.

"Mighty thoughtful, son," he said dryly.

Malachi flashed him a quick grimace. "Mr. and Mrs. Haywood, thank you again. Good night, now."

He nodded to the young maid and swept by her. He forced himself to walk slowly through the parlor and up the stairs. He glanced at the key. Room five.

It wasn't hard to find.

He took a deep breath outside the doorway, smiled again, and slipped the key into the lock. He heard her key fall out of the door on the other side as he pressed his in. He pushed open the door.

The most outrageous bathtub he'd ever seen sat before the fire. It was a long wooden tub with headrests rising up at both ends. It was decorated with copper and delft tiles, and at that particular moment, it was laden with bubbles...and with Shannon.

Her hair was curled high on top of her head, leaving the

slim porcelain column of her neck bare. Her shoulders and just a peak of her breasts rose out of the bubbles.

She turned on him, her eyes wide and startled and very blue. She almost leaped up, but then seemed to realize how much worse that would be. "Get out!"

"Darlin'!" he said softly, with taunting reproach. And he stepped into the room, closing the door behind him, leaning against it. His eyes stayed on her while he twisted the key in the lock.

She must have put on one hell of a performance with the Haywoods, he thought. She hadn't expected him that night. It was a pity that he hadn't gotten to see it.

Shannon sank farther into the tub, watching him as he sauntered coolly into the room.

"Don't you dare get comfortable," Shannon warned him. She felt herself burning all over, and it wasn't from the steam in the bath. It was caused just by the way his eyes fell upon her.

The nerve of him. How dare he be here. How dare he look at her like that. When he had just left his redheaded slut!

He tossed the key onto the side table and dropped down on Mrs. Haywood's beautiful crocheted bedspread, lacing his fingers behind his head and staring right at her. He smiled.

"Don't let me disturb you."

"You are disturbing me." She narrowed her eyes. "You've no right in this room. The Haywoods—"

"The Haywoods know that a man has a right to be with his wife—beloved."

"The Haywoods know that the man is a scoundrel and cad, seducing women from the Mississippi to the Pacific. They understood completely that you deserved a night in the livery stables."

"Tsk, tsk." His apparent relaxation had been deceptive. He moved all of a sudden, sleek and easy, twisting to stretch out on his stomach, facing her from the foot of the bed. There was no more than six feet between them. She could see the tension in his features and the pulses beating furiously against his throat and temple. There was a dangerous gleam in his eyes, and she was aware that he was angry with her—furious, probably, for her behavior in the saloon—and that he seemed to have forgotten any rules of fair play for the night.

She sank lower in the tub. He wouldn't force her into anything. She knew him, and she knew that he would never force any woman.

But what would he do?

And what would she do? If he touched her, she would scream, she thought, and not with horror, but because her flesh seemed to cry out to know his hands again. She was hot inside and out, and trembling fiercely. The scent of the lavender soap was all around her, the softness of the bed awaited…

And he had just spent hours and hours with a whore.

"Malachi—" She paused. "Sloan," she hissed. "This is my room. Get out."

He smiled, giving her a flash of white teeth against the golden strands of his mustache and beard. "I'm sorry, sweetheart. I may be a cad, but I wouldn't dream of leaving my sweet young wife alone for the entire night."

He rose and sat at the foot of the bed, nonchalantly kicking off his boots and peeling away his socks. Shannon watched him, stunned, as he proceeded to pull the tails of his shirt from his pants and unbutton his shirt and cast it aside.

"What are you doing?" she asked him quickly.

"I'm going to take a bath."

"No, you're not. This is my bath."

"Darlin', we've got to talk, and it looks like it's just the right place, to me."

"Malachi, if you touch me, I'll scream."

"You're my wife. They might shake their heads a bit downstairs, but they won't interfere."

"I'm not your wife!" Shannon swore, panicking. The look in his eyes caused shivers to streak along her spine. The sight of his bare chest, sleek and gleaming, brought her body alive with memory. She lowered her head, determined not to look at him.

But she could hear him.

She heard his pants fall to the floor, and she heard his footsteps as his bare feet padded behind her. He dropped to his knees and his lips touched her shoulders like a burning brand. She jerked away from him and wished she hadn't, for when she turned to him she saw his hungry eyes on her newly exposed breasts. Her nipples hardened instantly and flames seemed to rise to her cheeks, then sink back and lie deep in her core. She sank into the water. She wanted to be angry, indignant. Her voice came out as a husky whisper. "Malachi, I am not your wife!"

He was on his feet, naked as a jay, and his manhood flying proud and firm. She was determined not to stare, but her teeth were chattering, and she felt compelled to watch him, like a marionette jerked by strings. She loved the look of him, she realized. She felt some ancient and instinctive fascination, which lay deep below the level of her mind, something that caused her blood to race and heat and her breath to catch and come too quickly and that made her flesh come alive at the very thought of him. She could not draw her eyes from him. She could not help but respond to the naked length of him. She found him magnificent. From the breadth of bronzed shoulders to the lean hardness of his thighs, she found him so boldly and negligently male that she could not turn away.

He stepped into the tub, sitting behind her so that his feet brushed her bottom. He leaned back against the rim of the tub and sighed deeply. "This is just wonderful." He closed his eyes in complete comfort.

Hating him, hating herself, Shannon swore furiously. "Malachi, I am not your wife!"

His eyes flew open, glittering and dangerous. "That's not what you told Miss Andre when you so rudely doused her."

"I—I had to appear upset."

"Did you now?" He leaned forward. His hands dangled

over his knees. His fingers almost brushed the flesh of her breasts. She leaned against the tub, as far as she could go. It made no difference. "You're lucky she controlled her temper."

"You're damned lucky that I'm controlling mine right now."

"Am I? Why, beloved, is that a threat?"

She didn't answer him. She was shaking all over and she only hoped she had the bravado to make an escape. "If you're going to stay, Malachi, then I'm going to go." She started to rise. He was on his feet in an instant. He set his hands on her shoulders and pressed against them with relentless determination. Water and bubbles swished all around them. Her rear landed hard against the bottom of the tub, and he followed her quickly back down.

"Sit. You're not going anywhere."

"Don't you dare manhandle me! I've had it. I've simply had it! I'm not going to sit—" She tried to rise again. He caught her foot this time. She felt his free hand roaming the water for the soap. His fingers brushed her thighs and her rear and her flank and she gritted her teeth to keep from screaming out.

"Malachi—"

"Sit," he said pleasantly. "Just sit, darlin'."

"Malachi, you son of a bitch!" She tried to pull away. His grip upon her foot was firm. Softly humming "Dixie," he washed her foot with the lavender soap.

She leaned back and spoke through a clenched jaw. "Malachi, I want you out of here! Now! You left me cooling my heels to run off to a saloon. You spent the whole afternoon and evening with a whore. I had to act the way I did—"

"Jealous, darlin'?" He taunted huskily. She opened her eyes. Her foot was free and he had come close to her. Very close. Their limbs were all entangled. She could feel the shaft of his sex against her ankle, the hardness of his thighs against her toes. It was unbearable.

And she could see the pulse beating, beating, against his throat. His lips were close to hers as he spoke.

"Never!" she promised him in a heated panic. "I just can't stand the thought of being sullied by your touch."

"No?" He cocked his head, and his lashes fell lazily over his cheeks. "You didn't mind down in the store this afternoon."

"That was—that was necessary."

"No, I don't think so. I don't think so at all. Shannon, I haven't ever, not even by the most practiced whore, been kissed so provocatively in my entire life."

She leaped up. It had gone too far. Her cheeks were blazing and her breasts were heaving. The bubbles and water sluiced from her, bathing her in a seductive white foam.

Malachi leaned back. His eyes fell on the hardened dark peaks of her breasts as they thrust through the white foam of the bubbles. She saw that look in his eyes again, and she cried out softly as she stepped from the tub. She grabbed for the towel, but she had barely dried her face before he was up behind her. He lifted her cleanly from the ground and tossed her upon Mrs. Haywood's crocheted spread. She gasped for breath, trying to rise. It was impossible. He was down beside her within a split second, a leg cast over her hips and thighs, his arm a bar of steel across her.

"That kiss wasn't necessary at all," he told her.

"I am going to scream, Malachi. I'm going to scream so loudly that you'll be sorry."

"If you scream," he promised her, "it isn't going to be for help."

"You bastard!" She surged against him. "You can't come from a fancyhouse to me—" She broke off, straining against the muscles that held her. She tossed like a wild creature, but it served no purpose. It just put their bodies more fully in contact. Her breasts rubbed against his chest, and her limbs became more and more entangled with his. She felt the hard, searing heart of his desire against her thighs, against her belly.

She tried to kick him and failed, but he swore softly, knowing her intent. He straddled her, keeping himself safe from her rancor, and caught her hands, pinning them to her sides. Exhausted, she twisted her head from his, gasping desperately for breath.

She heard him chuckle softly and she opened her eyes, staring at him in fury. "I will scream, Malachi! You bastard!" Tears glazed her eyes. "Gentleman! Southern cavalier! The last of the flower of knighthood—"

"Shannon, I didn't touch her."

"What?" she breathed.

"She's a friend, and a good one. She's going to do some spying on Fitz for me."

"Fitz?"

"We're not far, not far at all now. Fitz has Kristin. She's in jail."

"Oh, no, Malachi!" She surged against him, bit her lip and fell back.

"But she's all right. Iris is going to go see her. She's going to help us."

"Or else turn you in," Shannon said softly.

He shook his head with irritating confidence. "She's a friend."

"I'll bet she is."

He lay over her, his head close to hers. "You are jealous, Miss McCahy. I told you; I didn't touch her.

"That—that doesn't mean anything at all," Shannon whispered against his lips. "I don't—"

His mouth closed upon hers with a curiously tender force, parting her lips, searing them, causing them to part sweetly beneath his. She lost contact with everything but the fire of his tongue, so hot and hard, thrusting into the depths of her soul and desire. She didn't feel the bed beneath her, or know that gentle candlelight filled the room. She could only taste the fever of his kiss.

She ceased to fight him. Her fingers curled around his. His

mouth lifted from hers, and touched down again upon the column of her throat. The brush of his mustache and beard feathered softly over her flesh, and she moaned, arching hard against him. He lowered his head, sweeping his face over her breasts, slowly encircling one mound with the tip of his tongue, then taking in the fullness of her nipple with the whole of his mouth. His teeth grazed the pebbled peak as he licked it in slow and leisurely fashion.

Her heart was beating like thunder; her blood seemed to hiss and boil and cascade through her, and she could not think of anything but the exquisite pleasure of his touch. Something deep inside her tried to warn her that it was wrong, that no great and everlasting love lay between them, that theirs was the heated and tempestuous passion forged from the hatred borne between sworn enemies.

But she did not hate him. Not at all...

She craved his touch with a basic, undeniable need. She felt the huge pulse of his passion, thundering against her, and she was sweetly excited, pleased that this time there would be no pain at all. She wanted to touch him. She wanted to explore his shoulders and run her fingers over his chest, and she even wanted to venture decadently downward, and touch with fascination the place from which his darkest desire sprung...

His lips moved over her, down to her belly. His tongue laved her with hot moisture, and his beard continued to caress her flesh and evoke a greater surge within her. She wanted him so desperately...

Suddenly he rose above her. His features were tight, but he smiled and he spoke lightly. "Good night, Shannon."

She stared at him in utter disbelief, then the color surged to her face and she tried to strike him in a raw fury. Once again, he secured her hands. He fell to her side and swept her against him. "We need to get some sleep."

"Sleep! I will never sleep with you, you Confederate snake! You rodent, you knave, scalawag! You bastard, you—"

"Enough, Shannon."

"Vulture, diseased rat! Rabid dog!"

"Enough!" He managed to land his hand on her derriere in a sharp slap. She swore again with the venom and expertise of a cowhand, and this time his hand landed over her mouth. "Darlin', let's go to sleep, or I will forget that I'm a gentleman."

"Gentleman!"

"A gentleman," he repeated. "You're the one who wants to be left alone," he reminded her gruffly.

She was quick and twisted around to see his face. His eyes were unreadable, his features taut, his jaw locked. And his eyes...he stared at her as if he hated her, and she found herself lowering her eyes in misery.

It was true. She had wanted to be left alone because...

"Oh, Malachi!" she said miserably, a sob catching in her throat. He was the one who had brought them to their present untenable position, but she had provoked him earlier. She had meant to stir him down in the store, and she had meant to provoke him over at the saloon. She had been sick, imagining him in the arms of the redhead...

"Malachi, I did love Robert," she whispered. "And if I did, then it can't be right, it just can't be right... I don't mean by Sunday-school morals, I mean in the soul, in the heart..."

She was near to tears. She couldn't possibly be speaking to Malachi this way, especially not when she lay naked in bed with him.

But something in his eyes softened, and his touch was very gentle as he drew her against him. "Shannon, I know that you loved him. You've taken nothing away from him by needing to feel warm again." He sighed. His beard brushed the top of her head. His hand lay against her midriff, but it was a tender touch, and not meant to seduce or capture. "Tell me about him."

"What?"

"Tell me about him. When did you meet? What was he like?"

She shook her head. She couldn't begin to imagine Malachi being interested in her deceased Yank fiancé. But he whispered against her hair softly. "Talk to me. It may feel good. You met when the house in Kansas City fell down."

She nodded, absurdly content to lie there, held by him. "I was arrested along with Kristin—for my relationship with Cole. I was arrested for harboring bushwhackers!"

"The Slater men haven't done much for you, have they?" he murmured quietly.

"I didn't mind that. Cole saved us. I always liked Cole. From the first moment I saw him."

Just like she always hated me, Malachi thought. He smoothed back a strand of her hair. What the hell was he doing here? He'd never been that much of a gentleman. Why had he let her go when she was welcoming him against her? He sighed softly.

"It was awful," Shannon said, shivering. "They had so many of us, stuffed into that terrible decrepit building. When the roof collapsed..." She paused. "I thought I was going to die. I was just hanging through the roof when the rafters broke apart. I could hear everyone screaming. And then Robert was there. He and Kristin made me jump. And he caught me. He was so brave and wonderful—a hero. I'll never forget looking into his eyes then. And then...then we heard all the screams again. Five of the women were killed. So many were hurt badly... It was odd. We were friends then, all of us. The other girls knew where my sympathies really lay, and they understood. Josephine Anderson was my friend. When she died, her brother went mad. That's when he really became Bloody Bill, after she died. Oh, Malachi! So many people died!"

"It's all right," he said softly. She was crying. Not sobbing hysterically, just crying very quietly. "It's all right," he said again.

He kept stroking her hair. She didn't speak again, and he didn't speak, either. He closed his eyes, just holding her. It was too painful for any of them to think of the war. North-erner, Southerner, it was just too damned painful to look back. Great men, kind men, good men, all of them dead. Gallant men, alone and moldering in gallant graves. He sighed and closed his eyes. He couldn't let it go on any longer. He had to find some way to free Kristin.

And then he had to find his brothers.

And run.

He opened his eyes. The candles were burning low. He had drifted to sleep. The room was cast in very soft shadows, and the light was pale and ethereal.

He wondered why he had awakened. Then he knew.

Her fingers were moving over his chest. Her nails lightly raked his flesh, and her hair fell over him like a brush with angel's wings. She traced tentative, soft patterns over him, exploring his rib cage and breast and collarbone.

He lay still. He kept his eyes open a slit, watching her. She rose slightly, watching him, watching the movement of her fingers. Her breasts peeked out from the golden glory of her long hair, and as she watched her fingers moving over him, she lightly moistened her lips with the tip of her tongue.

I'll be damned if I'll be a gentleman, he thought. Even cavaliers and knights of old surely had their needs.

He reached out, catching her hand where it lay over his heart. Her eyes darted to his in alarm.

"Go on. Touch me," he whispered.

"I—I didn't mean to wake you," she stuttered. They were both whispering. She must have known that he could not let her go, not this time. She was exquisite in the light, her breasts full and firm and ripe and her skin silky, shining in the candles' pale glow. Her eyes were so very blue…

"I'm awake," he told her.

"I've disturbed you—"

"Disturb me further, darlin'…please." His eyes remained locked with hers. He drew her hand along the length of his body. He heard her breath go ragged in her throat and her eyes followed the motion of their hands with a deadly fascination. Her fingers trailed over his flesh, over the soft hair that nestled around his sex. She tensed, and he felt her trembling. He sensed a certain fear within her, but he held her tight. She curved her hand around it hesitantly.

Rockets seemed to burst within his head and into his body. She gasped softly as she felt him swell huge and hard. She cried out softly. He reached up, slipping his hand around her neck to cup her head. He rose up on an elbow and kissed her slowly and fully, taking her lips, releasing them, hovering over them again just to brush them with the taste of his mouth and the seductive jut of his tongue.

Then he laid her flat and crawled aggressively over her. He kissed her again, easing away her hesitance.

He felt her fingers upon his shoulders again. Her body found a slow undulation beneath his. He set his hand upon her breast, and followed his touch with his kiss. He stroked her thighs and invaded her intimately with his touch.

With raw purpose he moved his body in a slow, bold sweep down the length of hers. He kept his eyes hard upon hers until he came to the juncture of her thighs, when he replaced his intimate touch there with the searing violation of his tongue.

She called out his name in a gasp as he brought her to the very edge of ecstasy, then withdrew. He found her eyes once more and she choked out incomprehensible words, reaching for him. She pulled him to her, seeking his shoulders with her lips and teeth. He pushed away again, demanding that she meet his eyes as he parted her thighs with the wedge of his knee and thrust deep and swiftly inside her.

She shuddered and whispered his name again.

That night, he gave little heed to finesse, and passion rose like a tempest within him. He caught her lips again with a savage passion, and as their bodies arched in an urgent rhythm, he caressed her with rough and demanding hunger.

Her legs wrapped high around him and her kisses fell upon him as she tasted the textures of his face and his throat. Her fingers trailed down his back to knot into the rigid muscles of his buttocks. At the end he cast back his head as a fierce shudder gripped his body, a hoarse cry escaping his lips. She sobbed out in turn, barely aware of the night, of time or place, barely conscious of reality.

Seconds later, she felt his touch, so absurdly gentle once again. Their harsh breathing could still be heard, and they were both covered in a soft sheen. "Malachi—"

"It's all right," he said gently. "You don't have to say anything." He lay back, bringing her down beside him. He whispered softly against her ear. "Just don't think to hop up and leave me. Don't deny me."

She lay there in silence. The darkness closed around them as the last of the candles burned out.

Much later, they crawled beneath the sheet. Shannon knew a moment of panic at this new intimacy, but then she relaxed again. There was nothing left to fear for that night. She hadn't meant what had happened. At least she didn't think that she did. She had thought he slept soundly, and she had not been able to resist temptation.

And temptation had definitely led to sin, she thought.

With his arms closed around her, she felt as if she might start crying again, because it felt so good. His arms offered warmth and security and a steel-hard strength, and she found she loved that. Just as she was coming to love the slant of his grin. And the way he would never let a man—or a woman—down. He had his code of honor.

And in his sweeping way, he was a cavalier.

She loved his courage, and his daring, just as she was coming to love the bronzed power of his arms, holding her close now. Just as she was coming to love the breadth of his golden-matted chest, and the hard, muscled length of his thighs...

And his impossible, immoral intimacy. She could not believe the way that he had touched and caressed her, and neither could she believe the sweet, unbearable ecstasy that he brought her with his sheer decadent purpose and determination. She was coming to care for him too much...

"Malachi," she whispered softly.

"What?" He moved his hand gently against her, beneath her breasts, idly, tenderly upon them.

"Have you ever been in love?"

He went still, then he moved away from her, his arm over his forehead as he rolled to his back, staring at the ceiling. "Yes. Once. Why?"

"I just...wondered."

He grunted, giving her no further answer.

"Malachi?"

"Yes?"

"Who was she?"

"A girl." It was a short, terse answer. He sighed. "It was a long, long time ago."

"What happened?"

"She died."

"The war—"

"A fever."

"I'm so sorry."

"I told you, it was a long, long time ago."

"It hurt you, though. Badly."

"Shannon, go to sleep."

"Malachi—"

"Shannon, go to sleep. It's night, and I'm tired." He started to rise. In the darkness, she saw the glitter in his eyes. "Unless you plan on entertaining me again, I suggest you go to sleep."

She closed her eyes quickly, turning from him and hugging her pillow. She couldn't...do it again. Not that night. She had to hug what had happened to herself, and she had to try to understand it, and live with it.

She felt him as he eased back down.

And later, when she was drifting off to sleep, she felt his arm come around her again, strong and sure, bringing her body close against his. It was warm, and it felt better than she ever might have imagined.

It felt...peaceful.

She opened her eyes and looked down at his hand, brown against the whiteness of her flesh in the moonlight.

It felt right, and though it might not be, she was tired. She was tired of the war, and tired of fighting. She didn't want to worry anymore. She wanted to take moments like these, and cling to them.

Her pa would be twisting and turning in his grave if he knew anything about her behavior in bed with this man, she thought ruefully. Gabriel McCahy had been a strong man—in his beliefs, in his ideals, in his morality. He'd liked his Irish whiskey, and he'd always been able to spin a fine tale, but he'd loved their mother, and when she had died, he'd been determined that his daughters would be ladies.

Of course, he'd never reckoned on the war.

And then, she reflected wistfully, maybe he wouldn't be so upset after all. He'd had an ability to judge men, and he might have understood that she had stumbled upon a good one, albeit, he came clothed in gray.

She closed her eyes and slept, her fingers falling lightly over Malachi's where they lay across her midriff.

"It is him! I told you it was him, Martha!"

Malachi woke abruptly, his eyes flashing open.

The bore of a sawed-off shotgun was stuck right beneath his nose. He jerked up. Shannon, curled against his chest, moaned in protest and went silent again. Instinctively, Malachi pulled the sheets high over her naked form as he stared respectfully into the face of the man carrying the shotgun.

"You're Malachi Slater," Mr. Haywood said. He barely dared glance at his wife, plump and pink in her nightgown and cap behind him. "Martha, you look now. It is him."

"Do you make a habit of bursting into your guests' bedrooms in the middle of the night?" Malachi demanded icily.

Beside him, Shannon stirred. Her eyes flew open and she saw the shotgun. "Oh!" she gasped, grasping the covers. She stared from Malachi to Haywood, and past him to his wife.

She stiffened, raising her chin, and her voice came out as imperiously as a queen's. "What is the meaning of this?"

"There's wanted posters out on him all over the countryside," Haywood said. "You're a dangerous man, Captain Slater. Captain! Hell! Bushwhackers shouldn't get no titles or rank!"

Shannon leaped from the bed, dragging the covers with her, and heedlessly leaving Malachi bare. "He isn't a bushwhacker!" she swore. "It's all a lie! You want to shoot somebody, you ought to go out and shoot Fitz!"

Malachi grimaced at her sudden, passionate loyalty and pulled his pillow around to his lap. "Mr. Haywood, what she's saying is true. I was never a bushwhacker. I was a captain under John Hood Morgan until he died. I signed surrender forms with my men, and we were all allowed to keep our horses, and I was even allowed to keep my arms. I didn't know anything about this until some Union sentries shot at me." He indicated the wound on his leg. The bandage had been lost during his impromptu swim in the stream, but the evidence of Shannon's quick surgery was still there, a jagged red scab.

"Well, I don't know, young man. You're worth an awful lot of money, you know. If this is the truth, you can tell it to Mr. Fitz," Haywood said.

"Fitz will hang him and ask questions later," Shannon said.

Both the Haywoods looked at Malachi again. Malachi barely saw Shannon move, but suddenly she was behind the chair and she was aiming her Colt at the two of them.

"Drop the shotgun," she said.

Mr. Haywood frowned. "Now, come on, little girl. You put that thing down. Those Colts can be mighty dangerous."

"You ever seen close hand what a shotgun does to a man?" she inquired sweetly.

Malachi was afraid of the outcome.

"Can she shoot that thing?" Haywood asked him.

"Better'n General Grant himself, I'm willing to bet," Malachi replied sagely.

He still didn't think it wise to wait. He leaped from the bed. Shannon watched in amazement as he swooped down on Mr. Haywood, bare as birth, and procured the shotgun. Mrs. Haywood gasped in astonishment, but didn't look away from the swaggering male body. Malachi bowed in response to her gasp. "Ma'am, excuse me." He tossed the shotgun to Shannon, reached for his pants and quickly limped into them.

"Oh, my goodness!" Mrs. Haywood gasped again. Her eyes closed and she promptly passed out.

"Oh, no!" Shannon wailed. Wrapping the sheet around herself, she hurried over to the fallen woman. Malachi stopped her, grabbing the Colt from her fingers. Shannon dropped down by Mrs. Haywood. "Malachi, Mr. Haywood, I need some water."

Mr. Haywood moved suddenly, as if rousing himself from shock. "Water. Water." He hurried to the washstand and brought over the pitcher. Nervous and disoriented, he poured the water over his wife's face. She came to, sputtering and coughing. She looked up at her husband. "Mr. Haywood!" she said reproachfully.

"Are you all right?" Shannon murmured.

"We've got to get out of here, Shannon!" Malachi warned her gruffly.

She ignored him. "Mrs. Haywood, I swear to you, I was telling you the truth. You've got to understand the whole story. Mr. Fitz had a brother who led a unit of jayhawkers, Mrs. Haywood—"

"I never could abide jayhawkers," Mr. Haywood said. "Never could abide them! Why, they were just as bad as the bushwhackers themselves."

Shannon nodded. "They killed Cole Slater's wife, Mrs. Haywood. She was expecting a child. She was innocent, and they came and they killed her, and they burned down the ranch... And, well, Cole ran into Henry Fitz toward the end of the war. It was a fair fight—even the Yanks there knew it. Cole killed him.''

"So now Hayden Fitz wants the whole lot of you Slaters, is that it?'' Mr. Haywood asked Malachi.

Malachi nodded. "But that doesn't matter. I want Hayden Fitz. He has Shannon's sister, Cole's new wife, in his jail. He's going to use her, another innocent woman, to lure my brother out of hiding. I'm sorry, Mr. Haywood, but I ain't going to be hunted down and murdered by the likes of Fitz. And I'm mighty sorry, 'cause you and your wife are fine people, but I'm going to have to tie you up so that Shannon and I can get out of here.''

"Shannon?'' Mr. Haywood looked her way, then sank down on the bed. He looked to his wife. "What do you say, mother?''

"I never could abide those jayhawkers. Killing women and innocent children. And that poor dear girl, locked in a jail cell. It ain't decent!''

"Ain't decent at all.''

Malachi looked uneasily from Shannon, kneeling by Mrs. Haywood, to Mr. Haywood, calmly sitting on the bed.

"What—''

"You don't need to tie us up, Captain Slater.''

"I'm sorry, but—''

"You're going to need us, I think. We're not going to turn you in. If what you tell us is true, we'll try to help you.''

"Why?''

"Why?'' Mrs. Haywood stood up, strangely noble despite the water that dripped from her nightcap over her bosom. "Why? 'Cause somewhere, Captain Slater, the healing has to start. Somewhere, it has to quit being North and South, and somewhere, we have to stand against the men going against the very rules of God!''

"Malachi!'' Shannon urged him. "We need them, if they will help us. We need this base. We need...we need the information that we're supposed to get in the next few days.''

Malachi thought furiously. Iris said that these were good folks. And Iris said that she could get to Fitz, and she could probably help him with information that he could never get on his own.

"Malachi! We have to trust them."

Slowly, he lowered the Colt. Then he tossed it onto the bed.

"Shannon, I pray you aren't going to get us both killed," he said savagely.

"Hmph." Mr. Haywood stood, as stout and proud as his wife. He went over and picked up his shotgun. He didn't wave it at Malachi, but he held it in his hand, shaking it.

"So you ain't a bushwhacker and you don't deserve to hang for that! But you aren't this young lady's husband, either, and you should be strung up for seducing an innocent, and that's a fact."

Shannon was surprised to see the flush that touched Malachi's cheeks. "That's none of your business, Mr. Haywood," he said.

"It is our business, captain," Martha Haywood warned him severely. "You were living in sin, right beneath our roof. What do you say, Papa?" she asked her husband.

"I say that he hangs."

"What?" Malachi exploded. He made a dive for the Colt. Mrs. Haywood moved faster. She grabbed the gun and aimed his way. "Now, captain, where are your manners? I never did meet a more gallant boy than a cavalry officer, and a Southern gentleman at that. You should be ashamed of yourself."

"Ashamed! Where have the values gone?" Mr. Haywood said fiercely. "Pride and gallantry and good Christian ethics. The war is over now, son."

"Sir—" Malachi took a step forward. A shot exploded in the room, and he stood dead still. Mrs. Haywood knew what she was doing with a Colt, too, so it seemed. The ball went straight by Malachi's head, nearly grazing his ear.

"Shannon," he said through his teeth, keeping his eyes

warily upon Mrs. Haywood. "Shannon, I am going to wring your neck!"

"No, captain, you're not. You're going to marry that girl, that's what you're going to do."

"I'm not going to be coerced into any marriage!" Malachi swore.

"Well, son, you can marry her or hang," Mr. Haywood guaranteed him. "Mrs. Haywood, would you like to go for the preacher? A Saturday morning wedding seems just right to me."

"No!" Shannon called out.

Malachi looked at her, startled. She was wrapped in the sheet, her hair a wild tangle around her delicate features and beautiful sloping shoulders.

Her eyes were filled with flashing blue anger. "Don't bother, Mrs. Haywood. I won't marry him."

"Well, well, dear, I'm afraid that you'll have to marry him," Mrs. Haywood insisted. "Right is right."

"That's right, young lady. You marry him, or we'll hang him."

Shannon smiled very sweetly, glaring straight at him. "I will not marry him. Mr. Haywood, you'll have to go right ahead. Hang him."

"Shannon!" Malachi swore. He swung around to stare at her in a fury. He was unaware of Mr. Haywood moving around behind him. He really did want to throttle her. His fingers were just itching to get around her neck.

His fury did him in.

He didn't see Mr. Haywood, and he certainly didn't see the water pitcher.

He didn't see anything at all. He simply felt the savage pain when the pitcher burst as Mr. Haywood cracked it hard over his skull.

He was still staring at Shannon, still seeing her standing there in white with her hair a golden, glowing halo streaming angelically all around her...when he fell to the floor.

And blackness consumed him.

Chapter Nine

Two hours later Shannon found herself in the store, standing on a stool, while Martha Haywood fixed the hem of the soft cream gown that Shannon wore.

It was a beautiful, if dated, bridal gown.

It had been Martha Haywood's own. A lace bodice was cut high to the throat with a delicate fichu collar over an undergown of soft pure satin. Ribands of blue silk were woven through the tight waistline, and the lace spilled out over the full wide skirt. Tiny faux pearls had been lovingly sewn into much of the lace.

"Mrs. Haywood, you don't understand," Shannon said urgently. She dropped down at last, catching the woman's nimble hands upon the hem. "Mrs. Haywood, you and your husband can't keep threatening Malachi. I don't want to marry him. And I don't believe you. You can't hang him if I refuse to marry him."

"We can, and we will," Mrs. Haywood said complacently.

"But I don't want to marry him. Please!"

Mrs. Haywood stared at her with her deep brown eyes. "Why? Why don't you want to marry him? You seem to be with him by choice."

"I am with him by choice. No...I mean, yes! But it's more circumstance than choice."

"That still doesn't explain why you don't want to marry him."

"Because...because he doesn't love me. I mean, I don't love him. It's just all—"

"Love comes," Mrs. Haywood told her. "If it isn't there already," she muttered. "The way you two came in here, the way we found you together... You explain yourself to me, young woman."

"I..."

"You just crawled into bed with him just like that...because of circumstances?" Martha Haywood's tone sent rivers of shame sweeping into Shannon. She felt as if she was trying to explain things to a doting and righteous aunt.

"You must have felt something for him. But then again, I'm not arguing that. Did you hear what you told me? You said that he didn't love you. So maybe you do love him. And maybe you're just afraid that he doesn't love you."

Shannon shook her head vehemently. "I promise you that he does not love me. And I do not love him. I was in love, once, during the war. I was engaged to marry a Yankee captain. He was killed...outside Centralia."

Mrs. Haywood finished with the hem and stood. "So you can't love again, and that's that. Why? You think that young man who did love you would want you spending your life in misery." She shook her head slowly and gravely. "The world has a lot of healing to do. And you should maybe start with your own heart. This Captain Slater seduced you under my roof, young lady. And you were curled up to him sweet as a princess bride this morning, so you're halfway there."

"Mrs. Haywood—"

"Papa has gone for the preacher. He is the local magistrate, so he's the law here. Oh, don't you worry none. Papa and me won't ever let on to anyone that we know your man's really a Slater. And the reverend will keep the secret, too. That is, if you two do the decent thing and marry up."

"You can't hang him for not marrying me!"

Mrs. Haywood laughed delightedly. "Maybe not, but there

ain't no law against hanging a criminal. Captain Slater under-
stands. Papa explained it to him real clearly.''

''Mrs. Haywood—''

''Lord love us, child, but you do look extraordinarily fine!''
She stepped back from the stool, gazing over Shannon and
her handiwork with rapture. Tears dampened her eyes.

''Mrs. Haywood, this dress is beautiful. Your kindness to
me is wonderful, but I still can't—''

''I had meant to see my own daughter in it one day. She
was such a pretty little thing. Blond, with blue eyes just like
you. And if I'd a caught her in bed with a Rebel captain, it'd
have been a shotgun wedding, too, I promise.''

''You…had a daughter?''

''Smallpox took Lorna away,'' Mrs. Haywood said softly.
She wiped a tear from her cheek. ''Never did think I'd put a
young lady in this dress, so it's quite a pleasure.''

Shannon sighed deeply. She should have just run away. She
should have run from the house, screaming insanely, and then
maybe the Haywoods would have understood.

But she just couldn't tell if they really intended to hang
Malachi or not. If they weren't going to hang him for being
a wanted man, surely they wouldn't for not being the marrying
kind.

Still, she couldn't just run away. Not when they had locked
him up. Not when they were holding all the weapons.

''Mrs. Haywood, please try to understand me—''

''Did you ever stop to think that Hayden Fitz just might get
his hands on your man?'' Martha asked her.

''What…do you mean?''

''Your man is going after your sister, his brother's wife. He
ain't going to stop until he has her. He'll succeed with his
mission, or he'll die in the attempt. I know his type. I saw all
kinds during the war. Men who would run under fire; men
who carried their honor more dear to their hearts than life.
Your boy is one of the latter, Miss Shannon. So you tell me,
what if Fitz gets his hands on the boy?''

"He...he won't," Shannon said.

"He could. I promise you, lots of folks wouldn't have paused like Papa and me. Fitz has power in these parts. Lots of it. He owns the mortgage on a dozen ranches, and he owns the ranchers, too. He owns the sheriff and he owns the deputies. So you tell me, what if Fitz gets his hands on this boy and kills him? What if you were free of us, and Fitz caught him and killed him anyway?"

"I don't...I don't understand what you're trying to say," Shannon protested.

"What if you're carrying that man's child and they hang him? What'll you tell your son or your daughter?"

Shannon felt herself growing pale, and she wasn't sure just what it was that Mrs. Haywood's grim words did to her. She had known all the while that they were entering into a dangerous world.

She knew that people died. She had been watching them die for years.

She felt ill and flushed and hot. Was she such a fool? Did everyone else think so rationally? The odds seemed so foolishly against them...

She still couldn't marry him. Not if she carried ten of his children, not if they were both about to be hanged in a matter of seconds. And suddenly she realized why.

She did feel for him. He had created a tempest deep within her heart, and it was with her always.

She didn't know how to put a name on the feeling. She didn't know if it was love or hatred or a combination of both. The thought of him with another woman had made her insanely jealous, and it had been humiliating to see how quickly he could still arouse her in the wake of her anger. Maybe their hatred had been mixed with love from the very beginning. Maybe circumstances were letting all her emotions explode here and now.

But she couldn't marry him.

She had heard herself. He didn't love her. And if he was

forced into marrying, he would never forgive her. Not in this lifetime, or the next, and he would escape her as soon as he possibly could. She didn't want the misery for either of them.

If she was ever to have him, it had to be of his own free will.

"Mrs. Haywood, I can't—"

"Let's go into the next room. I hear voices. Papa must be in there with the preacher, and it's high time that we got on with the ceremony."

"Mrs. Haywood—"

The woman stopped and turned to her, her hands folded serenely before her. "Papa is not a patient man, young lady. And I'll wager he's got the shotgun aimed right at your Captain Slater's heart. Don't tarry, now. I don't want him getting nervous. The poor fellow might move in the wrong direction and Papa might decide to shoot him in the kneecap just to make sure that he sticks around."

With a smile she turned and opened the shelved door and proceeded into the parlor. Shannon hurried behind her. They didn't mean it. They wouldn't shoot Malachi, and they wouldn't hang him, either.

Would they?

She stopped short when she came to the entrance of the parlor.

Malachi was there. He was standing right in the center of the parlor.

Mr. Haywood had apparently decided to dress Malachi for the occasion, as well. He was wearing a ruffled white shirt and a pin-striped suit with a red satin vest and a black-lapelled frock coat. She'd never seen him dressed so elegantly, and her breath caught in her throat as she saw him. The beauty of his costume was offset by the raw menace in his eyes and the rugged twist of his jaw. She had never seen him so coldly furious, nor had his eyes ever touched upon hers with such glaring hatred and with such a raw promise of revenge.

For a moment she couldn't move farther. She couldn't

breathe, and she believed that her heart had ceased to beat. Panic made her seize hold of the doorway, meeting the savage fury of his glare.

"Come in, come in!" Mr. Haywood called.

She still didn't move. Then she realized that the preacher was moving behind Malachi. He was a tall thin man with a stovepipe hat and black trousers and a black frock coat. He nodded to her grimly.

She heard a peculiar sound and looked at Malachi again...and saw that his wrists were shackled by a pair of handcuffs.

"Oh...really, please," she murmured. "Please, you all must understand..."

"Talk to her, captain. Talk to her quick," Mr. Haywood advised Malachi. He, too, was all spruced up in a silk shirt and brown trousers, which gave him a dignity he had lacked earlier. One arm was around his wife's shoulders; in the other, he carried the shotgun.

"Get over here!" Malachi snapped to Shannon.

The deep grate of his voice brought her temper surging to the fore. "Malachi, damn you, I am trying—"

She broke off with a gasp because he was striding her way with purpose and hostility. He might have been shackled but he managed to get a grip around her wrist, jerking her hard against him. She shivered as she felt the fire and tension and fury within him and felt his heated whisper against her cheeks.

"Get over here and marry me."

"Malachi, I don't believe them. I don't believe that they'll hang you if we don't marry."

He glared at her. "So you want to wait—and see?" he asked her slowly.

"I don't think—"

"You don't think! Do you want to wait until they tie the rope around my neck? Or maybe we should wait until I'm swinging in the breeze!"

"We could—"

"Shannon! Get over here and marry me now!"

"No! I will not—"

"You will, damn you!"

"I won't! Malachi, it wouldn't be right—"

"Right! You're talking about right? At a moment like this you're worried about right?"

"I don't love you!"

"And I don't love you, so maybe we're perfectly right!" His eyes narrowed to a razor's edge, raked hers with contempt. "They'll hang me, you bitch! Get over here and do it."

"What a wonderful way to ask!" she hissed sweetly.

His jaw twisted and set. "I'm not asking you, I'm telling you."

"And I'm afraid I'm not listening."

His fingers tightened around her wrist with such a vengeance that she cried out softly again.

"Captain Slater!" Martha Haywood protested, calling from the center of the parlor.

He didn't ease his hold. She found herself watching the pulse at the base of his throat with a deadly fascination. She felt weaker than she had ever felt in her life. She had thought she knew how to match her temper to his.

But maybe she didn't.

He pressed her up against the door frame, hard. "Shannon, you can get out of this later. You can say that you were coerced. But for the love of God, get over there now."

Some demon steamed inside her then, and she didn't know quite how to control it. All of her seemed awhirl in a tempest of hot blood and raw emotion. His anger fed her own. And for once, he was powerless against her.

"I don't like the way you're asking, captain," she told him icily.

He wasn't powerless, not in the least. With a swift turn on his heel, he dragged her along after him into the center of the room. She was stunned when he fell down on one knee, maintaining his firm grip on her before the preacher and the Haywoods. "Miss McCahy!" he hissed, the words dropping like sharp icicles from his mouth. "Dear Miss McCahy—beloved. Do me the honor this day of becoming my lawful wedded wife!"

"That wasn't exactly voiced the way I always thought that I'd hear the words!" Shannon retorted.

"Please, please, please, my beloved darlin'!" he said, rising swiftly, his eyes like knives that sliced through her. She was shaking, knowing that she pushed him. But he could have protested, too. He could have done more than he was doing.

"One more please, captain. And make it a good one."

"Please," he said. She had never heard anything that sounded less like an entreaty. He looked like some savage creature, and he didn't just want to chew her all up, he wanted to skin her alive first. But her demons told her they shouldn't be doing this.

He didn't wait for her answer, but turned to the reverend. "Go ahead, preacher man," he said dryly. "Get to it."

"No!" Shannon protested.

Mr. Haywood cocked the shotgun. The preacher began the ceremony.

Shannon listened to him in a daze. She could no longer run screaming into the street, because Malachi held her in a vise. Nor could she really risk it. Maybe Haywood would hang Malachi. She just didn't know.

The preacher was nervous. Looking at Malachi would probably make anyone nervous. Only the Haywoods seemed complacent.

Malachi answered the preacher in a cold raw fury, biting off each of his words. He spoke loudly and with a vengeance, enunciating each word. Love, honor and cherish. Till death did them part.

When her turn came, Shannon couldn't answer. She turned to him with one last fervent plea.

"Malachi, we can't do this—"

"Love, honor and obey!" he snapped at her.

"Malachi—"

"Say it!"

Shivering, she turned to the preacher. She stuttered out the words.

"The ring," the preacher said, clearing his throat.

"The ring?" Malachi said blankly.

"I've got it, Reverend Fuller," Mr. Haywood said. He stepped forward and placed a small gold band in Malachi's hand. Malachi stared at the man for a moment, fingering the gold. Then he slipped the ring on Shannon's finger, despite the fact that she was shaking so badly that her hands weren't still at all.

"We owe you again, Mr. Haywood," Malachi muttered.

"Don't worry. Price of the ring will be on your bill," Mr. Haywood said complacently.

"Hush, Papa! This is a beautiful rite!" Mrs. Haywood murmured.

It fit her tightly, snugly. Shannon felt the gold around her finger as smoothly and coldly as Malachi must feel the steel of the cuffs around his wrists. His eyes touched hers with a searing blue hatred and she thought that she could not wait to remove the ring.

Seconds later the preacher was saying that by the authority vested in him by the law of the great State of Kansas, and the greater authority vested in him by the glory of God on high, he now pronounced them man and wife.

Mrs. Haywood let out a long sob, startling them all. They stared at her. She blew her nose and smiled wistfully. "Don't mind me, dears, I always cry at weddings. Papa, release the groom from those shackles. He probably wants to kiss his bride. Reverend Fuller, could you do with a touch of Madeira? We've no champagne, I'm afraid. Maybe we've some across the way."

Reverend Fuller said that Madeira would be just fine. Malachi stared at Shannon venomously as Mr. Haywood came to him with a small key and freed him from the handcuffs.

"Captain Slater, a glass of Madeira?" Mrs. Haywood began.

But Malachi, freed, paid her no attention. He dragged Shannon into his arms and forced his mouth hard against hers with brutal purpose. His fingers raked her hair at her nape, holding her still for his onslaught. His tongue surged against her lips and forced them apart, raked against her teeth and invaded the whole of her mouth with ruthless abandon. Finally his mouth left hers and his lips touched her throat where it lay arched to him with deliberate possession. Then his mouth demanded hers again. His fingers trailed over the white lace of her gown with idle leisure and abandon, cupping lightly over her breast. The savage fury and heat of his kiss left her breathless, and with a searing sense of both clashing, tempestuous passion, and of deep, shattering humiliation that he would touch her so before others.

She felt the wrath in him deeply. It burned around him, and emitted from him in waves. She was amazed that he had married her; that he hadn't told the Haywoods to go ahead and hang him, and be damned. She hadn't thought that Malachi could be coerced into doing anything that he didn't want to do, but it seemed that they had managed to coerce him.

She tore away from him; he let her go. The back of her hand rose to her lips, as if she could wipe away his touch. "They should have hanged you!" she hissed.

He blinked, and opaque shadows fell over his eyes. He bowed to her in a deep mockery of courtesy.

"You were trying hard enough, weren't you?"

He didn't give her a chance to answer. He swung around to Mrs. Haywood. "I thank you for your hospitality, ma'am," he drawled with a sure trace of sarcasm, "but I think I've a mind for something a little stronger at the moment." He strode toward the front door, then paused, looking back. "I have fulfilled your requirements to escape the hangman, haven't I?"

"Sign your name on the license, and you're free to go," Mrs. Haywood said.

Malachi walked to the marble-topped table where the license lay. He signed his name with an impatient scrawl and looked at Mr. Haywood, his jaw twisted hard, his hands on his hips.

Mr. Haywood nodded to him grimly. Malachi cast Shannon one last glare and then he threw open the door, slamming it in his wake. Shannon stared after him as cold fingers seemed to close over her heart.

"Madeira?" Mrs. Haywood offered her with a winning smile.

Shannon mechanically accepted the glass of wine. She cast back her head and swallowed it down in a single gulp. It wasn't enough. Malachi was right about one thing—they both needed to head straight for the whiskey.

She set her glass down. The wine tasted like bitter acid in her present mood. "I'll give you your dress back, Mrs. Haywood," she said simply. She turned, nodded to the preacher and to Mr. Haywood, and ran up the stairs. She found both keys on the bedside table, and picked them up, biting into her lower lip with such force that she drew a trickle of blood.

Malachi might really be her husband now, but he wasn't coming into this room again. Ever.

Ever!

She couldn't admit it, not even to herself, that her fury came mainly from the fact that she was afraid that he wouldn't even try.

He had slipped a ring upon her finger, forcing her to issue vows, and then he had left her.

For a red-haired whore.

No, he wouldn't be coming in the room again. Ever...

"Why, Ma—Sloan!" Iris called out to him as he entered the saloon. She never would get accustomed to calling him by another name.

He nodded her way and walked up to the bar, tossing down

a coin. "Whiskey, Matey, if you would, sir. Whiskey, and lots of it."

Iris, pretty as a picture in a quiet gray dress and blue shawl, hurried over to him. She slipped her arm through his. "I was about to leave. I'm going to take the buggy and head for Sparks and see what I might find out about your sister-in-law. Is it still safe for me to leave? What's happened?"

He looked at Iris, at the concern naked in her eyes. He felt her soft touch on his arm, and some of the anger eased out of him.

"It's safe." He caught her to him and tenderly kissed her forehead. "You're a fine woman, Iris. Funny, ain't it? You really are such a fine damned woman no matter what your vocation. And her..."

"Your...traveling companion?"

"The little darlin'...yes. Shannon." He grimaced, staring at the ceiling, then he laughed bitterly. "My traveling companion. The curse of my life! The sweet little—hellcat!"

"What did she do now?"

"Damned little witch. I should have let you floor her yesterday, Iris. Hell." Matey put the whiskey bottle in front of him and he took a long, long swallow, gasping as the liquor sizzled its way down his throat to his stomach. He looked at the bottle reflectively. "I should have floored her myself."

"Malachi..." Iris realized that she had used his name, and she looked quickly around. The saloon was nearly empty. Only Matey might have heard her, and Matey minded his own business. "Let's go to my room, Mr. Gabriel," she said softly.

Malachi looked at her speculatively and picked up the whiskey bottle. "Yes, Iris, let's go to your room."

She led him up a flight of stairs in the rear and opened the first door.

She had a real nice room for a working girl, Malachi thought. There was a big bed with four carved posters and a quilted spread, a braided rug on the floor, a handsome dresser and a full-length mirror on a stand.

"Nice," Malachi murmured. He drank more of the whiskey. He drank deeply, then he crashed down on the bed. He reached out for Iris with a slow smile curving into his lips. She sat down by his side, but watched him speculatively. He stroked her arm, and soft, feathery tendrils of desire swept along her flesh. She wanted to be touched by him. She had almost forgotten the feeling of wanting to be touched.

She pulled her arm away. He swallowed more whiskey, leaving one last slug in the bottle. Then he just lay there, staring at the ceiling.

"I want to kill her, Iris. I want to close my fingers right around her lovely white throat, and I want to squeeze until she chokes. I want to take my hand..." He raised his right hand as he spoke, studying the length of his fingers and the breadth of his palm, flexing his fingers. "I want to smack my hand against her flesh until it's raw...I want to shake her until her damned teeth crack!"

"Malachi, what happened?" Iris asked him softly.

His eyes fell upon her. His lip curved into a twisted, wry grin. "I married her. For real."

Iris lowered her eyes, swallowing. "Why?"

"They said they'd hang me if I didn't. They're convinced that she's a sweet young innocent and that I seduced her."

"Didn't you?"

"No. Yes. Hell, she's almost twenty now, she's as sweet as raw acid, and as to her innocence..."

"Yes?"

"She seduced me equally. No one innocent has a right to look the way she does...naked."

Iris would have laughed if she didn't feel such a peculiar hurt deep inside.

It wasn't that he had married the girl. It was the way he spoke about her.

"Now who is it who thought that you weren't married to begin with? Who thought that she was...seduced?"

"The Haywoods. They said they'd hang me."

"Of course they would want to hang you! You're worth a lot of money, dead or alive. There's a bounty on your head. If they know that you're not married, then they know—"

"They don't care who I am. They don't intend to let the knowledge go past themselves—and the reverend, of course," he added bitterly.

Iris exhaled softly. "Thank God for that!"

Malachi grimaced. "They weren't going to hang me for being a Confederate, a bushwhacker, or Cole's brother. They wanted to hang me because I seduced Shannon!"

Iris inhaled deeply. She couldn't believe that she was going to defend the other woman, that beautiful young woman with the sky-colored eyes, alabaster skin and the sun-drenched fall of long, curling hair.

But she was.

"Malachi, if the Haywoods forced you into a marriage, you can't really blame her." She paused, frowning. "Did she tell them...who you really are? Did she demand that you marry her? I mean, they are real God-fearing folk. Did they do it? Or did she force and coerce you?"

"What?" He stared at her blankly.

"Malachi, you can't hate her if they forced it. Maybe you can't even really hate her if she did make them force you into it. She isn't...well, she isn't my kind of woman. If you took advantage of her, maybe she had a right to force you—"

"She didn't force me."

"Then—"

"The bitch!" he exploded. "They're sitting there swearing up and down that they will hang me—and she's refusing! She's sitting there arguing with a shotgun. I was barely able to make her spit out the words! She would have made me hang."

"Then..."

"She's a witch, Iris," he said softly. He swallowed the last slug of whiskey. Iris hoped he wasn't heading for one heavy drunken stupor; even an experienced drinker like him would have trouble with the amount he had swallowed in the last ten minutes. "She's a witch," Malachi continued. "I mean to touch her, and I'm furious, and I want to hurt her. And I don't quite understand it, 'cause I'm hurting myself. I dream of her eyes. I dream of her reaching out to me. And then sometimes she touches me and I feel everything in me exploding just to touch her back, to feel her softness, to see her smile, to see her eyes glaze with wanting... She teases and she taunts, and she loves like a wildcat, like a pagan temptress, then she bares her claws and she swipes out and she draws blood, Iris, blood."

Iris smiled slowly. He still wasn't looking at her. He was staring at the ceiling. He turned around and suddenly grasped her hand. He kissed her fingers, and she shivered, feeling the sensual movement of his lips and beard against her flesh. "She's not like you, Iris. She's not like you at all. You can't ever talk to her, you can't reason with her. She's a witch...I've been fighting her forever and forever, Iris. Always fighting. She would have let me hang, can you believe that?"

"They wouldn't have hanged you," Iris said.

"She didn't know that."

"Maybe she did."

"She didn't, and that's a fact." He sat up. His eyes glittered. "Well, she has married me now. And she's going to pay for it!"

"Malachi, you were mad because she wouldn't marry you."

"She wanted them to shoot my kneecaps, the witch! But now, now she's mine..."

He fell back. His eyes closed.

Iris watched him for a minute. He was asleep. She smiled ruefully. "She may be a witch, but you're in love with her," Iris said softly.

She set the empty whiskey bottle on the dressing table, and decided to leave him where he was. Let him sleep off the bottle of whiskey he had swallowed in ten minutes, and maybe he'd go back to his tender young bride in a better state of mind.

She picked up her portmanteau and hat, walked to the door and blew him a kiss sadly. "I'll be back tomorrow, captain," she said softly. "Even if you do love her, I've got to help you."

She turned around and left him. If she hurried, she could make it to Sparks, spend plenty of time there and still be back in Haywood by the morning with all the information she could gather. She had friends in Sparks. Friends of the best variety for what she needed now. They were smart, beautiful women. And they knew the men of Sparks.

She looked back with a wistful smile.

Malachi slept peacefully.

Iris shrugged. He probably needed the rest.

She left, letting him sleep on.

And on...

Shannon changed and returned Martha Haywood's gown immediately, thanking her. She didn't want to wear Malachi's shirt any longer than she had to, so she determined to go into the mercantile and find another. Martha followed beside her, talking about her own early years of marriage.

"They were a hoot and a holler, I do tell you. Why, we were madder 'n wet hens at each other time and again, but then, I don't really remember what one of those arguments was about."

Shannon found a pretty soft blue blouse with teal embroidery along the bodice. She set it on the counter with boxes of ammunition. "First off," she told Martha Haywood softly, "we've got the same conflicts between us that just set a whole country to war."

"The war is over," Martha reminded her.

"Secondly, I knew a man once who was always gentle. He never had a temper about him."

"You'd have been miserable in a year."

Shannon gasped in horror. "That's not true! I was in love with him, I was deeply in love with him—"

"And you can't let it go. Still, it's true. You'd have been miserable in a year. Now, I don't think that you and Captain Slater will be getting along real well for a long time to come. But I think you'll come to realize that you have more in common than can be seen."

Shannon flushed. She set her hands on her hips. "He's been over at the saloon all day, Mrs. Haywood."

"Well, go on over and get him then. If you want him back, go on over and get him."

Shannon bit her lip, pretending to study the beautiful new blouse. "It's wonderful embroidery," she said softly. Then she smiled at Mrs. Haywood. "I don't want him, Mrs. Haywood. I don't want him near me again, and I mean it. He's been over in that saloon all day..." She swallowed fiercely. "Mrs. Haywood, could I have a tray sent up to me? I think that I want to retire early."

"It was a hard tonic for him to swallow, Shannon, being manipulated by us and all. I'm amazed that he was as docile as he was. And it must have been darned hard on him when you turned him down—"

"He didn't want to marry me."

"You refused to marry him when we might have hanged him!"

"You wouldn't have hanged him. Thank you for trying, Mrs. Haywood. I need to lie down for a while."

"It's very early," Martha told her anxiously.

"Yes, I know. Now, you're running a tab on everything, right? I should be ashamed. We came out of the war much better than many folks. I do have money."

"We're running a tab, Mrs. Slater."

Mrs. Slater. The name sounded absurd, and she hated it!

Malachi had been in the saloon for hours and hours now. And if he tried to tell her that he wasn't with the redhead this time, she'd probably scream and go mad on the spot.

Impulsively, she kissed Mrs. Haywood on the cheek. "I really need to lie down," she said softly. "Thank you so much for everything."

Shannon stepped into the parlor. She realized that she was absently twisting the ring around her finger. She tried to wrench it off. It was too tight. Soap might take it off.

On impulse, she hurried to the door to the street and pushed it open. Things were quiet, very quiet. An old bloodhound lifted his head from his paws across the way on the saloon veranda. He looked at Shannon, then dropped his head again. Two men idly conversed down the way before the barber's shop, and that was it.

Shannon strode down the steps and across to the saloon. She entered the building, assuring herself that she wasn't going to do anything but order herself a brandy.

She pushed through the swinging doors. The saloon, she saw, as her eyes adjusted to the darkness, was almost as quiet as the street. A lone rancher sat in the back, his hat pulled low over his eyes, hiding his face. A blond harlot in crimson silk sat upon the bar, absently curling a strand of hair around her finger.

The barkeep was drying glasses. He looked at Shannon warily.

"May I have a brandy, please? And could you put it on my husband's tab?"

He shrugged uncertainly, found a glass, filled it and set it before Shannon. She nodded her thanks and swallowed the brandy down. She looked around the saloon again. Malachi was definitely not there.

Kristin would be horrified that she was standing in the saloon, Shannon thought. But then Kristin had always been more conventional, and Kristin had always had a better hold on her temper. Well, maybe not. Kristin had waged a few battles with Cole, and Cole was such a lamb in comparison with Malachi. None of that would matter to Kristin. A lady shouldn't be in a saloon like that.

Even if she was wondering what her husband of five hours was up to.

He wasn't in the saloon.

"Have you seen, er, Mr. Gabriel?" she asked the bartender sweetly.

The blond woman answered, looking her up and down and smiling sweetly. "He's still sleeping up in Iris's room, last I heard."

Shannon felt dizzy. It was as if the whole room went black, then seemed to be covered in a red haze.

"Thank you very much," she said pleasantly. "When you do see him again, please tell him that he is most welcome to remain where he is, and that he will not be at all welcome elsewhere. Thank you."

"Wait," the woman began.

But Shannon cut her off with a clipped, commanding tone, her chin high, her eyes a cutting, crystal blue. There was a note of warning in her voice. "Please, just see that he gets my message." She'd had no idea that she could speak quite so commandingly, but the woman's next words died on her lips and Shannon turned and left the saloon. In the middle of the street, she suddenly paused, doubled over and let out a deep, furious, and anguished scream.

Martha Haywood came running out of her parlor. "Oh, dear, oh dear, what is it?"

Shannon straightened. "Nothing. I'm fine, Mrs. Haywood."

"You're fine!" Mrs. Haywood exclaimed. "That didn't sound at all like fine to me!"

"Well, I wasn't fine until I did it. Now, I am fine. I promise you." She wasn't fine at all. She felt as if she was being ripped apart on the insides by sharp talons. She wanted to kill Malachi. Slowly. She wanted to stake him out on the plain and allow a herd of wild buffalo to trample him into the dust. She wanted to watch the vultures come down and chew him to pieces. She wanted...

She wanted him to come back so she could tell him just

how furious she was. And how hurt. How deeply, agoniz-ingly...hurt.

"I am fine, Mrs. Haywood," she repeated, smiling, stiff-ening. She clung to her temper. She would never forgive him. Never. She stood as tall as she could, straightening her shoul-ders. "Just fine. If you'll excuse me... Can you please see to it that I'm not disturbed until the morning?" She pushed past Martha and hurried into the house. She raced up the stairs and went into her room, locking the door and assuring herself that she had both keys.

She gasped, trembling, as she looked around.

Martha Haywood had tried so hard to make it welcoming!

Hot water steamed in the bath and there were fresh flowers beside the bed. A silver tray with cold meat and pastries sat on a table, and across the bed lay one of the most beautiful white satin nightgowns she had ever seen. There was a note on it. Shannon picked it up. "Every bride deserves a new thing of beauty. Wear it with our warmest wishes. Martha and Hank."

She set down the note and sank onto the bed, and suddenly she was softly sobbing. Every woman harbored and cherished dreams of just such a gown on her wedding night. And every woman cherished her dreams of a man, magnificent and gal-lant and handsome. A man who would hold her and love her...

She had the gown, and she had the man. But the dream had dispersed in the garish light of reality.

Malachi did not love her.

She lay on the bed and gave way to the flood of tears that overwhelmed her, and then, when her tears dried, she stared at the ceiling and she wondered just how long she had really been in love with Malachi. They'd never had a chance to be friends. From the start the war had come between them.

But she would never forgive him for this. Never. Come what may, he would never touch her again.

Whether he'd been coerced into marriage at gunpoint, it hadn't been her doing; she'd tried her best to stop it all. He'd had no right to go straight to the red-haired whore, and she would never forgive him.

After a while, the shadows of twilight played upon the windows. The bath had grown chilly, but she decided to indulge in it. She carefully set a chair under the doorhandle first; she wasn't taking any chances.

There was a bottle of wine with the food on the table. Shannon sipped a glass as she bathed quickly.

She even donned the beautiful satin gown.

In time, she stretched out in bed. She closed her eyes and she remembered him the evening before, coming into the room with a vengeance and a purpose. Sweeping her up, holding her.

Claiming his rights, when they weren't in truth married.

But now she was his bride.

Eventually, she closed her eyes. She had her Colt by her side, fully loaded. If he tried to return, she would demand that he leave quickly enough, and she would enforce her words.

But this night, their wedding night in truth, he did not return.

Toward dawn, she cried softly again.

He was her husband now. He did have certain rights.

But he wasn't coming back. Not that night.

Chapter Ten

At two in the morning, Malachi stirred. His head was killing him; his mouth tasted as if he had been poisoned, and his tongue felt as if it was swollen in his throat. A clock ticked with excruciating, heavy beats on the mantel.

He staggered out of bed and peered at the clock. When he saw the time he groaned and looked around the room. Iris was gone. She was a good kid. She had gone to Sparks, trying to help him. He was sleeping in her room, while Shannon...

Oh, hell.

His head pounded with a renewed and brutally savage fury. Shannon...

Shannon would be sleeping, too, by then. If she wasn't sleeping, it was even worse. She'd be furious, hotter than a range fire.

He threw himself back on the bed. The hell with her. They were going to have one fabulous fight, he was certain. It couldn't be helped.

He was going to be a rational man, he promised himself. He was going to be level and quiet. He was going to be a gentleman. Every bit as much a gentleman as the Yank she mourned.

The hero...

Well, hell, at this moment, it was easier for a Yank to be a hero. Rebs weren't doing very well. Just like she liked to tell him—they had lost the war.

Darlin'…the South will rise again, it will, it will, he vowed to himself. Then he remembered that he had just promised himself that he was gong to be reasonable.

They were married to one another.

His head started pounding worse as his blood picked up the rhythm, slamming against his veins. He was married to her…for real. If he had a mind to, he could walk right across that street and sweep her into his arms. He could do everything that the rampant pulse inside him demanded that he do. He could meet the blue sizzling fire in her eyes and dig his hands through her hair and bury his face against her breasts. He could touch her skin, softer than satin, sweeter than nectar, he could…

Rape his own wife, he thought dryly, for she sure as hell wasn't going to welcome him.

She would have let him hang! He was the one with the right to be furious. Granted, he would have come for Kristin with or without Shannon—he had meant to come without her—but it was still her sister he had traveled into enemy territory to save.

He could have been in Mexico by now. He could have been living it up in London or Paris. There was no more cause, no South left to save. It was over.

It should have been over.

He exhaled. He wasn't going to go to her now. She'd surely bolted the door against him. And the house would be silent. Dead silent. It just wasn't the time for a brawl, which is what it would be.

If she didn't just shoot him right off and get it over with.

She wouldn't shoot him. She was his wife now.

Yeah, a wife pining for a divorce, or pining to become a widow quick as a wink.

The turmoil and tempest were swirling inside him again. He didn't want to start drinking. He rose and went to the washstand and scrubbed his face and rinsed out his mouth, availing himself of Iris's rose water to gargle with. He felt a little better. No, he felt like hell. He felt like...

Racing across the street and breaking the door down and telling her that she was his and that she would never lock a door against him again, ever...

He groaned, burying his head in his hands. They were just a pair of heartfelt enemies, cast together by the most absurd whims of fate. She was in love with a dead man, and he wasn't in love at all. Or maybe he was in love with...with certain things about her. Maybe he was just in love. Maybe there really was a mighty thin line between love and hate, and maybe the two of them were walking it.

He walked to the window and stared at the night.

The new moon was coming in at long last, casting a curious glow upon the empty street.

They were forgetting their mission. Kristin...they had come all this way and met with physical danger, culminating with the last encounter with the Haywoods. They had come together in a burst of passion, and they had exchanged vows, and now they were legally wed, man and wife, and despite it all, they were still enemies, and despite it all, he could still never forget her, never cease to want her.

He walked over to the bed and lay down, folding his hands behind his head, staring at the ceiling. Iris would come back, and then he would have a better idea of what to do next. Cole must have heard what was happening by now. Jamie, too. And once they had heard about Kristin, they would have started moving this way.

He and Shannon had to start moving again. They had to cease the battle and come to a truce and worry about their personal problems later.

It was the only logical move...the only reasonable one.

He gritted his teeth hard against the fever and tremor that seized him again. He steeled himself against thoughts of her. He wanted her so badly...he could see her. He could see her as she had been in his dream, rising from the water, glimmering drops sluicing down her full, full breasts…water running sleek down the slimness of her flanks, down her thighs…

He could see her eyes, dusky blue, beautiful as they met his in the mists of passion. He could almost feel her moving against him, sweetly rhythmic. He could hear her whispering to him…whimpering, crying out softly and stirring him to a greater flame, a greater hunger…

Logical, reasonable. This was insane.

He was a gentleman, he reminded himself. He had been raised to be a Southern gentleman; he had fought a war to preserve the Southern way of life, perhaps the great Southern myth. He didn't know. But he had been taught certain things. He loved his brother; he would always honor his brother's wife. He believed in the sanctity of honor, and that in the stark horror of defeat, a man could still find honor.

Logic…reason. When the morning came, he would defy the very fires within him. She would not be able to ask for a more perfect gentleman. As long as she didn't touch him, he would be all right.

The perfect gentleman.

If not quite her hero.

Someone was turning the knob of her door.

Shannon didn't understand at first just what was awakening her. Something had penetrated the wall of sleep that had come to her at last.

She lifted her head and she listened. At first, she heard nothing.

Then she heard it. The knob was twisting. Slowly. Some weight came against the door. Then the knob twisted and turned again and again. Someone was trying to be quiet; stealthy.

She rose, biting into her lower lip.

It was Malachi, at last.

She leaped out of bed and ran to the Haywoods' lovely little

German porcelain clock. She brought it close to her eyes and looked at the time.

It was almost three in the morning.

She spun around. The knob was twisting...

Malachi. Damn him! He had finished with his whore, and now he wanted to come back to her to sleep! On her wedding day!

Oh, granted, it was no normal wedding day!

But still...

She hated him! She hated him with a vengeance! With everything inside her. How could he? How could he drag her—force her!—into this horrid mockery of marriage, and then spend the day with a harlot. After last night...

It was foolish to give in to him, ever.

She hadn't meant to give in to him.

Ever.

She had simply wanted him, and therefore, it had never been so much a matter of giving, it had been a matter of wanting. Of longing to touch, and to be touched in turn. Of needing his arms. Of needing his very height, and his strength. Of hearing his voice with the deep Southern drawl, of feeling his muscled nakedness close to her...

She had loved once.

And she loved now, again. Perhaps he could never understand. And if she valued not only her pride but her soul and her sanity, he could not know.

Not that it mattered. She could never let him in; she could never let him touch her again. He couldn't come straight from his whore to her. Whether emotion entered into it or not. He just couldn't do it, and that was the way that it was.

Her eyes narrowed; she was ready for battle.

But the doorknob twisted one last time, and then she heard footsteps—soft, soft footsteps!—moving away from her, down the hall and then down the stairs, fading away into the night.

"Malachi!" she murmured in misery.

So there would be no fight, and no words spoken. She could

not go to battle, and she could not give of herself or take, for he was gone, leaving her again.

She lay down and cast her head against the pillow in misery. She stared straight ahead and ached for what seemed like hours and hours.

He had gone back to her. Back to his old friend. Back to the red-haired harlot.

She could not sleep. She could only lie there and hurt.

At three in the morning, the last of the locals threw down their cards, finished off their beers or their whiskeys and grunted out their good-nights to Matey and to Reba, the golden blonde who played the piano at the Haywood saloon.

Reba started collecting glasses. Matey washed them, telling Joe, his helper, to go on and clear out for the night. Joe had a wife and new baby, and was grateful to get out early for the evening.

Reba tucked a straying tendril of her one natural beauty, her hair, back into the French knot she wore twisted at her nape. She looked across the saloon to the dark shadows and paused.

They had both forgotten the stranger. It was peculiar; she had thought that he had left earlier.

But he had not. He was still there, watching her now. She could feel it.

He raised his face, tilting back his hat.

He was a decent-looking fellow, Reba thought. Sexy, in a way. He was tall and wiry and lean, with dark hair and strange, compelling light eyes. The way he looked at her made her shiver. There was something cold in that look. But it made her grow hot all over, too, and there weren't many men who could make her feel anything at all anymore.

This one made her skin crawl. He also made her want to get a little closer to him. There was something dangerous about him. It was exciting, too.

"Mister," she called to him. "We're closing up for the night. Can I get you anything else?"

He smiled. The smile was as chilling as his eyes.

"Sure, pretty thing. I'll take me a shot and a chaser..." His voice trailed away. "A shot and a chaser and a room—and you."

"You hear that, Matey?" Reba called.

"Got it," Matey replied with a shrug. The drinks were his responsibility. It was Reba's choice, if she wanted to take on the drifter this time of night.

Reba brought the shot and the beer over to his table. He grasped her wrist so hard that she almost cried out and pulled her down beside him. She rubbed her wrist, but thought little of the pain. Lots of men liked to play rough. She didn't care too much. Just as long as they didn't get carried away and mar the flesh. If he wanted to be a tough guy, though, he could pay a little more.

"You got a room?" he asked her.

"That depends," she said.

"On what?"

He was a blunt one, Reba decided. She flashed him a beautiful smile, draping one long leg over the other, and displaying a long length of black-stockinged thigh. She ran a finger over the planes of his face, and found herself shivering inside again. His eyes were strange. They were so cold they might have been dead. They calculated every second. They were filled with something. She didn't quite recognize what it was.

Cruelty, maybe...

She shook away the thought. A lot of men looked at women that way. It made them feel big and important. Still...

She started to pull away from him. She almost forgot that she made her living as a whore, and that she didn't mind it too much, and that the pay was much better than what she had been making as a backwoods schoolteacher on the outskirts of Springfield.

Should she? She was tired; she wasn't in any desperate need

for money. She should just tell him that it was too darned late for her to take a man in for the night.

"I got gold," he told her. "Is that what it depends on?"

Gold. He wasn't going to try to pawn off any of that worthless Southern currency, and he wasn't even going to try to pay her with Union paper. He had gold.

"All right," she told him at last.

And unknowingly sealed her fate.

He stroked her cheek softly, and looked toward the stairs. He smiled at her, and Reba silently determined that she had been mistaken—he was just a tough guy, not a cruel one. And he was handsome. Not nearly as handsome as Iris's friend Sloan, but he had all his teeth, all his hair and all his limbs. And that wasn't so common these days.

A working girl could always use a little extra cash.

"Where's your friend?" he asked her.

"Who?"

"The redhead."

Strange, he was talking about Iris. Reba started to answer, but then she paused, stroking his arm. "Iris is occupied for the evening." She smiled.

The stranger lifted his glass toward the saloon doors. "The husband, eh? That the blushing little bride was looking for."

Reba chuckled. "It's a good thing the groom is occupied. The maid over at the Haywoods' told Curly—Curly's the barber—that Mrs. Gabriel has bolted down for the night. Sloan Gabriel would need four horses to ram the door down."

"Is that a fact?"

"'Course, Iris says he'll do it. When he—when he's good and ready, he'll go over and break right in. Determined type. He doesn't take nothing off of her."

"Doesn't he, now?"

"Not Sloan Gabriel."

The stranger's lip curled. "Sloan Gabriel, eh?"

"That's right. That's the man's name. Why?"

"No matter. It's just a good story. I watched the woman

earlier. She needs a lot of taming." He paused, sipping at his whiskey. "You think Mr. Gabriel will just break the door on down to get to her, eh?"

"To teach her a lesson."

"And he's here now. Right here in this fine establishment."

"Ain't that a laugh."

"Yeah. It's a laugh. But, hey, now..." He swallowed the whiskey in a gulp, then drained his beer. He set the glass down on the table hard. "No matter at all. What matters now is you and me. Let's find that room of yours, all right?"

Reba nodded swiftly, coming to her feet. She took the stranger's hand and called good night to Matey as they walked up the stairs. She passed by Iris's doorway and hid her smile of secret delight.

Sloan Gabriel was in there, all right. Still sleeping away, after consuming his own bottle of whiskey. Iris had asked her to look in on him now and then, and she had been glad to comply. He was still sleeping peacefully, and his golden wife assumed he was enjoying the daylights out of himself. She didn't know why she didn't tell the stranger. It was a funny story. It was great.

But Iris had acted as if she didn't want too many people to know where she was going.

Reba shrugged and hurried to her own door.

When they entered her room, the stranger closed the door. Reba turned around, smiling at him. "Want to help me with a few buttons, honey?" she asked. She sat down at the foot of the bed, a woman practiced with her craft, and slipped off her shoes. When that was done she slowly slid off her garters and started peeling away her stockings one by one. He watched her, standing by the door. Reba smiled with pleasure, certain that she had this drifter well in hand.

"What's your name, honey?" she asked him.

"Justin," he said.

"Justin what?"

"Justin is all that matters."

"All right, Justin, honey." She smiled and licked her tongue slowly over her lips, as if she gave grave attention to her stockings. He was quiet, then he spoke suddenly, pushing away from the door.

"Turn over," he told her.

"Now, honey, no funny stuff," she said. He didn't smile. She added nervously. "Honey, any deviation—any slight, slight deviation—will cost you a fortune." Little pricks of unease swept along her spine, but she kept smiling anyway.

Her smile faded when he suddenly strode across the room and jerked her around by the arm, pressing her down into the bed, face first. He tore at her chemise and petticoats, ripping them from her with a vengeance. Gasping, smothering, she tried to protest.

"Shut up," he warned her.

"No! No, please—"

Reba tried to twist around. He slapped her hard on the cheek, sending her head flying against the bedpost. Stunned, she still tried to resist. She hadn't the power. He shoved her over and down.

A scream rose in her throat when he sadistically drove into her. But her scream went unheard, muffled by her pillow.

In time, either the pain dulled, or she passed out cold.

When she awoke, it was morning. She felt the sun coming in through the window.

She tried to move, but everything about her hurt. Her cheek and eye were swollen where he had beaten her. She hurt inside, deep inside. She would have to see the doctor, and pray that nothing was busted up too bad. God, she was in agony.

She was afraid to open her eyes; he might still be there. She didn't feel him, though. She lifted her lashes just slightly. Then she dared to twist around.

He was out of the bed. He was dressed, and he was staring out her window, toward the Haywoods' store and hotel across the street.

Suddenly, he stiffened and straightened. She saw him set his hand on his gun at his hip.

"There he goes," he murmured. He swung around, as if sensing that Reba was awake. She closed her eyes, but not fast enough. He came over to her, wrenching her up. "You shut up, bitch!"

"I didn't say—"

He slapped her again. Reba gasped, screaming for all that she was worth. Matey would be up and about; someone would hear.

"Oh, no you don't!" He slammed her pillow down on her face, pressing hard. Reba twisted and gasped, and the pain entered her lungs as she could draw no air. He kept talking. As she grew dizzy, she could hear him. "You ain't ruinin' it for me, honey." He started to laugh. "What's one little whore, when the golden girl is right across the street? If you're right, Slater is in there, getting through to her for me right now. I tried to get to her last night, but I was afraid to bust the door down myself. I might have had the whole town down on me. I slipped out, and I slipped back in, and nobody knew it at all. I came back to the saloon...and to you, too, honey. I'm gonna kill Slater, and I'm gonna make her wish that she was dead. You can imagine how good I am at that, huh, honey?" Dimly, she heard him laugh. "You can imagine. You can just imagine." He pressed harder and harder upon the pillow.

Her struggles ceased.

Finally, he tossed the pillow aside. She was still and silent. "I wouldn't have had to kill you if you'd just known how to keep that whore's mouth of yours closed." He tipped his hat to her. "It's closed now, honey. Sure am sorry. It's just that you don't compare. No, ma'am, no way, you just don't compare. I'm gonna have me that girl, and I'm gonna kill that man."

He looked outside. Malachi Slater was heading across to the livery stable. Looked like time to take a walk himself.

* * *

"Shannon!"

She had awoken, hearing him call out her name in annoyance. He banged on the door. She pressed her fingers against her temple and ignored him.

"Shannon, open this door."

"No!"

"Don't give me a hard time now, Shannon McCahy. I've got to get in."

"It isn't McCahy anymore, is it?" she demanded bitterly through the door. "Get away from here!"

She waited. There was silence for a moment. "Shannon, open the door. Now."

"You arrogant Reb bastard!" she hissed at him. "Go away. I'll never open the door."

She heard his sigh even through the door. "Shannon, I am going to try not to fight with you. I am going to do my best to get along with you, Shannon, because—"

"Your best! Malachi, go!"

"Shannon, I really am trying. Now, open the door and—"

"You're an ass, Malachi. A complete ass!"

"Shannon, I am trying—darlin'. But keep it up, and you'll pay. I promise," he said very softly.

"Go away!"

"Shannon, I'm giving you ten seconds. One—"

"You should have knocked when you came last night."

"I didn't come here last night. You're dreaming."

"Nightmare, Mr. Slater. If I was dreaming, it was a nightmare." She paused, then said with disgust, "You liar!"

"I didn't come near you last night, Shannon. But so help me, I'll come near you now!"

It was a threat. A definite threat. After everything that he had done!

She spat out exactly what he should do with himself.

He slammed into the door. The noise brought her flying up

in panic, searching for the Colt. The wood splintered and sheared around the lock, and the door soared open.

Malachi stood in the doorway, looking much the worse for wear. His clothing was rumpled, his eyes were red, and his temper hadn't improved a hair.

Not that the night had done much for Shannon's.

She lifted the Colt and aimed it straight at his heart. "What do you think you're doing here?" she demanded huskily. She couldn't quite find her voice.

He eyed the Colt but ignored it. He stepped into the room, kicking the door shut behind him. "Shannon, I am going to try and talk reasonably. I—"

"Malachi, get out of here. Or else I will shoot you. I will not kill you. I will aim—"

"Don't you dare say it!" he snapped at her.

"Say what?"

"You know what!"

"All right! I'll shoot at—"

"Shannon!"

"Malachi, I don't want you here. I married you to save your damn neck and you can't even stay with me for two seconds."

"I had to beg you to—"

"You forced me to say those words."

"You know, I'm remembering right now just how bad it was. Dropping down on my knees to beg you to—"

"Beg! You get out, now! Or I will put a bullet right where it might count the most!"

"Why, darlin'," he drawled. "You are my beloved wife, and I can come to you whenever I choose."

"The hell you can."

"The law says I can," he told her softly.

"The law plans on stringing you up—darlin'. Maybe we ought not tempt fate."

"Well, then, Mrs. Slater, I say that I can." He crossed his arms over his chest, leaning back against the broken door. His lashes fell with a lazy nonchalance over his eyes, but she could see the slit of blue beneath them, wary and hard.

She was trembling. She couldn't let him see it. She kept her hand as steady as she could manage on the Colt.

"You chose your bed, captain. You just go on back to it."

"Darlin', I'm tired of you spying on me, and I'm damned tired of your being a brat. I didn't come to fight—"

"You shouldn't have come at all."

"Put the gun away, Shannon."

"Get out!"

"I can't, not now—"

"Malachi, get away from me, now!"

"Put the gun away, Shannon. Put it away now! I'm warning you as nicely as I can, but I mean it." It sounded as if he was growling at her. She gritted her teeth and smiled sweetly.

"Malachi, since I am the one with the gun, I'm warning you."

"You'll be damned sorry when you don't have the gun."

"Don't threaten me."

"You vowed to obey me."

"You vowed to cherish me. It was all lies. So no, captain, you go on back across the street to your whore. You're not going to touch me."

"You're one Yank I do intend to touch, my love."

She pulled back the trigger on the Colt, letting him hear the deadly click. "Get out. You know that I can aim."

"I haven't come to do anything to you. I've come because this is my room, and you are my wife. Put the gun down. I have every right here, and you won't shoot me."

"You have no rights here, and I will shoot you!"

He took a step toward her. She fired, with deadly accuracy. The bullet whizzed by his face, so close that it clipped his beard before embedding itself into the thick wood of the door behind him. He stopped, staring at her, the muscles in his jaw working. He was surprised, but he was not afraid. "You shot at me!'' he said, his voice harsh and low. "You actually shot at me!'' He took another step toward her.

"You fool!'' Shannon warned him, backing away. She fired again, and drew blood this time, nicking his ear.

But it did no good. He was upon her, wrenching the Colt from her hand. His fingers dug around her upper arms with a trembling force, and he picked her up and tossed her like a sack of wheat upon the bed. She struggled to rise, but he caught her and pushed her back. He straddled her, pinning her down, and she saw the naked amazement and wrath in his eyes. "You little bitch! You really would have killed me!''

She wriggled and kicked, struggling fiercely. "If I'd meant to kill you, you'd be dead, and you know it.''

He eased his hold on her to touch his ear, feeling the trickle of blood. She used the opportunity to surge against him, freeing her hands and swinging at him. She caught him on the jaw with a good punch, and he swore savagely, securing her beneath him again. The beautiful white satin bridal nightgown was twisting higher and higher around her hips with every fevered moment. "Let me go, Malachi.''

"Oh, no, Shannon, you're the one who wanted to play rough. Well, let's play rough, shall we?''

And he wrenched the gown up high on her thighs with his free hand. He released her to unbuckle his trousers, and she screeched, jumping up. He caught her arm, twisting her down.

"You shot at me!'' he hissed at her.

She swung forward, trying to hurt him, trying not to cry. "And you slept with the red-haired harlot, so leave me alone!'' She slammed against his chest and thrashed out with her legs. She heard him groan in pain and she knew that she had gotten him good.

But he fell against her again, and her hair caught and pulled in his fingers. "I didn't sleep with her—''

"Oh, no! Don't try to play me for a fool, Malachi.''

"I did not sleep with Iris. She's a real friend, an old friend. I should sleep with her. She is kind, and caring. And warm.

But I wasn't with her last night. I slept in her bed, but not with her."

"Liar!"

"No!"

He pushed her flat against the bed. Tears stung her eyes and she writhed and struggled against him. "Liar!" she accused him again. But his lips met hers, and she didn't understand what happened at all.

"I am not lying!" he swore, and his hatred contoured and marred his features.

"Please…"

He assaulted her…but she met his fury with her own. His mouth forced down hard upon hers…but her lips parted to his, and she met the invading thrust of his tongue with the passionate fury of her own. When his lips broke from hers, she cried out his name. She didn't know if it was a plea, a broken whisper, a beseechment that he leave her…or a prayer that he stay with her.

Whatever it was, it changed his touch. He went very still. Shannon was amazed that she had freed her hands, only to wind her arms around him, only to rake her fingers through his hair. She felt the touch of his fingers, slowly curling around her breasts over the satin of the gown.'

"I am not lying!" he vowed again, and softly. He rubbed her nipple between his thumb and forefinger and felt it swell to his touch. She felt the softness of his beard, and the sweet, burning tenderness of his kiss. He ravaged her body still, but with care, with passion, but with some strange lust gone, so gentle that she arched and writhed and twisted toward him, maddened to feel more and more of it…

Then he thrust into her, deep, full, grinding, and defying all his previous gentleness. Bold, determined, sure, his fingers and his eyes locked with hers as he claimed her completely and cast her shuddering to her depths with the ecstasy of feeling his body within her own, burning within her, a part of her mind, her heart, her frame…her soul.

"Malachi." She whispered his name again as he began to move within her. She held him, embraced him, caressed him. Fever and tempest were with them as they whirled and whirled in a dark and furious and timeless storm that stripped away pretense...

And even hatred...

Satisfaction burst upon them, as volatile as the burning cannon fire of the war that had raged around them.

He pulled from her when it was over. She lay silent; he lay looking at the ceiling.

"What are we doing to one another?" he said softly. But he didn't look her way. He rose. Shannon could not move, not even to adjust the satin of the gown over her hips. She heard him doffing his borrowed clothes, donning his own trousers and shirt and boots. She still did not move.

He paused at last. "We've got to go. Get up. Get dressed. I'll explain when you come down, but I've got some good news as far as freeing Kristin is concerned. Hurry. We need to get moving."

He walked to the door. When he reached it, he paused for several seconds.

"I'm sorry, Shannon. Really sorry. It...it won't happen again."

He was gone. She listened dully as his footsteps faded away on the staircase. Listlessly, she curled into herself. She had to get up. She had to get dressed and ready. They were going after Kristin. This was what it was all about...

She dragged herself up. Then she leaped up from the bed, anxious to call him back because she realized now she could still hear his footsteps. She had to tell him that she was sorry, too, so very sorry...

"Malachi!"

He was coming up the stairs, coming back to her. She raced to the doorway.

A man was coming up the stairs. He was wearing a feather hat, and his head was bowed low, and the brim covered his face. But it wasn't Malachi. A sense of danger suddenly sheared along her spine.

At that moment he reached the top step and raised his head.

She stared straight into the evil leering face of the bushwhacker, Justin Waller. "Howdy, Shannon. Excuse me—howdy, Mrs. Gabriel," he said softly. "My, my, my, I have been anxious to catch up with you. And you do look particularly pretty this morning."

"You!" she cried, swinging around to dive for the Colt.

"Me! Justin Waller, Mrs. Gabriel. Why, yes'm, I've turned up again, and I am...anxious!"

The Colt was on the floor somewhere. She groped frantically, opened her mouth to scream. The sound that issued from her was a breathy gasp. He caught her around the waist. She opened her mouth to scream again, and his hand clamped tight over her mouth. "No, no, my little darlin'," he crooned, his face taut against hers, his pleased grin displaying his teeth. "You do have to hush! The captain might have gone for the horses, but the Haywoods are downstairs, and I planned to leave kind of quiet like. I do want to deal with Malachi Slater, but not here. Not now. You're going to be real, real quiet for me."

Shannon tried desperately to inhale and bite his hand. He laughed, reaching into his pocket with his free hand, and produced a soaking, foul-smelling scarf. He removed his hand from her mouth. She gasped in quickly to scream, but before she could issue a sound, he dropped the scarf upon her face, and she inhaled the potent drug upon it.

The room spun and faded and went opaque, and then disappeared entirely from view.

Justin Waller waited. Her eyes fell shut; she went limp beneath him. He pulled the scarf from her face at last, and lifted her dead weight over his shoulder.

At the top of the staircase, he hesitated. He heard Slater talking in the kitchen.

Quickly, quietly, he ran down the stairs and out the front

door. The street was quiet. He smiled. He walked calmly to his horse, tossed Shannon over the animal's flanks, and mounted behind her lolling body.

And rode serenely out of town.

Chapter Eleven

When Malachi returned with the horses, Iris was already waiting for him, seated in a small buckboard wagon. She was wearing green brocade with a cocky little feathered hat, and the green went exceptionally well with her red hair.

Malachi tethered the horses and looked at her. "You're a beautiful woman, Iris," he told her.

She smiled and didn't flush. "Thanks, Malachi. You didn't need to say that."

"You don't need to come."

"Yes, I do," Iris said. "You don't know anything about the back entrance to Cindy's house. And you won't be able to run around in the town of Sparks, I promise you. You won't be able to do your brother one bit of good if you're arrested along with his wife."

"I don't like putting you into danger," he said softly.

"I won't be in any danger. Cindy's a friend of mine. I come into Sparks often enough. I'm known there."

"Still—"

"Malachi, I swear that I will be in no danger."

Malachi still didn't like it, but he knew he had no right to dictate to Iris. And her trip to Sparks had been monumentally important.

She had found Cole. He'd been sitting in the local saloon, his hat pulled low over his head. She hadn't recognized him herself at first, not until she'd leaned back and seen his silver gray eyes. He'd been wearing ranch clothes and a Mexican serape and his face had been covered with the rustic start of a beard and mustache. He hadn't looked at all like Cole.

He'd recognized Iris, though. Before she could talk to him, he'd come up quickly to buy her a drink, then he had told her he was going by the name of Jake Egan.

Iris had brought him to Cindy's place, a big gabled house her friend owned on the outskirts of town. It was a cathouse, of course, and Shannon was sure to hate it, but that was where they were going now.

Cole told Iris that Jamie was just over the border, and he had gotten word to him. The three of them planned to converge in Sparks, and take matters from there. Thanks to Iris and her friends, they would have a good place from which to plan and work.

Iris glanced toward the Haywoods. "Your wife ain't pleased, I take it?"

He shrugged. "I haven't told her yet."

Iris frowned. "But—"

"We had an argument. We didn't get that far," Malachi said briefly.

Iris lowered her head and a smile stole over her lips. "I hope you told her that I wasn't with you—"

"Iris, it doesn't matter—"

"It matters to me! I'd just as soon she not shoot me."

"She's not going to shoot you, Iris."

"Malachi—"

"Iris, the matter is solved."

"I don't think so, Malachi."

"And why is that?"

"Well, as you might have noticed, Mrs. Slater isn't out here yet."

Malachi swore softly. He started up the porch steps toward the front door.

"Malachi!" Iris called to him. "I'm going to run back in.

Reba might be up by now and I want to thank her for covering things for me yesterday.''

Malachi nodded to her and hurried up the steps and opened the door to the parlor. Mrs. Haywood was just coming out of the kitchen with a big parcel in her hands. "Here you are, Captain Slater. Some of my best summer sausages and biscuits. And when you're heading back through, you make sure to come and see us.''

Malachi nodded stiffly. "Surely, ma'am,'' he said, and he looked up the stairway. "Has she come down yet?''

Mrs. Haywood shook her head. "Maybe you should go on and hurry her along.''

He nodded again. Mrs. Haywood was still staring at him.

"We wouldn't have hanged you, captain, you know.''

"I'm glad to hear that, ma'am.''

"And we couldn't have forced you into marrying your lady—not unless you wanted to.''

He hesitated, staring at her. "Now, Mrs. Haywood—''

"Never mind. Maybe you're not ready to admit that. You go up and hurry her along. I'll take the vittles out to the buckboard. Iris is going with you?'' Mrs. Haywood's eyes danced with merriment. "What a lively trip. I wish I were going. I wish that I was twenty years younger!'' she said, and she laughed.

A slow smile curved Malachi's lip. He saluted her. "Yes, ma'am, it would have been nice to have you along.''

Mrs. Haywood, chuckling, headed toward the door. Malachi went to the steps and started up them, two at a time.

He came to the door and noticed the splinters around the broken lock. He had already paid Mr. Haywood for the damages, but seeing the door made him feel ill. He had sworn he wasn't going to lose his temper, and he had. He had sworn that he wouldn't touch her in anger...and he had. He wanted to leave this place now. More than anything, he wanted to leave this place. Nothing could really be solved between himself and Shannon until Kristin was rescued, or...

Until they all died in the attempt.

"Shannon!" he called out sharply.

He stepped into the room. She was nowhere around. Other than that, the room was exactly as he had left it, not half an hour ago. "Shannon?" he called out again.

Damn her. She was angry, and she was playing some trick. Never! He never could trust her, not for one damned moment! He thought she had understood how close they were coming to Kristin.

He wandered to the foot of the bed and sank down upon it with a weary sigh. Where had she gone? Mrs. Haywood hadn't seen her downstairs. And...

He looked across to the hall tree. Shannon's shirt and trousers were still hung on it.

He rose, a frown knitting his brow. He went over to their saddlebags and ripped hers open. Her dress was still there. Wherever she had gone, she had gone wearing the slinky satin nightdress she had worn this morning.

He jumped up, trying to tell himself that she might have run into the mercantile store to buy something. More underwear, a new shirt, perhaps. Another one of the embroidered blouses like the one on the hall tree...

Malachi ran down the steps. Just as he reached the parlor, he heard screaming from the street. He burst out of the door and ran down to the street, his booted footsteps clattering over the wood of the steps until he hit the dust.

Iris was in the middle of the street, her arms around the blond, Reba.

Reba was lying in the dust, wrapped in a blanket, and held tenderly by Iris. Her eyes were closed. Her face was parchment white. A trickle of blood seeped onto the blankets.

The Haywoods were there, bending over.

"What happened?" Malachi demanded.

"She shouldn't have moved. She was trying to get to you. She wants you to kill him," Iris said, her voice rising hysterically.

"Kill who?" He looked from Iris to Reba. Her eyes remained closed. He leaned down and picked her up. He glanced at Martha Haywood for assent, but the sturdy matron was already shooing him toward the house. "Right into the parlor, Malachi. Bring her to the couch. I'll send Papa for the doctor."

He hurried inside with the blond whore and laid her carefully on the sofa. He knelt beside her as Iris followed, smoothing back her hair. She had been beaten. Her lip was swollen, and one of her eyes was almost shut.

Her other eye opened slowly. She almost smiled, a caricature of a smile. "He wanted your wife, Mr. Gabriel. He wanted your wife."

"What?"

His heart thudded, then seemed to stop for a moment. Cold fear fell harshly upon him. He took Reba's hand in his. "Please, we know you're...hurting." The way the blood seeped from her, she was probably dying. Maybe she knew it; maybe she didn't. "Try to tell me."

She moistened her lips, nodding. "Kill him. You have to kill him. I saw him watching you. He was waiting for you to get to her; he couldn't make the noise to reach her. He tried...last night. Then he came up to my room with me." She paused. Tears trickled down her cheeks. "He's got your wife, Mr. Gabriel. He thinks I'm dead. He thinks he's safe... Get him. Kill him. He—" She tried to find breath to speak, and made one final effort. "He said that his name was Justin."

Malachi shot up. Iris and Mrs. Haywood stared at him. "Justin Waller," he said. "He followed us. I underestimated him. I thought I'd lost him."

He turned and strode toward his horse, checking that his Colts were in his gun belt. When he reached the bay, he leaped upon the animal, and then just sat there. He didn't even know which way to ride.

East. Back the way they'd come.

Justin Waller wouldn't dare head farther west into Kansas.

He'd killed a lot of men in Kansas. Maimed and wounded them. Someone might recognize him.

East. He had to return eastward.

He set off at a gallop, and realized a second later that he was being followed. He turned and saw that Iris had mounted Shannon's big black gelding. With her skirts and petticoats flying, her fine green dress bloodstreaked and ruined, she was racing after him.

He reined in. "Iris, go back! What do you think—"

"Malachi, she's dead. Reba just died."

"So go back! This man is an animal. I'm better off alone."

"Your wife may need me," Iris said quietly.

Malachi locked his jaw, he was suddenly shaking so hard. That Shannon might be touched by the madman hurt...hurt so badly that he couldn't help her...

"All right, come on," he told Iris.

He leaned forward over the bay's neck, urging the animal forward, and they galloped eastward again at a breakneck pace. How much time did Justin Waller have on him already? How much time did Justin Waller need?

He didn't dare think. He rode.

It was the sickness in Shannon's stomach that finally woke her. She didn't know what he had used in his scarf to knock her out, but the smell of it had invaded her system, and her mouth tasted horrible, and she was certain that she was going to be sick any minute. She didn't care much about being sick. It might make her feel better. Except that there was a gag in her mouth, tied so tightly over her lips that she was afraid that she would choke to death upon her own fluids.

She tried opening her eyes carefully. The sunshine shot into them like knives. She had thought that she was moving; she was not. Her wrists hurt her because she was tied to a tree. The sun was overhead, streaking through the leaves. She was in a copse, surrounded by rocks and foliage and trees. She couldn't move at all, for rough nooses looped both of her wrists, and her arms were pulled taut around the circumference of the tree.

She closed her eyes again. The dizziness still assailed her. She willed it to go away.

There was a sound in the woods. She opened her eyes quickly. Justin Waller was coming through the bushes. There was nothing she could do. Absolutely nothing but stare at him, and hate him with everything in her.

"Hello, little darlin'," he crooned. He hunkered down by her, smiling as he tossed his rifle down at her side. He ran his hand over her thigh, moving the satin of her gown upward to her hip. She kicked and thrashed at him, and the motion almost made her sick. He laughed, enjoying her inability to really do anything, anything at all.

"I'd like to remove that gag, honey, and hear everything that you have to say to old Justin. You're going to apologize, do you know that? You're going to tell me how sorry you are for everything you ever did to me. And then you're going to tell me that you'll never leave me again. And you're going to tell me how much you want me, you're going to ask me to be nice to you."

He lifted his hand to her cheek, and ran a finger down her throat. He idly stroked a line down to the rise of her breast, and he laughed again at the rage that filled her eyes when he cupped the mound.

"You're thinking that Slater will come and kill me, aren't you? Well, he's going to come. That's why you're here. I'm going to meet him on the road, and then I'm going to kill him. And then I'm going to come back for you. But do you know why you're here in this nice little cove? 'Cause if I die, Miss McCahy, you're going to die, too. He'll never find you. Only the snakes and the buzzards will know where you are. Maybe a rattler will come by. And maybe not. Maybe you'll just bake slowly in the sun...and you'll be glad to die, you'll want water so badly. Then the birds will come down and you know what they like to do first? They like to pluck out eyes..."

He sighed, letting his hand drop. "I'd really like to stay. But—"

He broke off, listening. From somewhere, Shannon could hear the sound of hoofbeats.

Justin's face went dark. "How the hell did he know so damned fast?" he muttered. "Must not have done in that whore properly..." He stared at Shannon. "No matter, darlin'. Don't fret. Don't miss me too much. I will be back."

He rose, clutching his gun, and thrashed his way through the undergrowth. The sound of the hoofbeats was coming closer and closer. Shannon closed her eyes.

Malachi.

He would never abandon her, she thought. No matter how mad she made him, no matter how they fought...

Even if he hated her. He would never abandon her.

But would Malachi be expecting Justin to ambush him? And Justin meant to do just that. Sit in wait to prey upon Malachi, shoot him down in cold blood from the shadows of the bracken on a summer's day.

Malachi was coming closer. Shannon could feel the hoofbeats pounding the earth. There was more than one horse. He wasn't alone. Maybe that was something that Justin hadn't counted on.

She tugged at the ropes that held her, but Justin could tie a secure knot. The more she twisted, the more hopelessly tightly she was bound. Tears stung her eyes. If she could just call out. If she could warn him that it was going to be an ambush.

Willing herself not to panic, not to give up, she twisted her head, biting at the gag. At first, she felt nothing.

Then she felt it loosening.

The sound of hoofbeats had slowed as the riders had entered the narrow trail through the forest. Shannon bit desperately against the material slicing her mouth. There was a give and then a tear. She twisted and spit again. The gag slipped enough for her to draw in a huge gulp of sweet air, and then scream for all she was worth.

"It's a trap, Malachi! Don't come any closer! It's an ambush! Be careful, for the love of God—"

As she screamed, Justin Waller suddenly appeared through the shrubs, and she saw the murderous hatred in his eyes.

"Stupid bitch!" he swore. His palm cracked across her cheek so hard that she was dazed.

She felt a little trickle of blood at her lip but that didn't deter him in the least. He stuffed the gag into her mouth and secured it, winding a strip of rawhide tightly around her head. It cut searingly into her mouth, and she could barely breathe, much less issue the softest cry.

He smiled, pleased with his handiwork. "Our time is coming, sweet thing," he promised her.

He jumped to his feet, carelessly holding his repeating rifle. The sound of hoofbeats had ceased. The forest seemed quiet.

"Slater!" Justin screamed.

Shannon took some small pleasure in realizing that she had ruined his original plan. He couldn't possibly ambush anyone. He was the one whose whereabouts were now known.

"Slater, I'm going to shoot her. Right through the head."

She couldn't help the shivering that seized her. Justin Waller would do it. He would shoot a human being just as quickly and easily as he would swat a fly. There would be very little difference to him.

He aimed the rifle at Shannon. She caught her breath, and her heart seemed to cease to beat. She wanted to pray; she wanted to ask God to forgive her all her sins, but she didn't seem to be able to think at all.

Malachi's face filled her thoughts. His slow, cynical smile curling into his lip beneath his mustache. His eyes, bluer than teal, deeper than cobalt, secretive beneath the honey and gold arches of his brows. In those seconds, she imagined his face. And she wished with all her heart that she could see him. She prayed at last, and she prayed that he not be fooled into giving his life for hers...

The rifle exploded with a loud blast. Dust flew up, blinding

Shannon. But she wasn't hit. He had aimed at the ground, right beside her feet. He aimed again, and she quickly closed her eyes as pieces of bark sheared from the tree and flew around at the impact of the explosion. Shannon choked and screamed deep in her throat. More shots exploded against the tree. She almost longed for him to hit her so that the torture of waiting for a bullet would end.

"Come on out, Slater. One of these shots is going to hit her! Or maybe one of them already has. Maybe she's screaming deep, deep down inside, and you can't hear her...but you can hear me. Come on out, Slater, you coward, damn you!"

There was a rustling sound behind them. Justin swung around, shooting at the bushes. Bracken broke and flew, and the earth was spewed up in a rain of dirt. But when the noise died away, there was nothing. Nothing at all.

Justin hunkered down in the dirt, looking anxiously around. The silence was awful. It dragged on forever.

Shannon thought that she might have passed out again. It seemed that she closed her eyes and opened them again, and the sun was falling. The sky was streaked with beautiful, dark colors. Twilight was coming on.

And she was still tied to the tree. Justin was less than ten feet away from her, his rifle over his knee. He still stared out into the bracken as the night fell.

A fly droned around Shannon's face, and landed on her arm. She leaned against the tree, desolate, despairing.

"I think I've killed him. I thought he was out there, but maybe I've killed him," Justin muttered to himself.

He twisted around and looked at Shannon and saw that her eyes were open. Low on the ground, he crawled to her. He reached up with his knife toward her head, and she wondered with horror what he intended to do. She tried not to shrink from him, but she was terrified, and she couldn't help it. He smiled, liking her fear.

But he didn't cut her. He slipped the blade into the rawhide tie that he had bound so tightly around her head. He slid it, and let the scarf gag fall from her face. She inhaled, gulping in air. She would have screamed, but it seemed like such a foolish thing to do. There was probably no one to hear her.

Maybe Malachi *was* dead. Justin had mowed down half the foliage around him, and sheared away rock and trees. He could easily have hit Malachi. He could be out there anywhere, lying injured, dead, dying...

Justin stretched his length against her body. She didn't kick him and she didn't speak. She stayed still, her head against the tree, and stared at him. He was insane, she decided. Some men would come back from the war and tremble through the night at the memories of the horrors they had seen...of the death they had themselves delivered. But Justin Waller had used the war. He had loved it, reveled in it. It had allowed him to rape and murder freely. And now it seemed that he had learned murder and rape as a way of life.

She would give him no satisfaction, she swore.

"You've nothing to say, sweet thing?" he whispered against her flesh. He touched her cheek and ran his hands down to her breast again. "Our time has come. Your lover is dead, and we have the whole night ahead of us. Your mouth is free. You can scream and scream and scream..."

She gazed at him. "You're pathetic," she said softly.

He grabbed her thigh, pinching it mercilessly. She wasn't going to cry out, but the pain came so fiercely that she did.

"Talk to me nicely, little girl. Talk to me nicely. Tell me that you won't take off again. No more tricks. And maybe, just maybe, if you're good, real, real good, I'll let you live."

She lifted her chin. She ignored his hand upon her thigh, inching up the satin of her gown. "Death might be very simple, Justin," she said.

He started to laugh again. "Yeah, it just might be. But you ain't going to die. Not until I'm through with you." He cupped her chin in a cruel grip and moved his face close to hers.

She managed to twist away. "I will throw up on you," she

threatened. "I swear, I will throw up all over you. That drug is heaving up and down inside of me."

He jerked away from her as if he had been burned. He stared at her, and then he chuckled and stroked her chin again. "You are a one, Miss Shannon McCahy. I've waited a long time for a woman the likes of you. A long time."

He leaned toward her again. She prayed that the earth would open up and swallow them whole.

The earth did not open up, but there was suddenly a massive rustling in the bushes near the road. Justin jerked away from her and stood up on the balls of his feet with his rifle ready. Shannon watched him with renewed fear. "Son of a bitch! Sit tight, sweetheart. I'll be back, and we won't waste any more time." He jumped close to the tree, then bent down and disappeared into the low brush.

Shannon strained frantically against the ropes that bound her. Maybe Malachi lived. Maybe he was out there thrashing around, needing help. Justin would hunt him down. He would hunt him down and shoot him between the eyes. Justin Waller might be a raving lunatic, but he had fought with the bushwhackers, and he had learned a lot about guerrilla warfare. He was wiry and athletic. He was an able opponent. And Malachi...

"Watch out!" she screamed aloud. "Malachi! If you're there, watch out!"

Justin did not return to shut her up. She bit her lip, looking into the bracken. Night was just starting to fall.

Suddenly, from around the tree, a hand fell over her mouth. Fear curdled within her again. With wide, startled eyes she twisted around.

It was Malachi. He had found his hat. It sat jauntily atop his head, the brim low, sheltering his eyes. He brought a finger to his lips, and she exhaled, so dizzy with relief that she nearly fell. Hunched down low beside her, he smiled the crooked, rueful smile that had stolen her heart.

"Are you all right?" he asked her swiftly.

She nodded. "Malachi—"

"He didn't—he didn't hurt you?"

"He hasn't had much time. He's been watching for you through the day. Oh, Malachi! Be careful! Please, just get me out of here. He's dangerous. He's sick. He's—"

"Shh!" He brought his finger to his lips again. He seemed to hear something that she could not. "Can you make it just a few minutes longer?"

"Malachi—"

"Can you?"

"Yes, of course, but—"

"Shh!" He didn't untie her. He slunk back into the brush behind the tree.

"No!" Shannon whispered. She heard the branches breaking and a soft tread upon the earth. Justin Waller was returning. He was returning, and Malachi had left her for him...

"Weren't nothing," Justin said. "Weren't nothing at all but a rabbit or a squirrel. I left you for a rabbit. Can you beat that? My nerves are raw, honey, but you're gonna fix that."

Laughing, he dropped the rifle. He fell down on his knees beside her, and he stroked her calf. She kicked out in a rage. He fell upon her, the whole of his length covering her, smothering her. She started to scream and writhe, and Justin smiled, bringing his leering features level with hers.

"Moment of truth, honey darling mine—"

He broke off at the sound of a gun cocking, right at the base of his ear.

"Moment of truth," Malachi said harshly. "Get up. Get off my wife."

Shannon watched as Justin Waller went as stiff as a poker and slowly rose. Malachi didn't miss a beat. The barrel of his Colt remained flush against the man's head.

"She ain't your wife. Not for real—Mr. Gabriel."

"She is my wife—for real, Mr. Waller. And I don't take kindly to you touching her. In fact, I don't take kindly to much that you've done."

There was another rustle in the trees. Malachi didn't move a hair. Justin sneered, and despite herself, Shannon stiffened. Iris Andre stepped in among them. She had a small pearl-handled knife in her hands. She hurried toward Shannon, knelt beside her and started sawing the ropes that held her.

"Just how many woman do you need, Slater?" Justin taunted.

Malachi walked around in front of him, aiming the Colt at his heart. Shannon looked gratefully to Iris as the red-haired woman freed her. Maybe she was a whore. Maybe she had been sleeping with Malachi. But they had come together to save her, and for that, she had to be grateful.

Iris flashed her an encouraging smile. Shannon rubbed her wrists.

"Can you stand, honey?" Iris asked.

"I—I think so."

But she couldn't. When she tried to rise, she fell back upon the tree. She was parched; she hadn't had water in hours. The nauseating taste of the drug remained.

Iris lent her an arm.

"Boy, captain, you do have it made. A whore and a wife, leaning on each other. That's mighty cute, Miss McCahy."

"It's Mrs. Slater," Shannon told him.

"Poor little fool. Can't you see what he's doing to you?"

"Iris, tie up his hands," Malachi directed.

Iris nodded, leaving Shannon against the tree. Shannon stood there, chafing her wrists, shivering as darkness fell and the coolness of the night came upon them. She watched as Iris walked toward Justin with firm purpose. Malachi tossed her a skein of rope.

But before Iris could reach him, Justin reached out, and grasped her and pulled her against him. He produced a knife from his calf, and caught it against her throat.

"Malachi, shoot him!" Iris called out.

Malachi didn't dare shoot; Justin would have slit her throat as easily as he breathed.

"Drop it, Slater," Justin advised.

Malachi reached out and dropped the Colt. But as he did so, he lunged.

Justin thrust Iris away from himself just as Malachi stormed against him. Justin had his knife; Malachi was unarmed. They rolled together. Malachi leaped to his feet. Justin swiped at him with the knife, and Malachi leaped again. The knife sliced through the air.

Malachi landed a blow against Justin's chin, but then Justin was swinging with the knife again.

Malachi was good. He was fast on his feet; he could whirl with the wind. But Justin was armed. Unless he was disarmed swiftly.

Shannon could barely move. She shook her head, trying to clear it, needing strength. Iris lay on the ground before her, trying to stagger up.

"Iris!"

The woman turned to look at her.

"The Colt. Give me the Colt."

"You'll hit...Malachi."

Shannon shook her head. She had to clear it. She crawled past the tree before falling to the ground. She couldn't quite reach Malachi's Colt.

Iris reached for it and swept it along the dirt to Shannon. For a brief moment their fingers touched. Shannon bit her lip, then smiled swiftly, encouragingly. Her fingers curled around the butt of the gun.

The men were still locked in deadly combat. Justin was on top of Malachi; Malachi was straining to hold the man's arm far above him, to escape the deadly silver blade of the razor-edged knife. Shannon blinked against the darkness and against her trembling fear and the nauseating aftereffects of the drug.

She aimed carefully, and then she fired.

She was a crack shot, and she proved it that night. She hit Justin right in the hand. His knife went flying as he screamed in pain, his fingers shattered.

Malachi pushed him away and reached for the knife. Stunned, he came up on the balls of his feet and looked at Shannon. He smiled slowly, smoothing back a lock of hair that had fallen over his eyes.

"Thanks...darlin'," he murmured.

He stood, dusting off his pants. Justin Waller was rolling on the ground screaming.

"Bitch! I'll kill you, I swear, I'll kill you—"

"You aren't killing anyone else, Waller," Malachi said softly. "We're taking you back to Haywood, and they'll see that you hang."

"There ain't no wanted posters out on me, Slater."

"They're going to hang you for murder. Reba died this morning," Malachi said.

Justin let out a howl. "Your wife wanted it, Slater. She was smooth as silk to touch. She was better than that blond whore back in town. She screamed and cried and asked me for more and more."

Malachi stood still.

"But then, you can't imagine that whore. She wanted to live so badly. She begged me to stop."

"I'm not going to kill you, Justin," Malachi said. He walked over to where the man lay. "I'm not going to kill you. The war is over. I'm done killing. They'll hang you, and you aren't going to say anything to make me kill you now and cheat the hangman."

"You shoulda seen her scream."

Malachi ignored him. He started walking toward Shannon again.

"I'm going to kill you, Slater!" Justin raged. He stumbled to his feet and came running toward them. Cupping his bleeding hand beneath his good arm, he stumbled toward them and fell upon his rifle where it lay by the tree. Malachi started to spring for him.

Then a shot rang out. Justin Waller fell down dead.

Malachi and Shannon stared at one another, then turned and

looked at Iris. She had a little ivory-handled pistol in her hand. A small waft of powder floated from it.

She looked from the dead man to Malachi. "You couldn't kill him, Malachi. I had to."

Malachi nodded at her. He walked over and retrieved his hat from where it had fallen in the dust, then he came back to Shannon.

"Can you ride with me?" he asked her.

She nodded.

"What about him?" Iris asked, referring to Waller.

"We'll put him on his horse and bring him back to Haywood. They can do what they want with him there. If they happened to know that he was at Centralia, they might butcher him up and feed him to the crows. I don't know. We're done here. We've got to get moving."

Iris nodded. Malachi brushed Shannon's forehead with a kiss, then nodded to Iris. Iris came forward and slipped her arm around Shannon while Malachi picked up the dead man, throwing him over his shoulder.

Shannon looked at Iris sickly. "He—he killed a woman?"

"A friend of mine," Iris said.

"The blond woman?"

Iris nodded. "Come on, honey. Let's get out of these woods. It's been a long day, and it's going to be a longer night."

Arm in arm with Iris, Shannon made her way through the bracken and trees. Malachi walked ahead of them.

They came to where a trail showed in the moonlight. The bay and her black gelding were there. Malachi tossed Justin's body over the bay and looked at the women. "I'm going to give the woods a look for his horse. Will you be all right?"

"Of course, sugar—er, uh, I mean, sure, Malachi," Iris said.

"I'm fine," Shannon added. She wasn't fine at all. She was sick to death and cold and shivering, but Justin was dead, and the danger was over. And Malachi had cared enough about her to come for her.

She had loved Robert Ellsworth. She had loved him very much.

But that didn't stop her from loving Malachi now. No matter what his relationship had been with Iris.

She couldn't even hate Iris anymore.

Malachi walked into the bushes and disappeared. Shannon must have weaved in the night breeze, because Iris quickly made a clucking sound. "Let's sit. It's all right here, I'm sure. We'd hear a rattler if there was one around anywhere."

"Iris," Shannon said softly, sitting down beside the red-head.

"What? I'm sure that there's really nothing to worry about—"

"Iris, I'm really sorry about the whiskey."

Iris inhaled sharply and her eyes fell on Shannon. "It's all right." She grimaced ruefully. "Most ladies do feel that way about whores."

"Oh, Iris, trust me! I didn't act like a lady!" She smiled, and then she laughed, and she realized she was glad because she had wondered if she would ever laugh again. Then she was afraid, because perhaps her laughter sounded hysterical. "Too bad you couldn't have met my pa, Iris. He would have explained in no uncertain terms that a lady wouldn't do things like that." She hesitated, then she smiled. "Pa would have said that you were quite a lady, Iris. Thank you for coming for me. You don't owe me anything. Even if you—even if you do sleep with my husband."

Iris squeezed her hand in return. "I didn't sleep with your husband. Well, not now, anyway. I had a thing on him once, years ago, in Springfield. It was before the war. It was—it doesn't matter what it was. It's over."

"You know that we're not really married," Shannon said softly.

"You are really married now, if I understand things right."

Shannon flushed. "He had to marry me or hang."

Iris shook her head, and her sage green eyes glittered knowingly. "You don't know your man very well, Mrs. Slater. No one ever forced Malachi to do anything that he wasn't willing to do already, deep down inside." She brought her finger to her lips. "Sh! He's coming back. And men are funny. They just hate to have women talk about them."

Shannon smiled. Malachi thrashed his way through the bushes with Justin Waller's buckskin horse.

"Shannon, can you ride with me?"

"Yes."

"Iris? You'll be all right on Shannon's black?"

"Yes, Malachi."

The two of them were meek, Malachi thought. Damned meek, for a pair of hellcats.

He walked over to Shannon and reached down to her, wishing that his hands would quit shaking. It had been the longest day of his life. He'd had to wait and watch and steel himself to be patient lest Waller killed them both. He had barely managed to keep still when Waller had started shooting at the tree and the ground.

He pulled Shannon to her feet. The once beautiful satin nightdress was mud-stained and torn. "We'll get you into a warm bath and dressed as soon as we get to the Haywoods'," he said gruffly.

She smiled tremulously and stumbled against him. Her eyes shone with their own crystal-blue radiance, and he couldn't look away from them. They had never been so softly blue upon him. They carried a look of innocence and knowledge, older than the hills, and they had never carried such tenderness.

He swept her into his arms. Her eyes remained locked with his. Her arms curled trustingly around his neck.

He set her atop his horse and mounted behind her. She leaned against his chest, and they were a silent party as they rode back to Haywood.

Chapter Twelve

Shannon was certain, upon their return to Haywood, that she had never been more cherished in her life.

They had been met on the steps of the inn by Martha and Mr. Haywood and what seemed like half the town. Cheers went up as they rode in. Malachi handed Shannon down to Matey. A woman quickly brought a blanket to wrap her in, and Martha Haywood brought her water, which she gulped down until Malachi warned her that she must go slowly. That was the last she saw of Malachi. The men dragged him off to the saloon.

It was the last she saw of Iris for the moment, too, but she didn't dwell on the thought.

Martha clucked like a mother hen and took her immediately beneath her wing. She fed her roast beef with hot gravy, potatoes and carrots. Hot tea was made with brandy, and the bathtub was filled with steaming water and French bubble powder.

Shannon bathed with a vengeance. She wanted to wash away so much. The dirt, Justin's touch upon her...and the blood that marred not only the night, but so much of the countryside. She scrubbed her flesh and her hair, and she wasn't happy until she had scrubbed both a second time. Martha stayed with her, helping her rinse out her hair. And when Shannon stepped out of the tub at last, Martha was there with a huge fluffy towel to wrap around her. When she was dried, Martha offered her a new nightgown.

It was entirely different from the first. It was soft flannel with little pink flowers and it buttoned all the way to the neck. It was warm and comfortable, and Shannon loved it. Combing out her clean but snarled hair, Shannon thanked Martha. "You've been so very good to us."

Martha waved a hand in the air. "We haven't done a thing, dear."

Shannon laughed. "You're harboring a man whose face graces dozens of wanted posters and you've treated me like a daughter."

Martha looked at the bed as she straightened the sheets and plumped the pillows. "I'd like to think that if my girl had lived, dear, she would have been a great deal like you."

Shannon came over and kissed her cheek. "Thank you. That's so very sweet."

Martha blushed. "Crawl in here now. Someone wants to see you."

Her heart fluttering, Shannon crawled into the bed. Malachi was coming. There were things she wanted to say to him. Things that she needed to say.

Martha smiled and left the room, closing the door behind her.

It didn't lock anymore.

Shannon sat back against her pillow, biting her lower lip and smoothing her fingers nervously over the covers. She heard a slight sound as the door opened and she looked up with anticipation.

Iris Andre walked into the room.

Shannon tried not to show her disappointment. She smiled as Iris came to the bed, pulling a chair over from the hearth. "How are you feeling?" Iris asked her. She smiled, and her eyes were bright with concern.

A moment's jealousy rose within Shannon, and she tried to swallow the feeling. Iris had such lovely flame-colored hair and bright green eyes. She had changed into a soft blue cotton dress, high-necked, decorated with rows of soft white lace. She looked beautiful and worldly and sophisticated, and somehow angelic, too. And once, Malachi had had a love affair with her. Iris denied that she had slept with him this time, but he had been with Iris far more than he had been with Shannon.

"I feel fine, Iris, thank you. The nausea has all gone away. Food helped."

"So you're none the worse for wear?"

Shannon ruefully pulled the sleeves back on her gown and showed where her wrists were chafed. She shivered, and her smile faded. "He killed your friend. I am so sorry."

"So am I," Iris said softly. "No one deserved to die that way, not even a...whore."

"Oh, Iris!" Shannon sat up and reached out for the woman's hand.

Iris smiled. "You are very sweet, do you know that?"

Shannon flushed. "There isn't a sweet bone in my body." She hesitated. "Ask Malachi. He'll tell you."

"Malachi!" Iris said, laughing. There was a sparkle about her eyes.

"Why are you laughing?" Shannon demanded.

"I'm enjoying this, I suppose," Iris said, and then she sighed. "He does say that you have a temper. And you are good with a Colt. I'm glad I never tempted you to shoot."

"I was very tempted to shoot when we met," Shannon admitted.

"I'm glad that you didn't," Iris said. She stood up abruptly. "I guess I had better go. Malachi is anxious to see you—"

"Iris?"

"Yes?"

"I don't understand." She had to force herself to look at the other woman. "He didn't come back here last night..." She couldn't help it. She lowered her eyes, and her voice trailed away.

"I wasn't here, honey. I went over to Sparks."

"Oh!" Shannon looked at her again.

"It's a long story. I'm sure that he wants to explain it to you himself. I'll see you tomorrow. Malachi is anxious to get on his way tonight—"

"He's leaving?"

"There I go again. He'll explain—"

"He's leaving me here?"

"No, not exactly. Please, let him explain." Iris didn't give Shannon another chance to question her. She smiled and hurried out of the room. Shannon's mind began to race. Something had happened, something that she didn't know about. They were getting closer and closer to Kristin, and Malachi meant to leave without her.

She started to crawl out of bed. If he was leaving that evening, so was she.

She started at the sound of a tap on the door. Malachi? She glanced at the door, remembering what had happened when she tried to keep him out. And now he was tapping quietly?

He didn't wait for her answer. He stepped into the room. Shannon quickly glanced his way. He had been at the saloon, but he hadn't been drinking, not much, anyway. He still wore his cavalry hat. He was taking chances here, she thought. But then, maybe it didn't matter in Haywood. Maybe the war had really ended here.

She loved him in that hat. She loved the way the brim shadowed his eyes and gave mystery to his face, and she loved the jaunty plume that flew with Rebel fervor.

She loved him...

His shirt was torn at the sleeve and covered with dirt from his fight with Justin Waller on the ground. His shoulder was visible through the tear, bronzed and muscular. There was a masculine appeal to him that made her heart ache to look at him—mussed and torn in her defense, ramrod straight and tall and lean and rugged. She felt that she stared at him for ages, but it could have been no more than seconds. He frowned as he realized that she had been about to crawl out of bed. "What do you think you're doing?"

"I'm going to get dressed. If we're leaving—"

"I'm leaving."

"But—"

"Shannon, I'm just going ahead of you by a day. I have to go tonight." He smiled, and his lip twisted with a certain amount of amusement rather than anger. He strode across the room to her and caught her by her shoulders, pushing her gently back down on the bed and sitting by her thigh. She opened her mouth to say something, but no words would come to her. She didn't feel like fighting him at that moment. She didn't feel like fighting at all.

She reached up and stroked his cheek, feeling the softness of his beard.

He caught her hand and kissed her fingers. "I was so damned scared today," he told her.

She smiled. "So was I."

"Are you really all right?"

She nodded. "You came in time."

He folded her fingers and set them down upon her midriff. He stood and wandered idly over to the window, leaning against the wall and staring out at the street. "Did Iris tell you? She found Cole."

"What?" Shannon shot up with pleasure. "Oh, Malachi, I'm so very glad. Where? Is that what—"

He turned around and walked back to her. She was kneeling at the end of the bed. Her hair was drying in soft, waving tendrils that curled over her shoulders and breasts and streamed down the length of her back. Her eyes were beautiful with enthusiasm. She looked completely recovered from the day, and exquisitely alive and vital.

She loved Cole, she reminded herself. She always had loved Cole. The bright enthusiasm in her eyes was for his brother.

"Cole is in Sparks."

"Oh, no!"

"It's all right. He's safe. Iris has a friend there named Cindy who has a—er—house...on the outskirts of town. Cole is there. He's safe. He's gotten word to Jamie. That's why I have to leave tonight."

Shannon started to crawl out of bed again. "Whoa!" he told her, catching her arm. "You aren't coming. Not tonight."

"But Malachi—"

He caught her chin and lifted it. He met the dazzling sapphire blue of her eyes, and smiled. "I'm not leaving you, Shannon. It's too much trouble to try. But I want you to stay here tonight, please. I want you to get one good night's rest. Iris will bring you in the morning with the buckboard. All right?"

"But Malachi—"

"Shannon, we have to figure out a way to free Kristin. There isn't going to be anything that you can do until we form some kind of a plan. Please, get some rest tonight. For me."

The last words were softly spoken. They were husky, and they seemed to touch her with tenderness.

If he had yelled or ordered her around, she would have fought him. But he wasn't yelling; he wasn't angry. His hand upon her was light, and she longed to grip it and kiss his fingers in return.

"Stay?" he said.

She nodded. He stroked her cheek before turning away from her. He tossed his hat onto the chair.

"Will you take good care of that for me? Bring it tomorrow in the buckboard. Pack it. They probably won't think too much of it in Sparks."

"I'll pack it carefully."

"Thanks."

He started to unbutton his shirt, then realized that it was torn beyond salvation. Grinning at her, he ripped open the buttons. "This one has bit the dust, don't you think?"

She nodded. She didn't care in the least about his shirt. She cared about his shoulders, bronze and hard and glimmering in candlelight. And dried blood showed on a cut on his arm.

Shannon leaped out of the bed. He started to frown at her again.

"Your arm," she told him softly, as she hurried past him to where a clean cloth lay over the rim of the bath. She picked it up and wet it and came back to his side, suddenly hesitant to touch him. She looked up, meeting his eyes, and she flushed.

"It's nothing," he told her. She nodded, then gently started to bathe the wound. It wasn't deep. She wiped away the blood, then she found herself rising on her toes to press her lips against his back, against his shoulder. He twisted around to look at her. She kept her eyes upon his, and kissed his upper arm, then jutted the tip of her tongue to spiral it slowly upward to his shoulder.

He turned and caught her elbow and pulled her against him. Against the flannel of her gown and through his breeches she felt the pulsing hardness of his body. She laid her head against his chest and touched the mat of hair that lay there. She brought her palm against his chest, over the muscle, and found his hard nipple amidst the mat of gold hair. She teased it between her fingers, then tentatively reached forward with her tongue and bathed it with warmth. His groan gave her new courage and a soaring, exciting sense of her own power. She pressed her lips against the furiously beating pulse in his throat, and over the width of him and breadth of him, burrowing low against him to tease the steel hardness of his midriff, and delve her tongue into the fascinating pit of his navel.

He groaned again, dragging her back to her feet, winding his fingers into her hair.

"You've had a rough day," he said jaggedly. "You're supposed to be in bed."

She smiled wickedly. "I'm trying to be in bed."

It was all the invitation that he needed. He smiled in response and swept her up high, depositing her on the bed. He leaned over her, working upon the nightgown's dozen tiny buttons. They gave at her throat, and she arched back as he kissed and stroked the length of the soft column while working away at the next buttons, those that went lower and lower against her breasts.

There would never be another night quite like it for her. Soft moonlight played through the window and a soft cool breeze caressed her flesh. He made her warm despite it.

He made love slowly, with a leisurely abandon. She touched him and he caught her hands. He kissed each finger individually, and he raked his tongue between them, and then suckled them gently into his mouth. He kissed her arms, and her knees. He loved her feet, and cherished her thighs, and he ravaged her intimately with his touch and with his tongue until she cried out, shaking, soaking and glistening with her release. Then he touched her again...

And they sat and stared at one another, their bodies glowing in the soft light. When they reached out again, it was like tentative strangers, allowing slow exploration. She knew she could dare anything, and found the thrill of feminine power. She shivered and died a little bit with the delight of hearing him groan as she possessively stroked his body, and held him with her hands, and with her kiss, and with all the warmth and welcoming heat of her body. Time lost all meaning. His whispers were sweet, and often urgent. Passion was stoked to a never-ending flame, but for that night, tenderness reigned.

Somewhere in it all, she fell against her pillow, and in exhaustion, she slept. She awoke, though, when he moved away from her.

She watched him dress in the moonlight, loving the length of him. His shoulders, broad and gleaming, his legs, long and muscular, his buttocks, tight and hard...

She smiled as her thoughts continued to his most intimate and personal parts, then her smile faded, because he was leaving her, and she was suddenly very afraid.

"Malachi."

Startled, he looked at her. He pulled on his breeches and went over to the bed. "I'm glad you're awake," he said softly. He kissed her lips. "Do you mind coming with Iris?"

She shook her head. "I mind that I'm not coming with you."

"You'll be safer coming with Iris." He rose and donned a clean shirt, buttoning it quickly and tucking the tails into his pants. "Shannon, I'm a wanted man. You're not, and neither is she. Just in case there turns out to be trouble."

"Malachi—"

"Shannon, we'll be staying in a brothel, you know."

"And that's where you're going now?"

He nodded.

She didn't say a word. She watched him finish dressing. He kept his eyes on her, and when he had pulled on his boots, he came over to her with the Colt. "If anyone bothers you on the way, shoot him. Don't hesitate, and don't ask questions, just shoot. You understand?"

She nodded, her lashes hiding her eyes. He caught her hands and pulled her into his arms. He kissed and touched her, as if he memorized her flesh and curves. Then he kissed her again and slowly released her. Shannon picked up her pillow and watched him as he walked to the door.

"Behave," she whispered softly at last.

He turned back, grinning slowly. "Why, ma'am, I'm a married man. I intend to be an angel."

She smiled, wanting to send him on his way without worry. It was difficult to smile. She didn't feel good about his leaving. She didn't know why, but she was scared.

"Be careful," he warned her.

"You be careful yourself."

"I'll be careful," he promised. He hesitated, as if he was going to say more. "I'll be very careful," he said after a moment, and then he turned away.

"Malachi!"

She leaped out of bed and raced to him naked. She didn't

want him to go because there were so many things to say. But suddenly, she couldn't say them. She simply threw herself against him and he held her very tightly for a moment.

"I'm afraid," she told him.

"Afraid, vixen?" he whispered. "The hellcat of the west is afraid?" he teased in a husky voice. "Darlin', if you had just been on our side, the South might have won the war."

"Malachi, I am afraid."

"We're going to get Kristin, and then we'll all be safe," he vowed softly. Then he kissed her swiftly on the lips again and was gone.

Shannon closed the door in his wake and slowly, mechanically went to the bed and slipped into the flannel nightgown. She sat on the bed, then stretched out, and she tried to tell herself that she would be with him soon. Her eyes would not close; she could not sleep. She stared at the ceiling, and gnawed upon her lower lip, and worried regretfully about all the things she had not said. She was in love with him. It would have been so easy to whisper the truth. To tell him that she believed in him...

He was on his way to a whorehouse, she reminded herself dryly, and he had spent two nights in a saloon. But Shannon believed Iris, and she believed Malachi, whether it was foolish or not.

That wasn't what mattered, she thought, staring out the window at the moonlit night. What mattered were the things that lay between them. He had been forced to marry her, and his fury had been obvious. She couldn't whisper that she loved him because he didn't love her. She might have forgotten her hatred of the past, but she didn't think that he could forget the years that had gone before. She was his wife, and they had exchanged vows, but that wasn't enough for a lifetime. She couldn't hold him to a marriage.

She didn't mind loving him; she craved to be with him. But she couldn't hold him to the marriage.

She twisted around, determined that she would sleep. She

started to shiver. All of a sudden, she was very afraid. She didn't like him out of her sight.

He was safe, she told herself.

But no matter how many times she repeated the words, she could not convince herself, and it was nearly dawn when she slept.

Mrs. Haywood was perplexed to see her go in the morning.

"You don't need to go traipsing off, young lady. Let the men settle things. You should stay right here, in Haywood."

Iris was already in the buckboard and they were packed. Chapperel was tied to the rear of the wagon, and they had a big basket of food and canteens of water and even a jug of wine.

"We're going to be just fine, Mrs. Haywood," Shannon assured her. "Iris and I can both take care of ourselves."

"Hmph!" Martha sniffed, and she wiped away a sudden tear. "You come back when things are all right again, you hear?"

Shannon nodded and gave her a fierce hug. "We'll come back, Martha, I promise." She hurried down the steps then and over to the buckboard. It was going to be a long ride.

She climbed into the buckboard and waved to Mrs. Haywood. Mr. Haywood was with her now, his arm around her. "You send for us if you need us!" Mr. Haywood called.

"Thank you! Thank you both so much!" Shannon returned. She smiled. What more could they possibly do for her? No one could help a man condemned as an outlaw without so much as a trial.

"Ready?" Iris asked her.

"Ready," Shannon said. Iris lifted the reins. They started off. Shannon waved until they had left the little one-road town behind them, and then she turned and leaned back and felt the noon sun on her face.

She felt Iris watching her and she opened her eyes. "Are you really all right?" Iris asked her.

"I am extremely well, really. I've never felt healthier. Never. Honest."

"It's a long ride, that's all."

"I've already come a very long way," Shannon told her.

They rode in silence for a while. Then Iris asked her about her home, and about the war, and Shannon tried very hard to explain the tangled events that had led her to be living in the South—and being a Union sympathizer.

Iris was silent when she finished. Shannon looked at the other woman curiously. "You knew Malachi before. And if you found Cole, I assume that you knew him before, too."

Iris smiled. "And Jamie. They all used to come into a place where I worked in Springfield. Before the war."

"I see."

Iris looked at her curiously. "No, you probably don't see. You were raised by a good man, and you loved him, I hear it in your voice when you talk about your pa. I was raised by a stepfather who sold me to a gambler on my thirteenth birthday. You can't begin to see."

"I'm sorry, Iris. I didn't mean to presume to judge you." She hesitated. "You speak so beautifully, and when you dress like you so often—"

"I don't look like a whore, is that it?"

Shannon flushed, but she didn't apologize. She looked at Iris and smiled. "I just think that you are too good and too fine a woman to end up...like Reba."

"You're going to try to make me go straight, huh?" Iris asked.

"You could, you know."

"And do what?"

"Open up an inn."

"Miss Andre's Room and Board for Young Ladies?" Iris asked.

"Why not?"

Iris laughed and flicked the reins. "All right. I'll think about it. And what about you?"

"What do you mean?"

"When it is over, what about you?"

"I—er—I'll go home."

"Alone?"

Shannon lowered her face. "You know he didn't mean to marry me," she murmured.

Iris was quiet for a minute. "I know that you're in love with him."

"He doesn't love me."

"How can you be so sure?"

"He—he's never said so. And...Iris, you can't imagine, we were enemies. I mean bitter enemies. Remember, the North and South will still clash for years to come. His favorite name for me is brat. There isn't a chance..."

Iris laughed delightedly. "You listen to me, young woman. If he were mine, if I had this chance, I would hang on for dear life. I would fight like a tiger. If you've any sense, and if you do love him, you'll do the same."

"But, Iris, I can't force him to stay with me!"

"Then sleep with your pride. Lie awake night after night, and remember that you have the cold glory of your pride to lie with you instead of the warmth of the man you love."

Shannon fell silent. They rode awhile longer, then Iris suggested they stop for lunch.

They found a brook, and as they dangled their feet in it, Shannon entertained Iris with stories about growing up with Kristin and Matthew.

"You'd like my brother," she said impulsively.

Iris sniffed. "A Yankee."

"I'm a Yankee, remember? And you're living in Kansas. Yankee territory."

"No. The whole country is Yankee territory now," Iris said. "And I'm a working girl. Confederate currency doesn't put much food on the table these days."

They left soon after.

They didn't pass a single soul on the road. Close to sunset, they came to a rise overlooking a valley. Shannon climbed down from the buckboard to look down at the town of Sparks.

It was obviously thriving. There were rows of new houses, and more rows of businesses. Ranches spread out behind the town, and the fields were green and yellow and rich beneath the sun. In the distance, she could see railroad tracks, and a big station painted red. Iris told her that the town was a major junction for the stagecoaches, too.

She came back to the buckboard and looked at Iris. "It's a big place," she murmured uneasily. "A very big place. And Hayden Fitz owns it all now?"

Iris nodded gravely. "He owns most of the land. And he owns two of the stagecoach lines. And the saloon and the barbershop. And the sheriff and the deputies. Come on. Climb back in." She pointed down the valley to a large house surrounded by a stable and barns. It was a fair distance from the town. "Cindy's place."

"Cindy's place," Shannon echoed. She shrugged, and a smile curved her lips. "Let's go."

In another thirty minutes they reached the house on the plain.

It was a beautiful, elegant place with cupolas and gables, numerous stained-glass windows, and even a swing on the porch. It looked like the home of a prosperous family.

But when Iris reined in, the front door opened and a woman burst out, running down the stairs and dispelling any vision of family life.

She was clad in high heels and stockings and garters and little else but a short pink robe. She had midnight-black hair and a gamine face, and it wasn't until she was almost at the buckboard that Shannon realized that she was not a young girl at all but a woman of nearly fifty. She was beautiful still, and outrageous in her dress, and when she laughed, the sound of her laughter was husky and appealing.

"Iris! You did make it back. And this must be Malachi's blushing little bride."

"I'm not little," Shannon protested, hopping down from the buckboard. She extended a hand to Cindy. She might be slim, but she was taller than Cindy by a good inch or two.

"I stand corrected," the woman said. "Come on down, Iris. Do come in before someone notices that Mrs. Slater here is a newcomer."

"You're right. Let's go in," Iris said.

They hurried up the steps to the house and came into a very elegant foyer. Shannon could hear laughter and the sounds of glasses clinking. Cindy cast her head to the right. "That's the gaming room, Mrs. Slater. I don't imagine you'll want to wander in there. And there—" She pointed to the left. "That's the bar. Don't wander in there, either. Not that you're not welcome—the men just might get the wrong idea about you, and I don't want to have to answer to Malachi. Come on, and I'll show you to your room. Then I'll show you the kitchen. You're perfectly safe there. It's Jeremiah's domain, and no male dares tread there."

Cindy started to lead them up a flight of stairs. Shannon caught her arm, stopping her.

"Excuse me, but where is Malachi?"

"He's, er, he's out at the moment," Cindy said. "Come on now, I've got to get you settled—"

Shannon caught her arm again. "I'm sorry, but he's out where? Is Cole here? Has Jamie slipped in yet?"

"Cole is just fine, and Jamie looks as good as gold," Cindy said.

She came to the second-floor landing and hurried down the hall, pushing open a door. "It's one of the nicest rooms in the house. See the little window seat? I think that you'll be very comfortable in here, Mrs. Slater."

Shannon stood in the center of the room. It was a beautiful room with a large bed, a marble mantel, chairs, and the promised window seat. It was missing one thing. Her husband.

"Thank you for the room, and for your help and hospitality,

for myself, my husband and my brothers-in-law. And excuse me for being persistent, but where is my husband, please?''

Cindy looked uneasily from Iris to Shannon.

''He's...''

''You might as well answer her,'' Iris advised. ''She won't give up asking you.''

''I won't,'' Shannon said.

''He's holding up a train.''

''What?'' Shannon gasped in astonishment.

''Wait a minute, I said that badly, didn't I?''

''Is there a good way to announce to his wife that a man is holding up a train?'' Iris demanded.

''Well, he isn't really holding it up—''

''What are you saying!'' Shannon demanded.

Cindy sighed and walked over to where a pretty little round cherry-wood side table held brandy and snifters. There were only two snifters—the room was planned for a party of two, and no more.

''We'll share,'' Cindy told Iris, and she drank a glass of brandy before pouring out two more and handing one glass to Shannon and the other to Iris.

''Cindy, explain about Malachi,'' Shannon insisted.

''All right. All right. Kristin is being held in the Hayden house. They've got bars on the windows, and at least twenty guards in and around the house. There was no way for the three men to break in and carry her away.'' She hesitated. ''The boys just might have some friends around here, but we don't really know that yet. A lot of decent folk aren't pleased that Hayden Fitz is holding a lady, no matter what legal shenanigans he tries to pull. Anyway, Jamie heard tell that some bushwhackers on the loose were planning to hold up the train south. And there's a Federal judge on that train. They're going to seize the train from the bushwhackers and then try to explain the whole story to the judge.''

''Oh, those fools!'' Shannon cried. ''They're going to get themselves killed.''

Iris slipped an arm around her. "Honey, come on! They aren't fools. They know what they're about."

"If the bushwhackers don't shoot them, the judge will!"

"Well," Cindy said dryly, "you can be sure of one thing."

"What's that?"

"If Cole Slater is killed, Hayden Fitz won't need your sister any more. He'll let her go."

"I don't know," Iris murmured miserably, staring at her glass. "Knowing the perversions of Hayden Fitz, I imagine—"

"Iris!" Cindy said.

Iris quickly looked at Shannon and flushed. "Oh, honey, I'm sorry. I really am..."

"It's all right, Iris. You don't need to hide the truth from me," Shannon said. She sank down on the bed. "Oh, God!" she murmured desperately. "He said that we'd be together tonight. He said that we'd be back together."

Iris and Cindy exchanged looks over her head. Shannon leaped up suddenly. "Iris, I can't just sit. here. Let's go into town."

"What?"

"Iris, you can get in to see Kristin, can't you? I would feel so much better if you saw her."

"Shannon, I don't know—"

"Iris, I can't just sit here. What if—" She hesitated, feeling her heart thunder hard against her chest. "What if Cole and Malachi don't make it? Iris, we have to discover some other way!"

"Malachi would hang me if—"

"Iris, I'm going with or without you."

Cindy shrugged, lifting her brandy glass. "You both look like respectable young women right now. Can't see how a ride into town could possibly hurt. Besides, if Hayden is around, he probably will let you in to see Kristin, Iris."

"Iris, I'm going with or without you. Iris, please. I'll go

mad sitting here wondering about Malachi and Jamie and Cole and that stupid train!''

Iris sighed. ''All right,'' she said at last. ''All right. Shannon, I hope to God that this works out! He'll flay me alive if it doesn't.''

''We'll be fine,'' Shannon assured her. ''Just fine.''

She would have plenty of time later to rue her confident words.

Maybe, if Shannon could have seen Malachi, seated comfortably in the club car of the train along with both his brothers, she might have felt a little better.

The three Slater brothers were seated in velvet-upholstered chairs around a handsome wood table drinking whiskey from crystal glasses at the judge's invitation. Cole was intense, straddled across his chair, leaning on the back, his eyes silver and his features taut as he spoke. Malachi leaned back, listening to his brother, more at ease. Jamie was, for all appearances, completely casual and negligent, accepting his drink with ease. He wore a broad-brimmed Mexican hat, chaps and boots, and looked every bit the rancher. Only the way his eyes narrowed now and then told Malachi that his younger brother was every bit as wary this night as he and Cole.

Two friends of Jamie's from Texas were playing lookout while the brothers spoke with Judge Sherman Woods. Cole, seated to Malachi's left, was earnestly explaining what had happened at the beginning of the war, how his wife had been killed, how the ranch had been burned and how, sick with grief, he had joined up with the bushwhackers for vengeance.

''But I never gunned down a man in cold blood in my life, judge,'' Cole said simply. ''Never. I always fought fair. I wasn't with Quantrill more than a few months, then I went regular cavalry. I was assigned as a scout. I took my orders directly from Lee. I was in Kansas, and I did kill Henry Fitz, but it was fair. Any man who was there could tell you that.''

Judge Woods lit up a cigar and sat back. Malachi liked the

man. He hadn't panicked when the masked bushwhackers had seized the train, and he had barely blinked when the Slaters had reseized it from the robbers at gunpoint, sending them on their way into the night. He was a tall thin man with a neatly trimmed mustache and iron-gray hair. He wore a stovepipe hat and a brocade vest and a handsome black frock coat and fancy shoes, but he seemed to be listening to Cole. He looked from one brother to the other. "What about you?" he asked Jamie.

Jamie smiled with innocent ease. "Judge, this is the first time I've been in Kansas since 1856. I was damned stunned to hear that I was a wanted man. And amazed that any fool could think that my brother was a murderer."

The judge arched one brow. He turned to Malachi. "And what about you, captain?"

Malachi shrugged. "I wasn't in Kansas. I spent most of the end of the war in Kentucky, then in Missouri. I would have come to Kansas, though, if I had thought that Cole might need me. Fitz was a murderer. He killed my sister-in-law. He killed lots of other people. And it seems to me, sir, that if we're really going to call a truce to this war, we have to prosecute all the murderers, the Yank murderers, too. Now Hayden Fitz is holding an innocent woman. God alone knows what he could want with her, and so help me, I can't understand what law he is using to get away with this legally."

The judge lifted his hands. "You do realize that what you're doing right now is illegal?"

"Yes, it is," Cole admitted.

"But we did stop those other fellows from robbing you blind," Malachi reminded him.

"Of course. All right, I've listened to your story. And God knows, gentlemen, I, for one, am anxious to see an end to the hostilities! I'm afraid we won't live to see it, but I'm a father of four, and I keep praying that maybe the next generation will see something good come to this land. You had best slip off this train and disappear into the night, the same way that you came. I give you my word of honor that I will look into this situation immediately. If you're patient, I'll see that your wife is freed, Cole Slater. But I suggest that the three of you remain out of sight for the time being. Understood? And, oh— stay away from Fitz. We don't want him finding you.''

Malachi looked at Cole, and Cole looked at Jamie. They all shrugged. They *were* in hiding. Just because they were hiding right beneath Fitz's nose...

They shook hands with the judge. Outside the club car, Jamie waved to his friends, and they jumped from where they were standing on the engine platform and the mail car. The five men hurried quietly for their waiting horses, then galloped away into the darkness of the night.

A half mile from the train, they left Jamie's friends, Cole and Malachi voicing their thanks earnestly. The two men had served with Jamie during the war. ''Don't mind helping a Slater,'' said the older of the two. ''Jamie pulled me out of a crater in December of '64. I owe him my life.''

''Thanks just the same,'' Jamie said, tilting his hat. Malachi and Cole echoed the words.

Then the brothers were alone together, riding through the night.

Malachi flashed Jamie a smile. ''Well, I admit, it seemed like a reckless plan to begin with, but it went fairly well.''

''Nothing really gained,'' Jamie murmured.

''Nothing lost,'' Cole said, sighing. Malachi saw his brother's frown in the moonlight. ''And we're close enough. If Fitz does threaten Kristin...''

''Then we are close, and we just get a little more reckless,'' Malachi said. He urged the bay along a little faster.

''Hey!'' Jamie called out to him. ''What's your hurry now? We're not being pursued.''

Malachi reined in. ''I...Shannon is supposed to be coming in tonight.''

Jamie started to laugh. ''That hellcat in a whorehouse? You're right. Let's hurry.''

Cole grinned. "It will be good to see her," he said softly. "I've missed Miss McCahy."

Malachi hesitated, then he muttered. "Mrs. Slater."

"What?" Both brothers queried him.

"Mrs. Slater," he repeated. He looked from Jamie to Cole. They stared at him in amazement.

"They were going to hang me," Malachi explained lamely. "I—er, we kind of had to do it."

"She married a Reb?" Jamie demanded.

"She married—you?" Cole said.

"I told you, they were going to hang me if we didn't. Damn it, quit staring at me like that!" He swore. He urged the bay forward. "It's a long, long story and I'm not in the mood for it tonight."

"Cole, come on now, hurry!" Jamie laughed. "I am anxious to hear this! The hellcat married to my brother! Mrs. Sweet-little-hellcat Slater, holed up in a whorehouse! I can't wait."

Malachi ignored his brother and urged his horse faster. He wanted to see Shannon. His heart was pounding; his body was aching. They would have to take some time. She would need to see and hug and hold Cole, and she would laugh and maybe cry and then hug Jamie fiercely, too. But then they would be alone.

And he was realizing more and more that he had come to live for the moments when they could be alone.

She was his wife...

And he was very anxious to lie down beside her that night.

He had no idea until they rode into the yard in the darkness of the night that he would be denied that simple pleasure.

Chapter Thirteen

Shannon breathed a sigh of relief as they reached town. No one thought to molest two women riding in a buckboard, and when Iris reined in just to the right of Hayden Fitz's massive dwelling, with its barred windows and guards, they were still left entirely alone. The man before the door raised a hand to Iris, and a grin broke out on his features.

"Why, Miss Andre. Nice to see you."

"Herb Tanner," Iris told Shannon with a sniff. She reached in back of her for the basket of food they had packed. "I think that you should sit tight—"

"Who's that you got with you?" the man called out.

"Never mind," Iris said beneath her breath. "You keep quiet. Let me do the talking." Iris looked at her and shook her head mournfully. "A beautiful young blue-eyed blonde. You could be in trouble just by being here. I wish I had a sheet to put over your head. Keep your mouth shut, you hear?"

"I'll be silent as a mouse," Shannon promised.

She crawled out of the buckboard behind Iris and followed the older woman toward the house. Herb Tanner was holding a repeating rifle, but he seemed to consider his guard duty a bit of a joke. He set the gun down to sweep his hat off to Iris.

"Hello, Herb," Iris said sweetly.

"Hello, Iris!" Herb said happily. "The boss man is engaged this evening, if you come to see him." He spoke to

Iris, but he looked over her shoulder to Shannon, offering her a broken-toothed and lascivious grin.

"Well, Herb, I really came for curiosity's sake."

Herb's grin widened. "You curious about me, Iris?"

Iris laughed and patted his chest and moved close to him. "Why, Herbie, you could make a woman just as curious as a prowling cat, you know that, boy? But that wasn't what I meant. Not at this particular moment." She moved closer against him. "I want to see the woman that old Fitz has locked up in the house. I have a bet with my friend Sara here that we can get in to see her. They say that she's the wife of that awful outlaw, Cole Slater. What do you think, Herbie? Could we get in? Just to give her some apple pie and chicken from Cindy's house."

"I don't know, Iris," Herbie said.

"Oh, Herbie, come on! Isn't it funny? A couple of girls from Cindy's place bringing vittles to that little bushwhacker's lady? Why, it's just plain ironic, it is. Fitz would laugh himself silly, I'm certain."

"Iris, Fitz is in a meeting with some of his boss people—"

"Herbie, I could promise you a real good time."

Shannon saw that Herb jumped and trembled like a dog with a juicy new bone, just from the sound of Iris's voice. She clamped a hand on Iris's arm. Annoyed, Iris turned to her. Shannon pulled her down the steps.

"Iris! I don't want you promising that man sexual favors to get us into that house!"

"It's probably the only way, Shannon."

"Iris—"

"Shannon, it's what I do for a living!"

"You told me you just might think about changing occupations."

"Honey—"

"Iris, don't make any promises, please."

Iris grinned and shrugged. "All right, honey. You can promise him the sexual favors."

"What!"

"Oh, for heaven's sake. I'll promise him for a later date, and we'll never get to it, all right?"

Shannon exhaled slowly. "All right."

They hurried back to Herb. "Little financial negotiation," Iris said sweetly to him. "Sara doesn't think I should be giving the business away. But if you can get us in to visit that bushwhacker's woman, I'll promise you...I'll promise you the time of your life next Friday night. What do you say, Herbie?"

Herb's Adam's apple bulged and he exhaled in a rush. "Gee, Iris, I didn't think I could ever afford you. Not in a month of Sundays!"

"Well, curiosity, you know..."

Herb's eyes narrowed in calculation. "It's a deal, Iris. But I want you both." He looked over at Shannon like a cat who had swallowed a mouse, a pleased gloat on his face.

"What?" she gasped.

Iris elbowed her in the ribs.

"Sure, Herbie. Let us in, huh?"

"Let me see your basket," Herb said. Iris produced the basket. Herb searched through it. Satisfied, he nodded. He stepped aside, opening the front door.

There was another armed man in the entryway. "Let 'em in, Joshua. They're all right. They're just bringing the prisoner a bite of food."

"All right, Herb."

Joshua nodded to them. Iris dazzled him with a sweet smile, and he pointed them up the steps.

Shannon ran alongside Iris. On the landing was another man sitting in a chair reading the newspaper. Joshua called up to him. "Fulton, it's just a pair of—er, ladies to see the prisoner."

Fulton looked up and spat tobacco into a brass spittoon. "Herb say it was all right?"

"Honey chile, Herbie let us in," Iris told him sweetly.

Fulton stood up and moved close behind her. "Is there anything left that you can promise me?'' he asked with a yellow-toothed smile.

''We'll see, darlin','' Iris promised. ''Now, if you'd just show us the bushwhacker's wife...''

Fulton shrugged and produced a set of keys. He walked down the hall to a door and twisted a key in the lock. ''You're looking good, Iris. So is your friend.'' He paused, staring at Shannon. ''You new in town, girl?''

Shannon nodded.

''Learning the ropes of the business,'' Iris supplied.

Fulton's eyes swept over Shannon. ''Well, I'll be savin' up my dimes, young lady. You can bet on that.''

''Fulton, for you, there will be a big discount,'' Iris promised.

Fulton smiled and pushed open the door. ''Company!'' he called. Iris hurried into the room. Fulton caught Shannon's arm. ''I'll be expecting a big discount, little lady.''

Shannon wrenched her arm away, then remembered to smile. ''Sure, sweetie,'' she promised, and batted her lashes his way. Iris grasped her arm and jerked her into the room. ''Enough is enough, Shannon!'' she hissed. ''You want to wind up serving the man right here in the hallway?''

But Shannon wasn't listening. While Iris closed the door, Shannon stared across the room.

Kristin was standing by the foot of the bed, tall, stiff and proud, and every inch the lady. Her facade broke as she saw Shannon. Both women cried out and raced across the room and into one another's arms.

''Shh!'' Iris begged them. ''They'll hear you!''

Shannon and Kristin went dutifully silent, but continued to grip each other fiercely. Finally Kristin drew away. Shannon surveyed her sister as anxiously as Kristin studied her.

Kristin seemed to be all right. Someone had supplied her with a change of clothing, and she wore a cotton day dress in a soft rich burgundy with a cream lace collar. She was thin and pale, but she was smiling, and there didn't seem to be a mark on her.

Kristin held Shannon's hands as she made her sit down at the foot of the bed. Amazed, she looked from Shannon to Iris. Then she whispered, "What are you doing here? Shannon, I have been ill with worry! I saw the bushwhackers take you away—"

"Malachi rescued me," Shannon said quickly, not wanting to talk about that experience or Justin Waller.

"Oh, Shannon, you see, he has a good heart."

"Yes, Kristin—"

"Shannon, you shouldn't be here," Kristin said anxiously.

"Kristin, if I hadn't followed, Malachi might have slipped you away from the Red Legs. So I have to make up for that. Iris and I had to come!"

Kristin looked at Iris again, smiling. She stood up and offered Iris her hand. "How do you do? I'm Kristin Slater," she said softly. "Whoever you are, thank you!"

"Iris Andre," Iris offered.

"How did you get in here?" Kristin asked.

Shannon looked at Iris and Iris looked at Shannon. "We made a few deals," Shannon said ruefully.

"What? Oh," Kristin said. Her eyes, wide and very blue, fell upon Iris.

"I'm sorry, Mrs. Slater, but you should know. I'm a whore. And your husband and her husband have been staying out at Cindy's place. It might not be fittin', but we're willing to help, and—"

"Sh!" Kristin cautioned, hurrying to Iris with a crooked smile. "I don't care what you do, Miss Andre. I thank you for caring. Did you say my husband? Cole? Is he there? He can't be!" She whirled around and stared at Shannon. "Nor Malachi. They wouldn't allow Shannon to do such a foolish thing as come here."

A small smile teased Iris's lips. "Mrs. Slater, I'm willing to bet that both Cole and Malachi are aware that there is not much that can stop your sister when her mind is set. But, yes, Mrs. Slater, your husband has been in town. So has Shannon's and so's your brother-in-law Jamie. They went out tonight to try to un-hold-up a train.''

''What?''

''Kristin, I had to come. I had to see you. We must come up with a way out of this awful situation!'' Shannon said.

Kristin was still staring at Iris, a frown marring her features. ''My husband,'' she murmured. She stared at Shannon. ''And her husband...Miss Andre, what husband?''

''Why, Malachi.''

''Malachi!''

''Shh!'' Shannon jumped to her feet.

Kristin sat at the foot of the bed, staring at Shannon incredulously. ''Malachi!'' she gasped. ''Shannon, that's impossible! The two of you are incapable of sharing a room for ten minutes without all hell breaking loose. You and... Malachi?''

Shannon smiled uneasily. ''It—er—it seemed like the thing to do at the time.''

''They had threatened to hang him,'' Iris supplied with a shrug.

''But—'' Kristin began.

''I'll tell you all about it at some other time,'' Shannon promised quickly. ''Kristin, are they treating you well?''

''Well enough.''

''No one has—''

''No one has physically abused me,'' Kristin said flatly. ''Fitz thinks that if he can't get Cole to come out of hiding by just holding on to me, he'll pass a rumor that he's willing to deal.'' She hesitated. ''So Cole is here. Oh, God, Shannon, don't let him do anything stupid! What is this about a train? Please, talk to him. Make him see that he can't win. Tell him to go home and get the baby and leave the country. Tell him—''

''Kristin! You know that he'll never do that.''

"I have the perfect plan," Iris said softly.

Kristin and Shannon spun around to look at her. She smiled. "It will be easy enough to find another night when Fitz is occupied. And if not, I know how to occupy Fitz. Then we come with more of the girls. And we bring a few shawls and the like. And we all leave together. We just walk away, all of us, together. I guarantee you, none of the men will feel like moving."

Kristin stared at her in silence, then burst into laughter. "Oh, Iris, it's wonderful. But I couldn't let you do something like that! Fitz would surely get even with you—"

"With all of us? What could he do?"

"Fitz would find something."

"No. Because he would never be able to prove it. He wouldn't discover you missing until the next morning, and you could all be halfway to Texas by then. He wouldn't know which of us were involved, and it would be hard to hang a whole whorehouse. I think the men of this town would finally rebel."

"Neither Cole, Malachi or Jamie will let you do it, either," Kristin warned.

"They won't know!" Shannon said.

"But—" Kristin began.

"Shh! We'll be back," Shannon told her.

"Be ready," Iris warned Kristin. She grabbed Shannon's arm and pulled her to her feet. "We've got to move now, or they'll suspect us of something tonight, and we don't want that."

"Take care!" Shannon warned her sister, and hugged her fiercely again. "We'll be back."

"Come on!" Iris tugged on her sleeve.

They hurried to the door together. There was no one on the upstairs landing and they hurried down the steps. When they reached the bottom, Fulton was blocking their way. Iris smiled at him. "Thanks, Fulton. We'll be seeing you soon."

"You bet you will, Iris."

"Why, Fulton, what's wrong with you, honey?"

Fulton stepped aside. Shannon gasped, stunned.

Bear stood there. He was the massive jayhawker who had carried Kristin away after the fighting between the jayhawkers and the bushwhackers, and it was obvious from the glint in his eyes that he remembered his brief glimpse of Shannon.

"What's going on?" Iris asked uneasily.

Shannon didn't say anything. The big man walked toward her with a wide grin plastered against his beefy features. "It is her," he said flatly. His arms crossed over his chest, he walked around Shannon. "Saw you when I was coming down the street, little miss. I thought I recognized you." He spun in a sudden fury and banged Fulton on the head with his hat. "Couldn't you see how much she looked like that Slater woman? They're as like as two peas from the same pod, you damned fool."

"Don't go beating at me, Bear!" Fulton protested. "Herbie said that the women were all right."

"Well, Herbie's going to have to answer to the boss, and that's that," Bear said. He grinned at Shannon and Iris. "Let's go and see the boss man, little lady."

Bear grasped Shannon by the arm. Iris slunk back against the wall. Shannon bit hard into Bear's fingers. When he screamed, Iris pulled out her small pistol.

"Let her go, Bear," Iris said.

Bear lifted up his hands. Shannon grabbed the Colt she was carrying from her skirt pocket. She drew the gun and held it on Fulton. "We're going to walk away. I'm going to go back up and get my sister out, and we're going to walk away."

"I think not, ma'am," a deep male voice called out.

Shannon spun around and looked up the stairs.

Kristin stood on the top step now, biting into her lip.

Behind her stood a tall, lean man with snow-white hair and cold gray eyes. He wore an elegant brocade vest and a frock coat and he held a small silver pistol to Kristin's skull. "Drop the gun," he told Shannon.

"Don't do it!" Kristin charged her. "Get out, Shannon, just get out—oh!"

The man cracked Kristin hard upon the head and she fell at his feet. He smiled at Shannon and aimed the gun toward her sister's back. "Drop it."

"Do it, Shannon," Iris advised wearily. "That's Fitz. And he will shoot her, without a thought."

"Why, thank you, Iris," Fitz drawled softly, "for that fine commendation. Girl, drop the gun."

Shannon inhaled and exhaled. Fitz cocked the gun. Shannon slowly bent and lay down her Colt.

"That was a very fine idea, young woman." He nodded to Bear. "Bring her to my office."

Bear set his arms upon Shannon. She tried to shake him off. "I can walk on my own!" she spat out.

"Fitz, you can't hold this girl—" Iris began.

"Iris, I am so disappointed in you!" Fitz said, shaking his head with a half smile. "Fulton, escort our friend Iris to my chamber, will you? Iris, I don't know what promises you made to get in here, but we'll just discuss them all. Later. And you will pay up."

Fulton grabbed Iris, sweeping her little pistol from her hands and jerking her around. "Come on, Iris. You heard the boss."

"Fitz, you can't hold her! Fitz, you—"

"I can, and I will, Iris," Fitz said. He stepped over Kristin and started down the stairs. "Get her out of here, Fulton. You'd better start worrying about yourself, Iris. Harboring a known criminal like this one here. Why, we could just shoot you down on the spot, Iris, and no court of law in the country could have a thing to say about it. Fulton, get her out of here!"

"Fitz, you'll pay!" Iris vowed as Fulton wrenched her arm behind her back. Iris cried out in pain. Shannon couldn't bear seeing Iris so hurt on her behalf. She flew at Fitz, her nails gouging his flesh.

"Let her alone, you bastard!" she hissed.

She didn't expect the iron grip of the man. He caught her flailing fists and pressed her against the banister. When she tried to kick him he lashed out, slapping her so hard that she staggered to her knees. He jerked her to her feet and prodded her before him. He threw her through a door in the foyer, and she fell to the ground.

He followed her into the office, stepping over her skirts. He closed the door behind him and walked around his desk to sit, idly watching her for several moments.

Shannon barely dared move. She stared at the man and waited.

"Well, well, well," he murmured at last. "My net is closing fast around all the little fishes."

"I don't know what you mean," Shannon said.

"Don't you?" he said, arching a distinguished white brow. "I think that you do. After all, my dear, you are here now, aren't you?" He smiled. "I hear things, you know. Nothing much happens in these parts that I don't hear about. Captain Malachi Slater was with you in Haywood."

Shannon shrugged. "I'm here on my own."

"Come, come, my dear. Malachi Slater gunned down half my men in the woods along with his bushwhacker friends. Bushwhackers. You never can trust them. I even heard that Malachi Slater gunned down a fellow Reb just the other day."

"He didn't gun down anyone," Shannon said.

"Ah, but he is near!" Hayden Fitz said. He smiled. "And your name is Shannon, and you're a Slater now, too. Is that true?"

Shannon shrugged. "Malachi despises me. If you hear everything, you must know that he and I are enemies. We were on different sides during the war, Mr. Fitz. Perhaps you should know, too, that my brother is a highly respected Union officer. When he gets his hands on you, you'll be really sorry."

Fitz laughed, delighted. "Don't fret, girl. Your brother will be too late to help you. Oh, young lady! I can't tell you just how happy I am to have you. The net does draw tighter and tighter. And I know you *are* Mrs. Malachi Slater.'' He stood up, coming around the desk. He looked down at her. ''You're even prettier than your sister, and I didn't think that possible. My men would really enjoy you. And they just might, you know. I could enjoy an evening with you myself—'' He broke off, shrugging. ''But I want the Slaters first. I want every last one of them dead.''

''You'll never do it,'' Shannon said defiantly. ''They'll kill you, and you know it. You're so damned afraid of them that you can barely stand it!''

''Those Slaters are cold-blooded murderers!''

''The Slaters! Your brother swept in and murdered innocent women! How dare you talk about cold-blooded murder?''

''Bushwhackers deserved to die.''

''There weren't any bushwhackers back when Cole's wife was killed! Just bastards like your brother!''

Fitz clenched his teeth and struck out at her with his booted foot. She screamed with the sudden pain.

The door burst open. Bear and Fulton rushed in.

''Trouble, boss?'' Bear asked. Fulton was frowning, staring at Shannon.

''Boss, you know you can't hold another woman here. Someone will protest—''

''Shut up, Fulton.''

''But boss, if this gets out, too, now...''

''Mary Surratt was hanged for complicity in the Lincoln assassination,'' Fitz said quietly, staring at Shannon. ''I'm sure that I can pin complicity on these lovely ladies, too.''

''But boss, what about Iris?''

''Fulton, are you questioning me?''

''Sir, it's just—''

''Bear, go out, will you? Check the street and see if we've got any other visitors running around tonight.''

''Yes, sir.''

Bear ran out. Fulton asked, ''Mr. Fitz, should I go out with him?''

Shannon should have seen the curious cold light in Fitz's strange gray eyes, but she wasn't prepared for what happened next.

"No, Fulton, you stay here," Fitz said. "I need you." Then he pulled out his little pistol and aimed it at Fulton.

"No!" Fulton gasped, his eyes widening with horror.

Fitz fired. Fulton dropped to the floor.

And Hayden Fitz threw himself on top of Shannon, pretending to struggle with her.

The door burst open. Bear was back.

"She shot him!" Fitz cried. "The little bitch came flying at me and stole my pistol and shot Fulton, shot him down dead, in cold blood."

"Liar!" Shannon raged, trying to free herself. Fitz held her tightly, meeting her eyes with a cold smile.

"Murderess!" He stood and dragged her to her feet. "Damned bushwhacker's murderess!" he swore. He held her very close in a deadly challenge. "You'll hang for this!" he promised, and shoved her toward Bear. "Lock her up. Lock her up with her sister. They can both hang for murder, and for conspiracy to do murder!"

"You can't get away with this!" Shannon cried.

"Watch me, Mrs. Slater. Just watch me. You'll feel the rope around your neck and then you'll know."

She escaped from Bear and flew at Fitz with such a rage that she managed to rake bloody scratches down his cheeks with her nails. He hissed out something, and Bear came up behind her. He struck her hard on the head with the butt of his gun.

Hayden Fitz went hazy before her. Then the world went black.

"Lock them both up," Fitz said. "And make sure poor Fulton is brought over to Darby's funeral parlor. See that he's done up right. Stupid, murdering bitch."

"Yes, sir, yes, sir," Bear said. He scooped Shannon up into his arms and left the office.

Hayden Fitz stepped over Fulton's body. He walked to the stairs and looked up them. He smiled.

Iris had yet to pay for her part in the night's proceedings. She had yet to pay...

But she would pay very dearly.

He set his hand upon the banister and started up the stairs.

"That's—that's all I know," Cindy said unhappily, staring at the three Slater brothers. "A friend of Bear's come in here about midnight, and told everyone what happened. We've got to move the three of you—they'll come here looking for you, and I'm gong to have to pretend to be innocent. I—"

Malachi stood up. "Cindy, you don't have to do anything. I'm going in tonight," he said softly.

"No! Malachi, no, that's just what Fitz wants!" Cindy protested. "If you go raging in—"

"He's got my wife," Malachi thundered.

Cole stood and clapped Malachi on the shoulder. "He's had my wife, Malachi, don't forget that. I admit, bursting in, guns blazing, was my first thought. But Fitz will kill them, Malachi."

Malachi slunk back into his chair. He stared across the room.

"We have to bide our time," Jamie murmured.

"There will be some kind of a trial," Cindy said. She looked unhappily at Malachi. "But Hayden's telling everybody that Shannon McCahy Slater shot one of his men in cold blood. The trial will be rigged. She'll be condemned, and unless he gets his hands on you, he will hang her. He'll hang them both."

Malachi stood again. He strode across the room and came back to stand before Cole.

"A hanging. A big crowd, ropes. Lots of confusion."

Cole smiled slowly. "A few sharpshooters could do a fair amount of damage in a crowd like that."

Malachi grinned his slow, crooked smile. Cole laughed, and as Cindy watched, even Jamie smiled with a leisurely pleasure.

"You've all lost your minds!" she told them.

"No, darlin'," Malachi drawled softly. "I think we've just found our way out of this mess."

"What are you—"

Cindy broke off. Someone was knocking at the door. A voice called, "Cindy! It's Gretchen. I need to see you."

The Slaters quickly stood. Malachi came around behind the bar. Cole and Jamie sank against the pillars. Gretchen pushed open the door. She was followed by a tall man clad in the dark blue uniform of the Union cavalry man.

"Cindy, this man insists he get to you!" Gretchen said, rubbing her wrist and looking at the stranger in the shadows. "He said that he knows the Slaters are around here some-where, and he wants Cole to know that the baby is fine." Pretty, sandy-haired, freckle-faced Gretchen looked at the man resentfully. "He said something about a house shouldn't be divided, not a family, and that the Slaters ought to know what he was talking about."

Malachi came around the bar. He looked closely at the stranger. He started to laugh. "Matthew! Matthew McCahy! How are you?"

Matthew stepped forward. "Well, Malachi!" Matthew pumped his hand firmly. "What in God's name is going on? I've been following a trail of the most absurd stories to get here. Red Legs and bushwhackers, corpses all over. I've got friends investigating Fitz, but I don't seem to be able to get to my sisters. What the hell is going on? I hear tell that they arrested Shannon today, too, for murder."

"It's all right," Malachi said. "We've got a plan."

Cole and Jamie stepped out of the shadows. Cindy sighed with relief. "Well, I think that this calls for drinks all around," she murmured.

"Drinks, then we've got to get out of here before we cause Cindy any trouble," Cole said.

He took a seat at the round table. The other men followed him. Matthew McCahy looked hard at Malachi. ''All right. What's the plan?''

''It's dangerous, Matthew. We might get ourselves shot up.''

''They're my sisters,'' Matthew said. ''My flesh and blood. I'll darned well get shot up for them if I feel like it.'' He narrowed his eyes. ''Kristin is Cole's wife. But I've got more of a stake in this thing than either of you have, Malachi and Jamie.''

Malachi shook his head. ''Shannon is my wife,'' he said, finding with surprise that breaking this news got easier with practice.

''What?'' Matthew said incredulously.

''Malachi married Shannon,'' Jamie answered, smiling with amusement.

''Yes, I married Shannon!'' Malachi said dryly. ''Now, if you all don't mind, think we could get on with this?''

''Sure,'' Matthew said.

Malachi leaned across the table and started talking. Matthew listened gravely. When Malachi was done, he sat back, nodding. ''Think we'll have any help on it?'' he asked.

''Jamie's got a couple of friends from Texas here,'' Malachi said.

''And I've met some people in the area,'' Cole added. ''Maybe they won't take a stand against Fitz alone, but if we give them half a chance, they'll help us.''

''It doesn't matter what we do or don't have,'' Malachi said. ''As far as I see it, it's our best shot. Are we agreed?''

All around the table, they nodded to him one by one. Jamie lifted his whiskey glass. ''What the hell. A man's gotta die sometime,'' he said cheerfully.

Malachi stood. ''Let's get out of here. Cindy, you'll keep us up on everything that happens. Everything.''

''Of course, Malachi. You know that.''

An hour later, the Slaters and Matthew McCahy had slipped away into the night.

When Fitz's men came to the house, there was no sign that they had ever been near.

The only benefit to being held was that she was with her sister.

For the first day, Shannon nervously paced the room, but she was grateful that they had at least been kept together. She hadn't really meant to say much about her own strained relationship with Malachi, but the hours dragged on and Shannon found herself telling her sister almost everything.

Almost...

She didn't tell her how easily she had fallen into her old enemy's arms, or how she had longed for him to touch her again and again. She didn't tell her that even as they waited now, prisoners in the room, she thought of her husband, longing to be with him, aching to see his slow, lazy grin and the spark it ignited in his eyes. She didn't speak about that longing...

But watching Kristin's smile, she thought that her sister read her mind, and her heart, and that she knew.

"Actually," Kristin said mischievously, "I think you just might be perfect for one another."

Shannon shook her head. "Kristin, I don't know. I should let him out of the marriage. But Iris says that I'm a fool if I don't fight for him."

"I agree with Iris," Kristin said. She took Shannon's hands. "I'll never forget how miserable I was about Cole! I was tied up in knots, hating him, loving him. But it worked out for us, Shannon. I didn't think that he would ever forget his first wife, but he did fall in love with me. Shannon, even when I gave birth to Gabe, I was so afraid that Cole would never, never love me. You have to fight sometimes, for anything in life that is good. Look at the two of us now. Things have worked out—"

She broke off and Shannon bit her lip, watching her sister. Nothing had worked out for any of them. They were in the midst of disaster.

"I'm so scared!" Kristin said softly.

Shannon threw her arms around her. "It's all right. It's going to be all right!"

The two sisters hugged one another, shivering. They didn't know if it would be all right at all.

The next day was the mock trial, which took place in the town courthouse. Hayden Fitz sat on the bench as judge; the jurors were selected from among his men. Shannon was accused of murder. She stood at the witness stand and listened silently to the charge, then turned scornfully upon Fitz.

"I didn't murder anyone. You shot down your friend, Mr. Fitz. You shot him down in cold blood because he was protesting your cruelty to me. You may own this town, Mr. Fitz, but I can't really believe that you own everyone in it. Someone will get to you. The war is over, Hayden Fitz. No one will let you do murder endlessly!"

There was a murmur among the crowd. Fitz stood, pointing his gavel at her. "You murdered Fulton. I saw you with my own eyes. You murdered him to free your outlaw sister. You shot down men in Missouri, too. You're in league with your husband, and the two of you rode around the country in Cole Slater's gang, bushwhacking, murdering innocent Union women and children."

"Never," Shannon said quietly.

Fitz slammed his gavel against his desk. "You may step down, Mrs. Slater."

She didn't step down; she was dragged down. Kristin was brought up. Kristin denied everything, and threw at Fitz his brother's activities as a jayhawker. She described graphically how Cole's first wife had died.

A murmur rose in the courtroom, but Fitz ignored it. Kristin was handcuffed and led back to Shannon. They were both returned to the room with the barred windows at Fitz's home while the carefully selected jury came to their decision.

By night, the verdict was brought back to them. They were both convicted of murder and conspiracy against the Union.

They were to be hanged one week from that night at dawn.

"One week," Kristin told Shannon bitterly. "They want to make sure to give Cole and Malachi and Jamie a chance to show up."

Shannon nodded. One week. She looked at her sister. It had already been three days since she had been captured.

"Kristin?"

"Yes?"

"Where do you suppose they are? I'm scared, too, Kristin. They *were* in town. And now it's so silent! What if they've already been caught, and been taken..." Her voice trailed away miserably.

"They haven't been taken," Kristin told her dryly. "Fitz would have men walking through the streets with their heads on stakes if he'd caught them."

That was true, Shannon thought.

But as the days passed, they still heard nothing. An ominous silence had settled over the town. A harsh, brooding silence, as if even the air and the earth waited...

And prayed.

Slowly, excruciatingly slowly, the week passed. Finally, the night before the scheduled hanging came. Kristin sat in the room's one chair; Shannon stood by the window.

The scaffold had been built beneath the window, right in the center of the street, because Fitz had wanted them to watch its building. Shannon stared at it with growing horror.

It was a long night.

Morning finally came. "I—I can't believe that they haven't tried to rescue us!" Shannon told Kristin.

Kristin stared at the ceiling. "I was wrong. They must be dead already," she said softly.

Shannon felt as if icy waters settled over her heart and her body. She had endured too much. If Malachi was dead, then so be it. She wanted no more of this earth, of the awful pain and suffering. He had just taught her how to live...

And now, it was over.

When Bear came for them, he tied their hands behind their backs and led them out. Kristin smiled at her sister as they walked into the pearly gray dawn. It was going to be an absurdly beautiful summer's day. "Pa will be there, I'm certain," she said. "It won't be so hard to die. Mother will be there, too. And Robert Ellsworth. Oh, Shannon! What about Gabe, what will happen to him?"

"Delilah will love him. Matthew will come home, and he will raise him like his own."

"Shannon, I love you."

"Courage!" Shannon whispered. She was going to start to cry. Courage was easy in the midst of safety. But as they walked up the steps of the scaffold and beneath the dangling nooses, it was much harder to find.

Fitz sat in front of the scaffold on his horse. "Have you any last words, ladies?" he asked them.

Shannon looked over the crowd. The people weren't smiling or cheerful; they looked troubled. "Yes!" she called out. "We're innocent! Your hatred and your vengeance have made a mockery of justice, Hayden Fitz. And if you do not pay, sir, in this lifetime, I am certain that you will pay in the next, in the bowels of hell forever!"

Fitz's cold eyes narrowed. "Hang them!" he ordered.

The ropes were fitted over their heads and around their necks.

Shannon bit back tears as she felt the rope chafe the tender flesh of her neck. In a second, it would be pulled taut. She would dangle and choke. If God were merciful, her neck would snap. And if he were not merciful, she would die slowly of suffocation. Her tongue would swell and protrude and she would die hideously...

Hayden Fitz lifted his hand. The executioner walked over to the lever that would snap open the trapdoor.

Hayden Fitz read off the charges, and the order that Kristin and Shannon Slater be hanged by the necks until dead.

He lifted his hand...

And let it fall.

The executioner flipped the lever, and the floor gave beneath them.

Suddenly, the street was alive with explosions.

Shannon was falling, but the rope did not tighten around her neck. Someone had cut it. She kept falling, and crashed hard upon the ground. Cindy was there, slitting the rope that bound her wrists. Shannon twisted around in the dust.

"Get up! Get out of here!" Cindy cried.

"Kristin—"

"I'm freeing Kristin. Get up, go! Both of you!"

Kristin did not ask questions. She grabbed Shannon's hand and the two of them crawled out from beneath the scaffold. Shannon peered through the rain of gunfire. The streets had gone mad. People were screaming and running.

And a group of horsemen was bearing down on them.

She raised her hand over her eyes to shade them from the sun.

Malachi rode straight at her on his bay mare, his cavalry sword glinting in the sun, a Rebel cry upon his lips. He wore his plumed hat, and his full gray and gold Confederate cavalry dress.

He was coming for her, fighting his way down the street. Any man fool enough to block his way was cut down. As he neared her, she saw his teal-blue eyes blazing.

"Shannon! Get ready!" he yelled, striking down the last of Fitz's men to stand between them. He was a golden hero, riding to save her.

The bay was rearing over her. He reached down and swept her up onto the saddle before him, and they thundered down the street together.

Chapter Fourteen

The morning had burst into madness as they fled the town. There were explosions of gunfire. Women were screaming; men were shouting. Held tight against Malachi on his bay, Shannon was dimly aware of a number of horses riding beside them. Her hair kept whipping against her face, blinding her, but she managed to see at last. Cole was to her left with Kristin, her brother Matthew was to her right, and numerous men she'd never seen before were riding behind her. Some of them were in tattered remnants of uniforms, both blue and gray. Some were dressed as ranchers.

They all rode grimly, not stopping until they were miles from the town. Then Malachi reined in, shouting over Shannon's head to Cole. "We'll kill the horses if we keep this up. Think we've come far enough?"

Cole shrugged, his arms tight around his wife, and looked back along the trail they had just taken. "Here's Jamie," he said.

Jamie Slater, on a huge dapple gray stallion, raced up behind them. He waved his hat in the air, a look of triumph on his face.

"Fitz is dead. And there isn't the first sign of pursuit. I think we can take it easier now."

"Not too easy!" A woman called. Shannon gasped as she saw Iris on a dark roan, riding up behind Jamie. "Fitz may not have been tremendously popular, but someone may seek to avenge him.''

"Iris!'' Shannon gasped when the redhead looked her way. She was, as always, impeccably dressed, and her hair was unrumpled. She looked unscathed by her imprisonment, except for the large blue circle beneath her right eye.

"I'm all right, honey,'' Iris said softly. "Thanks to Jamie. He pulled me away from Fitz.''

"Jamie, bless you!'' Kristin said.

"Always willing to oblige,'' Jamie drawled softly.

Shannon leaped down from in front of Malachi and ran over to Jamie, who also hopped down off his horse to meet her. "Hey, brat!'' He laughed, sweeping her up in a fast hug. Matthew and Kristin dismounted as well, and they all hugged one another with laughter and relief.

"Shannon, get back over here!'' Malachi commanded sharply. She glanced at him and saw that his features had become as threatening as a winter storm. She stiffened. Cole wasn't yelling that way. She stared at Malachi, defiant and hurt at once. Safe in the warmth of his arms, she had felt that the war between them was over. But now it seemed that nothing had changed. Did he still hate her?

"We do have to keep moving,'' he said.

Kristin turned and hurried back to Cole. He lifted her up before him. Jamie and Matthew mounted up again.

Shannon turned to the strangers who surrounded them. "I don't know who you are, but thank you, all of you. With all my heart, I thank you.''

"We all thank you,'' Kristin echoed.

Malachi looked around at the curious assortment of men with them. "Shannon is right—thank you all.'' He pointed to the right. "These are Sam Greenhow, Frank Bujold, Lennie Peterson and Ronnie Cordon—all friends of Jamie's from General Edmund Kirby-Smith's command down in Texas. And those boys there—'' he pointed to the left ''—are from Haywood.''

"Howdy," said one of the Confederates to Shannon, and he tipped his hat to Kristin. "I don't mean to be telling you all your business, but you were right, Malachi. You should keep moving. You need to put some mean space between you and Sparks."

Malachi nodded. He and Cole and Matthew thanked the men. Then Malachi called to Shannon again. "Shannon, get over here."

She didn't like his tone, but she could acknowledge he was right. She lifted her head and walked back to Malachi. He reached down for her, encircling her waist with his arm and pulling her up before him. They waved to the men who had risked their lives to fight against the corrupt rule in Sparks.

A silence fell as their curious little party started off: Cole and Kristin, Matthew, Jamie, Iris and Malachi and Shannon. Jamie rode in the lead, taking them south.

Shannon waited as the morning wore on, wanting to speak, not knowing what to say. She stared at Malachi's hand where it rested on her knee, and thought of how she had come to love that hand, how the texture of the bronze skin, the tiny tufts of gold hair on his long fingers now meant everything in the world to her.

She thought of the warmth of the man behind her, and she thought of the danger they had faced together time and time again. When she remembered the past she wanted to cry out all her pent-up fears and sorrows, but her recollections also made her think gravely of the future, too. Life was precious. It was dear, and could be so swiftly stolen away.

She and Malachi had life. This morning, they both had life. They had the sun over their heads, and the radiance of the blue sky, and they rode with people near and dear to them. God had been good to them that morning.

But Malachi was still as stiff and cold as steel. Shannon thought that perhaps he had decided that now he had carried out all obligations to her. He was angry, that much she knew. Maybe he was anxious, too, to be free.

But Iris had told her to fight for him. Could she do that?

Shannon moved her fingers gently over his hand. "Thank you," she told him softly.

He grunted in return. She thought that he would say no more, but then he growled in her ear. "I should thrash you within an inch of your life, young woman."

"What?" she demanded, startled.

"You were told to come to Cindy's. But oh, no, that wasn't good enough for you. You had to put yourself and Iris into a damn fool dangerous position—"

"*I* was foolish! You three were out holding up a train—"

"We went to un-hold-up that train—"

"There is no such thing as un-holding-up a train, Malachi Slater. If you had been killed, Kristin would have been on her own. I would have had to have done something—"

"You did real well," he drawled sarcastically.

Shannon clenched her teeth, trying not to break into ridiculous tears. She stared down at his hand, and noted that he was shaking. With anger, she assumed. "I was doing fine," she stormed. "Ask Iris. Then that horrible Bear recognized me."

"You could have been killed."

"And you could have been killed—un-holding-up a train!"

"I know what I'm doing, and you don't!"

"Lower your voice. Everyone can hear us."

"Can they now?"

"You're humiliating me, Malachi Slater."

"Humiliating you? I wish I had a switch."

"You're the one who should be taken to a woodshed, Captain Slater. Let me down."

"Let you down? You going to walk to Texas?"

"I'll go and ride with my brother."

"You'll ride with your husband, Mrs. Slater," he said, and the words were hard but the husky tension in his voice swept sweetly over her. There was a note of possession in his words that captivated and thrilled her. She didn't mind the demand in it at all.

She looked down at her own hands. They were trembling, too.

Jamie pulled up suddenly in front of them, extending his arm to point. "There's a river up here, and a natural cove. Shall we take a break and ride with the cooler air in the evening?"

"Yes, please!" Kristin answered him. They had ridden so hard at first, and now they had been in the saddle for hours and hours.

"All right with you, Matt? Malachi?" Cole asked.

Malachi nodded. Shannon leaped down quickly. Malachi dismounted behind her.

"Someone get a fire going," Jamie said. "I'll see if I can find something in the woods to cook."

He nodded to them all, pulled his rifle from his saddle and started into the woods.

"I'll join you," Matthew called after him. He looked at Iris, eyeing her from head to toe. "Start the fire."

"I don't know how to start the fire."

"Learn," Matthew said curtly. He started off after Jamie. Iris kicked the dirt.

"Learn!" she muttered. "Damned—Yank!"

Shannon started toward Iris, wanting to assure herself that the woman was all right and to help her build the fire. She didn't get far. Malachi caught her by the arm. She stared at him indignantly.

"We're going for a walk," he told her.

"But I don't want to go for a walk," she began.

She broke off with a startled scream as he swept her up into his arms. "I said that we're going for a walk."

Stunned, Shannon remained silent, staring up into his teal-blue eyes. In the background, Kristin laughed softly. She'd obviously heard the exchange.

Stung by her elder sister's amusement, Shannon started to

protest, but Malachi was already carrying her off. With long strides he followed the river's edge, beneath the shade of the huge old oaks. The sun rose high above them, the sky was blue, and the water was tinkling a delightful melody.

Shannon's arms had curled around his neck for self-preservation.She kept staring at him as he moved, unhurriedly but with purpose.

"Malachi...let me down!" she entreated him softly. They were far out of sight of the camp now, around a curve in the river. There might not have been a living soul in miles, and there was no sound except for the melody of the rushing water and songs of the birds and the whisper of the breeze through the leaves of the oaks.

"Malachi, put me down!"

This time he responded, laying her on a grassy spot upon the slope, and immediately throwing himself down next to her. He placed his knee casually over her legs, supported his weight on an elbow, and touched her cheek.

"I should tan your hide," he said softly. His fingers trailed over her flesh. He stroked her face and her throat. He leaned against her and kissed first her forehead, then the tip of her nose. He buried his face against hers, and kissed the lobe of her ear, nibbling the soft flesh, warming it with the heat of his breath.

She wrapped her arms around him, holding him close.

"Malachi..."

"I should...I should really tan your hide."

His face rose above hers. His eyes searched hers, and she smiled slowly, her own eyes wandering over his beloved features, his clipped beard, his mustache, seeing the fullness of his lips, the character in his eyes.

"Malachi..."

She reached up and threaded her fingers through his hair and pulled his head down to hers. She kissed him, then broke away, then teased his mouth with the tip of her tongue, then kissed him passionately once again. His lips parted to hers, and he took control with a tender and savage aggression that swept through her like heat lightning across a summer's sky.

She felt the passion deep within him, simmering, threatening to burst. He leaned over her intimately, his fingers trembling as he worked at the tiny buttons of her bodice.

Shannon caught his hand. Her lashes fell low and sultry over her eyes. "Malachi, you are something, you know. You're always yelling at me."

"I'm not always yelling at you." He shook away her hand. She made no further protest as he peeled back her bodice and kissed her breasts above the froth of her chemise. Shannon stroked his shoulders, inhaling swiftly as shivers of delight cascaded along her spine.

"You are always yelling at me," she corrected. She placed her hands on either side of his face and lifted his eyes to her.

"You are always doing foolish things," he said softly. "And if I yell at you..."

"Yes?"

He smiled slowly. "What do you want? A signed confession?"

Shannon nodded.

"If I yell at you..."

She caught her breath, waiting.

"It's because I love you."

"Oh, Malachi!" She threw her arms around him and they rolled in the grass, laughing. "Malachi, say it again!"

He caught her beneath him and laid his hand upon her breast over the thin material of the chemise. He stroked the nipple with his thumb until it hardened to a coral peak, and she moaned softly. "Malachi..."

"You were willing to let me hang rather than marry me!" he told her reproachfully.

"I didn't want you to be forced to marry me!"

"You didn't want to marry me."

"But I did. I really did."

"You were in love with a ghost. Are you still?"

She shook her head, biting into her lower lip as she met his eyes. His hands were still roaming sensually across her body. "I did love him. But...even on the awful day that we were married...I did want to marry you."

"Did you?"

He laid his head against her breast and used his tongue to stroke her through the soft fabric. Shannon forgot the question. Malachi did not.

"Did you?" he repeated.

"What?"

"Love me. You haven't said it, you know."

She smiled, trembling beneath him. "I love you, Captain Slater. I think I loved you all along."

"From that very first time you tried to shoot me?" he teased.

"Maybe. Malachi..."

"What?"

"Love me."

"It's been forever," he said huskily, lacing his fingers with hers, stretching out over her.

"It's been a week."

"A long week," he corrected her. And when he took her lips with his own, she saw he spoke the truth.

"Love me," she whispered to him once again.

So he did. The sound of the river came as the sweetest melody, and the grass beneath offered up the softest bedding. He laid his coat upon the ground and stripped her of her clothing piece by piece. She barely dared to move while he touched her, feeling as if time had come to a standstill between them, and that she might shatter some fantastic spell if she were to breathe. She waited. She waited for him to finish with her, and then to doff his own clothing, and to lie down beside her.

She wondered if anything would ever again be as beautiful as that day at that moment. The sun was warm upon her and the air was cool, and his body was a fervent flame of fire within and around her. He touched her with tenderness, and with searing passion. He led her to the brink of ecstasy, and back down, merely to stroke the flames one more time.

Then there was nothing while she soared. Climax burst upon her, and she felt the sweet rush of his release.

Once again, the earth existed. The sky, the river, the ground beneath them.

Shannon looked to her side and saw that his hat lay upon the ground, his fine, plumed Confederate cavalry captain's hat. She smiled, wondering how she had ever allowed the war to stand between them. She realized then that she loved him for everything that he was. A man, a Rebel, a knight in shining armor.

A hero.

No matter how many times she had needed him, he had come for her. He had never let her down.

She touched his cheek. "I do love you. I love you, Malachi Slater."

"Captain Slater."

She smiled.

"I can't change my part in the war, Shannon. Nor do I want to. I fought for what I believed."

"I know."

He hesitated, pulling her close beneath his chin. "The fighting isn't over, Shannon. Fitz is dead, but they'll still come for us." He paused again. "Matthew is going to ride for home tomorrow, Shannon. I'm going to send you with him."

"No!" she protested, sitting up.

He smiled and lazily ran a finger over her bare breast. "Shannon, Cole and Jamie and I have to leave the country. I don't know where we're going. I don't—"

"Kristin will go with Cole."

He shook his head gravely. "Kristin is going home to the baby, Shannon."

"Malachi—"

"No!" he said firmly. Standing up, he started to dress, tossing her her stockings. "Shannon, I have to know that you're safe. Do you understand? Get dressed. We should get back to the others."

"And what are we supposed to do?" Shannon demanded bitterly. "Just go home and wait for the years to go by?"

"We'll find a way to return."

"When?" Shannon demanded, wrenching her dress over her head. "Malachi, I don't mind—"

He caught her against him and kissed her. He broke away from her, smiling ruefully. "That is the only way to shut you up, you know."

"Malachi—"

"No." He kissed her again, then caught her hand, pulling her along.

"Wait!" Shannon cried. She pulled back, flushing as she did up the numerous little buttons on her gown.

He paused, looking around. Shannon was about to argue again when he suddenly went very tense and brought his fingers to his lip. He drew his gun, and pulling her behind him, crept along the trees.

A few minutes later, Shannon began to hear the sounds as well. There were men and horses deeper in the woods. She crept along beside Malachi until they neared a small encampment.

There were about fifteen of them, all dressed in clean blue uniforms. They were a cavalry unit, and a young group at that. Two of the men were cleaning their carbines; one leaned against a tree reading, and the others were finishing a meal, laughing and talking idly.

"Damn!" Malachi muttered. "We've got to slip back and get the others to move."

Shannon nodded. She turned around to hurry with him, then hesitated and looked back, anxious to see if they had been spotted. They had not. The men didn't even look up. She turned again to follow Malachi, well ahead of her now and running in a half crouch through the bracken. Suddenly, she screamed, crashing straight into a blue-clad soldier who appeared from behind a tree.

He gasped, as startled as she, and she realized that he had been taking care of personal business in the bushes.

"Excuse me!" Shannon muttered.

"Excuse me, ma'am," the man apologized. Then his eyes narrowed. "Hey, wait a minute," he began, his hand falling upon her shoulder.

"Let her go!" Malachi called out. He stood ahead of them, leveling his gun calmly at the man.

But by then all the young cavalry boys were up and stumbling around looking for their weapons, and the most prepared were already through the trees.

"Let her go!" Malachi insisted.

"Slater!" Someone called suddenly. Shannon saw that it was the officer in charge. And he must have known Malachi, because he raised his hands, displaying that he carried no weapon, and he walked forward.

"Captain Slater," the officer called, "I know you—"

"I don't know you."

"I know your brother Cole. I'm Major Kurt Taylor. We were together in the West before the war broke out." He hesitated. "I saw him in Kansas. Before he went up against Henry Fitz."

"Ain't that nice," Malachi drawled softly. "I don't want to hurt anybody, major. Tell him to let my wife go."

"Captain Slater, I know that you could shoot down half my boys in a matter of seconds."

"That's right. So let her go."

"Captain, we were sent to find you."

"What?" Malachi asked warily.

"Judge Sherman Woods sent us out. I can't make promises—"

"I wouldn't trust a promise from a Yank anyway," Malachi interrupted.

"You've got a beautiful wife, captain. Do you really want

to spend the rest of your life running? Or do you want to take a minute and listen to me?''

"Start talking.''

"I can't leave, captain. So to get away from me, you're going to have to kill these men. If you come in with me, I'll promise you and your brothers a fair trial.''

"What's to make me think the Union will keep this promise?''

"You'll have to trust Judge Woods, Captain Slater. You went to him for help, and he wants to help. But you have to give him the chance to do so.''

"I'm sorry—'' Malachi began.

"Malachi!'' Shannon cried in anguish. "Please! For God's sake, please! Give us this chance.''

He was very still for a long time. Tall, proud, his Confederate greatcoat over his shoulders, his plumed hat waving in the breeze. His jaw was hard, his eyes cold, his chin rigid and high.

Then he exhaled and tossed his gun down.

"I couldn't shoot those boys anyway,'' he said quietly. "I just couldn't kill any more damned children. They say that the war is over. Major, we'll have to see if it is.''

Major Taylor nodded. "Captain, will you do something for me?''

"What's that?''

"Go talk to your brothers. If I can, I'd like to avoid being a target for a Slater.''

Malachi nodded. He reached out a hand to Shannon, and she ran to his side. Together, they walked through the woods with Major Taylor behind them.

When they reached the others, Jamie instantly drew his gun. Cole and Matthew followed suit.

"Kurt!'' Cole said, slowly lowering his Colt. "What's going on?'' he asked Malachi.

"You do know this fellow?'' Malachi asked Cole.

Cole nodded. "What—''

"Judge Woods sent me out to find you. We'll give you a fair trial in Missouri. It will be fair, I swear it on my honor."

Cole looked at Malachi, a question in his eyes.

"I'm tired of running," Malachi said. "And honor is honor. Blue or gray. I believe this man has some. I've already surrendered to him."

"Well," said Cole, "it's what we wanted when we talked to Judge Woods. Jamie?"

Jamie shrugged his shoulders. "I don't trust Yankee honor much, but I'll go with you and Malachi, Cole."

The two men dropped their guns on the ground.

"I just hope I don't end up hanging," Jamie muttered.

"You won't hang!" Shannon cried. She clung to Malachi's hand. She wouldn't let him hang. She couldn't.

Malachi turned to her. He swept off his hat and took her into his arms and kissed her long and deep for everyone to see. Then he broke away from her, replacing his hat on his head. He strode over to the bay and mounted. "Whenever you're ready, major. Your prisoner, sir." He saluted sharply.

Major Taylor saluted in return.

Cole kissed Kristin, and he and Jamie followed Malachi's lead, mounting their horses.

Then they rode away, without looking back.

Kristin started to sob. Matthew came up to her and put his arm around her, and then he gathered Shannon to him, too. "It's going to be all right. I swear to you, it will be all right."

"It will be!" Shannon agreed fiercely. "It has to be."

Iris cleared her throat. "I managed to make the fire, and Jamie managed to shoot the rabbits. Let's sit down and eat. And then we can head back and plan some strategy."

"She learns really fast," Matthew said with a grin. "Let's eat."

She tried to smile. She could not. But she slipped her arm around Kristin's waist and led her to the fire.

They did eat. When they were done, Kristin mounted with Matthew and Shannon sat behind Iris, and they started their cold, lonely trek back home to Missouri.

Chapter Fifteen

The trial took place in Springfield. The courthouse was crowded with spectators, and with artists from *Harpers* and from every other leading paper and magazine.

Shannon had visited Malachi in jail, and she hated the experience. He was distant from her there. She knew that he loved her, and that he was in jail for her sake. But not even for her would he deny any of his brothers, and he explained to her that the brothers had determined to stand together. They would not opt for separate legal representation, nor would Jamie and Malachi seek lesser charges.

Malachi smiled ruefully to Shannon through the heavy iron bars of the jail. "We are all innocent."

"Cole wouldn't want you to hang because he rode with Quantrill."

"Tell me, Shannon, could you bear it if Cole were to hang because he sought to avenge the death of a beautiful and innocent bride? His wife, a woman carrying his child? She was my sister-in-law. I would have joined Cole at any time; I was already in the Confederate cavalry."

"Malachi—"

"If you love me, Shannon, you must love me for the man that I am. My brothers and I stand together."

She turned away, tears in her eyes. Cole already would have tried to convince Malachi and Jamie to save themselves. The Slaters were a stubborn lot.

And no...she could not bear it if Cole were to hang! They had all paid enough; the war was over. She could not accept any further horror—they had to win.

The first day of the trial was wretched, although their lawyer, Mr. Abernathy, was a skilled defender, with a sure belief in the Slater brothers' innocence. Shannon was pleased with him, even if he didn't pressure the men to stand alone. But Taylor Green, the prosecuting attorney, scared her. He seemed to personally want the Slater brothers to hang, all three.

When the trial started, Green immediately struck upon Cole Slater's association with William Quantrill. There were dozens of witnesses to testify to that association. But they weren't necessary, for at the end Cole quietly admitted to it. In a low, controlled voice he described the scene at his own ranch, years before, at the very outbreak of the war, when the jayhawkers had come to kill his wife. Shannon listened to him, and ached for him. He did not break or falter, but she saw it all through his eyes. She saw his young wife, she heard the woman screaming, and running, running, trying to reach her husband. He made them feel what it was like, to catch her as she fell, to feel her blood upon his hands...

The court was still when he finished. Not even Mr. Taylor Green managed to speak for several seconds.

And then there was a recess for the day.

Kristin came to the witness stand the next day and described in graphic detail how Zeke Moreau had murdered their father, and how Cole Slater had ridden to their rescue.

"Against the bushwhackers?" the prosecuting attorney asked her scathingly. "You want us to believe, Mrs. Slater, that your husband rode against his old comrades at arms? Maybe they just made a deal there instead, isn't that possible?"

"No, sir, it isn't possible at all," Kristin said. "He came and saved our lives. And he returned with Malachi and Jamie Slater to save the lives of half a Union company when Zeke Moreau came back again."

Kristin was fierce and beautiful and unfaltering. Taylor Green did not care to have her on the stand long.

Malachi was called.

He walked to the witness stand in full dress uniform, and Shannon's heart felt as if it had been torn. He was tall and straight, distinguished and ruggedly indomitable, and he was the handsome cavalier who had captured her heart.

"Captain Slater—well, of course, you are a civilian now, aren't you, sir?"

"The war is over," Malachi said flatly.

"But you choose to wear that uniform."

"We fought with honor."

"You still deny the Union?"

"The war is over," Malachi repeated.

"You would like it to continue? You still think that the South can rise again and whip the North, eh, captain?"

"No, sir. I think that the war is over, and I damned well would like it to end for good!"

A loud murmur rose in the courtroom. Shannon smiled. It seemed the first ray of hope. The people were with her husband.

"Did you ride with Quantrill?"

"No."

"Never?"

"No, never. But I would have ridden with my brother. If you'd seen his wife, lying in a pool of innocent blood, you'd have ridden, too."

"Captain, you seem to be an ornery sort."

"I'm telling you the truth, and that is all. This is a court of law, and we are sworn to the truth, right?"

"You're bold with your brand of truth."

"I have to be. And I have to believe that there is still justice in this land. If justice has not been lost, then my brother Cole is innocent, and so are James and I."

"You were regular army."

"Southern cavalry. Under John Hunt Morgan."

"Sounds like you avoided the border war, captain. So tell me, why don't you come clean, and give us the truth about Cole Slater."

"The truth is, Mr. Green," Malachi said, his eyes narrowed sharply, "that my brother is one of the finest men I've ever met in my life. In the North or the South. And if Cole is guilty for wanting to hunt down the man who murdered his wife, then I'm guilty, too. I would have been with him if I could have been."

"An admission, gentlemen of the jury, there you have it! You may step down, Captain Slater!"

"Admission!" Shannon didn't know that she was the one who had shouted until everyone turned to look her way. "Admission! Why, you Yankee bastard!"

There was an instant uproar. Some people were laughing, and some, the northern sympathizers, were offended. The judge slammed down his gavel. "Young woman, one more such outburst and I shall hold you in contempt! Are we understood?"

She sank into her chair. Only then did she realize that Malachi was watching her, too, and that a smile curled his lip. She lowered her eyes, then met his once again, and the smile warmed her and gave her courage.

Malachi walked down from the stand, and Jamie was called up for questioning. He was barely civil, but Taylor Green didn't manage to get a single rise out of him. Jamie could be as stubborn and proud a Slater as either of his brothers.

Shannon sat in the court with Kristin and Matthew and Iris, listening to it all. When the session broke, she was allowed to see Malachi for a few minutes.

"Yankee bastard?" Malachi teased her, his eyes dancing. "Did I hear you say that? You, Shannon McCahy Slater, called that man a Yankee bastard?"

"Malachi!"

"I could die happy, hearing those words upon your lips!"

"Don't you dare talk of dying!"

"I'm sorry."

"Damn your pride!" she told him savagely, tears glistening in her eyes. "You are innocent, and it's as if you're trying to make yourself sound guilty!"

He smiled, tilted her chin and kissed her. "I can only tell the truth, Shannon."

She wanted to say more. She wanted to argue and hit him and make him see reason, but an officer of the court came and took him away, and she wasn't able to say anything more.

The days went on, and the situation began to appear bleaker and bleaker.

It wasn't that it didn't seem to be a fair trial. It was just that Taylor Green seemed to know how to make a simple statement of fact sound like a full confession. And the fact remained that Cole *had* ridden with Quantrill. No matter how briefly he had done so, it was enough to condemn him in many hearts. Still, she knew that his first speech had also touched the hearts of many. The brutal slaying of a young woman was a heinous act to any ordinary man, be he a Yankee or a Rebel.

On the fourth night of the trial Shannon went to see Mr. Abernathy. He was at dinner, and his housekeeper nearly stopped her from reaching him, but she pushed by. He was just about to start eating his dinner—a lamb chop, peas and a roasted potato.

"What are you doing?" Shannon demanded. She was so distraught that she picked up his plate and tossed it into the corner of the room.

He arched his snowy brows, and cleaned his fingers on the napkin that was tied about his throat and covered his chest. He smiled slowly at her and glanced remorsefully toward his lamb. "Mrs. Slater, I could call this assault! At the very least, it's a case of assault against a very fine lamb chop!"

"I'm sorry," Shannon murmured swiftly. She was sorry. She drew up a chair at the table. "I'm just so worried—"

Mr. Abernathy smiled again and took her hand, patting it. "Trust me, Mrs. Slater. Trust me."

"They could hang, sir!"

"I'm not going to let them hang. Now you'll see, you'll see."

"When?"

"Why, tomorrow, I do believe. The prosecution seems to have finished. I'll start with my case tomorrow. And I'll wager you two lamb chops that I'll need but a day!"

Shannon couldn't believe that he could possibly undo all the harm that Mr. Green had done. But he gave her a glass of sherry, and shooed her out the door.

Shannon went back to the hotel, where she found Kristin red-eyed and puffy-faced from crying. Shannon hugged her sister and lied through her teeth. "It's going to be all right. Mr. Abernathy has it all well in hand. Why, he says he can have them freed by tomorrow!"

"He can?" Kristin wanted so badly to believe.

In the morning, Mr. Abernathy stood before the court and addressed the judge. "My defense is simple. I will prove that we've no case against any of these men, no foundation for a charge of murder. And, your Honor, I will request that the case be dismissed!"

The judge invited Mr. Abernathy to proceed. Mr. Taylor looked up in protest, and Mr. Abernathy bowed very politely to him. He looked around, opening his arms to the court.

Then Shannon realized that the courtroom was curiously filled with men, officers in blue and gray.

One by one they stood and addressed the judge.

"Sir, I'm Corporal Rad Higgins, U.S. cavalry. I came here to say that I rode with Malachi Slater back in April, against a horde of bushwhackers. I rode with Jamie and Cole Slater, too. I'd like to testify, sir, that I ain't ever rode with better men."

"Sir, I'm Samuel Smith. First Sergeant, Darton's brigade, Union army. I'd been left for dead when these fellows came riding in. The fought and beat Quantrill's offshoots, and they offered me the finest medical care. Their doc even saved my arm, and it had been shot up mighty bad.''

From a man with the stripes of an artillery sergeant on his arms: ''I knew Cole Slater in Kansas before the war. I never met a finer officer.''

One by one, the men stood. Soldiers in blue, soldiers in gray.

Then a woman stood up, plump, dignified, gray-haired.

''I'm Martha Haywood, and this is my husband, and I come to say that I ain't ever met finer people than Captain Malachi Slater and his bride, and that's a fact. And my husband will testify to that fact, too.'' Mr. Haywood stood alongside her.

Shannon looked around, incredulous. They were all there. Jamie's Confederate friends from Texas, the people from Haywood, even the professional gamblers from the saloon. And one by one they testified with moving stories to the honesty and honor of the Slater brothers.

When it was over, the judge stood. He slammed his gavel against his desk.

''I dismiss these cases,'' he told the prosecution. ''Lack of evidence,'' he said flatly.

And he walked away.

Silence reigned for a moment. Then there was a Rebel war whoop as hats were thrown high into the air. The crowd rushed forward to congratulate the Slaters.

Shannon pushed her way through until she reached Malachi. He drew her into his arms, and he kissed her warmly.

''It's over,'' he said softly. ''The war is really over.''

''All of our wars are over,'' she promised him. She slipped her hand into his hands, then turned around, searching for Mr. Abernathy. She hurried over to him and gave him a tremendous kiss on the jowl. ''Bless you! And I promise you a dozen lamb chops every year, as long as I live!''

''That would be right nice, Mrs. Slater, mighty nice.''

''What's this?'' Malachi demanded, shaking hands with his attorney.

"That's a mighty fine little woman you have there, captain." Mr. Abernathy said. "Some temper, though, huh?"

"It's a ghastly temper," Malachi agreed.

"Malachi!" she protested.

"I love it, though," he told Mr. Abernathy. "I wouldn't have her any other way. She's full of fire and sparks."

"Malachi—"

"In fact, I'm going to take her right home and see if we can't get a few sparks a-flying." His eyes fell on her. "Seems like a long, long time since I've been away."

"Scat!" Mr. Abernathy told them.

They still had to fight through the crowd. Malachi had to kiss Kristin, and Shannon had to kiss and hug Jamie and Cole, and the brothers embraced, and then Malachi and his brothers thanked each and every man and woman who had come to their defense. Shannon hugged Martha Haywood fiercely, and Martha told her with shimmering eyes that she should go. "And be happy, love! Be happy."

They came out into the sunshine at last.

Then Malachi kissed her. Slowly, surely, completely. He broke away. "Come on. We can go home. We can really go home."

"And start sparks flying?" she teased him.

"No," he whispered.

"No?"

His eyes danced, as blue and clear as the sky above them. "Sparks are already flying."

She smiled slowly, meeting his eyes, curling her fingers within his while he sun beat down upon them, warm and vibrant.

"Yes, let's go home!" she agreed in a fervent whisper.

Because they could. They could really go home.

Life and love were theirs, and they were only just beginning.

The war was more than over. Peace had truly begun.

Epilogue

June 18th, 1866
Haywood, Kansas

Martha Haywood had just locked up the house for the night. There were no guests at the hotel, so she thought she might as well lock up early. She wished that someone would come through. It was summer, and it was beautiful, and it would be nice to be busy and have company.

She felt a surge of nostalgia for the previous year. She smiled, remembering all the hustle and bustle when Captain Slater had come with his Miss McCahy. Maybe she had been wrong. Maybe she and Papa shouldn't have forced the two to enter into marriage.

People had a right to make up their own minds.

She hoped things had worked out. Captain Slater and Miss McCahy had been the perfect couple. A handsome, dashing hero and a damsel in distress. But she hadn't heard from the two of them in a while, not since the letter at Christmas…

Martha started, hearing a fierce pounding at the door. She hurried over as fast as she could, muttering to herself. "People should have more courtesy. Why, I have half a mind not to open the door. Stopping this late along the way…"

But she threw open the door anyway.

For a moment, she just stared, stunned.

"Martha, may we come in?" Shannon Slater asked her. She

looked like an angel on the porch, in her light blue traveling dress with a white lace collar. She held a big, blanketed bundle in her arms, and she stood next to her husband. He was as dashing as ever. His Confederate gray was gone, and he wore a well-tailored dark frock coat and a stovepipe hat. He was carrying a valise and held a squirming bundle as well.

Shannon didn't wait for an answer. Smiling, she stepped into the house, pressing her bundle into Martha's arms. "We are awfully late, aren't we? I'm so sorry. It's much harder traveling with the children."

"Children?" Martha sputtered at last.

"This one is Beau. And this—" she smiled, pulling back the blanket on Malachi's bundle "—is Nadine."

"Oh!" Martha said at last. "Oh, twins!"

"Twins," Malachi agreed, and he pressed his bundle, too, into Martha's arms.

"Twins!" Martha repeated, as if she could think of nothing else to say.

Malachi winked at Shannon, enjoying the woman's flustered pleasure. "This is our wedding anniversary, you know, Martha."

"Yes," Shannon said, stripping away her gloves. "So we've come back, eager for our honeymoon suite."

"Your honeymoon suite—of course!"

Beau gurgled. Martha laughed with delight. "Oh, he is precious!"

"Well, you see, Shannon's brother Matthew and Iris were married last week—"

"No!" Martha gasped.

"Oh, yes. We were all just wonderfully pleased. But they're setting up housekeeping now."

"And we've done what we can to pull the McCahy ranch together," Malachi said.

"So," Shannon continued, "Cole has gone to Texas with Kristin and Gabe and Jamie and Samson and Delilah."

"We're going to join them down that way, too," Malachi said.

"Malachi has been offered a job as sheriff in a little town west of Houston," Shannon said.

"Cole is ranching, and Jamie is—believe it or not—scouting for the cavalry."

"Oh, how wonderful!" Martha said. She looked from one of the squirming babies to the other. "Oh! They're just both so beautiful."

Malachi pinched Martha's cheek. "We're so glad that you like them, Martha."

"Like them? Why, captain, I love them!"

Shannon smiled sweetly and kissed Martha's cheek. "Good." She laughed mischievously. "Because we're going to sneak up to our honeymoon retreat."

"Oh, of course!" Martha giggled. "You two go right ahead."

Malachi swept Shannon off her feet, striding to the stairs. "Oh, we'd like to baptize them tomorrow, if we could. If you and Mr. Haywood wouldn't mind. And we want you and Mr. Haywood to be the godparents."

"Oh!" Martha would have clapped like a child except that her arms were full of squirming babies. She looked at them more closely. They both had soft ringlets of gold and immense blue eyes. Nadine was going to be a beauty like her mother, and Beau would be as handsome as his sire. "My godchildren!" Martha cried. She turned around quickly. "We won't mind. We won't mind at all."

She wasn't sure that Malachi and Shannon heard her. Their eyes were locked with one another's as he carried her up the stairs. She was glorious, with her hair streaming over his arms, and he was wonderful in his dark coat, tall and striking. It was so romantic, the way he held her.

"Of course, of course!" Martha repeated.

Shannon had heard her. She looked over her husband's

shoulder and winked. Martha waved. A second later the door—now repaired—closed at the top of the stairs.

"Oh, my!" Martha said. "Papa! Papa, wake up, Mr. Haywood. We've responsibilities tonight!"

She sat down with her two little bundles.

And she smiled. She had been right—she had been ever so right. They were the perfect couple, and it was just like a fairy tale…

Ending happily ever after!

* * * * *

Seize the Fire
Patricia Potter

Prologue

San Juan Mountains, Colorado,
June, 1865

The mournful wail of bagpipes wafted plaintively through the forest. There were few to hear, only a solitary Indian hunter seeking food, and he lifted his head in puzzlement at the strangely discordant but compelling sounds. The rest were animals, which scattered in fear—all except the gray wolf, which lay at the feet of the man breaking the forest peace.

The alien music grew louder as the old Scottish hymn came alive in highlands much like, but so very far from, its original home. The keening notes reflected struggle and sorrow, man's loneliness and, lastly, in a great surge of power—final victory.

The musician took the pipe from his mouth, listening to the echoes of the closing notes reverberating through the trees, his proud head tilted as they faded slowly into silence. There was a moment of complete stillness, then the forest creatures once more found their voices, each one a part of an ancient symphony that beggared any of man's creations.

Or so MacKenzie thought as he listened intently to the forest music. It would be a long time before he heard its alluring sound again on this mountain.

He looked at the platform he had built, the platform that bore the body—if no longer the soul—of his father. There was no sorrow in the gesture, only a measure of duty toward a man who had lived true to his own values. That those values had not included love was something MacKenzie had accepted many years ago. Like the wolf at his feet, MacKenzie was a lean, cautious, forest-wise creature raised merely to survive. He had never known love and he did not miss it.

He felt comfortable in the Scottish clothes he had donned this day—the wool shirt and kilt, the thick leather belt and the red and black tartan. They had belonged to—and long been revered by—Rob MacKenzie, and now his son recognized that heritage for one last time.

But it would end here—with the death of his father and this last concession to his father's obsession with the past—with injustices real and imagined. For MacKenzie knew that he was the last. There would be no more of the line to follow. He would not pass on a legacy of hate, the stigma of "half-breed." He had learned to be a man alone, and thus he would stay—needing no one, trusting none, except perhaps the wolf at his feet.

His hands busied themselves with the kindling under the platform, and he watched without expression as the fire took hold and the flames shot upward, beginning their hungry attack on the platform. His father had requested this—a Norseman's funeral. Rob MacKenzie had always taken pride in that part of his ancestry, in the wild and free plunderers who had explored the world. Past glories. They had been his father's life. That and the lonely solitude of the mountains, which he had craved as most men craved love. It seemed only fitting now that his ashes be spread by the wind among the peaks and valleys he had known better than any man.

MacKenzie looked on impassively as the platform was consumed by fire. He wondered, briefly, at his lack of feeling. But then there had never been much between Rob MacKenzie and the bastard half-breed son known by whites and Indians alike only as MacKenzie.

His mother had been a Shoshone Indian, bought as a convenience from another tribe, which had captured and brutalized her. She had suffered her lot as concubine and slave to the older MacKenzie in dumb, embittered silence until her death years earlier. MacKenzie had never known a tender gesture or word from either of his parents—indeed he had never expected any. It was an alien notion—love. He knew the word from the Bible—and the worn battered volume of Robert Burns poetry his father had brought with him from Scotland so many years earlier—but it had no real meaning to him. It was like the Burns stories, something faraway and fanciful.

His father had, grudgingly, taught his son to read—"'Tis no' so easy ta cheat a mon who can read"—as he taught him to hunt and live high in the often snow-covered mountains.

MacKenzie had been eager to learn, for the escape into words, and he had memorized much of the Burns poetry as well as long passages of the Bible, although he knew that enjoyment had not been his father's purpose. Rob MacKenzie had sought to instill in his son his own obsession with Scotland, with the past, and had dressed him in kilts and taught him the pipes. It had been the one way in which MacKenzie had pleased his father—the pipes—for he had a natural aptitude for music, for hearing a tune and remembering it.

Sometimes when Rob MacKenzie was very drunk, he would tell his son he must one day return to Scotland and reclaim the title of lord, forgetting that it was lost nearly a hundred years earlier. At other times he would get violent, and the child would escape to the woods. It was there, among the animals, that he found some measure of pleasure and peace. They were his playmates, his companions, and he had a special kind of understanding with them. They seemed to sense that he meant them no harm, that he was, in so many ways, like them. He had the same silent grace, the same watchful eyes, the same instinct for danger.

He had left the mountains occasionally, first to trade pelts for his father, then to find his own way, and each time he encountered a hostile world. His thick, raven-black hair and bronze skin proclaimed an Indian heritage that brought him scorn and trouble in a white world. He fared little better in the red one, which distrusted anyone with white blood. MacKenzie had learned long ago that he belonged nowhere, not to his father's Scottish past, nor to his mother's tortured Indian present. And he had schooled himself not to care. His own abilities, his own strength were all that mattered. He would have turned his back on all men, Indian and white, except for the dream that carried him time and again into a world he despised.

He had to walk among white men to achieve it, so he did...reluctantly, cautiously, emotionlessly. He steeled himself to rise above the insults and distrust, to silently return the scorn while he worked toward his goal.

He had been employed these past nine years as an Indian scout for General Ira Wakefield, one of only two white men he had ever respected. He had left several times for reasons he would rather forget, but had been lured back by promises of autonomy and money. This would be the last time. The next assignment would earn him enough money for a beginning...the realization of his long-nurtured plans.

MacKenzie undressed and changed into his familiar worn buckskins. He looked around at the spartan cabin once again before gathering the familiar Bible and his father's cherished copy of Burns's poetry. In a tanned buffalo hide he wrapped them carefully, along with the bagpipes, the Scottish dress and a purse of coins and bills—the remnants of his past and the hope of his future—and buried the bundle under a towering evergreen. He would be back to fetch them, and Wolf, after this one last tour with the Army.

He would leave his father's other sparse belongings—clothes, some worn blankets and skins and a few remaining food goods—where they were. Few knew of the isolated cabin, only a mountain man or two and several Utes, and they would be welcome to what was left.

MacKenzie waited until the fire died down to a bank of dull red coals and then crumbled into ashes. He would risk no chance of fire to *his* forest, his home. He said a terse farewell to Wolf, mounted his horse in one lithe leap and rode slowly from the clearing into the deep forest.

He didn't look back. The only sound in the evening silence was the quiet hoofbeats of his horse...and the long, mournful cry of the wolf. MacKenzie's hands tightened on the reins for he understood, and knew, the same lonely anguish.

Chapter One

Boston,
August, 1865

Freedom. The last warning blasts of the train whistle seemed to scream the word to April Manning. Freedom, it repeated. Freedom from darkness, from mourning, from blacks and grays. Freedom to once more see the colors of life: a gurgling blue stream, a golden sun, the fresh vivid green of a forest. They had been there, of course, for the past four years, but they had been veiled by somber disapproval.

Freedom. How wonderful the word sounded. Freedom to wear a bright dress, to smile, to laugh and, most of all, freedom to see her too-solemn young son grin, and play, and be a child.

April felt the first lurching of wheels under the train car and her heart made similar jerky movements as she looked at Davon...no, Davey. Davey now. A name for a boy. She had always thought Davon too heavy, but her husband's family would call him nothing else and she, too, had finally bent to their will. As she had, to her everlasting shame, to so many other things.

She would not look, now, at *their* stiff, accusing figures standing on the platform. The four of them were there, she knew. They wanted her to know of their violent disapproval to the very end. But she wouldn't give them that satisfaction.

Besides, she could see them only too clearly in her mind. Mrs. Manning, her late husband's mother, and his sisters—Emily, Dorothy and Margaret. All would be clad in the same heavy, ugly black they had worn for four years. Their mouths would be pursed in tight, grim expressions, each so alike in her fear of life, in her tight hold on grief.

Freedom from gloom. The last whistle accompanied the quickening chugs of the train. April's hand reached over to Davey, who sat so quietly across from her. Childhood, and what should have been its joy, had been drained from him in that house of sorrow. Laughter and play had been banned...mischief discouraged by scolding tirades. She had wanted to leave for months, for years, but David, her husband, was missing in the war, and she felt it her duty to wait where he had left her, to be there when he returned...she and David's son.

But he didn't return, and months turned into years. Long, agonizing years of waiting for some word. Word that never came. Not until the war ended, and one of his sergeants was released from Andersonville Prison. It had been a miracle that the man survived four years of Southern imprisonment, but he had, and his first action after healing was to visit Captain David Manning's family and tell them about David's last hours. The sergeant and Captain Manning had been the only survivors of a Confederate ambush. But the captain had been mortally wounded, and the sergeant stayed with him, and buried him, before his own capture. He had reported Captain Manning's death to Confederate authorities, but somehow the news had never reached federal headquarters.

April had felt pain, but it had been dulled by years of waiting, of secretly knowing. Otherwise there would have been some word. She had been a ghost for those four years, haunted by an aching loneliness. Every moment knowing but not knowing. Living in a netherworld where smiles and laughter were unknown, where hope lingered painfully, then died. The confirmation of what she had come to believe had been both torturous and freeing. The contradiction did not elude her. Never again, she told herself silently. Never again would she subject herself to such agony. She had had her love, and she would treasure it, but she wouldn't subject herself—or her child—to such hurt again.

"Come over here," April told her son, and Davey moved to her side, letting her hug him to her, not wriggling under the increased pressure as he sensed her need with his five-year-old instinct. He was such a good little boy. Too good, too solemn. Too wise, April thought as tiny tears clouded her cerulean blue eyes. Her arm tightened around him. He would have a chance now, a chance to run and ride, to get into mischief, to tease and grin. Her father would see to it. Doughty General Wakefield, fierce and proud, was but clay in a child's hands, she knew that well. He fought and loved with the same intensity. The thought of him filled April with warmth.

It was a warmth she badly needed after the years of coldness. But she had loved David, loved him as only a young, inexperienced girl could love. And they had had so little time together—barely time to get to know each other.

Her father had disapproved of the marriage—not because of David, who was one of his finest young officers, but because of the rush. April and David, who had courted only a month, decided to marry when David was transferred east. Already the clouds of war were on the horizon, and Wakefield knew David would soon be in the middle of the hostilities, but April had always been stubborn, and now she was unmovable. So they had married at her father's post in Arizona, then taken stages and a train to Charleston, where David was stationed at Fort Sumter. They had nearly a year and a half together, a happy time, particularly when Davey was born, before Southern enmity persuaded David to send his wife and son to his family in Boston. She never saw him again. The war started, and he was lost in one of the first engagements.

April had tried, for David's sake, to adjust. But Mrs. Manning was still mourning for a husband dead ten years past.

Two of April's sisters-in-law were in their late twenties, plain and unmarried. The third was married, also to an army officer, but he was killed early in the war, and she moved back into the Manning house, a bitter figure in black.

All had doted on David and disapproved of April. Her laughter offended them; her gaiety horrified them, and she felt more and more stifled until she feared becoming one of *them*. Still she worked desperately to please them, even after the news came that David was missing in the first few months of the war.

The train had reached the outskirts of Boston, and April looked toward the neat, tended fields with resurgent hope.

Spaces. Spaces to roam. Spaces to see. No more hot, closed, black-draped rooms. No more bitter words about the one activity that had so incensed the Manning family and that had given her purpose and satisfaction.

"You desecrate your marriage," Mrs. Manning had angrily told her, absolutely forbidding her to tend the Confederate wounded in the prison hospital in Boston.

Emily gave her the usual malevolent glare. "You never loved David, or you wouldn't do this."

But April did. It had been her first rebellion but not her last. In those moments, she had learned she could stand up for herself and fight for what she believed.

She had not, at first, meant to so infuriate her husband's family. She had merely wanted to help...someone. Anyone. Feeling trapped and useless, she at first volunteered at one Union hospital, but it had more volunteers than it needed. One of the doctors recognized her fierce need and told April of the wretched conditions at Fort Warren, which held Confederate prisoners of war. April had known many Southern officers on her father's staff; they had always been unfailingly gallant and, no matter what, she couldn't hate them for doing what they felt was right. Always the defender of the weak, April received permission to help at the hospital and went several times a week, taking what little food she could scrounge, writing letters, trying to spread a little comfort. She suffered for it because hate was as much a resident in the Manning house as grief. And she was afraid Davey suffered for it, too, but something within her compelled her actions. She tried to explain once.

"If David's in a Confederate prison, I would hope some Southern woman would try to help him."

"You're a fool," her mother-in-law said. "Not one of those traitors would lift a finger, and now you're giving comfort to our enemies…perhaps to the very Rebel who killed David."

But April couldn't blame the soldiers she saw and tended. So many of them were merely boys—starved, war-sick, mutilated boys who wanted only to go home…

Home. Arizona now. Arizona with its strange, stark beauty. Arizona was a beacon to her, a place of sun and warmth, and it was a shimmering glow that had remained in her memory during the frigid wet winters of an inhospitable north.

She was going home. It was her most difficult rebellion, as the Manning women had used every ounce of guilt in their formidable arsenal. David would have wanted Davey to stay in Boston and be raised by his family. How could she think of taking him? How could she so betray her husband?

But she persisted, knowing in her heart that her husband would want Davey to be raised happily, not weighed down by the bitterness that had already made its mark.

Could it really be over? The waiting, the hoping, the praying, the endless lectures, the hateful looks and wounding words? Would she and Davey, at long last, have their own life, to mold as they wished?

She would miss David, her husband of so few months. She would always miss him. He had been handsome and tender and, unlike the rest of his family, joyous. She had often wondered how that inherent gladness of spirit had survived the deep gloom of his family. But perhaps he had once given it a light, and that light had been quenched when he left. She had been nineteen the last time she saw him, and now she was twenty-three. It had been nearly five years, and sometimes she couldn't quite remember what he looked like. It frightened her, because she knew she should. At least, that way, she could keep part of him alive.

But he had left her a wondrous gift—Davey. Wonderful, serious, responsible Davey, with his father's green eyes and dark hair.

April looked down at him. He was sleeping, his head resting against her side. She leaned down and kissed his tousled head. Now, she promised silently, now you will know laughter.

April's optimism and hope faded slightly as the train moved west. It was late August, and the heat was oppressive. It strained the tempers of the passengers. Cinders and dust made it almost mandatory that windows remain closed.

April was the only woman in the car, and Davey the only child. The war was now more than four months over, but still most of the men were in uniform, or parts of uniforms—living reminders of the country's recent agonies. There was still turmoil as soldiers were slowly mustered out of the army and started for home or for a new life elsewhere. Everyone seemed to be on the move. Despite victory, a feeling of dissatisfaction hovered in the air. Four years of bitter fighting had changed so many, had made it impossible for them to settle into old jobs. The west beckoned now as never before.

Sprinkled among the travelers were two men clad in gray Confederate trousers, evidently ex-prisoners finally released and making their way home. They endured the constant taunts and challenges in silence. April studied them carefully, wondering at their forbearance, noting the way one visibly swallowed a fierce urge to retaliate. She couldn't help but wonder why they were just now traveling. Surely they would have been released months ago. Or why they hadn't worn something less likely to invite trouble?

After one particularly ugly verbal attack, intended, she

knew, to incite a fight the Southerners could not possible win, April told Davey to stay in his seat, and she rose, moving to where a growing number of men joined to bait the two ex-Rebs. The men parted as April reached the two victims. The passengers had been together for two days in the hot railroad car, and they all knew her story of a missing husband just recently known dead. They had played with Davey and shared food with them...all but the Rebs, who had stayed to themselves.

April ignored the stares of the men and completed her journey toward the two men who sat alone in the back. She saw the knotted hands of one; the second seemed oddly indifferent. She looked at the seat opposite them, a seat that had remained empty despite the overcrowded train.

"May I sit with you?" she asked softly.

Surprise darted over the face of the older Southerner. He, too, had overheard the young widow's story. He rose. "We would be pleasured, ma'am," he said, in a pleasant but wary drawl, his eyes never leaving his antagonists.

April looked around at the faces—some angered, some abashed, some puzzled. "The war's over," she said, her voice shaking slightly. "There's been enough violence, enough hate, enough death..." Her voice faltered on the last word, and that, more than anything, sent the Union veterans back to their seats. April leaned back in the seat, closed her eyes for a moment, opening them only when she felt Davey's small hand on hers.

"Mama?"

April looked at his earnest face and patted the seat next to her, inviting him to sit. "Everything's fine, Davey," she said comfortingly. She knew he must have felt the tension in the car; his face was puzzled and his little body stiff.

When he settled in the security of her arms, April's eyes met the quizzical ones of the Southerner who had risen. The other's remained curiously blank.

"Thank you, ma'am," the older man said with an almost

imperceptible smile. "I'm Blake Farrar, formerly a lieutenant with the Texas First Cavalry. This is my brother, Dan." His mouth tightened, and bitterness clouded dark brown eyes. His hand touched his brother's sleeve, but there was no response, not even a flicker, from the man next to him.

"He's been injured?" April questioned gently.

Farrar sighed. "In ways you can't see. In ways I'm afraid you can't heal."

April's eyes misted at his anguished words, surprising the Southerner once more. "So many," she whispered. "So many wounds and hurts...so many dead..."

A compassion Blake Farrar thought long destroyed surfaced. His voice was very low. "You, too, I've heard. Sometimes...we forget...the pain back home." His hand started to reach out, then dropped. His voice grew stronger. "Where are you going, ma'am?"

April straightened. "Home. Arizona."

"You have family there?"

"My father," April said with a slight smile, the thought of him reviving her. "And you?"

"Dan and I are for Texas. I have a wife. Two children." His hard look softened. "I haven't seen them in four years."

"You've been at..." April hesitated at the word.

"Fort Warren," Farrar confirmed, once more with deep bitterness. "Two years. Two long, miserable, hungry years."

Davey had been listening and at the familiar words, he spoke up. "Mama went there," he said. "Grandmother didn't want her to. They fought about it all the time."

Farrar's eyes widened. "I thought your husband..."

"Was Union?" April answered. "He was. But I hoped...had hoped—someone down South would try to help *him*."

The Reb's eyes gentled for the first time. "I didn't think anyone cared," he said slowly. "It was hell there, begging your pardon, ma'am."

"There were others," April said, embarrassed.

"Not many, I think," he replied.

"I didn't see your brother in the hospital," April said, anxious to change the subject.

"He didn't have the kind of wound they treated there," Blake said. "You see, Dan couldn't stand the killing. We were at Shiloh, and he shot a Yank…turned out to be nothing more than a boy. It destroyed something in him. He just walked away, right into a Union patrol, and I had to go with him. He hasn't spoken since."

"You've just been released?"

"Three months ago. I met a doctor, hoped he could help Dan." Farrar shrugged. "He helped me get a job at the docks, but that quickly ended when so many Union soldiers came home. And Dan wasn't getting any better. I thought going home might help, but we didn't have any money. The doctor, God bless him, loaned us enough money for the trip, but it wasn't enough for clothes, too." He looked wryly at his ragged Confederate trousers. "I thought the war was over. Now I wonder if it ever will be."

April looked at her son. He would grow up without a father because of the war. She squeezed Davey's arm.

"My boy's about his age," Blake said wistfully, his eyes intent on the small figure across from him. "He's very good."

"Too good," April replied. "We've been living with my husband's family, and I'm afraid they didn't know much about small boys. Sometimes I wish he would get into mischief like other children."

"I doubt it will take him long to learn," the Texan said with a real smile. His hand reached over to Davey. He touched the small face with gentleness and wonder. "If only we could all be so innocent…"

April and Davey spent the next several days with the Farrar brothers, Davey finding an instant friend in the silent one. Although Dan Farrar still kept his silence, his eyes warmed when Davey's sleepy head sometimes dropped into his lap.

And Davey listened with fascinated interest to Blake's tales of Texas and the Alamo.

They separated at St. Louis, April and Davey changing to a train that would travel over newly completed tracks to Kansas City. The Farrars caught a Butterfield stage headed south to Texas.

Blake bid April and Davey goodbye with gratitude and real regret. "If ever you need anything, need anyone, please remember us," he said, giving her the name of the town nearest his ranch. "Your Davey has helped Dan more than anything else could, I think... Perhaps my own children can do the rest. Thank you." He took her hands in his. "I hope you and Davey find the happiness you deserve." With that, he turned abruptly, and he and his brother climbed onto the stage.

At Kansas City, April and Davey also transferred to a coach. They would go to Fort Atkinson, then Santa Fe, and finally across the New Mexico territory to Arizona...

Would it never end? April did not remember the journey as being so long, but then the first time she had been a new bride, and everything had been so gloriously wonderful. She and David had never stopped talking, and it had all seemed such an adventure.

Even Davey was squirming restlessly in the Concord coach. There were another four passengers squeezed into its confines, and piles of mail were stacked in every corner. April felt she would never want to sit again after the constant jolting along the primitive roads. The only relief came when the horses were changed every twenty miles or so. Then she and Davey could stretch and walk during the few moments it took to change horses and drivers. Sometimes there would be a hot meal available, though it was usually little more than rancid bacon, bread and coffee that tasted like dishwater. It was still better than the hardtack and jerky that most passengers, including April and Davey, carried. The heat prevented any variety.

The other passengers were mostly a silent lot, all of them

men headed for the California gold fields. Of the four, two drank constantly, to April's quiet dismay. The smell of liquor and sweat made her want to gag, and only the approaching journey's end made it tolerable. She greeted the first sight of desert with joy, particularly at sunrise when the bright glimmering sands caught the serene beauty of a rising sun. Where others thought the desert stark and ugly, April had always found a quiet radiance in it. She had hungered for it for five years, and now not even her drunken companions could quiet the triumph growing within her.

At Santa Fe, she and Davey gratefully left the coach and rested in the frontier town for several days before continuing. There was a stage heading west, and a small army encampment on the border of the New Mexico-Arizona territories. She knew from her father's letter that she could get transportation from there to his headquarters. He had warned her about marauding Apaches, and made it clear she and Davey were not to travel into Arizona without adequate escort.

Already Davey was changing, his green eyes glistening with eagerness and curiosity. He was full of questions about this strange barren land, so different from the bright greens of the northeast.

Most intriguing to him was the thought of a horse. For his very own, April promised. And a dog. He should finally have a dog, his dearest desire for the past year. But the Mannings had been horrified at the thought of a "filthy beast" in their home. But now he would have both, and more.

April told him stories of her own childhood and pets. She had moved often as a child. Her father had been a career army officer, serving in a number of posts from Kansas to the northwest to Arizona. He had been assigned to Arizona as a colonel in 1858, and it was here that April's mother died, and where April's heart, for some reason, stayed. Wakefield was one of the few officers not called east during the war, although he did fight the Confederates when they crossed into New Mexico during the first year of the war. His real expertise was with the Indians, and he finally won his general's star at the war's end. April had not seen him in the past five years, but they had written frequently to each other. She knew he would adore Davey and give him the masculine influence and love the boy seemed to crave.

Only a few days now, perhaps a week at most, depending on the Army's schedule. Arizona. Home. Father. April shivered with anticipation as she and Davey boarded their last coach.

Chapter Two

Arizona,
September, 1865

MacKenzie, his eyes wary and his right hand taking the rifle from its scabbard, slid from his horse.

He stooped, studying the pony tracks carefully. They were from an unshod pony...and recent. And many. Too many. There had been several small groups of Apache renegades killing and burning in the southeast corner of the Arizona Territory. It appeared now that they might have joined forces, and that boded ill for both the settlers and the Army. And himself.

It meant he would have to stop by the small garrison on the Chaco River and give warning before heading back to Wakefield's headquarters. Not, he thought wryly, that his advice would be heeded. Not by Sergeant Peters, nor by Peters's friend, Terrell. And their shavetail lieutenant didn't have the sense God gave a chicken. But distasteful as it was, dealing with the two men who regarded Indian blood with bitter hatred was his job.

MacKenzie remounted his Appaloosa. He had selected the horse for its toughness and speed, but it was deceptively ugly and ungainly. It had often invited taunts, but MacKenzie knew the horse's endurance had saved his life more than once. He eased back in the saddle, wiping the sweat from his brow and taking one last sweeping look across the mesas. He pressed his knees against the horse's sides, urging it to a gallop. The sooner he reached the Chaco River, the sooner he would rid himself of a disagreeable duty.

Seven hours later, as dusk approached, MacKenzie reached the small cluster of buildings that comprised the Chaco post. Because of recent hostile outbreaks, it had been reinforced and should have had a commander of higher rank than Lieutenant Evan Pickering. But the captain who was in command had been abruptly recalled to Washington, and no replacement had yet arrived. So MacKenzie had to deal with a damn fool, a cocky West Point graduate who knew little about the West and less about Indians. And who depended almost entirely on his two top sergeants, both of whom hated MacKenzie and deeply suspected any and all of the Army's Indian scouts.

MacKenzie paused before riding in. He was bone tired and filthy. He had been in the saddle for two weeks, scouting alone. It was the way he wanted it. He didn't like depending on anyone else, nor did he enjoy being responsible for other scouts. He had repeatedly turned down Wakefield's offer to be named chief of the scouts. Besides, he had argued, some of the officers and enlisted men refused to listen to him because he was a 'breed. 'Breed. God, he hated that word. But he could expect to hear it repeatedly in the next few hours. He shifted in his saddle, his buckskin trousers straining against his muscular thighs. Because of the heat, he had replaced his usual buckskin shirt with a more comfortable cotton one, its sleeves rolled up and the neck open where a sweat-stained bandanna ringed bronze skin glistening now with beads of perspiration.

A hand went across his face, feeling the bristling beard. He would be eyed with disdainful disapproval by Pickering, who was always dressed like a rooster, flaunting his carefully pressed uniform like tail feathers. MacKenzie 'sighed. He would spend the night here, find a bath and hit the trail again early in the morning. The deserted mesas always held special appeal after the prejudice and hate at Chaco. He steeled himself for the coming confrontations and rode into the encampment.

"I don't believe it," the heavy, blue-coated figure blustered. "Those damned Apaches hate each other too much to band together."

"They may hate you more," MacKenzie replied coolly, eyeing Sergeant Peters with his usual contempt.

"Does that include you?" Peters sneered, his lips twisted with loathing.

"I don't think about you one way or another, sergeant," MacKenzie said with the small burr he had learned from his father and which was noticeable only when he was angry.

The implication that the sergeant merited no thought at all caused the man's face to go even redder. "You arrogant red bastard." He practically spit the words.

Only an almost imperceptible movement of a cheek muscle indicated MacKenzie had heard the words. He turned his back on the burly sergeant and once again faced the young lieutenant.

"Do as you will. I gave you the information. I'll be giving the same to General Wakefield. There could be a large uprisin' brewing and the ranchers should be brought in."

Lieutenant Pickering looked from the tall, lean scout to his sergeant. When he had first been assigned this post, he had been told to listen to his top sergeant. He did not like Sergeant Peters, but neither did he like the insolent half-breed who showed no respect for rank or, for that matter, the army. And the man's person was disgraceful. Unshaven. Dirty. Pickering didn't consider the fact the scout had been in the saddle nearly nineteen hours a day for the past fortnight or more. His nose twitched as he wondered, once more, why this particular man seemed to hold Wakefield's trust so firmly. *He* wouldn't trust him any farther than he could throw him. Which, he realized, looking at the animal power of MacKenzie, was exactly no distance at all. The thought added to his feeling of inadequacy, and he vented his frustration on the scout.

"I won't order the settlers in on your guess," he said. "They could lose everything."

"Not their lives," MacKenzie said very quietly, the soft burr even more pronounced as he emphasized the last words. *Damn their stupidity.*

"I'm in command here," the lieutenant said. "Not you."

"No," MacKenzie said in a low but openly contemptuous tone that infuriated both Peters and Pickering. "And it's on your shoulders, not mine. If I'm right, and they die, it'll be you the general blames." The implied accusation was his last weapon, and it was a measure of his concern that the burr had become very pronounced. It was the only indication of any emotion, and only he knew what it represented.

"You just want those ranchers to leave everything to your friends," Peters blustered.

"My friends?"

"Your Indian friends, MacKenzie. That way, they can take everything without a fight."

MacKenzie shook his head in disgust and turned to leave. "You're naught but a fool, Peters." He turned to Pickering. "And you're a bigger one if you don't do something. I'll be leaving at dawn."

Peters caught MacKenzie's shoulder. "You don't call me a fool, injun, and get away with it."

MacKenzie looked at him calmly, then looked at Pickering. "You're a witness, Lieutenant. I'm not fighting him. Not now, not ever. He's not worth it. I'm going to take a bath and leave." He turned to Peters. "Now take your hand off me."

"Sergeant Peters!" For once, Pickering's voice carried authority. He didn't understand it, but he knew General Wakefield valued this particular scout, and he wasn't going to jeopardize his career by seeing the man killed or badly hurt by one of his own men. Nor did he want Peters dead. He knew how Peters fought. And he knew MacKenzie's reputation.

"Damn it, sir," Peters said. "He needs a lesson in manners."

Pickering silently agreed as he saw MacKenzie's thin smile, which was really no smile at all. "Let him go," he ordered, and Peters reluctantly took his arm away.

Without another word, MacKenzie disappeared out the door and headed toward the bathhouse.

In answer to the sergeant's fury, Pickering tried to pacify him. "You can teach him a lesson someplace else, Sergeant. Not here."

"I'll kill that half-breed bastard," Peters promised before turning and leaving for his family quarters. His anger continued to mount, and he transferred part of it to his daughter, Ellen, when he reached the stark living area. Where in the hell was she this time, when his dinner should be ready? Fooling around again, he supposed. With one of the enlisted men? Officers? Was any man so plagued as he? Ellen couldn't seem to keep away from men...any man. He lifted a bottle from the messy table and took a long pull from it. If she wasn't home after a few drinks, he would go look for her. And then he would beat her within an inch of her life.

MacKenzie washed the grime from his body, taking brief satisfaction in being the solitary occupant of the small bathhouse. Exhausted from days of riding and nearly sleepless nights, he had paid one of the Indian women to fetch and heat some water. He sank in the tub, letting the hot water soothe his aching muscles.

He had planned to spend the night here, but now he would not. It meant trouble, and trouble was something he was trying to avoid. He cursed his own tongue. He shouldn't have let Peters get to him like that, but damn, they were fools. Dangerous fools. The only thing to do now was to get to Wakefield, and perhaps the general would order the area evacuated. MacKenzie could only hope it wouldn't be too late. There could be a bloodbath. He closed his eyes. God, he was tired. He dreaded the thought of remounting.

MacKenzie was so exhausted, so physically drained that his usually sharp ears didn't hear the slight noise as the door opened or the almost soundless footsteps that approached him. He was nearly asleep, all his warning instincts dulled. His first indication that someone was with him was the touch of a hand on his chest.

His eyes flew open. Ellen Peters was kneeling beside the tub, her fingers trailing across his wet chest, caressing it with knowledgeable intent.

MacKenzie shot up in the copper tub. "What in the hell are you doing here?" He shoved away the girl's probing hand.

Ellen's strangely colored eyes consumed him, and her mouth twisted into an inviting smile. Her hand sought his rock-hard bronze chest again, which she had coveted for so long.

"No one saw me," she whispered, an intense gleam in her eye. "It's just you and me."

MacKenzie glared at her. Ellen Peters, like her father, had been nothing but trouble since he'd first stopped at Chaco. She was pretty enough, but there was something not quite right about her. He had often found her staring at him with an intensity that made him uneasy. He had overheard talk that she was easily available, but the combination of her possessiveness and her father's rage had kept most of her liaisons very short indeed. In his brief stops at Chaco, he had not missed the ardent invitation in her eyes, and he had avoided her. No woman was worth the trouble he knew she represented. Once more, he shoved her hands away, and he rose, wrapping a towel around his waist.

"You have no business here, Miss Peters," he said, hoping the reserve in his voice might do what anger would not. "Your father will be angry." Anger, he swore silently, would be the least of it.

"To hell with my father," Ellen said. "All he wants is a

servant." Her hands reached for the towel and before MacKenzie could react, it was on the floor, and her hands were on his manhood. "I want you," she whispered softly.

MacKenzie felt himself instinctively harden under her touch, and he moved swiftly away, grabbing his buckskin trousers.

As one of her hands reached for him once more, he caught it. "No," he said succinctly. "Now get out of here."

"You're refusing me?" Ellen said with disbelief, her eyes narrowing and a strange glowing light invading them. "You... a half-breed...refusing me..." Her voice rose. "You should be grateful someone's willing to even touch you, you dirty..." A long flow of filth followed.

MacKenzie ignored her and continued dressing, his dismissal fueling the rage in her voice. He felt trapped as her words got louder and louder. He strode over and put his hand over her mouth. "Quiet," he warned softly, but the girl was beyond reason, and he felt her teeth on his hand. His other hand instinctively tightened around her shoulder, and he heard her scream.

MacKenzie sensed rather than heard the menacing presence of Peters, and he whirled toward the door, one arm still on Ellen. He heard the girl's shrill voice. "He's trying to rape me, Papa."

His arm propelled the girl away from him as he faced Peters. "That's a lie."

But Peters's face was frenzied, and his hand was reaching for the revolver at his side.

MacKenzie was too far away to reach him, but his knife was lying on a table next to him. With lightning speed, his hand reached for it and let it fly with one deceptively easy motion. It reached its target just as the pistol discharged.

Everything became a blur. MacKenzie could hear Ellen Peters screaming, and then the room was full of blue uniforms. He fought, but there were too many. He took a blow to the head, then his stomach, and he was on the floor, his body twisting in agony as one boot after another found its mark in his chest, his buttocks, his stomach, his groin, his legs. And then red—the color of pain—turned black as he slipped from consciousness.

Even the slightest movement was agonizing. Through a fiery haze of pain, MacKenzie slowly regained consciousness, his senses reviving one by one. There was not one part of him that didn't feel intense hurt. He tried to move to explore the wounds and their severity, but his hands were bound tightly together. So were, he knew instantly, his ankles. And not kindly. The ropes bit into his flesh, and the slightest struggle against them seemed only to make them tighter. The ropes around his wrists and ankles were apparently joined by another rope. If he tried to stretch, he only increased the pressure on both.

His eyes adjusted to the darkness until black became gray, and he could decipher shapes and forms. There was no guardhouse at Chaco, and he had been imprisoned in one of the several storerooms. There were boxes piled along the walls, and his allotted space was small. He could not straighten his body—if he had wanted to. And, at the moment, he didn't think he did. Not when a stabbing pain traveled through his chest as he struggled to relieve the pressure on his wrists.

There was silence. Complete silence. Only his own broken breathing echoed in the room. He couldn't hear movement outside, and didn't know if it was night or day. If he could feel his cheeks, he would know from his beard how long he had been here; he had shaved just before his bath. Was it four hours? Eight? More than that? And Peters. Was he dead? He must be. MacKenzie remembered those last few minutes with complete clarity. He seldom missed with a gun. Never with a knife.

He could smell blood and sweat. That told him something. He had been here, like this, more than several hours.

He could feel the dryness in his mouth. His throat was parched, and his body yearned for liquid.

Forget the thirst and the pain. He had killed a sergeant in the U.S. Army. He remembered Ellen Peters...the way she had screamed rape. Even Wakefield couldn't help him now. Not that he would expect him to, not that he even wanted him to. MacKenzie had always taken care of himself. He would this time, too.

Ignoring the torture of his torn wrists and the severe bruises that covered his body, he struggled to bring his bound hands up to his mouth, twisting his body to do so. Pushing his knees up to his chest, he started to chew on the knots.

Pickering could almost see his short career come to an abrupt halt. A murder and rape in his command! Committed by one of his general's top scouts. And now Sergeant Terrell was demanding the scout's death.

"He should hang...now," Terrell said. Peters had been his friend, his best friend. "Slowly," he added with relish.

Pickering paced the floor. There was no question of MacKenzie's guilt. Her face awash with tears, Ellen Peters had told the whole wretched story...how she had gone to fetch some soap, not knowing anyone was in the washhouse...how the 'breed had grabbed her and was forcing her to submit...how her father had attempted to rescue her and was callously knifed to death in front of her horrified eyes. She showed the dark bruises on her arm as proof. Despite her reputation, or lack of one, no one doubted her story. A white girl would never be attracted to a savage like MacKenzie.

But lynching?

At least, Pickering thought, General Wakefield would come to realize the true nature of the scout he had trusted so completely. In fact, Pickering would like to see the general's face when the charges were lodged.

"Lieutenant?" the sergeant probed. He already had a group of soldiers ready and willing to proceed. Many of them had seen the remains of tortured comrades, and it made little difference to them whether MacKenzie's Indian blood was Shoshone or Apache. Indian was Indian.

"No," Pickering said. "I'm sending him to Fort Defiance for a trial."

An ugly look came over Terrell's face. "Why can't we save ourselves the trouble, b'God? We all know he done it."

"There will be no lynchings under my command," the lieutenant reiterated. "You can take charge of him, if you want," he added, seeking to calm his now highest-ranking sergeant. "Just make sure he gets there alive."

"Barely?" Terrell said as if seeking approval.

Pickering shrugged. "You're in charge."

"And if he tries to escape?"

"Alive, sergeant. I said alive. I don't want any questions or investigations by General Wakefield."

"He'll wish to hell he was dead before I get through with him," Terrell said.

Pickering stared at him. "Handle it your way."

The sergeant saluted, making ready to leave when the lieutenant added as an afterthought, "Perhaps I'll go with you. Sergeant O'Hara can take care of matters here. Pick thirty men. Just in the event MacKenzie's right about the Apaches. We'll leave the day after tomorrow."

Terrell could feel his face flush. He would rather have had MacKenzie to himself. Regardless of what Pickering ordered, he had planned to hang the half-breed along the way and, as he had said earlier, slowly. Not the way the Army would do it, a clean break. No, MacKenzie would strangle to death, dancing to Terrell's music. Terrell had already selected the men who would keep their mouths shut. Now he would have to rethink the plan. But, he vowed, MacKenzie would die before he reached Fort Defiance, before Wakefield could interfere. Damned injun-lovin' general.

Pickering did not miss the fleeting disappointment on the sergeant's face. It strengthened his resolve. "That's all, Sergeant,'' he said curtly. Still, he would not wish to be Mac-Kenzie in the coming days. The whole affair just proved you could never tame an Indian.

Thinking bleakly about the next miserably hot days on the trail, he sat down at his desk, fingering the charges he had prepared against the scout. Anger boiled up inside him. As if he didn't already have enough problems in this godforsaken country. With the exception of MacKenzie's death, he would allow Terrell a free hand. A small smile played around his mouth as he anticipated MacKenzie's humbling.

The door to the small storeroom opened, and MacKenzie flinched against the sudden light.

Terrell stood there, flanked by two men, one of whom held a gun. As MacKenzie's eyes adjusted to the streaming light, he saw the other was the post blacksmith, and he was holding a length of chain. Damn his luck. He was almost through the rope. Only a few more moments, and his hands would have been free.

Terrell stooped and investigated the chewed ropes, his mouth straightening into a tight, cruel smile. ''Damned injuns will eat anything,'' he said. ''We'll see about chain.'' He nodded to the smithy. ''Bind his wrists tightly,'' he said.

MacKenzie struggled to sit up and maintain a shred of dignity despite the stabbing pain that violated every part of his body. He felt the rough rope fall from his wrists, then the chain links once more binding them together. The blacksmith used his tools to close them with an iron link that could be broken easily only by another blacksmith. Through the haze of pain, MacKenzie remembered an old trick he had once been shown, and turned his wrists in such a fashion that the chains would be looser than the blacksmith intended. Not loose enough that they would fall away, but sufficient, at least, to present the faint possibility of working out of them when the time was right. The rest of the length of chain dangled from his wrists, and he watched with an air of careless indifference as the blacksmith bolted a ring in the storeroom wall.

The bonds around his ankles were cut, and he was hoisted roughly to his feet.

"Take him to the latrine," Sergeant Terrell said. "Then chain him to the wall." He looked at MacKenzie with a small, malevolent smile. "Thirsty, 'breed?"

MacKenzie stood, swaying slightly as he fought against weakness. He would not give Terrell the pleasure of seeing him fall. In response to the sergeant's question, he merely stared impassively ahead, nothing in his face giving indication of need or desire.

His detachment infuriated Terrell. "You will be on your knees begging before I finish with you," he threatened. "We're taking you to Fort Defiance day after tomorrow, and you will walk every step of the way."

Still receiving no reaction, he angrily turned to the man with the gun. "Give him just enough water to wet his lips. I heard injuns can go days without water. We'll find out."

April stared at Lieutenant Pickering with puzzlement. She had not expected to be greeted with open arms, but neither had she expected to be regarded as something akin to a contagious disease.

She carried papers her father had arranged, which were signed by a major general in Washington, requesting that Mrs. Manning and her son receive every consideration and assistance from the army to reach Fort Defiance. They did not carry her maiden name, Wakefield. She had always felt awkward with the fawning and exaggerated courtesy the name produced. It was enough to let them think she was just an army widow, travelling home. For, after all, that was what she was. But she had not considered the possibility of resistance, particularly from the young lieutenant.

"It's too dangerous," he was saying for the fourth time.

"Not," April said succinctly, "with the company of an

army troop.'' She had heard there would be a detail leaving on the morrow for her father's headquarters.

Pickering looked at her with real dismay. She was obviously a person of some importance; she had extraordinary papers with her. He did not care for her to learn what had so recently transpired on *his* post. But now he had no choice.

''We're taking a dangerous prisoner to trial,'' he explained. ''It will be no place for a lady...such as yourself,'' he tried, hope in his eyes. God knew he needed no more problems.

But April merely looked at him with grim determination. ''Surely,'' she pressed, ''a troop of American soldiers is a match for one prisoner...and protection for myself and my son. Or,'' she challenged, ''am I wrong?''

Pickering silently cursed her. At any other time, he would have flirted with her. Though she wore a high-necked, long-sleeved dark blue dress, which showed the effects of long travel, and her rich, chestnut-colored hair was pulled back in a severe knot at the nape of her neck, she was pretty enough. There was a glimmer of gold in her hair, and her eyes were a deep, rich blue. They were, he thought uncomfortably, uncommonly direct for a woman.

''All right,'' he finally surrendered. ''You and your son can ride in the wagon with Miss Peters...she's going to testify.''

''Perhaps,'' April said softly, ''I can be of some assistance.'' Despite the lieutenant's reticence, she had already heard of the young girl who had almost been raped and who had lost her father. Her heart had contracted with sympathy when she learned the details. She remembered her own grief when she lost her mother, and how much it would hurt if she now lost her father. She would do what she could for Ellen Peters. As for the murderer, he would be well-guarded. She couldn't understand Pickering's concern.

It ended there. Pickering had no choice but to allow her to accompany them. His sallow face reflected his displeasure.

She and Davey were given use of one of the nicer officer's quarters. Both fresh water and food appeared, and Davey, par-

ticularly, ate the stew with a hearty appetite. Their recent diet
had been austere, to say the least, and it was bound to get bad
again on the trail. After eating, he clamored to go exploring.
Pleased at his excitement and interest, April readily consented.
Hand and hand, they left the hot, airless quarters and walked
toward the river. The temperature was rapidly cooling as the
sun disappeared. It was a strange time in the Southwest, a
time of blistering days and cool nights. Davey had skipped on
ahead when April stopped suddenly. Just in front of her, two
blue-coated soldiers led a man in buckskin trousers and torn
cotton shirt. His hands were bound by a chain in front of him,
and the end was being jerked first one way, then another by
his captors as they laughed. One vicious shove sent him
sprawling at her feet.

April stepped back. But she couldn't take her eyes from the
man as he struggled to rise. His eyes met hers...so briefly she
was stunned by the impact.

She had never seen such eyes. They were a deep, dark gray,
and completely impenetrable. Not that they were empty. She
had a fleeting impression of depth upon depth. Of currents
swirling, a bottomless vortex of complexity. But she blinked,
and when she looked again they were hooded. Calm. Emotionless.

She heard the laughter once more from the soldiers, and she
suddenly hated them, although the reason escaped her. This
must be the man who tried to rape an innocent young girl,
who had killed a sergeant in cold blood. She stepped back,
and her eyes swept him coldly.

His mouth twisted into a slight grim smile as he recognized
her evident repugnance. Back on his feet, he turned away from
her and, if she didn't know better, she would say it was pride
that held his shoulders so stiffly. But it couldn't be that. Not
a murderer and rapist. She watched as he was led to a shed
and pushed inside, the two guards still with him. They reappeared a moment later and carefully locked the door.

April didn't understand the chill that suddenly ran up her

back or the deep feeling of disquiet that swamped her. She bit her lip in confusion, then called for Davey and thoughtfully walked back to their temporary quarters.

An hour later, when Davey was asleep, April went several doors down the long building, which served as family quarters, to see Ellen Peters. She wanted to offer her sympathy and meet her travelling companion.

Something about the girl immediately rang false. April had started to put her arms around the young girl in sympathy, but Ellen had flinched and stepped back. To be expected, April thought, after a man had touched her with violence. Until Sergeant Terrell entered, and the girl flung herself into his arms. Again not unusual, April pondered. The sergeant was evidently a family friend. But then April saw the girl's glistening eyes. And they held neither grief nor fear.

The longer she stayed, the more uncomfortable April became. There was an atmosphere she remembered only too well from the Manning home—unadulterated hate. In the north, it was directed against Southerners. Now it was aimed at Indians—all Indians.

She was glad she had put Davey to bed. It didn't take long for her stomach to knot at the conversation. Hate. Vengeance. Murder. She remembered the calm gray eyes of the accused renegade and compared them, in her mind's eye, with the sly, malicious ones of the victim.

Don't do this, she told herself. Don't make a martyr out of a killer. There is no question of his guilt. Perhaps it was only the girl. She had seldom disliked a person on sight. Especially one who had been through what Ellen Peters had apparently endured. But the girl repulsed her as no one else ever had.

Sergeant Terrell, apparently assuming that April shared his prejudices, was telling the girl that he intended to make the half-breed suffer on the trip, that he had withheld water from the man to see how long he could go without it. The soldier apparently didn't see the distaste in April's eyes, for he laughed as he told Ellen how he intended to make his prisoner beg before reaching Fort Defiance. "If he doesn't die first!"

April could not stand their presence another moment. The trip ahead of them looked longer and longer, and she hated to think that Davey would be exposed to such cruelty. She would talk to Lieutenant Pickering in the morning. And, if she must, she would tell them exactly who she was.

She couldn't sleep that night. She kept seeing the man in buckskin trousers, and his eyes haunted the darkness. She recalled his battered face, the blood on his clothes and, most of all, the pride in his bearing. And the eyes. So fathomless.

You're romanticizing, April, she scolded herself. He's nothing but a rapist and a murderer, and he's bound for a hangman.

He's also a human being, a voice within her persisted. And they have no right to treat him, or anyone, like a mad dog.

But what if he is? What if he is no more than a rabid animal?

No! April knew. She knew with all the instincts she valued that he was not a merciless killer. Her father had always told her she was a good judge of character, like himself. He took great pride in the fact; he was seldom disappointed in the men he chose for leadership. He could quickly separate the weak from the strong, the judicious from the foolish. And this man, she had heard, was one of his personally selected scouts.

MacKenzie. She had heard the man's name during the evening, and it rang a bell somewhere in her mind. Now she searched for it, only slowly recalling a letter in which her father mentioned the name. "He's a strange man," she remembered him writing, "a man without loyalties. But once he gives his word, nothing deters him. I'm glad to have him back."

MacKenzie. She remembered now. She remembered being fascinated with her father's short portrait of a lone and independent mountain man who, he said, was the most savvy scout in the Southwest.

That man and the one described earlier in the evening didn't match. Didn't match at all. Something was wrong, very wrong. April shivered in the cool night. Her natural affinity for an underdog surfaced. She would not allow the sergeant to kill the man before her father could sort it all out. She didn't know how she would stop it, but stop it she would. Somehow she would.

Chapter Three

April couldn't take her eyes off the man walking behind the wagon. No matter how hard she concentrated or how many times she tried to turn her attention to Davey or to the stark beauty around her, her eyes continually wandered back to the man called MacKenzie.

She, Davey and Ellen Peters had already been settled in the back of a supply wagon when he had been led out. She hadn't missed the smug satisfaction in Ellen's eyes as the chain attached to MacKenzie's wrists was padlocked to another chain at the back of the wagon.

Once more, April was startled at his composure, his seeming indifference to his own discomfort. No emotion at all showed in those remarkable eyes as the punishing, humiliating chain was secured. His eyes locked with hers for just a second, a flicker of recognition crossing them quickly before going blank again. He didn't acknowledge her presence in any other way. He simply stood there, waiting stoically for the wagon to start moving.

His clothes were the same as the night before, still bloodstained and torn. He wore knee-high moccasins on his feet, and she flinched as she thought of the terrain they would be travelling.

Before the wagon started, she had a chance to study his face. It had none of the usual handsomeness, but was, instead, like a hewn piece of oak with strong, striking features that caught and held one's attention. Those deep-set gray eyes again continued to dominate her thoughts, but she also noted the high cheekbones, strong chin and firm mouth. His hair was midnight black, and straight. At the moment one tuft fell over his forehead, between his eyes. He seemed not to notice.

She couldn't decide if the rich oak color of his skin was due to his Indian blood or the fact that he had apparently lived his life out-of-doors. Black bristles covered his lower face but somehow they merely made him look more intriguing. Dangerous without being frightening. She knew her rapt attention was only too obvious to him, but again he bore her scrutiny with what seemed to be supreme indifference. Even when his eyes touched Ellen Peters, there was no emotion. April didn't understand that at all. There should have been something: anger, lust, shame. Something.

She had meant to talk to Lieutenant Pickering about Sergeant Terrell's intentions, but the lieutenant had ridden ahead before she was called, and April had had no opportunity to do so. She would, she decided, when they stopped. In the meantime, she watched MacKenzie walk behind the wagon, showing no strain or weariness. He was lean and tall and as graceful as a mountain lion, his steps light as they kept pace with the wagon, always keeping some slack in the chain so he wouldn't be thrown off balance by a sudden lurch. Despite the slimness of his hips, she could see muscles bunch under his shirt and the cloth of his trousers. She sensed an enormous amount of leashed power simmering under his calm exterior, and couldn't help but wonder what would happen when he exploded. April knew, from Sergeant Terrell's words, that he had probably had little or no water last night and this morning, and the sun was a bright ball of red fire. The coolness of the night had disappeared under its blistering rays, and she wondered how long the man could continue without water or rest.

Unfortunately, Davey, too, was watching with fascination. Unable to withhold his curiosity, he finally asked the question. "Why is that man chained?"

"He's being taken for trial, love."

"Is he a bad man?" Davey's green eyes were bright with interest. "He doesn't look bad."

April was startled at the boy's observation. She glanced at Ellen Peters. "That's yet to be decided," she said calmly, noting Ellen's face flushing with anger under the words. April did not hide her growing doubt.

The reply satisfied Davey, who went on to other questions, which April answered with half her attention. The other half was still focused on the enigmatic prisoner. She was suffering every step with him, probably more than he if his unchanging expression was any indication.

Noon came, and the sun glared like a shield of red-hot brass, its rays scorching the earth. Familiar with the heat and unwilling to suffer through stays and petticoats, April had donned a split riding skirt and cotton shirt she had owned before her marriage. But even with the lighter clothes, she felt the sweat trickling down her neck and between her breasts, and Davey was squirming with discomfort. Yet MacKenzie still showed little effect, although April knew each step must be torture. She and the other passengers, at least, had several canteens of water, all of which were nearing empty. She herself had declined the last offer of water, unable to tilt the canteen in front of MacKenzie's eyes, although she noticed Ellen took great delight in doing so, as well as in letting water drip onto a handkerchief and wiping her face with it. April had wanted to slap her.

At last, a halt was called, and the wagon rolled to a stop.

April had expected the Indian scout to drop when the wagon stilled, but he did not. He stood there defiantly, as if mocking Terrell's best efforts.

His relentless eyes fastened on hers, and she felt something tighten inside. She sensed he was measuring her against the background of his experience, and she was found wanting. She was surprised at how much the thought hurt. *He's a murderer, April.* Regardless of whether Ellen Peters told the truth, he had killed a sergeant. With a knife. No civilized man would do that.

And he was definitely not civilized. How could he radiate such danger, such mastery in his position? But he did. Even in chains, he seemed to dominate the group by his open contempt. His refusal to allow thirst or exhaustion to affect him taunted his captors and made him stronger than they. She could tell by Terrell's flushed face that he recognized the arrogant mockery.

April and Davey left the wagon to stretch their legs, but April kept one eye on MacKenzie as she searched for the lieutenant. She saw the horses being watered and fed, the men eating, and she and Davey were given water, bread and dried beef. She noticed the prisoner was given nothing.

Having made his point, MacKenzie settled on the ground, his long body folding into a sitting position. The chain was barely long enough to permit his wrists to reach the ground but, as always, he seemed to consider it merely inconvenient. Those hooded eyes, however, moved constantly, and she knew they missed little. His lips were cracked, and yet his tongue never tried to moisten them.

April watched as the large sergeant eyed the prisoner thoughtfully, then busied his hands with a rope. In minutes, he had fashioned a noose, and he approached MacKenzie.

"You can wear this the rest of the way, 'Breed. To remind you that every step you take brings you closer to the hangman." He dropped the circle around the scout's neck and tightened it, but MacKenzie didn't flinch or change his expression by so much as a blink as the rough rope cut and bruised his neck and the rope's end fell to the ground in front of him. If anything, April thought she caught a flash of victory in the man's eyes. His silence had goaded his enemy into action. He intended to goad him into mistakes. She didn't know how she knew that. But she did. MacKenzie had not given up...he was merely waiting. Waiting for what? Despite the heat, April felt shivers run up and down her spine.

Once more, her eyes met his, and she wondered at the depth, at the secrets in them. Something in her reached out to him, and she saw startled perception in his face. But like everything concerning him, it was gone so quickly she thought she'd only imagined it.

April could wait no longer. The soldiers were preparing to mount again, and still there was no lieutenant. She was at least going to see that MacKenzie received some water. Lieutenant or no lieutenant, she could stand his torture no longer.

Very resolutely, she took a cup and filled it with water from one of the barrels on the wagon and approached the prisoner. She saw his eyes watch every movement, saw their sudden warning as she felt a rough hand on her arm.

"He's not to have no water," Terrell said roughly.

April whirled around to face him. "He can't go any farther without it."

A grin broke out on Terrell's face. "I don't know. He seems fine to me. They say injuns don't need water, not much, no ways. They ain't human, you see, missy. More like dogs than men. He seems right natural down there with a collar round his neck. Anyway this ain't none of yer business. He killed my friend, tried to rape his baby girl..." His eyes narrowed as he looked at her. "Perhaps that's what you're after..."

April's hand went back and struck his face with all her force. Just as swiftly, his fist hit her, knocking her to the ground. April heard Davey cry out, along with a low vicious growl from the direction of the prisoner. She saw Davey attack the burly sergeant with all the small fury he possessed, only to be easily swatted aside. She grabbed him up, trying to protect him from another blow, heedless of the cut on her mouth. She clutched Davey to her, her whole body trembling with rage. When she finally looked up, the sergeant was standing, red-faced and unrepentant.

She heard him bluster, "You shouldn't go messing in Army business." She could only glare helplessly at him. She was no match for his strength.

"What in the hell is going on?"

April turned and saw Pickering riding up, his face white with anger.

"Your sergeant," April said tightly as she rubbed the growing bruise on her cheek, "seems to enjoy tormenting those who can't fight back. I wonder if he fights men as well as he does women and children."

Pickering looked at Terrell with horror. "You hit this lady? Her son?"

"I didn't mean to, sir. It was an accident. She was interfering with the pris'ner," Terrell said defensively. He didn't know exactly who the lady was, only that she was the widow of an Army captain, but he suddenly felt fear. "You know we can't let anyone near the prisoner...he's too dangerous. She just didn't understand that." He turned to April, hastening to make amends of some kind. "You understand that, don't you, missy? I was just trying to protect you."

April straightened. "*You're* the one I need protection from, Sergeant." She turned back to Pickering. "I want to lodge charges against this man."

Pickering looked at the angry, defiant woman in front of him, a line of blood now trickling down her cheek, and felt the tight ball in his stomach grow larger. This whole trip was a nightmare. His eyes moved to the Indian scout who had caused it all. The man was standing again, his fists knotted together in tight balls, his legs braced as if ready to pounce. There was something very menacing in his face.

"He hasn't given that man any water," April said. "It's inhuman."

Pickering, at the moment, was feeling none too lenient toward the man who had started it all. "Sergeant Terrell knows best," he said soothingly. "You can see he doesn't seem to be suffering. He's an Indian," he added as if that explained everything.

The statement only served to fuel April's anger. "If I hear

that once more..." She didn't know how to finish the sentence. She didn't know what she would do. Damn them.

She tried again. "He's a human being," April said quietly now, "and I'll not stand by and watch this...this bully of yours torture him. Look at that rope around his neck. How can you permit such a thing?"

Pickering flinched at the raw contempt in her voice. "Now, Mrs. Manning. There's only one way to deal with these murdering savages...wear them out. It's like the sergeant said, he's very dangerous." There was a note of finality in the lieutenant's voice.

April used her trump card with some reluctance. "Would your general agree with you? Would he condone the abuse of prisoners?"

"General Wakefield?" the lieutenant said. "He gives no quarter in the field."

"That's in the field," April said coldly. "Not against helpless prisoners. And I have occasion to know. I'm General Wakefield's daughter."

Both Pickering and Terrell went white. April glanced over at MacKenzie and saw what might have been amusement. She wasn't sure. She didn't know if anyone could ever be sure of what the man thought.

Pickering was the first to speak. "But why...didn't you say anything?"

"I didn't think I needed to," April replied with a sharp edge to her words. "I assumed, quite incorrectly as it turned out, that an army widow would be given the same respect as a general's daughter." Her glance went back to Terrell's now livid face. She wondered idly how one's complexion could go from stark white to bright red in a matter of seconds.

"And I assure you, Lieutenant, that my father would never tolerate...this." She looked at MacKenzie, who was lounging against the back of the wagon, the hideous rope falling almost to the ground. It occurred to her that he wore it as nonchalantly as most men would wear a scarf.

She leaned down and picked up the cup and returned to the water barrel, refilling it as the officer and sergeant, along with a score of other soldiers, watched her warily. When it was filled, she walked to MacKenzie and pressed it into his bound hands. She watched as he raised it carefully, awkwardly, and took slow sips. When the water was gone, he gave the cup back to her, one eyebrow raised quizzically.

"That wasn't necessary, Mrs. Manning," he said.

It was the first time she had heard his voice, and April was surprised at the soft, pleasant baritone sound and the small, but distinctive, Scottish burr that distinguished the words. It was gently, courteously said, but quite without thanks. Mesmerized by his steady gray gaze, she knew by the use of her name that he must have heard the full exchange.

"But it was," she said just as softly. "If not for you, then for myself...and Davey."

He merely nodded, understanding, as she stood there, thoroughly disconcerted by his insouciance. She eyed his wrists, torn open by the chain links, and turned her attention back to the rope around his neck. It had been cruelly tightened, and she could see it eat into his flesh. She winced.

"Do not let it worry you, Mrs. Manning," he said. "It doesn't me. You've done enough."

"No," she said. "Not nearly enough. You need food and more water."

He shrugged. "Leave it be," he said. "I don't need your help."

"I wouldn't let anyone treat a dog like this," she said without thinking. For the first time, she saw emotion flicker across his face. Pure rage. And she suddenly remembered Terrell's earlier words. She knew he must have heard them, and she had just compounded the injury.

The burr was very heavy when he finally spoke. "I'm nay a dog...not an object for your pity." He turned his back to her.

Mortified that her words were so misunderstood, she stared

at his back helplessly before turning to Pickering, who had watched the exchange with a satisfied smile. "You see, Mrs. Manning, you can't be decent to them."

"Take that rope from his neck," April said furiously, then took Davey's hand and returned to the wagon, knowing that a few ill-considered words had probably done more damage to MacKenzie than all the torment planned by Sergeant Terrell.

Step by step. Just think about the next step, not the one after that. MacKenzie fought to keep the spring in his walk, to show every one of them that they could never, never defeat him.

But the pain was terrible. He knew his feet were bloody inside the moccasins. He could feel the wash of blood as each foot touched the ground. The soft hide had not been designed for the punishment inflicted by the hard, rocky terrain. He wondered how long he could continue.

He had to keep pace with the wagon, or he would be jerked from his feet and dragged. That was what Terrell wanted, what he was waiting for. Well, Terrell would wait until he reached hell, and MacKenzie hoped to speed that journey.

Think about something else. Wakefield's daughter. That was a surprise. He knew the general had a married daughter somewhere east. The man had mentioned her once in a rare terse conversation. She had probably even been on a post when he had been there. But he never approached the living quarters and rarely stayed overnight. He usually came late and left early. His eyes went to the wagon. She was like her father—determined and combative. There had been no lack of courage, and his anger grew once more as he remembered the blow she took on his behalf. But he had not asked it, had not even wanted it, he assured himself. He had seen her watching him several times, and had wondered about it, for, unlike so many other women, she had not averted her gaze when caught by his own eyes. Nor had she looked at him with distaste or loathing. Just interest, and something close to sympathy. He should not have snapped at her. She had meant well, and he remembered the stricken look in her face at his cruel reply.

He could see her now, leaning over to talk with the cub. He liked the way she did it. As if the boy was a friend. There was a closeness about the two that brought forth a pang of regret. What would it have been like, he wondered, to have had that kind of a mother?

He was jerked by the chain. His thoughts had changed the rhythm of his feet, and the slack had run out. He had to brace himself to keep from falling, to hurry his movement to keep nearly abreast of the wagon.

Keep going. Tonight. Tonight, he hoped, Terrell would believe him too tired to require heavy guard. And he would soon start faltering to encourage that belief. He hated to give Terrell that satisfaction, but it could mean his freedom. And that meant everything!

He had thought about General Wakefield at Fort Defiance, about the possibility that the general might listen, and believe. But he soon discarded the idea. Terrell meant to see him dead before they reached Wakefield. And, even if he lived to reach the fort, who would believe a half-breed's words against a white girl's? Even Wakefield couldn't help him now...even if he could trust the man. And he didn't. Not entirely. He didn't trust anyone. It was a lesson he had learned early, and he had never found reason to doubt its wisdom.

Rape. Murder. He would surely hang. He remembered the feel of the rope around his neck before Pickering ordered it removed. It had taken all his strength, all his will, not to fight it. But the time wasn't right, and it would only have meant satisfaction for Terrell. Let Terrell think he was winning the battle between them.

The sun was going down, and some of the heat was receding. Before many more minutes, the cold air would hit him, chilling the sweat that caked his body in layers. They would call a halt before long. Lieutenant Pickering was never one for much effort.

One step...then another. And another.

He was right. Within the next hour, Pickering ordered a dry camp. MacKenzie had stumbled those last minutes, one time even being dragged several feet before catching his balance. It was planned, but it hadn't been difficult to do. God, but he hurt. All over. The long walk had done nothing to alleviate his other injuries.

With satisfaction, he noticed Terrell's malicious grin. Give him a few more hours of pleasure; it would be gone in the morning. One way or another, he would be free...or dead...by first light.

He was surprised when a private cautiously offered him both food and water—and a blanket. The blanket was greater appreciated because under its folds he could work his hands free. He glanced at the Manning woman, positive it was her doing, and was further convinced when he saw her arguing heatedly with Lieutenant Pickering. She apparently wasn't the type to quit, even after his bitter words. A most unusual female.

But that was the least of his interest now. His eyes scanned the camp as guards were posted. He was taken several yards away to attend to his private needs—apparently a courtesy offered only because of the women present. He was rechained to the wagon, his leash offering only one position in which to lie. His ankles were bound tightly with rope, but that didn't matter. They had not rechecked the chain around his wrists. Terrell, in his confidence, did not post a separate guard at the prisoner's side, a fact for which MacKenzie was supremely thankful. He studied the position of each of the pickets, the terrain he would have to crawl to reach them...and finally the horses. They had brought his own Appaloosa with them. Another unexpected gift.

Pickering was an idiot. There were not nearly sufficient guards in a country crawling with Apaches. And many of his men were not Indian-wise soldiers. Most of them were new to the West, recently arrived from an entirely different war in the East. One in which, MacKenzie understood, men stood up in waves and marched into cannon fire. He had thought that immensely stupid. But then the same had happened in Scotland so many years ago. He had heard the tales from his father.

The camp was finally silent. He didn't know where the Manning woman and her boy were sleeping. He had not been able to see them from his limited view. Not that it mattered. He knew every step he would take. But first his bonds. He moved his wrists, refusing to acknowledge the agony the struggle cost him. His wrists turned, and the chain slackened. He tested them. His hands almost, but not quite, found freedom. He needed moisture, something slippery, to help them slide loose. Without a moment's hesitation, he looked cautiously around him and then sat up, drawing his wrists to his mouth. They were already slightly bloody, with red lines going deep into the skin. But not enough. He bit hard into his left wrist, tasting blood, feeling it flow freely. He washed both wrists in it, and then he tried the chain again. It was slippery with the wetness, and he worked his wrists first this way, then another, until he felt one go free, then the second. He placed the chain quietly on the ground and started working on the ropes around his ankles.

He was free!

April stared at the silver moon in the black sky. There were wisps of clouds playing among the field of stars. She studied one that she fancied was winking at her; it was a particularly bright gem that seemed to hold some kind of promise. But what? She suddenly felt tired and depressed. Something special had left her life…the part of her that had always been so optimistic. More than four years of war had done its part in killing it. But today…today was even worse. She was seeing a meanness of spirit, an unreasoning hatred, a deliberate desire to inflict pain. It couldn't help but dull the world for her.

Her arm went tighter around Davey. She wished she could protect him from it. She had seen his confusion several times, and his small burst of fury when she had been hit. Poor Davey. He had known so little real happiness. She had wanted it so badly for him, particularly on this journey. But her interference on behalf of MacKenzie had completely isolated them from their companions. Ellen and Terrell looked at her with complete loathing, Pickering avoided her with deftness, and the other soldiers eyed her warily. Not only was she the general's daughter now, but she was an Indian lover.

She sighed, listening to the lonely howl of a coyote somewhere in the distance. Through eyes grown accustomed to the darkness, she saw the prairie grasses sway with the growing wind and the dwarfed pines standing like sentinels against the sky. She shivered in the cold night air, even with the three blankets she and Davey shared. And she wondered once more about MacKenzie. She had again joined battle to see he had some covering. She had also fought Pickering about tomorrow's trek. The prisoner should not be forced to walk, she insisted, but on this subject the lieutenant was adamant. There was no way, he told her, he would permit MacKenzie in the same wagon as his victim. Nor would he allow the man to ride. MacKenzie, he explained, was a superb horseman, the best he had ever seen and, even bound, might be able to escape on horseback. "He's half Indian," he repeated again as if that explained everything. "He's all Indian in heart."

April didn't even try to explain that she had been around Indians most of her life, much longer, in any case, than Lieutenant Pickering. She had grown up in frontier posts where Indians had often been employed in some capacity or another, or had come to trade goods, or even in surrender after some conflict. She had found them much like whites. Some good, some bad. Some kind, some cruel. She had even, on occasion, played with Indian children as a child, had known some of the scouts. She wondered now why she had never encountered MacKenzie. He apparently had been a scout for her father for some time. MacKenzie. He must have another name. Why did she care? Why did he so dominate her thoughts? No man had done that before. Except David. Damn MacKenzie. Damn him for ruining this trip, for invading her mind. She closed her eyes and willed herself to sleep. But it didn't work. She felt Davey wriggle beside her, and she recognized the symptoms. Sighing once more, she shook off the blankets and rose, gathering one around her son. She looked around. The camp was completely still. She didn't even see the sentries she knew had been posted earlier. But April wasn't worried. They were probably patrolling the area around the camp. Hand in hand, April and Davey walked to a small stand of trees in back of the picket line where the horses had been tethered for the night, and she turned her back, giving him some privacy. Her eyes once more swept the camp.

"Mama..."

She looked down on the small but sturdy figure.

"Cold, love?" she asked, feeling his fingers tighten in hers in agreement. April leaned down, pulling the blanket tighter around him. Her eyes still on her son, she started walking back to where they had bedded down for the night. They were passing the horses when she was startled by a sudden movement. She looked up.

It was a shadow. A tall, graceful shadow at the picket line, just three feet away from her. She had seen enough of MacKenzie that day to identify the shape immediately. A small cry of surprise escaped her mouth, and she felt a strong hand go over it, felt her body held closely by an arm that could have been steel.

"Quiet." She heard the whisper and stopped struggling. And then she was free, but Davey was in his arms, MacKenzie's hand now over her son's mouth. "Quiet," she heard him say again, "and you and the cub will not be hurt."

Her hand went to his arm. "Let him go. Please."

In that small gleam of moonlight, she saw pain flicker over his face. Deep reluctance. But also determination. "You will both go with me," he said, and his voice held none of its earlier softness.

"I won't say anything...just let us go."

He looked at her, and dark gray eyes seemed cold and merciless in the dim light. "I wouldn't trust anyone that much," he said in a tone laced with iron. "Can you saddle a horse?"

She nodded, then stared at him. "The sentries?"

"Unconscious," he said. "But probably not for long." He had already untied an Appaloosa on the string and he swung easily up on it, Davey securely in his arms. "You can come. Or you can stay," he said shortly, growing impatient. "But the boy goes with me till I'm sure of safety. If I hear you cry out, he'll die." MacKenzie detested his words, but he knew of no other way to insure her silence. It would take too long to tie them, and even then it would be risky.

April hated him in that moment, and her expression must have indicated it, for he said again, "You'll not be hurt, you and the boy, if you do as I say. I didn't want this, but now there's nothing for it. I cannot leave you here."

April knew nothing would change his mind, and she quickly saddled a horse. "Take that bedroll," he demanded, pointing to one near the picket line. She lifted it, feeling its weight, and placed it across the saddle. He also had one, she noticed, as well as a rifle slung across his shoulders and a gun belt around his waist.

"Quietly," he warned, and they walked the horses out of the silent camp. She saw one still form at the edge, and another not far from it. Again, she shivered. She didn't know if they were unconscious, as he claimed, or dead. How ruthless was he? Had she been so wrong? As they distanced themselves from the camp, MacKenzie finally spurred his horse into a gallop without saying a word.

He knew she would follow.

Chapter Four

Dawn was deceptively peaceful. Silver and pink tinged the earth in layers. The moon lagged behind in an azure sky as the sun rose above the craggy horizon. It was benevolent in these first few minutes of morning, drawing the chill from the air but not yet beating the earth with relentless rays.

April felt anger and outrage simmer inside her. Both emotions had burgeoned through the long night, overwhelming the body-numbing weariness. She now hated the man who rode so tirelessly in front of her, but strangely felt little fear of him. Instead, she knew a deep sense of helplessness, of being completely at the mercy of another person. She had thought herself free of such bonds, and now she was trapped deeper than ever before. April sensed that the man, MacKenzie, would not harm Davey, but she couldn't forget his harsh words or take the slightest chance with Davey's life.

She had followed him mindlessly through the cold night lit only by the slice of a new moon. She repeatedly blessed the fact that she had dressed warmly for the night with several layers of clothing, including a wool coat. But even then she was chilled to the bone. At one point she had urged her horse next to MacKenzie's and was slightly comforted by the fact that the man had wrapped Davey warmly in a blanket. Davey was sleeping easily in his arms.

April had asked to take her son, and MacKenzie merely shook his head in denial, his eyes impenetrable in the night.

She fell behind him, uncomfortable with his intense scrutiny and unwilling to indicate any sense of companionship. She was a prisoner now, as he had been hours earlier. He kept a steady pace, maintaining a fast walk for several miles, then a trot, then a walk again. She knew he was husbanding the strength of their horses and recognized the discipline such caution required in light of the urgency she knew he felt.

Every muscle in her body hurt. She had been an excellent rider years earlier, but she had not ridden astride in five years, and her body was protesting the brutal punishment. She kept praying MacKenzie would stop for a rest, but he showed no signs of weariness or pain, though she knew he must be feeling both. She had seen the livid bruises on his arms and chest, and his wrists, when he had seized her, had been scarlet with blood. He rode without stirrups, having sliced them from the saddle shortly after leaving camp. She supposed he used a saddle only because it was then easier to carry the extra rifle, saddlebags and bedroll that he had stolen from the camp.

Pickering had said he was a superb horseman, and April now knew the words were no exaggeration. He was beautiful on a horse, so much a part of the Appaloosa's easy gait that the two were one continuous fluid movement. He looked relaxed, but April could almost feel his taut wariness. She wondered if he ever relaxed. She doubted it.

What was he like? Did he feel even a twinge of guilt about taking Davey? He had seemed oddly gentle hours earlier with her son asleep in his arms. Or was she just trying to reassure herself?

She heard Davey's voice. "Mama?"

April's knees tightened against the horse's side, and she increased the pace until, once more, she was beside MacKenzie.

"I'm here, Davey," she said calmly, seeing his frantic searching look. He was wriggling, trying to free himself from MacKenzie's firm grip. "It's all right, I'm fine."

She looked up at MacKenzie's face, her eyes pleading, asking for confirmation, as she continued, ''We'll be stopping soon for a rest.''

The scout merely nodded, but his quick appraising look approved of her, and April, unwillingly, felt some of her quiet anger replaced by an unfamiliar tingling sensation. Why, she wondered, should she care whether she had his approval? But she knew the answer instantly, knew that it was probably very rare, and she felt a surge of pride in receiving it.

Don't, April. He's ruthless. He's threatened to kill Davey, and he will do anything...anything to get free. He's an outlaw. A renegade. He's killed a man, and probably won't hesitate to kill again—even Davey. How can you even think about pleasing him? You should be thinking about escaping.

But how? She didn't know where she was. There were hostile Indians in the area. Their safety—Davey's and her own—now lay completely in the hands of their kidnapper.

They stopped by a small stream. MacKenzie lifted Davey and leaned over the saddle, gently settling him on the ground. He again nodded to April, giving her permission to dismount. Once she was down, he, too, dismounted, taking the reins of both horses in his hand and leading them down to the water.

It took April several minutes to even try to walk. Her muscles complained in new ways, and she almost fell. But she straightened and grabbed Davey in her arms, hugging him to her until he protested.

''I'm thirsty,'' he complained, and April suddenly realized that she, too, was parched. She and Davey went to the stream, and leaned down to drink, savoring the water still cold from the night. She tore a piece of cloth from her skirt and washed his face with it, then her own. She marveled at how much better she felt. She had another need, and realized Davey did, too. He was contorting uncomfortably again. April looked up and found MacKenzie's eyes on them. He was standing some twenty feet away, pacing the horses' intake of water. His head inclined toward a small clump of trees, and April flushed as she realized he understood her necessity. Damn the man. It was as if he read her mind. But need overrode modesty, and she hurried over to the designated spot, waiting first for Davey before knowing relief of her own.

When her clothes were replaced, she took Davey's hand and returned to the stream. The horses were now hobbled, and MacKenzie was at the edge of the stream, washing feet that were torn and bleeding. When he finished, he took off what was left of his shirt and tore it into strips. April flinched as she thought of the dirty, sweat-soaked shirt binding the raw wounds.

Seized by a sudden compulsion she didn't understand, she went over to him and regarded him hesitantly. She had tried to help before and been rebuffed. April saw the sudden wariness in his eyes as she approached. He obviously didn't trust anyone, not even someone so completely in his control.

"You'll just get infection," she said bluntly.

MacKenzie only raised an eyebrow in question, his eyes cool and appraising.

April winced. Did the man ever speak? She had only heard him twice—first when she had offered him water, and his voice had been soft and attractive with the intriguing burr, and later when he threatened Davey, and it had been harsh and uncompromising. Which would it be now?

She steadily returned his gaze, shedding her jacket, then one of the extra shirts she had donned last night as protection against the cold. It was almost clean, worn only last night over another one. She handed it to him without a word.

His expression didn't change, but he took it and, with a knife, cut the garment into bandages and deftly wrapped them around his shredded feet. When he finished, he washed his wrists and tried to bandage the one he had bitten; it was still bleeding slightly.

April watched him struggle for several seconds as he tried to use his teeth to tie a knot. Finally, without a word, she stooped and took the bandage from his hand and, ignoring his now slightly perplexed look, she neatly wrapped it with experienced hands. When she had finished, she continued to stand there, searching his face for a sign of something.

"Where are you taking us?" she asked finally.

She was surprised when he actually replied. "There's a Navaho village a day's ride. I know them, and you and the boy will be safe there until Pickering arrives. I don't think," he added with a slight trace of irony, "he'll be too far behind...not with the general's daughter gone." Every word seemed carefully weighed but still held that soft, distinctive burr that, under other circumstances, would have completely charmed her.

April nodded, glancing at Davey. Apparently quite content with his new adventure, her son was exploring the bank, oblivious to the tense atmosphere between the two adults. Her attention turned back to the scout and his intriguing face.

She had never seen such strong features. It was as if they had been sculptured in stone. Or perhaps they seemed stronger because of his cryptic expression. April couldn't help but wonder if he ever smiled and, if he did, how it would affect a face so marbled in gravity. His watchful eyes were regarding her with the same intensity that she had focused on him, and there seemed a question in his look.

Her eyes fell to his naked chest. She had never thought a man's body could be such a thing of perfection. Corded muscles rippled with his slightest move, and his deeply tanned skin was the color of rich, glowing bronze. The only flaw were the large, ugly purple bruises that covered nearly every part of his upper body, and April recoiled as she thought of the pain he must have endured, both when he received them and on the long walk yesterday.

When her gaze traveled upward again, she noticed MacKenzie's eyes had not moved from her. She inwardly flinched, knowing that she had probably never looked worse in her life. During the long night, her hair had come loose from its usual neat coil, and it fell in undisciplined curls down her back. Her face was probably dirty, and she needed only to look to see the wretched state of her torn and stained clothes. *I don't care,* she tried to tell herself. *I don't care at all.* But she did. Terribly.

Suddenly angered by MacKenzie's close scrutiny and embarrassed by her own obvious examination of the man who held her and her son captive, she turned to leave. She stopped when she heard his low voice.

"I would not have harmed the boy."

She turned and stared at him, knowing it was probably as much of an apology or explanation as he was capable of offering.

Not wanting Davey to hear, April's reply was just as soft. "I didn't think you would."

"Then why...?"

"I couldn't take even the slightest chance with Davey's life." She met his eyes directly, not faltering.

He merely nodded. That seemed to be his response to most everything.

"It wasn't necessary," she couldn't help but add. "I wouldn't have warned anyone." And she knew she wouldn't have. She had, in spirit, been on his side since the moment he was chained to the wagon. Or perhaps even when she had first seen his eyes. They were not the eyes of a murderer.

"I didn't think so," he surprised her by saying. There was the smallest twitch of his lips. "But I couldn't take the slightest chance." April couldn't quite believe the hint of roguish mischief in his voice as he turned her own words around.

But such a thought died quickly as his face once more was shuttered, as if he regretted the brief confidence. He rose lightly despite the fact that his feet must be terribly painful. Yet there was no limp, no hesitation as he went to the horses.

She watched him check the contents of the bedrolls. She suspected they belonged to the pickets he had attacked. Each had the required hundred rounds of ammunition for the Spencer carbines he had stolen, along with several days' rations.

She saw quiet satisfaction dart across his face as he found a blue uniform shirt in one and a razor-sharp knife in the other.

He pulled the shirt over his heavily muscled back and chest, and April could see the cloth strain against the supple, hard body. He stooped down and with a piece of his old shirt quickly tied the knife to his ankle. Without a glance at her, MacKenzie took the canteens from the saddles and filled them. There was no wasted motion in his actions. Each sleek movement was precise and confident. April thought she had never seen such a self-assured man. Warmth flooded her with unexpected impact. And she fought it. Bitterly. She could not allow herself to feel anything for a man whose life span appeared anything but long, who had taken herself and her son hostage and forced them on this exhausting trek. But as hard as she tried, she couldn't shake a certain excitement as she watched him move like a graceful, dangerous forest animal.

MacKenzie took the hobbles from the horses and turned toward her. "It's time to go," he said, interrupting her wayward thoughts.

April wanted to protest. A few more moments. But one look at his face dissuaded her. She knew he felt they had already stayed too long.

"Can Davey ride with me?" April questioned instead.

"He's safer with me," he replied shortly, and she knew it would do no good to protest. Davey seemed to have no objections as he was once more lifted in MacKenzie's arms and swung onto the Appaloosa.

As they rode side by side from the stream, she thought she saw a look of sympathy, and even admiration, before MacKenzie's face settled into its usual implacable lines.

MacKenzie pushed as hard as he thought the horses—and April Manning—could endure. He wasn't overly worried now about immediate pursuit. Pickering would be far behind and probably falling farther. Most of his troopers were unused to the heat and lack of water in the southwest, and they had no good trackers. It would take them time to find the trail over rocky terrain. As long as he kept moving, he would be safe.

He wanted to maintain that distance, but he also wanted to see Mrs. Manning and her son safely settled with the Navahos. It was a small camp of several families MacKenzie had been able to save from the forced march of Navahos to Bosque Redona in eastern New Mexico. MacKenzie had more than a few regrets about his role as a scout for Kit Carson last year when the colorful colonel virtually starved the proud Navaho nation into submission. The subsequent march by the reluctant participants across New Mexico to barren lands had been a nightmare MacKenzie wanted to forget. But he had, through Wakefield, won exception for several families that had once sheltered him.

He looked at Mrs. Manning. She was doggedly keeping pace. Her grim expression, however, told him it was costing her much. He felt an unaccustomed guilt as her straight back and set features spoke of pride and determination—and of a courage unusual for a woman. She had not complained once during the journey, nor had she displayed any fear. There had been, at first, open anger, but even that had seemed to fade during the last hours. Or perhaps it had been dulled by weariness. She had every reason to detest him.

She had surprised him at the stream when once again she had tried to help. Even after he had threatened her son and forced them both to endure such discomfort, she had unselfishly offered her own clothing and quiet assistance. He had been too startled to refuse it, and had not known how to respond. Until he tried to tell her he had meant Davey no harm, and even that was offered awkwardly. No harm? He was dragging them through Indian country, scarcely allowing them enough water and food and rest. He had never consciously caused hurt to women or children before, and yet he was doing it now. To survive. There had been one other time when he had been responsible...but he had not known then what his actions would sow...

He did not welcome the reminder. He had tried to lock those moments from his mind. Except in the deep of night when they battered at his consciousness and kept him from resting.

But he had known exactly what he was doing when he took the boy...Davey. And he knew he would do it again—given the same circumstances. For that reason, he could not apologize. Words would mean little.

How had things gone so wrong? Everything was gone now. Everything he had worked for and longed for. He had been foolish from the beginning to believe things could be otherwise, that he could create and build something fine, something solely his. He would be hunted for the rest of his life now. And he would probably do as his father did...find an isolated spot on some mountain and live alone.

His hand felt good, resting on the boy. He had never known that something like this—the small body snuggling trustingly into his large one—could spark such confusing feelings. Feelings of tenderness and protectiveness that warmed the cold place inside. He didn't deserve them. He had subjected them—the boy and his mother—to hardship and danger.

But he couldn't be retaken. He would not let the bastards win. Not men like Peters and Terrell and Pickering. He would not die at the end of a rope or be caged like an animal. No matter what he had to do! But he would, somehow, see that the Mannings were safe.

He looked at April again. She looked untamed herself with the wild chestnut hair streaked with gold and the indomitable head arched stiffly. She was different. He had known that the moment he stumbled at her feet and had seen the anger that flickered across her face so fleetingly and realized it was not aimed at him, but at his guards. And later, when she defied Terrell. He had not wanted her hurt for him...so he had snapped at her like a trapped animal might. Now he was putting her through pain much worse than that quick blow of Terrell's.

She is so very pretty, even now, after a night and half a

day in the saddle, MacKenzie thought. Brave and pretty and very desirable. He felt a craving in his loins, a ravenous hunger combined with a slow, pulsating warmth that spread throughout his body. He wondered how it would feel—touching her. He had known few "good" women, and bedded none. His physical needs had been satisfied by whores or curious saloon women. Don't even think about it, MacKenzie told himself. Don't torture yourself. You've done enough harm to someone who doesn't deserve it. With supreme discipline, he tried to erase the thoughts from his mind, but his body wouldn't obey. To rid himself of the demons that were torturing him with burning, stinging stabs of desire, he tightened his hold on the boy and once more urged his horse into a trot.

MacKenzie's idea of a day's ride was not like anyone else's, April realized along about midafternoon. They had stopped several times but had not dismounted. He had merely offered her water and some hardtack, then pushed on again. She was pitiably grateful when he finally called a halt at a small water hole surrounded by several trees. She was beginning to think he would never stop. She had never known such weariness, such pain from harshly used muscles and bones. They had continued through the morning, sometimes at a walk, sometimes a trot. Davey had been uncomplaining, seemingly content in MacKenzie's arms. Only once had she heard a small whimper. She had kicked her horse forward, having lagged behind, but as she neared she heard a low, crooning sound. Pacing herself several lengths behind, she listened in amazement to an uncommonly rich voice. She didn't understand the words, but the unusual melody hung in the air like a gentle morning mist, softening the heat, gentling the landscape. And then he seemed to sense her nearness and the voice stopped, breaking the magic and hurtling her back into reality, into fatigue and pain and anger.

For the anger was still there. It was mixed with numerous other emotions, many of which she didn't understand. There was pity when she saw his wounds, a warm, inexplicable tingling when she watched his quick, sure movements, resentment as he moved tirelessly ahead while she grew numb with exhaustion. He had disrupted all her plans, but even more than that he had awakened something inside her, something she had tried hard to bury. Something she couldn't define, but which she knew was dangerous.

When the horses stopped, MacKenzie once again motioned to her to dismount first. As if, she thought bitterly, she could even think about escaping him. He was always so wary, so cautious.

She started to slide gratefully from her horse, but she kept going down. Her legs simply refused to hold her. Almost in a fog, she saw MacKenzie move, move so swiftly that he seemed almost a blur. She felt his hand at her elbow, gently guiding her to her feet and steadying her. The touch seemed to burn her, to spread from her arm to the inner core of her body. It was so strong, so confident, so *protective*. But when she looked at his face, it showed no emotion, and the eyes were hooded, and she knew she must have been mistaken. She was sure when she heard his words. They seemed as indifferent as his expression.

"Are you all right, ma'am?"

All her anger, frustration and hurt exploded at the insane question. She had had no sleep in two days. She was hungry and thirsty, and every bone in her body felt as if it had been on a rack in some ancient torture chamber. Her son had been threatened, she had been forced to ride through some of the roughest terrain this side of Hades, and he wanted to know if she was all right. She started to laugh, but there was no humor in it.

MacKenzie reached out for her again, and this time when she felt his touch, she recognized its gentleness, and she resented it, resented it with all her being. Instinctively, her hand went out and, with all her remaining strength, she slapped him, leaving a new red welt against the already battered face. The sound seemed to reverberate in the air, leaving a deafening stillness in its wake.

His hand dropped from her arm, and he stood back. There was complete silence and, for the first time, April felt fear of MacKenzie, and she was afraid to look at him. There was a palpable aura of violence and danger always around him, and she was deathly afraid she might have unleashed it.

"You're a brave woman, Mrs. Manning," he finally said, and despite herself she felt a spinning sensation that had nothing to do with weariness. There was no hint of anger in his voice or the slightest touch of reproach. There was, instead, a certain note of satisfaction.

She looked up at him. His mouth had softened ever so slightly, and he was regarding her with respect. "I was wondering when that was comin'." His expression was suddenly wry. "But I didn't think you had that much strength."

April stared with horror at the red splash of color that remained on his stubbled cheek. Before she had hit Terrell, she had never struck anyone in anger in her life. Now twice in as many days she had responded in a manner she'd always thought barbaric. And her blow must have been doubly painful against the bruised skin. Her deep blue eyes clouded with regret. "I'm sorry," she whispered.

"Don't," MacKenzie said in that deep voice she thought could charm birds from a tree. Foolish birds. Like her.

That strange Scottish inflection was more evident as he continued. "You had every right...and more."

There was something hesitant in that hard face, made harder now by the black beard that covered his jaw and cheeks. But the dark gray eyes were as unreadable as always.

Again MacKenzie broke the silence. "Get some rest, Mrs. Manning. I'll look after the boy."

April looked around and saw Davey standing there, regarding them both solemnly. He had seen his mother hit the tall man who had held him so comfortingly. Why was she angry?

April leaned down and held out her arms. When Davey walked into them, she whispered, "I'm just tired, Davey."

"Don't you like him, Mama? I do."

April hesitated, then looked at MacKenzie standing there, a strange expression on his face.

"Yes, love. I like him."

Davey brightened, feeling his world right again. "I'm hungry."

April's smile was brilliant. She had been blessed with this child. Did MacKenzie have anyone? Her father had said he was a loner. But he had such a way with Davey. She had never seen her son respond so readily to someone...unless perhaps the silent Confederate on the train. And that had been a sort of magic. A need they both had. Perhaps that was all it was now. Davey seemed to need a father so badly. Maybe it wasn't MacKenzie after all. But even as the thought flickered through her mind, she dismissed it. There was already something special between MacKenzie and her son. She sensed it.

April tried to stand, but once more her legs balked. She felt herself being lifted into strong, masculine arms, smelled the scent of him and heard the strong beat of his heart. The weakness in her legs seemed slight to the weakness that swept her body at his closeness. Weakness and yearning and a sweet aching. She closed her eyes and partially understood Davey's own contentment in this man's hold. She didn't know whether it was the sure confidence of his arms or the feeling of shelter or the unexpected gentleness of his hands. They were all there and, like Davey, she had seldom felt so safe, so protected. Even here in this tiny oasis in the middle of nowhere, surrounded, perhaps, by hostile Indians; kidnapped; and, by now, followed by angry troopers.

She felt herself being lowered under a tree where there was a trace of shade. MacKenzie surprisingly knelt next to her and, without asking permission, took off her boots and drew her riding skirt about her knees. Before she could protest, his strong hands were kneading her legs, moving surely from one set of aching muscles to another, and she started to feel wonderful relief even as his touch left searing brands on her skin and consciousness. She watched wonderingly at his deftness as gentle but sure fingers eased away the pain.

Too soon, the fingers left her. He was standing. "Get some rest," he said again. "I'll watch Davey."

Despite herself, April closed her eyes at the soft command, and almost immediately she was asleep. She had only a moment to wonder that she was so willingly leaving Davey in the care of an accused murderer.

Chapter Five

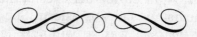

MacKenzie watched as April's eyes closed and her body relaxed. She should sleep well, now that some of her sore muscles were soothed. God knows she needed it.

He had been amazed at her uncomplaining endurance and more than a little chastened at her apology after she had struck him. He winced as he thought how much he deserved it—that and more.

She was indescribably beautiful to him now. Great golden-brown lashes shuttered her sometimes compassionate, sometimes fiery eyes, and her long hair fell in curls around her face. The face had strength and character, qualities made more apparent, he thought, by the smudges of dirt. She had withstood hardship without complaint and, after all he had done, still considered her son and even himself before her own needs and comfort. It was something he had never before encountered, and he didn't understand.

It struck him with sudden pain as he realized, for the first time, just a little of what he had missed and would continue to miss. He had relished the feel of Davey's small, trusting body against his, Mrs. Manning's odd concern, her touch this morning when she had bandaged his wrist. He had been oddly pleased when Davey told his mother he liked him, had heard Mrs. Manning's reluctant reply—even knowing, as he did, that it was for Davey's sake.

But he couldn't think about such things. They would reach

the Navaho camp sometime early this evening, and these few fleeting pleasures would become only memories.

His eyes moved from Mrs. Manning to Davey, who had sat and was watching him seriously.

"Would you like to help me?" he asked abruptly.

The boy's face brightened, and he nodded.

"Come, then, and we'll take care of the horses together." He started to walk away, but he felt a small hand on his, and he hesitated, then took it. Once more he felt an unusual twinge as the boy's hand rested comfortably in his large one.

He let Davey lead his Appaloosa to the water while he led the black gelding. He knew his own horse was steady; he wasn't as sure about the other. MacKenzie watched carefully, explaining to Davey that he must not let the horse drink too fast or he would have a bellyache. Davey's quick understanding and eagerness to help moved him once more. The boy was like his mother.

"Am I doing it right?" Davey asked, his face earnest and eager for approval.

"Aye," MacKenzie said. "You're a natural horseman. Both you and your mama." He was rewarded with a dazzling smile, the first he had seen on the boy's face. It was like sunshine after a storm.

When they were through, he asked Davey if he would like to help once more, and Davey eagerly agreed. MacKenzie went to one of the bedrolls and undid it, taking out some dried beef strips and hardtack, and a small mirror he had discovered.

He went to the stream, Davey at his heels, and sat cross-legged at the water's edge, watching as the boy imitated his every move. Using strips of his old shirt, MacKenzie washed his face and handed Davey the small mirror.

"Can you hold this very still?" he questioned, his lips smiling slightly at Davey's energetic nod.

MacKenzie slipped the knife from the band around his ankle and started shaving, watching the mirror intently. He had the Indian's contempt for facial hair even though his father's had grown long and unkempt. When he was through, he felt better than he had in several days. He also trimmed his hair around the sides and back. For convenience, his hair was short, shorter than that of most whites. If he didn't keep it short, it would fall in long shanks over his eyes, and he needed no distraction. Long hair was also easier to grab in a hand-to-hand fight. He had done it himself during several battles and was not willing to give his opponents that advantage.

God, he was tired. He didn't know when he had had more than a few moments of sleep, and that was fitful snatches in the storeroom. Pain had then kept him from more than an hour's release. But he couldn't sleep yet. Not until he delivered Mrs. Manning and Davey safely to the Navaho village. The horses' droppings would direct Pickering...slowly...to that destination, and then MacKenzie would disappear into the mountains.

He watched as Davey's head began to droop, and he reached down and picked up the boy. Carrying him to April's side, MacKenzie settled him down next to her. He then searched for green wood to carve a bow. He would not have time to prepare it properly, but it would have to do. For the next several days, he would not use a firearm, and he intended to leave most of the rations they had with Mrs. Manning and the Navahos. They needed them more than he; he was heading toward the high country, where game was plentiful. His hands moved knowledgeably over the wood.

He woke April as the sun was beginning its drop from the sky's apex. A slight breeze was cooling the air. Startled from a deep sleep, she was confused at first, then immediately awake as she remembered where she was. Her eyes frantically searched for Davey and found him curved beside her, a contented smile on his face.

"It's near time to go on, Mrs. Manning," MacKenzie announced.

She looked up at him, startled. He was clean-shaven, the

first time she had seen him without the dark bristles that had made his face appear so hard. It was still hard: the chin set and determined, the lips locked in a tight, grim line, the eyes still shuttered against invasion. But it seemed to have lost some of the savagery that marked it earlier.

He handed her a canteen and some food and watched as she slowly ate the poor fare. It was prepared for convenience, not for taste, and April had to force herself to eat. But she knew she needed her strength...both for herself and Davey. She didn't know how long she would be expected to continue today.

It was as if he read her mind. "We will reach the Navahos by nightfall," he said slowly. "Pickering should be there by noon tomorrow. Even he should manage that." He didn't try to hide his scorn.

"And then," April said with sudden insight, "he'll have to take us home...he won't be able to follow you."

The wariness in his face told her she was right.

"You had more than one reason for taking us," she accused him.

MacKenzie cursed her quickness. It had not been the main reason, but it had been in the back of his mind from the beginning. His lips tightened even more, but he nodded. He would not lie to her.

He saw a cloud gather in her eyes. For some reason, she was disappointed in him, and he was surprised at how much the thought troubled him. When he spoke, however, his voice was curt and indifferent. "There's no more time to waste. Wake the boy."

April watched as he filled the canteens, leaving one with her for Davey, along with some food. She woke her son and gently teased him into chewing some beef and drinking some water as her eyes continued to study MacKenzie's quick movements. He went to the horses and resaddled them. They, too, had needed a brief respite, and he had relieved them of the saddles and blankets after watering them. After taking off the hobbles, he stood impatiently, reins in his hands.

April rose painfully. MacKenzie's ministrations had helped some, but she was still stiff and sore. She thought Mac-Kenzie's mouth softened at her obvious discomfort but, as ever, any flicker of emotion was quickly gone. Unlike the other times, however, he did not mount first, but offered his hand for her foot and helped her into the saddle.

"You've decided I'm not going to run away?" she challenged, and was gratified at his brief wry look.

"Not without the boy," he replied.

"Why don't you let me have Davey? You could easily overtake me with your horse."

Again she surprised him. She was a better judge of horseflesh than most men. Although he had not spurred his horse to full speed, she had obviously seen its capabilities. Not many did, and his respect for her rose.

But he couldn't let her see it. She might use it against him. Instead, his words were curt. "I couldn't spare the time."

"Damn you," she said, and felt a certain satisfaction when she saw a muscle flex in his cheek. But he didn't say anything. He merely turned away, reached down, picked Davey up and placed him on the Appaloosa. With one easy movement, MacKenzie jumped behind Davey and nudged the horse into a trot. April followed, wondering whether she had only dreamed his gentleness earlier in the day.

MacKenzie's concentration was impeded by the woman. He knew he shouldn't be affected by her sudden disappointment in him. He was doing what he had to do. And he couldn't quite understand why she could accept that he had to take her and the boy to keep them from crying out at the camp, yet was upset over the other obvious benefit of their presence. It didn't make sense to him.

But he didn't have time to brood about it. An hour from the stream, they intersected pony tracks, dozens of them, and MacKenzie's entire attention was immediately riveted on them. His mind quickly ran through the possibilities. He doubted it would be the Navahos. They had given up hunting this far away from camp and were raising their own crops and animals now.

Apaches? They usually didn't come this far north. But they were on the warpath and might be ranging north in hopes of finding horses, food and slaves. They often took young men and women and even children from other tribes and sold them to Mexican ranchers. It was one way to raise money for rifles. MacKenzie involuntarily shivered. It would be worse than death to the freedom-loving Navaho.

Or it could be the Utes, reaching down from Colorado on a hunt or raid. They, too, took slaves and sold them.

But whoever and whatever made the tracks, they could mean trouble for his Navahos, for himself and for the Mannings. It was the last thing he needed now.

His hand tightened around Davey's waist, and he slowed his horse until Mrs. Manning caught up. He didn't want to frighten her, but he knew she should be aware of the danger.

When she was by his side, he pointed to the tracks. "It could be Apaches or it could be Utes. The Utes won't bother us. The Apaches..."

He didn't need to say more. April immediately understood. The Utes sometimes raided neighboring tribes and quarreled frequently among themselves, but they had worked with Kit Carson against the Navaho. They had no current grudge with the whites. Her father had kept her posted, in letters, of action in the area.

April paled a little at the thought of Apaches, but that was her only sign of concern. She looked at him questioningly.

"Stay close by my side," he said. "If I yell, ride like the devil's behind you. I won't leave you." He paused. "Can you shoot?"

She nodded. "I grew up on army posts, and my father thought I should learn... It's been a while, but I don't think it's something you forget."

He took the rifle from his back and started to hand it to her. He couldn't let himself think she might turn it on him. He wouldn't leave her undefended if anything happened to him.

"I'm better with a pistol," she said quietly and watched as he slung the rifle around his shoulders and, without a word, handed her the Colt from the gun belt around his waist. She felt it for a moment, trying to familiarize herself. She had forgotten how heavy it was, how ugly. It was an instrument of death, and while she had once mastered it she had never liked its purpose. Her father had insisted, however, since she often went riding by herself. She put it in one of the saddle-bags, leaving the top of the bag unbuckled.

She kept pace with him now, often turning to study his face for clues. It was watchful, and she saw his eyes darting rapidly over the horizon. It was ideal ground for an ambush: large, craggy rocks, hills, heavy underbrush. They were entering the mountain area, and there were thousands of hiding places.

April wondered why she didn't feel more fear. And why she had such a sense of security with this man. The feeling scared her more than the Apaches. It suddenly came to her how much she was trusting MacKenzie, how much faith she had in him. He might protect her physically, but emotionally he was doing things to her she'd never thought possible.

I have to get away from him. The thought hammered at her consciousness. She and Davey. She looked at Davey in his arms. Her son looked as if he belonged there. She remembered MacKenzie's warm touch earlier in the day and understood. MacKenzie, she reminded herself, is an accused murderer. He'll most certainly hang once they find him. And they *will* find him. They always do. And what will that do to Davey? And me? Pain curled inside her at the thought. She had never witnessed a hanging, but she had heard about them. She knew it wasn't a pleasant way to die, even when it was properly done, which didn't always happen. April's hand touched the saddlebag as she resolved to get away from her kidnapper...after this danger. If he didn't leave her and Davey with the Navahos as he promised, she would *make* him leave them there. Now that she had a gun, she could protect both herself and the boy until the soldiers came. And then she could forget MacKenzie. She *would* forget him.

MacKenzie's pace had slowed. If he had been cautious before, he was doubly so now. He rode alone to each rise, mounting it carefully, eyes searching for movement. It was dusk before they reached the outer edges of the Navaho land, much later than he'd anticipated arriving.

He knew immediately something was wrong. There were always sentries at this point. And there were masses of tracks, all made within the past twenty-four hours. Then his nostrils caught the smell.

His hand went up in silent command. One finger pointed to a hill at their left, and April obediently followed, understanding instantly that speech was not wise. MacKenzie studied the landscape, finally finding what he sought. With gentle pressure, MacKenzie covered Davey's mouth and slid from his horse with the boy in his arms. April followed his lead silently, taking the reins of her horse and almost soundlessly following MacKenzie's footsteps up a slight rise.

He pointed to a place surrounded on three sides by sheer rock. The front was covered by underbrush. His hand urged her down, and he placed Davey in her arms. "I want you to stay here," he said in a whisper. "No matter what happens, what you hear, stay here unless you hear my voice. Will you do that?"

She nodded. Her faith in his judgment—in this matter, anyway—was complete.

He looked at her black horse. At least the color was a blessing. But he was afraid to leave it with them. A whinny or the stamp of a hoof might lead an Apache right to them. Yet if anything happened to him, she needed to be able to find the horse quickly. "I'm taking your horse just around the side of the hill," he said. "There are a few trees there. I'll stake him out."

April did not want the horse to go. "Then why can't we hide there, too."

He sighed. "You're safer here among the rocks...with some protection. The horses would stand out. Please do as I say."

It was the "please" that decided her. She knew he wouldn't have said it if he weren't desperate. She nodded her assent.

"If I'm not back by morning, and you've heard no noises during the night, get the horse and try to follow our trail back. You should run into Pickering." He handed her a couple of canteens and some beef jerky and finally, after a brief hesitation, his gun belt with its ammunition.

He looked at her as if he would like to say something else, but didn't. She wanted to ask him not to leave her. But couldn't. His face was frozen with determination. Something was very wrong. She knew that, and she also knew he wasn't going to tell her what. He had made his decision, and he wasn't going to change it. She would not humiliate herself by asking.

In the growing darkness, he took one last look at her and marveled at her control, although he saw the fear in her eyes and the confusion in Davey's face. He felt something clutching at him in his gut, and he almost bent over with the pain. He didn't want to leave them. But something very bad had happened over the ridge, and for their sake he had to know what. He couldn't make any decisions until he did. Nor could he subject them to what he was afraid he was going to see.

His hand reached out to Davey's shoulder and, involuntarily, moved up to touch April's face. He withdrew it instantly. He had no right. Then he saw the slight reassuring gesture had relaxed both of them, and he felt somehow comforted. He had needed that touch. MacKenzie reluctantly left, his moccasins making no noise as he disappeared.

It was worse then he had feared. The stench came from dead bodies, now bloated by the heat and sun. Men. Women. Young children. Only the young men and women were gone, taken, he knew, as slaves. The huts had been burned, the dogs killed. All the livestock was gone. Crops had been trampled. MacKenzie felt sick. He had done these Navahos no favor a year ago when he had won them a reprieve. Apaches. He recognized the lances and arrows. And the mutilations. Apaches believed they gained strength from cutting their enemies. One of those so butchered had once saved MacKenzie's life.

He fell on his knees as he viewed the carnage. He wanted to beat the earth at the waste. He had seen it before—too many times. And each time it had taken a little more of his soul. The first time had been the worst, because then it had been his fault. He had led the soldiers to a small, peaceful village of mainly women and children. He had not known the lieutenant was a bloody bastard with a hunger for glory. When he saw what was intended, he had attacked the lieutenant, had been subdued by a score of soldiers and tied to a tree where he had watched the rape of an innocent village. It all came back now, every terrible minute. It had not helped that the lieutenant had been court-martialed, that a major named Bennett Morgan had seen the man dishonorably discharged. The memory still haunted him; he doubted that it would ever leave him. He had resigned then and disappeared into the mountains for several years until General Wakefield had found him once more. He had wanted to say no, but Wakefield knew him only too well, knew his dream, and he had offered it. And a certain freedom of action. So he had reluctantly agreed. He had had only a few months left…

"Damn," he whispered to the dead. "God damn this world." MacKenzie didn't know how long he remained there on his knees, nor did he know that wetness formed in his eyes and traveled down his cheeks.

It was dark when he rose. There was one hut left partially standing, and he dragged and carried the bodies into it. He would not let the animals have them. When he was finally finished, he placed wood around the hut, and twigs and dry pine needles. He lit the pile, remembering only too well the same ritual nearly a year earlier.

MacKenzie mounted his horse, knowing it would take time for the tiny flame to kindle and light the dark night. He had to get the Mannings and move fast, although he believed the Apaches had probably gone south with their newly gained slaves and livestock. Some might have lingered. He couldn't take the chance he was wrong, not with the woman and boy.

Only fleetingly did he think about leaving them here in case Pickering was closer than he believed. The blaze in the sky would certainly speed them. But curious Apaches or other renegades might also be drawn to the scene of death, and he would not risk that. Immediately, he thought of an alternative. Between here and the high mountains, there were several ranches and a Ute Village. In the meantime they would have to ride tonight, and ride hard.

He tried to think of ways to soften the news for the woman. He knew she was going on grit alone, and part of her strength, he thought, was because she knew the ordeal was soon to end. Now he could promise nothing, only more uncertainty, more discomfort, more pain. And yet, deep inside a place he wouldn't recognize, there was a sudden gladness that he wouldn't lose them yet.

The time seemed endless to April as she huddled in her tiny hiding place. Davey had gone to sleep, and as she listened to the night sounds, the least noise became magnified. The whispering breeze among the pines was a roar, the call of a faraway coyote seemed only yards away. She had never been so frightened. Perhaps she should have been, these past several days? She had wondered frequently why she was not. But MacKenzie's absence terrified her much more than his presence had.

MacKenzie. How could one man so shake her entire being in such a short time? Make her question everything she had planned? Make her feel shivery and wanting and tender at the same time? He had left her here. Alone. He had treated her indifferently from the beginning, unmindful of her discomfort and pain and hurt. He had been intent only on his own escape. So why should she give a care? Except to see him captured, and she and Davey returned safely. She should be glad to see him in irons, in jail. So why was the thought so completely abhorrent? And why could she think of nothing but his proud, lean grace and his striking eyes—and those few seconds in his arms?

April felt the pistol growing heavier, and she grasped it anew, steadying it. Where was MacKenzie? What was he doing? Why had he told her so little? Perhaps he planned to leave them here alone while he made his escape north. Terror struck her anew. She had thought several times that she would use the gun against him, force him to take her and Davey someplace safe, regardless whether it fit into *his* plans. And now, in her anger at him she started to consider the idea once more. If he *did* come back. God, please make him come back. She leaned against the rock and waited, her hand locked on the gun, her finger on the trigger.

The moon was still a sliver, but bright stars lit an unclouded night, and MacKenzie had no trouble adjusting his eyes. He often traveled at night, and seemed to have extraordinary vision during those hours. Whether it was practice or training or something else he did not question.

He had no trouble finding April and Davey Manning. In order not to frighten them, he called out softly, then approached. The rifle was in his hands but held carelessly now. He had scouted well before returning, and there was no sign of human life—or trouble—within miles.

Tired and still sickened by the recent violence, he did not anticipate trouble from another direction. He went easily into the place he had prepared for April Manning, only to find her hand firmly on the Colt and her finger taut on the trigger. And the gun was pointing straight at his heart.

Chapter Six

April's hand didn't waver, and through the very dim light MacKenzie saw the determined set of her chin. He stood absolutely still.

"Drop the rifle." The command came clear and loud in the quiet night. There was no hesitation or weakness in it.

Only the slight throbbing of a muscle in MacKenzie's cheek indicated he heard as he considered the order. He was in no hurry to obey.

He shifted the rifle in his hand—not toward her or in any threatening manner, but not toward the ground, either. He knew she wouldn't shoot unless he made a move. But he wasn't quite sure whether she might shoot if he reached for her gun. He simply didn't know to what lengths of desperation he had driven her.

MacKenzie realized he had been gone for hours, hours that must have terrified her. The fact that he had had no choice made little difference. It did not help his conscience that those hours had come after the kidnapping of her son, a bone-wrenching day of riding and uncertainty about his intentions despite his poor assurances. Why, after all, should she trust him at all? A man accused of murder and rape who had grabbed a small boy. His terrible weariness was swallowed by an aching hurt as he watched the strong, courageous face just feet away from him. In minutes she would crumble. He could tell from the too stiff posture, the almost desperate cast of her chin. And he didn't want that to happen. She needed that pride to keep her going.

She had told him she could shoot, and she certainly held the Colt as if it were familiar. Her finger was on the trigger just tight enough to prevent him from trying to jump her, but not tight enough so the pistol would go off without intent.

"You don't want to fire that gun now," he finally said quietly. "There's Apaches not long gone."

"The Navaho camp?" There was the first hint of uncertainty in her voice. He had told her that was their destination.

The silence answered her question.

"I want to go home. I want to go to Fort Defiance."

"I know," he said in a gentle voice.

"I can wait here for the soldiers. You said they wouldn't be far behind."

"It's too dangerous… I couldn't leave you and the boy alone. And I can't stay."

"Then where?" It was a cry of desperation, and MacKenzie's hand tightened around the rifle. What in God's name was he doing to her? But there was no alternative. None at all.

"I will see you safe." It was all he could say.

"No," she said. "Davey and I will stay here."

"I can't let you do that."

Her hand tightened on the gun. "I said, drop the rifle!"

"No, Mrs. Manning." The voice was soft and regretful, but absolute, and April knew she had lost. She slowly lowered the gun.

"Damn you," she whispered.

MacKenzie stood, wanting fiercely to reassure her, to comfort her, to touch her, but he had no right, and he knew she would reject it now. His mouth, always grim, tightened into an even firmer line. His hand balled into a fist as he fought the desire to take her into his arms.

Davey was mercifully asleep and had been spared the tense scene. MacKenzie's eyes went from the boy to his mother, and he saw the defeat and confusion, and it pierced him to the depths of his being. He turned abruptly.

''I'll be getting the horses,'' he said, forcing the words, hoping they didn't reveal his own uncertainty.

April made a move to hand him the gun, but he shook his head. ''Keep it,'' he said, his voice once more oddly gentle. As he disappeared, April leaned against the rock, trembling. She had been able to hold it in check while he was there in front of her, but now it rocked her body.

She had known, from the start, that she would not be able to shoot him. Her only chance was a bluff, and he had seen right through it. And now they would go on, and on, and on, and part of her was angry, and part terribly tired and part...relieved. She really had not wanted to stay alone, and she couldn't deny the feeling of safety she had with Mac-Kenzie. But she feared that feeling as much as she feared the Indians out there.

In the distance, she saw a glow, a golden halo reaching into the sky. It was in the direction from which MacKenzie had come, but she had no time to ponder its source, for she saw him approach, the two horses in tow. He silently handed the reins to her and helped her mount, his hand resting on hers a moment longer than necessary. She felt his warmth and strength, and she straightened her back.

MacKenzie picked up Davey, careful not to wake him, and swung up on his Appaloosa. Without any more words, they moved silently out, the golden glow behind them flaring in one last gasp, then slowly fading into nothingness.

April's fear during the long hours alone had dulled her to the biting cold, but now it attacked with ferocity. She shivered and tried to gather her jacket tighter around her. She was emotionally and physically drained, and she wondered if life would ever return to any kind of normalcy. She looked at MacKenzie's straight, unyielding back, and envied him his endurance. At least she had had several hours of sleep yesterday afternoon and could catnap on the horse. He had had none in two days, perhaps longer. How could he keep going? He would surely have to stop soon. No one could continue to maintain this pace.

April wondered what had happened during the hours he had been gone during the night. He was always grim-faced, but there had been something more when he returned. A stark bitterness. And, perhaps, sorrow. It was hard to tell with him. He guarded his feelings as most men guarded gold. If, that is, he had any. She was beginning to wonder about that. And with each step of her horse, she wondered more. Where was he taking her and Davey now? Where would it end?

The first hint of dawn broke the darkness, and black faded into a dull gray as clouds swarmed the sky, blocking even a hint of a warming sun.

MacKenzie stopped at another small stream. April didn't even puzzle any more at his uncanny ability to find water in this dry country but, instead, she slid gratefully from the horse, dropping where she landed. She didn't have the strength to take even one step.

Davey, now awake and bright-eyed, went to her, and MacKenzie followed. His eyes swept over her, missing nothing—not the droop in her shoulders or the infinite exhaustion in her face. He sighed. She had been stronger than he had any right to expect, but she couldn't go much farther. He looked at the threatening thunderheads beginning to form in the sky, and knew they had to find shelter. The rain would erase any trace of their trail, and he suspected Pickering would not pursue them much beyond the Navaho camp. The lieutenant would probably have to report to Fort Defiance, where they would send out additional search parties. He smiled wryly. He would not like to be in Pickering's boots when the lieutenant faced Wakefield. He could almost hear the roar now. Pickering's career had ended the moment MacKenzie took Mrs. Manning and Davey. But what in the hell was he going to do with them now?

There were several ranches between here and the high mountains that were now his goal. And if worse came to worst, there was a Ute village where the woman and boy would be safe while word was sent. The Utes had a strong treaty with the United States because of the leadership of Chief Ouray. And a daughter of a general would be well treated and protected.

But now he needed to find shelter. He saw April shiver in the cold morning air, and he took a blanket, slitting a hole in the middle. He offered his hand to her, and she took it, once more feeling its remarkable warm strength, which seemed to flow into her. She stood, swaying just a little as he settled the blanket around her. With another quick movement, he cut a piece of rope and tied it around her waist.

"That should help some," he said tersely as he felt her blue eyes on him. They seemed enormous now in a face pinched by exhaustion.

April didn't answer. She was simply too tired.

"An hour more," he said, and there was more than the usual softness in his speech. "An hour more and you can sleep as long as you wish."

April barely comprehended the words. An hour seemed a lifetime to legs screaming in agony, a mind crying for sleep. But she knew she could not fight him. There was a magnetic power in him that lured something inside her to obey, to go beyond what she thought she could do. She nodded and received a fleeting reward—a small, rueful smile that held an engaging hint of admiration. It disappeared quickly, but for a moment it eased his face, and she thought how attractive it was. If only he would do it more often.

She watched as once again he carefully tended the horses and filled their canteens. All too quickly, he was back. She felt his sure, confident hands around her waist, and she was being lifted effortlessly into the saddle. How assured those arms felt. She wondered, briefly, if she imagined a slight hesitation before his hands left her. Then she pondered the warm glow that started to burn within her at the thought. Foolish April. He was thinking of nothing but escape.

Then they were moving again, and she could only clutch the saddle horn and pray for a quick end to this. One hour. Sixty minutes. She started to count to keep her mind from absorbing the punishment. She never considered the fact he might have lied. One hour. Then fifty-nine minutes.

Half drugged with exhaustion, she didn't realize he had taken her reins, or that he was leading them through the middle of a small stream to hide their tracks. He was watching carefully for horse droppings and stopped once to disperse a pile near the edge of the stream. He didn't know how far he would have to take her, or how long they would have to rest, and he didn't want the cavalry on his tail now. He again doubted whether Pickering would continue this far, but he couldn't be sure. The threat of losing the general's daughter might just spur him on.

He looked at April, her head nodding, her hands clutched tightly to the saddle, as if locked there. The blanket made her shapeless, and her hair was a curly mass falling down her back, the rich chestnut brown streaked with hints of gold and red. She was a valiant one. And so was her boy. He never thought a small lad could be so good, so quiet, so completely trusting of a stranger. But Davey had burrowed a hole in MacKenzie's chest and seemed content. He was awake now, and watching everything, occasionally holding out a hand to point at something unfamiliar. MacKenzie would try to explain, at first simplifying his words, but then he realized it was not necessary. The boy was uncommonly bright and absorbed everything.

As they continued to climb the streambed, the clouds grew heavier and more ominous. MacKenzie knew exactly where he was going—a cave he had occasionally used on scouting trips. He finally saw the rocky face of the foothill he was seeking and left the streambed, carefully guiding the horses through tangled underbrush to an opening in the rock. He dismounted and went to April, noting her almost glazed eyes as she made no effort to move.

"We can rest here," he said, offering his hand, but she made no move to take it. He went around to her other side and released her foot from the stirrup and returned to the left side. His hands reached up to her waist and once more she was in his arms. Like Davey, she seemed to snuggle there for a moment, unaware of the sudden tautness of his body as it came in contact with hers. He carried her inside, Davey at his side, and he set her on the floor of the cave. It was deep, and he looked back into the dark interior. He doubted they had any animal companions; he would have heard or smelled them by now. But with the boy, he would take no chance. He lit a match and told Davey to stay with his mother while he searched the cave. There was nothing but some old animal bones and a few mostly broken pieces of ancient pottery. One jar, however, was virtually intact, and he brought it back with him.

The cave was cold, and MacKenzie saw Mrs. Manning shiver. He left and was back within minutes with an armful of firewood, and his hands quickly had a blaze going. He left once more and tended the horses, taking off the saddles, rubbing the backs where sores were beginning to show from the hard riding. He hobbled them, then returned to the cave, bringing the bedrolls with him. He fashioned one into a pillow for Mrs. Manning and took a blanket from the second, pulling it up around her.

"I'll watch the boy," he said as he had the day before. "You sleep."

"What about you?" April was barely able to mutter, but the thought nagged at her. He must be much more tired than she…if that were possible.

"I can rest with one eye open," he said with a slight smile. "I'm used to it."

April believed him. Her eyes closed and she was asleep almost instantly.

* * *

When she woke, Davey and MacKenzie were gone. She felt a moment's panic and forced herself to think. There was still light filtering into the cave, so she had not slept the entire day away. And the fire had obviously been frequently tended; the pile of ashes was substantial, and there was a stack of firewood against the wall of the cave. Once more, she was struck by conflicting feelings. She still couldn't quite comprehend that indefatigable energy that kept him going when most men would have fallen. It frustrated her that he could do so much, and she must appear so weak. And once more, there was that strange, warm feeling of protection, of knowing that she and Davey were in good hands.

But where were they—MacKenzie and her son?

She rose slowly, every muscle screaming in protest as she made her way to the cave's entrance. Clouds were boiling in the sky, large black and purple splotches reshaping themselves as they crossed overhead in great, hurrying masses. The wind was blowing hard, and her hair whipped around her face, and the leaves and limbs of nearby trees groaned and whistled as gusts bullied their way through them. There was an expectancy in the air because of the approaching storm, and April wondered why she wasn't frightened. She had always liked storms, but then she had always been well-protected by sturdy structures, not out in the middle of an untamed wilderness with only a cave for shelter. But now the elemental electricity excited her, and she felt a small flame start deep inside at the thought of sharing it with MacKenzie, even though she knew she shouldn't.

April saw a movement in the brush, and MacKenzie's rangy, graceful form appeared first. Davey was tagging behind, a large fish in his hands and a huge smile on his face. MacKenzie was carrying several fish on a thin piece of rope, a satisfied gleam in his eyes.

His eyes swept April, and she thought for a moment how much they resembled the gray, frothing sky. If only she could

read them. But she could only see the complexity, as she had
that first night. Nothing more.

"Dinner," MacKenzie proclaimed. And April thought to
herself it was the only unnecessary word she had ever heard
him utter.

"I caught a fish," Davey said with great pride as he showed
his treasure. "MacKenzie taught me how."

April's eyebrows lifted. "MacKenzie?"

"He said I could call him that. It's all right, isn't it,
Mama?"

Once more, April looked at the man who had so radically
changed her life in the past few days.

There was a tiny, almost indefinable glint of amusement in
his expression. "I didn't think Mr. MacKenzie sounded quite
right. Everyone just calls me MacKenzie."

"No other name?" April couldn't help but ask.

The brief amusement disappeared, and tiny bitter lines
formed at the corners of his mouth. "Many," he said, "but
none I would say in front of the boy."

April was stunned at the intensity of his words. They held
a deep, savage bitterness he had kept well-hidden until now.
She recalled Terrell's brutal treatment and wondered how
MacKenzie had held his temper. It must have taken superb
willpower to have endured what he had with so little show of
emotion or concern. She could sense the suppressed violence
in him.

MacKenzie turned away abruptly, obviously regretting that
brief lapse of control. "I'll clean them," he said shortly, taking the one fish from Davey and adding it to his own. He went
some twenty yards from the cave and sat, cross-legged, his
back stiff and hostile, the sharpening wind ruffling his thick
black hair.

April hesitated, wanting to say something. It was almost as
if she could feel the jagged wounds within him. He had revealed them for only the briefest of seconds, but she knew
they ran deep. She moved toward him, then took measure once

more of the tense, hard body and knew he wouldn't appreciate sympathy. And yet there was such a deep longing in her to comfort, to share, to soothe...her kidnapper? Davey's kidnapper? The man who had put her through such physical agony? It didn't make sense, but as she looked at him, his very strength and reserve seemed to magnify that brief image of vulnerability.

One fist clenched her side in an effort to keep her distance. She stood there for a moment, then retreated into the cave with Davey, who was chattering eagerly about the fish. He had never gone fishing before, and he was filled with enthusiasm. MacKenzie, he said, caught *his* fish with a spear he had made from his knife and a piece of wood.

"But I caught one all by myself with the pole. MacKenzie just helped a wee bit."

Every time Davey said "MacKenzie," his eyes shone with adoration, and April was flooded with new fear. She had never seen Davey so open, so flushed with excitement. Her son was already imitating MacKenzie's slight burr. What would happen when MacKenzie disappeared from their lives? As he undoubtedly would, and soon. Davey had adopted MacKenzie without reservation, without question.

And MacKenzie? He had been uncommonly patient with the boy. She had seen him whispering to her son on the long ride, and she remembered the haunting song that had filled the air with a misty loveliness of its own. Would he miss Davey? Or her? The last question sent a stab of warm longing coursing through her, leaving a bittersweet aftermath of anticipation and fear. She had thought herself immune to these kinds of feelings after four years of a purgatory of waiting. She thought she had successfully schooled herself against them, and now they frightened her with their raw intensity.

April fed the fire, welcoming the chance to busy her hands and take her mind away from the renegade scout. She *had* to think of him that way. The flames grabbed the new fodder and danced upward, sending a wave of warmth across the cave, but April didn't feel it. Instead, a sudden chill ran through her body, a fear so deep she felt her body shiver. But she couldn't identify it.

She tried to shake the feeling, taking Davey's hand and leading him to the blankets where she wrapped herself and him, listening all the time to his eager, happy words of his new adventures with MacKenzie. After what seemed hours, he quieted and went to sleep in her arms, and she searched the small face with a love so great it hurt. It was still flushed from the outdoors, and the fire, and memories of a happy day. There was a contented smile in place of the old, apprehensive look so often in place at the Manning home. April felt a surging tenderness for Davey and gratefulness to MacKenzie for the gift of joy he had given Davey this afternoon. Even as she knew it would end soon. And she and Davey would be going home. She tried to think happily about the prospect, about the moment she and Davey would be free, but she could only feel a deep emptiness at the prospect. Curled up with Davey, it was her last thought before she drifted into a troubled sleep.

April woke to the rumbling roar of thunder, the lonely sound of rain hitting earth and the savory smell of cooking fish. She opened her eyes slowly and knew it was evening. The cave was dark, lit only by the occasional spurt of flame from the fire. MacKenzie had let it almost die, apparently to cook the fish, which were skewered on a stick. It rested over two piles of rocks on each side of the fire. April felt Davey warm against her, and she didn't move as she adjusted her eyes to the darkness.

She saw the lithe, sinewy outline of MacKenzie's body, and wondered once more at the primal grace of it. Every movement was so sure, so confident. He seemed like one of the dancing shadows created by the flares of flame. She heard a new roll of thunder as it gained power and fury and crashed in great waves of tumultuous sound, followed by an immense flash of light, which illuminated the cave. It seemed to focus on MacKenzie's face, framing the hard, angular planes and his compelling masculinity, resting for a split second on eyes that looked like a storm-tossed ocean, restless and tormented. April felt a stab of longing that was becoming painfully familiar. She had never so wanted to touch someone...not even with David. She had loved David, but it had been a gentle, dreaming young love; she had never felt this overpowering need for contact, this aching in her body that stretched from its core to every nerve end. She shivered with her own need and drew her arm tighter around Davey.

"Mrs. Manning." His voice was so soft it was almost a whisper, but it was audible through the noise of hard, driving rain. She wondered how such a large man, such a strong man could have such a quiet voice. She also wondered how he knew she was awake. She was in the shadows, and she had not moved. He was uncanny about sensing things. He left her with few thoughts of her own. She could only hope that at least one of them was safe.

"Mrs. Manning," he said again. This time there was a command in it.

April reluctantly sat up, carefully unwrapping Davey from her arms without waking him. She knew MacKenzie must be conscious of the fact she had been watching him, studying him. She eased her son to the ground, saw that he was well covered and moved to where MacKenzie knelt before the fire.

"Yes?" she said coolly, willing reserve in her voice, even disdain. As befitting captive to captor, she thought. *I can't forget that! Please God, don't let me forget that.*

His gray eyes pierced her with the electric intensity that was so much a part of him. His body was tense, almost, April fancied, like a cougar's before striking. And that is what he reminded her of...a fascinating, dangerous mountain cat. Free and untamed and beautiful with its sleek sureness and power. But the image was suddenly broken when his hand went up to his hair and raked it in a gesture that denoted the first uncertainty she had seen in him. It was an almost boyish movement, and once more April detected the vulnerability that he tried so hard to hide.

"Yes?" she said again, this time in a softer tone.

MacKenzie hesitated, obviously trying to find words. "We'll stay here a day or two...so you and the boy can get rested."

April knelt beside him so she could meet his eyes. He was struggling to say more. She waited.

"You do not need to worry," he said finally, his face set as granite. "I'll not touch you."

April's face must have reflected her surprise for he continued. "I didn't hurt that girl back there."

MacKenzie's jaw was rigid, and April understood how difficult the words must have been. He was not a man who explained or apologized or justified. Yet he was trying, awkwardly, to reassure her. What small hostility she had tried to summon melted altogether.

"I know," she said, and there was so much conviction in her voice MacKenzie's mask broke and she saw open astonishment in his face.

"Davey's a very good judge of character," April continued. "And so is my father."

"Your father?" He couldn't hide his confusion.

"He wrote me about you. He trusts you."

"He *did*," MacKenzie said wryly. "I don't think so anymore."

April bit her lip, then summoned all her courage. "Go back with me," she said passionately. "Go to Defiance with me. You know my father. He'll see you get justice, that Ellen was lying."

There was no mistaking the pain in MacKenzie's face now. "I've also killed a sergeant."

"Self-defense," April guessed. "It was self-defense, wasn't it?"

He looked at her steadily, scarcely understanding that she

believed him, that she trusted him after all he had done to her and the boy.

"You don't understand," he said finally. "It makes no difference. The word of a half-breed would mean nothing against a white girl or Terrell or the others. I wouldn't stand a chance." His voice was once more bitter.

"But I could tell them what Terrell did..."

"Do you really think anyone cares...that it would matter? Then you're a fool." His face once more froze, and his eyes were like cold steel. It was as if he had placed a stone wall between them.

April couldn't let it go. "My father..."

"Your father would probably happily see me hang now." There was regret in his voice but no yielding. "I'll not go back."

Davey stirred then, and both MacKenzie and April quieted their voices although their eyes still battled.

It was MacKenzie who finally spoke. "The fish are cooked...and there's hardtack." A suspicion of a smile appeared at April's grimace. But she didn't say anything.

"You are a very unusual woman, Mrs. Manning. Do you never complain?"

"If I think it will do any good," she replied, her eyes lighting with mischief. "And you might call me April. After spending several nights together, I think it would be appropriate."

The cold reserve dropped from MacKenzie's face, and once more he seemed, for a second, at a loss. "April," he said, his senses savoring the sound. "It fits you well." But then he turned away from her, and April sensed the withdrawal, and she knew the wall was still there.

Chapter Seven

Daylight crept into the cave, moving slowly to encompass the entrance, then where the fire still burned, and finally to where April Manning and her son slept.

MacKenzie had been awake for hours. He had caught naps through the night, but was aware of the need to feed the fire, to keep his charges warm in the cold, damp air. He had lived for years on scattered pieces of sleep, knowing well the penalty in both the animal and human world for unawareness. He would wake at the slightest sound, or the cooling of a fire, or the rustle of an oncoming storm. His senses never slept, not even when he was totally exhausted.

The rain had stopped, but the air was still cold, unusually so for this time of the year. He shifted his gaze from the fire to the sleeping pair on the other side of the cave.

Mrs. Manning—he wouldn't let himself think of her as April, he couldn't—was still sleeping soundly. She had tamed her wild hair into a braid, which fell over her right breast, and one hand cradled Davey. Long lashes covered the blue eyes that hovered in his mind, and her wide, generous mouth was curved into a small smile. How gently she slept.

His prisoners. He did not think of them that way although he knew she must. He had listened to her plea the night before, when she suggested he return them to Defiance. He had even considered it for a moment, but he had had enough of "justice," and contempt and humiliation.

If he thought there would be the slightest chance...but there wasn't and never would be.

When he had taken the boy, he thought it would only be a matter of hours, but it had been days, and it might well be many more. He had not meant to hurt either of them, and now he was responsible for both, and he was astonished and dismayed at how quickly each had grabbed a piece of a heart he had thought hardened. Something happened when Davey stuck his hand in MacKenzie's and eyed him with such trust. He had never known what it meant to touch another's life and give it the bright happiness that glowed in the boy's face.

And April Manning. She warmed him as no other person had. She challenged him with her courage and endurance, eased him with her bewildering trust. He had sought to comfort her last night, and it was he who was comforted. Even if he couldn't show it.

He couldn't let her know how much he wanted to touch her, to hold her, to feel her warmth. For then, they would both be lost. He sensed in her a passion that, when fully awakened, would be all-consuming. And he could give her nothing. Less than nothing. Only hiding, and fear, and death.

With no little disgust at his self-indulgence, he quickly rose to his feet. They would stay half of the day to let Mrs. Manning's sore muscles adjust, then continue on to the Ute village. He and Davey would do some more fishing this morning, and perhaps he would even try to hunt with the rough bow and arrows he had fashioned. He knew he would have little range; the bow had none of the suppleness of a properly prepared one, but perhaps... They needed fresh meat, and such gifts would make them doubly welcomed by the Utes. He added enough wood to the fire to keep it going for another hour or two. He would not be gone any longer.

April felt Davey tugging on her. His face was gloomy. "MacKenzie's gone," he announced.

She felt a sudden apprehension, then studied the cave. The

fire had been recently fueled, and both saddles and bedrolls were still there. His one blanket was neatly folded near the wall. He had given three to April and Davey. Everything else was neat. The fish bones from the night before were gone. She smiled at the thought of MacKenzie cleaning the cave as carefully as any Boston housewife.

She stood and stretched and felt better than she had in days. Some of the pain in her bones and muscles was fading, and she felt well rested. She felt more alive than she had in years as she wondered which of the several MacKenzies she would encounter today. He had, unwillingly enough, showed them all yesterday: the terse, quiet loner, the gentle man who taught her son to fish, the intense, attractive man who said her name fit her. There had been something in the way he said it... something warm and approving.

In the meantime, she and Davey needed to make good use of the time. She had been far too tired in the past several days to do anything about their appearance. Now she would find the stream and try to remedy that. She wished desperately that she had a comb. Her hair was never easy to control and now it was a messy web of snarls.

April quickly looked through the saddlebags and MacKenzie's bedroll, where she found a bar of soap and a comb. She took two of the blankets to use as covering while she washed hers and Davey's clothes. Taking Davey's hand, she let him lead her to the stream where he and MacKenzie had fished the day before.

It was a beautiful rain-washed morning, even though there was a sharp bite to the wind. The sky was as deep and pure a blue as she remembered seeing, and the sun was spraying the water with freckles of gold. The mountains rose up in purple splendor in front of them, and even this stark, rocky hill country was colorful with an occasional wildflower. Against all common sense, April felt shivers of joy run up and down her spine. It was so incredibly peaceful, so lovely in its own lonely way. It seemed a place apart from violence and death, as if she and Davey and MacKenzie were the only people on earth and they were in harmony. MacKenzie. Her thoughts seldom strayed from him now, and her eyes anxiously searched for him. While fearing to find him.

Was it just because she and Davey were so dependent on him? She had no idea where they were, nor was she even sure they were in as much danger from Apaches as MacKenzie had indicated. Perhaps it was just his way to keep her from trying to run away. But why? He had made no move to hurt her, and she knew she and Davey were a burden to him. They slowed him down, and she sometimes fancied she sensed his impatience even though his face never showed the slightest anger or disapproval.

MacKenzie mystified her, taunted her with his apparent indifference to her as a woman. He had been kind enough that day when he had rubbed her sore muscles but that, she knew, was only so she could continue. She tried to convince herself that his gentleness with Davey came from that same concern...

Don't think about it. It's a short episode, a small adventure in your life, April told herself. Don't think about it as anything more. Still, she couldn't keep her eyes from searching for him, or quiet the expectation that hovered inside her. Davey, now convinced that MacKenzie would soon be back, squirmed free from her hand and tripped from one discovery to another. He beamed as he told April the name of a cactus MacKenzie had pointed out. "You can get water from that," he explained proudly. "MacKenzie said so."

April worried at the awe in Davey's voice. What would he do when MacKenzie was gone? Would he understand?

April stripped down to her chemise and pantalets, shivering a little in the cold. She washed both Davey and herself quickly, then her hair and finally their clothes. When she was through scrubbing them, she lay them out on rocks and bushes to dry in the sun and wrapped the two of them in the blankets as she told Davey a story about a prince and princess in a faraway country.

Only once did Davey interrupt. "Did he look like Mac-Kenzie?" he asked. "And did the princess look like you?"

April smiled at the thought of MacKenzie in armor, but not at all at the thought of him slaying a dragon.

"Yes, love," she whispered. "I think he might."

So absorbed were both of them that they didn't hear MacKenzie's soft footsteps, nor sense his presence as his longing eyes moved with fierce protectiveness from the slender blanket-clad woman to the child. He listened silently, hands knotted in fists and eyes filled with immeasurable pain. At the story's end, he moved away soundlessly.

When Davey and April returned to the cave, April smelled coffee and cooking meat. She wondered how long MacKenzie had been back. She felt self-conscious at her appearance. Her thick hair was still a little wet and curling in all directions. Her clothes were also damp and clung to her slender form. But at least she was clean.

She met his eyes when she entered and, almost shyly, held out the soap. "I borrowed your soap...I hope it's all right."

MacKenzie couldn't take his gaze from her. There was an uncertainty in her face that made him want to take her in his arms and quiet the questions and doubts in her eyes. Instead, he turned away. "Use anything you need."

April stared at his back, feeling the palpable tension between them. Despite his rough words, she knew he felt the surge of electricity between them, the flash of desire that burned her as nothing else had. It had been growing between them, day by day, and now she knew it frightened him as much as her.

"MacKenzie," she said softly. When he turned she knew she was right. His eyes were tormented in that one second before the protective shield was back in place.

His voice was cool when he finally replied, "Mrs. Manning?"

"April," she insisted.

"Mrs. Manning," he said in a tone that allowed no argument. It was obvious he was trying to keep distance between them. As if a name could do it, she thought with dry amusement. The electric current was even stronger now, and she felt her body tingling in reaction.

And his. She could see it stiffening, visibly see the control he was exercising over it. The expectancy in the air was several times greater than yesterday when the storm was whipping itself to a fever pitch. She felt it start in the core of her being and spread until all she wanted was to touch him, to feel his arms around her.

April was sinking in a quagmire of want and need. MacKenzie's eyes had lost their shield and reflected the same burning, aching agony she felt. She had never known anything like it before, this craving that made her forget everything else, every piece of respectability, her father, everything... everything but Davey.

Davey. She felt his hand pull on hers. "Mama?"

She heard his voice from a distance, and tore her eyes from MacKenzie's rigid form. She knew she had been holding her breath, and now she released it slowly, trying to find some sanity in the effort.

MacKenzie watched as tears formed at the corner of April's eyes and their usual clear color turned a misty violet that tore at his soul. He closed his own eyes, forcing himself to regain control, to steel himself against the growing vulnerability these two were creating within him. He could not afford it. He could not make mistakes now—for his sake or theirs. He had no future. He must make certain they did. If anything happened to them, he would be damned forever.

With the greatest effort he had ever made, MacKenzie swallowed and walked several steps away. He turned, his eyes avoiding April's. "You and the boy eat. I have things to do. We leave in a few hours." He spun around and left the cave without another word.

MacKenzie took the hobbles from his Appaloosa and adjusted the bit. He slipped his rifle over his shoulders and vaulted to the horse's back, tightening his knees against its side. He felt free without the saddle, more a part of the horse's fluid gait. His heels dug into the horse's flank and sent it into a gallop.

The tension inside him seethed and boiled, constricting his stomach into a ball, attacking his gut. He had come so close, so very close to reaching out to her, to taking her.

"Aah..." The anguished war cry tore from his mouth as he sought release from a hunger he had never known existed until now. The horse under him stretched its legs in even greater strides, sensing its rider's need and responding to it. MacKenzie was at one with the animal, his lithe form riding high on the neck, a portrait of grace and power.

He didn't know how far they went before he slowed the horse, feeling its lathered heat under him, seeing its foam-flecked mouth. He pulled up and dismounted, sliding his hand down the Appaloosa's neck in apology. The horse and Wolf...his friends. He needed no others. MacKenzie walked the Appaloosa, letting the horse cool slowly, letting his own fevered thoughts bathe in the cold, cleansing air.

There was a ranch not far away. He had ignored that possibility because, he admitted, he had not really wanted to relinquish Mrs. Manning and Davey. Not yet. But this morning showed how very important it was that he do so. He had had need of a woman before, but it had never been this sweet aching that overshadowed everything else. Perhaps it was because he had never really *liked* a woman before. And he liked April Manning. Very much.

And because he did, he was becoming careless. He should have been scouting the area rather than listening to nonsensical tales of princes and fairies. Or making coffee from their very limited supply. But he had wanted, in some way, to please her, to see the smile again.

MacKenzie swung back up on his horse and set his mind to the tasks at hand. He would check out the Ebert ranch, then make a wide arc south to see whether there were any signs of army or Indians. April Manning would be safe. He had left his pistol with her and, as far as he knew, no one knew of the cave. No one alive, anyway.

The sun was directly overhead, but still it was cold. An early winter, perhaps. He needed to get up into the mountains before the first snowfall. The passes, once swallowed by snow, were impassible, even to one who knew them well.

Wary and watchful, MacKenzie retraced his steps down the streambed they had climbed the day before. After an hour, he cut away and went west, setting a fast but not wearing pace. There were still no recent tracks, but he felt an unease, an edge that he had come to respect. It usually meant trouble. He didn't want to think it was there because of the woman and child, because they had, somehow, destroyed instinct, which had kept him alive this long.

He was five miles from the Ebert ranch when he saw the first signs. Numerous pony tracks, again from unshod ponies. Heading south from the ranch. The familiar sickness started in his stomach. The Eberts had two young children—a girl and a boy. He had warned them to leave several months ago, when the Apache raids moved farther north, but Tom Ebert had felt they were far enough away from the trouble. They had scratched out a living with a small corn crop and a few horses. It had been Ebert's plan, as it was MacKenzie's, to raise horses. It had been a small bond between two taciturn men.

Knowing it was too late, MacKenzie nonetheless pushed his horse into a gallop, seeking the bluff that overlooked the ranch. He dismounted half way up and crawled until he could see over its top.

MacKenzie closed his eyes when he saw the scene below. The ranch house was gone, burned to the ground. Bodies, including several in blue uniforms, lay scattered like broken dolls. He could pick out Mrs. Ebert because of the dress.

So some of Pickering's men did get this far. It was probably Corporal Patterson. Patterson was the most savvy and consci-

entious soldier in the small command. MacKenzie felt a wave
of regret. For Patterson. For the others. Most of all for the
Eberts. He studied the terrain, seeing nothing move. It must
have happened fairly recently. He supposed that the troops had
heard the shots and come to assist the settlers.

It had been another misjudgment on his part. Patterson had
followed his trail faster than he thought possible. The corporal had probably lost it someplace along the creek bed and
cut over to the Ebert ranch. MacKenzie realized he had been
a fool not to start out early this morning, but he knew his
charges had badly needed rest, and so did he. It didn't matter
now, he thought darkly. Pickering would have to go back
now.

MacKenzie considered the alternative of going down to the
killing ground. Apaches were thorough. There would be no
one left alive, and there was really nothing he could do. He
certainly couldn't take the time to bury them, and he supposed
Patterson's absence would soon bring additional troops. He
cursed roundly. He simply couldn't leave without checking.
Grimly, he half walked, half stumbled down to his horse and
mounted again, reluctantly turning his Appaloosa toward the
Ebert place.

He had been right. There was no one left alive, not even
the little Ebert girl. The boy was gone, taken, probably, to be
raised as an Apache brave. It *was* Patterson, and he had been
tortured before dying. It hadn't been more than several hours
earlier.

MacKenzie didn't even think about burying them. It would
take too long and now every minute was dangerous. He and
the Mannings were no longer safe in the cave, either. It was
too close to both the soldiers and the Apaches. He had mis-
judged Pickering's tenacity...or was it desperation? Mac-
Kenzie briefly considered the possibility of leaving Mrs. Manning and the boy to await the troops, but quickly dismissed
it. He could not leave them in this valley of death, nor could
he risk the possibility that Pickering might just give up the

chase when Patterson didn't return. The Ute village was still his best choice.

MacKenzie went down the hill to the Appaloosa and, moving cautiously over rocks that would not leave a trail, headed for the cave.

April paced the cave, which was quickly becoming a prison. Davey was asleep, and she dared not leave him alone. They had eaten part of the rabbit MacKenzie had prepared, but his abrupt departure and curt words had taken away her appetite, and she had merely picked at the food. The coffee, boiled in tin cups found in the bedrolls, was black and bitter, too bitter for her taste. She supposed MacKenzie was used to it so strong. It would keep him awake, alert. If it didn't kill him first, she thought wryly. Yet she knew he had made it for her. It would have been a small gesture for anyone else, but a large one for him. She suspected he was not used to doing things for others.

His presence haunted the cave. He was such a contradiction: harsh and gentle, strong and yet oddly vulnerable. A man accused of the worst possible crimes yet able to sing a lullaby to a child. *Where are you, MacKenzie? And who are you? Who are you really?*

MacKenzie was wondering that same question. The whole fabric of his life was changing. In only four days, he had discovered wants and needs he had scorned all his life. He was feeling real fear for someone else, realizing the richness of trust, the elusive joy of affection Davey gave so freely, the quiet pleasure of friendship offered by April Manning, the promise of rapture that shone so innocently in her eyes. He greedily wanted to seize them all, to seize the fire...

But he would not be the one burned. It would be the woman and child. And he would never, never let that happen.

Feelings of futility and bitterness swept over him, almost blinding him. He wiped his eyes with the dust-covered sleeve of his shirt, wishing for the old oblivion where survival was his only concern. The glimpse and the promise of something more were heavier chains to bear than any man could devise. And now he would wear them forever.

April's joy at seeing MacKenzie dimmed quickly at his almost savage expression. Even Davey drew back, sensing that something was very wrong.

"We're leaving now," he said abruptly, his gray eyes as cold and merciless as a winter sea.

"But you said…" April started, then stopped. It obviously no longer mattered what he *had* said. "What's happened?" she asked, searching his face, which revealed little.

MacKenzie stooped down until his face was level with Davey's. "My horse is just outside," he told the boy. "Can you start rubbing down his legs…like I showed you?"

"Just like you showed me," the boy affirmed.

"Go, off with you, then," MacKenzie said, "but no farther than the horses."

He turned to April, his gaze serious and hesitant, as if weighing how much he should tell her.

"What's happened?" she asked again. As the silence lengthened, anger crept into her voice. "I'm not a child."

"No," he agreed, somewhat to her surprise. "You're not. And you have a right to know." His eyes bored into hers. "I should never have taken Davey…and you." He sighed, then continued. "The night before last…when I left you…the Apaches had raided the Navaho camp and slaughtered everyone. Today…it was a ranch. Not far from here." The words came slow as if forced by sheer determination. "They're dead…along with an army patrol from Pickering's troop."

"Looking for us?" April whispered.

MacKenzie nodded. "I tried to warn them…I tried to tell them the Apaches were banding together. But they wouldn't believe a half-breed." His voice was low and bitter. "I didn't want this, none of it."

"What are you going to do now?" April asked quietly.

"I never thought the Apache would come this far north," he replied. "I thought I could find someplace safe for you." His words were tinged with a kind of pain, and April felt his quiet desperation. "I would take you back now, but you wouldn't be safe, even with Pickering's troop. There's hundreds of Apaches south of us now, and if Pickering has any sense he'll make for Defiance before they find him."

"You would take us back?" April repeated with a sort of wonder. He had said repeatedly he would not.

He gave her the slightest suggestion of a smile. "Not quite all the way," he amended. "Just far enough that they could find you and protect you. But I won't trust you and Davey to Pickering. They'll be damned lucky if they live through this."

"Then..."

"The Utes have a treaty with your father. They respect him. There's a village four days from here. Four hard days," he added, eying her speculatively. "They can get a message to Defiance."

Four days. Four more days with MacKenzie. Her clouded blue eyes met his, and she thought for the briefest moment that he, too, was savoring the idea. But no. She and Davey were nothing but burdens to him.

"I'll get ready," she said stiffly.

His hand reached out and touched her shoulder, and she felt seared by his touch. Seized by a sudden impulse to walk into his arms and be comforted, she did the opposite and jerked away, bewildered by her own action. His hand fell, and his eyes grew icy before he nodded and turned away.

MacKenzie understood her repugnance. He had promised her rest, and he was breaking that promise. He had promised her safety, and that, at the moment, was questionable. He had brought her and her son into terrible danger and subjected them to exhaustion, thirst and danger. She had every reason to despise him. But it hurt. God, it hurt.

*   *   *

By late afternoon, they were back on the trail, climbing up and up. April noticed the increased number of pines, no longer dwarfed but reaching for the sky. The streams were deeper and the temperature cooler. Afternoon became dusk, and the sky changed to a deep velvet blue that framed violet peaks haloed by moonlight and an infinite number of bright stars.

April rode with more confidence now, all the old assurance flooding back. Her muscles were adjusting themselves, and she felt a quiet joy, even in this dangerous country, in the loveliness of early night.

She looked at MacKenzie, who rode alongside her, one of his arms cradling a sleeping Davey. His body seemed relaxed although she knew his eyes were constantly moving, studying every tree, every rock. He never really rested. She was beginning to wonder if he ever slept. He had said he had last night, but she still had not seen him do so. She wondered what he would look like…asleep. Would some of that taut energy, that aura of barely leashed violence seep away? No. It was a part of him, as much as those finely honed muscles and suspicious eyes and casual elegance as he rode. April thought she had never seen anything quite as splendid as MacKenzie on a horse. There was a oneness about them, a fluidness that was very beautiful.

He turned suddenly, and his eyes met hers. The dim light made them impossible to read, but she felt them assess her, and she squared her shoulders and straightened in the saddle. She saw his mouth curve with a tenderness he usually reserved for Davey.

And she knew she would do anything for him, go any place he said. With frightening realization, she knew she didn't want the four days to end.

Chapter Eight

MacKenzie stared at the abandoned Ute campsite with something close to desperation. There was nothing remaining of the thriving camp of several months ago. He knew that the Utes were nomadic and seldom stayed in one place long, but this clan had seemed more settled than most, and when he was here five months earlier there had been no plans to follow the buffalo to the central plains.

He looked around hopelessly. They had not been gone long. The ground still showed signs of camp fires, and barren spots on the earth showed clearly where teepees recently stood. Just long enough, MacKenzie thought bitterly.

MacKenzie cursed silently to himself. It was as if fate itself was his opponent. Everything had gone wrong from the moment he had first entered the Chaco army camp. In total frustration, his right hand raked his hair before he turned and looked at Mrs. Manning and saw the question in her eyes.

He didn't have an answer. For the first time in his life, he was at a total loss. Behind him lay hostile Apaches and an army anxious to hang him. In front were the San Juan Mountains, a haven for him...but the Mannings? The mountains were treacherous even for one who knew them well; a mistake, even a minor one, could be fatal. They couldn't go back; they couldn't go forward. *The devil's playing with you for sure,* MacKenzie thought.

He dismounted. Davey had been riding with his mother this

morning. MacKenzie had wanted all his senses alert, and he had often spurred his horse ahead, making circles, checking for tracks. Nothing was as it should be. The Apaches had never come this far north before, not in his experience, anyway, and now he was beginning to wonder whether there could be some sort of alliance with the Utes. They had been allies years ago against the Comanches, but MacKenzie dismissed the idea almost immediately. The Utes had decided long before that their small number was no match for the might of the United States. They had negotiated repeatedly with military leaders, gaining concessions and land that no other tribe had been able to win. They wouldn't risk that now.

MacKenzie knew the Utes well. His mother had been Shoshone, and the Shoshone had ancient ties with the Ute. The Utes, the best horsemen of all the area tribes, respected MacKenzie's many skills. They had a common love of horseflesh, a common interest in crossbreeding. MacKenzie had, in fact, won his Appaloosa in a contest of horsemanship. It was the first time a Ute had been defeated in such a test, and the loser had challenged MacKenzie again. It was then that MacKenzie won possession of a small, lovely valley—the heart of his dream. His now dead dream.

The remainder of his hopes, now gone, sent a sudden shadow across his face and deepened his frown.

"MacKenzie?"

April's tentative question stung him back into reality. He looked up at her as she sat restlessly. His eyes were bleak as they noted her tired face, now furrowed with concern. The last four days had been torture for her, pure and simple. He had driven them relentlessly, pursued as he was by his own internal devils. It had been the only way he could keep from touching her, from quieting the want that plagued him constantly. And it had never been stronger than this minute, despite the new obstacles. Sitting on her horse now with ease, she was, to him, all that was proud and spirited and beautiful. Her back was straight, as it always was when he watched her. Her golden brown hair was twisted into one long braid that fell halfway down her back. But, as always, it was her eyes that held him. The deep clear blue of a mountain lake. Unafraid. Direct. Tired now...there were lines at the corners, but no blame or accusation clouded them. She seemed to face every hardship, ever obstacle with an uncomplaining acceptance that constantly astonished him. Yet there was fire there. He had seen it the night she pointed a gun at him, the day she defied Terrell, the afternoon she had slapped him despite her fear and exhaustion. And he had seen it constantly in her relationship with the boy. She laughed with Davey, teased him, challenged him as MacKenzie looked on with lonely, hungry eyes.

He saw something similar in the looks she furtively cast his way. He recognized the warmth in her eyes, the awakening desire, even as she tried to hide it, and it made everything more painful. He knew the mistreatment he'd suffered at Terrell's hands was nothing compared to what he was experiencing now. For he had never wanted anything as badly as April Manning, and his personal code, as well as his sanity, would not allow it. For her sake, for the boy's sake, for his own sake.

He felt a surging tenderness as he watched uncertainty wash across her face as her question went unanswered. His hands reached up for Davey. ''We'll rest here a while,'' he said, setting the boy on his feet. With one hand holding the bridle, he reached for her with the other hand. MacKenzie felt warmth flood him at her touch, and he treasured the trust inherent in it. When her feet touched the ground, his left hand left the bridle and settled on her arm, steadying her. At least that's what he told himself as his hands lingered there, unwilling to let go.

Their eyes locked, clouded, troubled gray searching blue ones suddenly alive with the electricity that sizzled between them. His hands tightened against her jacket with a need that had a life of its own. It deepened as MacKenzie saw her eager response and felt her hands on his chest, burning and searing through the shirt he wore. This was a magic he had never known before, and it made him lose the control that he had honed to an art. There was no meaning to anything but her touch, the look in her eyes and the tender smile on her lips. No one had ever looked at him like this, and he held it in his mind and locked it in his heart.

He slowly dropped his arms and backed away, his face twisting with the effort. At her look of painful confusion, his right hand went up and touched her cheek with such gentleness that April wanted to cry. It moved to cup her chin, and he lifted it until she gazed directly into his swirling thundercloud eyes.

"It cannot be," he said in a voice so low and sad that it pierced April's soul with its raw agony. "It cannot be," he repeated, as if trying to convince himself. His hand left her face, and he whirled around. He stood there alone for a moment, his hands knotting and unknotting, the muscles in his cheek throbbing as he sought to restore his self-discipline.

Tense and frightened at the sudden passion that had flamed between them, April watched as his stiff back slowly relaxed and his hands stopped their compulsive movements. She wondered at the mental strength that allowed it, for she felt caught like a butterfly on a pin by her own emotions. There was such a deep, sweet yearning inside her that she no longer cared about the consequences. She wanted only to touch him, to wipe away that loneliness she sensed in him, to feel that hard body against hers...

April closed her eyes. It was ridiculous. She had vowed not to love again, and now she was trembling like a lovesick schoolgirl over a man who had kidnapped her and her son, who was wanted for murder. *But it didn't matter. God help her, it didn't matter.* Something had happened to her in the past several days, had awakened senses dulled for so very long. Not only awakened them, but brought something new. She had loved David, but she had never felt this wild wanting that made her feel so alive.

April watched as MacKenzie took the two horses and

walked away, and she slowly, reluctantly turned toward Davey, who was happily exploring the clearing. They had climbed steadily for the past four days, and this place was nestled between the foothills and the high mountains, which seemed to reach in green and blue splendor to the sky. They had stopped just long enough to sleep and eat, MacKenzie always impatient to continue. She knew he only tolerated the pauses because of her and Davey, but he never said anything. His shortness of speech and constant tenseness said it for him.

His eyes had been as unreadable as always. Sometimes she had caught a brief change in his expression when she found him looking at her. But those times had been rare. He was, more often than not, looking any place else. She smiled now, knowing that it was not indifference that made him look away...as she first had thought.

A setting sun sent streams of gold shimmering through the trees, flooding the clearing with diffused light. The leaves of the oak and mountain mahogany were just now turning into muted shades of red and yellow and orange. April could smell the rich, spicy scent of the pine and juniper. She drank in every sight and smell, relishing them. Despite her deep weariness, she wanted to dance and sing with the simple, uncomplicated beauty of it and the wonderful, astonishing stirring of life within her. MacKenzie, in some way, had heightened all her senses, making them greedy for more.

"Davey," she called. "Let's go find MacKenzie." She was finding his name easier to say. Her lips seem to savor the sound.

They followed his path through the trees, to a deep, clear stream where he was watering the horses. She had learned the horses always came first when they established camp. Once the animals were tended, MacKenzie would then turn his efforts to a fire, or hunting, or the distribution of food.

He watched April and Davey warily as they approached. He felt as if he had given part of himself away earlier when he allowed April a glimpse of his need. But the bright joy in her face made indifference impossible, and he couldn't prevent a smile as he saw the woman and boy together, their feet barely touching the earth as they skipped over to him, their faces creased with laughter and their eyes filled with mischief and light.

"Can we stay here?" April asked with hope. "Just a little while. It's so lovely."

If all the demons in hell were after him, and MacKenzie was half convinced they were, he could not have said no. They should be safe enough here for several days. The Apache would not come this far into Ute territory, nor, he knew, would Pickering be tempted this far north, not with men dead four days back. And God knew they all needed more than the little rest they had had at the cave. He could hunt while trying to decide what next to do. Which reminded him of the impossible choices. But he would not let that spoil April's happy mood. Once more, he thought how like her name she was. Fresh and pretty and bursting with life and hope. He wondered about her husband...Davey's father. What had he been like? What had happened to him?

Like a child, April took off her boots and gingerly tried the water. She abruptly did a tiny, involuntary dance as the stream sent pinpricks of icy pain through her tired feet.

Amusement lit MacKenzie's eyes as Davey, ever curious, did the same. "It comes directly from the snow above," MacKenzie explained. "And it's deep enough not to be warmed much by the sun."

"Can we go fishing?" Davey asked hopefully. Fishing had become his joy, a private time together with MacKenzie, who made him feel very grown up.

"Aye. There should be some trout there, fat and just waiting for you. But first you can help with the horses."

"And me?" April asked. "What can I do?"

He eyed her speculatively. She must be bone tired, but she had the same eagerness to help as Davey. His breath came quickly, and he felt a lump setting in his throat. He tried, without success, to swallow and seemed, for a moment, to be suspended in time.

He could barely manage the next words, but he couldn't let her see how she affected him. "You can gather some wood for a fire and find us a good place to sleep tonight."

"Here," April said. "Right here, next to the stream." The streambed fell sharply just feet away, and she could hear the rush of water, the happy gurgling as it sped between the rocks and tumbled downward in a small fall.

Once again she saw a hint of a smile break the angular planes and hard lines of MacKenzie's face. Perhaps it was its rarity that gave it such enchantment. But everything in her warmed at the sight.

He nodded and went back to unsaddling the horses, hobbling them and rubbing them down with Davey happily assisting as far as his small size allowed. April looked at them both, her heart beating faster as she watched them work in tandem, a silent harmony between them. She watched until it hurt too much, and then she went to find wood. Even then he was still with her as MacKenzie's rich baritone voice hummed that haunting melody she had heard the first day of their strange journey.

Flames reached upward, casting eerie shadows over MacKenzie's freshly shaven face. His eyes were darker, more mysterious than ever to April, who couldn't take her eyes from him.

Davey had long ago succumbed to sleep after a day he had proclaimed the best in his whole life. He had caught several fish, with MacKenzie's assistance, and had helped clean and cook them. Pride was evident in his broad smile and tilted chin, and he hadn't stopped talking about it as the sun dipped behind a mountain in a spectacular sunset that left a warm pink glow bathing the valley. Nothing, April mused, was as pretty as a mountain sunset or sunrise. The mountains themselves changed colors as the golds and oranges and reds took their turns in framing them with first soft, then vivid tints, each more hauntingly lovely than the last.

From MacKenzie's expression, April knew he felt the same awe, although he said nothing. Their eyes met in silent appreciation, and it made her feel closer to him than ever.

She moved to the fire, seeking its heat. With the darkness came cold, and Davey was wrapped in two blankets settled on a pile of pine boughs MacKenzie had gathered for them. It would give protection from the cold ground, he explained, painstakingly working them so they would not scratch. He only shrugged when April asked why he did not do the same for himself. She guessed that he did not want to be too comfortable...that it would dull his natural wariness.

April's move toward the fire put her within inches of MacKenzie, who was staring into the flames, his face set as if carved in stone.

She reached out and touched his arm, and he drew back as if burned, his eyes meeting hers with hot intensity.

"I...I..." April said hesitantly as she met his glowering visage. "I just wanted to thank you for being so kind to Davey."

MacKenzie released a long breath, as if he had been holding it. "He's a good lad. You have reason to be proud."

It was unusual praise from MacKenzie, and April felt a wave of warm pleasure flooding her. She said nothing, not wanting to destroy the moment.

It was MacKenzie who finally spoke, and April was surprised at the quiet intensity of the question.

"His father...?" It was a question that had been plaguing him these past few days. Where was April Manning's husband? What happened to him? She had never mentioned him, yet there was a sadness in her eyes at times. He had known Wakefield's daughter had gone east, but he knew nothing else. He and the general had never indulged in a discussion of personal matters. Their contact had always been all business. It was the way MacKenzie had wanted it.

April bit her lip, and her eyes clouded. "He was killed in one of the first battles of the war...but we didn't know...not until the months after the surrender. He was just...missing. Davey never knew him."

MacKenzie felt a stab of pain, one of the few he had ever felt for another person. To have a husband killed outright was one thing, but not to know for years...

He couldn't stop the next question. "Did you love him?" Once it was out, he inwardly cursed himself. It was none of his business.

But all he saw on April Manning's face was a small, wistful smile. Her eyes met his directly. "Yes," she said softly. "I was eighteen and he was twenty-six and already a captain. He was kind and gentle and..." Her voice fell off. She was going to say strong, but now she hesitated. She had once thought so, but now she realized how dominated he had been by his family. Strange that she hadn't really understood before. Somehow MacKenzie's total self-reliance made her husband seem weak. "Yes," she said again, reassuring herself. "I loved him."

MacKenzie noted the hesitation, heard the tiny note of doubt and was surprisingly glad.

"You're just coming home now?" he questioned, once again startling himself with the need to know.

"I was," she said with that smile of mischief he had seen before. "Before I was waylaid." Her eyes twinkled with something like amusement, and he felt his heart lurch in an unfamiliar way. How very badly he wanted to explore the sweet promise that seemed to hover around her, to taste the gentleness she lavished on Davey.

As if it had a will of its own, his hard, callused hand moved toward April, touching her hand with feather lightness. He half expected her to jerk away, but she didn't, and his hand turned hers over, exploring its contours, relishing its feel. Until he felt the blisters. He drew it closer to the fire where he could see. His eyes moved to her face, and he noticed the raw red where her skin had peeled from exposure. Once again, he cursed, this time out loud.

"Why in the devil didn't you say something?" As always when he was angry, the burr was more noticeable. April had come to recognize those moments; it was usually the only way she knew something was bothering him. His facial muscles never seemed to change; nor did the tight grim line of his mouth.

"Why?" she answered simply. "We couldn't stop."

He closed his eyes. How could he have been so blind? In his headlong flight, he had completely ignored her discomfort. He thought of the several times she had inquired about his wounds...his feet, which had almost healed now, his wrists, which she had wrapped so carefully, not once but twice on this trip. He had looked, but he had not seen. Because he had not wanted to. Because it would have slowed him down.

"We could have bound them," he said, still fingering her hand as anger deepened his voice. Anger at himself, but April didn't know that. She just knew that the brief shining moment was gone, and she felt desolate. What was it about him that made her heart act in such totally unpredictable ways? She looked at his fierce expression and felt shivers run up and down her spine. Tingling, expectant shivers.

"I'm sorry," she said finally, seeking a way, any way, to break the silence.

There was complete quiet, like the stillness before a storm. His words, when they came, were as low and fierce as the first roll of thunder. "Don't ever, ever say you're sorry...not to me...never to me." He continued slowly. "My God, what I've one to you...you and the boy..." His voice faded, but like the thunder it left an echo. "Not ever," he repeated. He unwound his long-lean body and stood, his eyes for once revealing open wounds. "Not ever," he said once more, and April thought she heard a slight tremor in the sound as he swung around and disappeared into the trees.

April waited for him to return. She added wood several

times to the fire, watching it flame anew and studying the different shades of gold and red as the bright glow seemed to play and tease. There were only a few wisps of clouds in the sky and they laced the moon, whose crescent had increased in size. A week? Had it been only a week since her life and Davey's had become so intertwined with that of an outlaw? She watched as the clouds played hide-and-seek with the moon and the myriad stars that jeweled the heavens.

She remembered that first night, the night that had started it all, when one particular star seemed to wink at her with promise. She didn't know then the danger of losing her heart to a man who had no future, who wanted no attachments, who shied away from any emotion.

But those few moments together at the fire—his soft touch and his anger at her hurts—showed, if only briefly, another facet. He was not as unaffected as she thought. She had glimpsed a want and need as deep as her own, and she was determined to break the shell he had built around himself. So she waited. Even as her eyes tried to close and her head drooped, she waited. She finally lay beside the fire, still waiting until, unwillingly, her eyes closed.

MacKenzie had a purpose in leaving. Several, in fact. There was a plant, yarrow, which held a healing substance. He planned to gather enough tonight to soothe her hands, her burned face. But he would do it tomorrow. He didn't think he could be alone with her again. Not tonight. Not after seeing the warmth and desire flare in her face and feeling the responsive craving in the depth of his being. It had taken every ounce of control he had to keep from enfolding her in his arms, to keep his lips from reaching for hers.

Damn! What was happening to him? He should be thinking of flight, of how to rid himself of her instead of thinking how much he wanted her with him. With him, the outlaw. With him, the hunted.

He had never really recognized loneliness before. He had

been comfortable with his own company, with the wild things around him. He had never needed people, at least he had never believed he did. He had never wanted to depend on anyone, nor have anyone dependent on him. But now he had two, and he couldn't deny the satisfaction in providing for them, even when he did it poorly. As he had with April Manning.

Her blistered hands and burned face came back to haunt him. Why had she said nothing? Why had she not cried and pleaded like other women would have done? That, he knew, he could deal with. This stoic courage was something else altogether. And her eyes. The eyes that trusted, that searched, that...sought something he didn't have the right to give.

MacKenzie felt the chill of the wind and heard its lonely wail as it swept down from the high mountains through the trees. It would be an early winter. He could smell it. He could see it in the thickness of the animals' fur. The earlier the better. For him. But what about April? *He had to think about her in some other way. Not April. Mrs. Manning. The woman. A stranger.*

But she was that no longer. And neither was the boy. They had, in little more than a week, become part of him, and he didn't know how he could survive the rest of his life without them, without the radiance they seemed to carry with them. It had been better not knowing. For he could see hell clearly now, and it was not the fire and brimstone his father delved from the Bible. It was knowing affection and being denied it. It was feeling tenderness and having to stifle it. It was lighting a fire only to have it quenched as its first burst of warmth stretched toward him. He had devised his own hell when he had taken Davey, and now he would have to live in it.

MacKenzie was gone when April woke. He had been there. She knew that. His blanket had been spread carefully over her, and the pile of wood was substantially lower than when she had last fueled the fire. Damn him. He was like a ghost, a protective, elusive ghost.

Dawn was coloring the eastern sky with a golden haze, and a bright fiery orange sun lay close to the earth. Even so, she shivered in the cold air, despite the blanket, her jacket and riding skirt and several other layers of clothing. She wondered about MacKenzie. As far as she knew, he had only the one stolen shirt. They would need more covering if the air continued to get colder. If they stayed together. If....

Davey threw off his blankets, his hands rubbing his sleep-filled eyes. Then he searched the clearing, and April knew he sought MacKenzie. Always MacKenzie now. The Appaloosa was gone, so were the bow and arrows, but the rifle was there, leaning against a tree, and so were his saddlebags and the contents of the stolen bedroll. Protection? Had he left the rifle here for protection? She already had the pistol, tucked away in one of her own saddlebags. *He* should have it. One or the other. She felt sudden fear for him, even knowing he was the most capable, cautious man she had ever met.

She took some of the hardtack from MacKenzie's small hoard, and she and Davey chewed on it. There were several fish remaining on a string in the stream, and she supposed MacKenzie would cook them later. She suddenly wished she knew how to clean a fish, but she didn't. It was a chore always performed by her father's striker, an enlisted man paid extra to serve as a servant to officers, or, in Boston, by the cook. She had never realized quite how useless she was, not until now. She could take some pride in her riding ability, and even perhaps a few nursing skills, but that, she thought sadly, was about the extent of her accomplishments.

Davey was full of energy and eager for a walk. April shrugged off her feeling of inadequacy. MacKenzie would make anyone feel inadequate. They followed the stream for a brief time until they reached a pool shaded by mountain oaks. April sat, drinking in its cool perfection while Davey explored. His curiosity was boundless, and April enjoyed the endless chatter, thinking how much he had changed since leaving Boston, how much he had opened up. Part of it, she knew, was simply leaving Boston and its dreadful morbidity. But a larger part was due to MacKenzie. Davey had found someone to imitate, to look up to, and April was glad it was the quiet, aloof man who was so frustratingly competent at everything.

She closed her eyes but kept her ears open, listening to Davey and his little-boy sounds until they suddenly stopped. April could sense his fear even before her eyes opened, sense the menace that so completely shattered the peace.

Davey was twenty yards away, near the pool, and just feet away from him lumbered a huge brown bear, its teeth bared as it moved closer to her son, who was now frozen with fear.

The Colt. Why on earth had she left it in camp? But there was no time to think about it. "Davey," she called out softly. "Davey, move back, slowly." But he didn't hear, or couldn't obey. He just stood there, stiff, as the bear reared on his back legs and pawed the air with huge clawed feet and continued toward the boy.

April looked frantically around, her eyes finally resting on a large broken branch on the ground. She had to distract the animal, drive him away from Davey or attract him in her direction. She screamed, hoping MacKenzie would hear, hoping that the bear would turn her way, but it ignored her, all of its attention fixed on the boy.

April grabbed the branch and ran toward the great animal, all the time knowing she wasn't close enough, or strong enough, to do anything.

She didn't know what part of her recognized the hoofbeats, or how she knew instantly that it was MacKenzie. It all happened so fast, it was a blur of motion, of senses. She saw MacKenzie propel himself from the nervous, shying Appaloosa onto the bear, a knife glistening like silver in his hand. She saw the huge paws wrap around him in fury, and the knife go up, then down, and up again, no longer silver but a deep red. Suddenly everything was red. She saw the spurts of blood that washed the ground and didn't know its source...the bear or MacKenzie. *Please God, not MacKenzie.* And then the bear fell, MacKenzie with it, and with horror she saw the animal twitch in death throes while MacKenzie lay still, his body covered by one enormous paw as blood began to seep from the dozen small wounds on his body, and the huge jagged tear in his side.

Chapter Nine

April knew she had to do something, but the enormous animal was still twitching, a giant claw once more reaching mindlessly for MacKenzie, as Davey stood by in stunned terror.

She waited no longer. She reached where the two lay intertwined—the man and the bear—and with strength and determination she didn't know she had, she lifted the huge leg, crying in frustration as it landed once more on the still form beside it. She tried again, tears almost blinding her as she tugged and lifted and pulled until finally MacKenzie was free.

April went to his feet, grabbed them and pulled him away from the bear. But his weight was more than she could handle, and she could move him only inches, knowing that she was probably causing him to bleed more. But she had to get him away from the still moving animal. "Help me, damn it," she whispered desperately to him. "Help me."

MacKenzie's eyes flickered open, and the iron gray was glazed with pain. "Davey?" he said, his mouth contorting with the effort.

"He's safe." She leaned down, and tears washed her face. "Thank you. Thank you for my son."

MacKenzie relaxed, his eyes closing for a moment. "The bear?"

"Dead...dying." She didn't know exactly what; its legs were still twitching, but the eyes were empty. She paused, looking at MacKenzie's paling skin, the blood that was puddling under him. She pulled off her jacket, then her shirt and stuffed them against the wound; they were instantly soaked. "I have to stop the bleeding." Fear made her voice shaky.

His eyes remained shut, and for a moment she thought he had lost consciousness again, but then they opened, and they were clear. "You'll have to sear it."

"Cauterize?" she said with horror. She had worked in a hospital and had seen many unpleasant things. It was the reason now she could bear to see his blood. But to press white-hot metal against his torn flesh? She trembled.

"You must," he said relentlessly.

"I don't know if I can."

"You can do anything," he answered, and she knew she could. For him.

"What must I do?"

A muscle throbbed in his cheek as a new spasm of pain attacked him. "The knife...get the knife."

April shuddered. The knife was embedded in the bear. There was blood everywhere, but one look at MacKenzie's clenched teeth steeled her. Biting her lip, she approached the animal; his movement was slowing, and she had no doubt now he was dead. She saw the hilt of the knife in the region of his heart. April closed her eyes for a moment, praying for strength.

"You can do it."

She heard MacKenzie's words, and the confidence in them shamed her. It was her fault this had happened. She should not have taken her eyes from Davey. And MacKenzie would bleed to death if she didn't do something now. Her teeth piercing her lower lip, she leaned down, placing her fist around the slippery red hilt of the knife. *You can do it.* His words echoed in her mind. She pulled, and her hand slipped. She seized the knife again, this time with both hands, and pulled with all her strength, feeling it tear through muscles and tissue that didn't want to release it. And then it was free.

"Mrs. Manning!" She heard the weakening voice and realized she was still standing there, the knife in her hand, paralyzed by the horror of it.

"Mrs. Manning...my horse. Get my horse. Bring him over here."

Grateful for another order, April shook off the numbness and hurried to do his bidding. The Appaloosa was standing in the trees, half wild with the smell of bear and blood but too well trained to leave its master. Its fear was palpable, but it finally obeyed her insistent tugs. When they reached MacKenzie's side, she leaned down and gave him her hand. It seemed so fragile to her, so inadequate. But he took it, and rose shakily until his hand found his horse's neck and his arm went around it. April could feel the enormous effort it took him to move, to grasp the horse's mane.

"Go, boy," he whispered to the horse. "Help me. Back," he murmured to April. "Help me get back to the camp, to the fire..."

April pressed her shirt tightly against his side as MacKenzie let the horse's strength guide him along, his feet stumbling over the uneven ground, his face going whiter with each step. She could feel his skin growing clammy, and she grew cold at the realization. She knew what it meant. She turned around and saw Davey following, his face awash with tears and filled with guilt. Her heart died a little for him, but she couldn't comfort him now. MacKenzie needed her more.

Somehow they got back. April never really knew how, just that it was his tremendous willpower. As they neared the fire that was now little more than embers, he let go of the horse and fell to the ground, his face twisting in agony.

"The knife," he muttered. "Heat the knife."

April didn't even think now. She was caught in his urgency. She would not let him die.

She piled more wood on the fire and stuck the knife blade in the new flames, wincing at the sweet, cloying smell of burning blood. She wished she could have washed the knife first, but the fire would purify it.

April went over to MacKenzie. Davey was standing at his side, looking lost and scared. "Bring me a blanket," she told him, knowing that he also needed something to do. When Davey returned, she folded it and put it under MacKenzie's head. MacKenzie was holding the shirt close to his wound with his right hand, and Davey put his hand into the scout's left one.

MacKenzie suddenly knew a new fear, that he might crush the tiny fingers when the pain flared anew. He tried to smile at Davey, but it was more a grimace. He deciphered the boy's guilt-ridden face.

"It wasn't your fault," he whispered. "You can do something for me."

Davey's smudged, tear-stained face looked questioning.

"Find me a stone...a big, round, smooth stone. Can you do that?"

The boy nodded, releasing MacKenzie's hand as he ran to find the perfect stone. He didn't know why MacKenzie wanted a stone, but Davey was determined his friend would have the best there was.

MacKenzie saw April watching him as she waited for the knife to heat, and he met her gaze directly. He didn't want her to see his weakness; she needed what strength he could give her. He knew she could do what had to be done, but he also knew how difficult it would be for her. Her heart was too gentle for the agony she would be forced to inflict, but there was no choice. He had seen a core of iron in her that he doubted she yet totally realized. She was so much stronger than she knew.

"A piece of wood...I need a piece of wood to bite on."

April searched the ground with her eyes, glad of the momentary diversion. She found a branch, an inch in thickness, and broke off a piece. She handed it to MacKenzie wordlessly.

"The knife should be ready." His voice was expressionless, and April trembled, wondering how on God's good earth she could do what he was asking.

"You must." It was as if he were reading her doubts. "I'll bleed to death if you don't." He could feel the blood leaking from him, saturating the cloth that held the wound together.

April forced herself back to the fire. The steel was glowing white hot in the flames. She tore a piece of cloth from her riding skirt and reached down to pick up the handle, feeling it scorch her skin even through the layer of cloth. But the pain was minor next to what she knew was coming.

Davey was back, pressing something into MacKenzie's hand. She heard MacKenzie's weakening voice. "Help me hold it, Davey. Help me hold it, and close your eyes with me."

In that moment, she knew she loved MacKenzie. Even seconds away from a torment she knew would be terrible, he was more concerned about her son and his feelings than his own coming ordeal. It made her stronger, and she approached him with determination. She kneeled beside him, on the opposite side of Davey, and took the cloth from the deep, jagged tear, flinching as she saw torn muscle and tissue.

His gray eyes met hers, and he nodded, ready, his teeth now clamped on the piece of wood, his hand, with Davey's small one tightly covering it, clutching the stone.

She willed her shaking hands to be firm as she pressed the knife to the raw, gaping opening, feeling his compulsive jerk and hearing his soft, low moan as if it were a scream. She held the knife steady, searing the wound, shivering at the sound of sizzling skin and the stench of burning flesh. There was another jerk of his body, and then he fell back, and she blessed the unconsciousness that relieved him of pain. For now. When he woke again, it would be bad, very bad.

"Live, MacKenzie," she ordered. "Live."

Then she was aware of Davey again. His eyes were still closed, as MacKenzie had asked, but his face was pinched with misery and hurt.

April pried his fingers from MacKenzie's still hand. "Take the cups, Davey, and get some water for me. And this…" She unwrapped the torn cloth from her hand and gave it to him. "Wet this, so we can wash him."

Davey stood still before her. "Will MacKenzie be all right?" His lower lip quivered, and his eyes were swimming with tears.

"Yes, love, he'll be all right."

Davey wanted to believe. He looked at the pale face of the man. "It's my fault."

April took him in her arms, her hands stroking his dark hair, comforting. "No, love. It wasn't your fault. It was nothing you did. And he *will* be all right. I promise you."

The tears fell then, in huge torrents, and April felt the wetness in her own. She didn't even think it strange that she and Davey felt so strongly about this aloof man they had known little more than a week. It seemed a lifetime now. When Davey's tears were spent, she straightened. "Some water, Davey. He'll need some when he wakes."

Entrusted with doing something for MacKenzie, Davey obeyed, and April sat and stared at the scout while keeping one eye on her son.

It was the first time she had seen MacKenzie still. Thick black lashes shielded his eyes, and a lock of midnight black hair fell over his forehead. Tight lines of pain still controlled his face, and she wondered if she would ever see it relaxed. If she would ever see him smiling. Her hand went to his face, exploring its strong lean contours, trying to smooth the hard, uncompromising lines. His usually bronze skin was almost pale. His brow was clammy to the touch and wet with sweat. How could anyone lose so much blood and live? She knew a fierce protectiveness. "You have to live," she whispered. "There's so much for you to discover. Laughter and love, and peace. I know you don't believe it now. But there is. And I'll help you find it. We'll find it together."

When the knife touched his skin, MacKenzie felt his whole body arch with an agony so fierce he felt he was being torn apart. He was alive with fire, with pain greater than any he had ever felt. His fingers squeezed the stone until they were white; the fingers on the other hand dug into the earth with a frantic clawing movement. His teeth clamped down on the wood, stopping a scream that came from deep within him. Shadows came and went, a blessed darkness hovering just beyond them, but while part of him called out for oblivion, another part fought it. He needed his senses about him, the woman and boy needed them. But as he struggled to remain conscious, fought desperately against the weakness, he felt himself slipping irretrievably into a blurred haziness, then blackness. He carried with him the whisper of a soft voice, a promise buried some place deep inside him...

When he struggled to the surface of consciousness, MacKenzie thought he was again being consumed by fire. He fought against the heat that beaded his body in sweat and struggled against hands that tried to keep him still. His side was a torment where great swells of agony competed, each one greater than the one before. When his eyes finally opened, he saw April's weary, worried face.

"How long...?"

"Several hours," she said, and she flinched as she saw the ravages of pain in his face.

"I've got to..." MacKenzie tried to move, but fell back.

"You've got to do nothing but rest. We need you too badly to have you die on us." The last was accompanied by a small, tired smile. She sensed it was the only reason that would mean anything to him.

MacKenzie fell back, recognizing the sense of her words. Besides, he was too weak to do anything else. The heat turned into cold. Shivers shook his body, and he silently raged against his helplessness as the woman covered him with all their blankets and fueled the fire. He could only lie there, too weak to help, to make even a minor protest. Her clothing was still covered with blood, and her face was lined with worry. Yet there was a new strength and confidence about her that made her truly beautiful. Another wave of pain attacked him, starting in his side and forking throughout his body. And the heat came back, terrible, racking waves of heat that sucked the moisture from his body. He threw off the blankets, unable to bear their suffocating weight. The movement stoked the pain until he was drowning in it. Until, once more, he was falling, falling into a dark abyss of nothingness.

MacKenzie drifted in and out of consciousness, going from bouts of fever to racking shivers, never quite gaining complete rationality. April kept Davey going back and forth to the stream, filling their coffee cups with water as she sponged the scout's fevered body, then covered it with blankets when the icy cold attacked him. Day disappeared into evening, and still he seemed no better. If anything, he seemed even paler and more disoriented.

April's fear grew as the hours sped by and he grew worse. They were running low on food; the stolen rations were enough for perhaps one or two days longer. She had the rifle and pistol, but she had never tried to shoot game, only stationary targets. And even then she wouldn't know how to clean them. Once again, she cursed her own ignorance of the most rudimentary skills of survival.

And she couldn't leave the man on the ground. Not even for a few moments. Several times he had thrashed around in pain and fever, and she had to use her whole body to restrain him before he reopened the wound. He mumbled frequently but rarely could she understand him. The burr was now so thick as to make his words incomprehensible.

As she washed his face once more, she realized how very little she knew about him, how tightly he kept to himself. She didn't know where he came from, or what he wanted, or why he was with the army he seemed to despise and distrust. She didn't know what had carved those hard lines in his face, or what happiness he had had. Or if he had loved. Especially if he had loved.

Only once did she comprehend his words, and then they

were filled with a pain not born of his wounds. "It's women and children...only women and children...God damn you to hell...let me go, damn you. Let me go..."

Once more, he moved violently, as if trying to escape bonds. April tried to quiet him, her hands forcing him to the ground, her desperation making her strong enough to pin him down, her soft, soothing words somehow quieting him. When he stilled, April found his face wet once more, but this time from her own tears. There was so much pain in him. For all his strength and outward impassivity, there was so much pain...

MacKenzie woke to the first tenderness he had ever known.

He felt her hand against his cheek, and he didn't want it to leave, so his eyes remained shut as he carved the sensation in his mind.

And then he cursed himself for the weakness—even as he continued to hesitate to move and lose that precious contact.

His head pounded and his side throbbed, and he felt as weak as a newborn babe. But something wonderful and new surged in him as *her* touch, so light in its gentleness, caressed and loved and soothed. He could stand it no longer, and his eyes opened. Her face was right over his, and the wide, lake-blue eyes were filled with an emotion he had not seen before.

"MacKenzie," she said, and the sound was full of magic for him, so caring, so wistful.

He tried to answer, but no words came. He was confused, his world whirling around him. There was something in him that warred with his natural caution, with the protective walls he had constructed over the years. He tried to move, and once more pain and weakness stopped him. Baffled by his own feelings, by a vulnerability that appalled him, he retreated behind his old facade of detachment.

"How do you feel?" April asked, sensing his silent struggle for control. It had been a day and a half, and his color was better, and she knew now he would live. She felt his intense gaze, and she wanted to shrivel up inside as she thought how she must look. She had seen something in his face when he first woke, when his eyes opened, but it had quickly faded. Now his eyes were assessing, questioning, with no hint of anything more.

He tried to lift himself with one arm, but fell back.

"I'm so damned weak," he said, almost in condemnation of himself. He looked at the wound on his side. It was red and puckered and raw but already beginning the healing process. "You did well," he said, and the words restored her pride as nothing else could.

"I was so afraid," she admitted slowly. "I was so afraid you were going to die."

There was a bare, painful shadow of a smile on his lips. "I think I would have without you... I remember..." He stopped. What did he remember? Bits and pieces of images, a will stronger even than his own. Once again, he tried to move, succeeding only a little before waves of nausea and pain forced him down again.

"The boy?"

"He's been helping. Getting water. Getting firewood." April hesitated, then added, "Praying."

MacKenzie's eyes closed. There was a sweet hurt at her words. And guilt. A terrible, stabbing guilt. He had placed them, both of them, in terrible danger. They should feel anger, hate even, and yet they had given him loyalty and care and even affection. He didn't understand. He didn't understand at all.

And that made him angry. When he opened his eyes, they were fierce and forbidding, the tenuous bond between him and the woman sliced coldly...at least he thought so. But April saw the brief confusion and, with new awareness, understood his fear. Just as she understood there was now something between them that could never be broken—no matter how hard he tried. And that he *would* try, she knew and accepted. It would be, she knew, a battle of wills. And with determination forged from a strength she was just beginning to realize, April Wakefield Manning decided it was a battle she would win.

Chapter Ten

General Ira Wakefield's voice was deceptively gentle.

Only his adjutant, Bob Morris, suspected the fury behind it and felt a fleeting sympathy for the young lieutenant who, he knew, would be on his knees before he left this office.

"Tell me again," Wakefield said. "Tell me everything. From the beginning. From the time MacKenzie reached Chaco."

Wakefield didn't have to be told. He already knew everything, or almost everything. Every damning, mismanaged thing. He had personally interviewed each man on Pickering's detail from Chaco, and had had an earlier session with Pickering himself. Even then, he knew the lieutenant was conveniently omitting important details.

He knew because it was entirely incomprehensible that MacKenzie was responsible for the crimes he was charged with. Except for his flight—given reason enough. Wakefield was fully aware of the scout's distrust of the military. He had been burned once before. And if half of what was finally wormed out of Pickering's men was true, Wakefield could well understand MacKenzie's escape. But he couldn't accept the rest of it: the accused rape, the murder, the kidnapping of his daughter and grandson. MacKenzie had always steered clear of trouble, even, at times, at the cost of his very strong pride. The scout had something stronger driving him. The only time Wakefield had known MacKenzie to react violently was when an army detachment had massacred an Indian village of mainly women and children. Despite the scout's aloofness and almost fanatical independence, Wakefield had always felt he harbored a deep, unspoken compassion for the weak and victimized.

Rape? Impossible. Murder? Also impossible...unless it was to save his own life. Kidnapping? A woman and child? Unlikely. Unless he felt forced, and even then Wakefield doubted it. At least he had until he heard how MacKenzie had been chained to a wagon and dragged across desert lands. Wakefield's hands balled up in quiet rage as he listened to Pickering's faltering explanation.

"Let me understand," he asked in the same quiet tone. "My scout told you Apaches were massing, and you ignored it."

"Sergeant Peters said he was lying, sir."

"And you, in your youthful wisdom, thought I would employ a scout who wasn't to be trusted?"

Pickering felt the sword point in his gut. "No...no sir, but..."

"And so instead of heeding his warning, you saw fit to drag *my* scout across the desert without food or water...in front of women and a child."

"He raped..."

"He was accused, Lieutenant," Wakefield interrupted. "Accused. But even if he was guilty, we don't treat prisoners that way. Especially my men, my scouts."

Pickering was white now. "But Sergeant Terrell..."

"Tell me, Lieutenant, was Sergeant Terrell in command?"

"I...I..."

"I understand," Wakefield added, "that MacKenzie was never meant to arrive here. Alive, anyway."

"That's not true. I gave strict orders..."

"So it *was* by your orders that MacKenzie was treated as he was."

"No, sir."

"No? Make up your mind, Lieutenant. Because I damn well want to know what fool caused ten of my men to be slaughtered by Apaches and allowed this whole territory to go up in flames because he was too goddamned arrogant to listen.

"And," he added, his voice deadly quiet, "I want to know how my daughter and grandson disappeared from your camp. And why."

"MacKenzie..."

Wakefield visibly had to control himself. He had never wanted to hit a man so badly in his career. "You fool...you stupid, bumbling fool. I'm going to see you're assigned to the worst hellhole in this army. Now get out of here before I do something I regret."

Pickering needed no urging. His hand, when he saluted, was shaking. Wakefield did not return the salute but merely glared at him.

When the door closed behind him, Captain Morris turned to Wakefield. "What now, sir?"

"The girl and Terrell have already pressed charges. I don't have any choice but to file them. And send a detail after MacKenzie...and my daughter and Davon."

"Why do you think MacKenzie took them? It doesn't make sense."

"You're right, Bob. It doesn't. I think I know him better than anyone. Or as well as he'll allow anyone to know him. I just can't believe he would hurt April in any way."

"Unless he's turned completely loco."

"MacKenzie? Never."

"But if he was goaded enough...?"

Wakefield turned toward the window and stared at the desert that stretched endlessly before him. His voice was tortured when he finally spoke again.

"He didn't want to return to the army, but I convinced him things would be different, that Elbow Creek wouldn't be repeated. Damn, I need him. Especially now with this new outbreak." He paused. "Bob, I know it's not your job, but you know him. Maybe you can talk to him. Take a company. Try to find him. Try the cabin in that valley of his. I doubt if he goes there...he knows we're aware of it, but it's a beginning. Find April and Davon. And take MacKenzie alive!''

"If I can't?"

"Just do it, Bob. Do it."

"If he's guilty...or even if he's not...he may not give me a choice."

"The girl's lying. I can see it in her eyes. And Terrell's lying. And while you're gone, I'm damn well going to prove it. Tell him that."

Morris studied his commanding officer carefully. Wakefield had been a different person since hearing that April and Davon were coming. There had been a new spring to his step, a happy gleam in his eyes. Now they were gone, and there was only a deep weariness. "Yes, sir," he said. "I'll try my damndest."

Wakefield acknowledged the words with a brief salute, then turned back to the window. "Bring them back, Bob. The three of them."

April swallowed, trying to keep back the bile that kept rising in her throat. Her fist clutched the knife.

There is no choice, she told herself. The bear was lying there, and they needed food. The salt pork was gone, and only hardtack remained, scarcely the best diet for one who had lost so much blood.

MacKenzie had tried to rise again this morning, but could manage only several steps before paling to a pasty white and falling. April had scolded him, asking if he was going to complete what the bear had failed to. She used the only argument that had ever worked with him. "We need you too badly."

MacKenzie tried to argue. They needed food. But when he tried once more to move, his legs collapsed under him, and he went tumbling down, wincing at the new pain in his side. His eyes smoldered with frustration, and April once more felt the now familiar ache inside her. He was not a man used to helplessness, nor one to depend on another. But he was forced by his own body to do so. And he despised himself for it. She wanted to tell him it was nothing to be ashamed of. God knows, he had done far more than any other man could have when he attacked the bear. But she knew that meant little to him.

The bear! As much as the thought appalled her, she knew it offered what they needed most at the moment: meat.

She waited until he went to sleep, found the knife and went the nearly half mile to the bear.

She reluctantly approached the dead beast. It smelled even worse than it had three days ago. She had been told no animal smelled quite like a bear, and now she believed it.

It was not only the bear smell, but the added odor of dried blood. MacKenzie's and the bear's. She swallowed again.

Davey was with MacKenzie. Thank God for that, anyway. She finally reached the animal and stooped. She still remembered how it had twitched, and she halfway expected that it would come to life and take a swipe at her.

Where to start? The fur was thick and matted. For a moment, she wished she knew how to skin and cure it for it looked enormously warm, but that was out of the question. She would be doing very well if she could just carve a piece of meat from it. Something already had, she noticed, shivering with horror and distaste as she noticed rips in its body. She wondered if she was truly grateful that something was left.

The haunch. She knew about that. If only she could reach it. The stench would have emptied her stomach had there been anything in it. She wondered if she could, indeed, force herself to eat any bear meat at all. But perhaps it wouldn't be so bad cooked.

The bear was half on its side, and there was a part that looked untouched. She moved the knife, closing her eyes as it entered in flesh. She hacked and cut, not knowing quite what she was getting, until she freed a chunk of meat. She went deeper, trying to get some without fur attached, her stomach rebelling at every additional slice. At one point, she had to retreat to the trees where she kneeled over and retched what little there was inside her. Then she started to work again. It seemed like hours before she had three relatively large pieces of meat.

She cut them in smaller chunks and put them in the old jar that MacKenzie had found in the cave days earlier. She would add some water and wild onions and let it cook on the fire. She knew from watching MacKenzie how to build a little platform over the flames.

April retreated from the bear, hoping she would never have to see it again. It was far enough away from the camp that predators could feast without fear of humans. She hoped that this meat would be edible, but the Lord knew it wouldn't be in several more days. If she had to, she would go hunting. She wasn't quite sure how desperate she would have to be to kill something. More desperate, certainly, than she had to be to carve on a dead bear. As revolting as that was. Or perhaps she could fish. Except she didn't know how to clean fish. It couldn't be any worse than butchering the bear.

She couldn't ignore the sense of accomplishment. She had done the unthinkable. And she had done other things in the past three days, things she never thought herself capable of. In addition to searing MacKenzie's wound, she had washed the man nearly from head to toe, neglecting only his most private parts. Severe injury had shut many of his systems down, and there had been no need yet for anything horribly personal. But she had washed the sweat from his body and had made him a sort of rough shirt.

MacKenzie, she had told him with a small smile, was very hard on shirts. The last one had been torn to shreds by the bear.

And April did know how to sew. Even if she had no needle to sew with. She painstakingly used a knife to make laces from the torn shirt, and cut a new covering for MacKenzie from one of the blankets, using the remainder to make a coat for

Davey. She punched holes in the heavy, rough material and fastened the material with the laces. The garments were not very attractive and definitely not stylish, but they accomplished their purpose: they provided warmth.

MacKenzie had, predictably enough, protested. They would need the blankets. But she ignored him, knowing he was too weak to fight her on this. He had to have some kind of covering on his upper body.

She had done other things. She had found the yarrow plant MacKenzie described and, following his instructions, made a salve, which she smoothed on his wounds and on her own blistered hands. The Utes had used it for years, he told her.

And she had kept the fire going, even through the cold nights, and washed the blood from her clothes and from MacKenzie's deerskin trousers. He had protested again, but she insisted, turning her head as Davey helped him pull off his knee-high moccasins and then the trousers stiff with dried blood. When she turned back to him, his lower body was covered by a blanket, his eyes once more full of confusion...

She understood his confusion, for she was full of it herself. If anyone had told her a month ago she would be hacking her own dinner from a dead animal, or bathing a man wanted for rape and murder, she would have thought them entirely insane. She wasn't aware of the soft smile on her face as she thought of MacKenzie's hard, bronzed chest. She had washed it, wiping the blood from the many cuts and scratches while he was unconscious. It had given her time to admire his body without his knowledge. Even with its numerous wounds and the blackened, raw burn, it had been quite magnificent...broad, strong shoulders and upper chest corded with muscles before tapering to a lean, rock-hard waist. Her eyes had wandered further down, to the tight deerskin that molded the strong legs, the lean hips.

April felt the heat rise in her again as she recalled every contour of his body. They were well set in her mind, even as she chastised herself for such thoughts. Think about the bear meat, she told herself. But still she couldn't control the sweet wild blaze within her as she triumphantly approached him with her offering.

MacKenzie, who had awakened while she was gone, couldn't help but smile when he saw her. She looked like a lioness bringing its family dinner, her chestnut hair sparkling in the sunlight like a tawny mane. Davey looked at the jar quizzically.

"Bear meat," she announced in reply to both their unspoken questions.

She watched as the disbelief in his eyes turned to appreciation, then pride. His face gentled. "That must have been very difficult for you."

"I wasn't very good at it," she admitted shyly. "But it should make some soup. I thought about trying to shoot a rabbit, but..."

"It's never easy to kill," he said, in the same gentle, almost tender voice. "Especially the first time. In fact, for some, it's always hard—even when there's no choice. It's not weakness...it's respect."

April knew from the fleeting cloud in his eyes that he meant himself as well as her, and those few words told her more about him than a book. That he had said them to *her* meant even more. He was telling her he *trusted* her to understand, and that, she knew, was a rare gift indeed. Her heart twisted and melted like wax over a flame. A peculiar tingling numbness paralyzed her body as her eyes met his and the now familiar electric currents flowed and flamed between them.

She finally forced herself away from him and made a little platform over the fire. She felt his constant appraisal as she divided the meat, keeping some in the jar for her broth and placing the rest on a spit over the fire. When she looked up, her eyes locked with his, and she felt they could almost consume each other in the blast of heat that exploded between them.

"MacKenzie?" April's voice hung in the air like the soft

song of a hummingbird, and it was full of questions he couldn't answer.

"MacKenzie," she repeated. "What are we going to do? Where are we going to go?"

He didn't miss the implication of her words. It was no longer "you" but "we." He felt an infinite sadness growing within him, a tender yearning for something that was being offered but that could never be. He tore his eyes from her, and turned to Davey, who was, self-importantly, gathering pine needles and small twigs for the fire.

"Mrs. Manning," MacKenzie started.

"April," she insisted.

"Mrs. Manning..." It was a test of wills, and they both knew it...just as they knew the unspoken reasons behind it.

"It won't work, you know that. It doesn't change anything...whatever name you call me."

"I don't know what you mean," he lied, a muscle throbbing in his cheek.

He flinched inwardly at her look of disbelief. He had never been a coward before, nor had he consciously lied to anyone or, more importantly, to himself. MacKenzie turned away from the challenge in her probing eyes.

"I need...we need...to leave tomorrow," MacKenzie said, trying to reestablish the old lines of captor and captive, trying to stoke the resentment he knew she had had in the beginning, even as he knew they were far beyond that now. How had it ever gotten so turned around?

That she knew what he was doing was obvious. That he was failing miserably was equally obvious. It was in the lovely eyes that made him weaker than any loss of blood. They were more dangerous than all the Apaches, all the troops they had left behind.

Davey's small voice piped up. "I'm hungry," he complained, and MacKenzie blessed the interruption. His voice struggled for balance as he watched April take a piece of meat from the fire, smiling as Davey grimaced when he took the first taste. But he ate it. They all ate the rancid but nourishing meat, each quiet as they struggled to keep it down.

April said no more, but the determined tilt of her chin as she sat stubbornly chewing the terrible meat told MacKenzie it was only a momentary surrender.

There was no chance to speak later. The pile of firewood was rapidly disappearing, and the wind, howling now through the top of the trees, signaled another cold night. They had no ax and were completely reliant on fallen branches and pieces of decaying trees that had fallen to disease or lightning. April and Davey struggled during most of the afternoon to pile bits and pieces, knowing they would disappear rapidly in the greedy flames.

Later in the afternoon, they all had some of April's soup. It was a little better than the roasted meat, because some of the bitter taste was disguised by sweet wild onions. Restored slightly by the food, MacKenzie, leaning on April for support, managed to reach the stream where a pool promised fish. With a hook he had fashioned from a piece of metal on his saddle, he fished while the Mannings sought wood. Davey had, quite efficiently, found him some fat worms at the base of a cottonwood. He leaned against a tree trunk, willing strength into his body. The blanket shirt itched, but its warmth felt good in the increasingly cold air.

He turned his attention toward the pool. It was vital that they have more food. If he could catch enough fish, they could smoke some and carry them for the next several days. But where? They couldn't stay here much longer. He wondered if Pickering had reached Defiance yet and, if so, whether Wakefield had taken to the trail himself. He doubted it. If nothing else, Wakefield was a very competent commander, and with the territory aflame with Apache raids, his first duty would be to quiet the frontier. Even his daughter and grandson would come second, as painful as that might be. But he would send someone; of that, MacKenzie had no doubt. Probably Morris.

Morris had visited MacKenzie's valley once with Wakefield. That would be the first place they would look. The thought did not comfort him. Morris was a damned good officer, which was why he was Wakefield's adjutant. Wakefield did not tolerate inefficiency or failure.

MacKenzie knew they did not know about his father's cabin. He had never talked of it, nor had he ever mentioned his father to Wakefield. It had been an omission made partly because of his father's obsession for privacy, and partly because it was something MacKenzie did not care to remember or divulge. His origins were no one's business but his own. Out of duty, he had made the journey to the cabin twice a year, bringing flour, coffee, sugar and oats for the one horse his father kept. His father had been old, too old for the kind of life required of him on his mountaintop. The last time MacKenzie had climbed the mountain, he had found his father dead, an ax in his hand.

The line in his hand jerked, and MacKenzie was startled back to the present. He slowly pulled in the string, feeling the heavy weight fighting the hook. It was a game fish, he thought, wishing he had the choice of letting it go. He knew how it felt to be trapped, to be pulled inexorably against one's will. He knew why he had never taken up trapping, like his father. He felt too strongly about life, about its value, to kill wild things for coin.

There was something inherently satisfying about a morning frost glistening like pearls in the rays of an early sun, MacKenzie reflected as he baited the hook and returned it to the water. The smell and taste and sound of a cold clear mountain stream, the beauty of a canyon wall struck by the rosy glow of twilight. The images once more stirred regret. Nowhere were they more lovely than in his valley.

Instantly, his decision was made. They had time. He would visit the valley once more. There was more than one reason, more than his need to see it again. There were blankets there, and tools, and clothing. And they were in need of all three.

Perhaps he could even leave April and Davey there, knowing
that someone would be along soon. But the thought fled instantly. He could never leave them without protection, even
for a few hours. And he was just guessing about Wakefield's
moves. What if he didn't send anyone, what if he couldn't?
Or what if the Apaches killed the detachment? No, he could
not leave them alone.

But neither could he keep them with him. It was too dangerous for them—and for himself. He was much too susceptible to his emotions when they were around. He was already
afraid they were dulling his instincts, clouding his judgment.

Amos! Perhaps the answer was Amos Smith, an old des-
perado who had been his father's only friend. Like many
mountain men, the old man worshiped women and children.
Amos had fled some deep trouble in the past, but he never
spoke of it. When MacKenzie had left his father's cabin,
Amos had become Rob MacKenzie's one link to the outside
world, trading his furs for occasional food staples and other
goods. Amos frequently traded with the Utes, and from his
cabin word about April could be passed to General Wakefield.
He would never reveal the whereabouts of Rob MacKenzie's
cabin, and the woman and boy would be safe with him. Safer
than with himself, MacKenzie thought, as he remembered the
passion that had flared earlier between April and himself.

When April and Davey returned, MacKenzie was exhausted, but he had eight cleaned fish beside him. April could
feel the gnawing hunger rumbling in her stomach. Proud as
she had been of the bear meat, it had been truly awful, and
she had not looked forward to finishing it.

The smell of sizzling fish made April's mouth water. She
sniffed appreciatively as the bite of the wind caused her and
Davey to move closer to the fire.

After resting for a little while, MacKenzie insisted on taking
over care of the fire despite April's protests, and he was keeping it low while the fish cooked. In one corner, he had spread

the ashes, covering them with the extra fish, wrapped in water-soaked leaves, to smoke.

The sunset was even more spectacular than usual this evening, April observed with delight, as a host of clouds diffused the light into layers of brilliant color. Billowy puffs of white moved with purpose across the vast expanse as the daylight faded into the indigo gloom of the pines that covered the mountains rising to the north.

The stream next to them was almost alive, with flashes of gold and silver shimmering over its surface, and its bank on the opposite side was scarlet with patches of poison oak and Virginia creeper.

April felt humble in the midst of so much natural beauty and knew a hardly bearable joy at being here…sharing such magnificent riches with her son. And MacKenzie. She looked at the silent, intent man next to her. As their eyes met, she knew he was sharing the same tender anguish. It was evident he loved these hills and canyons and mountains. Her heart swelled with the knowledge, with his closeness, with the warmth she felt radiate from him.

All her senses were so alive. The air was pure and clean, and pungent with the smell of smoke and the surrounding pine. The silence was interrupted only by the sizzle of their dinner and the chirping sounds of grasshoppers. April knew at that moment there was no place she would rather be, no other person she would ever need. MacKenzie. He was so different from any man she had ever met: so quiet, so sure of himself, so at home in this world of color and challenge. So very alone.

April felt a shiver of fear. She had vowed never to give her heart again, and now it was offered quite openly and without shame to a man who had given no indication that he wanted it. To a man whose future was dubious at best. Was she willing to risk not only her own life but Davey's future as well? Was she willing to risk more years of fear and hurt and waiting?

Davey crawled into the crook of MacKenzie's left arm, and his dark head settled on MacKenzie's shirt as the small face looked up at the scout and asked a question. April saw pain flash across the man's face as the boy accidentally touched his wound, but it was gone instantly, as he bent down to answer. April watched the two together, Davey boyishly eager and MacKenzie murmuring softly in her ear. Her heart seemed to explode with sweet pain, and she knew she would risk anything, everything, to stay with this man.

In the next several days MacKenzie's strength slowly returned, though the wound remained ugly and raw. April would see it when he applied the yarrow salve; he would not let her do it. He would, in fact, let her do very little although he showed her how to clean fish, and she took over that small chore. She hadn't been able to make him rest nearly as much as she thought he should; he fished in the morning and had even gone hunting, bringing back two rabbits. He had been his usual reticent self, and any attempt at conversation on her part met mostly with a yes or no.

But his mere presence and the chance to watch him grow stronger were enough for the time being. April's eyes rarely left him when he was in camp, and Davey was his shadow.

The nights were growing colder, and the three of them usually stretched, like wagon spokes, from the fire, feet closest to its warmth. Davey and she shared two blankets, and MacKenzie took one and that only at her threat that if he didn't, she wouldn't use her two.

April seldom slept well. She was constantly tormented by her need for MacKenzie. She was at a loss about how to cope with it, particularly when he was so careful to keep his distance.

It was the fifth night since the bear attack when she first heard the wolf. Its lonely, long howl woke her from her usual troubled sleep. Davey was lying next to her, and they were both wrapped together in blankets against the cold. April blessed the pine boughs that made a fine mattress and kept them from the cold ground.

The howl came once more, joined by another. She was grateful Davey slept through the fearsome sound, amazed once more at the child's ability to sleep through almost anything.

Her slight movement alerted MacKenzie, who was once more piling wood on the fire. "There's naught to worry," he assured her with a soft burr. "They won't come near a fire."

"I haven't heard them before..."

"It's the weather...they feel winter coming."

"Winter? It's only September." Or was it October? She had lost all track of time.

"It often comes early in these mountains," he said with his usual brevity.

"When...?"

"Soon," he said. "I can almost smell it." He hesitated. "I want to see you safe...before it comes. We'll leave in the morning."

"Where?"

"There's a cabin in a...valley one day's ride from here."

April caught the momentary hesitation in his voice before he said "valley," and she wondered what it meant, but she had no time to think about it, for he was continuing.

"We can get some supplies there, some warmer clothes."

"And then?" April held her breath.

"There's a man in the mountains...you will be safe with him, and he can get word to your father."

April gently unwrapped herself from the blanket, careful not to disturb her son. She sat up and huddled near the fire. "I want to stay with you." She kept her face averted from his. She hadn't meant to say the words, not yet. They were muffled as she bit her lips against them. But she could withhold them no longer.

There was a long silence, and April was both afraid that he had understood her words...and that he hadn't.

She heard his deep sigh and then the infinite sadness in his voice as he answered her with regret.

"It cannot be."

"You don't want us?" Once more, April hadn't meant to say the words, but the hurt was suddenly too deep.

Again the silence seemed to stretch into hours, and she didn't think he would respond.

She couldn't miss the pain in his voice when he finally replied, and it sent ripples of anguish through her body.

"I will be hunted... I'll not have you and the boy hunted with me."

There was finality in the words, but April couldn't stop. She had already gone too far. "I don't care."

"But I do... I'll not have anything happen to you."

"Davey loves you." It was her last weapon.

Again there was a silence, and his jaw hardened with purpose. His words, when they finally came, were obviously painful. "He'll ha' no chance wi' me."

The Scottish pronunciation told her something about how much the statement cost him. She had discovered it only surfaced when he was deeply disturbed about something. She had kept her head down, avoiding his eyes as she'd so clumsily declared herself, but now she looked directly at him. His face, lean and handsome in the flickering firelight, was tormented, and his eyes, when the light hit them, seemed to hold a need as vast as her own.

Her hand went to his, partially covering its hard leatherlike surface. Her fingers stroked his, seeking their warmth, compulsively needing to touch some part of him. She turned his hand over until his palm was toward her and studied its callused strength with her fingers. Bringing it to her face, she pressed it against her cheek in a gesture of complete surrender, of infinite tenderness, and felt the wild desire rushing through her veins.

MacKenzie grew rigid as her soft caress ignited blazes more painful than that of the knife days earlier. The gentleness of her touch and all it represented filled him with a desolation larger than the barrenness of the great desert. He knew he should take his hand away before he was lost, but the velvet feel of her cheek transfixed him. He had no will as she moved his hand to her lips and he felt their soft touch. Without words, she was proclaiming her love for him, offering him everything she had without condition or expectation.

MacKenzie felt he was drowning in their combined need, and his body coiled like a tight spring as he struggled for restraint. But still he left his hand in hers, unable to tear it from her. Her touch was hypnotizing. Her lips were incredibly sweet as they spoke silently of a heaven he'd never suspected existed.

Both were barely aware of the fire, which crackled and flamed against the midnight-blue sky. The moon was laced by clouds, and only a slight streak of silver was visible. But April and MacKenzie were oblivious. Nothing mattered except each other, and the sensuous cry of their bodies, the silent scream of fettered emotions.

With a tremor that shook his entire being, MacKenzie turned her hand with his captured one and gently guided it to his side. Unable to help himself as he searched her wistful, longing eyes, he pulled her close, cupping her face with his free hand.

"If it were otherwise..." But what he was about to say was stopped, for her lips were near his, and he could no longer resist their promise. His mouth met hers with a gentleness that was almost ethereal as he savored the first taste of her. Their lips explored, teased, caressed until they both felt maddened, and the gentleness turned to hunger...insatiable hunger as each sought more and more of the other. More to hold. More to keep. More to remember.

MacKenzie's tongue entered the delectably soft mouth, feeling sensations he had never known before, feeling his heart welling with tenderness. He had never made love before, had only taken—quickly—relief for his body. He had never touched like this, or been touched, had never known the millions of pinpricks of fierce desire that could torture a body with exquisite pain. And the soul.

He felt the limits of his knowledge fall away, and the ground become a large pit in which he was falling in great spiraling circles. He reached for safety, but found none, only a bottomless vortex that he was powerless to fight. His hands tightened on her, and his lips moved to her cheeks, her eyes, her hair, her throat. They moved greedily, wanting to capture all of her, to taste all there was to taste, to know all there was to know. That she *wanted* him to know was obvious. She met caress with caress, hunger with hunger, her body straining toward his with primal need.

The long, mournful howl of the wolf came once more, joined by others, the chorus swelling with echoes in the cold black night. The woeful, lonely cries jerked MacKenzie back to reality, and to thoughts of a night a year earlier when he had said farewell to his father, to who he was and where he was going, and why. And to the plain undeniable fact that, for everyone's sake, he had to go alone.

A piece of molten lead seemed to lodge in his chest as his lips slowed their avaricious journey. A moan tore from his throat as he forced himself to pull away.

"MacKenzie...?" April's voice was like a whisper of a summer breeze. "Your...wound...? Did I hurt it?"

Better to let her think that. "It's...still tender."

He saw the guilt in her face and wanted to reassure her, but he couldn't. "I think," he said stiffly, "that we both need some rest."

Consumed by guilt, April could only nod. She touched his arm again, this time for reassurance that he was all right, but his face was once more closed and shuttered against her. The distance between them suddenly yawned enormously, and she wondered for a moment if she had only dreamed those wonderful caring moments. She saw him flinch under her hand

and she took it away, staring at him with tear-misted eyes. It was almost as though she now repulsed him.

She drew back, confused and wretched, her face so full of hurt that MacKenzie wanted to reach for her, comfort her. But with all the will remaining to him, he turned instead and refueled the fire, his shoulders denying her the smallest solace.

"MacKenzie...?" she tried again.

He faced her, but his eyes were empty. "Get some rest, Mrs. Manning. We leave for the valley at dawn."

Chapter Eleven

The night was the longest April had ever spent.

She was unable to sleep as she recounted, over and over, each word that had been said during those few moments with MacKenzie. She puzzled over his consistent withdrawal from her whenever she thought she was lowering the barriers, and relived the pleasure of his touch and the taste of his lips. But then her stomach would knot and churn with hurt at his rejection. Each minute seemed an hour and each hour an eternity, knowing as she did that he lay within feet of her, a distance that now seemed like miles. She could hear his own restless movements, and she wondered if they resulted from the continuing pain of the wound or regret over those few seconds of reluctant surrender.

Regret? She bitterly doubted whether he regretted anything or even, at this moment, whether he felt anything. She had offered everything she could, and he had rejected it. Rejected her. Rejected Davey.

She heard him move again and hid her face in the blanket, pretending a sleep that eluded her. She could hear him feeding the fire again, and then there was silence. She sensed his presence above her, and once more she was bewildered. A warmth encompassed her, even now in her despair, and she could almost see his eyes on her. They were engraved indelibly in her mind, like everything else about him. Only their mood escaped her. Indifference? Impatience? Curiosity?

Her heart pounded harder as she realized he was drawing closer, and she felt his hand, warm and tender, touch her hair and the back of her neck with feather lightness. It lingered there, and her heart seemed to stop as his fingers moved ever so gently against her skin. April tingled all over, and she was sure he must know she was awake, that he could feel the great waves of desire that he created with the slightest touch. The fingers stopped, and she intuitively knew he hesitated, that he didn't want to abandon contact. She felt the blanket being rearranged, as if he wanted to do something for her...even if it wasn't needed. And finally—as if their spirits were melded together by some invisible cord—she silently felt the regret and weariness that flowed from him, and thought her heart might break. He wasn't indifferent or impatient or angry. He was afraid, and the knowledge gave her even greater pain. Strong, indomitable MacKenzie, the man who attacked a bear without hesitation, was tortured by fear.

He stayed there for several moments and then the warmth disappeared, and April knew he was gone, although his moccasins made no sound in the still night. There was an emptiness and chill where he had been, and she curled up in a tight ball of misery and dug deeper in her blanket.

In the morning, April rose to gray skies. MacKenzie's eyes were the same bleak color, and his tone was once more cool and emotionless as he parceled out duties. April wondered once again whether she had dreamed everything that had happened last night. She saw MacKenzie wince several times as he leaned down, and she knew his injury was still painful. He should not be riding this soon, but she guessed from the hard jut of his jaw that he would not change his plans.

Her own anger grew at his obstinacy, obstinacy about his wound and about her. Even about Davey, because this morning he was cool to the boy, and she could scarcely bear the sight of her son's hurt puzzlement.

They ate the last of the hardtack taken from Pickering's

troops, along with smoked fish and bear berries they had picked the day before. MacKenzie ate hurriedly and alone, then saddled and packed the horses, pacing restlessly as April and Davey finished the sparse meal and took a few moments to attend to their private needs.

His hard, piercing eyes gentled only when Davey approached and asked if he could ride with him on the Appaloosa. April could see refusal in MacKenzie's face, but then his mouth seemed to relax as if giving in to something he really wanted anyway, and he lifted Davey to his saddle with a small wry twist of his lips.

It was as if there were two MacKenzies, April thought wistfully, each battling the other for supremacy. She pondered the sheer contradictions of the man...and the outcome of the war within him.

Mounting her own horse, she silently followed his lead from the clearing where she knew she had lost her heart. She looked back to the place where the fire had been, but even that was now bare. MacKenzie had taken great care to eliminate any sign of their presence. Once they were gone, the great bear carcass would soon be devoured by wolves. A sense of sadness encompassed her as she turned her head toward MacKenzie's stiff back. Despite the raw violence of the bear attack, she had known moments of unprecedented joy here. She wondered if she would experience them again. He seemed so determined she would not.

They climbed steadily, in silence, into the mountains, and by late afternoon April's mood was lifted by the sheer enchantment of the beauty that surrounded her. The threatening clouds had disappeared, leaving the sky a brilliant blue. Giant snow-covered peaks rose in sharp contrast to the sky, and a bright sun intensified their pristine cloaks and warmed the earth. They passed through gates of rock and alongside red-tinged canyon walls that fell sharply to dells of bright green grass. Crested blue jays darted through the dark pines, and scores of squirrels chattered merrily among the branches. A lone eagle soared gracefully overhead, reminding April of MacKenzie. Solitary, splendid and dangerous...and every bit at home in this wild untamed country.

They stopped beside a small lake and once more dined on smoked fish and berries they found. The water was cold and wonderfully refreshing after the tepid remainders of the canteens. Davey, eager to stretch his legs after so long on horseback, started his usual exploring, but after the bear attack he was careful to stay within sight of both his mother and MacKenzie, glancing at them frequently for reassurance.

MacKenzie was unnaturally stiff, and April knew he must be hurting. His normally clear gray eyes were fogged with pain, and he moved slowly, watering the horses and hobbling them so they could feed on the rich grass before he took any rest of his own. He finally sat and leaned against a cottonwood tree, unconsciously releasing a long, grateful sigh.

"You can't go any farther today," April said with combined concern and exasperation.

"We can." The reply was terse. "And we will. I just need a little rest."

"You need more than that," she said sharply, surprised that he'd admitted any need at all. She went over to him and kneeled. Without waiting for his consent, she pushed up the blanket shirt, revealing the bandage she had made from her pantalets. It was stained through with both salve and secretions from the wound.

He winced as she carefully untied the bandage and gently pried the soft cloth from the puckered burned skin, studying the discolored areas that surrounded it. MacKenzie was uncharacteristically docile, and the unique attitude worried her more than any other symptom. She looked with dismay at the purple bruises that still covered so much of his body. The last hours must have been torture.

"You are not going any farther today," she pronounced, "not if you want to be able to move tomorrow." Surprisingly,

MacKenzie didn't protest. She wondered how long such acquiescence would last.

"We need food," he observed mildly, his eyes never leaving her face as she studied his burn.

"I think I might be able to find something," she said.

"You've done enough," he said, his jaw tightening as her fingers soothed the skin around the burn.

The wound was secreting a watery yellow substance, but April didn't think it was infected. It didn't have the smell or look of the gangrene she had seen in the prison hospital. But it did look angry and painful.

"This wouldn't have happened if Davey and I hadn't wandered off," April replied.

"It could have happened just as easily in the clearing," he replied. "The bear was heading for it. There was something wrong...perhaps it had lost its cub or been wounded by an arrow earlier. It was nothing you did."

"Perhaps not, but you're still hurt because of us."

He flinched once more, not because of the physical pain but at the fear he remembered, the fear for the two of them when he had seen the bear. He had almost been too late, and he had realized only too well in the past several days that his actions in taking Davey in the beginning had almost killed them both. "You are not here by choice," he finally said.

"I am now," she answered softly.

"No...you're here because I kidnapped your son. And I put you both in great danger. Don't forget that, Mrs. Manning, because I can't."

"April," she said patiently.

He stared at her with chilly remote eyes that thawed gradually as he puzzled over her persistence. Then the side of his mouth twitched. She was a glorious woman. Maddening. Stubborn. Resourceful. Proud.

"I'll make some more of the salve and wash the bandage while you rest," she said, hating to leave him for even a moment, particularly when she saw the warmth in his eyes. She wanted to touch him again, like she had last night, but then she remembered how he had drawn away. She forced herself up.

MacKenzie had packed some of the yarrow plant, and now she made the salve with water. She spread it over the burn, all the time feeling the almost intimate touch of his eyes on her. She let her fingers linger on his skin after the chore was done. She knew the process had been painful, although he had said nothing, had not indicated his discomfort by even the slightest move or expression. April finally compelled herself to leave him and took his bandage to the lake where she scrubbed it and set it on a rock to dry. She sent Davey to look for firewood, warning him to keep within sight, and she started a fire.

April Manning learned fast, MacKenzie thought, as he watched her build the fire like an experienced woodsman. He felt its first blast of heat with something akin to gratitude. The air was cooling again, now that the sun was withdrawing toward the west. It would be even colder tonight, and tomorrow. He could almost smell snow. He knew they should be moving on; he had wanted to get to his cabin tonight, but his strength was gone, and he felt as weak as a newborn cub. Once he had sat down, his body had rebelled, and he couldn't seem to force himself up. The woman was right. He could go no farther today. He would only endanger them all even more. But it galled him that he could do so little now for April and her son, could not even provide them with a decent meal. He closed his eyes, willing his strength to return, but total exhaustion from pushing his body far beyond its endurance nudged him into a heavy sleep not far removed from unconsciousness.

April made a neat pile of firewood and searched the bedroll and saddlebags, taking inventory of the food supply. With the fish MacKenzie had smoked, and berries, they had enough for perhaps two days. But MacKenzie needed something more substantial. He was a large man, despite his rangy frame, and he had lost a great deal of blood.

She looked at him. The past few days had taken their toll. His face, even in sleep, was creased with pain and weariness. Lines of worry extended from his eyes now, incongruously sheltered by long black eyelashes. She sat down beside him, content for the moment to be near him, to hear his soft breathing and study the strong face covered by black stubble. Each severely chiseled feature had, in the past few days, become very dear to her. Sleep had softened the face only a little.

April felt a crippling weakness of her own. She had never known love could be so formidable, could affect every thought and every action. Each time she looked at him she seemed to turn into a puddle of wax, every sense melting with her need for him, a need that went far beyond physical touch although she ached and yearned for that, too, she thought ruefully. She came alive in his presence. The sky was bluer, the stars brighter, the sunsets more vivid. She also hurt more, but even that had an aching beauty to it. Her insides seemed to turn into a knot as she thought what he had brought her: a wonder she hadn't known existed, a joy that came with just being with him. She hungered to know everything about him, to know his pleasures, to share his pain. She had tasted his passion, however briefly; had seen his gentleness with Davey; had sensed his compassion for all living creatures; had felt his deep protectiveness toward her and her son.

As he had the night before, she leaned toward him, unable to keep from touching him any longer. His cheeks were bronze from the sun and weathered by the elements. The usual lock of midnight-black hair fell boyishly over his forehead, and she pushed it back, relishing its thick texture. In sleep, his mouth had lost its harsh tight line, and her fingers touched it, remembering its tender exploration just hours earlier. *MacKenzie. Whether you want it or not, I'm not going to let you go. Not ever.* He moved slightly, and she reluctantly moved her hand away. He needed as much rest as he could get. With one last long, searching gaze, she rose. There was much to do before nightfall.

When MacKenzie woke, the sun had disappeared behind the mountains, but its afterglow remained, coloring the horizon. Ribbons of gold and crimson framed the rugged canyon walls. The dark pines were mirrored in the silent lake, and as he watched, the entire sky turned a muted violet, which seemed to blend heaven and earth. MacKenzie knew the same reverence he always did when confronted with God's craftsmanship in his beloved mountains. He had been away for too long. He thought of the hangman's noose that awaited him...or, at the very least, prison. And he knew the latter would be for him far worse than the cessation of life. To be caged like an animal. Never to see the sun rise or set or smell the fresh clean scent of the forest. Never to feel the serenity and purity of a world untouched by man-inspired violence or hate. He felt a coldness inside, and it steeled his determination to make good his escape.

The bitter thoughts contrasted with the calm, silent tranquility of the evening. The world seemed stilled now. It was a time of profound silence, when the day creatures had retreated and the night ones had not yet emerged. It was a time of expectancy and change, and MacKenzie felt its old elemental pull. It was the time he had always loved best.

The silence was pierced by a sharp crack as a large piece of wood fell farther into the fire. He was now aware of the tart smell of smoke and the savory aroma of cooking fish. He turned his head and watched as April, unaware that he was awake, bent over the fire, her long braid caught against the red flames. He could see her profile, like a fine sculpture, in the sun's afterglow. There was a smudge on her nose, and her lips were pressed tightly together in concentration.

He wondered briefly how the fish had been obtained. He didn't think Davey had yet mastered the art of fishing, and he had gained the impression that April had never fished. She was full of surprises, an endless spring of ingenuity and resourcefulness. He was awed at the deep, warm pride he felt in that discovery.

MacKenzie tried to rise, but his body did not cooperate. It was stiff and painful, every movement agony. He had tried to go too far too early, but he was determined to reach his valley before the army; then he would go to Amos's cabin, where he could safely leave April and Davey. Another kind of anguish attacked him at the thought. The woman and child had become a part of his life, a wonderful, joyful part that warmed and delighted him as nothing else in his experience. The exquisite pain of tenderness, the trusting touch of Davey's hand, the light in April's eyes and the gentle touch of her fingers on his face were all gifts of such great magnitude that he didn't know if he could bear them...or their loss. He thought of the years of loneliness that stretched before him, years when the only warmth would be the memories. And his heart hurt far worse than his body.

April heard the slight movement and turned, her lips flashing a brilliant smile, which seemed to embrace him in its radiance. Her blue eyes touched him with such concerned gentleness that he once more felt himself falling into a pit of hopeless yearning. He felt blood in his mouth where his teeth bit into his lip, and he struggled to rise again, to escape the trap of that smile, of that look, of the love he wanted so badly but could not take. Because now, he realized, he loved her, too much to ruin her life—and Davey's.

MacKenzie rose slowly, awkwardly, welcoming the waves of pain that flooded him...anything to distract him, to jar his eyes from April's face. He did not want to turn from the love written there, or the bright seductive promise of her lips, the eager expectation in her eyes.

"You shouldn't move," she said. "You should let your body rest more."

A wry smile twisted his lips. How he longed to touch her.

He hoped that wish wasn't in his eyes, but he was afraid it might be. He could no longer control them. His voice was very low, the burr heavy. "We cannot stay here…and I cannot let my side get too stiff. We must leave on the morrow."

Some of the brightness left her eyes, and she turned back to the fire, turning the fish on a makeshift spit much like the one he had designed several days earlier.

"You caught those?"

April looked at Davey, who was sitting cross-legged near the fire. "Davey helped…he found the worms." She grinned. "And put them on the hook."

Her quick, self-depreciating smile touched him. She had done so much more than he thought possible of a woman of her background.

"You're a very unpredictable woman…"

"April," she prompted.

"April," he surrendered, and April's heart did a quiet little dance.

Their eyes locked on one other, and it was as if a cyclone had snatched them up, sending them spiralling to its eye and holding them there in a deceptive calm charged with electricity.

The enchantment was such that MacKenzie was almost unaware as his hands went to her shoulders and hovered there. She glided into him, and his hands moved to her back, holding her tightly against him, taking comfort in the soft yielding body and the sheer pleasure of having it pressing close to his. He could feel her shiver, and knew she must be hearing the pounding of his heart as her head lay so trustingly against his chest. Nothing else was necessary at the moment, only this gentle embrace. MacKenzie felt his heart expand, and when April looked at him with unabashed love, he knew there was no greater heaven.

Neither knew how long they stood there, oblivious to the fire and Davey who sat with fascinated wonder at the utter intensity binding his two favorite people in all the world. He didn't understand what he was seeing or feeling, but he sensed the currents and somehow felt a new security. He had been afraid they did not like each other, that MacKenzie would leave them. He didn't want MacKenzie to leave, not ever.

Neither did April. She told him so silently, and only the raw anguish in his eyes answered her. It was so agonized that she stepped back, and as his hands fell from her she grabbed one, refusing to release it.

"Never," she whispered. "I'm not going to let you go."

MacKenzie could do nothing but stare into the bottomless blue eyes that asked him only to love. The silence was pregnant with thoughts unsaid, with needs unmet.

His free hand touched her face. "You're beautiful... beautiful and strong." He buried his lips in her hair. He had wanted to continue, to say that she would meet a man who could give her and Davey a home, but he couldn't force the words. The very thought cut to the bone, so he just stood there, unable to relinquish her, although he knew he was making everything worse. For everyone.

"Whither thou goest..." she started.

"You cannot go," he interrupted. The few words from the Bible shattered the illusion he had momentarily permitted. He took a step backward, his hand falling from her face to her shoulder, holding her away. "If you don't think about yourself, think about Davey."

"He loves you," she said. "He needs you."

"He needs a father who can give him safety, and a home, and education."

"We can do that..."

"Not safety...not ever safety. Not now. I'll not have a bullet meant for me destroy him...or you."

"We can solve this...together. Some way. Father will help."

"I could not stand a cage, April. Not for a moment. I'll never again let anyone do what they did in Chaco." He hesitated, then added softly, "Not even for you." His strong proud face tensed, and she knew for the first time the full extent of what that terrible journey had cost him in dignity and pride.

"I love you," she whispered.

He could not answer, could not offer the words he wished he could return. He had not the right. Instead, his mouth quirked in a self-mocking smile and his grave gray eyes fastened on something beyond her, as if he could no longer bear her gaze. April felt the tears well up in her eyes and brim over. It shamed her that such was the case, but she couldn't prevent them. And then she felt his eyes on her again, and she blinked under their intent stare. Surprisingly, his hand went up and wiped the tears from her face with gentleness.

"Don't cry, April. I don't think I can stand remembering your tears." He smiled, a real smile, and it was breathtaking. "I want to remember you bringing in the bear meat so proudly, and bullying me and...defying Terrell. You're strong enough for anything. Always remember that, because I will. Your strength."

The tears were coming faster now despite, or perhaps because of, his words. She turned away, not wanting him to see them. Her voice was shaking with emotion, but she tried to regain some measure of dignity. "I won't change my mind."

"Neither will I," he said in a low voice. "I'll not risk your lives."

Her teeth bit into her lower lip. "You'd best eat," she said finally. "You need to build your strength." Her voice told him she would never surrender.

"Yes, ma'am," he said, trying in some way to lessen the tension that stood between them, like a living thing. He started to lean down to take the spit, but the pain in his side at the sudden movement was so great he couldn't withhold a small groan.

"Go sit down," she ordered, and like an obedient child he did. He knew he needed his strength, now more than ever. He had to get the Mannings to safety. And for his sanity it had

462   *Seize the Fire*

to be as soon as possible. April Manning was as debilitating to him as his wound. And every day it grew worse.

The three ate in silence. Davey crept over to MacKenzie's side, realizing that the closeness he had sensed between MacKenzie and his mother had turned into something else. He had not heard all the words, but he had seen his mother's tears and the pain on MacKenzie's face.

"Are we going with you?" he asked.

"For a little while," his friend answered slowly.

"Why not forever?"

"Because," MacKenzie tried to explain, "we're going in different directions. You want to see your grandfather, don't you?"

"I want to stay with you," Davey said stubbornly, his lips in a rare pout.

"And I would like that...very much," MacKenzie said, "but you must go with your mother to Defiance, and go to school and meet other boys. I think I know how much your grandfather wants you with him. You don't want to disappoint him."

"I don't know him," Davey said belligerently, and there was a little fear in his voice. "I want to stay with you, both Mama and I. Please. Please."

Once more, MacKenzie felt mortally wounded. How could he comfort Davey when there was no comfort for himself?

This time it was April who assisted him. She had gone to the lake for some water and heard only the last of the conversation, but could tell from MacKenzie's face some of the ache he was feeling.

She held out her hand to Davey. "Come on, Davey, we need some more wood for tonight. Will you help me?"

Davey's eyes went from one to the other. Neither smiled, although his mother tried. Something was very wrong. But he saw the plea in her eyes, and he slowly consented. He looked back at MacKenzie who, with a nod, urged him on. He took his mother's hand, and together they faded into darkness.

MacKenzie watched them go, knowing they would not venture beyond the flames. He moved closer to the fire for warmth and closed his eyes, willing himself to sleep once more. It was, he reasoned, to build his strength, not simply because he couldn't bear to watch April and Davey, to know that they wanted him and he could not have them.

But no matter how hard he tried, he couldn't block out the sight of soft tears falling from April's eyes or Davey's pleading face. He did not realize when a tear of his own trickled down his hard bronze cheek.

Chapter Twelve

The valley lay below like a polished emerald.

April had moved her horse up beside MacKenzie's and gazed down at the wonder below. Beneath the steep cliff was a plain of blue-green grass fed by a stream that fell from a high cliff into a pool at its base, then meandered gently through the tall grass. There were hundreds of aspens, their white bark and slender trunks contrasting with the vivid colors they held—ruby to topaz—moving slightly in the breeze so that each tree seemed to be magically shimmering in the bright sunlight. It was splendid in its perfection, as tranquil a picture as April could envision.

She glanced at MacKenzie and knew that he was lost in the same enchantment that had overwhelmed her. Yet there was something more. It was as if the sight enveloped every part of him. His eyes drank it in hungrily, and his mouth softened. A muscle throbbed in his cheek as he stared intently at every piece that composed the whole, like a person who had painstakingly put a puzzle together and now rejoiced in its completion. It was a look of love, of ownership.

"This is the valley you mentioned? The one with the cabin?" She asked hesitantly, timid to interrupt such deep emotions. But her curiosity could not be stilled. This valley was obviously very important to MacKenzie, and she wanted to know everything about him.

He looked at April, his eyes naked for a change. There was love and pain and a certain despair in them. And pride.

"It's mine," he said softly with a kind of reverence.

"But I thought the Utes owned all this...by treaty."

"They do...except for this valley," he said slowly. "And legally I suppose they own this, too. But I won use of it in a contest with a Ute chief...for me, for my children, for my children's children."

"What kind of contest?" April asked, fascinated.

MacKenzie smiled, and the smile lit his face in a way she hadn't seen before. The angular planes eased and the mouth became vulnerable...approachable.

"A horse race."

"Just a horse race?" From the unexpected mischief in his eyes, she knew there was more to it. Much more.

"A very different kind of horse race," he said, but then his face closed again, and the reserve, which had been there since daybreak, was back.

"Can we get down there?"

He nodded, but his attention was once again focused on the scene below. In his mind, he saw the future he had intended: a valley of a new strain of horses—a cross between the hardy, surefooted mountain horses like his Appaloosa and swift-blooded eastern stock. He saw them now in his mind: young fillies and colts frolicking beside their dams; stallions, their heads tossing with freedom, asserting their dominance among the mares and yearlings. It was a dream that had inspired him for more than ten years, that had spurred him to do many things he detested. The softness left his face, and his mouth pressed in a grim line. It did no good to think of it now. And he couldn't waste time. General Wakefield was only too aware of this valley and its importance to him. It would be the first place he would look. Which was part of MacKenzie's plan.

He turned to April, who was riding with Davey to prevent any more hurt to MacKenzie's wounded side. "I'll take the boy," he said curtly. "It's a steep ride. You have to be careful.'' He did not worry about her safety. She was a fine rider, but he knew it would be easier for her without worrying about Davey.

After taking the boy, MacKenzie turned his horse toward some pines hovering over the cliff. As they entered the trees April was startled to see a path that led downward. She noted that it was not visible unless you knew exactly where to look. MacKenzie had not exaggerated. It was a difficult passage, but the sturdy horses nimbly picked their way through the rocks and branches. The path was wide enough for two horses, but they went single file to avoid coming close to the edge of the precipice. April said a brief prayer as she leaned over and looked down the sheer cliff, and was humiliated when MacKenzie picked that time to look back and see her apprehensive expression.

Once more that day, his eyes softened. ''Don't look down,'' he said. ''You're doing very well.''

The words restored her courage, and she took his advice, keeping her eyes on the trail in front, seldom moving them to MacKenzie's back. His usual easy grace was missing, and she knew he was once more pushing himself unmercifully.

April was grateful when they reached the bottom, and the majestic plain lay before them like a magic carpet. ''It's beautiful,'' she whispered with no little awe.

''Aye,'' he said. ''It is that.'' He turned his horse and they rode to a corner of the valley that could not be seen from overhead. A small, neat cabin stood with its back to the rock of the canyon wall.

MacKenzie placed Davey on the ground and dismounted slowly, as if in pain. He went to assist April, but she was only too aware of his injury and she slipped down easily without any assistance. MacKenzie took both pairs of reins and tied them to the branch of a nearby tree.

April watched and waited, her eyes following his every move as he went from the horses to the door of the cabin and opened it, nodding for her and Davey to enter before him.

She didn't know what she expected but certainly not the interior that met her gaze.

It was whimsical. No other word could quite describe it, and the cabin said more about MacKenzie than anything he had revealed in the past two weeks or more. She had expected its neatness, for he was meticulous in everything he did. But in addition, it had color and character and charm. Blankets woven with intricate designs and bright colors decorated the walls and bed. A woven rug of various shades of blue covered the wood floor. A mantel over a huge fireplace held several wooden carvings of horses. In addition to the bed, the furniture included a finely carved chest, and a table with two chairs. The overall feeling was one of warmth.

April turned and looked at MacKenzie's half-expectant, half-wary expression. "It's wonderful," she said, and was rewarded with a brief smile. She went over to the carvings and fingered them with appreciation. They were roughly carved, almost primitive, yet each had its own charm. It was almost as if they were alive, so well did the creator capture the fluid movement of a horse in motion. She turned to MacKenzie. "Did you do these?"

He nodded. "When I was a boy."

"The blankets?"

"Navahos." His mouth became grim again. They had come from the small band massacred by the Apaches.

April looked around again, taking in everything. How much it revealed of him. How much it belied the stoic, harsh exterior he seemed to have mastered. But she didn't have time to ponder the discovery because he was moving around, reaching for tins on shelves and selecting several food items.

"Can we stay here?" April asked, wanting very much for the answer to be affirmative.

A muscle throbbed in his cheek before he answered. "No." The answer was abrupt, and April sensed the reluctance behind it.

"We'll eat," he continued, "then pack some of these blankets. We need them. And clothes. There're some in the chest. See if there's anything warm you can cut down for Davey and yourself. We have two more days' ride, straight up, and it will be cold."

"But why can't we stay here?"

MacKenzie looked at her carefully. "Your father knows of this cabin and how to reach it. He'll send someone here. But I can't leave you. Not alone. With the Apaches on the move, he may not be able to send anyone right away or, if he does, they might be slowed by Indians." Or massacred, he thought to himself. Damn. He was running out of alternatives, and the very thought of April's presence for additional days was pure torture, almost as great as the thought of losing her.

April bit her lip, wishing she hadn't asked as she realized he believed he was giving up this place he loved, possibly forever. "Where are we going?" April pleaded. "Where are *you* going?"

"I'm going to leave a note for your father and tell him I'm leaving you and Davey with Amos Smith. He's an old mountain man. You will be safe with him."

"And you?" she whispered.

"I'll be going on, up into the high country where I can get lost," he said frankly.

"We'll go with you," she offered once more, forsaking her pride completely.

"I know," he replied. "I know you would, but I can give you nothing. Less than nothing. Only hardship and danger, constant danger, and running. Always running."

"I don't care."

"You must...for Davey, if not yourself."

She knew he was right, although she had been avoiding the fact. She had to think about Davey. But Davey loved Mac-Kenzie.

MacKenzie saw the flickering emotions cross her face. He gave her his last argument. "And it would be dangerous to me," he said. "A man alone can lose himself, but a half-breed with a white woman and child. Even in the mountains, whispers travel.'' April's eyes clouded, and he knew he was, at last, winning. It gave him no satisfaction.

"Eat," he ordered as he opened some tinned peaches with his knife.

If April's stomach wasn't in her throat, she might have enjoyed the treat. Especially after so many days of fish, hardtack and dried beef. But all she could do was move the morsels around in her mouth. Davey, who didn't quite understand everything, had no such reservations and in minutes the tin was empty, and another was opened, and another.

MacKenzie was, as usual, impatient, and as April and Davey ate, he busied himself. Not bothering with false modesty, he discarded his awkward blanket jacket and found a clean buckskin shirt in the chest. He knew April had already seen him in several states of undress. He then packed another shirt and pair of cotton pants in saddlebags, and pulled out some clothes he thought April and Davey might be able to adapt. He scooped flour from a barrel and tied it in a bag, grateful that he always left supplies in the cabin; he never knew when he would return, and the supplies had been safe there. Only the Utes and a few acquaintances knew of the cabin and how to reach the valley floor. He added the colorful blankets to the bedrolls, along with several cooking utensils. When he'd completed packing, the cabin looked bare. He handed one of the carved horses to Davey, whose face lit at the gift as his hands fondled it possessively.

MacKenzie urged April to select the clothing she needed, then sat down to write a note. It was short and abrupt, saying only that April and Davey were safe and could be found at Amos Smith's cabin. He offered no excuses or explanations. For, in his opinion, he had none. Although he had not committed the crimes of murder and rape, he was responsible for equally unforgivable ones, including the kidnapping of a woman and child. He did not expect General Wakefield to forgive or forget.

When he finished, he found April watching him, her dark
blue eyes steady.

"May I write my father?"

MacKenzie winced at the question. She didn't need permission for anything. That had ceased days ago. But he merely
nodded at the several sheets of paper he had taken from the
chest. He purposely moved away so that she wouldn't think
he didn't trust her.

April hesitated. She knew what she wanted to say, but not
quite how to say it. She wanted her father to know she and
Davey were well, but mostly that MacKenzie was innocent
and should not be hunted. She finally dipped a pen in ink
MacKenzie supplied, and carefully wrote:

Please don't blame MacKenzie. We went with him willingly to keep Sergeant Terrell from killing him. He saved
Davey's life with grave injury to himself. If anything
happens to me, please know he's innocent and has done
everything possible to protect us.

Your Loving Daughter

She looked at MacKenzie. "Do you want to read it?"

MacKenzie shook his head. "It's time we left."

April sighed. She wished they could stay here a day or two,
at least until MacKenzie had healed a bit more, but she had
not missed the tenseness in his body or the forbidding set of
his jaw.

He gave her a sheepskin coat that had been in the chest and
took a lighter one for himself. He made sure Davey was
wrapped in several layers of heavy clothes and gave April a
giant pair of leather gloves obviously meant to fit himself. Her
fingers were lost in them, but she suspected she would be
grateful for them later.

The sun was halfway down the horizon when they remounted their horses. MacKenzie believed they would have
at least four hours of daylight. He wouldn't hide their tracks,

not until after he left Amos's. It would be then he would become the fox.

Captain Bob Morris, twenty men riding behind him, pushed his horse as hard as he could in the rocky terrain. He recognized several of the natural landmarks, and he knew he was only hours from MacKenzie's valley. He was tired, dog-tired, and he guessed each of his troopers shared the same affliction, for they had stopped only for brief rests in the past four days.

He also knew his only chance was to find MacKenzie at the valley. The damned scout could be a wisp of wind when he wanted, and the only hope they had was that the woman and child might have slowed him down.

Morris had been astonished at Pickering's and Terrell's tale. He himself had never cared much for MacKenzie, not because he was half-breed, but more because of MacKenzie's own distant attitude. His take-it-or-leave-it arrogance did not make things easy for those who employed him. It had not bothered General Wakefield, however, whom Morris suspected harbored a deep affection for the scout, as well as respect. It was, all personalities aside, a respect Morris shared. He knew his life had been saved more than once by MacKenzie's instinct and knowledge. And he had never doubted MacKenzie's intelligence and loyalty once he undertook an assignment. Morris agreed with his commanding officer that Pickering was a fool, and his rage grew as he saw burned-out ranches and farms along his way. Some of it could have been avoided had MacKenzie's warning been heeded immediately. His detail had already been weaned by the necessity of sending escorts back with the fleeing settlers.

He wondered about April Manning and the boy...and how they were faring in this rough country. It was no place for women and children, especially when they had been east for so long. He had seen April's portrait frequently since he had been assigned to General Wakefield two years earlier, and he had looked forward to her arrival. More than a little, he admitted. There were few women at Defiance, and most of them were married. The others were mainly laundresses and whores. Which reminded him of Ellen Peters.

Wakefield had been unable to shake her story, despite several interviews. She clung to her tale of rape and murder, and insisted on charges being pressed and MacKenzie apprehended. But she certainly seemed to have no sorrow over her father's death or even the slightest fear of men. Because she was a material witness and because Wakefield wasn't through with her by any means, Ellen had been allowed to stay as a laundress, a very unpleasant job in the sweltering Arizona heat. But she apparently had no other place to go. What Ellen didn't know was that Wakefield wanted her to stay, to watch her...and break her.

But that was not Morris's problem. His was to find MacKenzie and April and the boy. He knew MacKenzie had a substantial head start, but the scout would have to take roundabout ways where he was taking the most direct route. And MacKenzie had the woman and boy to slow him. Like his commanding officer, Morris was sure of one thing: MacKenzie would see they would not come to harm. If it were possible! In this hard country, nothing was certain, nothing was safe...even with MacKenzie's bloody competence. Morris saw a level stretch of country, and spurred his horse into a gallop.

Morris and his men reached the rim of MacKenzie's valley just as the sun was setting. The captain had visited it previously with Wakefield when the general had sought once more to obtain MacKenzie's rare talents. He had sent for MacKenzie to no avail and decided to take matters into his own hands. Wakefield had known of MacKenzie's valley, although he did not know its exact location. He had employed a Ute to guide him, and both Wakefield and Morris had been astounded by the beauty of the valley and the comfort of MacKenzie's cabin. They had not, Morris remembered, been exactly welcomed—either by a big gray wolf that bared its teeth and never took its eyes from them, or by MacKenzie, whose whole demeanor told them he resented their intrusion—but after a day's discussion, Wakefield's persuasion finally won...

Like MacKenzie and April not many hours earlier, Morris gazed down at the valley with something akin to awe. In the faltering light, it was indescribably lovely. The various hues of the sunset seem to inflame the falling water on the opposite cliff wall, and silver and gold danced in the pool below. The color of the grass seemed even richer in the muted light. He could find no sign of activity. It seemed an empty painting...too beautiful, too peaceful to be real.

He sighed, sensing he was too late, but gave the order to descend. He could only hope there was some kind of sign, some indication of where MacKenzie was heading.

The cabin was much as Morris recalled, although it seemed emptier than before. He had remembered more color. His eyes immediately saw the paper on the table and in three easy strides he was fingering the notes. He quickly read MacKenzie's note, swearing as he did. Smith's cabin was a good two day's ride. His men and horses were exhausted, as was he. And the territory MacKenzie was entering was even more treacherous than this. It was no place for a lady and boy. Morris wondered how long ago MacKenzie had been here. He saw an empty tin in a corner and took it, smelling the residue. It hadn't been long. No more than a day if that long. God damn it. If only they had arrived a little sooner, MacKenzie would have been trapped. The man was as elusive as a damned ghost.

Morris took the second note and scanned it. He wondered briefly if the woman had been forced to write it, but he quickly discarded the idea. MacKenzie wouldn't have bothered. Two words particularly caught his attention. ''Grave injury.'' So that was why he had almost caught up with the scout. He wondered how badly injured. How much it was slowing him? How much it would continue to slow him? Perhaps he could find April and Davon Manning. And maybe, just maybe, he would bring in MacKenzie as well.

Captain Morris gave the order to dismount and make camp. He could not risk going up the steep trail at night, and they all needed rest. In these mountains, MacKenzie would also have to stop at night, particularly with a serious injury. Tomorrow his men would be fresh and able to move fast. He wanted to catch up with MacKenzie before he reached Smith's cabin…while he was still slowed by the woman and child and before he could erase his tracks. Morris knew once MacKenzie was alone, he would be impossible to find.

April, Davey and MacKenzie dined on dried fish, berries and another can of sweetened peaches. MacKenzie had located a deep cave just as twilight surrendered to darkness, and they had settled in for the night. The moon was now almost full but MacKenzie couldn't risk April's and Davey's lives by continuing after dark. The steep trails fell to deep canyons; bushes blocked the paths, and the footing was often treacherous. Several times they had had to dismount and lead their nervous mounts through cramped passages or across narrow ledges.

Davey helped MacKenzie take care of the horses, and then both fell to the cave floor in exhaustion, Davey after a full day of fresh air and activity, and MacKenzie because of his continuing weakness and lingering pain. With the addition of extra blankets, MacKenzie decided not to build a fire. He did not know how far behind any pursuers were; he had risked a great deal by stopping at the valley but had deemed it necessary—both to obtain warmer clothing and to provide for April's safe return. But he did not care to offer Wakefield any additional help by providing a beacon if anyone were determined enough to travel at night. The moonlight would permit it, dangerous as movement might be, and were it not for his wound and his two charges he would have attempted it himself. He stood and walked outside the cave, watching the moon play over mountaintops dressed in white. The stars seemed incredibly bright against the blue-black sky, and the cold pure air of the mountains invigorated him. He lifted his head toward the sky, trying to toss aside the melancholy that had plagued him since leaving the valley. He used to take pleasure from such a scene, but now there was only a deep loneliness. He had discovered the joy of sharing such gifts. And soon the sharing would be over.

He sensed April's presence before seeing her. She, too, had been quiet during the past hours. He wondered whether she felt the same bittersweet emptiness, and knew she did as she slipped a hand in his. Despite his best intentions, he turned to face her, and he felt his heart contract at the love that was so openly expressed in her face. How hard it would be to leave her.

"Tell me more about the valley," April probed gently.

And suddenly he wanted to, needed to.

He guided her, and they both sat in the moonlight, staring at the infinity above, which seem to make them very small indeed. But what flowed between them was strong as steel and, April knew, as enduring. "Tell me," she said again.

MacKenzie started slowly. He was unused to revealing anything about himself. It was a habit difficult to break, even with April. "I had planned to raise horses." Each word was carefully spoken as if difficult to extract. And April knew each was a victory for her. "There was a major I knew...Bennett Morgan. One of the few really good officers, the only one to take the time or trouble to learn to track, to learn Indian ways. He had a blooded horse that could outrun any on the post. Even," he added wryly, "my own mountain pony, which had always won races before. But it didn't have my horse's endurance. I thought then, and so did Major Morgan, that a cross between the two would be unbeatable. It was a dream for a long time, but I didn't think there was any hope for it. I didn't have the money to buy stock or land, and I doubted I would be welcome anyplace." His words were bitter, more bitter than any she had heard. "I didn't care what anyone thought," he continued slowly, "but I didn't want to have to fight all my life."

The words faded in the night air, and April felt the stillness. But the peace was gone. His anger simmered below the surface. It was several minutes before he continued.

"It was always there...the idea...in the back of my mind...and then it became possible. I was challenged to a horse race by a Ute chief. He had never lost and thought he never would...not to a half white anyway." There was a small, rueful smile on MacKenzie's face as he remembered the chief's chagrin and fury when he lost his favorite horse—the Appaloosa. The chief threw out a second challenge, this time a more difficult one. They would race bareback with a weapon to be picked up from the ground. MacKenzie would never forget that race, leaning down to grab a tomahawk, his face close to the horse's hooves, his balance maintained only by a handful of mane. But the prize was a great one—the valley; and he had won. There was also a fight, a bloody one, and again MacKenzie had triumphed. He had won the respect, if not friendship, of the Utes. They had honored the wager.

But he said little of this to April, only that he had won both the horse and the valley. And it had given him the start he needed. He'd continued scouting to earn enough money to buy the blooded stock he wanted. He had figured he would have enough after this last assignment with the army.

MacKenzie paused. "I had planned to go to Texas, ask Bennett Morgan to help select stock and bring them to the valley. It's a natural corral, and the grass is rich. It's protected from the wind by the canyon walls. I could easily round up wild mountain horses for breeding. It all seemed so possible...just a few more months."

April let several seconds go by. She could feel his anguish, the loss of something vitally important to him. She was startled he had let her see it. Startled and pleased and infinitely sad. There had to be some way she could help.

"This Major Morgan...he is a friend?"

MacKenzie hesitated. ''Not a friend... I think he was as cautious about trusting as I was...but I think we respected each other. There's not many I feel that way about...perhaps your father...'' His voice trailed off as he remembered exactly what he had done to her father, how worried he must be about his daughter and grandson.

And April knew she couldn't offer any comfort. She, too, thought about her father, knew how much he had looked forward to her coming, to seeing his grandson for the first time. She had tried not to think about it, but it had been there, in the back of her mind, since the beginning. She had considered it when she asked to go with MacKenzie, had battled with her loyalties.

A shooting star flamed its way across the sky, and both MacKenzie and April watched it silently, each wondering whether it was an omen, and if so, what it portended. April laid her head against his chest, and it was enough, just then, to be together.

Chapter Thirteen

Long before they reached Amos Smith's cabin, MacKenzie knew it had been another futile effort.

Amos's dog, as faithful as his own wolf, always sounded an early warning of strangers. There was nothing now but silence. And MacKenzie didn't know whether he was blessed or damned. He did know he would have to make a decision immediately. He had insured that by leaving the note in his cabin. He could not linger here, not unless he wanted to be taken back to Defiance in chains, and that he had sworn would not happen. Yet he had promised Wakefield his daughter and grandson would be waiting here.

He was unaware that his face reflected his dismay and that his back had stiffened even more rigidly. Somewhere in the past few days his protective shields had ceased to work. He heard April draw abreast of him and saw her puzzled face. It was full of questions.

He could only shake his head and shrug in reply. He pushed his horse into a trot and within minutes they saw the dried mud roof of a rough cabin. There was an air of desertion about it.

April watched while MacKenzie slung a leg over the saddle and slid easily to the ground. He dropped the reins, knowing the Appaloosa would stand quiet for the few minutes he needed. He unhitched the latch holding the door closed and entered the cabin, his eyes immediately assessing the interior.

The dust was not heavy, and MacKenzie knew Amos had not been gone long, perhaps not more than a week or so. He could only surmise that Amos had headed for Denver to trade furs for winter supplies. Of all the damned bad luck! His had to be the worst. He left the cabin and strode to the side of April's horse, first taking Davey down, then offering a hand to her. The touch was like fire to both of them, burning like a brand through their skin, the heat racing through their blood like fast-flowing lava.

MacKenzie looked at their hands, still entangled together, hesitating to relinquish the brief contact even as the heat magnified. His gray eyes became smoldering coal, and hers were the color of an inviting mountain pool. Both probed and queried and explored, finally locking in an understanding and knowledge that shook them with their strength.

There was some satisfaction in April's voice when at last she spoke, piercing the tense silence. "He's not here," she said, stating the obvious. "You'll have to take us on with you now."

The words jerked MacKenzie back to reality and the terrible dilemma facing him. He could take April and the boy higher into the mountains and hope he could find someone to whom he could entrust their safety. Or he could stay here with them and allow himself to be captured.

April read the indecision in his face. "No," she said. "I will not stay and let you be taken."

Despite his worry, MacKenzie had to smile slightly at the fierceness in her voice. "I thought," he reminded her wryly, "that's what you were urging me to do."

It had been, April admitted to herself, but that was before she knew MacKenzie so well. She was no longer willing to take even the slightest chance with his life...or freedom. The latter, she had discovered, meant more to him than breathing. She had seen it in every restless movement and every loving look he cast on his mountains. And she wanted to be with him. Oh, how she wanted that! Every moment she could borrow or steal. She tore her eyes from his face and looked down at Davey. Did she have the right to make this decision? But then she saw the look of trust and worship in Davey's face as her son looked at MacKenzie, and she knew no more doubts. Only her father gave her pause. She was being so unfair to him. Yet she had no choice. Her heart was giving her none. It was as if MacKenzie, in the space of three weeks, had become her life. And she would be a hollow, empty thing without him.

"I will not stay and let you be taken," she repeated, this time even stronger. "Davey and I go with you."

MacKenzie fought himself. She had never been so beautiful. Her eyes sparked with the light of battle; her chin jutted defiantly. The thought of losing her and the boy was excruciating; yet what could he offer them? Once more he weighed his alternatives. They were so damned few.

He could not leave them here alone, any more than he could have left them in the valley. He believed with all the instincts that kept him alive this long that there were troops behind him—and not long behind. But he could not be sure, and he could not gamble April's and Davey's lives on it. The second choice—the mountains ahead—was what his heart was arguing. More days, more time with April and Davey. Time to explore these new feelings that gave grace to a life previously untouched by love, or trust, or giving. But didn't that also mean sacrificing? Sacrificing his happiness, even his life, for their safety?

But they would be safe with him...for a while...until he could find a haven for them. No one knew of his father's mountaintop cabin. He could readily supply them with the food, shelter and clothing they needed until he found a way to get them home. And he could collect memories, store them and treasure them for when he was, once more, alone. Need and greed—need for belonging, greed for love—swamped him, drowning his reservations and his usual calm, dispassionate judgment.

Ignoring the warning sick feeling in his stomach, he made his decision.

His hand touched her cheek, and he gave her a rare smile. "I think the Fates are making the decisions for us," he said softly. "We'll go on together."

Spontaneously, she reached up and kissed him, and MacKenzie was swept up in it. The kiss was at first hard, then sweet and lingering as neither wanted to let go. It was MacKenzie who remembered Davey, and pulled back, reluctantly releasing her.

"I really didn't want to leave you," he admitted wryly as he watched her face light with happiness. Suddenly, he felt like the boy he had never had a chance to be, and his smile broadened, reminding April of the brilliance of a rainbow after a storm. The hard lines smoothed out, and his eyes flashed silver with an openness and anticipation she had never seen before.

Elation filled April, chasing any specters that remained. Love filled her so thoroughly she thought she might explode of it. "We should hurry," she said, afraid now that something or someone would alter his decision.

MacKenzie nodded. Now the decision, for better or for worse, was made, he was caught up in an urgency of his own. But first there was something that must be done. He could not leave Wakefield with no word or explanation; he had put the general through enough already. There was no pen or paper in Amos's cabin; the mountain man could not read or write. And MacKenzie had taken no writing materials with him. With all he needed, that seemed the most useless. Asking April and Davey to stay outside, he went back into the cabin. With his knife, he cut a small trail in his wrist, and let drops of blood fall on the table. With a finger, he wrote the words which he hoped would explain, if not excuse.

When he returned outside, he saw April eye his bloody wrist, but he shook his head as if it were no matter. He helped her mount once more, then mounted himself, leaning down and lifting Davey in front of him.

Without looking back, they trotted away.

Captain Morris eyed the vacated cabin with frustration. He had pushed his men until they were ready to drop, but still they had not been able to overtake MacKenzie. His growing anger, spawned of one disappointment after another, increased tenfold when he failed to find the general's daughter and grandson at Smith's cabin as promised. The rough table caught his attention, and he strode over to it. His fingers traced the bloody letters. Only MacKenzie, he thought, would communicate in quite this fashion. He read, with difficulty, the brief message: "Amos gone. Couldn't leave Mannings alone. Safe."

"Damn the man's eyes," Morris whispered under his breath. "Damn his soul."

He strode outside, carefully observing the manure that lay just outside the cabin. He leaned down and touched it. Fresh. He had missed them by hours.

Morris looked up at the lemon-colored sky. There was something about it that alarmed him. The wind had increased and now was making low moaning sounds as it swept through the trees. He pulled his greatcoat tighter, shivering. He thought of the woman and child caught in one of the furious snowstorms that sometimes isolated entire mountain areas for weeks and even months at a time.

"Damn MacKenzie," he cursed once more. He had been entrapped in one of these storms before, and he didn't want to repeat the experience. He and a small detail had watched their horses freeze and had almost starved to death before eating horseflesh. Morris had come close to dying that time, closer than he wanted to remember. He knew MacKenzie came from these mountains and that probably no one was better equipped to survive a hard winter, but what about Mrs. Manning and her son? He dreaded returning to Defiance without them...and without MacKenzie. His right fist, gloved in warm leather, balled and unballed before he made his decision. "Get mounted," he told his sergeant. "We're going after them."

MacKenzie's eyes searched the sky warily. In the past few hours great gray-black clouds had swept across the sky, blocking the sun and shrouding the mountain peaks. Although only midday, it was growing so dark it looked like dusk.

The wind was rising rapidly and there was an electric tension in the air that always foreshadowed a mountain storm. He considered returning to Amos's cabin, and then thought about his father's place just a day and a half ahead. It was straight up, and the trail split at several places, the last segment so rarely traveled as to be practically invisible if one didn't know it well. If he eliminated any sign of their presence, there would be no way to find him. And if it did snow heavily, the passage would be blocked as thoroughly as if by an iron gate.

MacKenzie did not worry about the storm once they made it to his destination. Rob MacKenzie's cabin was sturdy, like the man who had built it, and as in his own cabin, there should be tinned goods and flour to keep them until he could hunt. There had been plenty a year ago and he doubted whether anyone had been there since. It was simply too isolated. The question was whether he could reach the cabin before snow made travel too dangerous. He was avoiding the other nagging problem. How could he live closely in a cabin with April and Davey without becoming further ensnared in a web that had no escape? The thought both alarmed and elated him.

He looked at April who was riding abreast of him and was also anxiously scanning the sky. He answered her unspoken question. "It's another day away..."

They were even beginning to think alike now, April thought. They were so in tune with each other that spoken words were almost unnecessary.

"We can't go back," she said, dismissing the very idea. She was not going to give him up now.

"It could be dangerous...Davey..."

She shook her head. Her faith in him was absolute. Nothing would happen to them with MacKenzie.

He read her expression and once more smiled, though it did not ease the worry lines around his eyes. He might have hesitated, if he did not know these mountains so well. But he knew every rock and cranny, every hiding place and every trail in the area. He had roamed it incessantly as a boy and young man. He knew he could find the cabin even with the snow...if they reached Devil's Fall first. He would not even attempt the treacherous pass with April and Davey if they did not outrace the snow. It was dangerous enough without ice.

MacKenzie tightened his hold on Davey and spurred his Appaloosa forward with new urgency.

An icy rain began to fall as the three reached Devil's Fall. April gazed with trepidation at the steep winding path that fell sharply off on one side. It made the descent into MacKenzie's valley look like a cow path.

MacKenzie dismounted and eyed the trail dubiously. It had never looked quite as dangerous as it did now. It was a short passage, to be sure, and they would be well over it before the rain froze, but still....

April shivered from both cold and fear, but she had come too far to falter now. She looked at MacKenzie's grim visage. "I'm not giving up," she said, trying to keep the tremor out of her voice.

MacKenzie knew he could not hesitate. Each second counted. In an hour, the trail would be impassable. To him or to anyone following. It was that knowledge that decided him. He could get the Mannings over safely...now. He had no doubt of that...but he loathed the fear he saw in April's eyes, fear he knew would worsen when they continued.

Her chin lifted as if she could read his mind. "We can't stay here," she said, her voice stronger.

"You'll have to trust me completely...do whatever I say when I say it..."

She nodded, her hands tightening on the reins.

His mouth relaxed. He reached up and took Davey from his saddle. He quickly unrolled his bedroll and took out a blanket, wrapping it around the boy. He then lifted Davey up and placed him at the front of April's saddle.

April watched as MacKenzie tied the reins of his horse to his saddle horn, taking just a second to run a hand down the horse's neck in reassurance. He then took the reins to April's horse and started walking, knowing the sure-footed Appaloosa would follow behind them.

The path narrowed even more, and April felt the icy rain pelting down, soaking the sheepskin jacket that until now had kept her warm. She knew MacKenzie, with his lighter coat and moccasins, must be freezing, and she shivered uncontrollably. Remembering the brief fear she felt descending into the valley, she forced her eyes away from the sheer drop on her right side and hugged Davey closer.

The climb seemed to go on forever. April wanted to close her eyes, but couldn't. Instead, she fastened them on MacKenzie who moved surely but cautiously along the path, seemingly unaware of any discomfort or fear. She felt her horse stumble, and froze, but MacKenzie merely turned, his hand quieting the horse as he whispered soothing words. And then they were going on again. This time she shut her eyes tightly, listening to the cadence of her horse's iron shoes against the rock. It was a comforting sound among the other noises—the wailing of wind and the cold beat of rain against the canyon walls. Davey seemed to try to burrow himself further into her, and her hands, now nearly lost in MacKenzie's large leather gloves, found Davey's, which had been wrapped in the blanket. She helped them wriggle inside her gloves, and held them tightly as her arms continued to wrap around him, sharing warmth and courage.

The horse stopped, and April opened her eyes. MacKenzie's

eyes were on her, a victorious smile on a face dripping with rain. She looked around. The path had leveled and widened, and trees now rose where previously there had been only dark yawning space.

"It's over?" she whispered, hating the fear that lingered in her voice.

He nodded. "There's a cave not far... I'll try to build a fire." He looked back at the pass. In an hour, it would be sheer ice. If there were pursuers, they would come no further. Not for days. The trail from here on was rough but passable, unless the coming snow was unusually heavy. Approaching snow or not, they couldn't travel much longer; what little light remained of day was fading fast, and he was freezing.

Captain Morris and his scout stared at the fork in the trail. They had left Smith's cabin two hours earlier, and MacKenzie's path had been easy to follow until now. At this point, there was no indication as to which way the half-breed and his two prisoners had gone. The ground was rocky, and there were no hoof marks. In fact, there was nothing. Morris's scout had tried both directions and found no evidence of passage. It was as if their quarry had simply vanished into thin air. A rain was falling now, rain mixed with sleet, and Morris knew everything would soon be washed away...if MacKenzie was careless enough to leave any trace at all. Morris doubted it. But he had come this far, and he was not ready to stop. He called his sergeant over.

"Take ten men and try the left trail. I'll take the right. We'll both go about two miles. If you don't find anything, come back here and wait an hour. If I'm not back by then, follow me. I'll follow the same procedure. Look for the smallest thing...a piece of cloth, a broken branch. You won't find anything else...not with MacKenzie."

The sergeant nodded, wishing he were anyplace but in these mountains. He, too, knew MacKenzie and felt the whole thing was an exercise in futility. Yet he also understood a woman and child were at risk. He would do his best. He hunkered down in his coat, and signaled the other men, cursing under his breath. What damned miserable weather!

It was Morris's detail that reached Devil's Fall.

He had found nothing, not the slightest clue when he reached the steep trail upward. Rain had turned to sleet, and his horse was already having difficulty keeping its balance. He looked at the icy trail and knew it was hopeless to go any farther. He also sincerely doubted whether MacKenzie had gone this way. It would take a mountain goat. And while MacKenzie might attempt it alone, he doubted if even the scout would try it with a woman and child. Morris sunk his chin in the collar of his heavy coat and turned around. He hoped like hell his sergeant had found something. Otherwise they had no choice but to start back to Defiance. They couldn't wander around these mountains blind in a snowstorm, and he knew one was right behind the sleet. He shook his head. How in bloody Hades would he ever explain his failure to General Wakefield? One eloquent curse followed another as he turned his horse around and started back.

He wasn't surprised when his sergeant had no more luck than he had. With heavy hearts, the twenty men made for Smith's cabin. They would warm themselves, and eat, before turning back toward the fort.

It took MacKenzie more than an hour to kindle a fire. He had sought dry wood under heavily laden trees where there would have been some protection, but all of it was at least damp and resisted his attempt to light it. He finally urged a spark from some juniper needles and the wood began to smoke reluctantly, igniting into flames.

April couldn't stop trembling...from both the cold and a delayed reaction to the fear. She wondered if she would ever be warm again, yet most of her concern was for MacKenzie. Davey was already wrapped in layers of blankets and was drowsily nodding. But MacKenzie! His clothes were soaked through and his black hair was still wet with icy moisture. His face was red from the wind and cold, and his lips had turned blue. His eyebrows seemed like tiny silvery icicles in the cave's dark interior. He had worked ceaselessly since they'd arrived, bringing the horses in from the now howling wind and braving the stinging sleet to find wood. Now she knew it was catching up with him. His entire body was shaking with cold and exhaustion.

April took one of the least wet blankets and drew it around him tightly, her hands going around his wide shoulders. She hugged him with her arms, trying to share some of her warmth. She felt him shuddering under her touch and lay her head against the iciness of his hair. One of his hands reached for hers, and she felt its chill. It was so large and hers so small, she doubted what little body heat she had was doing him any good. His head turned and in the slight glow of the struggling fire his eyes were enigmatic silver. Her arms tightened around him once more and she felt the hard tense muscles in his arms and chest. "I love you, MacKenzie," she whispered under her breath so he wouldn't hear. She knew he didn't want to hear it again, that he was fighting it, but she couldn't stop the words. The feeling was too deep. She felt him react, felt his body stiffen and saw something new in his eyes when once more they met hers.

"You mustn't," he rasped, his gray eyes now steely with determination.

Now it was out, April decided she would not retreat, not any more. "I'm afraid you can't do anything about it," she said. "It's done." Her tone held finality, and he could only stare at her with a kind of hopelessness.

April did not give him time to ponder her words or to speak. She took her arms away and searched in the saddlebags for something dry. When she found a shirt she had taken from his cabin, she returned to his side and used it to towel his hair and try to at least take some of the freezing moisture from it. He was unexpectedly still under her ministrations, and she didn't know whether it was acceptance of her pronouncement or simply fatigue.

The fire was catching now, finally offering some heat and light. The flames danced merrily against the dark walls of the cave, and April felt the shivering of MacKenzie's body gradually abate. She slipped down beside him and, without words, he opened the blanket and included April in its warmth. Side by side, silently, they shared the blanket and the fire, listening to the howl of the wind and the sound of sleet pounding a tattoo on the side of the mountain. The words were gone now; none were needed. Both felt comfort at the simple pleasure of being close to one other while the elements warred outside. They disregarded the nervous stamping of the horses and the quiet breathing of the sleeping boy. For those few moments, only the two of them existed in a world made exceptional by the depth of their emotions. The simple touch of their bodies spoke of love, so strong was the electricity that sparked and burned and illuminated.

April snuggled closer to him, feeling as if she belonged there in his warm curves and protective arm. Her hand wandered to his shirt and inside the still damp cloth to his chest. She rubbed its cold hardness until it strained and trembled under her touch. She looked up at his face, and his eyes were now like molten steel, fiery and impassioned. April melted under the gaze, her body almost uncontrollable as it seemed to reach of its own volition toward his, her lips inviting, then demanding with their expectancy.

MacKenzie groaned and surrendered.

He could no longer deny himself, any more than he could stop breathing. He wanted April Manning more than he ever wanted anything in his life, and he was tired of fighting. Of fighting the world; of the exquisite agony of fighting her...and the feelings she aroused in him. At this moment the only thing that existed was the fierce, heated passion that raged between them.

His lips reached down and touched hers with a barely restrained hunger that stoked her own. They seemed to question at first and, finding the answer, sought more. His mouth played with her lips and, feeling them open to him, his tongue reached out and explored greedily. Her tongue met his, and they teased each other in a dance that sent all their senses reeling and crying for more...

MacKenzie knew a craving he had never felt before...and so many other complicated feelings. He had never felt so alive as he did this minute, so completely enveloped in waves of sensation as he felt April's body press against him with a need as elemental as the storm outside and the warmth of a summer sun. The combination was irresistible. As if, he thought wryly, he had any will left to resist.

His lips kissed and caressed with a possessiveness that jolted him, and he drew away for a moment, his eyes assessing. God, how he wanted her. In so many ways. Even while he knew it meant disaster. But at this particular moment, he didn't care. He knew somewhere deep inside that he had been waiting for this all his life. This caring. This gentle, aching link to another person, a puzzling mixture of sweetness and ferocity, of the need to give and take at the same time. Suddenly, nothing existed except this moment. And it had to continue.

MacKenzie saw the question in April's face, and in response he shook his head in defeat and saw the joy leap in her eyes, unaware that it was reflected in his own. He only knew the exultation of feelings acknowledged and returned and treasured.

He felt her hand on his face, exploring its planes, and his hand captured it, bringing it to his mouth. He kissed it simply, first on the palm, then on the back, and he was plunged into waves of longing, longing that could no more be suppressed.

April knew the moment it happened. It was as if a shade had been lifted from his eyes, and he had finally decided to reach out. She felt his hands, both tender and urgent as they reached for her clothes, resting for a moment on her breasts before continuing.

Don't stop, she willed him as she sensed the momentary hesitation.

She felt his hands moving once more to remove the clothing, and she wanted to help as her innermost part quivered and quaked with the need to join with him, to become one, to feel his strength and innate gentleness in the deepest core of her body.

April touched her lips to his cheek, then nuzzled his ear, rejoicing in the rushing momentum of passion that she felt rising in him...and in her. She could barely lay still under his hands, but she was afraid to move, afraid that he might once more distance himself. She didn't think she could stand that, not now when her body was afire and her heart drowning in love for him...and the need to express it in the most intimate and elemental way.

Somehow he had taken his coat off as well as hers, and they lay wrapped in the blanket, skin searing skin. For the moment April wondered how she could have been so cold earlier. For now she felt like rivers of fire as his lips found her breasts and fondled them as waves of pleasure swept through her. She felt him trembling as he moved closer to her, and she could hear the pounding of his heart. Through her torn riding skirt, she felt the throbbing of his need as he pressed even closer to her, igniting wildfires throughout her body, each feeding a giant conflagration, which greedily demanded more and more sensation, more and more touch, more and more everything. She had never known such raging need, or understood how powerful, how all-consuming it could be.

She could not suppress a small moan of desire, of urgency and she felt him stiffen with a passion as deep and compelling as her own. His lips touched her skin, and caressed it, then licked it, leaving trails of liquid fire as he went from one breast to another, the sensations multiplying until April thought she would die if he did not enter her and fulfill the promises he was making with every touch. Her hand went to the mound between his legs, a mound straining against the buckskin, hot and pulsating and full of the same imperative demand that so tormented her, with the necessity to become one, to explore the full eruption of colors and sounds and feelings each teased and awoke in the other. Most of all, she wanted the comfort of his body connected and bound to the deepest essence of her own, for then, and only then, would she truly feel she would know him, would become a part of him, and his life. And this she wanted more than she had ever wanted anything before.

She untied the rawhide thongs on his trousers and felt them giving way, releasing his straining manhood. It seemed so natural to caress him, her fingers touching and exploring, feeling the power and strength...and raw need. Almost from a distance, she heard him moan and shudder with desire barely held in check, and his lips hungrily attacked her mouth as his hands now searched to free her intimate entrance, as *she* had released him.

He groaned once more in frustration as his fingers swept away her riding skirt, only to find pantalets barring his way. Finally, he found the tie, and then he felt her sleek bare stomach. His hands wandered softly down her curved hips to a patch of hair, and he tangled his fingers in it, feeling her body rise and arch in response to his touch...

MacKenzie felt a kind of fear he had never experienced before. He knew there was a magic between them, and he was deathly afraid that he would do something to destroy it, to hurt her, to break the spell that wove them in its golden threads. Every fiber of his being was tingling with anticipation and a sweet gnawing hunger. He had always taken his pleasure quickly, without preliminaries; his partners having had little more interest than he did in anything but the quick physical act, whether it was done for money or lust. But now he ached to prolong each moment, to savor the waves of tenderness that swept him just by touching, to give April the same unconditional love and joy she was now offering him with such complete trust. *He loved her.* He knew it now, without question. And for these few priceless moments he wanted to tell her in every way possible.

His body lowered to hers with a control that required all his massive will to maintain. He let his manhood touch the most sensitive and tender part of her, and he felt her tremble under him. Her hands went around his shoulders, trying to draw him closer, but still he hesitated, wanting to prolong every second, every minute until the fire within them would brook no more delay. His lips once more touched her face, moving with a reverent tenderness from her eyes to her lips as he gently allowed his manhood to probe and caress and finally enter the soft velvet opening that was so irresistibly welcoming. MacKenzie tried to go slowly, to extract every exquisite rush of pleasure as their bodies came together in a symphony of sweet giving, then a burning passion that knew no limits. He thrust deeper and deeper as her body arched upward for more and more, each knowing they had not yet reached the limits of the comet that streaked across their consciousness with such great brilliance. The crescendo built, their bodies moving in tandem, exploring and filling hollows in their lives and knowledge and feelings. They were reaching for the moon, and the stars, and they carried ecstasy with them. With one final, wild, desperate plunge that reached into the core of April's being, they were flooded with billows of fulfillment, one great surge after another, and their world exploded with millions of lights falling around them, trapping them in a radiant glory that shook them both with its grandeur. And love. And belonging. And peace.

They lay together, MacKenzie still warm within her. April felt every after quake as her body quivered at his slightest movement, as her womanhood contracted and moved, seeking every sensation he offered, refusing to relinquish the joy of her body fused with his.

MacKenzie was equally reluctant to move. His tranquillity

was like a drug…her possession of that most sensitive part of him a priceless gift. He felt his shaft growing hard again within April's pulsating core, and he felt her own renewed awareness and hunger. Once more, they came together with a tender ferocity, in a primal rhythm that became a song as they reached new summits of pure, uncomplicated bliss…

April and MacKenzie remained locked together until he felt her shiver and knew the fire was dying. Reluctantly, he finally moved, gently disengaging her and pulling on his buckskin britches. He looked at Davey, wondering how the boy could have slept through the howling storm outside and the intense one inside the cave…but grateful that he had.

He quickly refueled the fire, his eyes rarely leaving April. He piled on enough to keep them until morning and regarded April with quizzical eyes. The invitation was too great to resist. He gathered another blanket, now almost dry, and draped it around her. Without a word, he dropped next to her and held out his arms. She rolled into them and nestled deep into his body, her mouth kissing the arm that held her. She knew he would not be there in the morning, but she was grateful for these minutes and hours. It was strange, she thought. She was in the mountains in the midst of a winter storm, and she had never felt safer. She snuggled even deeper into his curves and closed her eyes.

Chapter Fourteen

MacKenzie woke to an unfamiliar warmth. His arms were still wound tightly around April, and he felt both tenderness and desire rising within him. He did not welcome either of them this morning, but neither did he have regret. It had been too incredible an experience, too miraculous, to regret. But he did know it could not happen again. He could not risk leaving April with child, a quarter-breed bastard of an outlaw. Some of the old bitterness chewed at him as he remembered the few times he had encountered civilization as a child. Civilization! He had felt the hatred. He hadn't understood at first but it was soon made clear to him. He had the scars to remember. And because of all that had happened in the past weeks, a child of his would have a greater burden...a father labeled a rapist and a murderer.

He lay there quietly for minutes, relishing the feel of April in his arms. He wished he could tell her he loved her, but he could not. That would only make things more difficult. For both of them. Instead, his mouth gently touched the curly hair that had escaped the braid. He listened to her quiet breathing, and forced himself to keep from tightening his hold on her. Sweet Jesus, he wanted to keep her there forever.

MacKenzie could hear the wind outside, and he felt the growing chill in the cave. The fire was once more fading, and he needed to stoke it. It was, he judged, near dawn. A faint gray light was snaking its way into the cave. They needed to leave early if they were to reach his father's cabin before dark. His eyes fastened on the cave entrance, and he saw the snow flurries and knew they could not delay.

He carefully unraveled himself from April and the blankets, covering her up. He pulled his shirt on quickly as the cold hit him with a frigid blast. He found his coat, now dry from the fire, and slipped it on. After feeding the fire and watching it roar with new vigor, he walked to the cave entrance and stood there in lonely solitude.

Gray was spreading over a sky churning with rapidly moving clouds. They were threatening-looking lumps this morning, purple and black and fat with moisture...moisture he knew would become snow and ice and freezing rain. The first few flakes of snow were already settling on the earth, like sugar on a cake, but not nearly as benevolent. It would not be an easy journey today. But then, he reminded himself, none of it had been easy. For any of them.

He didn't know exactly how long he stood there, watching the snow's lazy pattern, knowing from experience it could soon change into a blizzard. He felt a strange lassitude. He did not want to leave this place where he had found such warmth and happiness and all-consuming pleasure. He did not want to leave because it must end here. And, God help him, he didn't want it to end, didn't know if he could make it end. Not with the days ahead when they would be forced together by weather and circumstance.

MacKenzie felt April next to him, felt her head leaning on his shoulder. He looked down, thinking how right it felt, having her there. She had the blanket wrapped around her, and his mind disobediently reminded him there was nothing under it. He stiffened with the knowledge, feeling his manhood swell once more within the confining britches.

"It's beautiful," she whispered, looking out at the softly falling snow.

"And dangerous," he replied grimly.

"Like you."

Damn. She could make him feel like a trembling child. His lips pressed tightly together. He wondered how he could keep from touching her.

But April had no such compunctions, and while one hand clutched the blanket, the other reached out and touched his hand. She wasn't ready to relinquish the MacKenzie who had introduced her to such dazzling feelings and emotions.

MacKenzie tried to keep his gaze from her, but the black velvet eyelashes banked her challenging blue eyes, and her mouth was swollen with the passion they had shared…and that both remembered. In every vivid detail.

He jerked away as if touched by a burning brand. And he was. His whole being was on fire. Once more, he felt himself tremble, felt the shudders that ripped through his body at her nearness.

"We must go," he said, self-anger making his voice harsh. "Get the boy." He stalked out of the cave, into the frozen world he knew and understood. *What in hell was happening to him?*

The horses struggled against a howling wind and snow that was becoming denser by the minute. They had been on the trail nearly eight hours, and MacKenzie knew they would be hard put to reach the cabin. Wrapping a blanket tighter around Davey, he kneed his horse, stepping up the pace despite the treacherous footing. It was becoming a race, and MacKenzie didn't intend to lose. There was too much at stake. The weather was worsening faster than he had ever seen it, and for the first time he knew a real fear of the mountains. He could no longer make out the trail that, in the best of times, was only slightly visible. He used landmarks instead…the cliff shaped like the bow of a ship, the knotted, gnarled trunk of an ancient juniper, but even those were disappearing in the swirling snow. He was moving by instinct more than anything else…and prayer, as unfamiliar as it was to him after years of rejecting it completely. It had been his father's refuge…as much as the mountains had been…but his father's religion had been cold and harsh, as merciless as the mountains and their many moods. Retribution had been its keystone. MacKenzie could still hear the echo of his father's curses of damnation against those who had sinned against his family and taken that which should have been his.

MacKenzie had heard the story often enough.

His father's family, an old clan with a wild and proud history, was proscribed in the 1700s…outlawed by the British for their constant attempts to restore the Stuarts to the British throne. Their lands were taken and their leaders beheaded or sold as slaves. It was called transportation, but the title made no difference. It was still slavery, which was worse than death to the proud Scots…to be auctioned off and forced to labor in another man's fields or home. The clan members who escaped such a fate became outlaws and remained outlaws when other clans submitted to British rule.

MacKenzie's grandfather had been publicly hanged by the family that usurped the MacKenzie lands, and Rob MacKenzie had fled Scotland for France, then America, with little more than his pipes and kilts. He retreated to the Kentucky mountains, then moved farther west where, he heard, the mountains resembled the craggy Scotland highlands. But he never forgot the injustices he felt had been inflicted on his family, or the tales of old days when clans raided one another for sport. His background was thievery when he and his father had robbed for their needs, and it was a practice he continued in America until he was caught and almost hung like his father. He had escaped and climbed to a place where no white man would ever find him…unless he wanted them to. He had found refuge for a short time with an Indian tribe where he learned many of the skills he needed in return for teaching them to use the white man's rifles they had stolen. It was 1834, and Rob MacKenzie became one of the first of the mountain men, following Jeremiah Smith by only a few years. Now the men were spotted throughout the Rocky Mountains, nearly all of them hiding or running from something. MacKenzie had always understood them, but had not felt a part of their suspicious brotherhood...until now.

MacKenzie brushed away the bitter thoughts as he sought familiar sights. He felt Davey wriggle with cold in his arms, and he wrapped his arms tighter around the boy. And prayed.

April was numb. The cold had seeped through every layer of her clothes and into her bones. Her hands, in the heavy leather gloves, could hardly cling to the reins as her horse wearily followed MacKenzie's Appaloosa. Her eyes fastened on MacKenzie's back but now, more often than not, it disappeared in the snow and she depended upon the horse to follow. She knew MacKenzie was breaking the trail, which was now high with snow. He frequently looked behind, but still she was seized by numbing fear. What if she got lost? She scolded herself. MacKenzie would never let it happen, but still...it was so cold. So very, very cold. She looked around, wondering how MacKenzie knew where he was going. Everything looked the same to her, like an icy blanket, white and pale and deadly. *Dear God, how much longer?* She felt her horse stumble, then sidestep as it tried to regain its balance. She grabbed for the saddle as she felt herself falling. She screamed.

Everything was fuzzy. Why was it so fuzzy? April tried to lift her head, but it wouldn't cooperate. She heard the thrashing horse next to her, and she tried to reach out and touch it but she felt as if someone had tied her down. *MacKenzie.* Where was MacKenzie? And then he was beside her, his hands, wrapped in torn cloth to keep them warm, fondling her face and running expertly over her body. MacKenzie. She felt a warmth flood her. He was here. He would take care of her. She felt his lips on her face, saw what looked like tears before they froze on his cheek like scars, she thought, as she tried to respond. She finally struggled half upright with supreme effort. She had to help him. She couldn't bear to see his ravaged face.

"April." How nice her name sounded on his lips, she thought sleepily. But just as she savored the sound, she felt pain on cheeks she thought numb, and she realized he had slapped her. She looked at him with astonishment.

"April," he said again, urgency in his voice. "You have to help me."

"Help...?"

"Can you stand?"

She would have died for him, but she didn't know if she could stand. She took his hand and, using his strength, slowly rose, feeling her legs quake under her. She saw the horse thrashing in the snow, and her gloved hand tightened against MacKenzie's as she stared at him questioningly.

"His leg's broken," MacKenzie said, his voice oddly restrained. His hand reached out and stroked the horse's neck, and it quieted under his touch. He stayed there a moment, still rubbing the horse gently. With bleak eyes, he turned to April.

"You take my horse," he said as he moved away from the horse that lay quiet now. He made her walk, knowing she needed the movement to revive her legs, her body. When they reached the patiently waiting Appaloosa, he lifted her into the saddle behind Davey. He walked the horse several feet, then tied the reins to a tree.

His face etched in gravity, he turned back to her. "I won't be long," he said, and the words seemed forced from his throat.

April sat on the horse, clutching Davey, knowing what was coming. She wasn't quite prepared, however, for the sound of gunfire, which echoed through the cold, frozen forest like thunder. Nor was she prepared for MacKenzie's expression when he materialized next to her. It was harder than she had ever seen it. She hadn't thought it possible. Even as thick, driving snowflakes clouded her vision, she could see the agony in his eyes. He took the reins in his hands and started walking. He didn't look back.

MacKenzie led the Appaloosa through drifts two and three feet high. He stumbled and fell but still he kept going, his feet like burning embers under the layers of cloth he had added to the moccasins. He had stopped only once, to cut a blanket and wrap pieces around the inadequate footwear. Ice coated his cheeks and made icicles of his eyelashes. As he had done in the desert, MacKenzie put one foot in front of the other, hoping they would support him a little longer...just a little longer. Where in God's name was the cabin?

April saw it first...a shadow in the distance. At first she thought it a mirage in the graying light, and then the outlines became clearer and clearer. She didn't even try to think how MacKenzie had found it. It was enough that it was here. She looked at MacKenzie, and slowly realized, even in her own cold and tired daze, that he was plodding on as before, completely unaware that they had found safety.

"MacKenzie," she called, but there was no answer, nor did he slow. It seemed as if he would lead them straight past the shelter. She jerked the reins, nearly spilling Davey, and finally MacKenzie responded, turning to her with a puzzled face. She stretched out her arm toward the cabin, and saw realization grow on his face. Without a word, he changed direction and moved toward the cabin, his face grimly shuttered as he released the reins and worked the latch on the door. It didn't want to open under the fumbling of his frozen fingers. April, now unmindful of her own cold agony, lifted Davey from the horse and slipped down, making her own way laboriously through the heavy snow. She took off one of the huge gloves and awkwardly unlatched the door.

April fetched Davey, who had sat down in the snow, too tired and cold to do anything else, and pushed him into the cabin. She watched as MacKenzie entered slowly behind her, every movement impossibly slow and deliberate, and she knew he must be in great pain. Frostbite? Please, no!

Her own immense discomfort meant nothing. Davey and MacKenzie needed her help.

She looked around the cabin, noting its neat, spartan nature, looking for anything that she could use. Thank God, firewood was piled neatly in one corner.

The matches. Where were the matches? Out of one eye, she saw Davey crawl into MacKenzie's lap and saw MacKenzie's arms, almost unconsciously, wrap around the boy. But both were so cold and wet, there was no warmth in either of them.

Matches, April reminded herself. Where...? MacKenzie's coat. She searched frantically, feeling his shivers through material never meant for such intense temperatures. He tried to stand, to help her, but he simply couldn't move again. His legs collapsed under him and he stumbled as she reached to catch him and, with strength she didn't know she had, lowered him onto the rope bed. She tried his pockets again, finally triumphantly coming up with several long matches. She piled wood in the fireplace and tried to light it. The flame sputtered and died, and she tried again. This time a tiny spark hit the dry wood, and she watched as a small red glow inched along a juniper log. She stood there for a moment, incredibly grateful as the thick gum on the log sizzled and sparked and flamed, spreading golden light and the first surge of warmth into the cabin's icy interior.

Disregarding her own overwhelming need to stay close to the fire and soak up a little of its heat, she once more studied the cabin and its meager furnishings. It had been deserted for longer than a little while. Dust and dirt clung to the otherwise flawlessly neat interior. The smell of mold and disuse was heavy. Her eyes finally settled on several worn blankets piled at the end of the bed, and her indecision ended immediately. She pushed aside the enervation caused by cold and weariness, which threatened to paralyze her.

Lifting Davey from MacKenzie's lap, she placed him in

front of the fire, as close as she could safely set him. Then she turned to the man who had once more risked his life for theirs. She carefully unwrapped the freezing wet cloth from around his moccasins, and with great difficulty loosened the frozen thongs, finally pulling the leather from his legs. She looked at them with worried eyes; they were blue and purple, and altogether unnatural looking. April looked up, and saw MacKenzie's eyes on her face. His whole body was shaking with cold, and she was seized by a terrible urgency. She took one of the dry blankets at the end of the rough cot and wrapped it around him, then took the second and wrapped it tightly around his feet and legs. She wanted to rub them, but knew she could not. She had learned that much from a surgeon when her father had been posted in the cold northwest. The frozen limbs would have to warm gradually. MacKenzie silently endured her efforts, not even a facial muscle reflecting the burning pain she knew he must be feeling. His eyes were as hooded and unfathomable as the first time she had seen him.

The first time! It seemed like years ago, now he was so much a part of her life. Her life and soul. Tears gathered at the corners of her eyes as love and tenderness and desperation flooded her. He had to be all right. He had to. Her hands increased the pressure on the blanket, pressing it against his feet, trying to speed the warmth.

MacKenzie watched her helplessly. He knew the danger of frostbite, of subsequent gangrene, but he couldn't move if he wanted to. Every part of him seemed frozen stiff, and his fatigue rendered him powerless. But she should be seeing to Davey, and herself. He tried to tell her that, but she ignored his half-frozen muttering. He didn't know how long she stayed beside him, keeping the blankets tight against his legs, his feet, but finally he felt a tiny warmth creep into them, and the burning sensation diminished in intensity.

Heat from the now roaring fire seeped through the room, gradually replacing some of the fierce icy cold. The cabin, he knew, was tightly built and once warmed would stay that way as long as the fire was continually fed and tended. His father had been nothing if not meticulous. Still, MacKenzie could hear the wild howl of the wind outside, and knew they were not yet safe. Their food supply was low, and they would be in real peril if he could not soon hunt. And the wood...it, too, was in short supply. His expression grew even grimmer as he realized the extreme danger in which he had placed April and Davey. He silently cursed himself for not staying with them at Amos's cabin...to wait for troops, which could guarantee their safety. But he had let his own selfish desires rule his judgment, allowed his compelling need for April to place her in intolerable danger. He had, he knew, almost killed them once more, and he hated himself for it. He had always had a certain pride in himself, he realized ruefully, in his own skills and detachment. It was what had made him a good scout and kept him alive these past years. But that often arrogant objectivity was gone now...destroyed within a matter of weeks until he no longer knew who or what he was.

April's head was leaning over his legs, her chestnut hair glowing in the firelight. Her tenacity and strength astounded him, though he knew by now it should not. She had surprised him over and over again. Surprised and amused and delighted him, and frustrated him. He had never met anyone like her. She must be tired beyond reason, and yet she had not stopped moving since they reached the cabin. Just then she looked up, and he caught the triumph in her eyes and the smile on her lips, and he felt his heart ache. He could never mean anything but death and misery to her. He wanted to give her happiness, but had brought her nothing but hardship and trouble. If he had not fully realized it before, he did now. He moved slightly, retreating from her touch.

"Look after the boy," he said shortly. "And yourself. My legs will be fine now." He hesitated. "Thank you," he added stiffly.

The formal words were like a blow to April. She knew he

was once again moving away from her. She had hoped, believed, they were beyond that now, that their common danger had bonded them even tighter. But it was the opposite, and she thought she knew why. He was blaming himself for what had nearly happened. She would not let him.

"I begged to come," she said. "And I don't regret it."

"You should," MacKenzie rasped. "If not for yourself, for the boy. You don't belong here. You never did. You never will." The words were purposely cruel. He had to break this link between them, had to make her understand there was no future together. Even a short one.

April's face grew taut with stubbornness. "You're wrong. I belong with you. We belong with you. I don't care what you say," she said. "You can't change how I feel." She turned away from him and went closer to the fire, her face easing as she saw Davey asleep on the floor. She wanted to join him, Lord, how she wanted to join him. She was so tired. But the cabin creaked with the force of the blizzard outside, and she remembered the horse. She looked at MacKenzie and knew he had the same thought. He tried to stand but stumbled, and April knew he could not walk yet. Firming her shoulders, she tucked her chin into MacKenzie's heavy sheepskin jacket and started for the door. "I'll take care of the horse."

"Like hell you will," he replied and tried again. But once more his body failed him, and he fell back on the cot, his grizzled face now savage with frustration. He watched with rage as she ignored his words and unbolted the door, disappearing into the gray evening.

April had seen the small shed when they rode in, and now she took the Appaloosa's reins and led him into the stall of what was little more than a lean-to. At least he would have some shelter from the snow and wind. She angrily berated herself for not bringing MacKenzie's gloves, but then she probably wouldn't have been able to do anything anyway. They were altogether too large and bulky. But still...her hands were getting colder by the moment, slowing down each of her motions. She awkwardly unclenched the saddle, and was barely able to catch it as it fell, precious saddlebags, bedrolls and all. She took just an extra second to unwrap a blanket and settle it on the horse. After all, she and Davey and MacKenzie had a fire. April put her face against his muzzle in comfort, wishing she had some oats or an apple or anything. He had done well today. His breath looked like smoke in the air, and she hoped he would be all right. MacKenzie should be better in the morning and he would know what to do. He always did. With that comforting thought, she headed back to the cabin, bedrolls tucked under her arm while cold red hands buried themselves in MacKenzie's sheepskin jacket. She sniffed it appreciatively. It smelled like him. Leathery and masculine and woodsy.

April hesitated before going in despite the cold. She knew he would still be angry. He was always angry when he allowed any emotion to show. Almost always, she amended with a small smile as she thought of the previous night.

She pushed open the door, allowing a blast of cold air to enter with her before she could push it shut again and drop the bar across it. Davey was still asleep, and MacKenzie was sitting up, his back against the wall as he eyed the door impatiently, his lips compressed in their usual tight line. He had obviously not mellowed in the few minutes she was gone; he seemed, in fact, even more frustrated. From the mess of blankets on the floor, it was obvious that he had tried to walk again—and failed.

April dropped her burdens on the floor and unwrapped them, placing the wet things near the fire and drawing a dry blanket around Davey. She then handed a blanket to MacKenzie. "You need some rest," she said, and braced herself for the sparks she knew she would see.

She was not disappointed. "You expect me to sleep here like a wee babe while you and the boy sleep on the floor?"

"Davey's content," she answered, "and I don't want to disturb him, and as for me...I thought..." She looked at one side of the bed longingly. She wanted to sit, to lie down. The weariness was catching up with her now...the fatigue and the fear and the cold. She knew she would always remember the bone-aching cold. And more than anything she wanted the comfort of his presence, of his body. She wanted to share her warmth with him and know they were safe. Her legs almost gave under her, and she took a step toward him before they gave way completely and she felt herself falling. Her eyes closed before she saw him quickly lean forward and catch her in his arms, but she felt their power...and gentleness. She barely heard his soft, crooning voice. "Such a brave girl." She felt his lips on her brow, and she didn't want to open her eyes. Not ever.

She fell asleep there, finally captured by complete exhaustion and by the comfort of his closeness. She didn't know he held her there for minutes that turned into hours, unmindful of anything but the light, courageous bundle in his arms and the strange feeling of contentment that spread within him. He waited until her breathing deepened and he knew she would not wake easily.

MacKenzie finally shifted his burden, lying her flat on the bed and covering her with blankets. He used the side of the bed to help him rise, feeling once more the sharp pain in his feet and the exhaustion that had numbed his body and made it useless. He stumbled, more than walked, to the fireplace, piling new logs on the still blazing fire. He then took one of the drying blankets, wrapped it around himself and lay down next to Davey. He thought of April on the bed and hungered for the feel of her. It was a hunger he would tame. He had to. But Lord, at what price? He didn't know how long they would be here; they could be snowed in for days, weeks, even months. The very thought was torture. Despite his complete exhaustion, MacKenzie lay awake for hours...wondering what in the hell he would do. He listened to the lonely wail of the wind and a faraway coyote and the crackle of burning wood, and he wondered...

Chapter Fifteen

The next two days were among the most miserable April had ever spent.

The blizzard continued unabated, and they were forced to remain together in the small cabin but, as far as MacKenzie and April were concerned, they might have been hundreds of miles apart.

No matter what April tried, MacKenzie seemed to withdraw further and further. Neither she nor Davey seemed able to coax even the smallest smile from him, although in the evenings, MacKenzie would spend hours with Davey, telling of Scottish adventures and legends and history. They constituted most of the stories he knew, stories that he thought would distract an active young boy confined to a small cabin. But he never smiled. Never.

Once in a while, April would catch his eyes fastened on her, but they were always hooded, and she couldn't tell what he was thinking. Or feeling. Then he would slowly turn away, not quickly as if caught unexpectedly, but slowly, deliberately. It hurt, but then she suspected that in some way it was meant to. That he was warning her in the only way he thought she might understand. Words certainly hadn't done it.

The morning after their arrival, April had awakened cold and alone, her hands stretched out for someone who wasn't there. In her half-awake state, she was seized by fear and emptiness...such a great emptiness. Her eyes flew open, but the room was dark, lit only by the flickering flames of the fire. Her eyes adjusted to the dim light as her heart pounded with a sudden panic. Where was Davey? MacKenzie?

It slowed only slightly as she saw the two forms on the floor, one small and one large, each sleeping peacefully. Why had he left her? She remembered his arms around her last night, the comforting warmth of his body, the tender feel of his lips on her forehead. Why had he left? There was room for both of them. She drew her blankets closer around her as she felt the chill. She wasn't quite sure whether it was from the cold that was once more invading the cabin or from the loneliness she instantly felt at MacKenzie's abandonment. She huddled on the bed, wondering what was happening outside. Was it still night or had dawn come? Was it still snowing or had it stopped? It was impossible to tell with the two windows shuttered and barred, but she no longer heard the battering of the wind against wood. There was only complete quiet except for the occasional tiny explosion from the fire as it found a pocket of sap in the wood.

She knew she should get up and put new logs on the fire, but she felt an unusual languor, created, she thought, from a combination of leftover weariness and disappointment at finding herself alone on the bed. She wanted MacKenzie next to her. She yearned to fit into his hard, muscled body and feel his arms protectively around her. *Get up, April. Don't torture yourself.*

April moved slowly, trying to infuse herself with the old energy. Somehow, MacKenzie had taken her coat off, but all her other clothes remained and she felt heavy and burdensome, even while grateful for the warmth they provided. How could he be attracted to her? She knew her hair must be tangled despite the ugly practical braid, and strands had come loose, matting around her face. She had not had a bath in days and suspected her face was smudged and dirty. She felt woefully lacking in every way. She buried her head in the blanket like a child, trying to escape the reality of a misdeed.

Another need cropped up, one that wouldn't be denied. She would have to get up and make a trip outdoors. She dreaded it. If she opened the door, she would wake MacKenzie, and she wasn't quite sure if she wanted to face him at the moment. And she shivered at the thought of baring even a part of herself in the frigid temperatures.

But it had to be done.

She finally struggled to her feet, feeling the chill in the cabin that even the fire couldn't alleviate completely. Reluctantly she moved to the diminishing pile of logs and added two to the blaze. She found the sheepskin coat next to the bed and pulled it on. When she reached the door, she looked at MacKenzie before unbarring it and saw that his eyes were open and steady on her.

She went over to him, stooping down. "How are you?"

He gave her only an almost imperceptible nod in answer as he cautiously sat up. His face had settled into its old, grim, implacable lines. "You're not to go out alone," he said, rougher than he intended. Then his voice gentled as he tried to explain. "You don't know this area...there could be crevices just barely covered over, or you could easily get lost." He hadn't lost that terrible fear from yesterday when he was afraid April and Davey might die in the storm. He didn't want to take any more chances.

"You can't go with me," she replied, a small, embarrassed smile on her lips, and he immediately understood.

He used a corner of a chair to help himself stand, then limped painfully to the door. He took the bar down and opened the door. The snow was still falling in huge thick flakes. April could barely see the shed.

He closed it again, then fetched his coat, shrugging it on before reopening the door. He took her arm protectively and headed toward the shed, then nodded for her to go to its side. April flushed, remembering that first morning after they had been taken by MacKenzie. She had been mortified when he so nonchalantly acknowledged bodily functions. After so many years of pretending they really didn't exist, particularly in the presence of men, she found it awkward, if not difficult, to understand his casual acceptance of such needs even while she knew it was an absurd social custom not to do so. Without another word, she did what she was told. For the sake of her chilled flesh and her mental discomfort, she quickly took care of her physical needs, straightened her clothes and, with as much dignity as she could muster, returned to MacKenzie, who was looking after his horse.

His veiled eyes might have held a second of amusement at her obviously wounded modesty despite their weeks together, but the severity of his facial expression did not change, and she wondered if she'd imagined it.

"Why did you leave me last night?" she asked bluntly, deciding to attack.

"Because it's best," he replied with a deep frown.

"I needed you," she said, throwing her pride to the winds. She found it meant little compared to her overwhelming need for him.

"You don't need anyone, April," he said, his eyes fierce, blazing with something April couldn't identify. "Much less me or the trouble I carry."

"You didn't do anything..."

"Damn it, April. I have led you into one danger after another. You and Davey have nearly died several times because of my selfishness, because I took him when I had no right. Because I didn't stay with you at Amos's cabin. Do you know how close you both came to freezing to death yesterday?" She flinched at the bitter self-condemnation in his voice as he continued slowly, painfully. "I wanted you...wanted you both...just a little longer, and I almost killed you." A muscle flexed in his jaw. "We have to forget what happened...back there at the cave. And when it's clear enough, I'm taking you back."

She stared at him. "But you can't..."

His voice was harsh. "I can and I will...and I'll not leave

you with a bastard child, a part-Indian bastard.'' He turned to her, his expression fierce. ''Do you understand, April? It can never happen again.''

''No,'' she said defiantly. ''You can't change the way I feel, no matter how hard you try.''

She could barely hear his words, but she knew they were a long, frustrated curse. ''It won't happen again,'' he repeated with finality.

He took her arm and, ignoring a brief moment of resistance, led her back to the cabin.

He was as good as his words in the next few days as the snow continued to fall heavily. Confined to the cabin, they ate the remaining food, and any conversation was between Davey and MacKenzie, who was unfailingly gentle with the boy. He virtually ignored April except for a few polite words. On his occasional short trips to get wood and see to the horse, he had found a place under a stand of trees where the snow was not as thick and the animal could dig for grass under the snow with his hoofs. There were also oats and a little fodder in the shed from his father's time.

But even MacKenzie was reluctant to venture far in the blinding snow, and tension in the small cabin continued to grow.

On the third day, April rose after a sleepless, lonely night and opened the cabin door to find that the snow had finally stopped falling. Instead, there seemed an unearthly peace this morning. Fresh snow glistened and sparkled in the first glimmers of a rising sun. The sky, frothy yesterday with dark clouds, was now pink and gold and the palest pristine blue. The pines were wreathed with crowns of white, tinted by the gentle colors of dawn, and their branches dipped with silver ornaments. It seemed a fairyland. Pure and untouched and lovely. April almost forgave the blast of freezing air that accompanied it.

She stood in awe, unable to say meaningless words. And then she felt MacKenzie's presence.

MacKenzie understood her silence. Only too well. The scene seemed entirely too perfect to be real. But he also knew the beauty disguised the dangers: drifts that covered chasms, hunger that lured the predators; the blanket of white that hid landmarks and could easily deceive; a numbing cold that could kill silently. "You're not to go alone," MacKenzie reminded April. His voice was harsh, without tenderness.

Davey was just waking when they reentered the cabin, eyes crusted with sleep, and April knew she would have to make a trip outside, but MacKenzie moved quicker, putting his lighter coat on and bundling Davey up. April eyed him speculatively, then gave him, instead, the sheepskin coat. "You'll need this," she said, meeting his direct gaze with one of her own, refusing to back down. MacKenzie shrugged and took it.

MacKenzie's scarcity of words continued for the rest of the morning. After he and Davey returned, he distributed what little food they had to Davey and April despite her protests that he had kept nothing for himself.

"I'll find some game," he said shortly. "Stay inside the cabin until I return." His tone permitted no argument, and April nodded, any rebellion quelled by the hungry rumbling of her stomach. She watched him disappear out the door without further words.

The day seemed endless. Occasionally April would unbar the door and look out, but each time a blast of cold air would blow in, and it would take hours for the fire to reheat the cabin. She would have been frightened if she had not, by now, known MacKenzie so well. Despite his pronounced limp, she knew he would bring food back.

April used part of the time to take some snow from outside the cabin and heat it in a large pot she found in the corner. She poured some of it in a pitcher for drinking water and used the remainder to wash both herself and Davey. He still looked like a chimney sweep, and she knew she didn't look much better, despite a similar attempt to wash clean the day before.

She had felt self-conscious then, trying to wash in front of MacKenzie, and had just rearranged the dirt. April found the mirror MacKenzie had used earlier to shave. There had been a strange intimacy in watching him perform such a personal task. She had tried to avert her eyes, but couldn't, and she knew he was watching her through the mirror. Now she looked in it, and promptly wished she hadn't.

Her face was red and raw, first, she supposed, from exposure from the sun, then the cold. Her hair, which she usually kept washed and tamed in a neat knot at her neck, had escaped much of the braid and went in all sorts of odd directions. It had lost its reddish shine and looked dark and heavy and ugly. Her hands were likewise far from the soft white skin she had previously pampered. They, too, were raw-looking and covered with calluses. April regarded herself sorrowfully, wishing for the luxury of sitting down to cry, but there was Davey, restless Davey, to think about. *How could MacKenzie care for her at all?*

She steeled herself against self-pity. MacKenzie certainly hadn't asked her to fall in love with him. She had all but thrown herself at him. And if she was completely honest with herself, which she was loath to be, she could delete the words ''all but.''

April didn't understand how quickly she had fallen in love with a man who didn't want to be loved. After David's death, after four years of complete purgatory, of waiting, she had vowed never to subject herself to such agony again. And now she was in love with a man whose life expectancy was probably even lower than her husband's had been.

And yet, she would do anything, sacrifice anything, to be with him. Anything but Davey. Deep in her soul, she knew MacKenzie would never allow anything to happen to her son. Which was why she was so ready to give her heart, to journey with him anyplace, under any conditions. But despite that night before the storm, he had given no further indication he felt the same. He had never, ever mentioned the word "love." He had merely taken what was offered.

She missed him even now, even that glowering presence that held her at arm's length. She missed the masculine scent of him, the way he dominated the cabin, the catlike grace with which he moved. She missed everything about him. And she always would, no matter where she was, or where he might go.

April played absentmindedly with Davey. He had brought out MacKenzie's carved horse and they discussed, most solemnly, a name for it.

"Horse," Davey finally said.

"That's no name," April scoffed. She thought she had offered some much better ones.

"That's what MacKenzie calls his horse," Davey insisted.

"He does?" April said. Come to think of it, she had never heard him call his horse much of anything. She wrinkled her nose. "Horse?"

"Well, he says that's what it is. No sense putting fancy names on it, he said. It'll do the same no matter what you call him."

April sighed. MacKenzie didn't even want to get familiar with his damned horse. What chance had she? She supposed she was lucky that he called her April. When he wasn't calling her Mrs. Manning. Thank God that, at least, had stopped.

"I still think," she insisted, "that *this* horse would like a name. Devil take MacKenzie."

"That's it," Davey grinned like a pleased gremlin. "I'll call him Devil."

It wasn't exactly what April had had in mind, but her son looked so pleased with himself she didn't protest.

"I can't wait to tell MacKenzie," Davey ran on. "When do you think he'll be back?"

April flinched. It would be just like Davey to explain exactly how Devil had been named. "It shouldn't be long...let's look outside." She sincerely hoped it wouldn't be long for many reasons. She could hear her stomach growl and churn with hunger, and she knew Davey must be feeling the same empty feeling. They still had some flour, but without lard or fat or meat she didn't know quite what to do with it.

She and Davey bundled in their heavy clothes and opened the door, going out quickly and closing it behind them to keep the cold air from snaking its way inside. Once again, she thought how beautiful it was as the snow glistened in the sun. Davey was silent. He had seen snow in Boston, but never like this, never so purely white.

"Let's build a fort," he said suddenly, his face aglow with excitement. He had never been allowed to play in the snow in Boston, not unless he and April sneaked out. Even then they had faced disapproving stares when they returned... which had spoiled everything.

April remembered MacKenzie's warning, but at the moment she decided not to heed it. *He* had gone out, and had been away for nearly half a day, and she, as well as Davey, already had cabin fever. It wasn't fair that he could roam the woods while she and Davey stayed penned in the sparse cabin. Besides, she reasoned, they were almost at the door of the cabin. The eagerness on Davey's face precluded any additional caution. She caught her son's excitement, and together they started building their own peculiar version of a fortification.

Busy packing the walls with the same diligence her five-year-old had, April didn't realize that Davey had moved farther and farther afield in his search for branches to use as cannons. She heard his frightened voice before she even noticed he was not at her side.

"Mama."

April looked up, and her body turned numb as she saw a wolf approach from the woods, its fangs bared and a small growl coming from deep in its throat.

Oh, God, not again. Why had she not heeded MacKenzie's words?

The wolf was approaching cautiously, all menacing, lean

grace. Davey was between her and the animal. April very carefully stood and took one slow step after another toward her son, afraid any quick movement might bring a similar response from the wolf. Perhaps her size might frighten the animal...she knew they usually went after smaller game. Like her son.

The wolf stopped but didn't retreat. April continued, one terrified step after another, all the time whispering to Davey to keep him still, keep him calm. She saw the wolf's fierce dark eyes follow every step and almost felt the lithe power of the beast when it seemed to tense as if ready to spring. Still she continued, fearful her legs would buckle under her. It seemed like hours but she finally reached Davey and very deliberately picked him up. She took one step backward, then another, and her throat caught when she saw the wolf stalking them like a rabbit or a young deer. If only she could get to the door. She heard the growl again. It came from deep within the animal, and she shuddered at its vicious sound. Why hadn't she at least brought the pistol? She imagined it was still in the shed where she had left it last night. Only ten more feet, then eight, then six. The wolf poised for attack, and April knew she wouldn't make it in time. She could only hope to divert the animal until Davey escaped inside.

She whispered to Davey, "When I put you down, go inside and bar the door, no matter what. Wait until MacKenzie gets back before you open it. Do you understand?"

Davey didn't. Not exactly. But his mother's tone was more grim than he had ever heard it. He nodded.

He was halfway to the door when April heard a low whistle and saw the wolf pause, then turn in the direction of the sound. In numb amazement, April saw the beast bound toward MacKenzie who stood at the edge of the clearing. For a moment, her heart stopped as she expected the wolf to lunge at MacKenzie. But the scout's rifle was at his side and he stood there unconcerned, a rare smile on his face.

The wolf stopped at MacKenzie's feet and sat, his previously lethal-looking teeth bared in what could be nothing but a grin. April's eyes went from animal to man, almost feeling the affection flowing between the two, although MacKenzie made no move to touch the beast.

April felt herself trembling almost uncontrollably. She felt Davey's hand snake itself into her glove, and knew he was also suffering from the aftermath of fear.

MacKenzie faced them both, the slight smile still on his face, his eyes warm. She had done it again, risking her life for her son's. He thought he had seldom seen such courage as he came into the clearing. April Manning had been willing to be torn apart for Davey's safety. He had thought her beautiful before but never quite so much as now.

"You need not worry," he said gently now. "The wolf will not hurt you...he was just guarding the cabin. He would not have attacked unless someone attacked me." He took a step toward Davey, and the wolf rose and followed at MacKenzie's heel. Davey stepped back, but MacKenzie stretched out his hand toward the boy, and Davey hesitantly, fearfully, took a trusting step toward him.

MacKenzie's hand reached Davey's and took the small one, urging him even closer, until boy and wolf were almost together. He could feel the trembling of Davey's grasp, and he felt brief pleasure that the boy so trusted him. He stooped until the three of them were all at the same height. "Let him sniff you," MacKenzie told Davey quietly, and Davey bravely withstood the animal's inspection. "Now you," he said, looking at April who stood, still mute and almost in shock. When she didn't react, he reached out his other hand for her, and she took it, following his example and stooping. She tried to hide her fear as the huge, lean animal sniffed her, its tongue flopping out of the side of its fierce-looking mouth.

MacKenzie stood, pulling her up. "He'll protect both of you now...with his life if necessary."

April couldn't rid herself of fear quite that easily. "I don't understand."

"I raised him from a cub...his mother had been killed," MacKenzie said slowly. "I take him when I go to the valley, but when I'm scouting I bring him here...to his old home. I think he's safer here. People...hunters...wouldn't understand a tame wolf."

"Tame?" April finally managed. The wolf had seemed anything but tame to her.

"He's not afraid of men, not like other wolves. He would be easy prey. Sometimes I wonder if I shouldn't have taken him back to the wilds sooner. There's no place for a wild thing in civilization."

April wondered for a brief moment if MacKenzie was thinking only of the wolf. She looked at the animal and sensed why MacKenzie and the wolf appeared so well matched. They were alike, these two. Both creatures of the forest: lean, graceful and cautious.

She felt Davey move next to her, and she saw his small hand touch the wolf, who now tolerated it with an air of complete indifference.

"Does he have a name?" April asked, feeling foolish as MacKenzie raised his eyebrows quizzically.

"Name?" he questioned.

April remembered Davey's earlier revelation about the horse. Her mouth turned up in a sudden smile. "Wolf, I suppose?" she said mischievously.

MacKenzie's throat constricted. He liked her more every day. Liked? Loved! He longed to reach out and touch her, to place his fingers at the corner of her smiling lips and taste her sweetness again. His hand started to reach out, then fell back to his side. He nodded curtly and forced anger into his voice. "I thought I told you to stay inside."

April's smile faded, and MacKenzie felt he had just tortured a young live thing. But there was no help for it. He had to keep a distance. He had to...for both their sakes. He had to keep control, and he had to make sure she obeyed his commands...for her own safety.

"I...I...thought...we were just outside the cabin door."

"Damn it," he exploded. "Anything could happen just outside. You didn't even bring the gun with you."

"And if I had, your...pet...would be dead," she retorted, her anger growing at his sudden arrogance.

MacKenzie had no easy answer to that. He did not doubt it for a moment. April handled herself well in emergencies, and he knew by now she had not boasted when she had said she could use a pistol.

He looked at Davey. The boy's eyes were going from MacKenzie's face to his mother's. He sensed the sudden hostility and didn't understand it. His hand went to the wolf and buried itself in the deep, thick fur, his eyes clouded.

"We won't discuss it in front of the boy," MacKenzie said abruptly and turned away.

"Damn you, MacKenzie. You won't discuss anything. Ever. You just order."

He whirled around, astounded at the sudden fury in April's voice. Even the night of his escape, he had not heard such angry depths. He winced as she cautioned.

"You can't keep running from everything forever..."

"I'm not..." he started to say, then stopped. He *was* running away from her...as much as he was running from those who would take him to Defiance. Even if it was for her sake and Davey's, it was still running. Despite her words, he was not used to it. Yet it seemed all he was doing now. Running from the army. From his own tumultuous emotions. From April. Retreating. He was suddenly uncertain.

His right hand knotted in frustration. "I'm trying to keep you alive, damn it," he growled. "And you don't make it easy."

April's indignant face relaxed. That soft, telling burr was back in his voice, and she saw the shadow of pain flit across his eyes. She sought to break the tense silence. "Did you find some game?"

"Aye," he said. "An elk. I brought back what I could. I hung up the rest...to keep it from the wolves."

"Does that include your wolf?"

"He roams with them at times...when I'm not here. He'll stay close now to the cabin." He looked at her. "I meant what I said. Davey will be as safe with Wolf as with me. He's very protective..."

"I noticed," April said wryly. "I was sure he was going to attack." She shuddered, remembering those few horrible moments.

"I should have warned you," MacKenzie said. "But I thought I would see him before you did. If you had stayed in the cabin..."

April bit her lip in exasperation. "I know," she said. "But you can't expect us to remain locked up inside forever."

He nodded, knowing she was right. He should have realized how difficult it would be for an active young woman and child to stay inside, particularly when the outside was so inviting in the sunlight. It had been his fault, not hers. He was not used to women and children, and it had not occurred to him that their restlessness might override their obedience. It was just another example of why he needed to see them safely home. He couldn't protect them here, no matter how hard he tried.

MacKenzie, the wolf at his heels, turned and limped to where the Appaloosa was standing at the fringe of the clearing. He had been walking most of the morning, and each step worsened the pain in one of his feet. It still had not quite healed. He remembered the moment he had approached the clearing and had seen April's terrified face as she had whispered to Davey and turned to face the wolf alone...

Now he lifted two haunches of meat from the saddle. He set one on the ground while he took a knife to the other, cutting two large pieces of meat. He deliberated over what to do with the remaining carcass, finally deciding to hang it from a tree just outside the clearing. He wanted it no place near the shed where the Appaloosa stayed, in case it attracted wolves.

He looked up and saw April standing there, ready to take the meat. "I can cook it," she said. She looked at his feet, still clad in the knee-high moccasins. "You need to sit down, or lie down, or..."

April was a bit surprised when he handed her his bounty without comment. "I'll take care of the meat and horse first," he said. "Davey should get inside. The cold is deceptive."

"For you, too," she warned and was rewarded with a small, rueful smile and a nod.

"Soon," he agreed, and her heart caught at how the small smile relieved the harsh, uncompromising lines of his face. It was such a strong face, and yet it could be gentle and compassionate. When he would let it. With an effort, she forced herself to turn toward the cabin, ushering a reluctant Davey inside. Now that Davey's fear of the wolf was gone, he wanted to stay with the huge beast.

Compared to the food of the past few days, dinner was wonderful. April had roasted a large piece of elk on a spit, and had already started a soup, which she thought would be just right in the morning. There were no spices other than some salt that MacKenzie had brought from his own cabin in the valley, but she could thicken the soup with some flour and it would be warm and hearty. They all ate well, including MacKenzie, who had finally appeared and agreed to sit while she tended the fire. He said little, but April could feel his eyes on her.

She thought of the wolf. That a wolf should be his sole friend and companion seemed tragic to her. And yet, as she thought of them together there was a rightness about it. They *were* alike: fierce yet unexpectedly gentle, wild yet protective. She wondered how long it had taken MacKenzie to tame the wolf, and how long it would take her to gentle MacKenzie? Or even if she wanted to. Perhaps that was what attracted her so...that wild free spirit. And she wondered if it could ever, completely, be done? And whether some day either one— MacKenzie or the wolf—would turn on the one that limited their freedom?

Chapter Sixteen

The tension between April and MacKenzie was always there, live and sizzling, as October turned into November and November into December. Although there was no additional snow, except for an occasional flurry, the temperatures froze what was on the ground, and MacKenzie knew there was no way through the passes that led to his mountain hideout.

For him, it was a time of supreme joy and supreme agony.

He treasured every moment during the day with the boy and April, but each night was a long, hellish torment as he warred with himself. So far his iron determination to stay away from April had won, but just barely. And the open, wanting invitation in her eyes had not helped matters.

At his insistence, April slept in the bed with Davey, and he continued to use the floor. It did not bother him. He was used to sleeping on the ground, and the floor next to a fire was almost a luxury in itself. At least it would have been had April not been inches away.

He would often rise in the middle of the night and sit, watching her sleep and feeling himself grow rigid with need and desire. Her black lashes swept the eyes he could never dismiss from his thoughts, and her mouth beckoned him. What was always so agonizing was that he knew she was there for him…waiting, willing, needing. It was only his own willpower that kept him from the bed.

After minutes, even hours, of thus torturing himself, he

would sometimes get up and go inside, letting the cold air douse a body nearly ready for explosion. Wolf would join him, and he would stare at the myriad stars haloing the white-clad mountains and wonder what had happened to him...to the man who had never needed or wanted anyone. One part of him longed to lose himself in the old protective isolation, but another knew he had been immeasurably enriched. He had been given unqualified love and trust by both April and Davey, and it had made him whole for the first time in his life.

Although the days had settled into a routine of activity, they were routine in no other way. So many moments were joyful treasures to be hoarded and remembered. All but the persistent ache in his loins that wouldn't go away. It was a constant reminder of the barrier between April and himself, of the potential disaster if he weakened in his resolve. A child. At times he would fantasize about having a child with April, and he would briefly allow his heart to soar. And then it would come plummeting down as he considered the consequences, the uncertain future such a child would have, the danger to April. And he would place the thought aside in some secret place within him and berate himself for his foolishness.

In the meantime, there were times of great sweetness and a belonging he had never known. Realizing the stark truth of April's accusing words the afternoon Wolf appeared, he started taking Davey and April for long walks every morning. With Wolf beside them, MacKenzie and Davey would explore fresh tracks in the snow, search for patches of grass for the Appaloosa and even indulge in occasional moments of snowball pelting.

April would usually stand back and watch, content with the sight of boy and man enjoying each other so completely, feeling the joy bubbling inside her that such was so. She had never seen MacKenzie so relaxed or Davey so happy. The scout even smiled on occasion, sometimes forgetting to catch himself, she thought impishly. Her only misery was his continued insistence that they stay apart at night. He recoiled from her slightest touch, shying as if burned when their fingers accidentally met at mealtimes. She would have been hurt and angered were it not for the fierce hunger his eyes could no longer hide, or the nights she woke and sensed his gaze on her and heard the frustrated closing of the door as he went outside.

She knew him well enough to realize that the only thing holding him back was pride, that deep, fierce pride that demanded he keep her and Davey safe. He mistakenly thought the danger lay within himself. It was a belief April intended to dissolve; to make him see that happiness also lay there. But she had decided to move slowly, to let him learn bit by bit what it meant to love. She had the time, she thought, as she looked at the icy cliffs and ravines still filled with snow, although the sun had washed some patches of earth clear. And the reward would be worth it. The future would take care of itself. She had to believe that...for she could no longer think of a life without MacKenzie.

MacKenzie continued to hunt alone in the afternoons, leaving Wolf with April and Davey. He thought they were safe enough from predators when guarded by the huge, protective beast. But he still warned them not to venture out of sight of the cabin. They had plenty of elk meat remaining, but MacKenzie didn't know how long they would be here, or whether they might be victim to another blizzard. He wanted skins for warmth and a sure supply of food. He brought back rabbit and venison, and he and April and Davey would smoke some, as well as dry strips of meat.

There was a warm intimacy about these days despite MacKenzie's grave reserve. April saw new sides of him daily: a sly sense of humor as he recited some Burns verse; a curiosity about everything that matched Davey's own; a tender playfulness as he wrestled with Davey on the cabin floor.

But she was restless, and MacKenzie recognized it. She was

intrigued when one day he brought home something that would have appalled her months earlier: a bloody animal skin.

He cautiously watched her expression, a combination of interest and horror, and he gave her that rare slight smile. "I thought you might learn to dress a skin."

April eyed the bloody mess dubiously, wondering how it could ever become anything useful, especially under her hands. But she had been complaining she had little to do, and she could hardly decline. Besides, she had done much worse. She shuddered as she thought of the bear so many months ago, and how she had butchered it.

So she nodded and was immediately pleased she had. His eyes warmed to a rich charcoal, and the twist of his mouth grew a trace wider.

"What do I do first?" she said.

"I think we'll wash it first," he said, his eyes conveying a small twinkle as she continued to eye his prize dubiously.

April accompanied him to the stream near the cabin. It was iced over, but MacKenzie had chopped a hole on the first day and kept it open by breaking the ice every morning. It was here he fished and drew their water. He filled a pail, and they rinsed the skin together, their hands tingling with the cold before they finished.

Strangely enough in this new world of hers, April particularly cherished the next step, for she and MacKenzie worked in tandem, and even Davey helped. The three of them laid the skin on the floor of the cabin, and she and Davey spread ashes over the hair side of the hide, which lay stretched on the floor. They then poured water over the ashes, according to MacKenzie's instructions, and in three or four days they were easily able to pull the hair from the skin.

Davey found the process a game, piling his hair in a neat lump and challenging April and MacKenzie to match his growing pile. Before long they were all speeding along, laughing as they sought to outdo each other. MacKenzie was uncharacteristically clumsy; and April grinned inside at his obvious attempt to give Davey a victory.

Their hands met occasionally, and for once MacKenzie didn't pull away, but let his hand rest against hers for a fraction of a second as his eyes glinted in a way she had not seen before. She swallowed, forcing the breath through the thick lump that settled in her throat so frequently now. She loved these rare moments when he relaxed and the angular planes in his face smoothed out in a smile. It was dazzling to her, like the first rays of sun striking the ice-covered stream and sending paths of gold and silver skittering over it. Or the rainbow over a rain-washed forest.

She wondered, but only for seconds, how a chore so inherently distasteful as this could be such a joy. But then almost everything accomplished with MacKenzie was a pleasure.

Davey won the hair-pulling race, and he swaggered with no little pride, MacKenzie's amused eyes on him as he sought a reward. They finally settled on one: a song, one of Davey's favorites, about a frog courting a mouse.

"How could a frog speak to a mouse?" Davey asked after the song. "They wouldn't speak the same way, would they?"

"He croaks and she squeaks," MacKenzie answered with the mischief worthy of a small boy. "I guess they just gradually learn to understand each other."

"But how?"

MacKenzie cast a pleading look at April. He was still not completely used to little-boy questions.

"When you love someone," April said with mischief of her own sparking in her eyes, "you just naturally understand." The message was aimed at MacKenzie as much as at Davey.

"But..." Davey persisted.

"There are ways you understand," April said. "The look in an eye, the touch of a hand. Like when you touched Wolf. You didn't speak the same language, but you knew when you became friends."

Davey smiled, finally satisfied. Wolf and he *did* talk in their own peculiar fashion.

April looked at MacKenzie, who wore an expression of part admiration, part wry understanding.

"I think," he said slowly to Davey, obviously trying to change the subject, "that you might like to learn to speak like a Scot."

Davey's eagerness was only too apparent. He hadn't understood some of MacKenzie's stories before, but he had known from his tone whether it was funny or sad. Now he soaked up his first Gaelic words, and laughed as MacKenzie rolled off some that he had heard before, taking heed of what his mother had told him.

He listened carefully as MacKenzie explained that "rantin" meant merry, and "hae" meant "have," and "warl'" meant world. And then MacKenzie's wonderful deep voice enriched the room as he recited with a lilt in his voice:

"O Willie, come sell your fiddle,
O sell your fiddle sae fine
O Willie, come sell your fiddle,
And buy a pint of wine;

If I should sell my fiddle,
The warl' would think I was mad,
For many a rantin day
My fiddle and I hae had."

It was an exquisite evening for April, and she hugged it to herself, afraid it might flee along with MacKenzie's rare mood. There was a light in his eyes, and she could tell he was thoroughly enjoying himself. Once she caught his eye and he even smiled, as if, for this evening anyway, he had cast aside all his devils.

She had hoped, in some part of her, that he would join her in bed, but though he didn't hide the longing in his face, he placed a sleepy, happy Davey on the bed and, without a final word, rolled up in his blanket beside the fire.

But April had something to keep her warm. MacKenzie was changing, slowly. He was letting himself relax, feel, smile. It was no little progress, she thought, and she went to sleep, still hearing his "Froggy Went A'Courtin'" song.

The deerskin continued to keep them occupied over the next several days.

Once the hair was removed, MacKenzie placed the skin in a large pail of water and animal fat and let it cure for a few days. After that he showed her how to work it and beat it over a stump or log until it dried. The whole process, messy though it was, gave April a tremendous sense of accomplishment. She blushed under MacKenzie's sparse praise and watched with satisfaction as the skin emerged as something beautiful and useful. In three months, there were several such skins, and they used them for additional covering.

One evening after a skin was completely dried, April sat in the one chair near the fire, fingering the soft, supple leather, which she was stitching into new moccasins for MacKenzie. MacKenzie was on the floor with Davey, the two dark heads bent together as MacKenzie recited another poem. She had ceased to wonder about his uncanny ability to remember so many and the expressive way he relayed them. She listened closely as his soft burr once more deepened into the taste of the Scottish tongue. She could make out a few words, "The Twa Dogs," but not much more, and she doubted whether Davey could, either, but MacKenzie's deep voice was mesmerizing, and she felt shivers as it rose and fell according to the content of the poem.

His voice was humorous and wistful by turns, and April felt herself melting at the complete delight of it. MacKenzie was such a strange man, so full of contradictions and unexpected depths and riches. Each day she discovered a new facet, and she fell deeper in love until she thought her love could be no greater. But then something else would happen...he would whistle with a bird, or tempt a squirrel to his hand, or wrestle ever so gently with Davey, and she knew what she felt would grow every day of her life, and the thought made her eyes mist. More than anything else in the world, she wanted to bring him joy and laughter and love. Gifts that he continued to reject.

When he finished his poem, he glanced at April, his lips smiling. Like the night they had pulled hair from the first deer hide, his eyes were completely unguarded, and the wistfulness so recently in his voice was in his eyes for her to see.

"Bobbie Burns," he said with a slight abashed smile that looked like one Davey frequently had. "I grew up with him...and the Bible. I think I can recite from memory every word he wrote. He became a very good friend." April's heart raced. It was one of his longest speeches, and one of the few that revealed anything.

"Your father taught you to read?"

MacKenzie's smile disappeared, and April wanted to kick herself for sending it away, even if she didn't know why. She wished again she knew more about him.

"Aye," he said shortly, then turned back to Davey.

"He lived here long?" she probed gently.

"I was born here," MacKenzie said, not entirely answering her question.

"And your mother?" April ignored the growing frostiness in his eyes. She had to know. Perhaps then she could better understand him...and his iron determination not to care, not to love.

"She died when I was Davey's age," he said shortly, then sprung up. "I'll see about some wood," he muttered, all the time knowing that it was obvious they needed none. Logs were piled high on both sides of the fireplace.

"MacKenzie?" April pleaded.

He hesitated. "Get your coat," he ordered suddenly, and April hurried to comply. Davey also stirred, but MacKenzie shook his head, and Davey, already half asleep, nodded.

The night was clear and pure, the midnight-blue sky a perfect backdrop for the brightly shining stars and the moon, which rode full and high. April tucked her hand in MacKenzie's and was surprised when he didn't pull away. But neither did he encourage her any further.

They walked to the edge of the trees, and MacKenzie stood there, the creases that stretched outward from his eyes deeper than she had ever seen them. Still and silent in the moonlight, he seemed completely lost in thought, removed from her in so many ways she didn't understand. Looking up at the strong, solemn profile, she felt a knife twist deep inside her with longing, with the need to erase some of the gravity that was always so much a part of him.

Had she ever been carefree? Had he laughed as a boy, and teased and loved as little boys should? She doubted it. He often seemed seized with wonder at Davey's delighted grin. He wasn't aware that not many weeks ago, Davey had some of that same solemnity. He didn't realize it was he who had given Davey that laughter and childhood, nor how much April wanted to gift him with it in return.

"I'm sorry," she said. "I shouldn't have pried."

He withdrew his hand from hers and clasped both his hands behind his back as if to bind them there. His now silvery eyes pierced her. She saw both desolation and determination in them. It was time that she realized the full extent of the differences between them, he thought.

"My father," he said slowly, "was a very bitter man. He came from Scotland, from a famous clan, which had lost everything in their support of the Stuarts. He was an outlaw there, fighting fruitlessly to regain something that had been gone for a hundred years. When he was forced to flee to America he became an outlaw here. He disappeared in these mountains to escape the law...and, I think, to recapture a part of Scotland that obsessed him to the day he died."

MacKenzie studied April's rapt face. "He was so full of bitterness for what he felt was taken from him that he had no room for anything else. Certainly not love."

"Your mother?"

She could feel his bitterness when he replied.

"A Shoshone stolen from her people and made a slave by the Comanches. After they had used her, they sold her to my father for a horse. One horse. Which showed her value to both! She was nothing more than a slave to my father, a concubine to use and ignore. There was nothing left in her when I was born. I don't remember her ever speaking one word. She did as my father commanded. Nothing more. I think she willed herself to die when I was Davey's age."

April ached for the child, and for the man who still carried the burden of those years. It must have been a horribly lonely life for a small boy and later...

Her hand crept to his arm, and even through his coat he could feel its warmth. She still didn't understand. He continued.

"My father taught me to read and write, mainly because he needed me. I did the trading for him, and he didn't want to be cheated. And he taught me the pipes." His eyes fastened on hers. "Can you imagine anything more senseless? He would sit there and listen, and he would be back in Scotland, the laird of a great clan." This time the bitterness was thick in his voice. "But he did teach me the mountains...and how to survive...and how to be alone."

MacKenzie's face was suddenly blazoned with determination. "Do you understand, April? Do you understand any of this? I thought I could break the circle of hatred and bitterness. I thought I had a chance with the valley, but I don't, and I'll end up just like him...living with dead hopes and bitter dreams...running from the law, unable to ever meet a man without wondering whether he brings death. I will *not* give that kind of life to Davey. Or you.''

His voice broke, and April could feel a hot tear running down her cheek. She had never realized the depth of his loneliness. How could she? What he was saying was so foreign to her. Not to have had any love at all.

''You're not like that,'' she whispered. ''You're not like your father at all. You have so much love to give...I've seen it with Davey... Don't give it up.''

''Do you think I want to?'' His voice was more a groan than anything else. ''But I could never live with myself if I hurt...''

April's hand moved up to his face, as she thought once more how strong and beautiful it was. ''I love you, Mac-Kenzie. I love you more than I thought it possible to love another person. I hurt all the time because of it, but it would be far worse if I lost you. I don't know if I could stand that.''

His next words were purposely cruel. ''Your husband...you survived that...'' Could he never make her understand that he could bring her and the boy nothing but pain? Either way. If he went back, he would hang. It was that simple. And she would be there to see it. That was the course he had already chosen. He had made his decision. He had to see them to safety, back to her father, Davey's grandfather. The more she became involved with him, the more terrible it would be...for all three of them. The other way, the way he had already weighed and discarded, would be to give her the same life he had, to constantly subject the only two people he had ever loved to constant danger and isolation.

Love. He had never thought anything could give so much joy, so much pain. April's face, lifted to his, was now dotted with tears, and he shivered at the glowing love that shone so unashamedly from it.

Unable to resist despite his fierce will, his lips reached down and his tongue tasted the tears from her face before moving to her mouth and claiming it. In one violent movement, his arms seized her and pulled her body tight against his with a need so desperate that, at the moment, nothing else mattered. Time seemed to stop as he hungrily sought to bind her to him, to capture a moment in time and hold it forever.

April melted into his arms, feeling his strength and his weakness, understanding him as she never had before, loving him even more, if that were possible. She met his passion with one every bit as fierce, every bit as uncontrollable. Her body strained to feel him, to know once more the hard feel of his manhood, which had swept her to such sublime heights. More than anything else, she wanted him to become one with her again, to relive that fervent ecstasy, to taste his lips as he thrust deeper and deeper inside...

"Oh, God," he whispered, and April could merely cling tighter to him. "We can't stay here...and Davey..."

"Davey will probably be asleep...it won't be long..."

MacKenzie shook himself, as if from a dream. He felt his heart in a vise. His body was trembling with need, his arousal full and demanding. His breath caught somewhere in his throat, and he shuddered as caution warred with need, responsibility with desire. "We cannot risk a child," he said finally, but his hands still kept their hold on her.

"I want your child," April said.

Those words, lovingly said, stunned him. And made him drop his hands as nothing else could have done. "No," he growled. "No, damn it." Raw agony was in his face, and his eyes blazed with silver fire.

April watched as his jaw set and he turned away, striding from her and the cabin, and she wanted to kick herself. One step at a time. She watched him disappear among the trees and knew she should not follow. He had to fight his own demons. As she had to fight hers, for she had never known her body to ache so painfully, to cry so for release.

She slowly walked to the cabin, damning MacKenzie's father with every step.

Ellen Peters lowered her eyes in a way meant to be both innocent and seductive, but they no longer had the power they once had over Phillip Downs.

Sitting on the ground behind some outbuildings where there was a semblance of privacy at Fort Defiance, at least during this time in early evening, Lieutenant Downs just felt disgust. Disgust with himself, disgust with the clinging woman next to him.

My God, but he had been a fool. He had found out just how much of one the night before, when he had heard other officers snickering. Apparently, everyone had known about Ellen but him.

He had thought her a victim, a girl raped against her will who had then watched her father die at the hands of the half-breed rapist. He had been kind and gentle and had refrained from seeking much more than a kiss. He had treated her as a lady, though he was puzzled at times with the strange, bright light in her eyes. He had even, at her not so subtle hints, considered marriage. Marriage!

Phillip shied away from her hand, and she glanced at him with surprise. He had arrived at Fort Defiance several weeks earlier, and she had met him when he brought his uniform to be washed. He had been gallant and sympathetic when she had poured out her story. She thought she had played her role of despoiled maiden well, for he had sought her out and asked to court her, stating awkwardly that he would give her time to recover from her most terrible experience.

In the next several weeks, Ellen displayed acting talents that had been honed well. Between tears and feigned bravery she went after the young lieutenant with a campaign that would have done a general proud. More than anything else in the world she wanted to be an officer's wife, and she would do anything to accomplish that. To her, that was the greatest prize a woman could earn. After being an enlisted man's brat, she was obsessed both with improving her station and with men in uniform. She loved army posts, despite the heat and discomfort. She knew nothing else, wanted nothing else than to be among so many men, men who carried an aura of violence and danger with them. It excited her, made her body tingle and shiver with anticipation. It was why she had become a laundress, one of the nastiest and hardest jobs on any post. She knew she would eventually find a husband. Women were at a premium here, and many men wanted a lusty woman. She had, in fact, had several offers. But never from an officer.

And then Phillip Downs appeared. He had known nothing of her reputation, and his standoffish personality kept him from mingling with the other officers and hearing the gossip. If only she could get him to marry her before he did.

So she had played the innocent, trembling when he neared as if still frightened from the rape. It had produced a protectiveness in young Downs that kept him from seeing her as she really was. Until he had taken a walk last night after leaving her in a barracks reserved for the laundresses.

As he had turned a corner, he heard three officers laughing.

"Did you see old Downs...actually courting Ellen Peters?"

"Serves him right...thinks he's too good for the rest of us and here he's treating the biggest whore on the post like a princess. I hope he does marry her...make him the laughingstock of the army."

"I think he actually believes she was raped...as if anyone would need to rape her, even that damned half-breed. Never did believe that part of the tale, not after she'd been here two weeks. No woman who'd been raped would jump that fast into someone's bed."

"You, too?"

"Are you surprised? Anyone among us ain't been in her bed?"

There was laughter. Then another voice. "She's easy and hot, all right."

"But trouble. I stopped going. Kept remembering MacKenzie. I can't say I ever liked him, but damn if I don't think he got one hell of a raw deal. She probably egged him on, and then cried rape when her father found them."

"That's what Bob Morris says the general believes."

"What about Morris?"

"Don't know. He doesn't say. He was mad as hell when he came back without the general's daughter."

There was a more thoughtful voice. "I'm with you, Sam. I didn't like MacKenzie, either, but damn it, when he rode scout you knew what was going to be there. Not like now. Carter's detail...the one that bungled into an ambush just a week ago...that wouldn't have happened with MacKenzie."

"Have you heard what the general's going to do?"

"Can't do anything now...that whole mountain area's impassable. Probably stay that way most of the winter."

"Damn if I don't feel sorry for him. He sure was looking forward to seeing that daughter of his."

"So was I." The words came with the amused chuckle of one of the men. "Haven't seen a good-looking available lady in more months than I want to count. I think every unmarried officer in Fort Defiance would like to go after the half-breed for stealing her away."

"Don't let General Wakefield hear you call him that," came the thoughtful voice again. "He dressed me down well for using it."

"That attitude might well have changed since then."

"I doubt it," the voice continued. "I heard him and Sergeant Terrell having a go at it. I think he blames the sergeant more than MacKenzie..."

"I wonder where he's gone...Terrell? He sure was angry when he resigned... I heard he had a choice of that or a court-martial. And after seeing General Wakefield's fury, I think he was damned lucky to get off that light. Losing the general's daughter and grandson, for God's sake.'' There was a note of thanks in his voice that he had not been attached to the ill-fated patrol.

''Pickering might as well resign. He was assigned to that prison island off Florida...where they're holding that doctor who was in the conspiracy to kill Lincoln. I hear it's a hell-hole.''

There was another laugh. ''Another of Ellen's victims. I wonder if Downs will actually marry her. You think he's that big a fool?''

''Aye,'' said one voice to general laughter.

''I'll make a small wager...''

Phillip Downs had cringed against the side of the building as he heard the wagers being made. How could he have been so foolish? He was also hurt, by Ellen's deception and by the general contempt in which he was apparently held. His aloofness came not from arrogance but from insecurity and shyness. Which, he thought, probably made him so susceptible to Miss Peters. Starting tomorrow, he vowed, he would disengage himself from her, and try to establish a rapport with his fellow officers. If the damage hadn't already been done...

Now, as he looked at Ellen, he wondered how he had missed all the signs, how he had misinterpreted that too bright gleam in her eyes, the touches that he had believed accidental...

Had she really falsely accused someone of rape? Was she responsible for her father's death? He shuddered. As he thought of it he realized she had never shown any indication of grief over her parent.

''What's the matter, honey?'' she said. ''You seem different tonight.''

''Perhaps I am,'' he answered cryptically.

She snuggled closer. ''When are we going to get married?''

Downs jerked away. "I don't think marriage is something to jump into," he replied cautiously.

"But you said you wanted to take care of me..."

Raw anger tinged Downs's words. "Like others have?" he said softly.

Ellen blinked. "I don't know what you mean."

"I think you do."

Ellen Peters, unfortunately, did. Somehow he had heard things. She started to defend herself. "You've heard talk...because I was raped." Somehow, in Ellen's mind, her claim of attempted rape had turned into the actual thing. "No one will ever forget I was raped by a dirty half-breed; they all think I should kill myself or something. Is that it? Because I didn't have any choice but to lie with an Indian? They say all sorts of things because of that...that I'm loose. I'm not, Phillip, I was raped, and it wasn't my fault." There was a note of panic in her voice. She was losing everything.

"Were you, Ellen? Were you, really? That's not what I hear."

"I don't know what you heard, but it's a lie. It's all lies. I was a virgin until I was raped. I swear it." A dangerous gleam came into her eye. Just as it had with MacKenzie, an uncontrollable fury was working up within her. She was being rejected again...just as she thought she was reaching her goal. Reason fled, and she would do anything, anything, to hold onto her dream.

Her face became almost feral as Downs watched in horror. Her eyes were calculating and cruel, all of their feigned innocence gone. "You promised to marry me," she said flatly.

"I promised nothing. We simply discussed the possibility, but surely you see now it's impossible."

"Impossible?" she said in a tone that almost made Downs shudder with its malignancy. My God, what had he gotten into?

"Impossible," he confirmed.

"No, it isn't," she said, all reason gone. She only remembered what had worked before. Her hands suddenly started tearing at her clothes.

He watched in horror, too startled to react physically.

"If you don't keep your promise, I'll scream and say you raped me. That you said if a half-breed was good enough, you were, too. I'll ruin your career, see you hang. Not good enough for you?" she spit. "I'll make sure *you'll* not be good enough for anyone else." Her rising voice calmed slightly. "But if you keep your promise…"

"You're crazy," Downs sputtered without thinking, wondering whatever happened to that sweet brave girl he thought he was courting. He *had* been a fool. All of a sudden, he felt a surge of sympathy for the Indian scout he had been hating.

Her face tightened, but she persisted. "Will you marry me?"

"When hell freezes," he answered coldly.

He was not quite prepared for the scream that followed, or the crowd of soldiers that appeared, or Ellen's panicked accusations. A superior officer, a captain, came, and a stunned Phillip Downs was confined to quarters until an investigation could be conducted. As he was led to his spartan officer's quarters, he turned to his escort and asked that General Wakefield be informed that Downs had information of importance to the general.

The next morning a sullen Ellen Peters was ushered into Wakefield's office. With Captain Morris as a witness and a sergeant to take down the words, Ira Wakefield offered her a chair and started gently. "I'm sorry for all your trouble with my command, Miss Peters."

Ellen eyed him suspiciously. He had, she knew, doubted her story about the half-breed.

"Two attempted rapes, Miss Peters?" His eyebrow rose in disbelief. "One perhaps, but two? I would think you'd be a little wary of being alone with any of my men."

"I thought Lieutenant Downs was a gentleman, an officer," Ellen replied. "I was wrong."

Wakefield pulled his chair over to where she sat, and folded himself into it, his eyes now level with hers. "I was rather surprised at the charge," he said. "Lieutenant Downs has an estimable record. This will probably destroy his career, if not send him to prison." He watched her carefully. "Is that what you want?"

"Yes," she said vindictively. "He attacked me."

"Did he, Miss Peters? He says not."

Ellen's face blushed. "Of course he would deny it."

"Did MacKenzie also deny it?" He didn't miss the further heightening of her color or the guilt that flashed across her face.

"No," she said triumphantly. "He never did."

Wakefield's face moved closer to her own. "But then he never had a chance...because you and Sergeant Terrell planned not to give him a chance."

"He killed my father..."

"Why did he kill your father? Because your father was trying to kill him?"

"Yes...no...he was trying to protect me."

"Protect you from what, Miss Peters?"

"That half-breed raped me...he did..."

"Did he rape you...or did he try? Make up your mind, Ellen." His voice softened as he used her first name, and Captain Morris knew his general was getting ready to strike.

"He raped me..."

"Like Phillip Downs?"

"Yes, like Lieutenant Downs," she said defensively.

He sat back in his chair and half closed his eyes. "You've been a busy little lady," he said.

"I don't know what you mean!"

Wakefield rose and went to his desk, where he picked up several sheets of paper. "I have a few statements here," he said. "There are Lieutenants Canfield, Harding and Davie, Sergeant Edwards, Corporal Brown. Among others. Do you know any of these men?"

Ellen's face had gone from red to white in seconds. She started to answer, then thought better of it.

"Each," Wakefield said, "said they had intimate relations with you." He leaned forward. "Do you know the penalty for perjury, Miss Peters? Do you? You can go to prison, and I don't think you would like it there."

"I didn't do anything," Ellen protested.

"No?" Wakefield said. "Your accusation killed your father, caused my daughter and grandson to be lost, cost the lives of at least ten men and God knows what else. Now you're trying to ruin another soldier. You are a very dangerous young woman."

Ellen started to fold as she kept glancing at the papers in Wakefield's hands. She thought about everything she had heard about prison and shivered in fear. "Not prison," she whispered. "Please don't send me to prison."

"Then tell me what happened that night at Chaco, and last night. The truth...if you know how...and perhaps I can do something."

"I wasn't lying about MacKenzie. He was going to rape me. I know he was!"

"Going to?"

Ellen burst into tears.

General Wakefield looked at her without sympathy. My God, the damage she had done to good men. "Why were you in the bathhouse?"

"I was bringing some clean towels."

"And yet when you saw it was occupied you didn't leave...you went inside."

Ellen Peters looked around helplessly. "I...didn't think anyone would be there...it was mess time."

"And where was MacKenzie?"

She hung her head. They had been over this before...when they had first arrived. Why in heaven's name had she accused Phillip Downs? What a fool she had been. Now she knew General Wakefield wouldn't stop.

Patiently, as if talking to a child, Wakefield drilled her. Over and over again until she no longer knew what she was saying.

"All right," he said finally. "So MacKenzie didn't touch you. You just thought he would. And your father came in. Did he draw on MacKenzie first? The truth, Ellen, or I'll make sure you go to prison."

"Yes, damn you." She almost spit the words out.

With no satisfaction, Wakefield leaned back again. "So it was self-defense."

"He's a dirty Indian," she said. "He doesn't have the right to kill a white man, no matter what."

"Just what did he do to you, Ellen? Turn you down?"

It was so softly said, Ellen just sat there, the truth written all over her face.

"And Lieutenant Downs...did he turn you down, too?"

Her expression confirmed his charge.

Wakefield sighed. "You will sign the statement Sergeant Evans took down. Captain Morris and I will witness it. And then you will leave Fort Defiance. God help you if I ever hear of you on an army post again, for I will make very sure you pay for all the damned misery you've caused." He stood and left the room as if he could no longer bear the odor of it.

Captain Morris was right behind him, and once they reached fresh air both men stopped.

"You were right, General."

"That gives me damned little pleasure at the moment."

"Where does this leave MacKenzie?"

General Wakefield's mouth was rueful as he considered the question. "Only with a few capital charges like horse theft and kidnapping."

"The letter your daughter left..."

"He shouldn't have taken them...he knew the dangers."

"Then why did you go after Ellen Peters?"

"I don't want him for what he didn't do. But God knows I want him for what he did do!"

"I thought you wanted him back as a scout."

"It's been three months, Bob. Three months without word." Wakefield's voice was strained. "I never thought MacKenzie would go this far. I thought he would find a way to send them home. His fists clenched as he thought of April and Davey in the mountains. "I want him," Wakefield repeated through clenched teeth. "I want him very, very badly."

Chapter Seventeen

April peered out the door with dismay.

The sky was lemony, just as it had been the day before the blizzard that had almost killed them all.

MacKenzie had left minutes earlier. She had seen his tense, tight face when he had returned from a short walk. His words had been even more clipped than usual. "It looks like another bad storm. I'm going after some fresh meat. I'm taking Wolf so you and Davey stay inside. All the way inside. Do you understand?"

April felt a rush of resentment at being treated like a child. Then she remembered the last time she'd disobeyed him. "Yes," she consented, although there was a defiant note in her voice, which he ignored with a half smile at her truculent tone. He had left, and April knew it was partly because he wanted to be away from her. He had, since that evening several days earlier, avoided her as much as possible and cautiously spared his words when he could not.

It had hurt at first, but then she realized that she should have expected it. MacKenzie obviously didn't find sharing thoughts or feelings easy. She knew he wanted her as much as she wanted him, and there would be another opportunity. She was sure of it, and she waited, not willing to push. Not yet.

She watched him disappear through the trees, wearing the Colt in a gun belt around his waist and carrying a rifle. With

Wolf at his side, he appeared untamed and savage, and April smiled softly. Only she and Davey knew the gentleness that was so abundant under that proud and free exterior. She had closed the door against the cold and worked with Davey on his numbers.

But as the wind increased and the temperature inside the cabin grew colder despite a roaring fire, she occasionally looked out. Snow flurries started and grew in intensity until they became as large as pebbles and the trees on the other side of the clearing disappeared in a white shower. She watched anxiously for MacKenzie, but her view was becoming more and more limited.

April glanced at the wood piled on both sides of the fireplace. MacKenzie had left plenty, but perhaps she should bring in a few more logs while she still could. It would keep him from having to do it later; he still hadn't totally regained his strength, partly, she thought, because he kept pushing himself. He never seemed to rest. At night, his face was creased with deep lines of exhaustion and even pain.

In her desire to make things a little easier for MacKenzie, she conveniently forgot her promise to him. The woodpile, after all, was less than a hundred feet away. Nothing could happen in that distance.

She put on MacKenzie's lighter coat; he had taken the sheepskin jacket and gloves. Extracting her own promise from Davey that he stay before the fire until she returned, April opened the door a crack and darted out, fastening the bar on the outside so it wouldn't blow open. She shivered. It was freezing. She buried her hands in pockets in the jacket and started toward the woodpile, stumbling several times in the howling wind. She could barely see the woodpile. The wind and cold and snow almost blinded her, forcing tears from her eyes, that immediately froze on her face.

April didn't know how long it took her to reach the woodpile...forever, it seemed. This storm was even worse than the one on the way here. How could the snow envelop everything so quickly? MacKenzie. Where was he? Anyone could get lost in this white cloud. Even him, she feared. She filled her arms with wood and looked the way she had come. Her footprints were already gone, and the cabin...where was the cabin? All she could see was snow. But she knew the direction...it was straight back from the woodpile...she remembered that. But she had moved around the pile, trying to find logs easy to handle. It had to be in front of her... or was it to the left? Why didn't the snow slow a moment, just long enough for her to get her bearings? Her hands grew colder as they clutched the precious pieces of wood, and snow covered her chestnut hair. She would have to guess. After all, if she went in the wrong direction, she would run into some trees, and all she would have to do was go in the other direction. She would be all right if she kept moving. But it was cold, so terribly cold.

Still holding the wood, she struggled against the wind that was already creating drifts. She took one step, and her foot kept going down. She stumbled, and the wood went flying from her hands. As she sprawled on the ground, her head struck one of the fallen logs. White turned into black as the blow whirled her into a spinning void.

The storm's fury came even faster than MacKenzie had anticipated. He had had little luck, only two rabbits. The other animals, sensing the storm, seemed to have disappeared from the earth, each finding its own shelter. He was nearly back when the snow became blinding, and he blessed the fact he had taken Wolf. The animal unerringly moved ahead, and MacKenzie knew his companion would get him to the cabin. April and Davey should both be safe there. She had promised not to leave it.

God, he was cold. He thought about the roaring fire awaiting him, Davey's welcome and April's bright blue eyes. He tried to push back the wild joy that always welled inside when he returned to the cabin, to home. Strange to think he never thought of it as home before. Inside the leather gloves, his fingers reached and stretched and clenched in anticipation. His heart was speaking a new language, and he was just beginning to understand its complexities. He had tried not to, had tried deliberately to ignore its call, but little by little he felt his barriers breached. He smiled, thinking of April, of the long chestnut braid and the warmth of the blue eyes. "Come on, Wolf," he said. "Let's hurry," and the animal seemed to catch his urgency, quickening the pace through the deepening snow.

As he moved steadily behind the wolf, he wondered whether April was still angry. She had been this morning when he had been so short with her. But he had needed to leave, and he wanted to know she would be safe. The atmosphere between them in the past few days had been uneasy at best. He had not returned until late that night he had revealed much. She was on the bed and appeared asleep, but his instinct told him she was as wide awake as he was. He nonetheless had settled before the fire without a word, and spent a sleepless night. *If only he didn't want her so badly.*

But he had survived the night and the next days with a minimum of words, and was grateful that she didn't mention that night or what they had discussed. She seemed, in fact, preoccupied with something else altogether. While part of him was thankful, another incomprehensible part was strangely wounded. It didn't make any sense. The only cure, he knew, was to get her and the boy back home. And before this storm, he had thought it might be possible in the next few days. He had stopped thinking about himself weeks ago. The only important thing, his driving force, was to return April and Davey safely.

While he still walked with Davey and April in the mornings, he would disappear in the afternoons without so much as a word. He had not told April he had been checking the passes every several days. The sun's rays were slowly melting the icy surface, despite the freezing temperatures. He thought it might be safe enough within days. But he had said nothing to April, sensing she would protest or attempt something foolish. What, he didn't know. But he had in the past weeks learned something about her determination and stubbornness.

Now it seemed his plans were once more being thwarted by outside forces, and he couldn't bridle the feeling of elation that swept through him. He had never before felt such delight at failing to accomplish something he had set out to do. More hours, more days with April and Davey.

Wolf stopped, and MacKenzie could barely make out the outline of the cabin just inches away. The snow was that dense. His hand sought the door and his heart stilled as he saw the bar across it. How could it be barred unless someone was outside? But she had promised!

His hands fumbled with the bar, and he pushed the door open. Davey was alone, his face white and terrified.

"Mama," he whispered.

"Where did she go?"

"To get some wood."

MacKenzie cursed under his breath. "How long ago, Davey? How long?"

Davey shook his head, but MacKenzie saw the dried tears on his face, and knew it must have been a while. Damn. Why did he leave this morning? He should have realized she still didn't understand all the dangers of these mountains, how quickly a storm could cover everything, how deadly the snow was. She wouldn't have thought the woodpile so far. What could have happened?

His hand went down to Davey's shoulders and he stooped to the boy's height. "Don't worry," he whispered. "Wolf and I will find her. You stay right in front of the fire. We can't lose you, too. A bargain?"

Davey nodded.

"You promise?"

Again, the boy nodded, his anguished eyes pleading with MacKenzie.

''I'll find her,'' MacKenzie said again. He grabbed a piece of clothing and opened the door again.

Wolf was still there, seemingly waiting to be invited inside. MacKenzie once more stooped down. ''Find her, Wolf, find April.''

The wolf sniffed the garment and looked questioningly at MacKenzie.

''Find her,'' MacKenzie urged again, and felt hope mix with fear as the animal moved away from the cabin. After endless steps he spotted the woodpile at his immediate left, but the wolf continued on. MacKenzie's foot kicked against a log and then Wolf stopped and he heard the animal's soft whine. He leaned down, brushed snow off a mound and felt April's body. She was completely covered, and her face and hands were like blocks of ice. He took off his jacket and wrapped it around her, burying her hands in its folds. He picked her up. ''Take me back,'' he ordered the wolf, and the animal turned and headed back, MacKenzie no more than inches behind.

When they reached the cabin, MacKenzie placed April on the bed. She was unconscious but still breathing. Davey approached, his eyes full of fear. ''Is she...is Mama going to be all right?''

''I think so, Davey, but we have to warm her as quickly as possible.''

MacKenzie took the cold jacket from her and carefully stripped off the other wet and frozen clothes, wrapping her in blankets while allowing Davey to wrap her hands with one of his shirts. The boy needed to do something, and the faster he could get warmth back into her hands and feet, the better chance she would have to escape without permanent harm. When he had dried and wrapped her to his satisfaction, he picked her up and took her to a chair next to the fire, where he sat, holding her tightly against him, sharing his own warmth.

One hand gently rubbed her frozen cheeks, and his fingers

found a large bump on her head, and some dry blood. He knew it was important that she wake and move around, but he was loathe to let her go. She was so impossibly light that he felt as if he were holding a spirit in his arms. She had lost weight during this journey, and he felt desolated, knowing that he was responsible. Like he was responsible for all the other discomforts and dangers. He loved her, and he had almost killed her. Not once but over and over again. He hugged her even closer to him, as if he could transfer his strength and warmth to her, but her body kept shivering, sometimes in spasms. "Fight, April. Fight," he whispered, his mouth burying itself in her hair, still wet from snow.

When another series of spasms hit her body, he lifted her and carried her to the bed. As Davey watched, MacKenzie covered her with everything he could find, then told Davey to snuggle up in front of her. MacKenzie also reclined on the bed, pulling her into his arms and bringing her to him as tightly as possible until April was like a piece of meat between two pieces of bread, soaking up the warmth of both.

MacKenzie didn't know how long they stayed like that. Davey eventually went to sleep, but he could not. He could feel her body gradually relax and the shivers decrease in intensity, but her skin still felt cold, and she had not yet gained full consciousness, although she seemed to try to move a little. His hands stroked her, and he felt new tremors and wondered if they came from the lingering cold or from some other unconscious response. His own hands shook. He loved her so much, and if he had been just minutes later...

He didn't move until he felt her harsh breathing soften and felt her mold herself securely into the curves of his body. He rejoiced when he heard her whisper, "I love you," and he clutched her even tighter as he felt her body relax and knew she had fallen into an easy sleep.

For those few moments when he thought he might lose her, he had felt an emptiness as vast as the mountains. He didn't think now he could ever let her go.

* * *

It took three days before April was back to normal. She continued to shiver the next day, and her head hurt from the blow. When she tried to rise, she felt dizzy, and MacKenzie finally decreed she lay still.

The snow continued to fall hard, though not as densely as the first day. MacKenzie, who kept the area around the door clear, said it was as high as the roof in some places. He strung a blanket up to give April a little privacy and though he did not join her in bed again, he frequently touched her...as if she might be a miracle he didn't quite believe.

In fact, April couldn't quite believe he had been there in bed before, anyway. She thought it must have been a dream...those arms around her so possessively. She remembered bits and pieces of that day...the walk, her fall, then, perhaps, his arms. But he said nothing about it, and she and Davey were alone on the bed when she woke the next morning. MacKenzie was feeding the fire and had a broth bubbling in a big kettle.

Nothing had ever tasted so good as that rabbit broth. Perhaps it was because she remembered how cold she had been and thought she would never be warm again. Or perhaps it was because MacKenzie had made it.

Whether or not he had been in bed with her, something in him had changed. He no longer hid his concern or his tenderness under the blank mask. He had even smiled at her when she complimented his soup.

"I wonder," he said with a small twinkle, "if you are ever going to do as I ask?"

"I truly thought it was safe...it was such a little way...and I didn't want you to have to do it when you got back."

MacKenzie grimaced and shook his head. "Mrs. Manning, your father should have taken a switch to you long ago." His eyes and their tender expression belied his words, and April's heart did funny little flip-flops. He was regarding her so fondly, even after all the trouble she had caused. It seemed she was always doing that to him. The bear. Her horse falling. The snowstorm. She had been nothing but trouble from the beginning.

"I'm sorry," she said. "I am. And thank you for finding me."

"You can thank Wolf for that."

"I can thank him for finding me, and I can thank you for taking such good care of me."

"As you did me...twice," he said softly. His voice broke. "I am so sorry, April. I'm so damned sorry for everything I've put you through, you and Davey."

April was stunned. There was a stiffness in his voice that told her the apology was rare indeed. Her hand crept over to his and found its way into its hard callused interior. Instinctively, his hand closed around hers with a tenderness that would have surprised her if she hadn't seen it with Davey. She would never really understand how his gentleness had taken root and survived during his childhood. But he was the most exceptional man she had ever met.

"Don't," she said. "Don't say that. You've given us both something special. You've shared your world with us, and you gave Davey wonder...something that I allowed to be stolen from him," she said. "Almost since the beginning, we came because we wanted to. And you've protected us over and over again. We're alive because of you."

"But if I didn't take him in the beginning..."

"Our lives would be empty...even with my father. Don't you understand, MacKenzie? You gave us both love. You may not have planned to, or even wanted to, but you did." Tears glazed her eyes. She wanted so badly for him to understand, to believe, to accept.

A muscle throbbed in his cheek. "I have...nothing..."

"You have more than any man I know...you just won't accept it."

"You...and the boy will be in danger."

"We can go away...where no one can find us. I don't care where...not as long as we're with you. Mexico, perhaps."

There was a glimmer of hope in his eyes. "It's impossible," he said but for the first time there was a hint of indecision in his voice. "It's impossible," he repeated.

"It's impossible to kill a bear with a knife, and to find your way in these mountains during a blizzard. But you did it, MacKenzie. You did it." She was fighting for her life now, for hers and Davey's.

"Your father..."

"I can write him. He'll understand. He loved my mother very much. He knows what it's like."

For the first time, his eyes were completely naked. She saw hope struggling with fear, love with his sense of duty. They were so perfectly beautiful to her, the silver streaks mixed with such deep gray wells.

"A child...would be part Indian. He would never be accepted."

"By those who count, he would. Tell me truly, MacKenzie, my father accepted you...the major you mentioned...there must have been more. Do you really care about the others...like Lieutenant Pickering and Sergeant Terrell?"

For the first time, MacKenzie grinned. "I can't say I do, little wise one."

"Then..." she said triumphantly.

"You forget," he reminded her gently. "I'm wanted. There will be an army of bounty hunters. There will never be any peace, any security."

"You are all the security I want."

He turned away from her, and April was immediately glad there was a blizzard outside. Otherwise, she knew, he would be out the door. It was a victory that his hand continued to grasp hers. "Do something for me?" she requested.

His face turned back to hers in question.

"That first day on the trail. You sang to Davey. It was so beautiful, so haunting. What was it?"

MacKenzie's face relaxed slightly. "An old Scottish song...about a bonnie young prince who had to flee Scotland..." His face tensed again as he recognized some similarities.

"Will you sing it for me?" she said, refusing to give up.

MacKenzie hesitated, but it was a small thing after what she had gone through. She had never asked anything, not really, and at least he could give her a song. But in doing so, he knew, deep inside, he would be giving her something else. A piece of himself. But he could no more refuse her than he could stop breathing.

April had almost thought he was refusing until she heard the first light hum. It grew until it filled the room with the haunting melody, and April listened to the wonderful, soft, sad voice as it told of a ship carrying a young prince from his home. Davey came over and crawled up on the bed with her, his eyes rapt. When MacKenzie finished the song hovered in the cabin, and April felt the tears in her eyes.

MacKenzie suddenly smiled, and his face crinkled in a way she had not seen before. His voice took on a lilt and he sang an enchanting little song about a squirrel, a partridge and a possum. There was so much humor and affection for his subjects that April and Davey regarded him with awe. They could almost hear the squirrel's chattering, see the speckle-breasted partridge who steals the farmer's corn and sympathize with the possum who isn't afraid of anything till he hears the hound dog's bark.

They begged once more for the frog and mouse tale, and they both giggled as he trilled the mouse's part, and Davey clapped his hands in delight.

MacKenzie looked very pleased with himself when he finished.

"Where," April asked with fascinated laughter, "did you learn all that?"

"I listen," he said. "There's a lot of musicians in the army."

"Ah, MacKenzie. How many other surprises do you have for us?"

"Sing another," chimed Davey.

He did, and April was completely charmed by his thoroughly unusual mood. For the first time since she had known him, he seemed totally relaxed. And happy. Perhaps that was it. She lay down and reveled in the spell he was weaving.

All too soon he stopped, and some of the severity returned to his face, but there was something else now, too. Something lighter.

And so the next two days went. They were locked in together, and MacKenzie seemed determined to make it as pleasant as possible for both Davey and April. It had been his fault, all of it, and he was trying in some small way to make amends. For despite those few moments of hope, he doubted it would ever work. He was still determined to take her back. He would probably die for it. But for now, he was taking what he could and giving what little he had.

Christmas came to the small cabin tucked in the heart of the mountains.

For MacKenzie, it was a singularly new experience.

He had never observed Christmas. It had always just been another day, although he had sometimes curiously watched the often elaborate preparations at some of the army posts to which he was attached. It was a quiet time with fewer details, and he generally used the opportunity to ride out and enjoy the solitude. He was never invited to any of the celebrations, nor would he have attended if he had been. Crowds held no interest or pleasure for him. And, to him, religion was empty words. Good will toward man was a philosophy that seemed to last one day.

But where he had always regarded Christmas with indifference, April was the opposite. She loved Christmas. When she was a child, Christmas had been a wonderful, magical time, full of love and surprises. She wanted it to mean the same to Davey. And to MacKenzie. Whether he wanted it or not.

But how? They had little but the necessities of life, and not too many of those. And she had lost track of time. She could only guess the correct date. But that she did. And she announced to MacKenzie that Christmas would be held in the cabin in ten days.

He could only eye her warily, wondering what was expected of him. He was damned if he knew.

But he couldn't help but be affected by her enthusiasm and Davey's anticipation. And he would try...for them.

The days since the second blizzard had been the best he had ever known. Having made the choice, he decided to enjoy it, and time passed in a haze of belonging and love. There was no more talk of the future, and though a tiny voice in the back of his mind nagged at him to be careful he pushed it away. There was not even the slightest possibility now of getting through the mountains, not with the snow piled in drifts of ten and twelve feet and higher in some places. And there probably wouldn't be until spring.

MacKenzie took every moment as a gift. The only blemish was the unrelieved tension of his body. For although he relaxed with April, he remained adamant that they would not join together again. He would not leave her with a child. Davey's constant presence made the vow easier to keep, but it did nothing to cool his body, which constantly ached to merge once more with April's. He couldn't forget that one night when he felt so vividly, wonderfully alive, when every sense had exploded with such total fulfillment. He often lay awake at night, feeling his manhood swell with memory and desire.

When April mentioned Christmas, he at first wondered how and why she would observe it, but he was soon caught up in her enthusiasm. He found himself seeking a small tree and picking berries and watching as she carefully used her needle to string them together with a piece of yarn she'd unraveled from a blanket.

He would return from a hunting trip and find April and Davey giggling together and hiding things, and was astounded at his own excitement. Soon he was sneaking off by himself to carve a small boy for April, and a wolf for Davey. He had not carved anything since he was a child, but a rough skill was still there and he was not unproud of his efforts. He wanted to please as he had never wanted anything before.

So did Davey and April.

"What can I give MacKenzie?" Davey asked one day when they were alone.

"I don't think you need to give him anything at all, love," April said. "Just yourself."

Davey made a face. "That's nothing..."

"It's a great deal, Davey," she assured him, but he looked anything but comforted.

She finally came up with an idea and presented it to Davey, who grinned with delight. She had bits and pieces of her riding skirt left, and Davey could make MacKenzie a scarf with it. She showed him how to turn the edges and sew them, and while the stitches were not particularly even, Davey spent hours and hours trying to make it as perfect as possible. When his mother wasn't looking, he used his new, albeit somewhat unperfected, skill to make a ribbon for her hair.

April's Christmas dawned bright and clear. As usual, MacKenzie had woken earlier than anyone else and stoked the fire before leaving to attend to his personal needs. On his way back he stopped at the small stable and took the two carved figures he had hidden there. He touched them, wishing they were better. Almost shyly, he hid them in his large hands and returned to the cabin. He put them under the tree, and watched April and Davey as they continued to sleep.

His heart swelled with an aching tenderness. Both looked so young, so vulnerable in their sleep. Davey's hair was mussed, and his long, dark eyelashes swept over an expectant face. And April. How beautiful she was with her arms around her son, her chestnut hair framing her exquisite face. She was his, no matter how temporarily. She was his. He watched as her eyelashes finally fluttered open, her eyes caught and held his and a slow, sleepy smile bid him a good morning.

"It's Christmas," she said unnecessarily.

"Aye...I guess it is, and there's two lazy shakes still abed."

She grinned at him, delighted. He had recently started to tease her, and she loved the mischievous light that lit his eyes when he did. That and the soft affection that always accompanied it.

"I suppose," she replied, snuggling deeper under the blankets, "you want me to do something about that."

"'Tis no matter. I enjoy watching you just like that. It's *your* Christmas!" But April didn't miss a certain anticipation in his voice, as though he might have a few secrets of his own. But it couldn't be. He had been dragged, somewhat reluctantly, along with her plans.

Her hand tousled Davey's hair, and he wriggled, and then his eyes sprang open as he remembered what day it was.

MacKenzie turned away to give April some privacy as she slowly unwound herself from the blankets. He knew she was wearing one of his father's old shirts and a pair of trousers held up by a piece of rope. Her own clothes had disintegrated weeks ago, not long after she was caught in the blizzard. He knew she despaired of the garments, but he thought she would be beautiful in sackcloth.

MacKenzie tried to look unconcerned as April and Davey rose, but Davey's eyes caught the small tree in the corner and then the two little figures, and he squealed with joy as he picked up the one that looked like Wolf. MacKenzie felt April's hand on his arm, and he heard her whisper, "Thank you, MacKenzie." There was such quiet amazement in her voice he almost smiled.

"The other one's for you," he said.

April looked under the tree and saw the tiny carved boy. It

had Davey's smile and stance. She had never understood crying with happiness before, but now she did. A tear welled up in her eyes and splashed down her face. Nothing in the world spoke more eloquently of MacKenzie's feeling than the two small, imperfectly carved figures.

When she could finally bear it, she looked up at him, finding his face crestfallen, like Davey's when he had disappointed her.

"I know they're not very good..." he started, then turned toward the door, ready to escape.

"It's the most beautiful thing I have ever seen," she said slowly. "It's the most wonderful present in the world." Another tear formed.

"But..." MacKenzie stopped, and his hand wiped away the tear.

"Oh, MacKenzie, I love you. By all the saints, I love you." She flung herself into MacKenzie's arms, and after a second's hesitation they closed around her. She savored his gentle warmth, felt his lips touch her lightly on the lips and his hand tangle itself in her hair. They stood there like that, silently exchanging feelings too strong to utter. She lay her head against his heart and heard its strong beat and felt the heat of his body. The tears made hot paths down her cheeks even as she tried to halt them, for she knew MacKenzie didn't understand. He backed away, just a little, to study her tear-stained face.

"This Christmas of yours," he teased, "does it always make you so sad?"

"Happy sad," she answered. "Oh, so very happy..."

MacKenzie saw the bright light in her eyes and thought he understood, for he, too, felt an agonizing, bittersweet torment, which apparently came with loving.

April left the comfort of his arms to present her own surprises. MacKenzie knew she had sewn a deerskin shirt for Davey...she had done it at night when the boy was asleep. And Davey had known she was sewing one for MacKenzie.

But neither knew they were receiving one of their own...each identical except for size. She had unraveled more yarn from the blanket to bind them together, and they were handsome. April had always been able to sew well, and these were labors of love.

And then it was Davey's turn, and with great pride he presented his treasures to April and an astonished MacKenzie, who could only stand there, completely silent. Only the possessive workings of his fingers over the new garments showed his emotion. But it was enough for April and Davey, who now knew him and understood.

As for MacKenzie, they were the first presents he had ever received, and he looked at the shirt and crooked scarf with disbelief mixed with a sharp anguish as he now understood April's recent tears. "Thank you," he said quietly and, sure that he could not withhold the bubbling emotions within him, he turned around and went out the door. He stood there, leaning against the wood, his hands still wrapped tight in the shirt as tears glistened in deep gray eyes.

Chapter Eighteen

Spring came unexpectedly early. Too early for April. In fact, never would have been too early.

The winter in the small cabin had been a time of happiness, of joys small and large, marred only by MacKenzie's refusal to join with her physically. But he had showed his love in so many other ways. She laughed as she pulled at a soft blade of new grass.

After that wonderful Christmas day, MacKenzie no longer fled from her. It was as if he had made a bargain with himself. She didn't know exactly what that bargain was, and she feared its ultimate outcome, but in the meantime MacKenzie had shed his cloak of solitude and severity and had joined wondrously in their lives. He made no mention of the past or the future, and the three of them simply took each moment for its own sake and squeezed it to extract as much from the precious time as possible.

April's laughter floated over the hill, catching in the soft, chilly breeze that rustled through the pines. MacKenzie and Davey and Wolf had gone out early this morning. She had stayed behind, intending to wash their clothes, and herself, in the stream under a warming sun. And she wanted Davey to have this time alone with MacKenzie. He loved the man so. As did she.

She lay in the new grass, studying the clear cerulean sky. Was the sun's new warmth, its golden promise, going to take

MacKenzie away? Already his smile was fading, and the glow in his eyes was waning. It seemed several times in the past few days as if he were trying to say something, but couldn't quite force the words.

MacKenzie. How she loved the name. How she loved everything about him: his strength and determination, his courage and gentleness, and the quiet vulnerability within him that touched her heart and made it ache. And that unique ability to communicate with almost every living thing except his fellow humans.

Her smile disappeared. She had learned much about him in the past months, probably more than he had ever intended. But once he had opened his heart and mind to her, bits and pieces had come out, albeit slowly.

She recalled one afternoon when Davey was sleeping. She and MacKenzie had taken a short walk, leaving Wolf guarding the cabin. The earth then had been a mixture of snow shining brilliant in the sun and patches of emerald-colored new grass, and the trees stood proudly like sentinels guarding treasure. Everything was always brighter with MacKenzie. Brighter and shimmering with life.

April had tried to extract information from him, asking about the man Bennett Morgan he had mentioned weeks earlier. She wanted to know more about the one man MacKenzie considered a friend. Perhaps he could help in some way. MacKenzie, she had learned well, did not give his trust easily, or fleetingly. But there had always been something else there, too, when he mentioned the army officer. A deep bitterness and an undercurrent of sadness.

And so she had probed, even as she saw a strange haunted look drain his eyes. And when he finally spoke, the old bitterness was thick in his voice. "I was a scout in the northern plains," he said finally. "Your father was in Washington, and Ben Morgan was temporarily in command. He sent me out on a patrol commanded by a young lieutenant with an itch for glory. Like Pickering he was, without an ounce of sense in his head. There had been several attacks on supply trains, and we were sent to see if we could find any sign of those responsible. I found the tracks and stupidly led them to an Indian village." He stopped, and his jaw tensed as he remembered the horror that followed. The hostile Indians apparently had stopped there and then traveled on, for there were only women and children and a few old men. He had watched for several hours before reporting to the lieutenant.

"There were naught but women and children," he said, "and I told the lieutenant that. But he ordered an attack, saying they had sheltered the renegades. I tried to stop it, but he ordered me under arrest, and I was bound." He didn't tell her he was tied to a tree where he could see and hear everything. He didn't tell her about the screams of women as their children were skewered with bayonets before they themselves fell. He had watched the killing and the burning and wondered exactly who were the savages as he fought the ropes until his blood ran freely.

"They were all killed," he said in a toneless voice, "and I was charged with interfering with an officer, dereliction of duty, cowardice..."

April had winced at the last. She knew MacKenzie's pride. Only too well.

MacKenzie hesitated, before continuing slowly. "Major Morgan was probably the best officer I have ever known...along with your father. He wanted to learn everything he could about the tribes in the area, and he learned to track...the only officer who ever took the trouble. They relied on us...their Indian scouts...though they didn't trust us." Once more his grim mouth twitched with bitter irony.

"When we returned, Morgan was out on patrol himself, and the lieutenant lied to the second in command. He said the village harbored the fugitives and that they had killed many braves. I was branded a liar and renegade and thrown in the stockade." His whole body was rigid with tension. "I learned then," he said, "not to trust white justice or to contest the word of whites, not when it was theirs against mine. And I swore I would never be caged again...never."

April bit her lip. She now thoroughly understood his single-minded determination to escape Terrell. But there was more to this story; there had to be. He had spoken of Morgan with respect. "What happened?"

"I was there a week before Morgan returned." Mac-Kenzie's face relaxed slightly, and there was almost a note of disbelief in his voice. "He believed me...questioned all the men on the detail until one finally broke and told the truth. He ordered me released and the lieutenant court-martialed. He asked me to stay, but I couldn't forget those children. I still can't. I left and remained in the mountains until your father found me two years ago. By then I had the valley and I wanted to stock it. So I went back." There was a pause. "Nothing changes, April. I should have known that. I saw them destroy the Navaho, and I was a part of it." There was self-loathing in his voice now. "But I wanted to build something, something of my own."

April's hand crept into his. "It would have happened anyway. You know it. The Navaho wouldn't stop fighting."

"No," MacKenzie agreed. "They had too much pride..."

April knew he wasn't just talking about the Navaho. She leaned her head against his chest, trying to give him comfort from the pain simmering inside him...

But that had been weeks ago, and the black mood had passed. Only infrequently after that had it returned until the last several days, and then it was only a shadow that clouded MacKenzie's face when he thought he was going unnoticed. She knew he continued to worry about their safety, but he had said no more about taking them back. And she, afraid of the answer, had not asked.

She had tread lightly, never requesting more than she thought he could give. But she sensed the time was growing short, and she wasn't going to let him go without a fight. She yearned deep inside for a child who would, perhaps, bind him to her, but they had been together only that one time, and she had not conceived...

April washed the clothes, then her hair in water she heated over the fire. She still wasn't quite brave enough to use the water icy cold from the stream, although she enjoyed basking on the bank. She knew MacKenzie was taking his baths in the stream, and she shivered at the thought.

She leaned against the bank, where the sun blessed the earth with its warmth, and combed her thick chestnut hair, allowing it to flow down her back instead of twisting it into the braid. There was little she could do with her clothes...other than wash them. She wondered if she would ever be comfortable in a dress again after a winter of wearing trousers, large and baggy as they were. It was wonderful not being squeezed tight in stays and petticoats. But she thought it would be nice to look pretty for MacKenzie. He had seen her in a dress but once, and that was the night at Chaco when he had stumbled in front of her. She doubted very much if he had noticed then. After that she had worn the practical riding clothes. Had it been only six months ago? It seemed a lifetime.

The sun reached its zenith before MacKenzie and Davey returned, the boy happy and tired.

"We saw a deer and its baby, and we got nearly close enough to touch," he exclaimed with excitement, his words running into each other. "And there's flowers...almost next to the snow." His voice was full of wonder and his eyes bright with enchantment at the miracles.

He was still so excited, he missed the glance that passed between MacKenzie and his mother...a guarded look that asked and answered. It would no longer be safe here.

"The ice is all gone?" April questioned.

MacKenzie nodded, his expression unfathomable.

"The pass?"

"Clear."

"They still can't find us, can they? You said no one knew about this cabin."

"I don't think they ever had reason enough to really look," he replied. "Your father will turn these mountains inside out now."

"Then we'll leave...go someplace else."

MacKenzie looked at Davey, who was listening intently. "I think this young cub needs some sleep. Then he can help me catch some fish. All right, Davey?"

Davey nodded his head in assent. Fishing had become his greatest joy in the past few days. While he dearly loved his mother, he treasured the hours alone with MacKenzie, and their grown-up talks. And besides, he was indeed sleepy. "Can Wolf stay inside with me?"

"I was just going to suggest that," MacKenzie said as they walked to the cabin. "You two take good care of each other."

"We do, don't we?" Davey agreed seriously, and Mac-Kenzie could barely restrain a smile despite the confrontation he knew was coming with April.

"Yep," he agreed and watched as Davey downed a bowl of simmering soup and then climbed on the bed while Wolf settled on the floor next to him. His wild wolf had become like a puppy with Davey. What would become of the animal now? He didn't wander as he once did, disappearing for days at a time, but stayed close to the cabin and close to Davey.

MacKenzie waited until the boy's eyes closed and his body relaxed. He put his hand on April's shoulder and guided her out. They no longer needed coats, but April wore two shirts against the nip in the air. MacKenzie wore only his buckskins. They walked to the stream, to where it started its meandering path through the trees. Finally freed of the ice, it now seemed to rejoice in its freedom and babbled happily among the rocks.

MacKenzie's fist knotted, and April felt the tension reflected in the straining muscles of his arm. "It's time to leave, April," he said, his voice harsh.

"Where?"

There was a long silence. His voice was a whisper when he finally spoke. "To where you belong."

"That's with you."

"No."

"Damn you, MacKenzie," April said. "I'm not a child to simply say no to. It's my decision, too, and I won't go."

"You will, if I have to hogtie you up."

April pushed out of his arm's reach. "I love you, Mac-Kenzie."

"You'll forget about me. You're a beautiful woman; there will be many men eager to wed you."

April went white. "After they hang you, you mean. I'm to watch you go meekly to your death, then pick a substitute. Like a cherry pie when the apple pie is stolen. Is that it?" She was enraged, and her hand went flying toward his cheek, and she heard the impact as from a distance. "Is that what you think of me?"

Tears rushed from her eyes and she sank to the ground, her arms going around her knees and clutching them to stop the waves of pain that assaulted her.

Hopelessly, MacKenzie looked at her. God, he had been clumsy. How could he let her know he wanted only the best for her? For the boy? He knew he should leave her, *now,* but he couldn't.

Instead, he knelt next to her and took her in his arms, holding her tightly against him and trying to kiss the tears away. He might as well have tried to stop a waterfall from flowing, as all her withheld fears and uncertainty and wild desperate longing for him poured out. Her body was heaving with great spasms of grief, and her arms dug into his back. At that moment he was completely defenseless. He wrapped his arms tighter around her, and crooned to her as he had once done to

Davey. She smelled like flowers, and his lips tasted the newly washed silk of her hair. He was lost. Completely. His hand found her chin and gently brought it upward so his mouth could meet hers, and it did, eagerly and greedily. All the months of denial had built in him a colossal demand, and now it exploded.

"April," he said in the ragged, desperate whisper of a man no longer able to prevent himself from doing what he considered a great wrong. His lips met hers with a fierce tenderness, and he was scarcely able to keep from ravaging them, so great was his need for her.

Her mouth opened to him, and his tongue explored its sweetness. He would never be able to get enough of her, he knew, and he tried to curb his raw, hungry desire, but he could not. He felt the throbbing, aching arousal of his manhood, and once more thought how different it was now from the other times when he had merely taken relief. He was consumed with the compulsion to give pleasure, to make April feel the same soaring elation, the exquisite torment that made his body a miracle of blinding sensations.

Somewhere, a warning pounded at him, but he was beyond that now. He could no more stop than he could hold back the sun.

His lips slipped from her mouth, and his tongue played up and down her neck, savoring the nectar of her taste, the light, soft flavor of her skin. He felt her react to the slow sensuous movement, felt her body tense and move under his touch, then arch toward his in an agony of her own repressed need. For the moment there was only the two of them, and nothing else mattered, not the past, not the future...only the fierce, sweet love they exchanged in each touch, in each look, in each soft caress that turned deliciously savage as they sought to become one in every possible way.

Somehow their clothes were removed; neither exactly knew how, nor did they care. It was enough that their bodies were touching, searing each other to their very souls, sending ripples of ecstasy through every nerve. They moved together, his maleness gently probing her before moving, with incredible restraint, into the warmth he craved with all his being. He moved within her, like a sensual dancer, awakening and teasing every tingling nerve end until April thought she could bear no more and her body arched up in a desperate plea. He plunged deeper and deeper, filling her with the most glorious wonder even while she ached for more. He moved rhythmically within her, each time exploring even farther, sweeping both of them into a frenzied, whirling world pierced by bursts of supreme pleasure that spread like sun rays to every part of their physical and emotional being.

But still April reached, unwilling to release him even as rushes of ecstasy flooded her and exhausted her body; even then she craved the feel of him inside her, the wonderful, gentle yet irresistibly probing intensity of his body merged so deeply with hers. She felt his maleness quiver inside her with renewed strength, and once more she was transported on a journey that held new and miraculous surprises at every sensuous movement. When she thought there could be no greater pleasure, he moved with deliberate, savage grace within her until her body was a roaring inferno. She felt the tiny explosions building until it seemed her whole body erupted with sensations so great, so rapturous that she thought she would drown in them. Her body filled with his seed, and she felt its warmth mingle with her own, and she exulted in it.

April felt his soft stroke on her face, the whisper-light caress of his lips as he told her he loved her in ways more meaningful than words...

Afraid he might hurt her with his weight, MacKenzie rolled over, keeping her at his side, still joined to her in the most intimate way. He was loath to let her go, to relinquish the delight and peace...and utter blissful lust that had done such peculiarly wonderful things with his body and spirit. His heart sang with such joyous music it engulfed the ominous warnings of his mind. She was like the rain to his thirst-ravaged soul, like the sun to newly planted seeds. She gave him life.

And he couldn't let her go. God help him, he couldn't let her go.

Ex-Sergeant Terrell jerked his reins, unmindful of the hurt to the horse's mouth. His spurs dug into the animal's side as he raced out of the Ute village. It had taken him all winter, but at last he had what he wanted: the probable location of the goddamn 'Breed.

The man had eluded him for months, despite his intensive search. He had a score to settle and, if it took the remainder of his life, he would see it done.

Terrell had lost everything.

Since he was eighteen, the army had been his life. He had joined in the fifties and fought Indians on the plains where he forged a deep hatred for any of their kind. He had seen men he had served with massacred and mutilated in the most horrible ways, and he felt, no, knew, that none of the damned redskins were any more than animals. Including the children. "Nits grow into lice," he had frequently said, echoing a widely held belief among soldiers. He had been transferred to the Army of the Potomac during the War Between the States, and if any compassion had remained in his soul it had been trampled in the four years of slaughter. His life had been complete when he was promoted to sergeant, a position of respect, and he relished the company of men like him, men who enjoyed the camaraderie of a life spiced by hardship and danger.

MacKenzie had robbed him of that by killing one of his closest friends and getting Terrell himself thrown out of the army. A damned redskin who paraded as a white man. Hate festered in the bitter man as he remembered his meeting with General Wakefield. He could recall every word, and it spurred the rage inside him.

The damned turncoat general had taken the 'Breed's part.

Terrell had stood there in disbelief as the general told him he was a disgrace to the army. *That* after serving loyally and faithfully for more than fifteen years. A court-martial, the general had threatened. Humiliation in front of men he had led. Or he could resign.

Terrell knew a court-martial panel would include Wakefield's handpicked men. He had no desire to go to prison for perjury or to be publicly drummed out of the service, his buttons and sergeant's stripes ripped from his uniform in front of the assembled troops. So he had resigned, vowing to get both Wakefield and the 'Breed. But the 'Breed came first, and then perhaps he would get Wakefield through his daughter, the Indian-loving bitch. It had been all her fault. If she hadn't interfered in the beginning, if she hadn't showed up, MacKenzie would be dead, hung by the trail and left for the buzzards. Terrell smiled tightly at the thought. It was his one pleasure now, thinking of what he would do to the 'Breed. Cripple him first, perhaps. Watch him crawl. Terrell had little doubt that he could do it. As good as the 'Breed might be at fighting, Terrell was confident in his own skills. He was a born killer, and few were his equal with the rifle. It was just a matter of finding MacKenzie. Finding him and waiting for the right moment to ambush him.

Finding him had been the obstacle. After his resignation, Terrell had followed Captain Morris's detail until the trail narrowed and he could not continue undetected. So he had waited and watched as Captain Morris returned without MacKenzie or the girl. After the captain started toward Amos Smith's cabin, Terrell followed the trail Morris had abandoned and reached the same fork that had so concerned the army captain. With snow falling in great clumps, he realized it was senseless to go any farther.

The snow kept him out of the mountains, but it didn't deter his search. Tossing aside his hatred of Indians, he searched them out. The Utes knew this area better than anyone; he suspected if anyone knew MacKenzie's whereabouts, they would. And they were at peace, so he could easily enter their camp. He hid his hatred and purchased gallons of cheap whiskey, which he took by packhorse into one Ute camp after another. The Utes were nomads, and he spent his winter going from the plains to the hills to the mountains. Family groups formed small bands, and he learned about one from another. Finally he found one that was familiar with MacKenzie.

The braves were, at first, reluctant to talk to a white man. But whiskey loosened the tongue of one who remembered the horse race between his chief and a white man. The chief was humiliated when the white man won both his horse and his land. The fact that the man was half Indian meant little. The Ute was only too eager to win favor—and Terrell's whiskey—by betraying the man who bested his leader.

He told of the valley, but Terrell already knew about that. There had to be another place. The brave said he had heard rumors of a place high in the mountains where few traveled.

"Can you draw me a map?"

In response, the Indian took a stick and drew a rough map, nodding his head at various questions. Terrell felt a malignant satisfaction. He knew he could find his quarry, and the weather was no longer a deterrent. The ice and snow had melted, and most of the passes were safe to travel. MacKenzie was his. He would bring him back dead, and prove his worth to Wakefield. He would say the half-breed killed the general's daughter and grandson. It was, he thought, a fitting revenge all the way around.

Captain Bob Morris supervised the packing of provisions. It was usually a job left to his sergeant, but he was determined to go as long as necessary to find MacKenzie and the general's daughter. The man was not going to elude him again.

General Wakefield had been uncommonly understanding when he had returned months ago empty-handed. It was almost as if he had expected Morris to fail, which, in retrospect, did nothing to soothe Morris's raw anger or pride. It was bad enough to fail; it was worse to know that he only fulfilled expectations.

But this time he would not stop until he found April and Davon Manning.

He had chafed as the winter wore on, and he and General Wakefield knew any attempt to penetrate the mountains would be useless. But after thinking about it for months, Morris had become more and more convinced that MacKenzie had taken the steep path he had earlier discarded as a possible route.

He had studied the few available maps of the mountains. The maps were incomplete and fragmented, and sometimes nearly indecipherable. But he persevered and finally reached the conclusion that MacKenzie had taken the high route. Everything he knew, or had heard, of MacKenzie told him the scout had gone higher. And while Morris knew he could not breach the mountains in winter, neither could MacKenzie move. Morris knew he had to reach the fugitive while the scout still felt safe, which was, he suspected, only as long as he thought the range impassable.

Morris had, in the past few months, become obsessed with MacKenzie and the liberation of April Manning. Not a night went by that he didn't dream of her, that the picture on his general's desk didn't haunt him. He didn't share Wakefield's rather paradoxical opinion of MacKenzie. While his commanding officer was undeniably enraged about his daughter's disappearance, he still seemed to feel in some way that she and his grandson were safe.

But Morris didn't have the same confidence. A man who would take a woman and child up into the mountains in the height of winter was capable of anything. Including rape. The two of them were, after all, alone for months and months, except for the boy. His stomach tightened into a ball every time he thought about it.

Finally satisfied with the provisions, Bob Morris gave the

order to mount. A troop of thirty men followed him out of a gate that consisted of nothing more than two posts and a crossbar. Impatiently, his hand went up and forward, and the riders pressed their horses into a trot.

MacKenzie, his arm around April, watched as Davey and Wolf wrestled in the meadow among the wildflowers. The wolf growled menacingly, but none of them took it seriously. Not when the great tongue lolled happily out one side of his mouth. MacKenzie looked down at April's laughing face and wondered at his good fortune. He was still fascinated that his life had changed so radically, that there was so much easy joy and quiet pleasure in it. He no longer fought it. His surrender had been unconditional. He knew he should probably move on, and he had decided to take April and Davey with him, but he was caught by an unusual languor. This was where he'd discovered a happiness he had never expected, and he was reluctant to leave. The cabin, he convinced himself, was safe...at least for a while.

"You're worrying again," April said as she put an arm around him and pulled him closer. "Do you think we should leave?"

His lips touched the top of her head. She tasted so wonderfully delicious. He didn't know if he could wait until tonight to pull her tight against him, kiss her breasts, her neck, feel her strain toward him with a passion that equaled his own.

It had been delicately suggested to Davey that he might like his own bed, and the three of them had designed a bed of boughs, cushioned by skins and blankets. Davey felt very grown-up because of it. He barely noticed that MacKenzie took his place beside his mother, and since he had always slept very soundly, he never woke during the muffled happy sounds coming from the bed. The days passed with frightening speed, and April watched as the last vestiges of snow disappeared and wildflowers grew in number...

MacKenzie pondered her question. They should leave. He

knew it. But there was something he had to do first. His mouth twisted into a crooked grin.

April couldn't suppress a smile of her own. He could look more like a small boy than Davey at times. She had discovered in him a talent for mischief that never failed to delight her. It was as if all that had been suppressed for so long was now welling forth.

"What are you plotting?" she asked.

His gray eyes twinkled. "Stay here," he ordered. "I'll be back soon. Don't move."

April had never seen expectation in him before, but, unless she was very wrong, that was what was in his face.

She watched him disappear through the woods, his long legs consuming the distance with graceful speed. She smiled with elation, thinking about the changes in him in the past months. His hand often touched her lingeringly, and his eyes were soft when she found them on her. Like him, she refused to consider the future.

April sat down, her back against the tree, and closed her eyes. Wolf, she knew, would watch Davey as well as she could. Perhaps even better. What a peculiar circumstance! Trusting a wolf to guard one's son. But then everything was topsy-turvy since she'd encountered MacKenzie. Up was down, and down was up. And she would have it no other way.

Suddenly tired of waiting and curious beyond tolerance, she traced MacKenzie's footsteps toward the cabin and leaned against a tree as she watched him dig.

The ground was still hard, and sweat dripped from his face. She heard a grunt of satisfaction, and he stooped on the ground, bringing up a hide crusted in dirt. Still unaware that April was watching, he carefully unwrapped it.

April approached, and MacKenzie swung around. But there was no frown on his face at her disobedience, only triumph. He held a book in his hand, and April immediately saw it was an old worn Bible. There were other items lying on the hide, but she noticed none of it, only the intensity on his face.

He took her hand. "April..." He hesitated.

She looked up at him, her clear blue eyes meeting his now cloudy mysterious gray ones. "MacKenzie?" It was a love word. It was always a love word.

"We need to leave in the next several days," he tried again. April nodded.

"We could...I mean it's possible..." Again he stopped.

"What's possible?" April asked, her eyes now sparkling with amusement. She had never seen him quite as uncertain.

"A baby," he finally blurted.

She tried to repress a grin. "Yes," she admitted with a slight smile. "I think it's entirely possible, considering..."

"I don't want him to be a bastard." The words seemed forced out by pure determination.

"Or her," April said, her mouth now twitching with amusement at his difficulty.

He scowled as if he hadn't considered the possibility. It was bad enough to raise a boy if they were fugitives, but a girl... He wondered why he had not thought of that. A girl. Like April. With the same honest blue eyes and impish smile and stubborn set of the chin. His heart contracted.

"I thought...I mean...that is, if you will..."

She looked at the Bible in his hand and suddenly understood. But the mischievous side of her was not going to make it easy for him. He had avoided words of love.

"It would be a mountain marriage...it's legal if there's no authority around...no one will have to know...that is, if there's no child..."

April's amusement fled. "You mean I can deny it on whim. Damn you, MacKenzie. Won't you ever understand? I love you. I would never be ashamed of you, or your child, or the time we have together."

Her fierce look pierced him. He knew she was hurt by his

words, but he had had to say them. Their future was too uncertain.

"You'll do it then?"

"MacKenzie," she sighed. "That is probably the worst proposal in history, but let's go tell Davey."

He took her arm. "Are you sure, April?"

Her hand touched the worry lines in his face. "I have never been so sure of anything in my life."

MacKenzie smiled then, a slow, sad smile that almost broke her heart, and his lips touched hers with a soft, sweet poignancy.

Davey was, as predicted, delighted, and felt very important as MacKenzie and his mother stood in the meadow, their hands jointly on the worn MacKenzie Bible, and exchanged short vows.

April thought there couldn't be a more perfect chapel. The sky was the purest blue and the mountains were majestic with their robes of white. The sun had never shone so brightly, nor had the choir of birds trilled quite as sweetly. Only their tightly clasped hands indicated the fear behind the words, the terror of potential loss.

But the undertones escaped Davey, who shivered with excitement. "You're really and truly my daddy now," Davey said immediately.

"Really and truly," agreed MacKenzie.

"What should I call you then?"

"I think I'm used to MacKenzie," he replied.

Davey gave him a brilliant smile. "Me, too," he said. "And Wolf...he's my family, too?"

"Oh, I think he adopted you long ago," MacKenzie said, leaning down and picking up the boy.

"I suppose," Davey said with a considering look, "that I'm the happiest boy anywhere."

Only April saw the sudden misery and apprehension on

MacKenzie's face, and she couldn't repress her own premonition. She would be relieved when they left.

It was only later that night, after they had made love with a frantic, needful urgency and MacKenzie lay sleeping beside her, that April realized that he had never mentioned the word love.

Chapter Nineteen

April looked around the cabin helplessly. She didn't know what to pack.

They had only the one horse now, and they were limited in what they could take. She had made several bundles, each of which she knew was too cumbersome. She wanted to sit down and cry.

Part of the problem, she knew, was that she really didn't want to leave this austere cabin with all its memories. It would be like leaving part of her heart. Despite its plainness, she had been happier here than any place in her life. MacKenzie had filled it with his own peculiar brand of enchantment.

Now she didn't know where they were going or what would become home.

She dismissed her sudden misgivings. Nothing was important as long as MacKenzie was beside her.

She tried again, sighing as she attempted to roll three blankets and two hides together along with several pieces of clothing. And then there were the pot and the cups and the dried beef and…the bagpipes. MacKenzie had unearthed them along with the Bible, and she had pleaded with him to play them. He had acquiesced without pleasure, but once he put them to his mouth, they made wonderful music…full and majestic and hauntingly lovely. She could tell from his eyes that he both loved and hated them.

And then there were the guns. MacKenzie had taken one

rifle with him and left the other rifle and Colt with her; both were hanging on hooks out of Davey's reach. MacKenzie had already mentioned teaching Davey about them, but April wanted to wait. It was soon, much too soon for her son to learn about death. Davey. Where had Davey gone? He was six now and feeling all too confident and grown up. Wolf had gone with MacKenzie to dismantle the snares he had set, and April had been keeping half an eye on her son. Through the open door, she heard his happy chatter as he conversed with MacKenzie's horse. April shook her head. He was growing more like MacKenzie every day, with the same love and instinct for animals.

April gave up. She would let MacKenzie do it. He knew better than she what they would need. Instead she would take these last few hours of sun and play with Davey. Tomorrow, at dawn, they would leave.

Humming the irresistible lonely melody she had learned from MacKenzie, she walked over to Davey. Perhaps they would make up some stories while they waited for his return.

Terrell moved cautiously through the underbrush. There had been one false lead after another, but he finally found a faint trail...if it could be called that. He felt as if he had been going around in circles, but then he saw the twisted tree that had been drawn by the Ute and he was heartened.

He knew MacKenzie well enough to be very careful. The only way he would take the man was by ambush, and at a distance. When he reached another point described by the Indian, he tied his horse and moved stealthily by foot. Minutes went by, then, he reckoned by the sun, an hour before he saw an opening in the trees. He got down on his knees and crawled forward until he saw a small, neat cabin. Above it were some rocks; they were the perfect place for an ambush.

Terrell circled, every instinct alert. He moved low and slowly, his rifle clasped tightly in his hands. Where was MacKenzie? He finally reached the rocks and spread out be-

hind their protective covering, releasing one long breath. He
stayed there several seconds, trying to calm his jangled nerves,
then he peered between two boulders.

He still didn't see MacKenzie, but he did see the woman.
She and the boy were sitting in the grass, their faces rapt as
they talked. He sighted the rifle, judging the range. The barrel
of his seven-shot Spencer found April's breast, then the boy's
heart, then wandered back to the woman. He thought about
firing; he had already decided he had to kill both of them, but
then he hesitated. The sound of gunfire might warn Mac-
Kenzie, and *he* was the greatest danger. No, he would wait.
Then after wounding MacKenzie he might take the woman
while the 'Breed watched. Terrell remembered how the girl
had slapped him on behalf of the damned Indian, and his finger tightened once more on the trigger. It took all his control
not to pull it.

The sun was behind him, and he hoped MacKenzie would
hurry. If his first shot missed, MacKenzie would be blinded
by the blazing sun, and he would have a chance for another
shot before the bastard could find his position. Impatiently, he
awaited his quarry.

MacKenzie dismantled the last snare. There had been one
rabbit, and that they would have for dinner. He took his time
in returning, he and Wolf. This might be the last time he
would wander these woods he knew so well. He studied them
without regret. April and Davey were his future now and
somehow, somewhere, they would find peace. He knew it. He
could not allow himself to think otherwise, for there was no
way he could turn back. He realized he had a stupidly happy
grin on his face. It seemed to be there quite often these days.
It had quite stunned him that anyone could be this happy, this
content...even with the problems that faced them. But April
had made him believe...

He pointed the rifle at the ground, his fingers away from
the trigger as he hurried his pace. April would be waiting, and

in his mind's eye he could already see the welcoming sparkle she always had for him. He knew he would never understand his miracle, his great luck in finding her and Davey.

The grin turned wry. It was well they were leaving this place. He knew his normal caution had been dulled, that his feelings for April had blinded him to everything else. But it was difficult to think of danger after the bliss of April's arms. He turned his mind to tomorrow's journey. It would be a difficult trip with only the one horse for three of them. But he had the gold he had saved, and he hoped they would find two other mounts on some isolated ranch. He had thought about going to Denver but quickly dismissed the idea. He was known there, and surely word would have traveled. All of a sudden, guilt attacked him. They would have to avoid all settlements from now on. It was so damned unfair to April and Davey...and yet she swore it was what she wanted. And after the last miraculous weeks he was too selfish to say nay. Just thinking about them brought the smile back to his face, and a whistle to his lips. His eagerness to reach April blinded him to the flash of the sun on a rifle barrel. As he left the shelter of the trees, he had eyes only for April, who stood at the cabin door. The sun had turned her chestnut hair to flaming gold, and her eyes were so blue...so very blue...and dancing with delight at seeing him.

The noise and the pain came together. MacKenzie felt his leg crumble as agony flooded him, and the rifle went skittering from his hands. He tried to look toward the direction of the shot but the sun blinded him, and he knew complete helplessness. Somewhere his mind registered the low growl of the wolf as the animal sought to find the danger, and he saw Davey running toward him.

"No," he yelled to the boy. "Go back," but Davey kept coming. He heard another shot and saw the boy go down, and suddenly the wolf was streaking toward the rocks above the cabin. MacKenzie tried to crawl to Davey, to protect him with his body. April. Where was she? He looked up and saw a man standing up against the sun, his rifle pointed toward the animal hurtling at him. He heard another shot and saw the man fall just as the wolf sprang. There was a terrible scream, then silence. He tried to locate his rifle. Was there just the one man? Or more? Davey or the gun? He had to protect the boy...the boy and April. *What a fool he had been to think he could take care of them.* He sacrificed the gun to crawl to Davey, noticing the blood pouring from a wound on the boy's scalp. *Oh, God, please let him be all right.* And then he saw April kneeling beside him, a rifle still in her hand and tears snaking down her fear-stunned face.

"Davey?" It was a whisper.

"Get him inside," MacKenzie grimaced. "Give me the rifle."

"But..."

"Get him inside, there may be others." The pained desperation in his voice convinced her. And there was another gun in the cabin. She gathered Davey in her arms and ran toward the cabin.

The rifle clutched in his hands, MacKenzie rolled over, the pain momentarily dulled by his fear for April and the boy. His eyes searched the rocks, the woods. He whistled and Wolf appeared, his muzzle covered in blood. "Any more, boy?" he asked, and the wolf's ears perked upward, but the animal showed only wariness, not a warning.

Finally convinced the danger was over, MacKenzie checked his wound. It was bleeding profusely and hurt like Hades. The shot had ripped into muscle and tissue but he was thankful that it had gone through his leg without shattering a bone. He took the bandanna from around his neck and tied it tightly around the upper part of his leg to staunch the flow of blood. Using the rifle, he tried to stand. God, but it hurt. Only determination brought him to his feet. He stumbled across the rocks, then crawled up until he came to the body.

It was hard to tell anything. There was a bullet hole in the man's shoulder, and his throat was ripped. There was so much blood that, at first, MacKenzie didn't recognize him. But the burly build struck a memory, and he leaned down and wiped some of the blood from the man's face.

Terrell!

Why was he alone? Where were the others? Then he saw the civilian clothes. What had happened?

He heard the low growl of wolf.

"It's all right," MacKenzie said. "He's dead." There was no doubt of that. No one could survive that kind of wound or the loss of so much blood. MacKenzie's jaw tightened. The man had purposely shot a small boy. May he roast in hell.

Davey!

He would have to do something about Terrell's body, but that could wait. He had to see about the boy. Using the rifle as a crutch, he climbed down and limped painfully to the cabin.

The pistol lay on the table where April had left it after realizing the danger was gone. Now she was bent over Davey, her hands wiping away the blood with a wet cloth.

MacKenzie's voice was ragged. "How is he?"

"Stunned, I think," April whispered. "And the bullet...I don't think it's dangerous but..." Her voice faltered. "Oh, MacKenzie, there's so much blood."

"It's my fault," MacKenzie rasped and April could scarcely stand the agony in his voice. "Damn, but it's all my fault. I was a fool. A damned stupid fool." He took a step and fell, and April whirled around, her eyes going to his bloody trousers.

"MacKenzie," she whispered, her desperate eyes going from him to Davey.

"Stay with the boy," MacKenzie ordered harshly, and April obeyed. The sooner she finished with Davey, the quicker she could care for MacKenzie. She knew he would not let her touch him until then. Thank God, Davey was still unconscious. His breathing, however, was deep and even. She threaded a needle and tried to keep her hands from trembling as she sewed his wound together.

When she was finished, she turned to MacKenzie. "Who was it?"

"Sergeant Terrell," MacKenzie said through clenched teeth.

"Dead?" Her voice was surprisingly calm.

"Yes."

"Was it my shot?" Her face was tense as she waited for the answer. He had tried to kill her son, and MacKenzie, but she shuddered inwardly at the thought of actually killing someone.

MacKenzie heard revulsion in her voice, and understood, and it did nothing to ease his self-hatred. Christ, what had he done to her? "No," he said in a voice meant to be gentle but which, instead, was raw with guilt and rage. "Wolf," he explained shortly.

April's eyes closed as she remembered the scream, and MacKenzie felt his heart shatter. If there had been even a small part left intact, it was destroyed at her next words. "We have to leave quickly. If Sergeant Terrell found you..." Her words died, their meaning hanging thickly between them. If Terrell found them, then others would.

"Do you think you can travel soon?" she asked dispassionately as her hands busied themselves, cutting his trousers with a knife, eyeing the two holes in his leg cautiously.

The silence was deafening. When MacKenzie finally spoke his words were like those of a dead man. "I'm taking you back."

April looked up from the wound. MacKenzie's jaw was set...and not just with physical pain. His eyes were as they used to be. Hooded. Secret. Unyielding.

"No." It was a desperate cry. And she knew it would do no good."

"Mama."

April spun around at Davey's cry.

"I hurt, Mama," the boy said, and her eyes quickly went to MacKenzie's face. He couldn't curtain it fast enough, and it was filled with such raw, naked emotion that she felt herself turn to stone. She knew from his anguished expression that this time he would not change his mind.

"See to him," he said in a choked voice. "I can take care of these myself." He wanted to feel the pain. He deserved every second of it. He deserved to die. He deserved anything they did to him. His fingers angrily jerked the bandanna from his leg, and he wiped the wounds with it. He didn't really care if he bled to death or not. Except for one thing. He had to get April and Davey home. And nothing, and no one, was going to stop him from doing that.

April looked at him hopelessly. She wanted to soothe his hurts, ease his pain, but she knew now that it would only increase his suffering. With an instinct born of loving him, she knew he needed, at this moment, to do exactly what he said, to take care of himself. He would accept no help from her, and if she tried, she would only make things worse for him. She turned away as he patched himself together, wincing at his sometimes awkward efforts, which she caught in sideways glances. And she died a little from wanting to help. Wanting so very much to help. And knowing she could not.

It was as if the last few months had never happened, April thought the next day. MacKenzie was as detached and cold as he had been the day he had taken Davey. Perhaps even more so, if that were possible.

He was also drinking.

April had not realized there was any liquor around the cabin, but after Terrell's attack MacKenzie had limped to the shed that sheltered his Appaloosa and returned with a jug. After pouring a goodly portion on his wound, he sat on the floor morosely and drank.

She did not say anything because she knew he must be in a great deal of pain. He had not let her touch his wound but had sewn it himself after washing it with the raw liquor. She knew the agony must have been terrible, but he didn't flinch once. Indeed, he seemed to take grim satisfaction in the pain, and when the cabin fell dark he did not return to her bed but simply lay on the floor, leaving her lonely and aching and frightened.

The next day was no better. She had hoped that he would at least talk to her, but he didn't. He was gone when she woke and when she looked outside, he was sitting motionless on a boulder, a shovel at his side. She immediately sensed he had buried Terrell. She wondered how he had done it with his injured leg, but then nothing he did surprised her anymore. He had a will unlike any other.

She remembered the last time he had used the shovel, and how happy they had been. Would they ever be happy again?

Despite his shadowed look, she went over to him. "Davey's better," she offered, and he merely nodded.

"He was not that badly hurt," she tried again.

MacKenzie didn't look at her. Neither did he answer. There was nothing to say.

April wanted to scream at him, to climb the barrier that he had resurrected, but it was higher than ever. "Don't do this, MacKenzie," she pleaded. "Davey's ever so much better, and he's asking for you."

MacKenzie looked at her then, the mask firmly locked in place. His expression didn't change. "He's better off not seeing me. You, too. I'll be sleeping out here until I think we're both fit enough to travel. I'll not risk you again."

"You *can't* go back. They will hang you."

He shrugged with indifference.

"Damn you. Don't do this to us."

He whirled on her. "I've already *done* everything to you except get you killed, and I've come damned close to that several times. Do you want to see that boy dead? Two inches. Just two inches, and he would have been. God knows what could have happened to you, to the boy, if Terrell had aimed a little better and killed me straightaway. Even if Wolf did kill him, do you really think you and Davey could survive in the mountains...or find your way out? We've all been dreaming fools. It's no good, April. And if you care for me at all, you'll leave me alone. When we get to Fort Defiance, I don't want to see you again...neither you nor Davey.'' His hand caught her chin, forcing her to look in his cold, determined eyes. ''Do you understand, April? Do you?''

April jerked away, unable to continue looking at the icy eyes, so different from yesterday morning when they had twinkled and laughed with her, when hope and happiness had turned his mouth into such wonderful shapes.

''No,'' she whispered defiantly. ''I won't let you go. I won't ever let you go. I will go wherever you go, be with you no matter what happens. I'm your wife. Do *you* understand?''

MacKenzie groaned. He had tried to forget those moments. How could he have done this to her? ''It is easily remedied,'' he said, forcing a coldness into his voice. ''It's not been sanctioned by legal authorities. I will deny it.''

April was furious now. ''Deny all you want, MacKenzie, but it's done and everyone will know it if you're stubborn enough to commit suicide by going back.'' Too angry to continue, she stood and stalked to the cabin.

She didn't know where he went after that, but he took the Appaloosa and didn't return until dusk. He had another horse with him. Terrell's, she surmised joylessly. It would make it only that much easier for MacKenzie to take them back. Back to what? She would be as lifeless as MacKenzie without him.

When he finally entered the cabin, he took some dried meat and lifted the jug. His limp was much more pronounced than it had been in the morning, and he couldn't hide the tiny lines of pain in his face. His face gentled only momentarily when his hand touched Davey's hair and then, jug in hand, he painfully left the cabin. He didn't return, and April could only believe he had settled in the shed. Soundlessly, so as not to disturb Davey, she cried herself to sleep. MacKenzie had filled her life, and now he was draining it, leaving her hollow and aching. She could only go with him now and do what she could to save him. He obviously had no intentions of trying to save himself.

MacKenzie settled himself down in the corner of the shed and took a long draw from the jug. His father had made the liquor, probably not long before he died. Rob MacKenzie had liked whiskey and often drunk himself into a stupor. When he hadn't turned mean, that was...which had happened frequently. Both MacKenzie and his mother had felt his father's hand in a drunken rage. Because of that, MacKenzie had never had a taste for drink. He knew it clouded his judgment, and that was something he could not afford. Until now, he thought bitterly. Now he didn't have anything to lose. But April did, a voice inside him said. She depended on him. He buried his head in his hands. What in the hell was he doing? He had never wallowed in self-pity before. April and Davey would need his strength in the coming days. It was the least he could do after everything, see them safely home even if it broke his heart to do so.

He cast the jug aside, watching the last remnants of alcohol seep out, and stretched lengthwise in the shed. The horses were hobbled outside, but the wind was still cold at night and the walls of the rough structure gave him some protection. He needed to sleep, to regain his strength. He planned to leave the day after tomorrow. He figured his leg would be well enough then to tolerate the endless ride back. How could he bear being alone with April and Davey for so many miles, so many nights? And how would he ever be able to see those nights end?

And, in God's name, how could he ever make April let him go when he didn't know how he could do so himself?

Plagued by physical and mental pain, he stayed awake much of the night until finally his will triumphed and he fell into a short, troubled sleep.

* * *

Captain Morris stopped at Amos Smith's cabin for a short rest. He had been delayed repeatedly along his journey. General Wakefield's troops had captured a number of hostiles during the winter, but there were still a few roaming bands. Morris and his men had found the tracks of one band near two ranches, and he detoured to warn the settlers, only to find them under siege. He had ordered an attack and then sent his men after the escaping Apaches. It had taken the better part of a week to find them, and then he had had to divide his force to take his captives to Fort Defiance. He was down to ten men now. His fear was not of MacKenzie, if he could ever find the damned elusive renegade, but of the trip back through Indian territory with the woman and boy. But he was not turning back, not this time.

Smith was at his cabin, but he was silent and unfriendly. He didn't like the army. He didn't like authority and, most of all, didn't like anyone who was going after MacKenzie. Rob MacKenzie had been his friend, and he had always admired his independent son who asked nothing of anyone. Smith didn't believe a damn word Morris said...not about MacKenzie.

Bob Morris found his questions answered with a blank stare.

When asked about MacKenzie's possible destination, Amos Smith eyed him with contempt. "I don't know nothin' and even if I did I ain't tellin' you little blue boys."

Captain Morris knew complete frustration. "He took a woman and child...doesn't that mean anything to you? They could be in danger."

"Not with MacKenzie," the old man said calmly. "Now git out of here. You ain't welcome."

Morris wasn't ready to give up. "There's a pass not far from here, real steep. Is that where they would go?"

There was a flicker in the old man's eyes. "That ain't no pass. It falls off. Sheer drop."

Morris allowed himself a small smile. The man was lying. He had been right. That was the trail MacKenzie had taken. "Thank you," he said with ironic courtesy. He turned to his sergeant. "Tell the men to mount. I know MacKenzie's direction."

Amos cursed himself as he watched the blue boys wearily throw themselves back into the saddle and take the trail toward Devil's Fall. Then he shrugged. MacKenzie could take care of himself. He was probably a hundred miles away by now. A woman and child, huh? MacKenzie must have finally taken a wife, or else he would have had nothing to do with such a thing. The boy had always been too damned honorable for his own good. Not like his pa or even himself. Well, it was none of his business. Nonetheless, he felt a certain apprehension for one of the few men he called friend. "God speed," he whispered to the wind.

MacKenzie packed with the silent efficiency April remembered from their first few days together. If he felt any regret at leaving he didn't show it. His limp was better, except when he didn't know she was watching. Then he would sag wearily against a wall or tree, and she knew the pain must be great. But he would not let her near him, much less look at his wound. She didn't know when he tended it, or even if he bothered. It worried her constantly, but after two or three attempts to help she gave up.

Davey was much better. His wound had not been deep, and while it would leave a small scar on the side of his head, there was no sign of infection. Even the pain seemed to disappear completely, except when he rolled on it in his sleep. Then April would hear a small whimper, and she would take him in her arms and hold tightly. He, too, was feeling the hurt of MacKenzie's rejection, although it was not as obvious as her own. MacKenzie would tousle his hair or smile faintly, almost distantly, at him, but there were no more walks, no more songs, no more private talks. Davey would look at him with hurt confusion, and if her heart hadn't already broken, that look would have done it. However was she going to explain everything to Davey? What if MacKenzie was executed? How would she and Davey survive? They were questions she couldn't answer.

MacKenzie had decreed they would leave in the morning. April thought about trying to take one of the horses and Davey and run away, forcing him to come after them. But Mac-Kenzie, almost as if he sensed such a plan, seemed to appear every time she went near the animals. Besides, she knew deep inside she could never get far enough to do any good. He would find her within hours, and nothing would be accomplished. Damn. She felt so completely helpless. This afternoon, she would make one last attempt to talk to him, to change his mind. She had to. She just had to.

MacKenzie was at the stream when she found him. Wolf was with Davey at the cabin, and she had made him promise he would not leave.

When MacKenzie sensed her presence, he turned and faced her, and instinct told April he had expected her. But his eyes were unfathomable, his face held firmly in control. She wished that she had the same ability. She knew her heart was in her face, and she could already feel the hot rush of tears in her eyes. She had never cried much before she met MacKenzie, she realized with a sort of detached observation. He must think her weak and emotional. The thought hurt, but did nothing to alleviate the trail of tears.

His hands remained at his side, and something flickered in his eyes. "Don't, April," he finally said. "Please, don't cry. I can take anything but that." His voice broke on the last word, but April heard every excruciating syllable. She saw his strong jaw tremble with effort and a muscle throb in his cheek. His whole body was tense with the steely determination that controlled his life.

"I will have nothing without you," she said simply.

"You have Davey. You have your father. You have your life."

"Not at the expense of yours. I may go on living...I have to because of Davey, but it will not be life. It will be existence."

MacKenzie knew about existence, and probably nothing else she said could have made the impact that word did. He opened his arms, and April went into them. They held each other closely, each seeking strength from the other, for both knew MacKenzie had not changed his mind, nor would he. It was Davey's life as well as their own.

"Once more, MacKenzie," April whispered. "Fill me with glory once more, and I will do what you say." She knew she had no other choice.

His large hand tenderly pushed a curl from her face and his lips touched her forehead, then the eyes awash with tears. His hands had never been so gentle as when they cupped her face and lifted it so he could memorize everything as it was this moment. There was so much brave love shining from it. And neither for her sake nor his own could he deny the deep aching need to join once more, to feel hearts and blood and sorrow flow together for one last time. There was no urgency, only a measured poignancy that demanded that every touch, every movement be treasured and remembered.

When at last he entered her, he did so with a slow magic that enraptured and enslaved her. He moved deliberately, teasing every sense and reveling in the sweet agonizing pain of his core melding with hers, of going deeper until they were both lost in the depths of a bittersweet mixture of joy and fear, of rhapsody and discord...until the sensations became so thunderous, so fiery, so brilliant that everything else was forgotten...and they were left with exploding stars, bits and pieces slowly floating to earth...

Like broken pieces of a heart, April thought as MacKenzie slowly withdrew from her, leaving her still throbbing with fulfillment, still hungry for more. She would always be hungry for him, for his touch. Forever.

They said nothing as they dressed. There was nothing more to say.

It was gray the next morning. The usual subtle pastel colors of dawn were lost in dullness. It fitted April's mood.

Without a will of her own, she watched MacKenzie's preparations as through a haze. It was as if she had known but it hadn't really become real. Now it did. They were leaving. They were returning to Fort Defiance.

She watched with deep hurt as Davey said goodbye to Wolf, his face streaked with tears. He didn't know where they were going or suspect what would happen. She had said only that he would see his grandpa, and her words were accepted. As long as MacKenzie was going...

But his departure from the animal who had become his friend, his protector, was almost more than April could stand. She knew that MacKenzie had planned to take the animal earlier, when they thought they would find another place in the mountains. But there was no way he could take Wolf to the fort. It would be a death sentence for the animal as well as... *Don't think, April. Don't think of it.*

Finally they were ready. Davey had asked to ride with MacKenzie and with that sad wry smile, he agreed. MacKenzie told Wolf to stay, and they rode out of the clearing, Davey looking back to see the animal sitting there, as told, anxiety in every tense muscle.

This time, April didn't even care as the tears poured down her face.

The trail was narrow, and branches slapped at her, scratching her flesh and tearing her clothes. She was still wearing Rob MacKenzie's old worn-out trousers and shirt. There was nothing else. She looked ahead at MacKenzie. He was just as disreputable. He wore the deerskin shirt she had made, but his trousers were of coarse cotton. His buckskin ones had been ruined by Terrell's shot and the subsequent blood. He had also neglected shaving for the past couple of days, and his face was covered with black stubble that made him look more dangerous than usual.

He sat on his horse with his usual grace, but his shoulders were uncharacteristically slumped. His eyes were wary, but his face, when he turned toward her, was lined and hollow. She knew he hated what he was doing...giving up without a fight...but she also knew he felt he had no other choice. What had she done to him?

MacKenzie's hands still burned with Davey's tears as they left Wolf. Now the boy's head rested against his chest, and he could feel the bulky bandage still covering the boy's head. He had turned around once, after a particularly difficult part of the trail, and watched April struggling against the branches that stung her body. Her expression was lifeless, unlike any he had seen on her face before. All the laughter was gone. The determined courage. Oh, God, what had he done to her? To her and Davey. No matter what happened, he would never forgive himself for the misery and pain he had caused them.

He was so lost in regret, in guilt, that he didn't see the first patch of blue against the brown of the brush as they rode directly into Captain Bob Morris and his small command.

Chapter Twenty

It was difficult to determine who was more surprised.

But it took only seconds for Bob Morris's men to surround them, and MacKenzie found several guns pointed directly at him. He leaned back in the saddle, one hand still on Davey, the other relaxing with the reins on the saddle horn.

"Morris," he observed with a crooked, ironic twist of his mouth. "If you had waited a few days, I would have saved you a ride."

Bob Morris felt ire flooding his face and fought to control it. MacKenzie never had paid any attention to rank, except perhaps for Wakefield. And the scout's cool insolence now didn't mollify the anger that had been quietly building within Morris during the past six months of frustration.

"Hand the boy over to the sergeant," Morris said, his voice sharp. He turned his head to indicate the intended recipient. "Take him, Sergeant."

The sergeant moved his horse with difficulty along the narrow trail and leaned over to obey, but the boy tried to squirm away. "No," he insisted. "I want to stay with MacKenzie."

Morris saw MacKenzie whisper something to the boy, and the child stopped protesting. Reluctantly, Davon Manning let MacKenzie pass him over.

"Now you, MacKenzie. Give me your pistol and rifle...and do it slowly."

MacKenzie obeyed without comment. In some secret part

of him, he felt a measure of unexpected relief. It was over! There was no longer a choice; he was no longer waging a war between what he wanted to do and what he had to do, a war that had tormented and crippled his defenses. The fact that he had wandered unawares on Morris showed exactly how much. Or perhaps it had not been entirely unawares. Somewhere in his mind, he had heard the faint hoofbeats, had seen the fragments of blue through the trees, but he had disregarded them. Perhaps part of him had welcomed them. Davey and April would be safe now. He knew Morris was a competent officer.

"Keep both hands on the reins," Morris said, "and move slowly until we get to a clearing."

Receiving no reply, he added sharply, "MacKenzie, I want an answer."

"I didn't think it was a question," MacKenzie said, his jaw locking with sudden anger. He hadn't wanted Davey to see this. The boy, sitting stiffly with the sergeant, was regarding the captain with wide, rebellious eyes.

"Damn you," Morris said. "You make the slightest move to escape, and my men have orders to shoot you."

MacKenzie again didn't answer, but his thighs pressed the sides of his horse, and he moved into line in back of a trooper, leaving Morris to fume silently. Morris moved his horse to the side of the trail, enabling the others to pass until the young woman came abreast of him.

Even dressed in a man's clothes, she was a beauty. Perhaps it was the defiant sparkle in her eyes, or the proud tilt of her head, or the way the sun caught the red-gold flame in her hair. Perhaps it was his obsession with finding her, with the picture in Wakefield's office, with all the fears he had harbored for her for so long. He had, he supposed, expected gratitude, but what he found was anger. She was glowering at him. Nothing less. Instead of thanks, there was a deep, simmering antagonism that scorched him with its contempt. He almost flinched under her gaze.

He sought to reassure her. "Mrs. Manning...are you all

right? We've been trying to find you, you and your son. Your father's been very worried.''

She looked at him coldly. He had taken away time during which she might have changed MacKenzie's mind. She hated him at that moment. "Why?" she asked frankly. "My father knew I was with MacKenzie.''

"For God's sake, Mrs...." He stopped when he realized what he had said, and his face went red. "Beg your pardon, Mrs. Manning, but he kidnapped you.''

She had already decided on her defense. "He did nothing of the kind," she said. "I knew Sergeant Terrell was going to kill him, and I went with him willingly. And he didn't try to rape that girl, or kill anyone except in self-defense. Didn't my father get my note?''

"Yes...but he could have forced you...''

"Do I look forced, Captain?" she said, permitting only a trace of amused irritation in her voice. She wanted to tell him that she and MacKenzie were married, at least in the sight of God, but she decided she owed it to her father to tell him first. It would also, she knew, be her greatest ammunition, and she wanted to use it in her own way.

Morris didn't reply. MacKenzie had obviously influenced the woman in his behalf...along with the boy, if those first few minutes meant anything. He would have to keep them apart during the trip back, and hope she would see MacKenzie for what he was: a half wild renegade who had used her.

They finally rode into a small clearing, and Morris ordered MacKenzie to dismount. "Search him," he snapped despite April's protest, and a grim smile appeared when MacKenzie's knife was found in his boot.

"Put the handcuffs on," Morris told the sergeant as April and Davey looked on, Davey with bewilderment, April with vivid anger.

"No," she protested. "He was giving himself up.''

It was as if Morris hadn't heard. He nodded to the sergeant to continue and watched as MacKenzie held out his hands and the iron bands were locked around his wrists. April started toward him, but MacKenzie glared, stopping her as effectively as any hand. "Stay away from me, Mrs. Manning." He whirled toward Morris. "Are we going on?"

Morris nodded, feeling as if his command had just been taken away from him by his own prisoner. "But you take that black horse over there. The sergeant will ride your Appaloosa."

MacKenzie's eyes sparked icy fire, but he understood the reasoning. He could ride his Appaloosa with the mere touch of his legs, and everyone knew it. Morris wasn't taking any chances. Without another word, he limped to the designated horse and mounted, watching carefully as the reins were taken by a trooper. He stared straight ahead until everyone had remounted. His back straightened, and he focused his attention on the trooper who led his horse. He was damned if he would give them any satisfaction.

They rode until the sun set and the going became too difficult to manage in semidarkness. The horses were secured in a picket line and a fire was started. MacKenzie was allowed a few minutes of privacy before being chained to a slender pine. The left cuff was unlocked and circled around the pine to clasp the chain near his right wrist. It left one hand free to eat, but made escape impossible. He saw April trying to approach him, but she was stopped by Morris. They spoke for a few moments, then Morris approached him with a plate of beans and bacon and a cup of coffee. He set it down and stared at MacKenzie.

"I saw your limp...and the boy's head...what happened?"

"Your Sergeant Terrell. He tried to ambush us."

"And..."

"I killed him," MacKenzie said flatly. He didn't think it a lie. His wolf did it, and if he hadn't, MacKenzie would have. He wouldn't bring April into it. "Another charge you can add," he said with seeming indifference.

"Were you really bringing them back...Mrs. Manning and the boy?"

"What difference does it make?"

"Maybe a lot..."

"I don't think so," MacKenzie said. There was no bitterness in his voice, only a calm acceptance, and Morris wondered at it. It certainly wasn't what he expected, but then he had never known the scout well. The man had never let anyone know him well.

Morris's thoughts were interrupted once more by MacKenzie. "You will never know now anyway, will you?" It was almost a taunt.

"Mrs. Manning wants to talk to you," Morris said, trying to hold his anger.

"No," MacKenzie said sharply.

"And the boy?"

The cold mockery left MacKenzie's face and for the first time Morris saw real suffering. It surprised him to realize it was for the boy. Damn, could Wakefield have been right? And was it true that MacKenzie was coming in on his own? He thought for a moment of telling the scout about Ellen Peters, but felt it wasn't his place. The rape charge had been dismissed, but the death of her father was still active. It would be Wakefield's decision, not his, and he didn't want to feed false hope. He knew Wakefield's anger had increased over the endless winter months.

"I would be obliged if you kept him away, too. It's better for him." It was probably the first time, Morris thought, that anyone had heard MacKenzie ask a favor.

Morris nodded. He asked one of his men to get some blankets for the prisoner, and the army captain spent much of the rest of the night staring thoughtfully into the fire.

Morris paced his horse next to April's in the morning. He could actually feel the hostility brimming from her. Every time he attempted a pleasantry, he was pierced by daggers in her eyes. It hadn't helped when he told her she couldn't talk to MacKenzie and had placed several soldiers between them to make sure she didn't.

"The boy seems fond of MacKenzie," he finally said.

"Of course," she said, as if he were not very intelligent. "MacKenzie saved his life several times, was almost killed when he jumped a bear to protect Davey. My son wouldn't be here, nor would I, if it wasn't for him." She turned to him. "Captain, let him go. Let *us* go."

So much for rescues and gratitude, Morris thought bitterly. "I'm sorry, Mrs. Manning. I can't do that."

"Then let me talk to him, be with him," she said desperately.

"It's his decision, not mine," Morris said stiffly.

"At least take those handcuffs off him."

"You ask the impossible, Mrs. Manning. If you're right, if he was coming in, what's to stop him from changing his mind now you're safe? Your father wants him."

"My father wouldn't chain him."

"Your father gave me my orders."

"Because my father didn't know what happened."

Morris's voice softened. "We know what Terrell tried to do. We know about Ellen Peters..." He hadn't meant to say the last, but the suffering in her face prompted the words.

"You know..."

"We know part of it. Your father kept expecting you and Davon to appear..."

"He tried. MacKenzie tried. Over and over again, he tried to find someplace safe for us. But there were Apaches everywhere, and the Ute village was deserted, and then Amos was gone, and..."

"The storm came..."

April stared at him. "How did you know?"

"I was right behind you. Mad as hell, beg your pardon."

"Then you know he tried..."

"Do you have any idea how old your father has grown in

the past months? At first, he was sure MacKenzie would get you back, and then months went by, and he didn't know if you and his grandson were dead or alive.''

April grew quiet. She had known but had tried to push the knowledge away from her.

"I love him, Captain,'' she said finally.

Morris pushed his dreams away and sighed. "I know,'' he said. "And I wish I could help you, but I can't.'' He put his finger to his campaign hat and pressed his horse into a gallop.

The next few days were misery for everyone, except perhaps for MacKenzie, who had locked himself tight in a shell of his own. He rode with the familiar easy grace. His eyes were always hooded now, and he stared straight ahead day after day. Several times, April had managed to ease next to him, but he didn't acknowledge her existence with either words or looks. Davey was different. He couldn't lock the boy out, not when the green eyes were so beseeching. Davey would often elude Morris's guard and find his way to MacKenzie's side, resisting any attempt to stop him. Mac-Kenzie would reach out to touch, to reassure, his jaw tightening as the handcuffs restricted his movements. He had never wanted Davey to see him like this.

Bob Morris watched it all. He saw MacKenzie's eyes on April when he thought no one was observing. And April's open, unashamed ones on MacKenzie. He saw the boy's adoration of the half-breed, and MacKenzie's rather futile attempt to hide his own love for the boy. And he knew a fierce envy despite MacKenzie's precarious position. No one had ever looked at him like that.

Nights were worse, he thought. He supervised securing MacKenzie to whatever was available, all the time feeling the condemning eyes of April and Davey hard upon him. MacKenzie was the only one who didn't seem to object, and Morris had to admit to a growing fascination with the man. Most of the arrogance he remembered was gone, although

MacKenzie's disregard for rank or authority still seemed firmly in place.

More often than not, Morris took his meals with the prisoner, who was less hostile than Mrs. Manning and the boy. At first, MacKenzie was silent, regarding Morris with open indifference. But Morris prodded him with carefully phrased questions, focusing on MacKenzie's knowledge of the area tribes. At first, MacKenzie answered in monosyllables when he answered at all, and then his own curiosity was provoked by the captain, and his answers became more detailed. He wanted to know what had happened in the six months of winter isolation. What of the Apache?

"We caught the ones who killed your Navahos," Morris said. "They're on a reservation." He shrugged. "I don't know how long they will stay there."

"The children?" Again Morris was struck by MacKenzie's inconsistencies. Prior to this assignment, he had never seen this side of the scout. He knew, as did everyone who had been on the post for several years, that MacKenzie had fought for one particular family of Navahos, but no one knew the reason.

"I'm sorry," he said, and meant it as he saw MacKenzie's tense expression. "We didn't find them. They had probably been sold already."

Morris saw the brief interest fade from his prisoner's eyes, replaced by bleakness as MacKenzie leaned against the tree to which he was attached. The man's face was dark with stubble, and his black hair was falling on his forehead. He looked savage, but Morris was finding, day by day, sides to the man he never thought existed. What he didn't understand was MacKenzie's inexplicable passivity. He was wary of it. Even while he discovered, to his amazement, he was beginning to like the man.

MacKenzie was, indeed, biding his time. Now that Davey and April were reasonably safe, he started thinking of escape. He wanted to wait, though, until they were through Apache country. He had to be sure, absolutely sure, that the two would reach Fort Defiance safely.

And he had to be sure April, along with Davey, wouldn't try to follow him, that Morris could prevent it. He had been studying and testing Morris, just as he knew Morris had been studying him. The thought amused him in a cold, wry way.

He had shaken the lethargy the second day, but he had not allowed it to show. He was not going to let anyone hang him. Or imprison him. Though he may not be able to have April and Davey, he would, by God, have his freedom, what freedom there was now. He wondered how much it would mean without them, and his throat choked with emptiness when he thought of it, but he would not leave them with the image of him defeated.

He would wait until they reached the great massive towers called Ship Rock because of its resemblance to a sailing ship. Once past there, they would move into the Arizona territory where there would be more patrols, more safety for April. And then, somehow, he would make good his escape. And disappear. He already knew how.

April clutched Davey like a lifeline. They had been six days on the trail, and MacKenzie had not spoken a word to her. It was almost as if she ceased existing for him. The forest had turned from twisted pines and brush to thick oak and mahogany, and finally to cactus and brush. It seemed as though the trip into the mountains, when she had fallen so deeply in love with MacKenzie, was being kaleidoscoped in rapidly moving, mocking images. The hours of watching him ahead, his broad shoulders straining against the shirt, his head still held proud, were miserably slow, and yet they went too fast, for she couldn't bear to think of their end, of what might await them at Fort Defiance.

She thought constantly about helping him escape, even knowing he would probably refuse any help. During the long hours on horseback, she schemed. Possibly sensing her intentions, Morris had taken the rifle from her saddle, and she knew she was watched. Discreetly, yes, but undeniably. She would somehow have to steal a gun. MacKenzie would never survive without one. But how, without alerting someone? Perhaps Morris. Her initial repugnance to the captain had faded in the past several days. It was difficult to hate someone who was so unfailingly kind to her and her son and, though she disliked admitting it, fair to MacKenzie, despite the fact he wouldn't change his mind about the handcuffs. She had seen the two men talking, almost as if they were friends, and she felt an ache deep inside that MacKenzie would lock her out while opening himself to someone else.

She knew it was that damned stubbornness. He had, once more, convinced himself he was dangerous to her and Davey, and he had withdrawn, as he had so many other times. And, she knew, it was also pride. How many times had he vowed to her he wouldn't be taken again? She sensed it was excruciating to him to be a prisoner before her and Davey. But was he really so helpless? The thought suddenly struck her. He was being a little too cooperative. Even after the events of the past week, he was being very unlike any of the MacKenzies she knew. Hope suddenly seeded, grew and blossomed inside her. He was planning something. She knew it. There was a momentary agony when she realized she was probably no part of his plans. She couldn't restrain a small smile. She would make herself a part of them...she and Davey.

Her campaign started immediately. She started by pulling up alongside Captain Morris and, disregarding his inquisitive look, graced him with the first smile he had seen in the days they had been together. It was tentative, to be sure, but April was afraid to offer more. She didn't want to make him too suspicious. Even then, there was a slight wary look in his eyes as he returned it.

"Tell me about my father, Captain," she said, hoping the innocence rang true. It should. She did care. Desperately. But she had been too hostile earlier to voice her concern to Morris.

He was, after all, the man who was taking MacKenzie from her, and she had hated him desperately. Even Davey had picked up the hostile vibrations and had been unusually cold to Morris, despite the captain's many attempts to make friends.

An eyebrow raised, and she saw his skepticism.

Go slow, April, she told herself. Don't arouse his suspicions. She felt Davey stiffen in her arms, and knew he felt her own tension, though he didn't understand why. She forced herself to relax.

"Captain?" she said, pretending not to notice his hesitation.

"General Wakefield is fine…though worried…as I mentioned. I know how he was looking forward to meeting his grandson." Morris's eyes went to Davey and he wished he could do something to remove the dislike in the boy's eyes.

April saw the regret, and part of her mellowed. Morris, after all, was only doing his duty. But that did not sway her from her plans. It merely made her smile a little more sincere, and Morris, despite his inner caution, responded.

"I'm sorry, Captain," she said slowly. "I've been rude and difficult. MacKenzie has been…he's risked his life numerous times for us…and I hope you understand that…"

"I know you must feel gratitude, Mrs. Manning," Morris broke in. "There's no need to apologize."

He was making it altogether too easy for her. April suffered under his warm smile. Deception did not come easily to her. Even for MacKenzie.

"Truce?" she said.

"Truce," he confirmed. But he was far too experienced not to notice the flicker in her eye. He knew he should be angry, but he wasn't. He suddenly realized he would be disappointed with anything else. Yet…it was his duty to bring in MacKenzie. It was proving, he thought, to be a much more complex, and unpleasant, task then he had first thought.

Ship Rock stood majestically against the blue sky and silvery sand floor. The small group of riders was dwarfed by its size and the barrenness of the landscape. While the cool wind still ruffled the highlands, an early summer had hit the desert floor, and the heat made the riders miserable.

Except, possibly, for MacKenzie. He relished it. He knew it was draining the others, making them careless. Only Morris seemed alert.

Unlike his experience during the earlier trip through the desert, this time he was being kept well supplied with food and water. And he didn't have any of the duties Morris's small group was saddled with...tending the horses, scouting, sentry details. He found himself growing stronger as his guards grew weaker. His eyes occasionally found April, and he felt a sharp knife twist in his gut when he saw her with Morris. He could envision the smile in her eyes, the smile that had been reserved for him. He tried to tell himself that Morris would be good for her, for Davey, but reason couldn't stop the fire within him, the longing. He knew he would have to tame it to survive.

That night...the first evening past Ship Rock...they stopped at dusk. There was not so much as a cactus to secure MacKenzie, and Morris, after allowing his prisoner dinner and a short walk, almost apologetically had MacKenzie's hands handcuffed behind him, and his feet tied.

It was exactly what MacKenzie had been waiting for.

April, with the instinct that came with love, knew it.

Bob Morris could smell it.

The sound of a harmonica in the night broke the almost leaden silence of the desert. April moved closer to Bob Morris and shuddered with the loneliness inherent in the plaintive music.

"Davey?" the captain asked.

"Asleep...at last. He misses MacKenzie's singing."

"Singing?"

"He's a half-breed...he doesn't know songs...he can't be kind to a boy...is that it, Captain?"

"No," Morris said softly. "That's not it, Mrs. Manning...April. I think you've condemned me without a hearing. Tell me about him.''

April squeezed her eyes shut. She could stand anything but his kindness. She didn't know what would be required of her this night, but she knew she would do anything necessary to be with MacKenzie.

''I'm tired,'' she said, dismissing him, and he gave her a long, measuring look.

Morris watched as she took several blankets and wrapped them around herself and her son. She was so pretty. So blamed pretty. And so unreachable. He strode over to MacKenzie, who lay quietly under a blanket, and checked the bonds. He had the key to the handcuffs tucked securely in his boot, and the ropes around the ankles were firm. Why then did he feel such damned disquiet? He remembered Pickering's carelessness. And the lieutenant's fate.

He posted guards, one more than usual although he knew all his men to be immensely tired, then finally settled down in his own bedroll. The harmonica was silent, the night very still. He knew the slightest noise would awaken him, especially tonight. But he was spooked, and it took hours before he went to sleep.

MacKenzie waited until the deep of the night. Only a sliver of a moon showed itself in a partly cloudy sky. His careful eyes studied the guard set to watch him, and he could see the man's head nodding. There was another on the edge of the camp. Cautiously he strained under the blanket, twisting his body to slide his handcuffed hands down under his buttocks and up under his legs until they were in front of him. He quickly untied his ankles. He lay there for minutes, hoping no one had noticed the strange contortions under the blanket. But all was silent.

His tameness in the past days had apparently disarmed at least some of the patrol. He didn't think he had entirely fooled Morris, but the man couldn't stay awake all the time. MacKenzie eyed the captain's sleeping form. He had waited hours for the man to sleep, and even now knew it would take little to wake him. April was not far. He looked at her...for the last time...knowing he was leaving his heart here. She and the boy would be better off without him.

Tearing his eyes away, he discarded the blanket and crept toward the guard. He had to reach him before the man heard a sound. It would be awkward to take him with the handcuffs, but he had no choice but to try it. He could rid himself of the shackles later; there was no way of getting the key from Morris without waking the whole camp.

Deftly, his hands slid over the picket's head, clasping the mouth shut. He had just enough chain between the iron bands to deliver a short but potent blow to the side of the head. The man would live, but he would have a whopping headache the next morning.

MacKenzie snaked his way over to the other sentry. This one was more alert and turned just in time to receive a blow to his head. The man's intended cry never reached his mouth. MacKenzie went to the horses and untied his Appaloosa. He didn't want the sound of hoofbeats in the deep silence of night...not yet...and he led the horse a distance from the camp before leaping to its back and pressing his knees in its side.

April had watched it all, and now she woke Davey. If they were lucky she and Davey could follow without waking the camp. She moved carefully, pressing a finger on Davey's lip and smiling when he nodded with understanding. She saw Morris's revolver lying next to him and knew she and MacKenzie would need all the guns they could get. She imagined MacKenzie had relieved the guards of theirs. Her hand slipped into Morris's holster, hoping she would not disturb him. She had just freed it, and it lay in her hand, when Morris woke, jerking fully awake.

The captain took only a moment to adjust his eyes and see MacKenzie, low on the neck of his horse, streaking across the desert. He reached for his pistol, and instead found its barrel in his side.

April shook her head. "No, Captain," she said softly.

"You won't shoot." His voice was low and level.

She regarded him sadly. She had lost MacKenzie now. She could not follow. But she would make sure he made good his escape. "Not to kill, perhaps, Captain," she said slowly but in a very determined voice. "But I would put a bullet in your leg...it would give him enough time to get away."

Morris looked at her tense face and believed her.

He stood carefully, keeping his eyes on the steadily held gun. "We will get him, you know."

She smiled slightly. It was a wistful smile, but there was also a hint of elation in it as MacKenzie and his Appaloosa disappeared in the black night.

He was free!

Chapter Twenty-One

MacKenzie raced his horse, feeling the cool breeze ruffle his hair and tease his skin. He had hoped to regain that old sense of exhilaration he had always had when he and his horse were one, running like the wind across the plains.

But it wasn't there, not any more. There was only a tightening in his gut, the feeling that nothing would ever be the same again.

He felt the Appaloosa's muscles straining under his legs. He had taken no saddle, but he was riding as he had always liked to ride, unfettered by leather and bulk, the communication between him and his horse direct and easy. He had not even taken the time to place the bit and reins in the horse's mouth, and his fingers wound themselves in the horse's mane while his knees issued directions.

He cursed the handcuffs, hating the limiting of freedom, but he would break the chain with his pistol handle when he reached the hills. The sentry's pistol and ammunition belt were slung around his neck; he had no way of buckling it on with the chain binding his wrists. He had to leave the rifle, having no way of carrying it. Later he would find a way to rid himself of the iron bands. One hand fingered the chain. It was the last time, by God. The last time anyone would bind him again.

Knowing he was too far away now to be caught, MacKenzie threw back his head and a savage yell, half elation, half anguish, echoed through the silent desert, its sound just barely reaching April and Morris, who still stood there silently with a pistol between them.

The sound woke the troopers, and they were on their feet almost instantly, weapons drawn, only to find their captain disarmed and held at pistol point by the general's daughter.

"Sir?" said the sergeant, not quite sure what to make of the situation and even less sure of what to do.

Morris, his mouth crooked into a rueful smile, looked at April. "The young lady says she'll shoot me. I believe her."

April's hand wavered for a moment at Morris's almost gentle tone, but then it steadied again, and Morris's expression grew grim. "May the sergeant check the sentries?" He nodded toward the silent forms.

April nodded. "After he drops his gun...along with the rest of them."

Morris's eyes pierced her, his jaw tightening. Then he shrugged. It was too late now, anyway. MacKenzie had a long lead, and the Appaloosa, he knew, could outrun any of their horses. At least he had the woman and boy. He would go after MacKenzie later. He wondered briefly if she would try to go after the scout, but realized instantly she could not. She would only lead them to him. She had made her choice when she held him at gunpoint. Morris couldn't help but admire her, even as he swallowed his chagrin. He would probably never live this episode down, his command shanghaied by a woman. And how in the devil would he explain it to Wakefield?

He nodded at his men, and they dropped their weapons. The sergeant carefully approached the fallen guards who were now returning to consciousness and wondering what in the hell had happened. At April's orders, the ten men sat while she carefully kept her gun aimed directly at Bob Morris until the first glimmers of dawn appeared in the east. She then, quite simply and without words, handed it back to him.

MacKenzie barely saw the flash of light in the gray haze of dawn. He squinted his eyes, wondering whether he had merely caught a ray of sun against the mesa, but no...there it was again. Soldiers or Indians? The Indians had easily picked up the art of signals, much to the army's discomfort. They had even used signaling once to lure a detail into ambush.

He put one leg over the horse's neck, resting for a moment as he pondered the meaning of the flashes. Morris had told him a number of the Apache renegades had been captured, and their attempt to mass had been foiled by their own internal feuds, but there were still roving bands that eluded capture. And, MacKenzie knew, they would like nothing more than sleek army horses. Damn. How long had Morris's little group been under surveillance? And why, for God's sake, had MacKenzie not noticed it?

But he sure as hell had been noticed, and he realized instantly they knew that he had seen something, that he suspected their ambush in the arroyo ahead. He saw the mounted figures sweep down toward him. He could race for the mountains...and freedom. Or return and warn Morris. He looked at his chained wrists and, longingly, at the distant peaks.

And turned his horse back, leaning low on its neck. "Go, boy," he whispered, and felt the valiant power beneath him as the horse raced back to the handful of army troopers...and April and Davey.

Morris's small detail was preparing to mount when Davey saw MacKenzie, and he yelled and pointed. He had not understood anything earlier, except, perhaps, that MacKenzie had left him. There had been tears, then little-boy bravery.

But now he saw the Appaloosa rushing toward him, and a trail of dust behind, and he tugged at April with a wide grin on his face.

His smile was the only one. April, fear filling her with dread, saw the troopers grab their rifles, and one was preparing to shoot when Morris told them to hold their fire as he saw additional clouds of dust whirling behind MacKenzie.

Almost before April could breathe again, MacKenzie was

in their midst, sliding off his horse while yelling to Morris. "Thirty Apaches, at least...behind me...they were waiting in ambush."

Morris nodded, giving orders immediately. One man was told to hold the reins of the horses; the others to spread out on the sand. MacKenzie shouted at April and Davey to get behind him, and he, too, lay nearly flat on the sand as his hand jerked the pistol from the holster on his shoulder.

April had no time to think. None of them did. Screaming painted Apaches were bearing down on them, and bullets were already peppering the oncoming riders. The troopers had the seven-shot rifles and were deadly accurate. Morris had selected only the best for this detail, and each made every shot count. MacKenzie didn't have the range with his pistol, but he, too, brought several men down as some of the most daring of the Apaches were able to approach the perimeter of Morris's circle. Almost as soon as it started, it was over. The Apaches had thought the small group easy prey, and had no appetite for the type of punishment they'd received. A third of their number lay dead on the ground.

When Morris was sure there wouldn't be a second attack, he stood and inventoried his small command. Two were dead, two wounded. His eyes wandered over to MacKenzie, who also stood slowly. His wrists were still cuffed together, and his pistol hung from one hand. He looked at Morris with a crooked smile on his lips, and eyes full of self-mockery. He offered the gun to Morris. "I'm afraid it's empty."

"If it wasn't?"

MacKenzie shrugged.

"You didn't have to come back."

MacKenzie looked toward April and Davey. "Didn't I?"

Morris sat down and pulled off his boot, tipping it upside down to retrieve the key to MacKenzie's handcuffs. He stood and unlocked them, watching as MacKenzie, his gray eyes questioning, rubbed his wrists.

"Get the hell out of here, MacKenzie," Morris said.

MacKenzie turned to April, who was holding Davey tightly. Her eyes hadn't left him.

"They stay with us," Morris said, correctly interpreting MacKenzie's look.

MacKenzie surveyed Morris's diminished force before locking eyes with the captain in a contest of wills. "You can't make it with what you have," he said finally. "Especially without a scout."

He looked out to where the dust was still settling. "They haven't given up; they'll just look for a better spot."

"I'm all out of scouts at the moment," Morris replied.

"Maybe not."

"I can't promise you anything."

"I know," MacKenzie said softly. "But I'm damned tired of running."

Morris let a small whistle pass his lips. "You should know...Wakefield's mad as hell."

"I would guess as much."

"But he knows you didn't rape the Peters girl, and Sergeant Peters...well, the general sort of figured that out, too."

MacKenzie lifted an eyebrow.

"But there are still a number of charges..." He looked at April and her boy. "You could still go to prison or...even hang."

MacKenzie's mouth straightened in the old grim line. "I know. But I can't leave them...or you...out here now, God damn it. Now will you get ready before those Apaches change their minds?"

Morris nodded and quickly gave orders. April helped tend the wounded while the two dead men were buried. It was midmorning when the small group mounted and headed west. MacKenzie had left an hour earlier to scout the trail.

Morris, who rode next to April, couldn't help but question his own actions. He had risked his bars when he'd offered to let MacKenzie go, and now he was trusting his small command to a renegade half-breed who was wanted for any number of criminal acts. He shook his head as he realized he had seldom felt in better hands.

April and Davey saw little of MacKenzie in the next several days. He was out scouting most of the time and only rarely rode in, and then only to confer briefly with Morris. They were taking a zigzag path, and whenever they seemed low on water, MacKenzie would almost magically find a muddy hole. The water was never very appetizing, but at least it kept thirst at bay.

They saw no more Indians, although there were sometimes tracks. And then, they stopped, and April knew they were approaching Fort Defiance. She had tried to talk to MacKenzie the few times they had stopped to make camp, but he had avoided her.

It was a pattern that continued until the night before she was told they would reach the fort. Much to her surprise, MacKenzie sought her out. His eyes dark and hooded, he spoke briefly to Morris, then approached her.

"I want to talk to you," he said without preamble, his face harsh.

Vacillating between hope and fear, April could only nod, and she followed him out of camp, beyond hearing range.

"I want to say goodbye," he said abruptly. "Now. I'll be arrested tomorrow, and I want your promise you won't try to see me."

"You can leave tonight...we can leave tonight," she said. "Captain Morris won't try to stop you."

"It would just be someone else then," he said tiredly. "Make it easy for me, April."

"Captain Morris will help you...I'll help you. And I know Father will help...when he knows everything..."

"Stay out of it, April. Please."

"Do you always have to be so damned independent, so damned alone?" she cried in frustration, a hot tear forming in her eye.

"You don't understand...your name can't be linked to mine...it will brand you...you and Davey."

"You are my husband," she said, her fury mounting as she saw him wince at the reminder. "Do you think I can just walk away? It may not have meant anything to you, but..." His rejection hurt more than anything in her life, and she turned so he couldn't see the aching pain and misery she knew must be plain in her face.

He didn't have to see her face. It was in the slumped shoulders and the head bent low, the proud courageous head, which should always be held high. He had brought her to this...and it could only worsen...if he couldn't make her let go. He wondered if anyone could ever invent a torture more agonizing than this. It was as if his heart had been lifted from his chest as it still beat and was being shredded piece by piece. "You must forget it, April. If not for yourself, then for Davey."

She whirled around, her voice ragged with emotion. "No, I love you. I'll always love you...and I'll yell it to the world."

His arms caught her, and his hand cupped her chin, forcing her to look up. "If you love me, if you really love me, you will do as I ask."

"You can't do that to me," she cried rebelliously. "I won't accept that."

Tears glistened in the moonlight, and he put his head down on hers to hide his own agony. She must not know how much this was costing him.

"Even," he said slowly, letting every hurting word be understood, "if I don't go to prison, you can't be with me. There's no room in my life for a wife and child. I want to be free...free...in every way..."

"I don't believe you."

"Damn it, April. I don't want you. Can't you understand that?"

"The marriage..."

"Was a mistake. I thought it would make you happy...but now it's over. All of it."

It was the cold emptiness of his voice that finally made an impact on her. The voice and the hostile eyes. There was no trace of the familiar warmth, of the tender protectiveness. He was a stranger. A cold, antagonistic stranger, and she believed none of it. The voice, the words, the eyes were all made liars by the gentleness of the hands. There were some things he could hide, but others he could not. She hadn't imagined the pain in his earlier words.

She straightened, her eyes filling with secrets of her own. She realized there was no way she could tell him he was wrong, not now. He had decided he had to do this for her, and she would let him think he had convinced her, even though it sent a dagger through her heart to do so.

April cried inside for him, for all the wounds he was afraid to show, for everything that made him feel his love was a hurtful thing rather than the bright and warming glow it really was. He was trying to give her the only gift he thought he had, and she knew, because she knew him, that it was tearing him apart to do so.

The only thing she could do, at this moment, was to make it easier for him...until she could talk to her father, until she could, in some way, making things right, make it possible for him to accept that they could live together in happiness and peace, that there were more men like her father, and Bob Morris and Ben Morgan, that they all weren't like Peters and Terrell. And she had to do it. As she looked into the gray eyes struggling to remain cold, into the face creased with lines that shouldn't be there, she felt her heart swell and expand until she thought it would crush the flimsy shell that held it. She wanted to touch him, to love him, to share her faith.

And she could not. Not now, not tonight. For it would make his pain unbearable. Her hand trembled as she sought the courage to make him believe she accepted his words.

Her chin went up proudly and her eyes sparked. "And you want me just to forget everything?"

It was all he could do to nod.

"And Davey?"

"He's young...he'll forget soon enough."

"Forgive abandonment...I doubt it." In her own churning confusion, the words escaped before she could stop them and she immediately knew the depth of the blow she'd delivered.

She saw the hurt he couldn't hide this time, the agonized twist of his mouth as he recognized the truth of her words.

The tears in her eyes had dried. She needed the same strength he had to continue the fable.

For him.

She turned her back and walked away, every step a feat of extraordinary struggle between her needs and his.

For him, she told herself, she could do anything.

April didn't sleep at all, and she knew from MacKenzie's too still form that neither did he.

Even then, morning came too soon with its seductively soft golden light that promised so much and offered so little.

She tried to keep Davey from MacKenzie, but he slipped away. MacKenzie had been gone most of the last several days. He had left early and seldom returned until Davey was asleep. But he wasn't going to get away from the boy today. Davey had been waiting to pounce. He delivered himself at Mac-Kenzie's side as the scout prepared to mount. With six-year-old determination, he spread his legs with all the belligerence of a young bull.

"I want to ride with you," he pronounced, his confidence belied only by the trembling of his lips.

It would have been easier for MacKenzie to shoot a puppy than refuse. His hands reached down and picked Davey up, holding him close for an infinitesimal time before settling him in the saddle and swinging up behind him. Without any words, he moved away from the rest of the group, once more placing an invisible wall between him and others. Only a small hand on his arm said anything different.

When they were within hailing distance of the fort at midday, MacKenzie rode to April and, his face hard and unyielding, handed Davey to her.

"Morris and I are going ahead," he said curtly. "Stay here with the other soldiers."

Her arms tightened around Davey, and her hands squeezed the leather reins so tight she thought the horse would spook. But it was as tired and exhausted as she and merely stamped in protest. She nodded, and he turned.

"MacKenzie..." She couldn't prevent uttering his name.

He turned, his eyes swirling with something she couldn't identify.

"Thank you for taking Davey."

His jaw worked for a second, then he turned and pressed his horse into a gallop. He and Morris disappeared behind a churning cloud of dust.

General Ira Wakefield was waiting at the gate for his daughter and grandson.

He had been in his office when Morris and MacKenzie rode in. Despite Morris's objections, the officer of the day had immediately ordered MacKenzie confined in the guardhouse. There were standing orders for his arrest.

Morris angrily strode over to Wakefield's office to have those orders changed. If nothing else, he wanted MacKenzie to share his own quarters...under house arrest if there was no alternative. MacKenzie, he felt, had saved his patrol when he could have made good his escape. In the past few days, his initial grudging acceptance of the half-breed had turned into a somewhat wary friendship.

But he had no chance. Wakefield's concerns at the moment were his daughter and grandson. Before Morris could utter a word, Wakefield had left his desk and was glowering at him.

"April and Davon?"

"We found them, sir, or," he admitted wryly, "they found us. MacKenzie was bringing them back. They're following us by just a few minutes."

It was enough for Wakefield. He was buttoning his coat and out the door before Morris could say any more.

"General Wakefield!" The general turned at Morris's unusually sharp voice.

"Yes?" He said impatiently.

"About MacKenzie...he's been taken to the guardhouse..."

"Good," Wakefield said with satisfaction. His anger had grown throughout the long months of uncertainty. It was, in fact, explosive. At the moment, he would have cheerfully pulled the man apart with his own hands.

"General Wakefield...he was bringing them back, and he saved my patrol from Indians...I think..."

"Later, Captain...I'll deal with MacKenzie later. Now I just want to see my daughter. And I'll want a full report in three hours. In the meantime, MacKenzie stays where he is."

"Yes, sir, but..."

"Captain!"

Morris was effectively gagged, and he knew it.

"I would suggest," Wakefield continued, "that you get yourself cleaned up. You're dismissed."

"Yes, sir," Morris conceded, and saluted. He started planning his defense of MacKenzie as Wakefield hurriedly left the room.

Despite April's deep fear for MacKenzie, she couldn't restrain a wide grin when she saw her father standing stiffly beside the gate. She would always see him this way, tall and straight. But his face was older, worn-looking, and the twinkle in his eye was not as bright as she'd remembered.

She brought her horse to a stop before him and handed Davey down to him. "Your grandson, sir."

Wakefield took the boy, and held him out for a moment, studying every feature. How he had longed to hold the boy. But it was, he sensed, too soon. The boy was stiff, and his look suspicious. Wakefield set him on the ground, and kneeled to the boy's height. "I'm glad to make your acquaintance,

Davon," he said formally, and the words brought a slight smile to the boy's face, and he relaxed a little.

"Is MacKenzie here?" the boy asked, his eyes searching the parade ground.

Wakefield stiffened, then looked at April, who had just dismounted. She had the same question in her eye.

Wakefield held his tongue and opened his arms, taking April into them and holding her tighter than he ever had before. There had been days and weeks and even months when he wondered whether he would ever see her again.

"MacKenzie," Davey insisted, his concern for his friend overpowering his awe of the tall authority in blue.

"He's resting," Wakefield replied gently as he noted April's similarly questing eyes. He looked at his daughter. Her coarse clothes had been designed for a man substantially larger than her, and they were coated with layers of grime and dust. Her face was smudged, and her chestnut hair dull and messy in a braid hanging down the back. But her eyes were bright and her skin healthy and glowing. It had been more than six years since he had seen her last, and he had expected change, but not quite the strength and maturity now facing him.

She had left him a girl, and returned a woman. A beautiful, glowing woman. And a determined one, if he was right about the stubborn jut of her jaw whenever Davey mentioned MacKenzie.

"Come to my quarters," he said, placing one hand on her shoulder and the other on Davey's. "I've waited for this moment for a long, long time."

His house was fairly plain, but large. Large clay jars hung both inside and outside. They were filled with water, which evaporated rapidly in the heat to provide some cooling, but still the air was stifling at this time of day. April and Davey were greeted by the general's striker, a soldier who served as cook and housekeeper.

He, like everyone by now, had heard that the general's daughter and grandson had arrived, and he had already prepared some lemonade. He grinned happily, hoping that the general's dour moods would disappear.

But Wakefield's joy was dimmed by Davey's quiet reservation and April's reticence.

April finally got Davey to take a nap, and she and her father sat in the parlor together.

"Tell me what happened," Wakefield said gently. "Everything. Did MacKenzie hurt you in any way?"

April started slowly, telling him about the first night she had seen the scout, the terrible day in the desert as MacKenzie was dragged without food or water.

"He didn't have a choice, Papa. He truly didn't have a choice, and he thought it would just be a matter of hours, or a day at most, before he could...get rid of us safely." She told him about the Navahos, and the bear attack, and the blizzard when he had saved her life, and finally Terrell's attack.

"He saved our lives over and over again," she said, "and then when he could have gone free he did it again...on the way here. Even then, he could have gotten away, but something...wouldn't let him."

"He may have saved your lives," Wakefield said, "but he put them in danger in the beginning. I don't know if I can forgive that."

"Neither can he, Papa. I think that's why he came back. I offered to go with him. Anyplace." She saw her father wince at the words. "I love him. There are so many sides to him, so many gentle places he tries to hide."

"He's part Indian," Wakefield said. "You know what that means in the west. Some people will never understand."

"I don't care about them!"

"You must...if not for yourself, for your children."

"He's the most decent man I have ever met, the most compassionate, the most caring," April said, tears misting her eyes. "And Davey loves him."

"I've noticed," her father said dryly. As for the rest...were they talking about the same MacKenzie?

"What are you going to do with him?"

He studied her anguished face. "I don't know, April. Ellen Peters confessed to lying, and admitted MacKenzie killed her father in self-defense. If he hadn't escaped, we could have straightened it all out. Now there's horse theft and kidnapping, theft of government property and any number of other things. When I sent Bob Morris after you, I couldn't keep it quiet. It's gone farther now than this post."

"Sergeant Terrell never meant for him to arrive here alive," she countered. "And it was his own horse."

"Two were missing."

"I stole one," she said defiantly. "And I wasn't kidnapped, and I would testify to that."

Wakefield shook his head in defeat. "I don't suppose it would look very good for a general's daughter to admit to stealing a horse." He took her hand. "I'm not promising anything, April. Not until I talk to him. Even then I don't know what I can do."

"Father...there's something else..."

He looked at her with some wariness.

"We were married...in the mountains...according to mountain law. Davey was a witness."

There was a long silence. "I'm not sure how legal that is."

"I don't care whether it's legal. I'm his wife in my heart. And that will never change."

"And MacKenzie?"

"He's afraid Davey and I will be hurt."

"Not an altogether unreasonable assumption."

"Not if he's cleared of charges, not if we can go to his valley..."

He sighed wearily. "I love you, April. I want you and Davey to be happy more than anything in the world. I know how terrible those years were...when you waited for news of David. I don't want to see you hurt again."

"Nothing will ever change the way I feel. MacKenzie is my life. He's Davey's life. They adore each other, and he's been so good for my son. It will break Davey's heart if he's taken away.''

''Are you sure about the way MacKenzie feels?''

''He's afraid right now,'' April said. ''He's afraid of caring, afraid of hoping, afraid of hurting...but yes, I think I know how he feels.''

Wakefield looked at his daughter. Her love and compassion and understanding were quite beyond him. They filled him with a certain awe that he had helped produce her.

But still he hesitated. Some of his anger had seeped from him during April's recital of events, but nothing could really block out the months of agony, of not knowing what had happened to the only two people he had in the world. He understood most of MacKenzie's moves, but not the one at Amos Smith's cabin, not the one in which the scout had consciously taken his daughter and grandson up into the mountains. But then he realized why he didn't understand. It had been a human decision, a humanly selfish decision, one he had not expected MacKenzie to make. He had long ago stopped expecting weaknesses in the man, but apparently his daughter and grandson had wreaked havoc with his iron reserve. Wakefield could almost smile. Almost. MacKenzie must have gone through hell.

It was a different aspect of MacKenzie. But a husband for his daughter and a father for his grandson? The notion was too new for him to readily accept. April had said he was gentle and tender, but those were sides he had never seen in his scout, though he had observed a sometimes contradictory streak of stubborn defense of those weaker than MacKenzie.

''I'll talk to Morris, then to MacKenzie,'' he said. ''We'll discuss it again later. In the meantime, Mrs. Forbes, one of my officers' wives, will help find you some dresses, and I think you probably want a bath.'' He took her hand. ''I love you, April. I'll do what I can. I promise.''

Morris was anything but objective during the interview, and Wakefield wondered at his captain's heated defense of a man he had never previously liked. It was, in a sense, gratifying to find his own judgment so resoundingly echoed, but Wakefield still had his reservations and wasn't sure he wanted to forgive MacKenzie quite so easily. The charges would be easy enough to dismiss; they had stayed within the military system thus far, and Wakefield's influence was considerable. But a part deep inside, a part he wasn't particularly proud of, wanted the scout to suffer just a little of what he had been suffering these past months. It was also difficult to reconcile April's description and Davey's hero-worship with the cold, aloof and arrogant traits of the scout he had so valued for his objective ruthlessness.

After dismissing Morris without comment, Wakefield made his way to the guardhouse.

Without being told, he would have known which of the two cells held MacKenzie by the restless stalking within. A guard hovered near him and, with an impatient wave of the hand, Wakefield banished him.

With a trace of ironic humor, Wakefield regarded MacKenzie carefully. "If you're going to stay here long, it seems we'll have to replace the boards."

MacKenzie stopped his pacing. "Am I?" He had wondered if and when he would be turned over to civilian authorities. The sooner the better. He did not want to be this close to April and Davey. It hurt too damned much.

"Going to stay here long? I haven't decided." After months of agony, he wasn't going to make this interview easy for the scout. Besides, he wanted to make his own judgment on April's choice of a husband.

MacKenzie met his direct stare. He had surrendered his freedom but not his pride, not his spirit. He dominated the small cell.

"I could easily, and quite happily at the moment, shred your skin for the worry and trouble you've caused," Wakefield said slowly, emphasizing every word.

MacKenzie's gaze didn't waver. "I'm sorry," he said, and

somehow Wakefield knew it was a unique announcement. "I'm sorry for that," MacKenzie repeated. "You didn't deserve it."

"Humility, MacKenzie?"

A small smile lit the scout's face as he considered the question. "Perhaps."

"Well, maybe the past months did accomplish something, then," Wakefield observed. MacKenzie's face *was* different. Only a hint of the old arrogance remained, and there was a sort of puzzled humanity that Wakefield had sensed but had never actually seen there before.

"Most of the charges have been dismissed," Wakefield continued abruptly. "The Peters girl finally told the truth. April says she went with you willingly. There remain the small matters of stolen property, assault on army personnel, escape... I could continue."

MacKenzie, feeling his gut tighten into a knot, acknowledged the words with a grim set of his mouth. "I suppose you could," he conceded.

The two men stood there in tense silence. Weighing each other carefully.

It was several minutes before Wakefield began again. "My daughter says she stole one of the horses...not a very good admission for a general's daughter, do you think?"

A muscle throbbed in MacKenzie's cheek. "She did not, and I will say she did not. I forced her through the boy. She is guilty of nothing except..."

"Except what?"

MacKenzie's voice shook just a little. "Of being too kind, too caring."

"Strange," Wakefield said. "That's what she says about you. Somehow I never expected it."

MacKenzie strode to the bars, and his hands clasped them desperately. "Send me away from here...I don't care where. Just get me away. It's better for them."

"Is it?" Wakefield said coldly. "Or is it better for you, MacKenzie?"

Only the raw agony in the scout's face answered him.

"My daughter says she married you. She considers it binding. Apparently you don't," Wakefield added with ice still glinting in his eyes.

MacKenzie's hands were white as they strained against the bars. "She...shouldn't have..."

"I am finding my daughter every bit as stubborn as you, MacKenzie. I don't think I envy either one of you."

MacKenzie slowly absorbed the words, a seed of hope growing within. "I don't...understand..."

"Do you want my daughter and grandson?" The words were purposely blunt.

MacKenzie's eyes closed with sudden wild, elated confusion. It couldn't be happening. When he opened them, Wakefield had his answer. Longing and love were so very obvious in his face. It was, indeed...tender.

"I'll see that all the charges are dropped," Wakefield said, somewhat more softly than he meant to. "I do expect a more...traditional ceremony..."

"General...?"

"Of course," Wakefield continued, halfway enjoying the rare confusion in MacKenzie's face, "I will probably be losing a good scout..."

"Not so good anymore," MacKenzie commented wryly. "I stumbled right into Morris."

"Distracted?"

"A little," the scout admitted. "Your daughter has a tendency to do that to me."

The bantering tone left Wakefield's voice, and it became harsh. "Can you make her happy?"

"I don't know," MacKenzie said with some of the old doubt. "I just know I would try like hell."

"You're not exactly the son-in-law I would pick."

This time, MacKenzie's mouth spread in a wide arc. The

sunbeam inside had spread to a miraculous sunrise...a blinding glow of light and promise. "I can understand that," he said in a voice that Wakefield thought came close to sounding humble. MacKenzie?

"I love her, MacKenzie. And she loves you. And so, obviously, does Davey. I trust her judgment. But by God, if you cause her one more moment of unhappiness..."

MacKenzie's eyes were haunted. "I don't know..."

"More humility. I think I could learn to like that in you." Wakefield grinned. "Morris has offered to share his quarters with you. I take it I can accept your word that you'll stay at Fort Defiance until I can work everything out."

"I still don't understand...why you're doing this..."

"Because I don't want to be tarred and feathered by my own family. And, believe it or not, MacKenzie, I've always sort of liked you."

MacKenzie was released several hours later, and April was waiting for him in the guardhouse office. She had taken a bath and changed to a borrowed pink dress. She had always been beautiful to MacKenzie, even in the worst of times, but now her happiness gave her a special radiance. He was still a bit disbelieving at his sudden change of fortune, but holding April helped make it real. He wondered how she could abide him. His whiskers were thick on his face, and his clothes were the same ones he had worn for the past several weeks. Still, she drew as close to him as possible while she looked at him with such naked love that he thought his heart would burst. They stayed like that, as the guard self-consciously found other duties to attend to, until General Wakefield entered. Only his lifted eyebrows commented, and MacKenzie and April separated a little, their hands still tightly intertwined.

"I've taken the liberty of talking to the post chaplain," he announced. "You can marry tomorrow if you're both still of the inclination." He sighed as he saw, very obviously, that they were. "He did say he needed MacKenzie's full name."

There was complete silence. Wakefield had never known it. April had never heard it. MacKenzie was not pleased about sharing it.

"MacKenzie?" Wakefield questioned.

MacKenzie hesitated, his mouth twitching. Finally, he admitted wryly, "Burns MacKenzie," as he eyed April for a hint of distaste.

Her hand cupped in his, April could barely restrain a giggle. She looked up at him, laughter and love and joy lighting her face. "I think it's perfect," she whispered. "Just like you."

MacKenzie felt a flood of warmth and belonging and tenderness he had thought he would never know. "It's you, my love," he replied quietly. "You gave me a miracle."

The miracle continued. MacKenzie first went to Wakefield's home where he was reunited with Davey. After bounding into MacKenzie's arms and receiving a bear hug unlike any MacKenzie had previously offered, Davey stepped back, a very serious expression on his face. "Are you all right now, MacKenzie? Are you really all right?"

April and MacKenzie stared at each other. Apparently everything they had been trying to keep from Davey had communicated itself, in some way, to the boy.

MacKenzie slowly smiled, a wide smile full of joy. April trembled from its impact. It *needed* to be used sparingly, she suddenly thought, or she would remain in a state of perpetual idiocy. She could barely stand now, so weak were her legs, so trembling her body.

But it was nothing compared to the next few moments. MacKenzie got down on his knees and regarded Davey solemnly. "I have a request to make," he said in his wonderfully soft burred voice.

Davey looked at him with his head tipped, curiosity in every feature.

"I want your permission to marry your mother again..."

If heaven was ever in a little boy's face, it was in Davey's that moment, and now April's heart joined the quaking and general disability of her body. She struggled to keep back the tears as Davey whispered, "Yes...oh, yes."

The rest of the evening went by in a blur...every moment a wonder in itself, until MacKenzie finally left for Morris's quarters. Lost in a happy daze, April prepared for bed and, for the first time in days, slipped easily into a sleep no longer dominated by fear but by a soft happy contentment.

Some of MacKenzie's reserve returned as he approached Morris's quarters. He had, more or less, been ordered to stay there by Wakefield, but he felt awkward and uncomfortable in doing so. He would have preferred a piece of ground someplace, he thought, where he could be alone and consider the last few hours. He wanted, with all his heart, to marry April, but he couldn't dismiss all his fears about what it meant for her, or the misery it might bring.

He didn't exactly know how he felt about Morris. Their relationship thus far had been wary, that of captor and prisoner, then scout and officer. He had to admit a grudging respect for the man, and Wakefield had told him Morris had been almost insubordinate in his defense of MacKenzie. But MacKenzie still couldn't quite dismiss that warning voice inside, the one that told him not to trust.

Morris was reading, a glass of whiskey at his side. Any doubts MacKenzie had about his welcome were quickly dispelled by the wide smile.

"I hear congratulations are in order."

"Thanks to you, I'm told," MacKenzie said hesitantly. "I understand you..."

"To hell with that. The old man had already made up his mind. He's always liked you." Morris grinned disarmingly. "I could never quite understand why." He offered MacKenzie a glass. "Until recently, that is. I've found children are seldom wrong." He held out his hand, and MacKenzie took it firmly, and both men knew, somehow, it would be a lasting friendship.

MacKenzie, still new to the idea, hesitated, then very slowly, very carefully asked, "I don't suppose...I mean I think I need someone to stand with me tomorrow..."

Morris's grin extended even farther. "I would be delighted."

MacKenzie didn't sleep nearly as well as April. A thought nagged at him throughout the night, and it continued to nag him the next day.

The wedding was set for the post chapel, and he was tense and wary, not for himself but for April and Davey. He knew Wakefield had invited some people, and he feared they would snub her. It simply was not acceptable for a white woman and a half-breed to marry.

But the chapel was respectably filled and the faces, far from malicious, were sympathetic and warming. There were even tears. Everyone, by now, had learned much of the story, and it had touched their romantic souls. The image of MacKenzie attacking a bear with a knife to save the general's grandson did what little else could do. That and the fact that the scout had sacrificed his own freedom to save some of their own. The obvious love in the eyes of all three participants did the rest.

And MacKenzie looked devilishly handsome. There were even a few sighs from the women in the chapel when he entered. He had borrowed dress clothes from Morris, and their black starkness emphasized his gray eyes and black hair. But it was the look in his face and eyes when he visually caressed his bride that affected everyone. The hard, austere face had softened in some mysterious way, and the mouth folded into a shy smile that held a wealth of charm. Hearts fluttered and eyes teared. The men wondered if this was the same arrogant scout they had served with. And April...April was beautiful in her borrowed blue dress, her eyes glowing like a lake shimmering with the rays of the sun.

Afterward, MacKenzie accepted their congratulations awkwardly, amazed at their apparent sincerity. He clutched April's hand like a lifeline, and his eyes laughed only when they touched April or Davey.

April kept looking at him, and not only with fascination. There was something bothering him, something that was beyond the things she already knew. There was a strange light in his eyes that had not been there before. She could feel the tension in his body.

As soon as she thought it polite, she made excuses, and she and MacKenzie left, leaving Davey in his grandfather's proud care. They would use the general's house tonight, while he stayed in one of the vacant officer's quarters. Tomorrow they would switch, until all of MacKenzie's legal problems were put to rest. And then they planned to leave for MacKenzie's valley.

It was twilight, and the first stars were blinking above while the earth was bathed in muted gold and pink. For a land that could be so savage and unforgiving, it was incredibly peaceful, April thought. Her hand tightened around MacKenzie's as a sweet pain struck her.

"It wasn't so bad, was it?" she said teasingly.

"I think I would rather had fought that bear again," he answered, and April smiled inwardly at the wry self-mockery in his voice. But it held none of the old bitterness, and there was a new note in it. Something light and hopeful.

She looked up at him. "MacKenzie?"

There was a painful self-searching in his face. "I've been wrong all these years, haven't I?" It hurt him to say the words, to admit that so much of his life had been based on a lie.

April's hand squeezed his, sensing the wounds and uncertainty.

"My father...he taught me, made me believe, all men were like Terrell and Peters and Pickering. I never gave anyone a chance to prove otherwise...not even your father, or Ben Morgan. I was always so afraid of being betrayed that I betrayed myself." Each word was hesitant, like the steps of a man walking in the dark. "I wouldn't let myself see people like Morris...or those today."

April thought her heart would break, and she was heedless of the tears snaking down her face. But she could say nothing. He had to do it. He had to do it all.

"April." He released her hand and cupped her face in his hands. "I didn't know what I missed until I met you, until Davey put his hand in mine, until Bob Morris risked his career for me."

Now there were tears in his eyes. "Teach me, April. Teach me to trust." There was such anguished yearning in his eyes that April couldn't, at first, speak.

But she knew she didn't have to. He had already started to learn, and while she knew it might be slow, the seed was well planted. "Ah, my love," she said, "you've already started. So well. So very well."

His eyes were searching as he sought reassurance, as he sought her own confidence. He found it in her face, and he knew that no matter what happened, what their future might hold, he would never be alone again. He would have her. He would have her love. And because of it, he would have so much more.

MacKenzie's lips turned upward in the first untroubled smile they had known. And they touched April's.

Oh, so gently.

Oh, so hopefully.

And oh, so completely!

Epilogue

The sun was setting as MacKenzie and April reached the path to his valley.

Without speaking, they stopped and dismounted and went to the place they had stood once before so many months ago. MacKenzie put his arm around her shoulders, and together they watched the huge red ball dip slowly behind the golden cliffs. Its lingering, caressing rays painted the blue-green valley floor with rich strokes of rose and gold and coral, mixing with the thin column of smoke that came from the cabin. Davey was down there. Davey and her father.

April leaned against MacKenzie's lean, hard body, a body she had gotten to know well in the past month. And yet there was always something new about it, and the incredible responses it brought forth from her own. It had been a month of discovery and supreme happiness. A time of loving without fear, without doubts, without ghosts. It had been a time of gentleness, of fierce splendor, of incredible sweetness.

April looked up at MacKenzie's face, hardly crediting the changes in it. His mouth smiled easily now, and his eyes were alive with eagerness and anticipation. They had relished this time alone, but now both were eager to see Davey again, to begin a life that held so much promise...

Wolf whined anxiously. He had been waiting at the mountain cabin when MacKenzie and April had arrived, his onyx eyes full of welcome.

It had been partly for Wolf that April and MacKenzie had retraced their steps. And partly, April thought, to rid MacKenzie of the last vestige of a haunted childhood, a sort of cleansing. He had gathered the last of the items he had unearthed several months earlier and stared at them for a long time before reburying all but the Bible. This time, they would stay there. He had taken the money with him to Fort Defiance, intending to see that April and Davey received it. It had now been sent to Ben Morgan in Texas, to purchase some blooded stock. The horses would be here soon. Here in his valley.

April and MacKenzie had needed this time alone, to learn about each other without the fear that had haunted them earlier. It had been a time of golden treasures for both...every shared sunrise and sunset, the carefree swims in mountain brooks, the teasing times before they united in fiery, loving embraces and the aftermaths when they lay contented on the sweet-smelling pine needles.

Davey had stayed with his grandfather. Once he had learned that the stern man in blue meant no harm to MacKenzie, he had readily succumbed to Wakefield's rough affection, and Wakefield had hungered for the chance to get to know his grandson.

The sun disappeared completely behind the craggy mountain peaks, and only a misty pink glow remained. The waterfall seemed to beckon them down, and Wolf whined once more with eagerness.

MacKenzie looked down at April, his face bathed in the soft twilight, and his hand tightened around her shoulder. He wondered how anyone could be this happy, this content.

"Come, love," he said finally as the music welling up inside him threatened to erupt and overwhelm him. "Let's go home."

*   *   *   *   *

Sweet Song of Love
Merline Lovelace

Chapter One

Lady Mellisynt of Trémont drew in a deep breath and raised wide, steady eyes to the towering stranger before her.

"I will wed with you, my lord."

"You understand you have a choice," he growled. "You may take your widow's portion with you to a nunnery. With such riches to buy your entry, you would enjoy a life of restful ease."

"I understand."

Piercing blue eyes, the color of a winter sky washed with rain, stared down at her. He had removed his helmet, revealing a lean, sun-darkened face and thick black hair threaded with faint traces of silver at the temples. Lines of weariness bracketed his mouth and eyes, and his dark brows drew together over a nose that had been broken more than once, by a mailed fist or an oaken staff. He looked exactly like the ruthless warrior Mellisynt knew him to be.

His jaw tightened, as if he had come to a decision that afforded him little pleasure.

"So be it. Summon your household priest and arrange for the betrothal ceremony within the hour. We'll leave for Nantes at first light on the morrow. I would have you safe within the city walls before I rejoin the duke."

Mellisynt nodded, her heart pounding. She knew well the knight's spoken words masked their real meaning. He intended to carry his wealthy prize to the city because he dared not leave her here. He feared she might repudiate their betrothal in his absence and seal herself within Trémont's formidable walls. He could not know she would have walked naked across a bed of hot coals to leave this place.

"Do you wish to wash and refresh yourself in my lord's— in Lord Henri's chambers? I will attend to you immediately I speak with Father Anselem."

He glanced down at his mud-spattered surcoat and leggings, then shook his head. "Nay, I must see to the keep's defenses while there is yet light. My squire will attend to my needs before I take you to the chapel."

Mellisynt stood silent while he took his leave and strode across the dim, cavernous hall. A cowering servant threw open the doors that led to the bailey, and for a moment the knight stood silhouetted against thin winter twilight. His broad back, made immense by his mailed armour and fur-lined surcoat, filled the doorframe. Sudden doubt swamped Mellisynt, and she drew her mantle tight around her shoulders. Sweet Mother of God, what had she done? He was so huge and stern of face! How could she have agreed to bind herself to such a one?

The door closed behind him, cutting off the light and plunging the hall back into its customary gloom. A rustle of activity at the far end of the great room stilled her incipient panic. She straightened, not wanting her people to see her fears. They'd been frightened enough at the appearance of a heavily armed troop whose fierce leader demanded entry by order of their overlord, the duke of Brittany. When the knight had identified himself as Sir Richard FitzHugh, their fear had turned to terror. Since war had broken out this summer, in the year of our Lord 1184, FitzHugh had left a trail of charred villages and subdued castles in his relentless wake. But on this cold November day, at least, he'd laid aside his sword and ridden alone up the steep incline to Trémont's gates.

Even from the high perspective of the castle walls, Mellisynt had seen at once the knight's raw strength. When she'd learned his business, she'd allowed him entry into the keep.

And into her life. Surely such a man could give her the child she longed for. And he would remove her from Trémont. Were he twice as large and even more fierce, she would take him to husband for those two reasons alone.

She wrapped her arms tighter around her chest, knowing she should go to Father Anselem, but loath to move. Her eyes roamed the vast hall, now bathed in dark shadows lightened at intervals by flickering, pitch-soaked torches. Soon, she told herself, soon she would walk out of this keep that had housed her for most of her girlhood and all of her adult life. Soon she would be free of its gray stone walls. A rush of joy washed through her veins, stilling the last of her fears. With a steady step, she crossed the rushes to the narrow corridor leading to the chapel.

Father Anselem paced back and forth before a side altar, his embroidered chasuble slapping against well-padded thighs. Annoyance at being excluded from her meeting with the knight showed plainly in the scowl darkening his pudgy face.

Mellisynt paused in the shadows of the vestibule, took a deep breath, then stepped into the small chapel.

"'Tis indeed the FitzHugh, Father."

The cleric's breath hissed out and pale, watery eyes narrowed to spiteful slits. "The English bastard! The duke would wed you to the son of a common whore."

"Aye, the duke is ever solicitous of his subject's welfare," she agreed dryly.

At her sarcasm, the priest's face filled with the choleric red it habitually assumed whenever he dealt with her. "Mind your speech," he sputtered. "Brittany is your overlord, after all. It is his right to dispose of your person where he thinks best."

"Aye, just as he did when he bestowed me on Henri of Trémont." Try as she might, Mellisynt couldn't keep the scorn from her tone.

"'Tis your choice to take another husband," the priest snapped. "If you were a dutiful wife, you would accede to

Henri's dying wish and retire to the nunnery he chose for you. The documents were signed, the fees agreed upon.''

She shook her head. "Nay, I've had enough of walls."

"But think, my lady, think! To bind yourself to this black knight!"

She folded her arms across her chest and met his agitated glare with a wry smile. "My experience of husbands has not been such that I expect overmuch. This one will do as well as any. At least he will give me children."

The priest strode forward, leaning so close she could see the candlelight gleaming on his tonsured head. Her nostrils quivered at the mingled odor of incense and garlic he always carried.

"This is God's punishment for your willfulness, woman. If you had served Henri more faithfully, you might have been blessed with a child of his loins. Then you need not have taken a new lord, nor ceded Henri's lands and wealth to this bastard.''

"Nor put your comfortable living in jeopardy, Father?"

The priest's high color deepened, and he stepped back. It had been many years since he'd left the primitive simplicity of his Cistercian monastery to become Henri's confessor. And just as many years, Mellisynt suspected, since he'd held to his vows of poverty and chastity. More than one castle maidservant had born a babe with his pale eyes. For a moment she enjoyed his sputtering indignation, but then she sighed. As many uncomfortable hours on her knees as this vindictive little man had cost her, he was not, nor had he ever been, worthy of her spite.

"You need not fear as yet, Father. We leave at first light for Nantes. 'Twill likely be some months before this war is done, and FitzHugh turns his attention to ordering the livings within Trémont."

The cleric's face lost some of its mottled hue.

Mellisynt gathered her skirts to leave. "He would sanctify the betrothal this night, within the hour."

"'Tis not right," the priest muttered. "Henri's barely shriven."

"What's done is God's will, Father."

His mouth sagged as she recited the words he'd so often parroted to her. Before he could frame a reply, Mellisynt turned and left the chapel. Inside the keep, she stopped beside a pillar darkened with age. Soon, she told herself. Soon.

Shaking off the tight knot of disgust Father Anselem always raised within her, Mellisynt spurred herself to action. A quick summons sent four men-at-arms to the dank, locked cellars where Henri had stored his less valuable goods, with orders to locate her bride chests and bring them to her *solar*. When the panting men placed the chests in the center of her tiny room some time later, Mellisynt knelt beside them. She ran her fingers over the great iron hasps, then fumbled through Henri's heavy key ring to find the ones that would unlock her youth.

"Ahh, my lady, what colors!" her elderly maid gasped when the lid lifted to reveal a rainbow of shimmering silks.

Mellisynt reached out to stroke the rich cerulean and amber and crimson brocades. She tried not to think of the child bride who'd stood, excited and nervous, while a bevy of chattering maids fitted her trousseau. That girl had disappeared, along with the colorful gowns, within weeks of arriving at Trémont.

"Oh, no," the maid cried as she held a heavy damask outer robe up to the flickering oil lamp. "The worms have been at them. This bliaut is falling apart."

"Aye, so it is."

With a sigh, Mellisynt sat back on her heels. Her bride clothes, riddled with rot, seemed to symbolize her life. Like the rich, glowing garments, she'd been locked away these ten years and more to wither and decay. She reached out to stroke the figured silk. It felt cool and smooth under her fingertips. Despite its wretched condition, the emerald fabric shone in the weak light. Taking strength from its brave color, Mellisynt gave the maid a determined smile.

"Open the other chest, Maude. Mayhap we can find some gowns that careful stitching can make whole."

Between them, she and Maude salvaged two serviceable sets of robes. Knowing nothing of current styles, Mellisynt could only hope her bliauts, with their flowing, many-gored skirts and side-laced bodices, would not disgrace her in her new lord's eyes. The gowns would require careful stitching and patching to hide time's depredations, stitching that she and Maude would have to do by candle later that night. She spread them across a narrow wooden bench to air.

Buried in the bottom of one chest she found a chainse of fine bleached wool, still in its protective sheeting. She stroked the delicate gold embroidery embellishing its sleeves and hem. She was tempted to disrobe and don it now, if only to go to her betrothal with an elegant shift under her shapeless gray robe. At that moment, a breathless maid came running with the announcement that the FitzHugh awaited below. Mellisynt put the chainse aside, a smile curving her lips. Soon, she told herself, with a last look at the bright gold stitchery.

"And thereto I plight thee my troth."

FitzHugh eyed the still woman who knelt beside him as he slipped the heavy gold betrothal ring onto her thin finger. The folds of her old-fashioned wimple hung forward, hiding her face from view. As if from a distance, he heard his promise to care for her person and possessions echo against the dank chapel walls. His jaw clenched, and he released her hand. The priest gave a thin-lipped nod and continued the service.

Sweet Jesu, FitzHugh swore under his breath, if only the pompous cleric would cease his pontificating about the sanctity of marriage and a wife's duty. The man was dragging out what should have been a short exchange of promises into a high sermon. He should know this ceremony was a mere formality, a sop to the lady's estate and the power of the church. The duke of Brittany himself had signed the betrothal documents last eventide. FitzHugh had left immediately afterward to claim the lady. He didn't need this red-faced priest's sermonizing to sanctify what he already held as his own.

Cold from the stone floor seeped through his furred surcoat and into his bones. FitzHugh stifled a grimace. If he knelt much longer, the half-healed wound in his left knee would stiffen, and he'd be lucky to rise unassisted. He closed his ears to the cleric's droning and fastened his attention instead on a small tapestry hanging above the altar. Illuminated by tall candles, its rose, blue and gold threads glowed like jewels and added a touch of light and beauty to the dark chapel. The only touch, FitzHugh thought, shifting on the hard floor. Old Henri obviously hadn't shared much of his huge wealth with the church.

"And so, too, I plight thee my troth."

Lady Mellisynt spoke her vows in a low, steady voice. FitzHugh glanced down once more, but her bent head and heavy wimple obscured her face. His gaze caught only the tip of a short, rounded nose. He frowned, realizing that he had just joined his life to that of a woman he would scarce have recognized in a crowd. He tried to recall some distinguishing feature from their brief meeting in the dim, shadow-filled hall. The fact that he couldn't remember the color of her eyes, or even the shape of her face, added to his disgruntlement.

Nor could he discern much of her figure from the gray robe that hung, loose and formless, from her shoulders to trail the floor. Unadorned with even a single stitch of embroidery or patch of color, the gown completely enveloped the woman beside him. Lord Henri had spent as little on his wife as on his surroundings, FitzHugh thought with wry derision. And now the old man's relic, in the person of this same Lady Mellisynt, would bring all that hoarded wealth to him.

She was just the bride he needed, the duke had crowed. A rich widow, with no children, and no bothersome father or brothers to claim her estate. A recluse, from all reports, shut away from the world, caring for her elderly, infirm husband.

Not in the first flush of youth, certainly, but still well within her prime childbearing years.

The duke had ruthlessly overridden FitzHugh's vehement assertion that he had no desire to take another wife, his first having given him a taste of marriage that made the bloody flux seem pleasant by comparison. At length, his liege had admitted what FitzHugh had suspected all along. In addition to rewarding his friend for faithful service, Duke Geoffrey wanted to make sure a loyal vassal held the border fortress of Trémont. FitzHugh shifted once more on the stone floor, firmly suppressing the wish that the lady of Trémont had chosen the cloister instead of marriage, and so spared him the necessity of taking her to wife. 'Twas done now; he'd make the best of it. He sent the priest an impatient look, willing him to be done.

At long last, the friar granted them a reluctant blessing and concluded the ceremony. Clenching his teeth against the ache in his knee, FitzHugh rose and offered the lady his hand. She placed her half-mittened fingers over his, gathered her voluminous skirts in her other hand, and rose. Her fingers were cold as ice. Together, they walked through the dim corridor and into the great hall. The small crowd of FitzHugh's men and Trémont retainers who had been hastily gathered to witness the ceremony followed.

Lady Mellisynt lifted her face to his. "I've ordered wine and meats set out. If you do not object, I would ask my people to join us to...to honor the occasion."

Her eyes were green, FitzHugh noted, flecked with bits of brown and surrounded by thick sable lashes. They provided the only color in a pale face framed by an unbecoming white linen chinstrap and headrail. The outmoded head covering made her look older than the two-and-twenty years he knew her to be.

"They are welcome," he responded, willing back a mind-dulling weariness. Two savage days of fighting, followed by a relentless ride to claim the widow, had sapped even his endurance. He ached to shed his mail and tumble headlong into the soft bed he'd seen in old Henri's apartments, but a lady of her rank deserved what little celebration this hurried repast would provide.

She stood beside him as they accepted the nervous good wishes of the castle folk and hearty congratulations of his own men. A stooped old knight who served as Trémont's steward was among the last to greet them. FitzHugh gave Sir Bertrand a brief nod of mingled respect and caution. He'd spent the previous hour with the man, reviewing the castle's defenses. The knight's knees might be bowed by age and years in the saddle, and his hands so arthritic that they would wield a weapon only with great pain, but FitzHugh didn't doubt he could still put a sword to good use, aches or no.

"Are you sure this marriage is to your wishes, my lady?" Sir Bertrand asked, with the bluntness of an old retainer. "I have not many moves left in me, but I would use them gladly in combat with this mountain disguised as a man, do you say the word."

The lady cast FitzHugh a quick glance, then turned back to the old knight.

"Nay, Sir Bertrand," she said, laying a firm hand on his arm. "There's no need to fight. I spoke the vows of my free will."

"Harrumph," the steward grunted, clearly not quite convinced.

"Truly," she told him. "I...I am well served."

"Well, if not now, ye soon will be," he muttered, running his eyes over FitzHugh's massive form. "At least that much will come of this hasty union."

The old man stumped away, and FitzHugh watched as a wave of color washed over his lady's face. Biting her lips, she stared straight ahead.

"Thank you, my lord," she managed after a few moments.

"For what?"

"For not taking umbrage at Sir Bertrand," she replied

stiffly. "He's stood as friend and protector to me for many years."

"Why would I fault a man for holding true to his oath to serve you and Trémont? If he swears allegiance to me, as your lord, I will be well satisfied. I plan to leave him in charge during our absence. One of my own men will stand lieutenant to him."

A rueful smile curved her lips. "And your 'lieutenant' will see that your orders are obeyed, although Sir Bertrand is nominally in charge."

FitzHugh nodded, thinking that perhaps this pale, demure woman was not such a mouse after all. "I said I didn't fault him for holding true to you and Trémont. I did not say I trusted him completely."

"In any case, I thank you," she said once more.

"There's no need for thanks," FitzHugh told her. Weariness rasped through his voice like the sound of a rusty boot nail scraped across cobbles, making it sound harsher than he intended. "I know well enough a good soldier when I meet one."

Her green eyes flashed at his curt tone, deepening to a color that reminded him of a forest glen at the edge of a summer's night. Almost immediately, thick lashes swept down to brush against her cheeks. FitzHugh was left to wonder if he'd imagined the glow that had infused her pale face with something approaching comeliness.

He eyed her speculatively before turning to respond to the priest's greeting. Lady Mellisynt slipped away with a murmured excuse about needing to see to the tapping of another wine cask.

"I am informed that you leave Trémont immediately, my lord," the cleric offered, his sausagelike fingers wrapped around a goblet of wine as if he feared someone would wrest it from him.

"Aye," FitzHugh responded coolly. His knee still ached from this man's damned sermonizing. Moreover, he had little respect for one who appeared to value his dinner more than he did his flock.

"I've long kept the castle records and accounts," Father Anselem continued. "Henri, God rest his soul, entrusted me with most decisions concerning the business of the keep. I am prepared to continue such office for you, as well."

"Such duties are usually a steward's responsibility," FitzHugh observed, taking a sip of his wine.

The priest bent forward, bringing with him a waft of garlic. "Lord Henri lost faith in Sir Bertrand. He intended to send him away. The man grew too particular in his attentions."

Father Anselem nodded across the hall, to where the old knight stood in conversation with the lady of the keep. The steward's stooped frame leaned over the Lady Mellisynt in a protective manner.

FitzHugh eyed the pair for a long moment, before turning back to the priest. When he spoke, his voice held a coldness that had set more than one man-at-arms to trembling. "My impression of Sir Bertrand is that he is a worthy knight."

"He is, he is," the priest sputtered, his color draining. "'Tis not his fault, after all. Most men are weak when a daughter of Eve beckons with warm smiles and sin in her eyes."

FitzHugh set his cup down on the wooden table with a slow, deliberate movement. "Do you imply that the Lady Mellisynt encourages him to dishonor himself and her?"

The cleric took a hasty step back, as if a chasm yawned suddenly at his feet. "Nay, she does not," he gasped. "No more than she did with any of the others Henri sent away. She cannot help what she is."

He stumbled backward as FitzHugh moved toward him with the silent menace of a panther.

"She is my betrothed wife, priest. I will hear no more of what rightly belongs in a confessional, if anywhere."

FitzHugh stood stiff and silent while the man scuttled away. A sour taste filled his mouth, and memories echoed in his mind of other, equally sanctimonious holy men reviling the woman who had born him for her loose, immoral ways. He picked up his goblet once more, draining it in one long swallow. His knee throbbed with a sharp, steady pain, his eyes felt gritty from lack of sleep, and his patience was suddenly worn thin.

The Lady Mellisynt cast him an uncertain look from across the hall. She began wending her way through dispersing servitors, scattered benches, and boar hounds rooting in the rushes. In her shapeless gown and confining head covering, she looked like a damn nun, FitzHugh thought. There was little in either her manner or her person to credit the wanton the priest had hinted at. If he hadn't seen that brief flash of green fire in her eyes, quickly hidden, he would have thought her too dull to raise any man's interest, let alone his rod. Yet now, for the first time, he found himself seeing her as a woman, not simply a widow.

"I ask your permission to retire, my lord. I have packing yet to do if we are to leave at dawn."

"Granted," FitzHugh replied, running his eyes over her impassive face. "I bid thee good-night."

He lifted her hand and gave it a quick salute. Her skin was soft and surprisingly warm under his lips. He caught a brief, elusive fragrance of gillyflowers. The old miser had trained his young wife well, he thought cynically. She didn't squander his coins on expensive perfumes of musk or sandalwood. As he watched her climb the winding stone staircase that led to her *solar,* FitzHugh wondered why the thought didn't bring the satisfaction it should.

Chapter Two

Mellisynt rose before dawn the next day. Shivering in the damp cold, she threw a thin wool mantle across her shoulders and knelt for her morning prayers. Hard stone cut into her knees and added fervency to her plea for God's blessing this day. Scrambling to her feet, she poked through the layer of ice crusting her water bowl and splashed her face. For a moment she toyed with the idea of summoning Maude to attend her, but excitement and years of habit quickly overrode the impulse. She'd dressed herself in the dark before tending to her husband for too many years to need any assistance from the old woman now.

Weak, gray sunlight drifted through the window slits as she pulled on layers of garments. Over a thigh-length linen tunic, she donned the embroidered chainse, reveling in the sinfully soft feeling of it. Its long, tight sleeves hugged her thin wrists and came down over the backs of her hands in decorated points. With a heady sense of anticipation, Mellisynt pulled on one of her refurbished robes. The heavy silk settled over her like a thick amber cloud. She tugged at the bodice ties, frowning at the extra folds of material around her waist. The gold brocade, shot through with colored threads, had once flattered her rounded, girlish figure. Now it hung as loose as a sack from shoulder to hips and dragged the stone floor. Her frown disappeared as she swished the material around, and a dimpled smile creased her cheeks. 'Twas more like a feed bag than a gown, but at least it had color other than the accursed gray she'd worn all these years.

Slipping on a pair of warm hose, Mellisynt slid her feet into serviceable leather boots. From long custom, she reached for the starched headrail and chinstrap lying on the wooden bench. Her fingers grasped the stiff linen, then stilled. She hated the constrictive head covering, but had long worn it at Henri's explicit wish. Drawing in a deep breath, she crushed the stiff fabric between her fingers. She opened her fist and watched the crumpled headrail fall, to lie like a broken blossom on the stone floor. Nudging it aside with one foot, Mellisynt tossed a light veil over her braided hair. A thin circlet of hammered bronze secured the veil over her forehead and her thick, coiled braids. She grabbed a heavy wool mantle and hurried out of the tower chamber without a backward glance.

FitzHugh awaited her in the inner bailey. Mellisynt stood on the steps of the keep, her eyes narrowed against the morning sun, and watched him approach. Sweet Mother, he was big! He strode across the cobbled bailey, carrying the weight of his chain mail as if it were no more than light cloth. Over the armor he wore a squirrel-lined surcoat in deep azure velvet, slit high on either side for ease in riding. The rich velvet was emblazoned on the front with a snarling black bear sewn in glittering ebony and gold threads. As he approached, a winter breeze ruffled through hair so dark it seemed to throw back the sun's light.

"Good morrow, lady wife."

He bent to give her the kiss of greeting, and his lips felt warm and rough against her skin. A faint aura of leather, damp wool and raw maleness teased her nostrils.

"Have you broken your fast?" she asked, swallowing.

"Aye, before the sun came up. Sir Bertrand and I wanted to inspect the men. We'll leave as soon as you're ready."

Her heart pounded. "I'm ready."

Mellisynt turned to take her leave of the men and women who had been her sole companions for so long. Maude, too old and too wedded to Trémont to journey with her lady, wept copious tears and fell into Mellisynt's arms.

Surprised at the painful tug it gave her to bid farewell to the castle people, she held Maude tight. She had dreamed of leaving this keep for so long she hadn't expected to feel any regret at all. Still, these people were all the family she had. She gave Maude a last hug and accepted Sir Bertrand's gruff farewell with a warm smile. As she turned to the priest, her lips thinned, then tilted upward in a determined curve.

"May God keep you, Father Anselem."

"And you, lady." His curt rejoinder held little affection. "Remember well all I have taught you."

"How could I not?" she responded, lifting wide, innocent eyes to his. "You've been most diligent in your instruction."

Father Anselem's brow creased, and the familiar red began to rise up the rolls of flesh swaddling his neck.

"We must make haste."

FitzHugh's deep voice spurred the priest to reluctant action. He laid his hands on Mellisynt's bowed head and muttered a brief prayer for her safety on the journey. He ended with the grudging hope that she fulfill her creator's purpose and proved more fertile in this marriage than her first.

Mellisynt added her silent, fervent prayer to his, then rose, as gracefully as she could in her heavy skirts and cloak. Her breath caught when FitzHugh took her arm and led her to the stone mounting block. A nervous fluttering began in her stomach as she eyed the caparisoned horse, held in place by a man-at-arms. Surely the animal was not as large or evil-natured as it appeared. Just because the gray gelding watched her approach with a small, mean eye, that was no reason to be afraid. And if it refused to sidle up to the block, despite repeated slaps on a huge, muscled rump, she shouldn't suppose it was as reluctant to take her on its back as she was to mount it. Mellisynt wiped her suddenly moist palms down the sides of her cloak.

"Help the lady mount."

FitzHugh's growled order to a waiting page made both the young boy and Mellisynt jump. The golden-haired youth moved forward to hold a wooden stirrup and looked at her expectantly. Taking a deep breath, she ascended the stairs. She slid her left foot into the stirrup, then whipped it out again quickly when the beast shied away.

FitzHugh's brows drew together as he walked around to heave his shoulder into the gray's far side. It snorted and sidled back to the block. Once more the page held out the stirrup. This time Mellisynt got her foot well in and both hands on the curved pommel before the horse danced away. Hanging on with grim determination, she managed to wrap her right knee around the wooden hook designed to give purchase on the precarious sidesaddle. Her buttocks landed in the leather seat with an audible thump.

FitzHugh glanced up, a look of pained resignation adding to the lines in his face, not quite erased by a night's sleep. Mellisynt managed a tight smile before he shook his head and turned away. He swung onto his own mount with a smooth grace that belied his size and the deadweight of his armor.

Mellisynt didn't look back as her horse clattered over the drawbridge. She couldn't, even had she wished to, since the swaying, shifting mountain of muscle under her claimed all her attention. Clinging to the pommel with both hands, she braced herself against the steep descent. Small, sharp stones rattled under her horse's hooves. Occasionally one pitched over the side of the track and down the sheer hundred foot drop to the river below. When her horse edged terrifyingly close to the side, FitzHugh jerked the gray in with a sharp oath and flung a hard look over his shoulder.

"By the saints, woman, can you not control your horse?"

"Nay," she said simply.

His dark brows furrowed. "How the devil did you get into the town to do your trading if you don't ride? Surely you didn't attempt a wagon or litter on this narrow path."

"I didn't go into the town," she answered with breathless

distraction, peering at the sheer drop with the fascination a rabbit might give to the widening jaws of a serpent. She heard FitzHugh's disbelieving snort, but was too busy watching the perilous placement of her horse's hooves near the path's edge to essay any response.

Gradually the track widened enough for Mellisynt to relax and enjoy the soaring vista. The river Vilaine lay below them, a slice of silver meandering through winter-browned earth. All around her stretched a pale blue sky, unimpeded by walls. Her breath came in little excited pants that hung on the crisp air, like the puffs of clouds in the distance. When the cavalcade rounded the last turn and the road flattened out before them, she was almost sorry to lose the breathtaking view.

She was most definitely sorry when they had passed through the huddle of mud huts and timbered buildings that nestled at the foot of Trémont and FitzHugh quickened the pace. The beast beneath her broke into a canter, causing the saddle to slap against her with a jolting rhythm that jarred her teeth. Grimly Mellisynt set her jaw and tried to fit her body's movement to that of the horse, without notable success. Reminding herself that a little discomfort was a small price to pay for her freedom, she concentrated on the scenery once more.

By the second hour, she'd lost any interest in the view. Her sole focus was the gathering soreness between her lower extremities. With her mount's every step, the chainse, bunched under her thighs, rubbed against her skin. The thin wool, which had seemed so soft and fine only hours before, now scratched like the roughest serge. She shifted precariously, trying to ease her aching buttocks and sore thighs, only to shrink back in the saddle when FitzHugh cast her a frowning look over his shoulder.

"Are you all right?" he asked, a sharp edge to his voice.

The inclination to tell him just how not right she was slipped away. Mellisynt straightened her aching back.

"I'm fine."

"There's a stream up ahead where you can rest and refresh yourself."

A surge of relief rushed through her, followed immediately by doubt. She feared that once off this thrice-damned beast, she'd never be able to climb back on again.

FitzHugh drew up a short time later in a wide clearing crossed by a narrow, ice-encrusted stream. With a brusque order, he sent men to guard the road's approaches, then slid from his saddle and tossed his reins to his squire. Two long strides brought him to her side.

"I would suggest you stretch your legs and make use of the bushes while you may. We've many miles yet to travel."

Huge hands closed around her waist and lifted her easily from the saddle. Mellisynt opened her mouth to give thanks, only to close it on a squeak of dismay when her legs crumpled beneath her. She grabbed his surcoat with two fists to keep from tumbling to the rutted road. FitzHugh swept her up in his arms and carried her to the icy stream.

"I'm sorry," she said in a stiff voice as he set her down on a fallen log and bent on one knee to break the stream's crust with his dagger's hilt.

He paused in the act of filling a horn cup with clear, sparkling water. "The fault is mine, not yours. I should have inquired whether you are used to riding, and made proper arrangements."

He passed her the cup and leaned a forearm across his knee, watching as she sipped. The water slid down Mellisynt's throat with a sharp, painful coldness.

"I have no excuse for such carelessness," he continued slowly, "except that I've been so long in the company of soldiers and mercenaries I seem to have forgotten the simple courtesies women require. Rest a few moments, and I'll rig a pillion for you."

She stayed motionless, held as much by surprise as by the ache in her legs. The last thing she'd expected from this man, whose fierce demeanor matched his reputation, was forebearance. Her eyes narrowed against the sun, she watched as he bent at the waist for his squire to pull off his surcoat. Folding the furred velvet robe once, then again, FitzHugh strapped it behind his saddle. As he labored, Mellisynt ran her eyes up and down his body. In his thigh-length mailed shirt, with its hood pushed back around the strong column of his throat, he looked like one of the giants of childhood tales, all scaled in silver. If she'd searched throughout Brittany, she couldn't have found a husband more different from the thin-shanked, white-haired Henri of Trémont. The thought sent a thrill deep into her belly. Before she could decide whether the sensation betokened fear or joy, he returned to her side.

"Come, I'll take you into the bushes." One massive, mailed fist reached down for her hand.

"Nay," Mellisynt gasped, gripping the gauntlet and struggling to her feet. "I'll see to my own needs."

"There's no room for false modesty between us," he said, his patience obviously waning. "We are husband and wife, after all."

"We are not yet husband and wife," Mellisynt replied, lifting her chin. "I would have privacy."

Wide green eyes met narrowed blue ones in an unspoken contest of wills. FitzHugh took a step forward, then stopped abruptly as a shout rang across the clearing.

"Surrender your arms. You are surrounded."

FitzHugh whirled, his hand flying to his sword. He pulled it free of the scabbard and held it low in front of him, in a movement so swift and instinctive Mellisynt stepped back startled. Her legs wobbled under her, and only the sheerest effort of will kept her upright. A vicious curse seared her ears as FitzHugh reached back and grabbed her wrist in an iron vise. He gave a swift tug, pulling her behind his mail-clad body.

At the far side of the clearing, a band of foot soldiers stepped from behind the trees. Each man held a drawn bow, arrow notched, string taut. Their ranks parted, and a mounted knight rode forward. The morning sun glinted on his armor and his visored helmet. A gilded swan, silver on a field of gold, shimmered on his emerald surcoat.

"We wish you no harm. Yield the lady, and I'll allow you and your men to depart."

Mellisynt's heart slammed against her breast. Her fingers curled against the chill of FitzHugh's mail, and she sucked sharp, icy air into her lungs in a painful gasp. The rattle of metal behind her made her head jerk around. FitzHugh's men-at-arms drew up beside their lord, swords ready, shields high.

"I yield to no man." Her lord's voice rang sure and strong across the winter air.

"Then I will take her, FitzHugh."

Mellisynt glanced up at the man beside her. His blue eyes were narrowed against the sun, and his jaw was set in a rigid line. A muscle worked in his cheek, and a slow, dangerous smile lifted one corner of his lip.

"She is mine, Beauchamp. What I have, I hold."

"You'll not hold her long, bastard, nor Trémont, either. Prince Richard sent me to claim her and her lands for Normandy."

FitzHugh nodded to his squire, a solemn, brown-haired youth standing at his shoulder.

"Take the lady back to the horses, out of harm's way. Guard her well."

As she stumbled toward the rear with the squire, Mellisynt swung between fear and a slow, growing sense of outrage. She was beginning to feel much like a soup bone tossed to the floor between two snarling boar hounds. Her heart pounded, and she peered over the youth's shoulder to see how her fate would be decided.

The knight rode farther into the clearing, his horse lifting its hooves high to pick a way across the winter stubble. He stopped halfway to the small stream and raised his visor. White teeth gleamed through a thick, silky brown mustache, and his eyes fixed on FitzHugh with mocking challenge.

"My men ring the clearing. We outnumber you twice over. Surrender the lady now, without bloodshed, and go your way."

"She is my betrothed wife, Beauchamp. 'Twill take more than your puny force to wrest from me what is mine."

A surprised expression crossed the knight's face, visible even to Mellisynt's nervous gaze.

"Jesu, you wasted no time."

"And you wasted too much. You were ever one to dally late abed with the wenches."

At FitzHugh's lazy drawl, a rueful grin twisted the other man's face.

"Well, I suppose there's nothing for it. I shall have to make the lady a widow before she's yet again a wife."

"You may try, Beauchamp. Swords or lances?"

Mellisynt's breath caught in her throat as the knight slid his sword out of his scabbard and lifted the hilt to his face in a mock salute. Her frightened glance flew to FitzHugh. He stood straight in the morning light, his dark head bare, his mail glinting in the sun. He turned to take his shield from the man-at-arms who had brought it forward. To her astonishment, a grin creased his tanned cheeks. He looked for all the world like a man about to engage in a game of spillikins instead of a fight to the death!

Her eyes whipped to the other knight, now dismounted and advancing to the center of the field. He, too, wore a smile of gleeful anticipation. Holy Mary, they were enjoying themselves! Her life hung in the balance, her future, and these two thought 'twas a matter of sport!

A pounding echo of thudding hooves far down the road cut off her chaotic thoughts. FitzHugh caught the sound, as well, and paused in the act of pulling on his helmet.

"Reinforcements, Beauchamp?" he taunted. "Do you have so little faith in your skills you must call for help?"

"They're not mine," the other knight responded with a frown. He called a low command to his men, and they formed into two ranks, spread in a semicircle on either side of their leader. The front rank knelt, the rear stood with bows aimed over the heads of their companions. FitzHugh's men split into two groups and moved to either flank. Totally bewildered, Mellisynt watched the two opposing forces melt into one, all poised to meet the new threat.

"Come, lady," the squire said urgently. "You must get to the center, among the baggage horses. Your lord and this knight have fought together many times before. They will protect you."

Within seconds, Mellisynt found herself surrounded by a solid wall of men and horses. The two knights, both mounted now, all but blocked her view of the road. As the steady drum of approaching hooves grew louder, she clenched her fists into the folds of her wool cloak. Through the thin half mittens, her nails cut sharp crescents into her palms. Fear, sharp and metallic, rose in her throat. A sudden longing for the safety of Trémont's thick walls rose, only to be quashed instantly. She'd wanted to be outside those walls these ten years. She'd not whimper in terror at the first hint of danger. She unclenched her fingers, one by one.

A small troop pounded into the clearing. Three golden lions on a field of red were clearly visible through the mud spattering the leader's surcoat.

"My lord, 'tis the king's courier!"

FitzHugh nodded at his squire's relieved exclamation and slid the lethal shaft of hammered damascened steel back into its leather casing. The knight beside him did the same. Both waited while the messenger drew to a halt in front of them.

"The king demands an end to the war and has called his sons to England to negotiate peace," he said, panting. "Duke Geoffrey and Richard Lionheart have declared truce. Couriers ride to the far borders with orders to cease all hostilities."

Mellisynt felt a breath she hadn't realized she was holding rush from her constricted lungs.

The courier rubbed a weary hand over his face and turned

to FitzHugh. "Duke Geoffrey is in Nantes. He asks that you come to the city straightaway so that he can witness your marriage before he sails with the evening tide. He bade me give you word if we should meet on the road."

FitzHugh stared thoughtfully at the courier for a few moments, then thanked him with a silver coin drawn from the pouch attached to his leather sword belt. Turning to the knight at his side, he gave him a look that was half regret, half amusement.

"Well, Beauchamp, 'twould appear we must postpone our meeting."

The other man leaned a forearm across his pommel. "It would appear so. 'Tis just as well. The last time we met in the lists, you sent me tumbling from my horse."

He hesitated, his rogue's smile fading. "This is an accursed war. With you sworn to the duke, and me to the prince, I knew we'd have to meet eventually. I much dreaded it."

FitzHugh nodded. "I'm glad the war is done. Godspeed, Roger."

The other knight raised his hand in farewell and wheeled his mount. He rode through the ranks, stopping beside Mellisynt. Merry brown eyes gleamed down at her.

"I'm sorry I was too late to keep you from pledging yourself to such an ugly, distempered rogue as FitzHugh. Mayhap I will see you at court and offer consolation on your lot."

Mellisynt gasped at the laughing invitation in his eyes. She now understood FitzHugh's earlier taunt about this man's dallying with the wenches. His devilish grin and glinting eyes would turn any maid's head.

She stammered something in reply, and he was gone.

Her legs wobbly, Mellisynt leaned against one of the packhorses and waited for her turbulent emotions to subside. Truly, she had not anticipated that her first day outside Trémont's gray walls would be quite so full of excitement. The men-at-arms dispersed slowly to check gear and girths in preparation for departure.

After a few moments, FitzHugh approached her, his dark brows drawn together in what Mellisynt was coming to believe was his habitual expression. In the midst of her inner turmoil, she wondered what he'd look like if those chiseled lips once smiled at her. He took her arm in a firm grasp and led her aside, away from the men.

"Were you part of this?"

The low, growled question took her by surprise.

"Part of what?"

"This ambush. 'Twas well planned, my lady. Beauchamp knew he could not take you from Trémont once I secured it. He knew, also, I would leave half my force to garrison the castle. 'Twas logical he would try to take you while we were on the road."

Stunned, she stared up at the harsh planes of his face. "Why...why would you think I had aught to do with such a plan?"

"You were most anxious to go into the bushes alone. Did you expect him here, in this clearing?"

Mellisynt's jaw dropped. Recovering quickly, she closed it with a snap and gave him an icy glare.

"I will tell you once, my lord, and this once only. I knew naught of any ambush. I pledged you my troth, and I hold to my word."

His blue eyes narrowed on her face for a long moment. Mellisynt felt a surge of fury at his scrutiny.

"Is a woman's oath of so little value that you do not believe me?" she asked, her voice cold with disdain.

"I've found it wise not to place my trust in any woman's words, lady wife."

"I am not any woman," Mellisynt snapped. "You'd do well to remember that, if our union is to proceed."

A flicker of surprise crossed his face, as if a puppy had suddenly turned and bitten him on the ankle. His hand reached out to cup her chin, the mailed gauntlet bruising against her skin.

"Our union proceeds. You are mine now, and what I have, I hold. 'Tis the motto of my house. You'd do well to remember *that*."

Mellisynt blinked at the lazy menace in his voice. For a long moment, silence hung heavy between them. At last the hard grip on her chin loosened. Bending, FitzHugh swept her once more into his arms and headed toward his sorrel stallion.

"You have a most forward manner," he observed casually. "Did Lord Henri beat you often?"

Mellisynt's chin lifted. "Nay, never," she replied. Henri's way had been to lock her in her bare, stone-walled *solar* for days of fasting and prayer, but this arrogant knight didn't need to know that, she decided.

"Hold, Voyager," he ordered the huge destrier as he lifted her up onto the pillion rigged behind his saddle. His hands gripped her thighs, steadying her until she found a secure seat. With a terse order to hold fast, he mounted and set off at a loping canter.

By the time they crested the last hill outside Nantes, Mellisynt clung to him with aching, cold-deadened hands. Both legs were blessedly numb, and her feet felt like blocks of ice. She managed to ignore her discomfort enough to lean around FitzHugh's bulk and survey the sprawling city, displayed to advantage in the early-afternoon sunlight. A crenellated tower, a relic of an earlier age, stood in solitary splendor on a high hill, watching over the city below like a careful parent. The city itself was enclosed by high stone walls and crisscrossed with spacious streets. In the distance the Loire flowed, muddy and sluggish with winter's ebb as it wound its last few miles to the sea. Quays lined the river's wide banks and sported ships of every size and description, from fishing vessels to merchant transports.

A short time later, FitzHugh carried her out of the frost-filled air into a two-story timbered house on a narrow side street. Warmth from a roaring fire in the great room reached out to welcome her, and Mellisynt settled into a cushioned chair with a grateful sigh. Waiting servants brought cups of hot, spiced ale, and a rolled parchment for FitzHugh. He leaned toward the fire, straining to see the scribbled words, then rolled the document up with a snap.

"You have two hours, lady, before we must be at the abbey. The duke will stand witness for you, as he is your overlord, as well as mine. I am requested to meet with him immediately. Can you manage?"

"Aye," Mellisynt told him, knowing she had no choice. She prayed she'd have back the use of her legs by then. She would not face the duke weak and trembling, as she had so many years before. Her hands tightened on the chair arms as she recalled her long-held image of the flame-haired man who had laughed as he handed a frightened girl to Henri of Trémont for his use.

"Good," FitzHugh responded. "I'll leave my squire to assist you. Ian will escort you to the abbey when you're ready."

Mellisynt watched his broad shoulders disappear through the door, then rested her head against the chair's high back and released a long sigh. If ever there had been a bride who felt less like wedding and bedding this night, she'd be much surprised.

Chapter Three

FitzHugh led his small escort through the cobbled streets, his thoughts on the white-faced, wilting woman he'd just left. God's blood, he hoped she would recover from the grueling ride. He had no desire to take a limp, unmoving lump of flesh to his bed this night. Nor any night, he grimaced, thinking of his first wife.

His horse slipped on a cobble, dipping its powerful shoulders. FitzHugh shifted in the saddle and let the stallion find its footing. With deliberate effort, he forced his thoughts from his last wife to his next.

A thoughtful frown creased his brow as he remembered the pale, quiet woman who had exchanged vows with him last eventide. He was beginning to suspect there was a more complex creature than he'd first supposed swaddled in those baggy robes. The nagging suspicion that she'd known about the ambush would not be dismissed. Her eyes had sparked with a pure green flame when he challenged her, and she'd sworn she held to her pledge. Still, he had little faith in women's oaths.

As his troop clattered into the courtyard of the duke's château, FitzHugh shrugged off the aborted ambush. If the Lady Mellisynt had thought to avoid her fate, she'd missed the chance. He'd ensure she had no other in the future. He strode through the château's maze of corridors, his spurs clicking against white-and-black tiles.

"FitzHugh! I began to think you stopped to bed your rich widow before you wedded her!"

Geoffrey Plantagenet, duke of Brittany, earl of Richmond, fourth son of King Henry II and Queen Eleanor of England, detached himself from a group of battle-stained knights. He greeted his vassal with a slap on the back that nearly sent him to his knees.

"Nay, lord," FitzHugh ground out. Much as he loved Geoffrey, he often wondered how he'd survived their friendship. Tall, boisterous, possessed of his father's red hair and his mother's smiling charm, Geoffrey had the strength of two oxen in tandem, and the bullheadedness to match.

FitzHugh rolled his shoulders to ease the ache of Geoffrey's greeting. "We traveled more slowly than I had planned, as the lady was unused to riding."

"Well, if she was unused before to the feel of a horse between her legs, she'll soon grow accustomed," the duke told him, his voice booming. "To a damned rutting stallion."

FitzHugh shook his head at the laughter that rose around him. "More like the lady will refuse to let me in the same room, let alone her bed, if I don't get your final orders and retire to the baths. I've been so long in the saddle, my horse smells sweeter."

Geoffrey buffeted FitzHugh on the arm with high good humor. "Come, there's hot water aplenty in my chambers. You can bathe while we talk."

FitzHugh groaned in pure pleasure as he sank to his chin in hot, steaming water. Built especially to accommodate the duke's magnificent bulk, the tub took his long frame easily. Pages scurried out to clean his discarded armour and clothing while Geoffrey sprawled in a carved chair and surveyed his friend.

"Tell me true, Richard, is she bearable? I saw her only once, when she was but a mite. 'Twas a shame to give such tender flesh to Henri, but the old goat paid well for it, as you can imagine. How does she suit you?''

"She'll do.'' FitzHugh shrugged, then added dryly, "Though 'tis a little late to be worrying about it, after all but forcing the woman on me.''

"You ungrateful sod,'' Geoffrey said, laughing. "Most men would jump at the chance for such a prize. And I know damn well you wouldn't have taken her, whether I wished it or nay, if you hadn't been satisfied with the woman.''

FitzHugh merely grunted through the soap on his face. "I took her, but almost lost her on the road.'' He related briefly the aborted ambush attempt.

"You and Beauchamp! That would have been a contest worth seeing!''

"You wouldn't have thought the contest so sporting if I'd lost the lady and her lands to your brother,'' FitzHugh said with some dryness.

The duke waved a beefy hand, dismissing the possibility. "You've yet to lose in single combat, except to me, and then only because you held your hand. The woman's fate was as good as sealed.'' He paused, one brow arching in inquiry. "Why didn't you bring her here, to your apartments at the palace?''

"With your duchess and her ladies in the north, and you set to depart this night, I thought it best to settle her in someplace less grand.''

"Hah,'' Geoffrey snorted. "You thought to avoid the trappings of a wedding feast and ceremonial bedding. You know full well those rogues out there, disguised as knights of the realm, would've filled your gut with meat, your head with wine and your lady with a disgust of all mankind by the time they were through.''

FitzHugh grinned. "Aye, that thought did occur to me. I still remember the crack your own sweet-tempered duchess gave my skull when we carried you, drunk and slobbering, to her bed.''

"'Tis a wonder I survived that bedding," Geoffrey recalled, his golden eyes gleaming. "The little witch has talons sharper than any falcon's."

FitzHugh ducked his head under the water, then began to soap the sweat and dirt from his arms and chest.

"Pull your thoughts from between your legs, my lord duke, and tell me where we stand on this matter of a truce. Do you yield the castles we've taken or wish me to hold them until the peace is settled?"

"We give them back. While you were off collecting your bride, I sent word to my brother that I'll restore his keeps, with suitable recompense, of course. The ransoms will make a goodly dent in the wealth he's collecting for his precious Crusade." Geoffrey smiled in grim satisfaction. "Richard Lionheart will think twice before daring to raise his sword in my lands again."

"He'll dare that, and more, when you threaten what is his," FitzHugh said quietly. "As would you."

The duke's smile faded, and he sprang up to pace the spacious apartment.

FitzHugh rubbed his scarred knee and listened with half an ear as Geoffrey began a lengthy catalogue of his older brother's iniquities. He was intimately familiar with the tangled web of strained loyalties and twisted allegiances that drove the Anjevin brood. He'd joined the royal household as a young man, having saved the duke's life in battle when they were both untried squires. Since that day, the bastard issue of a landless knight and the son of a king had been friends, as well as companions. For some twenty of his thirty-six years, FitzHugh had taken his sword and his heart willingly into battle beside Geoffrey. Only of late, as war followed insult and intrigue piled upon deception, had he begun to have doubts.

This latest war had added to his disquiet. Since Richard Lionheart had become heir to the throne of England, as well as to his ducal holdings of Normandy, Aquitaine, Maine and

Anjou, he'd grown too powerful for his father's peace of mind. In an attempt to curb his strength, the king had commanded that he cede some of his lands to his youngest, landless brother, John. The Lionheart, of course, had refused. To enforce his command, the king had sent Geoffrey to the Continent to take the disputed lands by force. In retaliation, the prince had struck ferociously into Geoffrey's own domains, savaging the land and luring border vassals to rebellion with promises of future gains.

Lords holding lands in vassalage to the two brothers had suddenly found themselves in the precarious position of having to choose sides between their next king and the emissary of the present king. 'Twas a tangled war of conflicting alliances, one that pitted vassal against overlord and friend against friend. It had raged for months, ravaging lands on both sides of the borders. Thank God the king had finally realized the fury he'd unleashed and demanded this halt to what was now a deadly feud between his sons. One that Geoffrey would someday carry further, FitzHugh feared, whatever the king's wishes. He closed his eyes and leaned against the headrest, wondering how he would choose if Geoffrey openly rebelled against his father. How could he choose between his king and his friend? He drew in a deep breath, reminding himself of all he owed the duke—including the rich widow even now awaiting him, he realized with a start.

"Jesu," he swore, hauling his dripping frame out of the tub. "If I don't move quickly, I'm like to keep the bride waiting at the abbey."

Geoffrey's eyes filled with laughter. "B'God, FitzHugh, already you dance to the woman's tune. I grow anxious to meet her once more."

"Come and meet her, then. And hurry."

When he and Geoffrey and the duke's inevitable entourage crowded into the south transept of the abbey, it was empty of all save a patient bishop and his acolytes. FitzHugh sent a page with a polite summons and took his place in front of the altar.

Lady Mellisynt and her escort arrived within moments. Coming forward at a slow, almost halting pace, she paused before the duke and sank into a shallow curtsy. It was a brief salute, the kind a serving maid might give a fat merchant, not the obeisance a lady would give her overlord and a prince of the realm.

FitzHugh's eyes narrowed at the deliberate slight, but the duke ignored it. With a strong hand and a warm smile, Geoffrey raised her from her curtsy.

"'Tis many years since last we met, my lady. How fortuitous that we do so again."

Her brow arched delicately. "Fortuitous, my lord? That Henri of Trémont died and gave me once more into your keeping? I suppose some might consider it so."

Geoffrey blinked at the irony in the lady's deliberate words. Still, his charm had carried him through more than one encounter with a difficult female. He smiled and led her forward, toward the waiting knight.

"It grieves me that your marriage should be so rushed, lady. When you journey to England, we'll celebrate with feasting, and all due ceremony."

"This suits me well, my lord," Mellisynt told him, her tone cool.

His smile slipped, and a hint of regal condescension edged his voice. "But not me. Richard FitzHugh is my friend, as well as my loyal knight. I would see him, and you, fittingly honored."

"Let's just see the thing done," FitzHugh suggested dryly.

The marriage took much less time than the betrothal had. Within the hour, they were wed. With the prelate and other vassals as witness, FitzHugh knelt, placed his hands between the duke's and gave homage for the fief of Trémont. They then bid Geoffrey farewell and retired to share wine and a hastily assembled wedding supper with the knights invited to join them.

After a round of ribald toasts that brought a rush of blood to Mellisynt's cheeks, the company settled down to the serious business of eating. Servants carried a steady parade of fragrant, steaming dishes from the kitchens below, and the knights' conversation picked up in volume with the flow of wine and hot dishes. Having come from the battlefield, the men were eager still to talk of booty and the satisfying ease with which the rebels' keeps crumbled under their determined assault. Caught up in the conversation, FitzHugh leaned forward, his bride all but forgotten.

Mellisynt picked at the trencher she shared with her new lord and listened to the talk of battles won and lost. Although she lived in a time when war was the accepted means of settling every quarrel, she had never experienced the violence these men seemed to relish. Henri of Trémont had paid scutage to his overlord, pleading age and infirmity as an excuse to avoid his knightly duties. He, and his wife, had stayed locked within his castle walls. The closest she had come to the edges of war were those heart-stopping moments in the clearing this morning.

Mellisynt listened to these knights' gruesome tales and tasted sparingly of the dishes set before her. She but sampled a bite of braised lamb served in a ring of truffles, artichokes and peas, and waved aside sauced sea bass and pickled herring. Only a bowl of delicate Bélon oysters tempted her. She pried a few of the flavorful, succulent mollusks from their half-opened shells and sopped up the sauce with a crust of thick wheat bread. The fire flickered low in the fireplace at the end of the hall, and still the men talked. Leaning both elbows on the cloth-covered table, she felt the weariness and emotion of the long day wash over her.

"Come, wife. I'd best take you to bed before you fall asleep in the sweetmeats."

Mellisynt blinked as a strong, firm hand took her arm and

lifted her from the bench. A last round of hearty toasts and explicit advice followed them out of the main room. As they made their way down a narrow passage toward the private bedchambers, Mellisynt felt the glutinous oysters congeal within her stomach. Every stricture Henri had thrown at her, every virulent lecture Father Anselem had ever delivered on the subject of a wife's duty, echoed in her mind. She swallowed, telling herself that this husband was different from the first, that she could perform her duties without feeling the edges of her soul curl in despair. Even if his use of her body proved as loathsome as had Henri's, she would endure. She took a deep breath when FitzHugh closed the heavy wooden door behind them.

"Would you like wine?"

"Yes," she whispered. Flushing at her own timidity, she swallowed and said again, more steadily. "Yes, if you please."

FitzHugh's thick brows drew together as he poured a stream of amber wine into a silver goblet.

"There's no need to fear me, lady. I know I'm overlarge, and not comely of face, but I won't hurt you if you give me no cause. Show yourself a dutiful wife, and we will contrive."

Mellisynt stiffened. Not yet wed three hours, and already he must needs instruct her in her wifely obligations. She took a deep, steadying swallow of wine. Placing the goblet on a high chest inlaid with ivory and gold mosaics, she nodded.

"I'll do my duty," she assured him in a level voice.

Reaching up, she tugged the veil from her head and pulled out the wooden pins that held her braids. Reddish ropes, thick as a man's wrist, tumbled down her back. Laying the veil across the chest, she began to work the ties that held her gown at either side.

"Do you wish me to ring for the women to help you prepare?"

Mellisynt looked up, surprise widening her eyes. "Prepare?"

"Forgive me, lady" came the sardonic reply. "I supposed you would wish privacy to ready yourself."

Uncertainty threaded through her. Was she supposed to don some special garment or apply some unguent? Henri had made her use what he called medicaments at first, but none had succeeded in sustaining the strength of his rod for very long. She'd not thought she would need such aids this night, with this man.

"I...I have no need... Nothing to prepare," she finally got out.

When FitzHugh shrugged, she shed her gown and chainse. Her hands reached for the edge of her undershift, then stilled. She cast a fleeting glance at the figure leaning against the far wall, his blue eyes surveying her body with interest, if not with the heated lust she'd often seen in Henri's avid stares. A shaft of feminine pique drove the unease from her belly. She might not have the soft curves of her youth, but her body was firm, and not totally despicable. She would not cower like some frightened virgin before his cool, assessing gaze.

Straightening, she pulled the shift over her head. The drafty air brought goose bumps to her naked flesh and puckered her nipples. Hastily removing her boots and woolen stockings, she climbed between the sheets. Her chin lifted a fraction as her eyes met FitzHugh's across the dim room.

He set his wine aside and crossed the room, working the buckle of his belt. Through half-lowered lids she watched him shrug out of the surcoat and the quilted gambeson beneath. He'd left off his mail shirt in honor of the occasion, she supposed. Untying the tapes of his chausses with quick, sure movements, he rolled them down, along with his braies. When he turned toward the bed, Mellisynt resisted the urge to shrink back against the pillows. In the dim firelight, he loomed huge and menacing. Where Henri had been all bone and white, withered flesh, this man was solid muscle covered with dark, curling hair. She dropped her eyes from his massive shoulders, down a chest marked by a tracery of faded scars, to a root lying thick and flaccid against his thigh. She bit back a gasp at its size.

FitzHugh tossed back the coverlet and slid into bed. The corn-husk mattress rustled and sagged with his weight. When he stretched his long legs out beside her, Mellisynt sucked in a ragged breath. Slowly she came up on her knees. Taking his manhood in both hands, she wet her lips and bent over him.

"What the devil are you doing?"

He grabbed her arm and jerked her upright. Mellisynt turned to him in blank astonishment.

"I but seek to raise your seed."

"Jesu," he swore. His grip on her arm tightened as he edged himself back to sit upright. "Just where did you learn that little whore's trick?"

"Whore's trick?" she gasped, pulling against the hurtful hold. Her uncovered breasts quivered with the cold and her awkward position. "I know not what whores do to swell a man's root! I know only that failure to rouse a husband is a sin. One I have done penance for often enough," she ended on a low, mutinous note.

A thunderous scowl darkened his features. "Do you tell me you were punished because your husband couldn't rise?"

Embarrassed and angry, she jerked her arm, but couldn't break his iron grip. His other hand shot out to take her chin and force her head around.

"Aye, my lord," she finally muttered. "I spent as many hours on my knees in the chapel as I did in my lord's bed."

Releasing her, FitzHugh threw the covers to one side and rose. With a hamlike fist on either hip, he growled down at her.

"Listen to me, lady wife. I don't need your mouth on me to make me swell."

He hesitated, then added, somewhat less forcefully. "Not unless you wish it. And from the look on your face, you did not."

Mellisynt wrapped the down coverlet around her chest and

stared in bewildered consternation at the figure towering above her. Sweet Mother, did he give her a choice? After a long pause, she responded hesitantly.

"I will admit I went to Henri's bed with great reluctance. But that had much to do with the fact that he smelled like rancid cheese and oft made me gag."

She paused, biting her lower lip. A slow tide of heat rose up her neck, and she looked away. "Your scent is passing pleasant, my lord."

When long moments passed in silence, Mellisynt looked up to see a tinge of red coloring FitzHugh's prominent cheekbones. His mouth curled in a wry smile that altered the harsh planes of his face into something resembling handsomeness.

"I will admit to bathing and dousing myself in Geoffrey's costliest perfume in your honor." The smile widened into a lopsided grin.

To her amazement, Mellisynt felt an answering smile tug at her lips. In all her years, she'd experienced many emotions in the marriage bed. Fear, revulsion, anger, and stubborn resistance had often taken hold. But she could not remember ever feeling the least inclination to laugh.

"I, too, bathed," she told him, biting her lower lip.

"Well, then, wife, let us not waste all that effort. Lay yourself down, and mayhap we can pleasure each other without gagging."

FitzHugh slid back into bed and turned her stiff body against his. As his hands stroked lean flanks and small, high breasts, he tried to sort his jumbled thoughts.

When she'd first bent over him and taken him in hand, the priest's ugly insinuations had flashed through his mind. For a startled moment, he'd believed the widow had a wider knowledge of men than he'd suspected. Her blank surprise and mumbled explanation had soon put that notion to rest. She'd only done what her decrepit old husband had taught her.

Although FitzHugh's mind revolted at the thought of how she'd been made to service the aged Henri, his shaft stiffened at the memory of her soft, moist lips brushing him so intimately. Deliberately his hand closed over her breast and plucked at the hardened tip. When she gasped and arched under him, he bent to take the nipple in his mouth.

"Sweet Mother," she breathed.

He took his time, worrying the tender flesh with small, teasing nips, then laving it with his tongue. A tang of milky sweetness rose from her nipple, and the taste made his loins throb. Lifting his head from her turgid flesh, he looked down at her face. Wide, luminous eyes met his. He could see a question in their green depths, and curiosity, and the first smoky edges of desire. He bent and took her lips with his.

FitzHugh felt his blood begin to pulse with a slow, sweet heat as he sampled her. She might be too thin and pale to arouse a man with her looks, but by the saints, she tasted of warm, dark honey and sweet wine. He ran his tongue over the smooth flesh of her inner lips, then thrust against her teeth until she opened for him. FitzHugh explored her mouth, and his loins began to ache in earnest. He tightened his hold, crushing her breasts against his chest and her hip against his swollen member.

When she moaned and writhed under him, he slanted his lips across hers more fully and slid his hand down her belly. With one knee, he pried her legs apart, opening her center to his touch.

"Oh!" She jerked her head back, breaking the contact of their mouths.

Smug male satisfaction coursed through him at her startled reaction. She might have learned a few unnatural tricks from the old lecher she'd been wed to, but she bucked under his questing hand like an unbroken filly. FitzHugh buried his face in her neck, breathing in once more the elusive scent of gillyflowers and spring. His fingers rubbed against her core.

This time her gasp accompanied an involuntary shift of her hips, away from his hand. A muted cry pierced his absorption. He raised his head.

"Do I crush you?" he growled, his hand on her moist flesh.

"*Nooo....*" The single drawn-out syllable wavered in the stillness.

Even through the heat clouding his mind, he could hear the tears in her voice. With a slight shock, he realized it was not passion that was making her writhe under his hand. He levered himself up on one elbow, grimacing at the ache in his loins.

"What ails you, lady?" Sweat beaded on his brow from the effort of holding back, but he would not force her unless he had to.

"The saddle, my lord," she said with a small gulp.

FitzHugh frowned down at her. "Saddle? What saddle?"

Her eyes slid away in embarrassment. "The one that took the skin from my thighs."

His scowl deepened. Sitting upright, he thrust the coverlet aside and parted her legs. Even in the dim light, he could see the raw, angry skin that darkened each slender thigh.

"God's blood, why didn't you say something? We could have stopped and bound your hurts."

Embarrassed, she tried to close her legs against his hand. "You stressed the need for haste, and I didn't wish to slow us. In truth, I didn't feel the pain after the first few hours. My legs were numb."

FitzHugh felt the last remnants of desire drain as he eyed the fruits of his own carelessness. He cursed himself for putting her astride a horse when he could see she was no experienced rider. Christ's bones, he gave his veriest recruits more consideration than he'd given the woman he'd sworn to protect and defend! Stifling another curse, he swung out of bed and stalked to the door.

Shaking awake the page who slept on a pallet outside the threshold, he sent him scrambling with a terse order. He shut the door once more and crossed to the fire. With quick efficiency, he tossed wood shavings and dry logs onto the smoldering embers. While the fire hissed to a roaring blaze, he picked up a glazed ceramic basin and water jug and brought them back to the bed.

"Those blisters need tending lest they fester. Let me cleanse them."

"Nay," Mellisynt gasped, scurrying back, away from his looming presence. Embarrassment stained her cheeks, and she dragged the sheets across her chest.

"Don't be more foolish than you've been already," FitzHugh snapped. He leaned down, intending to lay her flat, but a sharp rap on the door forestalled him.

He strode to the door and took a shallow covered bowl from the young page. The boy craned his neck, trying to see around his lord's massive frame. Mellisynt had a quick glimpse of curious brown eyes and tousled golden curls before the door shut with a slam.

"This should ease the pain," FitzHugh declared, setting the bowl on the floor. He looked around, then picked up the chainse lying beside the bed. With one sure tug, he ripped it from hem to neck.

"My lord!" Mellisynt gasped, her eyes wide with dismay.

"Don't fear," he told her. "I've bound enough wounds on the battlefield to know what I'm about."

"Aye," she said weakly.

"Bare yourself and let me tend your hurts."

Hearing the hint of impatience in his voice, Mellisynt responded with great reluctance. Waves of mortification swept over her as his dark head bent to examine her injuries. The intimacy of her position shamed her to her core. She turned her face away, and he lifted first one, then the other leg, washing them with amazing gentleness.

After a few moments, he set the water aside and removed the lid on the bowl the page had brought. Mellisynt's nostrils flared as a nauseous odor, redolent of onions, fenster oil and sour mead filled the room. Her eyes began to water with the reek. FitzHugh plunged his hand into the oozing mess and turned toward her.

"My lord!" she shrieked, wriggling away. "You do not mean to put that noxious mixture on me!"

"I do. 'Tis the best poultice I know for saddle sores. My squire always carries a goodly supply when we travel. It should work as well on you as on the horses."

"Do not speak to me of horses!" Mellisynt muttered, refusing to move. "Truly, I thank you for your attentions, but the aroma makes my head spin."

A roguish gleam lightened the blue of his eyes. "Consider the odor punishment for your stubbornness in refusing to reveal your hurts earlier. Come, spread your legs."

Mellisynt measured the determination in those glinting eyes. Accepting defeat, she heaved a resigned sigh and pushed aside the coverlet.

The poultice brought immediate relief. She gave a low, thankful groan as the searing pain in her thighs eased to a slow burn.

FitzHugh's dark brows drew together. Without speaking, he wrapped clean linen over the salved area. His hands stilled finally, and he sat back on his haunches.

"You must have been in agony most of the day. How in God's name did you walk to the abbey and back?"

Her lips twisted into a wry grimace. "With great care."

At his considering look, she gave a little shrug. "I thought it was God's punishment for my eagerness to be gone from Trémont. I would have endured pain many times more severe to be away."

His eyes thoughtful, FitzHugh tossed the used rags into the bowl and set it aside. Binding each leg with clean linen, he finished the job with quick efficiency, then washed his hands with the remaining water in the jug. That done, he climbed back into bed. Stretching out his long legs beside her, he raised both arms to link his fingers under his head. Stillness descended between them, broken only by the hiss and crackle of pinecones in the flickering fire.

"'Tis clear you had no joy of your first husband." His deep

voice drifted across the quiet. "But you had a choice this time. Why did you wed with me?"

Mellisynt turned her head toward him, her cheek brushing against the wool-stuffed pillow.

"The choice was you or a nunnery," she reminded him. "I spent most of my life behind Trémont's walls, my lord. I didn't want to spend the rest in a cloister."

"You need not have accepted those choices," he commented after a few moments. "You could have closed the gates and held Trémont for Prince Richard. He would gladly have taken you into his keeping for such a prize."

"I thought of doing so," she admitted, propping herself up on one elbow.

FitzHugh's blood began to pulse at the thought of how close it had been. If he'd left to claim the lady even a day later, he might have arrived at Trémont to find the gates closed and Beauchamp's pennant waving from its turret.

"But I had no way of knowing who Richard Lionheart would give me to," she continued candidly. "I decided I would as well take you. You are young enough, and strong, and you are a bastard."

He didn't move, yet his muscles seemed to harden under her very eyes. Mellisynt clutched the coverlet to her chest, aware that she had stumbled, badly. Hesitant, she tried to explain.

"Henri could trace his line back to Charlemagne, and even before. He boasted often that his veins ran with the purest, noblest blood in the land. Yet he was weak and infirm and could give me no children."

FitzHugh's face settled into sharp planes and shadowed angles. Despite his grim expression, Mellisynt forced herself to finish what she'd started.

"Many would scorn the fact that your mother was a leman, kept by your father for his pleasure, but she brought new, fresh blood to your line. I would pass that blood to my children."

She paused, then continued on a low, throbbing note. "I want children, my lord."

For long moments, silence hung heavy between them. Mellisynt swallowed, certain she'd spoken too rashly. She rued her forward tongue, as Father Anselem had so many times, but could not unsay the words.

When the silence had stretched her nerves to wire thinness, FitzHugh finally drew down his arms. With one huge fist, he closed the bed curtains on his side, then reached across to draw them on her side as well. Darkness welcomed them.

"Well, wife, it doesn't appear we can do aught to make you a babe this night. Go to sleep."

Chapter Four

The next days passed slowly for Mellisynt. Accustomed to tending Henri from earliest cock's crow, she felt a nagging sense of guilt at staying abed, even if it was at her lord's express order.

FitzHugh was absent most of the time, seeing to his duties as Geoffrey's chief lieutenant. With the duke en route to England to meet with his father and brothers at the peace council, it fell to FitzHugh to disband the armies. The lords of Brittany dispersed to their various keeps, replete with booty taken from subdued rebels. The English vassals enfeoffed by Geoffrey in his mien as earl of Richmond grumbled as cold, damp mist closed the harbors and prevented their departure for home. FitzHugh spent as much time settling violent disputes between the bored, idle knights as he did finalizing the details for transporting over a thousand men, animals and camp followers back to England.

Mellisynt learned little of his responsibilities from FitzHugh himself. The few times he repaired to their rented house to see to her welfare and grab a hurried meal, he was preoccupied and curt. When he returned, most often late at night, he fell into bed with a grunt and was soon asleep. Although he would take her in his arms and curl her into him for warmth, he brushed aside her halting offer to perform her duties with a brusque order to heal herself first.

The little page, Bartholomew by name, supplied Mellisynt

with most of her information as to her lord's activities. Shy and round-eyed, the youngster blushed when FitzHugh told him he was to see to his lady's care. Mellisynt guessed his age at around eight years. As unused to dealing with children as the boy was to a lady's company, she made awkward attempts to converse with him. He kept his eyes cast down, answering in one-syllable mumbles. She'd almost given up hope of drawing him out when she discovered a chessboard in the cupboard beside the bed. In bored desperation, Mellisynt moved to a low couch in front of the fire and began to place the pieces.

"Do you play, Bartholomew?"

"Some," he replied, his eyes shying away from hers. "Sir Richard has tried to teach me, but my moves oft try his patience."

Stifling the thought that most things tried her lord's thin patience, Mellisynt patted the couch. "Come, help me pass this dreary day."

It took more gentle coaxing before the boy shed his diffidence enough to seat himself on a low stool beside the couch. Cold, dismal rain splashed against the casement windows and filled the corners of the chamber with dampness. But, swaddled as she was in thick blankets and tucked close to the fire, Mellisynt felt a rare contentment. She smiled inwardly as the boy agonized over each move. Henri had not given her much joy in life, but at least his passion for chess had challenged her mind during her years at his bedside. Her hand passed over the bishop that would have placed the boy's king in check and, instead, moved a pawn forward.

"Have you served long with Sir Richard?" she asked idly.

"Nigh onto a year." Boyish pride glowed in his eager brown eyes. "My father is a freedman, a tanner. He like to pissed in his braies when the lord agreed to take me in service."

Mellisynt bit her lip. "Aye, of a certainty, he would be proud," she agreed.

Bartholomew had just moved a rook forward with reckless daring when a commotion sounded outside the windows. Dashing to the casement, the boy pushed it open to peer down into the street.

"There's a great train below, lady," he exclaimed. "I can't see the markings, but the horses' trappings are above order grand!"

Mellisynt began to gather the discarded chess pieces. Before she had them back in the board's fitted drawer, her chamber door opened and a diminutive figure draped in rich furs swept in.

"I bid you good-day, Lady Mellisynt. I am Constance, of Brittany."

The words rang with unconscious arrogance, but were softened by a smiling face framed by silver fox fur. While not beautiful, the lady's countenance shone with subtle rose tints and sparkling violet eyes.

"My lady," Mellisynt stammered, struggling to unwind the swaddling blankets.

"Nay, do not rise. I returned to Nantes this morn to find not only had my lord's most trusted vassal married in a shameful, hurried ceremony, but his wife was ill and abed in some damp little house. 'Tis why I came." She paused, her nose wrinkling delicately. "Do you have a putrid fever?"

Mellisynt shook her head.

"What is that evil smell?" Constance came forward a few cautious paces. "Tell me straight, lady, do you need the court physician?"

"Nay. The head groom, mayhap, but not the physician."

At the other woman's look of utter confusion, Mellisynt sighed. "My illness is naught but raw legs from an unaccustomed saddle. My lord doctored them with a remedy he claims is most efficacious with horses. In truth, it worked wondrously, but I fear this chamber will bear the scent of the cure for months to come."

Constance stared, eyes wide with disbelief. After a moment,

her mouth quirked, then opened in lilting laughter. "If that's not typical of FitzHugh! He always did know more about horses than women."

Her violet eyes alive with merriment, she studied Mellisynt from the tip of her hair to the toes peeping out from the twisted blankets.

"I've come to carry you to the château. Tell your women to gather your things."

Mellisynt frowned, nibbling at her lower lip. "My lord said nothing of moving."

"Pah! He used my absence as an excuse to avoid the court. But I'm returned now, and will not have the wife of my husband's most loyal knight housed without. I've sent FitzHugh word that he may attend you this eve at the château. Come, a litter awaits below stairs."

Mellisynt hesitated, having no desire for closer concourse with the duke or his court. Yet Geoffrey was gone, and his lady wife commanded her presence. She was debating what she should do when one of FitzHugh's men-at-arms rapped on the door of the chamber.

"Your pardon, milady." The man's Adam's apple bobbed nervously. "Sir Richard sends word you are to expect the Lady Constance and should do her bidding." He gave the women a quick, awkward bow, then slipped out the door.

Constance grinned in triumph. "There, you see! Even FitzHugh, stubborn as he is, bows to my authority—on some things. Come, my men will carry you down the stairs."

Before she quite knew how it happened, Mellisynt found herself ensconced in a litter, the like of which she had never imagined, much less seen. Intricately carved and inlaid with gold leaf, it was drawn by a pair of perfectly matched bays. Heavy velvet curtains of rich burgundy shut out the rain, and high-piled furs kept her warm throughout the short trip. Still bundled in her confining blankets, she was carried up wide marble steps and settled in a high-ceilinged apartment.

"You'll be more comfortable in here," Constance told her briskly.

Awed by the magnificence around her, Mellisynt could only nod. Her eyes roamed over the vaulted, gilded ceilings, past the rich tapestries hanging on each wall, to the wide canopied bed draped in burgundy-and-gold cloth. She stood, uncertain, still cocooned in her blankets, while Constance shooed the male attendants out.

"Get you to bed," she ordered. "But first remove those foul-smelling bandages. I'll not have my fine linens imbued with Richard FitzHugh's horse poultice."

Wondering that such a tiny woman could be so domineering, Mellisynt obediently unwrapped her coverings and reached under her thigh-length shift to strip off the offending bindings.

"Take these and burn them." Constance held the bandages out at arm's length and passed them to a reluctant maid. Mellisynt swallowed a sigh as she watched the remains of her only good shift being borne away.

"I'll leave you now to rest. My maids will tend your hurts with a cream of my own making. I trust you'll find it somewhat more aromatic than FitzHugh's," Constance drawled. "When you feel well enough, you may join me in my *solar* during the afternoons. 'Tis when we have our entertainment."

She was gone in a whirl of color and a cloud of tantalizing scent.

Mellisynt submitted with embarrassed reluctance to the attendants' ministrations. Not even with her old maid, Maude, had she allowed any woman to tend her so intimately. She protested in vain that her hurts were sufficiently healed, but the duchess's word was law. Not one of the determined serving women would leave until she was seen to.

Red-faced, Mellisynt finally settled into the wide bed. The equally red-faced and exasperated maids left, but one returned almost immediately.

"There is a page without, milady. He says he is yours and would speak with you."

At Mellisynt's nod, she stood back to allow in a wet, thoroughly bedraggled young boy. Water dripped from his flattened gold curls and squished in his shoes as he crossed the room.

"Bartholomew! How came you here?"

"I walked behind your litter, lady."

"In this freezing rain? Why didn't you wait at the house until Sir Richard returned?"

The boy's lower lip stuck out belligerently. "My lord bade me stay by you."

Mellisynt's eyes widened, and she turned a pleading look on the maidservant still hovering by the door.

"I'll send dry clothes for him, milady."

She gave the woman a wide, grateful smile.

A runnel of icy rain ran beneath the mail covering Fitz-Hugh's neck and slid down his back. The dampness added weight to the quilted gambeson beneath his armour and seeped into his bones. Wrapping his surcoat more closely about his body, he slumped, wet and weary, in the saddle. Sweet Jesu, if one more of Geoffrey's damned vassals challenged his authority to order the departure, he'd toss the lot of them into the Loire's muddy waters. As it was, half the ships scheduled to depart on the morrow were yet to be loaded. And now, instead of a quick meal and peaceful sleep in the quietude of his rented apartments, he had to wend his way through Nantes's crowded streets to the château to claim his rooms and his wife.

When he arrived at the palace, FitzHugh gave his horse, helmet and gauntlets into his squire's keeping and mounted the marble steps. After passing through a series of long, drafty corridors, he opened the door to his assigned apartments. He stopped short at the scene that greeted him.

Two children sat cross-legged before a blazing hearth, a

clutter of half-filled plates around them. One of them FitzHugh recognized immediately. Bartholomew's golden curls, the bane of his existence and the butt of older pages' taunts, identified him. But it took a few moments longer to recognize his wife.

Her unbraided hair cascaded over her shoulders in a cloud of undulating chestnut waves. Startled green eyes stared out of a face as scrubbed and pale as any child's, and a voluminous white nightshirt enveloped her slender frame like an oversized tent. She held a roasted chicken leg in one hand and wore what appeared to be a smear of grease on her left cheek.

While FitzHugh stood frowning at the unfamiliar creature who scrambled up and offered him a hesitant smile, Bartholomew jumped to his feet and came to greet him. Accepting the boy's welcome with an absent nod, FitzHugh dismissed him.

"I see you are well settled," he said finally.

"Aye, the duchess has been most kind." Mellisynt crossed the tile floor on bare feet to help him disrobe.

"Get back to the fire," he growled. "My squire will attend to this."

"Nay, my lord, I can help."

He shrugged off her light hand. "I'm wet to the bone, and will drench you, as well. Leave it."

FitzHugh cursed his clumsy tongue as Mellisynt's thick lashes swept down over her eyes and she went back to stand beside the fire.

"I don't want you to take a chill," he offered in a gruff tone, as unused to explaining himself to a wife who would see to his comfort. In a heavy-handed attempt at humor, he continued. "I would not be a widower before I'm yet a husband."

Mellisynt's back stiffened. "I am well enough now to...to tend to your needs."

Her offended tone made FitzHugh pause in the act of shrugging out of his sodden cloak. He glanced across at the woman standing in bare feet and rigid dignity. God's bones, with her thick, unruly hair and wide green eyes, she looked like a stray cat, one whose fur had been stroked the wrong way. Leaping flames silhouetted her body through the wool nightshirt, and FitzHugh felt a sudden flicker of heat deep in his belly.

"Are you sure? Your hurts are healed?"

Her tongue darted out to wet her lips, and the flicker grew to a low flame.

"Aye," she said, her eyes steady on his.

FitzHugh studied her through heavy-lidded eyes and decided at that moment to consummate their union. In truth, he'd been hard put to restrain himself these past nights, when her slender frame had fitted itself to his and they'd shared their bodies' warmth.

His initial reluctance to take this woman to wife had faded the past few days. Despite her barely veiled dislike of the duke, and FitzHugh's own lingering suspicions of her loyalty, she'd shown no other signs of rebelling against her fate. While he couldn't quite bring himself to trust her, he had to admit she'd not tried to interfere in his ordering of Trémont's men and moneys. He was already benefitting from the widow's rich inheritance, having outfitted his men and hers with new weapons and armour. 'Twas time he lived up to his side of this marriage bargain, he thought, remembering her admission that she'd given herself to a bastard knight to milk the strength of his loins. His loins were more than ready to be milked, he decided grimly. They ached. Bellowing for his squire, he finished undressing.

In short order, he'd wrapped himself in a clean, dry robe and joined his wife in front of the fire. She resumed her seat, knees tucked decorously under the nightshirt, and spread an assortment of cold meats, pasties and cheeses before him. When she leaned forward to pour him wine, her hair swung down in a curtain of dancing russet and gold lights. FitzHugh gave in to an unconscious urge and reached out to touch the thick, silky mane.

"Your hair is most unusual in color," he told her, fingering the fiery strands.

"Aye." She sighed. "Father Anselem reminded me often that red's the symbol of sin and wickedness."

She paused, then took a quick breath. "I dislike mightily the head coverings I was used to wear, but will don them if the color offends you. Or I could dye my hair black, as is the fashion here."

"Nay, it's fine. 'Tis like the coat of a newborn colt I once helped birth, all slick and shiny and filled with copper lights."

FitzHugh let her hair fall and grimaced to himself at his gauche reply. Few ladies of his acquaintance would appreciate being compared to a just-birthed horse. For the first time he wondered if Lady Constance was right. The duchess had often, and at great length, insisted he would benefit mightily from more exposure to her court, where the troubadours sang of courtly love and knights fashioned poetic tributes to their ladies. FitzHugh had little time and less use for such pursuits. Still, he knew wellborn ladies had come to expect flowery phrases and smooth songs of praise. He glanced at his wife.

The Lady Mellisynt didn't appear offended at his less-than-poetic comment about her hair. Her lips curved in a small smile, and she passed him a dish of salted fish.

Through the screen of her lashes, Mellisynt watched her husband consume the contents of the heaped plate she placed before him, then explore the remains of the other dishes. And to think she had protested when the servants left such heaping platters as would have made Henri screech in protest at the excess! She ran an assessing glance down FitzHugh's massive frame, displayed to advantage in a short velvet robe and wool chausses. He bent one knee and rested an elbow on it while his strong white teeth cleaned a pheasant leg. Mellisynt's eyes lingered on his muscled calf and trunklike thigh, before skittering over the pouch cupping his manhood. She felt heat stain her cheeks as she remembered her first sight of her husband's maleness. An unfamiliar tingling began, low in her belly, and she glanced impatiently at the scattered dishes to see how much remained to be consumed.

When FitzHugh finished a short time later and pushed aside the empty plates, Mellisynt's shivery sense of anticipation dimmed somewhat. She'd had little joy in what passed between husband and wife in the past, but she reminded herself of FitzHugh's restraint the night of their marriage. Instinctively she knew she need not fear this man, who would put a woman's hurts before his own desires. Still, she couldn't control the strange trembling in her hand when he took it and drew her across the furs to his side.

"Are you cold?" he asked, his big fingers fumbling with the drawstring that held the neck of her borrowed nightshirt.

"No. Yes. A bit," she stammered.

She looked up to see amusement glinting in his shadowed blue eyes. Did this man always find humor in the bedchamber! she wondered. She sat still while he pushed the nightshirt down her shoulders and off her hips, then stopped wondering, stopped thinking at all, as he slipped an arm around her waist and brought her naked body onto his thighs. When he dipped his head and nuzzled her ear, she stopped breathing, as well.

"I will warm you, wife."

His breath filled her ear with hot, moist promise. He took the lobe between his teeth, as if to taste her very flesh, and ran his tongue around the outer shell. While his mouth wreaked its depredations on her ear, his hand began a slow, deliberate exploration, from breast to hip and back again.

Mellisynt hunched her shoulder and wiggled, trying to evade the half-sensual, wholly disturbing sensations. Held firmly in his lap, her front to the fire and her backside tucked against his thigh, she heard him suck in his breath sharply.

"By the saints, I hope you are truly whole," he rasped. "Lie down and let me check before we go too far to stop."

Flames hotter than any in the fireplace leapt into her cheeks. "Nay, my lord, I'm fine, I swear it. Your remedy worked well. Please!"

She grabbed the fist, covered with fine dark hair, that reached for her thighs.

"The formula is my own," FitzHugh told her with a touch of smugness as he laid her down on the furs spread before the fire, then covered her body with his.

Conditioned by past experience, Mellisynt held herself rigid and still. The few times Henri had managed to mount her, he'd snarled at her to lie quiet lest she sap his seed prematurely with her wanton movements. But as FitzHugh's mouth pressed against hers with hot demand and his hands toyed with her nipples, she felt an overwhelming urge to move against him. Her hands loosed their death grip on the pelt beneath her and lifted slowly, tentatively, to grasp his arms. Muscles bunched under her fingers, like thick ropes of steel sheathed in warm satin. She ran the pads of her fingers along his arms and over his shoulders. Following an instinct older than time, she shifted beneath his weight to cradle his root against her cleft.

With one hand beneath her head, FitzHugh held her steady while he took her mouth. Mellisynt tasted wine, dark and sweet, and a masculine hunger that was as unfamiliar as it was arousing. A slow, steady pressure began to build between her legs. To ease it, she moved against him, lifting her hips to his.

The hand in her hair tightened to a hard fist, and he drew in a ragged breath. Mellisynt's own breath caught as his other hand reached between their bodies to rub against her core. When he slid his fingers into her, she bucked in startled surprise.

"What are you doing?"

"Sweet—! Do you hurt?"

"No!" she gasped.

"Then lie still and let me ready you," he ground out, "because my sword must bury itself in your sheath soon or I will disgrace myself."

Mellisynt stared, wide-eyed, at the vaulted ceiling above her. She had a good idea what he meant by disgracing himself, and was no more eager than he to have it happen. Ceding to his command, she held herself still. For the space of three heartbeats. Then she writhed under his hand. And thrust her hips up to meet him as he entered her.

When he rolled off later, much later, Mellisynt lay bathed in a fine sheen of perspiration. Her breath matched his in its ragged unevenness. FitzHugh sprawled beside her on the furs, his bulk shielding her from the cold drafts, his shoulder pinning her hair. He bent one leg to rub absently at his knee.

"It seems I owe you yet another apology." His voice broke the stillness between them.

Mellisynt turned her head as far as her trapped hair would allow. "For what?"

His lips turned down in a self-mocking smile. "I've been too many weeks without release. In my incontinence, I did not bring you to your pleasure."

Her eyes widened. The silence between them lengthened. Finally she shook her head.

"'Twould appear I have much yet to learn of marriage with you, my lord," she said in a small, confused voice. "I thought myself well pleasured."

FitzHugh gave a low groan and rolled to his feet. Scooping her up, he carried her to the bed. Curling her back into his body, he wrapped a strong arm around her waist. Her breast rested in the palm of his hand, and he played idly with its still-sensitive peak. His other hand splayed possessively across her belly and tangled in the curls at the apex of her thighs.

Mellisynt sucked in her breath as his lazy fondlings grew more deliberate and began to stoke the fires she thought well banked. She stiffened against him, her buttocks pushing into his loins. To her amazement, she felt his shaft begin to harden against her.

Sweet Mother, did he think to spill himself yet again? This same night? She tried to turn, but his hand tightened on her breast.

"Be still, wife, and relax against my hand. You don't need

to work so hard this time. Do we give it time, my rod will gain the strength to do its duty. Just close your eyes and let yourself feel where my fingers play.''

Mellisynt squeezed her eyes shut so tight she saw bright points of light behind her lids. And then, when he entered her, slow, rising stars. And, finally, a blinding flash of light that tore a ragged moan from deep in her throat.

Her last thought, before she drifted off to sleep, was that she'd better make her way to the chapel on the morrow. If Father Anselem had chastised her for unseemly demands on Henri, she shuddered to think what penance the priest here would impose on a wife who required a husband to service her not once, but twice, in one night!

Chapter Five

"Sir Richard!"

A loud pounding thrust them both into wakefulness. Darkness cloaked the room, except for a dim glow from the fire's embers. FitzHugh sprang out of bed, his hand groping for the dagger he'd laid beneath the mattress the night before.

"Sir Richard, a courier has just arrived. The news is urgent."

Mellisynt propped herself up on one elbow and watched as her husband stalked to the door, totally unconscious of his nakedness. When he flung it open, the oil lamp held by his squire wavered in the draft.

"What news?"

"The lord of Bellamy has broken the truce. He let a force of mercenaries into his keep, and they overran our garrison. Even now he barricades himself within the walls and defies all orders to surrender." Ian paused to catch his breath. "The duchess has called a council of all senior knights within the hour. She desires you attend her before the council."

"Tell her I'll be there immediately. And send the pages with my armor."

Mellisynt clutched the thick coverlet to her breast as FitzHugh threw logs onto the fire and used an iron rod to prod the smoldering embers into flames. Her clothes and his lay scattered before the hearth. As he bent to pull on his braies, two pages came with fresh clothing and armour. Bartholomew cast Mellisynt a quick, proud grin and he staggered in under the weight of his lord's precious mail shirt. Mellisynt suspected the forged iron links, threaded at intervals with silver gossets, weighed almost as much as the boy himself.

FitzHugh drew on his hose and his padded protective tunic, then knelt so that the two pages could lift the heavy mail shirt over his head and fasten the detached sleeves at the shoulders. Straightening, he threw the blue surcoat over his head. His long, blunt fingers fastened a sword belt low over his hips with the ease of long practice.

He strode for the door, the boys trailing behind him carrying gauntlets and shin guards. At the threshold he stopped abruptly, and Bartholomew crashed pell-mell into his back. With a muttered curse, he put the boy aside and came back to Mellisynt.

"'Twould do you better to stay with the duchess," he told her. "I know not how long I'll be gone. Draw upon her exchequer for your needs." He hesitated, then bent and brushed his lips across her cheek. "God keep you, wife."

"And you," she whispered.

FitzHugh followed the scurrying pages through the tall corridors. Flambeaux, set high on the walls in iron holders, cast patterns of light and dark on the smooth, tiled walkway. He was expected. A servant ushered him into a brightly lit *solar* where Constance paced. Geoffrey's chief minister for his French possessions, Roland de Dinan, a quiet, competent man of Breton birth, stood to one side.

Constance whirled when he entered. "That whoreson Bellamy! He waits only until Geoffrey is half across the sea before he recants his oath. You should have decorated the castle walls with his head when you subdued his rebellion the first time."

FitzHugh bit back a sharp reply and marshaled his patience. He knew well this tiny duchess was fiercer than any of the panthers in the king's menagerie when it came to her lands.

Geoffrey had married into a line that had held Brittany since the Charlemagne's time.

"I will rectify the error," FitzHugh told her.

"I want not one of his blood to see the new moon," Constance seethed.

"He has children."

"Put them to the sword!"

FitzHugh cast a quick glance at the minister. Roland shrugged and shook his head.

"Sheathe your claws, lady," FitzHugh said, with the bluntness of long service. "The count has only daughters. You know as well as I, 'tis more sensible to use them to your advantage. Give the girls in marriage to loyal knights who will hold Bellamy's land for the duke."

Deep violet eyes narrowed to angry slits. "Do you dare to tell me how to manage my lands, FitzHugh? If you and that doltish husband of mine had treated these rebels as they deserved, we'd not now have to send out more men."

"Geoffrey knew beheading the captured rebels would only stiffen the resistance of those who yet held out. That so many had surrendered without battle proved him right. You should be glad the rebellion was put down with so little loss of lives and livestock, instead of shrieking like a fishwife over the loss of one cod's head."

Constance glared at him a full minute longer. FitzHugh folded his arms and waited for her temper to ebb, as it always did.

"Don't give my husband credit for such clear thinking," she said finally. "He may be wondrously brave and a born leader of men, but he has the brains of a stillborn ass."

FitzHugh shot Roland de Dinan a quick look, and both men smothered their grins. They'd heard Constance say the same words to her laughing, infuriating husband on more than one occasion. Unfortunately, they were true.

"'Twas you who curbed his bloodlust, even as you do

mine,'' she conceded. "You've stood good friend to both of us these many years."

FitzHugh shrugged. "I owe Geoffrey much. And you, as well, my lady."

"The debt goes both ways. I was pleased Geoffrey had the rare sense to offer you Trémont's widow. Her wealth will help you restore that rambling ruin you claim as home."

"Aye," FitzHugh replied, noncommittal. He knew his tenacious hold on the small keep in England irritated Constance. She much preferred her native Brittany, and schemed endlessly to keep Geoffrey and his knights in France as much as possible.

"I like your bride, FitzHugh."

"She'll do well enough," he replied, itching to get back to the urgent business at hand.

The duchess's eyes narrowed at his offhand remark, but she followed his lead when he directed the conversation to the imminent council. FitzHugh gave her a list of the barons still remaining within quick recall of Nantes, and those yet awaiting transport. Although Constance would play no open role in directing the battle, FitzHugh knew she had a shrewder grasp of which nobles would respond than Geoffrey ever would. With Roland de Dinan's able assistance, they drew up an order of march. Lady and knights then repaired to the main hall for the council of war, in perfect accord on a battle plan.

The morning sun rose over the hills by the time FitzHugh led the advance guard through the city gates and headed north by east. He set a forced march, hoping to catch the wily lord of Bellamy before he could rally a force of any size to his side. The foot soldiers accompanying the mounted knights would have to trot to keep up, but FitzHugh knew they would do so easily. In their lighter mail and leather coverings, they could hold the pace longer than the knights, whose weighty armour wore down even their huge war-horses.

He felt a twinge of reluctance as the spires of Nantes faded in the distance behind them. For the first time in all his years of soldiering, FitzHugh regretted leaving a warm bed, and an even warmer wife. By all the saints, the Lady Mellisynt had surprised him last night. With her fire-kissed hair and uninhibited, untutored responses, she'd pulled the seed from his loins far sooner than he'd intended. FitzHugh couldn't remember the last time he'd lost control like that.

He shifted uncomfortably in the saddle as his groin tightened at the memory of their couplings. The discomfort annoyed him. He was unused to experiencing a lingering lust for any woman, especially one who was his wife. As his well-trained war-horse set one heavy hoof in front of the other, FitzHugh found himself pondering the Lady Mellisynt. After a week of marriage, he still did not know her well, nor know for sure where she stood. Most women were apolitical, amoral creatures, he knew. They would do what served their needs, regardless of oaths or duties. As would many men these days, FitzHugh was forced to acknowledge. In these troubled times, loyalties shifted with the tide. He straightened in the saddle and forced his attention from such troubling thoughts to the coming offensive.

By sunset, the troop had covered half the distance to Bellamy. Couriers brought reassuring word that the disaffected lord was caught within his keep, reinforced by a strong force of mercenaries. FitzHugh gave the men a brief rest while he conferred with the other senior commanders.

"If we push through this night, we have him."

FitzHugh nodded at Simon de Lacy. The old knight was descended from a long, illustrious line of robber barons whose principal keep dominated a strategic trade route between Brittany and Normandy. The senior knight who was technically in charge of the punitive force in Geoffrey's absence, de Lacy had great courage, but little skill at organizing or planning. He was shrewd enough to cede military decisions to FitzHugh while retaining the appearance of leadership—and the greatest share of the spoils, of course. FitzHugh wished some of Geoffrey's other vassals were as cooperative.

"We can't expect to take Bellamy as easily as we did before," another knight grunted. "This time he's brought in mercenaries. Those bastard sons and ragtag ruffians will want the chance to take booty and rise in circumstance."

FitzHugh ignored the sideways looks the other knights gave him. He was too used to the jealousies of Geoffrey's more nobly born vassals to let the slur affect him. Besides, the man spoke the truth.

"If Bellamy's defenders ride out for battle, so much the better. We are stronger and better equipped," Simon de Lacy asserted.

"Aye," FitzHugh agreed slowly. "For that reason, Bellamy will probably curb them and use their strength to hold the keep until Richard Lionheart sends reinforcements."

"If he will," another man interjected. "With the peace documents all but signed, and both princes en route to England, will Richard send men to support Bellamy?"

"If it gave him a foothold in Brittany, he would," Simon said. "Peace documents between the Angevin brothers last about as long as it takes the ink to dry. We can expect to sit on our thumbs outside the castle walls until the prince's troops arrive to force the issue or Bellamy is starved out."

FitzHugh surveyed the ring of men gathered around old Simon. They were a colorful lot, in polished armour and furred surcoats decorated with heraldic devices in bright shades of gold and crimson and azure. But FitzHugh saw beyond their varied plumage and rich fabrics, to the hardened knights who wore, as well, the scars of many battles. These men owed Geoffrey forty days' service at arms each year, and they, at least, had held to their oaths. FitzHugh knew to a day how much service remained on each man's duty, and how difficult it would be to keep them beyond their allotted time. As great lords with their own lands to manage, they could not stay away indefinitely. It would take promises of further fiefs and riches to keep them here for very long. Geoffrey would not be pleased if FitzHugh allowed his forces to settle in for a protracted siege.

"Bellamy is of earth and timber construction," he said with quiet authority. "We'll take it by fire if the lord will not fight."

A long, heated discussion followed, but in the end Fitz-Hugh's plan prevailed. By midmorning, he reined in his mount at the edge of the thick forest that surrounded the rebel keep. He gazed at the stronghold, set high on a mound of earth in the center of a broad clearing hacked out of the wood. Weariness and the throbbing ache in his knee faded as a slow surge of anticipation coursed through his veins. Within an hour he had the troops dispersed and the siege engines in place according to his will and Sir Simon's instructions. Within another half hour, he had Bellamy's contemptuous response to the order to surrender in hand.

Before the sun reached its zenith, the first balls of fire arced across the sky, trailing a shower of sparks from the catapults to the wooden palisade.

Mellisynt left the château's sumptuously appointed chapel, her head whirling. She'd skulked in her apartments for days, hesitant to leave, even to attend morning mass, because of a reluctance to visit the confessor. Finally, her conscience and long-ingrained habit drove her to seek out the priest. Her face burned as she remembered the list of offenses she'd whispered to the lean, ascetic prelate. Topping the list was the wanton way she'd responded to her husband!

Mellisynt knew full well the pleasure she had taken at FitzHugh's hands and lips was a grievous sin. Father Anselem had schooled her often enough on a wife's duty to receive her lord's seed without sinful, unholy passions. Especially when any kind of energetic response caused old Henri to spill himself prematurely, or lose his erection altogether. She knew by heart the passage from the book of penances, which punished the venial sin of desire within the marriage bed by forty days and nights of fasting.

To Mellisynt's amazed relief, the château priest had listened to her halting confession with a small smile. Such strictures against overindulgence and unseemly passion between husband and wife were intended to restrain men and lessen the burden of childbearing on women, he explained, as were the specified periods each month when no relations were allowed. Although he cautioned her against responding too immoderately, he sent her off with a light penance and the hope that she would soon bear the fruit of her marriage bed. Still stunned at the priest's leniency, Mellisynt wound her way through the maze of drafty halls.

Mayhap FitzHugh's seed had already taken root in her womb, she thought. A painful hope clutched at her heart. Her arms ached to hold her child, a tiny scrap of humanity all her own, to love without fear and without restraint. She hugged the thought to herself and continued, more slowly. After several wrong turns, she finally stood on the threshold of the duchess's *solar*.

Eyes wide and wondering, Mellisynt surveyed the colorful scene. Oil lamps augmented the light filtering in through rows of tall, leaded windows and illuminated a crowd of bright plumed courtiers scattered about the room. A richly gowned knight stood with one foot planted on a bench, picking out a melody on a strange, gourd-shaped instrument. Sleek greyhounds patrolled the room, their claws clicking against black and white tiles in counterpoint to the haunting tune. Used to floors covered by thick rushes, filled with fleas and the remains of bones thrown to the boar hounds, Mellisynt's eyes lingered on the clean, bright tiles. They gave the room an airy, spacious look. Bartholomew had told her they were an innovation from Moorish Spain and much copied in noble houses, even if they did make a page's life a misery. More than one youngster serving at the table had lost both his dignity and his lord's dinner when his pointed felt shoes slipped out from under him on the slick tiles.

Mellisynt drew in a quick breath as she surveyed the ladies' high-waisted gowns, trimmed in rich miniver and ermine and sable. Laced tight at the front to display the ladies' figures, the gowns gapped only enough to hint at the elaborate embroidered wool shifts underneath. Instead of fitted sleeves with pointed tips that served as half mittens against the cold, these ladies' robes sported cuffs so long that many had tied knots in the ends to keep them from dragging on the floor.

Trying to ignore the tongues of envy flicking up her spine, Mellisynt gathered her baggy gown in two firm hands and stepped into the *solar*. Constance looked up and smiled a warm greeting. "Welcome, Lady Mellisynt. Come, sit beside me and tell me how you fare."

"I am well, my lady," she replied, settling herself on a low, padded stool beside the duchess's chair. A buzz of interest rippled through the crowd. Mellisynt heard her name whispered, and FitzHugh's. Men and women alike surveyed her from head to toe, and she caught a flash of derision in more than one glance. She folded her hands together within the concealing swath of her gown and lifted her chin.

Constance saw the gesture and cast a frowning glance around her immediate circle. "You must excuse us, lady. The court's been shut away during these times of trouble. Any new face piques our interest. They would stare, even were you not the bride of FitzHugh."

Mellisynt turned questioning eyes at the woman's dry comment.

"We had long despaired of seeing him attached," the tiny, dark-haired duchess explained. "Tell me true now, are you well?"

"Yes, my aches are gone."

Mellisynt felt a twinge of guilt at the small lie, especially having just come from the confessional! If the truth be told, she carried a whole new set of aches. But this lingering soreness between her thighs had nothing to do with the horse she had ridden and everything to do with the man who had ridden her. She vowed to perish in flames, however, before she would ever admit to more pains of any sort.

"Well, while FitzHugh's gone you must rest and enjoy yourself. When he returns and carts you off to that dingy little keep he calls home, you'll have little enough time for pleasures."

Constance patted Mellisynt's hand and introduced her to those within her immediate circle. After a time, the courtiers picked up their individual conversations. When the plaintive melody resumed and drifted across the hall, Constance called out to the player.

"Sing your rondeau for us, Sir Guy. I'm most anxious to hear the song you've composed to your mysterious love."

The golden-haired knight smiled and crossed the hall. Constance whispered to Mellisynt that Guy de Claire's songs had won him almost as much renown as his exploits in battle. Mellisynt ran admiring eyes over the glorious embroidered device on de Claire's red velvet surcoat. It depicted three gilded lilies on a field of green. But when her gaze dropped to the knight's feet, she felt her mouth fall open in astonishment. The knight wore shoes with the longest, most pointed toes she'd ever seen. The tips protruded a good half foot in front of him, and their straw stuffing thumped against the tiles when he walked. Laughter gurgled in her throat. She covered it with a choked cough and glanced hastily around the room.

Over the heads of the other courtiers, a pair of merry brown eyes caught hers. Set in a well-shaped head crowned by curling brown hair, they invited her to share her mirth. Their owner, a tall, lean knight with a luxuriant mustache, smiled conspiratorially.

Mellisynt gasped, recognizing the face at once. It was the knight from the clearing, the one who had tried to take her

from FitzHugh. Her head whirled, and she wondered what a
knight sworn to Richard Lionheart was doing at the court of
Duke Geoffrey. Confused, she missed most of the trouba-
dour's song. Only when his pleasant baritone deepened in
pitch and intensity did his words register.

> My love's face is as a new bloom'd rose,
> Her breath as soft and fair as spring.
> Yet within such beauty lies a heart
> Cruel and unyielding to the one
> Who has loved her long from afar.

The singer's expressive eyes lingered on the duchess's face.
She smiled up at him and arched her dainty brows.

> Yet only to her do I sing of my feelings,
> Such is the love that keeps me discreet.

"La, Sir Guy," one of the ladies tittered, "you'd certainly
better be discreet. The last lady you pledged yourself to had
a most jealous husband."

The knight smiled. "A husband has no rights to his wife's
true love, or cause to be jealous. Marriage is a dull business,
after all."

"Especially when you're wed to a ten-year-old boy with
pustules still marking his face," another woman chimed in
grumpily. "Would that I had a lover my own age, one who
doesn't bury his face in my breasts and call me Mama. I hope
you win your lady's love, Sir Guy."

The lords and ladies of the court added their opinions as to
the worthiness of de Claire's suit, debating whether the unknown lady should yield to his advances. Mellisynt's ears began to burn at some of the franker suggestions to the aspiring
lover.

She listened to their badinage with growing amazement.
Stories of the cult of courtly love and the persuasive songs of

troubadours had reached even remote Trémont. But never in her wildest imagination would she have believed that men and women would discuss love and…and passion so openly. Her eyes rounded as she thought of what Father Anselem's reaction to such verses would have been, and the amount of time she'd have spent on her knees had she dared flutter her lashes at any man, as the duchess was now doing.

"What think you, Lady Mellisynt?" Constance turned, a mischievous light twinkling in her eyes. "You're the newest to the court, and most unbiased. Should Sir Guy win his lady's love?"

"Nay, my lady," Mellisynt protested, stammering. "I couldn't say."

"But surely you have an opinion?" the singer asked with a slight, mocking smile.

"Nay, truly. I know naught of love…of passion…of such emotions."

"Wed to the bastard FitzHugh, I'm not surprised," Sir Guy drawled.

Constance snapped her brows together, but not in time to stop the low laughter that rippled through the court.

Mellisynt straightened slowly on her stool and met the knight's malicious look with a steady gaze. She might know naught of the love he sang about, but she'd allow no insult to her lord.

"Indeed," she agreed coolly, "you *should* not be surprised. Little as I yet know my husband, I misdoubt he would countenance the adultery you espouse in your song. He holds true to his oaths of honor and virtue and loyalty."

A startled silence fell. The ugly word *adultery* seemed to hang on the air and clash with the concept of delicious, forbidden love. Sir Guy's grin slipped, then hardened into a thin, tight line.

"'Tis only a song after all," a lazy voice drawled. "And not a very good one, de Claire. You'll have to work on the last verse."

A tall, lean figure detached himself from the crowd and sauntered forward. Mellisynt looked up into the brown eyes that had mirrored her laughter only minutes before.

"I am Beauchamp, Lady Mellisynt. We met before, while you were...en route to Nantes."

"I remember," Mellisynt told him, her voice dry.

"FitzHugh and I shared a campfire more than once, before this latest war put us on opposite sides. Will you walk with me and tell me how the devil an ugly, distempered rogue like that convinced you to wed him?"

Mellisynt felt a smile tug at her lips. Where only moments before Sir Guy's sneering comments had raised her hackles, Beauchamp's good-natured insults invited mirth. She glanced at Constance for permission, then took his outstretched hand and allowed him to pull her to her feet. When the babble of voices rose behind them, Beauchamp gave her hand a friendly squeeze.

"I know not if you intended to put Sir Guy in his place, but 'twas well and surely done. He's most proud of his poetry."

Mellisynt glanced up and saw the silky mustache part in a smile.

"I would be careful, though," the knight continued. "However much he may look the languid courtier, de Claire has a swift, sure sword. He's long carried malice toward your lord for unseating him in a tourney some years ago. He's a prideful little cock. You'd best watch him."

Mellisynt gave a choking laugh. "Pray, excuse me. I find it somewhat strange to be taking advice from one who but a week ago crossed swords with my husband."

"Ah, but he wasn't your husband then." Beauchamp grinned, leading her to a window seat at the far end of the hall. "Had I been but a day sooner, mayhap he would not be, even now."

"What do you here?" Mellisynt asked, pulling her hand

free of the knight's light grasp. "How came you to the court of your enemy?"

"Geoffrey was my enemy last week. With the truce, he's once again my overlord."

At Mellisynt's startled gasp, he leaned back against the stone window casing and grinned.

"I know, 'tis most damnably difficult to keep it all straight. Like many old families, mine stole or acquired by marriage lands scattered across all of France and half of England. I owe Richard Lionheart allegiance for holdings in Aquitaine and Anjou, and Geoffrey for holdings in Brittany. I came this week to renew my pledge to Constance, in Geoffrey's absence."

"And she accepted?"

"Aye, of course. Until this last madness, I paid my knight's fees faithfully to Geoffrey and fought beside him in many a skirmish. And beside your lord."

Mellisynt shook her head at the confused logic of men. How could they so easily forget the enmity of just a week ago? To be sure, she didn't forget or forgive her grudges as easily. She grimaced, thinking of the hard kernel of resentment toward the duke she'd carried in her breast for so long.

With a connoisseur's eye, Beauchamp watched the emotions play across the pale face before him. By the saints, there was something more to this little widow than just her reputed inheritance. Those lashes framed eyes of startling depth and intelligence, though she kept them shielded most of the time. His gaze flicked over her dowdy dress, discerning the trim figure beneath. He felt a fleeting regret he'd not carried her off and discovered what else lay buried under those absurd gowns. He hooked a finger under Mellisynt's chin and turned her face up to his.

"If I can do aught to help you, or ease your way at court, I would be honored."

"Thank you, my lord."

Mellisynt pulled her chin away and rose. Friendship was

one thing. Allowing a man to put hands on her was another. She shuddered to think of the penance that small touch would have earned her at Trémont. With a tight smile, she drifted back to the crowd of courtiers and took a seat in a secluded niche.

She found it easy to stay in the background in the days that followed. Embarrassed as much by her outmoded wardrobe as by her naiveté concerning noble manners and mores, she dwelt at the fringes of the gay group surrounding Constance. She found much to entertain her in simply watching and listening. Beauchamp joined her occasionally, making her laugh with his droll interpretation of the court's antics.

Gradually, she grew more accustomed to, and less shocked by, the concept of a noble, physical love outside the vows of marriage. Still, however much the ladies might sigh over their chivalrous lovers and troubadours might sing of the purity of their passion, Mellisynt struggled with the whole idea. She'd experienced little love in her first marriage, to be sure, nor did she expect any in this one. Yet still she shrank from the thought of violating her holy vows.

The duchess treated Mellisynt with kindness, when she noticed her at all. The burdens of administering Brittany in Geoffrey's absence consumed most of her time. And word soon circulated that Constance quickened with her first child. Mellisynt offered warm congratulations, and sternly repressed a shaft of envy. Seated before the fire in her own apartments late one night, she wondered when she, too, would carry the spark of life within her. By imperceptible degrees, she found herself thinking less of the child she wanted and more of the process that would produce it.

Despite her stern admonition not to dwell on such carnal matters, memories of how FitzHugh had taken her there, on that very hearth, warmed her blood. Her face tingled with heat, as did her belly. Hugging her arms around her middle, she slid into bed.

She awoke the next morning to Bartholomew's hasty pounding on her door.

"My lady, Sir Richard returns this day."

Mellisynt scrambled out of bed and threw on a mantle to cover her shift. Her toes curled against the cold tiles as she ran to admit the breathless page.

"Truly, lady, a messenger just arrived and was closeted with the duchess. Word is that Bellamy surrendered after mere token resistance, and the lord's eldest was given as hostage."

"And he's taken no injury or hurt?"

Bartholomew's brows furrowed. "The lord of Bellamy?"

"Nay, Sir Richard!"

The boy shrugged. "None that were reported. Even if he's wounded, it can't be that bad, since he rides."

Mellisynt marveled at the page's cheerful unconcern as she dressed. Her own heart hammered, both in anticipation and in relief. Never having been exposed to the ravages of war, she had only a vague idea of the death and destruction it involved. The thought that her husband had been in the midst of such carnage made her queasy. Still, she'd married FitzHugh for his strength and vigor. She couldn't expect a man of his temperament to sit behind castle walls and hire mercenaries to fight his battles, as old Henri had.

The heralds announced FitzHugh's arrival just as the squires were clearing the boards from the noon meal. Constance herself headed the welcoming party that surged out onto the castle steps to greet him. She tugged Mellisynt with her to the front of the crowd.

"God's blessing, Sir Richard. Your safe arrival is as welcome as the news that you've taken Bellamy."

FitzHugh climbed down from his mount, his movements stiff and weary. He knelt to kiss the duchess's extended hand.

Mellisynt's little rehearsed greeting died on her lips as he rose, gave her an absent nod, then turned away. She watched him stride to a docile palfrey and lift down a heavily cloaked, hooded figure. Leading the figure forward, he stepped aside. The woman threw back her hood and knelt before Constance.

A collective gasp floated on the thin winter air. Mellisynt felt her own breath catch in her throat as she surveyed the most stunningly beautiful girl she had ever seen.

Chapter Six

"I am Isabeau of Bellamy, my lady. I come in surety of my father's obedience to your will."

The words identified the girl as a political hostage, but neither her voice nor her manner carried any hint of submission. She held her head high, its curling masses of blue-black hair catching the sun's light. Under delicate, arched brows, eyes the color of Brittany's storm-tossed seas met those of the duchess squarely. Her skin was smooth and white, with rose tints where the winter cold had kissed it. As the silence about her lengthened, the girl's tongue came out to wet one corner of her red lips, but she displayed no other sign of nervousness.

Constance gave her head a slight shake, as if rousing herself from a trance. Holding out a hand, she lifted the girl to her feet.

"Your father is fortunate to have so beauteous a daughter to send as hostage," she said, a hint of acid in her tone. "Mayhap you can soften the duke's fury with your recreant sire. When Duke Geoffrey returns, we shall decide your fate, and that of your father."

The duchess turned to give FitzHugh a warm smile. "Attend me later, when you have rested and soaked the chill from your bones. The rest of the knights will have returned by then. This night we shall have a special feast in honor of your victory."

Mellisynt stood quietly while her husband gave orders to

the troop to disperse. When he turned and started, as if surprised at her presence, she forced a greeting through stiff lips.

"I bid you welcome, my lord."

FitzHugh bent down to press a quick salute on her chilled cheek.

"Thank you."

Turning to lead the way inside, Mellisynt told herself she should be grateful that he had returned whole. 'Twas silly to expect effusive greetings from one who looked as tired and drawn as he did. Still, she felt a small niggle of feminine pique at the absentmindedness of his salute. Inside their rooms, she gave the servants orders for immediate hot water and went to help him disrobe.

"You don't need to sully yourself with my dirt," he told her, unbuckling his sword belt. "My squire will be here shortly."

"Nay, 'tis my duty," Mellisynt told him. She reached for the hem of his sodden surcoat.

FitzHugh shrugged and bent at the waist so that she could pull it off. She had laid it across a bench and was tugging at his heavy mail shirt when Ian arrived. The squire was as muddy and tired-looking as his lord, but he was well trained in his duties. He gave Mellisynt a respectful nod and stepped forward to finish the disrobing. FitzHugh grunted when his mail shirt came off, then quickly shed the rest of his clothes. A short time later he folded his bulk into a round copper tub, giving a low groan of pleasure as the hot water soaked into his chilled skin. The squire departed to clean his precious mail and heavy sword.

Mellisynt moved forward to kneel beside the tub. Picking up a rag, she spread it with soft soap and began to cleanse his back.

"Sweet Mother!"

"What?" FitzHugh opened his eyes and threw a quick glance over his shoulder.

"You have a bruise the size of a pomegranate on your back. 'Tis discolored and embedded with bits of mail."

"God's bones," FitzHugh cursed. "'Twill cost a fistful of silver pennies to repair that mail."

"'Twill cost more to repair your back, should it fester," Mellisynt responded tartly. "Lean forward, so that I may cleanse the wound."

With steady fingers, she picked the twisted bits of metal out of his inflamed flesh. While he finished his bath, she sent a page for ointment and clean linen. Positioning her lord before the fire, she doctored the lesion.

As she bent to wrap linen bandages around his chest, FitzHugh glanced down at his wife's neatly braided auburn hair. The memory of its thick, silky feel teased at his mind and chased the weariness from his body.

When she finished, he pulled on dry clothes with a grateful sigh, then crossed to his discarded surcoat.

Pulling a small leather pouch from a side pocket, he held it out.

"Here."

Her eyes opened wide.

"'Tis your bride gift. I had not time to find something suitable sooner." He pushed the pouch into her slack hand.

She opened the drawstring and gasped when a heavy gold brooch tumbled into her palm. Golden wires, twisted together to the thickness of a man's little finger, formed an intricate knot around a glittering square-cut emerald. Mellisynt touched the gem's faceted surface with trembling fingers. When she lifted her eyes to his, they glowed a brighter, deeper green than the stone.

"I've never had such a gift," she breathed.

Embarrassed, he shrugged. "The lady of Bellamy was most reluctant to part with it, but I thought you would like it."

The glow left her eyes like snow melting under an early spring sun. Thick black lashes swept down to hide her gaze from his view. FitzHugh placed his knuckles under her chin and tipped her face to his.

"Do you disdain the pin because it was taken as booty?" he asked, a harsh edge to his voice. "You need not. Bellamy knew he placed himself at risk when he broke his sworn oath to Geoffrey. He's lucky he lost only his possessions, and not his head."

Her closed, still face pricked at his pride. He had nothing to offer this woman but what he earned by the strength of his arm.

"I will not have you scorn what trinkets I choose to bring you. Such booty is the prize of battle."

"And you ever fight the duke's battles."

The disdain in her voice took him aback, then lit a slow anger in his gut.

"Aye," he told her, the word a soft warning. "I do."

She tried to jerk her chin away. His grip tightened.

"And you will wear the baubles I bring you from such battles."

Rebellion flared in her eyes before her dark lashes swept down to hide them from his scrutiny. She held herself rigid and unmoving while FitzHugh studied her set face. Finally his hand loosened. He scowled at the red marks on the fragile skin of her jaw. Annoyance at her stubbornness and anger at himself for marking her so roughened his voice.

"I must give the duchess my report. I'll see you at the evening meal."

When FitzHugh entered the main hall with Constance some hours later, he scanned the crowded benches for his lady. Irritation at his mishandling of her earlier lingered in his mind. Instead of setting up her stubborn back, he should have drawn her out, explored the reasons behind her simmering dislike of Geoffrey. FitzHugh had let pass her barely veiled discourtesy to the duke at their wedding, ascribing it to the stress of the day, but now he wondered at Mellisynt's animosity. Was it but a woman's resentment at being used as a pawn? Did it run so deep she would betray the duke, and her husband, given the chance? Surprised at how much the thought disturbed him, FitzHugh moved through the milling throng.

He spotted Mellisynt seated on a crowded bench beside a plump older woman. He started toward her, then stopped, a disbelieving scowl settling on his face. His wife wore a plain amber gown, unadorned by any touch of color. And bare of all jewelry. She dared scorn his gift. He felt the muscles beside his jaw tighten, and he moved forward once more.

A low, musical greeting stopped him halfway across the hall.

"God give you good even, Sir Richard."

After two days of travel in Isabeau of Bellamy's company, he would have recognized her voice blindfolded. And her scent. She wore a heady musk, redolent of the East and exotic nights. FitzHugh turned and acknowledged her greeting.

"And you, my lady. Are you settled and housed to your liking?"

Isabeau pouted prettily, a mischievous sparkle in her aquamarine eyes. "I'm put with three young girls. They are but children, in service to the duchess. I would rather be with women my age, to learn the secrets of the court and the choicest gossip."

FitzHugh felt his face relax into the makings of a smile. "I misdoubt you'll ferret out the gossip, regardless of your roommates. You have but to flash your eyes and you'll have all the courtiers at your feet, as you did half my troop."

"But not you, my lord," she murmured, slanting him a coquette's look from under kohl-darkened eyes. "You seemed most impervious to my charms."

FitzHugh bit back a grin at the chit's precocious femininity. In truth, her antics had kept him quietly amused throughout the two-day journey from Bellamy. His troop had barely ridden out of her father's keep before the supposed prisoner began testing her wiles on his men. His squire, Ian, had all but fallen off his horse helping the girl to dismount when they stopped to rest. More than one begrimed man-at-arms had tugged his forelock in bumbling awe at her sultry looks and luring smiles.

"Nay, Lady Isabeau, a man would have to be dead to be impervious to your wiles. But you should practice them on someone younger, less graybeard."

"Surely you, who made your fortune in the lists, know how much more challenging it is to attempt the harder target," she purred. She placed a soft white hand on his arm. "Please, will you not share a trencher with me? I know none of these people here, only you."

FitzHugh glanced over at his wife. She caught his look, lifted a haughty eyebrow, and turned away to speak to the woman beside her. With a slight shrug, he escorted the girl to a nearby seat. He'd deal with the Lady Mellisynt later.

Not even Isabeau's innocently provocative remarks could keep FitzHugh's attention from wandering as the meal progressed. As promised, Constance had turned the occasion into a banquet in honor of the returning knights. Doughty old Simon de Lacy, the senior vassal present, sat beside the duchess in the place of honor. Squires in puffed sleeves and pointed shoes served to the sound of pipes as course followed course and minstrels entertained the chattering crowd.

More used to simple soldier's fare than heavily spiced sauces and towering pasties in the shape of castles and cathedrals, FitzHugh had soon had his fill. He stretched his long legs under the table and recognized anew why he avoided Geoffrey's court whenever possible. A man couldn't even eat his supper without some damned doves bursting out of a pie and flapping around his ears.

He gave muttered thanks when Constance called for the boards to be cleared, the silverware counted and the leftovers distributed to the servants. Working the ache out of his left knee, he rose.

"Will there be dancing, do you think?" Isabeau sounded more little girl than budding woman in her excitement.

"Unfortunately so."

Her smile slipped at his disgruntled reply, and FitzHugh relented. "I believe the dancing master has some new steps to show the court. Come, I'll take you to him so you can meet him before the music begins."

From the corner of one eye, Mellisynt saw FitzHugh lead the Lady Isabeau to a far alcove. His dark head was bent over shining curls of a similar shade, and the chit smiled up at him shamelessly. Mellisynt clenched her fists in the folds of her skirts. An emotion as unfamiliar as it was fierce rushed through her. Only after a succession of deep breaths did she recognize the feeling for what it was. Jealousy. Pure, unadulterated jealousy.

Startled by the intensity of her disquiet, Mellisynt tried to banish it. What did it matter to her, after all, if FitzHugh chose to dally with this girl? She was welcome to the brute. Mellisynt rubbed her still-tender jaw, trying to whip up the anger and resentment she'd felt but a few hours ago, when he'd tried to impose his will upon her. But the anger wouldn't come. Instead, an insidious hurt wrapped its coils around her heart.

She traced a pattern in the table's cloth with the tip of one finger and berated herself for feeling hurt. So FitzHugh had been kind on occasion? So he'd been most thorough in their coupling, teaching her more about her body in one night than Henri had ever managed in all his years of fumbling? So he employed his hands and mouth in ways that left her feeling breathless just to think on them? She mustn't attach too much importance to their physical activities. 'Twas a natural function, after all, an expected part of marriage.

Theirs was a political joining, she reminded herself. He wed to secure lands and wealth, she to escape Trémont's walls and take a babe from his seed. FitzHugh was but fulfilling his duty when he took her to his bed. Just because she'd enjoyed the experience mightily, that was no reason to feel this searing jealousy when he smiled down at an overripe, forward piece of baggage.

"I see FitzHugh has brought us a pretty child."

Mellisynt glanced up from her study of the woven tablecloth to see Roger Beauchamp at her shoulder. She followed his bland look to where FitzHugh and the girl stood in intimate conversation with another courtier.

"The Lady Isabeau is passing beauteous," she agreed.

"But still a child," he said, dismissing the court's newest addition with a lazy smile. "Not to be compared with—"

A fanfare from the balcony above cut him off. The household seneschal stepped forward and thumped the tiled floor with his staff. Murmurs of delight greeted his announcement of the rigaudon, a gay, rollicking dance new to the court.

"Come, lady, I would partner you in this dance." Beauchamp took her hand in a warm, sure grip.

"Nay, my lord, I do not dance."

He ignored her urgent protests. With a steady tug, he brought her to her feet. Mellisynt tried to hold back, but, short of throwing herself to the floor, she couldn't stop him. Grimfaced, she caught her heavy skirts up over one arm and took a place in the ring of dancers.

"Just listen to the music and step with it," he told her, his voice light and teasing. "And try not to look as if you swallowed a bowl of curdled milk."

Mellisynt gave an involuntary laugh, then looked helplessly about as the music sounded and the dancers began to circle. The woman to her right stumbled into her.

"Move!" the woman snapped, giving her a little shove.

Mellisynt caught Beauchamp's wide grin and moved. Slowly at first, then with gathering confidence as she began to discern the pattern. Her eyes followed the dancers' nimble movements, watching how the ladies managed their swirling skirts, and the men their long, pointed shoes with grace and skill. In line with the ladies, she took a few skipping steps across the tile. Gradually she caught the rhythm, and her

movements became more elaborate. When she executed a dipping, swaying turn in time with her partner, she gave a little
laugh of triumph.

"Well, well," Beauchamp murmured, surveying her flushed
face and glowing eyes. "There's fire under that demure exterior."

"'Tis only breathlessness, my lord," Mellisynt responded,
laughing.

When the first round ended, she tingled with unaccustomed
pleasure. She'd never danced before in her life. Indeed, Father
Anselem had often decried the evil of such abandoned activity,
and had once read a text from the bishop of Rennes expressly
forbidding dancing in the church aisles by peasants. But, by
the saints, it made her heart gallop and her blood race most
feverishly.

Beauchamp bowed low over her hand. "Your grace and
spirit are delightful, my lady. Will you dance the second round
with me?"

"Nay, she will not."

Mellisynt felt the hairs on the nape of her neck lift at
FitzHugh's deliberate drawl. Her pleasure evaporated, and a
sick feeling rose in her stomach. She swallowed and turned to
face her husband.

"I was about to refuse him, my lord."

"Good." FitzHugh's blue eyes glinted. "I would not have
my wife in the company of such a smooth-tongued, pretty-
faced courtier."

"Then you should guard her better." Beauchamp's light,
mocking voice drew her husband's gaze. "The lady's too
charming to be satisfied for long with a heavy-handed dolt of
a husband such as you, FitzHugh."

Mellisynt gasped and cast her husband a frightened look.
"He's...he's but making sport. Please, my lord, I wish to retire. May we leave now?"

She bent to gather the weight of her skirt, and completely

missed the startled look the two men exchanged above her head.

"Has this churl in knight's clothing been bothering you?" FitzHugh asked, frowning.

"No! No, I swear!" She clutched his arm.

Beauchamp straightened slowly. "By all the saints, Fitz-Hugh, I knew you lacked address with anything not on four legs. But to cause such unease in just a week of marriage is something of an achievement, even for you."

"Begone, Roger," FitzHugh told him quietly, his eyes on Mellisynt's white face. He took her arm and started to lead her toward the dim corridor. Beauchamp took an involuntary step forward.

FitzHugh gave the other knight a hard, level look. "I'll see to my wife, Beauchamp."

After a long pause, the younger man nodded once, stiffly, then stood aside.

FitzHugh could feel the tremor in her arm as he guided his lady through the dim corridors. Icy drafts whistled along the vaulted ceilings, raising acrid gusts of smoke from the flickering flambeaux. He knew full well, however, that it wasn't the cold that made the lady tremble. He glanced down at the woman stumbling along beside him. She was pale and pinched of face now, but just moments before he had seen her laughing up at Beauchamp with a beguiling liveliness. Like creeping, insidious tendrils of mist, the castle priest's words crept into FitzHugh's head. Was this woman the wanton the fat little cleric had hinted at? Did she laugh so merrily with other men to lead them into dalliance?

He dismissed the idea immediately. Mellisynt's untutored responses during their coupling told their own story. Thoughts of that night, and the way her trim, taut body had arched against his own, hesitantly at first, then with growing enthusiasm, crowded out the priest's ugly insinuations. They also made FitzHugh revise instantly the punishment he'd decided upon for his wife's insolence in rejecting his bride gift. First, however, he needed to deal with the fear still darkening her eyes.

He released her when they entered their apartments. Ian was polishing an assortment of armour beside the fire, and was sent from the room with a quick jerk of his master's head. The door closed firmly behind the squire, and FitzHugh shot the bolt.

"Tell me what makes your hands shake so and your face pale," he ordered softly.

His wife whirled to face him. "Nothing. Nothing, I swear. 'Tis just the cold."

"It can't be nothing and the cold, both. Make up your mind, lady wife."

Moving slowly, so as not to frighten her more, FitzHugh crossed the room and poured wine into chased silver goblets. He swirled the rich Burgundian red around in one cup a few times, then handed it to the still, pale woman before him.

"Tell me," he ordered.

The wine splashed over the rim onto Mellisynt's gown. Taking a deep breath, she plunged into speech.

"He only touched me in the dance, my lord, I swear it! I tried to refuse, but did not want to make too much disturbance with my protests. There was nothing else between us, upon my soul."

"I didn't think there was."

His calm response brought her up short.

"You didn't?" Disbelief and fear edged her voice.

"Nay. I saw you clearly across the hall. Beauchamp has a well-deserved reputation with women, but even he couldn't manage to seduce you in a crowded hall while prancing around in circles like a silly jackanapes."

FitzHugh could see her tension ease with his casual words. Some of the rigidity flowed from her body, and the fright from her eyes. He went forward to lead her to the chairs before the fire, then halted abruptly when she stumbled backward, away from him.

His eyes narrowed, and then he moved toward her again with a steady, unhurried tread. Taking her arm, he settled first her, then himself, in the chairs.

Mellisynt sat stiff and uncomfortable, chewing on her lower lip. Her eyes stared unseeing at the snapping fire while her mind churned with FitzHugh's last words.

"Did you really not take umbrage at my dancing with Sir Roger?"

"I did not."

His calm words gave her pause. That he was not jealous of the handsome, devilish Beauchamp reassured her. Perversely, it also added to her little store of hurt. Telling herself that she should be glad this husband viewed their marriage dispassionately, as a business arrangement, Mellisynt stared into the fire.

"I take it Sir Henri objected to such activities rather strenuously?"

She flashed him a wary look. He sprawled, loose and long-limbed and totally at ease.

"Aye," she said, slowly.

"Or to any activity that put you in the way of other men?"

"To any other men at all," she admitted finally. "He was most…"

"Jealous of his young wife," FitzHugh finished when she seemed disinclined to.

"Aye." She sighed, then relaxed against the padded chair back. "I lost count of the number of men he had banished from the castle and his lands because he thought they gave me too warm a look, or because they dared to kiss my hand. Men whose livelihood depended on Henri's goodwill were turned out with their families to starve."

She turned her head and regarded him steadily. "Some took more than just his ill wishes with them. One poor knight swilled too much ale and pressed on me the embraces he thought my infirm husband could not. He carried away two broken thumbs and a fine web of lash marks on his back."

FitzHugh stretched his long legs out and crossed his ankles.

"I cannot fault Henri for that. Any man who dared insult you so would fare far worse at my hands." He paused as a log crackled and gave off a shower of sparks. "And you? Did you not take some hurt from his jealousies, as well?"

Her mouth turned down in a rueful smile.

"No, no real hurt. Just fasts and penances, and they were scarce noticeable among all the other days and weeks I spent on my knees. I seemed to collect such punishments regularly."

"Aye, I would guess that you did."

Mellisynt decided to ignore his observation. A slumbrous silence descended, punctuated only by the hiss and crackle of the fire. Finally, driven by curiosity, she turned to him once more.

"If you were truly not angry, my lord, why did you sound so...so harsh when you came upon us?"

"I didn't say I was not angry. Just that I was not disturbed by your dancing."

Mellisynt straightened, her brows drawing together in confusion. "Then what caused your anger?"

"Your willfulness, lady wife."

"What?"

FitzHugh took a slow sip of wine. "You heard me."

"What willfulness?"

"Did I not tell you I wished you to wear the bride gift I brought you?"

"Aye," she said, caution threading her voice. "But you didn't say I should wear it this night."

One dark eyebrow quirked. "Do you truly mistake my meaning so?"

Mellisynt felt the heat of the fire on her cheeks. "No."

"I thought as much." He set his wine aside and folded his hands across his stomach.

She waited, her breath caught in her throat, while the silence stretched between them. When her nerves could bear it no longer, she broke the stillness.

"All right, I admit my temper ran away with me! I didn't

wear the brooch because I hated that you won it on...on the duke's business.''

FitzHugh surveyed her thoughtfully. ''Aye, I thought as much. Tell me why you carry this hatred for Geoffrey in your breast. He is your overlord, as well as mine.''

''Aye.'' She sneered. ''And a fine protector he is, too. He would sell a child to one like Henri of Trémont, then ride off with his pockets full of gold and nary a backward glance, like the veriest whoremaster.''

The simmering resentment in her voice startled even Mellisynt. She sat back, her hands grasping the wooden chair arms, expecting FitzHugh's censure for such disrespect.

To her surprise, he simply nodded. ''′Tis the way of the world, to arrange marriages that bring the most advantage. Geoffrey gave a girl in his wardship to the lord of a strategic castle, one that guards his borders. Just as he gave you to me, to hold and protect that same castle.''

His even, measured tone, and the steady way he regarded her from beneath his dark brows, took much of the heat from Mellisynt's argument. All that was left was the pain of her lost youth. The tight knot of resentment, buried so long in her heart, loosened, but did not completely disappear.

''And you, my lord, would do the same? If we have daughters, will you give them to any man who can bring you gold or lands? Will you care if they ever again see the sun or hear a voice raised in song?''

FitzHugh frowned, and Mellisynt saw a flash of uncertainty cross his face. This stern warrior had not thought in terms of daughters, only sons, she realized.

''Is that what you endured?''

Mellisynt brushed aside her years at Trémont with an impatient hand. ''Aye, but I don't seek your pity. I want only your understanding.'' She paused, taking a deep breath. ''And your pledge that you will not use our daughters so, should we have any. I ask your promise that you will allow them joy and...and love in their marriages, if possible.''

His blue eyes settled on her face in a considering look. At length, he shook his head. "Love is an ill-defined emotion at best, found only in the troubadours' songs. Like you, I've seen little enough of it in my life. If we find trust and respect, and a touch of lust, in our marriage, we may count ourselves fortunate."

He held up a hand when Mellisynt would have protested. "I can't promise that the husbands chosen for our daughters will bring them more. But I do promise that I will consult with you before entering into an agreement for our children, do you wish it."

Mellisynt's eyes widened in stunned surprise. That Fitz-Hugh would grant her a say in the disposition of their children was beyond anything she'd imagined or hoped for. The knot of anger she'd carried for so long loosened even more.

"Aye," she breathed. "I wish it."

She slanted her husband an assessing look. His forbearance astounded her. For a man of his fearsome reputation in the field, he'd been remarkably restrained with her throughout their short betrothal and marriage. Except for his spurt of anger earlier, when she'd refused his gift, he'd treated her with respect and gentle hands. And that one incident had been as much her fault as his, Mellisynt decided magnanimously. Thinking to reward his remarkable promise with one of her own, she smiled across the small space separating their chairs.

"I apologize for letting my temper lead me to spurn your bride gift this eve. I'll wear it in all graciousness, if you will pardon my willfulness."

"No."

Her smile slipped. "No?"

"No, 'tis not enough." He turned his head. "You must learn that I don't make unreasonable demands, and those I make I expect to be obeyed. Take off your clothes."

"What?"

"Do you have a disorder of the ear, as well as a willful temper, wife?"

He rose with a loose-limbed grace that belied his size and reached for the buckle of his belt.

Mellisynt sprang up. "You puling caitiff! You would beat me?"

"The idea does hold some appeal," FitzHugh replied. "Now take off your clothes, loose your hair and lay yourself down in the bed before I decide to do so."

Chapter Seven

Mellisynt awoke the next morning feeling most properly chastised. And wondrously well used. She was discovering there was much more to this business of coupling than she'd ever dreamed possible. Lifting the deadweight of FitzHugh's arm from her chest, she slipped out of bed. Muscles she had never known she had protested as she groped her way through the dark to the pile of clothing scattered about the floor. She pulled her shift over her head, grateful for its thin warmth, then wrapped FitzHugh's discarded surcoat around her like a blanket. With a small groan, she sank down beside the hearth and began to feed the banked embers bits of kindling. Propping her chin on arms folded across her knees, she watched the coals begin to glow, then catch the kindling in tiny flames.

Sweet Mother of God, how she ached. A heat having nothing to do with the small, hissing fire suffused her face. Who would have thought a man's body could be the instrument of such exquisite punishment? That it could stretch and invade and fill her until she thought she'd burst? Only to be withdrawn and replaced by hands and lips that drove her to panting, sweating, groaning madness. For the first time, Mellisynt had experienced a male in full rut, a magnificent, sleekly muscled, powerful male who sought to demonstrate his dominance in the most elemental way possible.

Her face burned as she remembered FitzHugh's deliberate assault on her senses, his slow, determined pacing, her own gasping panic as he pushed her into a vortex of sensation the like of which she'd never dreamed of, let alone experienced, in all her life. She would have felt shamed by her wild, uninhibited responses if his low, rasping moans hadn't grown in volume toward the end until they matched hers, and he seemed to lose control of his own movements. What had begun as a lesson for one had ended in an explosion of erotic sensation for both.

As she studied the dancing flames, Mellisynt began to understand the courtiers' preoccupation with this business of love. To combine such...such passion with a fine, noble dedication of one's heart to another must surely be a worthy goal, even if unattainable.

With a small groan, she struggled to her feet. Shrugging off the heavy surcoat, she reached for her discarded robe.

"The aches ease with time and repeated effort."

She jumped and clutched her gown to her chest. Turning, she discovered her husband stretched comfortably in bed, his head pillowed on his hands.

"Do we repeat last night, I will not ache. I will be dead," she told him with a grimace only half feigned.

White teeth gleamed in his stubble-darkened face. "'Tis how many refer to the act of joining—*la petite mort,* the little death."

"There was nothing little about it, as I recall."

Her tart rejoinder brought what looked suspiciously like smug satisfaction to his face. She turned away, unwilling to pander to such masculine conceit. Pulling on her much-worn amber bliaut, she attacked its tangled ties with cold, stiff fingers.

"Did Henri force you to robe yourself, thus, in such shapeless rags?"

She glanced over to find him surveying her gown with distaste.

"Nay, he had me dress in gray wool habits so nunlike that at times I near forgot I was not a bride of Christ." Her fingers stroked the faithful yellow silk. "This was one of the gowns I brought with me to Trémont as a bride. 'Tis a bit outmoded, but has use yet in it."

The mattress stuffing rustled as FitzHugh brought his arms down and pushed aside the covers. Magnificent in his nakedness, he crossed the room. Faint fingers of dawn creeping through the high windows painted his body in shadow and light. Mellisynt ran new, experienced eyes over his massive torso and swallowed. Sweet Mother, what he could do with...

"Did the lickpenny you were wed to teach you his miserly ways?" His voice rumbled in her ear like a distant summer storm. "Why do you not buy yourself new gowns? The markets here in Nantes have goods from the four corners of the world."

Mellisynt looked up at him, her eyes wide. "I didn't think... I didn't know you wished it."

His brows knitted. "List to me, lady wife," he began. "I'm not Henri of Trémont. I—"

Mellisynt's indelicate snort interrupted him. "If I were not already aware of that, my lord, last night would have certainly made it clear."

She flicked a quick glance down his chest, lingered for a moment at his loins, then brought her gaze back to his face once more. His lips twitched, and he turned away to pick up his braies. Mellisynt surveyed two taut white buttocks with considerable attention. When he had covered them, and other parts of similar interest, he turned to face her once more.

"I'm no weak old man, lady. I'm fully capable of managing my most valued possessions, whether they be lands or armour or war-horses or wife. I don't require you to dress in rags to discourage overardent swains."

Mellisynt stiffened. "I'm not sure I care to be considered a possession of somewhat lesser worth than your horse, my lord."

One corner of FitzHugh's mouth lifted. "That's because you know nothing of horses, let alone destriers. A good one is much more difficult to obtain, and takes far longer to break in, than a wife.''

He laughed outright at her indignant gasp. ''Much as I value them, however, I will not have my horses better caparisoned than my lady. Outfit yourself as befits your station. Spend your coins on whatever women's fripperies you wish.''

''I would spend my coins most willingly,'' she snapped, ''had I any.''

The glint of amusement faded from FitzHugh's eyes. ''You have moneys. Use them.''

''I hesitate to contradict you and risk another lessoning, but I cannot use what I do not have.''

''Do you imply I've misused your inheritance, Lady of Trémont? That I've denied you your portion?'' His slow, dangerous drawl made the hairs on Mellisynt's arms prickle.

''Nay!'' she protested, confused by his sudden hostility.

He took a deliberate step forward. ''For most of my life, I've had little but the strength of my arm and my honor to claim as my own. It's held me steady in a world filled with men who twist with the wind and break their sacred oaths on the least provocation. I'll not have you imply that I dishonored myself, and you, in greed for Henri's estate.''

Mellisynt gaped at his grim countenance. ''I did not think you denied my portion. It's yours, after all, to manage for me and mine.''

For a long, hard moment, FitzHugh glared down at her. His jaw worked, and he made an obvious effort to rein in his anger. ''Did you not read the betrothal documents? Your revenues are in your name, to use as you see fit.''

Mellisynt thought of the parchments lying at the bottom of her traveling basket, totally incomprehensible to her untutored mind. She swallowed, and shook her head.

Disgust wiped the anger from FitzHugh's eyes. ''Do you not know which manors were put in your name? How much of the forestry fees and shearing tariffs come to you?''

Mute, she could only shake her head once more.

FitzHugh swore, low and long and colorfully. "We'll go over the documents this night. You need to know what is yours, and what comes to me to manage. For now, know that you have a goodly income of your own. You may spend it as you please."

"But I have no coins, nor silver marks," Mellisynt protested in muddled confusion.

"Did I not tell you to draw upon the duchess's exchequer?" he bit out, exasperation and impatience drawing his brows together in a familiar scowl.

"Aye." Her voice wavered, then gathered strength. "But I did not do so, not realizing I had moneys of my own nor wishing to spend your coin without permission."

FitzHugh expelled a long drawn-out breath. "I'll give you coins enough to take care of your needs until you are comfortable with managing your own accounts."

Mellisynt nodded, her thoughts churning. The idea that she had rents and fees and income of her own, to do with as she would, astounded her almost as much as FitzHugh's assumption that she could manage these moneys herself. And on top of those startling revelations, visions of bright silks and thick furs danced in her mind.

"I'll visit the markets this day, my lord."

He paused in the act of attaching the tapes of his chausses to his braies. "I recall your mentioning that you went little into town before. Are you used to haggling and buying?"

"Nay." An eager gleam entered her eyes. "But I'll learn."

"Mayhap you should take another lady with you, to show you the best shops," FitzHugh suggested. He paused, his shirt dangling from one hand. "Or take the girl, Isabeau. She's new to the court, and knows few other women as yet. No doubt she would enjoy a visit to the markets. And she is most pleasingly dressed. She can show you the latest styles."

Mellisynt bit her lip and turned away while her lord finished dressing. Her amazement at discovering she was mistress of her own funds and the shivery anticipation of exploring the shops had slipped away by imperceptible degrees.

"I still don't see why we couldn't have taken a litter."

Isabeau lifted one velvet-shod foot, protected by a heavy wooden patten, over a pile of snowy slush and gave her companion a disgruntled glare.

Mellisynt sent a silent prayer to the Virgin for strength. "I told you. I would not keep the men-at-arms standing about in the cold all day while we dawdled in the warmth of the shops."

"So instead we must pick our way through this— Oh!"

Isabeau jumped back as a shower of snow fell from the steep roof overhead. Pulling her fur-lined cloak closer, she hugged the inside of the narrow walk. The little page, Bartholomew, pressed into service with another youngster to carry whatever bundles Mellisynt might acquire, smothered a laugh. The two boys fell back when Isabeau whirled on them.

"You little toads, I'm tired of your snickering and laughing. If you don't know how to treat a lady with respect, I'll learn you right enough." She started toward them with one hand upraised.

Mellisynt sighed and put herself between the irate beauty and the unrepentant boys.

"Such agitation will leave lines upon your brow," she said mildly. She hid an amused grin as Isabeau halted in midstride and smoothed the anger from her face.

Having spent a full afternoon with the spoiled beauty and the two high-spirited boys, Mellisynt had learned quickly enough to handle them. She pandered to the girl's vanity and ignored all but the most outrageous of the boy's giggling pranks. 'Twas a wonder she'd managed to make any purchases at all, between admiring how a succession of colors looked against Isabeau's fair skin and keeping one eye on the boys as they enjoyed their unexpected freedom from the esquire who served as tutor and trainer.

"The little wretches," Isabeau muttered.

"They're just children, only a little younger than you yourself," Mellisynt commented, not for the first time that long afternoon. Indeed, at times she'd found the boys more mature, and certainly more companionable, than the budding girl-woman.

"I'm far from a child." Isabeau sniffed. "I would have been wed a year and more ago if my betrothed hadn't taken an arrow in the neck at Limoges. I had prepared all my bride clothes, too. 'Twas most inconvenient."

"No doubt your betrothed thought so, as well," Mellisynt commented.

Isabeau's delicate eyebrows drew together, and then she shrugged. "I met the man only once, at our betrothal. Now the duchess is to pick another husband for me, one who will hold Bellamy in my father's stead. I hope she chooses soon."

Mellisynt hoped so, too, most fervently, and continued her plodding path through the slush. She and Isabeau had just stepped around a pile of snow-covered garbage when a cacophony of shouts and high-pitched yelps made them both jump. She turned to see Bartholomew and the other page drop their bundles and hurl themselves at a milling, shouting group of street children. Both boys rapidly disappeared in a flurry of fists and thrashing legs.

"Holy Mother! What in heaven's name—?" Mellisynt thrust her own bundles into Isabeau's arms and picked up her skirts in both hands. Her pattens slid on the wet cobbles as she ran across the street and tried to make some sense of the swirling mass of shouting boys. Plucking at one ragged mantle, she tugged at it with both hands. A stocky urchin stumbled back and fell against her. Mellisynt and the boy both landed on their backsides in the slush.

Picking herself up with grim determination, she waded into the fray once more. She lost her veil and felt the pins slip from her hair as she struggled with the teeming mass. After a few breathless moments, she caught hold of Bartholomew's collar and managed to yank him upright. The other boys fell back at her fury.

"What in God's name are you about?" She jerked the boy's collar so hard his golden curls danced.

"They were stoning him," Bartholomew gasped.

"Him? Who?"

"Him."

He held out a begrimed hand and pointed to a huge, furred creature the size of a small pony, tied to a stone wall. The dog, if it was one, was the sorriest-looking animal Mellisynt had ever seen. Mud coated its brindled coat, half of one ear appeared to have been chewed off in a long-ago fight, and every rib stood out in stark relief against its ragged hide. One of its hind legs was missing, and it stood awkwardly on the remaining three. A rope cut cruelly into its neck and was tethered to a ring bolt in the wall.

"Whose dog is this?"

Keeping a firm grasp on Bartholomew's collar, she surveyed the assembled crowd. In addition to the boys, the circle around them now included interested passersby and shopkeepers drawn out into the street by the noise. Isabeau hovered at the edge of the crowd, a disgusted expression on her face.

"'Tis naught but a stray," one of the boys answered in a surly voice. "He's been digging in the garbage heaps and making a nuisance of hisself."

Mellisynt chewed her lower lip. No more than Bartholomew did she like to see a poor creature tormented. But a maimed animal such as this could not earn its keep, and was of no use to anyone.

"He's been hurt, Bartholomew."

"Yes, but see how he still manages on three legs. He's game, my lady. Look at his eyes."

She did, and knew at once it was a mistake. The hound's great brown eyes seemed to fasten on hers with a pathetic dignity, as if it sensed a savior from its torment but was unwilling to beg for salvation.

"He's filthy, and flea-ridden," Isabeau put in, shouldering her way through the crowd.

"So would you be if you had to sleep in the streets and eat garbage," Bartholomew told her indignantly.

"This is absurd. Leave him and let us return to the château, Lady Mellisynt. It's cold, and my shoes are wet."

Mellisynt looked from Bartholomew's pleading eyes to Isabeau's furious ones, and then to the crowd that surrounded them. The teeming mass waited with avid interest for the next act in this little drama. She bit her lip, then glanced up hopefully as a clatter of iron-shod hooves echoed over the heads of the crowd. A standard-bearer with Brittany's pennant rode into the square, followed by a troop of mounted men. When she recognized the unmistakable figure in the lead, she felt a rush of relief.

"What in the name of all the saints goes on here?"

FitzHugh's furious voice thundered across the winter air. He pushed his mailed hood back and surveyed the scene with a disbelieving scowl. Beside him, Sir Roger looked over the crowd, a grin of unholy amusement on his face.

Mellisynt's surge of welcome relief at the sight of her lord faded at the stunned incredulity on his face. Suddenly conscious of her straggling hair and mudstained cloak, she essayed a hesitant smile.

FitzHugh nudged his mount forward, parting the crowd. His eyes glinted dangerously as they scanned the throng, then came to rest on her.

"Would you care to tell me why I find my lady in the midst of a street brawl, with mud on her knees and face, surrounded by a bunch of ragtag ruffians and merchants?"

Mellisynt swallowed. Like leaves scattering before a cold wind, the crowd began to disperse, glancing nervously at the dark knight as they slipped away. Bartholomew moved closer to her side, and the other page scrambled to his feet.

"'Twas the dog, my lord," Mellisynt replied, with what

dignity she could salvage. "The boys were stoning it, and Bar—and we thought to save it from such a fate."

FitzHugh's eyes slid to the animal, and a pained look crossed his face.

"You appear to have accomplished your goal, at least for the moment. Come, I'll take you back to the château." He reached down to lift her up before him.

Mellisynt looked at the mailed fist, then flicked a quick glance back at the hound.

"No, my lady," FitzHugh told her softly. "Geoffrey would not be best pleased were I to add such a creature to his kennels."

She stiffened at the name, and FitzHugh silently cursed his blunder.

"We would not have to add him to the castle runs," Mellisynt offered, her chin high. "We can send him back to Trémont, when he's been tended to."

"Aye, my lord." Bartholomew stepped forward confidently. "I'll tend him myself till he's well enough."

"You'll be too busy seeing to your own hurts to worry about anyone else's," FitzHugh growled. "If this is how you care for your lady, you haven't learned much at your trainer's hand. I'll make sure he applies his lessons more forcefully."

The boy's face crumpled, and Mellisynt laid a protective hand on his shoulder. FitzHugh did not miss the instinctive gesture. Nor was his simmering anger proof against the unconscious plea in his wife's wide green eyes. His irritation began to subside.

In truth, until he'd rounded the corner and discovered his lady in such straits, he'd been feeling an uncharacteristic sense of goodwill toward her. He'd left their chamber sated—replete, in fact. He'd never dreamed that this pale, slender woman would light such fires in his blood that they'd all but consume him. That his deliberate assault on her senses would send his own reeling. He suspected his attempt to demonstrate his absolute mastery had missed its mark.

As he surveyed Mellisynt's mud-streaked face, he could see

it had. 'Twas obvious her spirit was intact, if the combination of appeal and stubborn determination filling her eyes was any indication. A grudging respect dawned. To have lived the life she had and kept her courage bespoke a stronger woman than he'd first supposed her to be. He shook his head, wondering at the nature of a woman who would wed a baseborn knight to get a child, one who would take a rascally page and a flea-bitten mongrel into her heart.

Isabeau interrupted his thoughts, stepping forward with her arms full of bundles and a thoroughly disgruntled look on her face.

"For pity's sake, my lord, I've stood here in this snow and wet too long as it is because of that misbegotten cur. My feet are frozen. Please, take us back to the castle."

"Beauchamp, see to the Lady Isabeau." FitzHugh leaned a forearm across the pommel and kept his gaze locked on his wife's dirt streaked face.

Beauchamp kneed his horse forward.

"Come, wench, 'tis clear this is a family discussion."

Leaning down, he wrapped a strong arm around the girl's waist and hauled her, packages and all, into the saddle before him. Flashing a wry grin over the beauty's dark head, he kicked his mount into a loping canter.

"My lord!" Isabeau gasped, struggling for purchase. "You go too fast! I cannot get my seat!"

Beauchamp tightened his hold, savoring the press of her full breasts against his arm through thick layers of clothing. Her bottom cheeks, soft and full and lush, bounced against his thigh. A wicked grin split his face. "Nay, girl. You most assuredly have your seat. I can feel the full weight of it, and very solid it is, too."

Isabeau's mouth dropped. "How—how dare you address me so!"

"When you get to know me better, you'll find I dare most anything, child."

"I'm not a child!" Isabeau snapped back.

* * *

Mellisynt swept into the great hall that evening, fully recovered from her street adventure. She glanced around the crowded room, looking for her husband's dark head above the milling throng. As she stood on tiptoe, one hand braced against a tall column, a lilting laugh floated across the air. Turning, Mellisynt saw the Lady Isabeau in the midst of a group of admiring courtiers. The elegant, golden-haired knight whose poetry so enchanted the court hung over the girl. He was as finely dressed as always, in a tunic of golden velvet and shoes so long and pointed they brushed Isabeau's very skirts.

"Nay, Sir Guy," Isabeau cooed, "I'm not yet ready to accept an *entendedor*. I've not been at court long enough for any knight to do duty as aspirant or supplicant, let alone be permitted to dedicate songs to me."

She softened her rebuff with a provocative smile that promised so much more than a girl her age and single status should.

"You're a cruel, heartless beauty," de Claire said with a sigh, lifting her hand to stroke it sensuously.

"Nay, she's just a silly, overpadded wench."

Mellisynt jumped at the mocking voice just behind her. She shushed Beauchamp with a smothered laugh, praying that his words hadn't carried to the group surrounding Isabeau.

They had. Guy de Claire stiffened. Isabeau turned, fury flaring in her huge aquamarine eyes.

"Sir Guy," she choked out. "Mayhap I would accept a suitor, if he were able to assure that ill-bred knaves do not bandy about comments on my person."

"None shall, my lady," de Claire said. He moved past Isabeau, putting the girl behind him with a steady hand.

Mellisynt's embarrassed amusement drained at the sight of the knight's face. His mouth curled in an evil smile that matched the feral gleam in his eyes. She suddenly remembered Beauchamp's warning after her own clash with de Claire, that the knight masked a vicious temper behind his courtier's facade. Glancing worriedly up at the man beside her, she discovered a devilish glee dancing in his brown eyes. Beauchamp was enjoying this, she realized, dismayed. The idiot didn't appear in the least daunted at the prospect of taking a dagger in his gut right in the middle of the duchess's crowded great room!

De Claire moved forward with a sinister grace that belied his elegant appearance. Mellisynt bit her lip, then gathered her skirts and made as if to move out of his way. In the process, her foot came down firmly on the tip of his pointed shoe. The man's eyes widened in surprise as his weight shifted. He wavered, then fell forward over his own feet and hit the tiles with a crash that made many of those nearby jump. Muffled oaths sounded, then gave way to sputtered laughter as the courtiers saw Guy de Claire, count of Almay, sprawled flat on his face.

De Claire levered himself up on one knee. His murderous glare told Mellisynt that wounding a knight's dignity was a far worse crime than disparaging his poetry. Evading Beauchamp's restraining hand, she rushed forward.

"Oh, Sir Guy, I'm so sorry. I swear, I'm as clumsy as a cow." She bent to take hold of one arm and help him rise. He shook off her hand.

"You did that apurpose, you little—"

"Do you address my wife, de Claire?"

The hairs on the back of Mellisynt's neck stood on end at the lazy menace in FitzHugh's voice. He pushed his way casually through the crowd, and stepped around his wife. With a firm hand, he set her to one side, out of the circle of his sword arm. Beauchamp moved up on silent feet to stand beside him, and the courtiers at the scene backed away.

The count straightened, his lips lifting in a sneer.

"'Twould appear you've taken an awkward wife, Sir Richard."

"Nay, de Claire," FitzHugh drawled. "'Twas you who

tumbled to the tiles, after all. You can't seem to keep your balance on your feet any better than you keep your seat in the tourney.''

A tide of red swept up the count's neck. "Bastard!"

"'Tis most unchivalrous of you both to discomfit a lady so." Constance swept between the men. With her dainty figure and haughty brow, she was every inch the duchess. "I'm sure the Lady Mellisynt does not wish a simple accident to cause such a disturbance.''

"Don't intervene in this, my lady," FitzHugh warned.

Constance stiffened, and ice dripped from her voice. "Do you think to order me in my own castle?"

FitzHugh swallowed a curse. He knew Constance when she assumed that frigid mien and drew the dignity of her rank around her like a shield. If he persisted now and took satisfaction of de Claire, the damned woman wouldn't hesitate to call the castle guards down on them both. In a fit of temper, she'd once kicked a drunken Geoffrey from her bed and locked him naked in the corridor.

FitzHugh straightened slowly. He had no desire to have the long-simmering quarrel between him and de Claire end so farcically. Besides, Constance was well within her rights to keep order among her husband's vassals. Reining in his anger, he bowed to the tiny duchess.

"Forgive my presumption. Sir Guy and I will resolve this matter at another time and place.''

Her eyes shooting violet sparks, Constance moved to de Claire's side. Deliberately, she took his arm. The rigid knight sent FitzHugh a look of hard promise over the duchess's head, then allowed her to lead him away.

"I'm sorry!"

"'Twas not your lady's fault.''

Mellisynt and Beauchamp both spoke as one, then stopped. The knight flashed his rogue's smile and bent over Mellisynt's hand.

"I thank you for trying to save me from the folly of my words, my lady, but 'twas not at all necessary."

"No," Mellisynt replied, nerves sharpening her voice. "You would have much preferred to spill his blood right here, on the duchess's Moorish tiles."

He grinned. "Well, if I do not, FitzHugh will most like to do so, and soon."

She turned and laid a hand on her husband's arm. "I would not have you at daggers drawn over this silly incident, my lord. Truly, I was most clumsy."

"Aye, you were," FitzHugh agreed.

Beauchamp smothered a laugh at her openmouthed indignation.

FitzHugh nodded. "Very clumsy. Although I applaud your intent, don't intervene again in the affairs of men. You could get hurt."

Mellisynt's eyes narrowed to glittering green slits. She turned away with a swish of her skirts and plopped down on a nearby bench, determined to ignore the two men who stood behind her and conversed casually, as if near-bloodshed in the midst of dinner were a most common occurrence, and one of little import.

Later, after the servants cleared the boards from the evening meal and the crowd began to mingle, Constance moved to Mellisynt's side.

"I saw your attempt to intervene between Beauchamp and de Claire," she murmured. "That was well done, even if your method was a trifle crude and had unexpected consequences. What caused the disturbance?"

Mellisynt hesitated. "Sir Guy took exception to Beauchamp's...ah...comments about the Lady Isabeau."

"I knew it," Constance said, seething. "Men take almost as much pleasure in fighting over a woman's skirts as trying to get up them!"

Her eyes roved to where Isabeau, still somewhat flushed, held her usual court. "I need to do something about that one."

Chapter Eight

"I tell you, you must go!"

Constance tapped an angry foot against the floor. The staccato beat matched the tempo of FitzHugh's furious pacing.

"Is this a ruse?" he ground out. "Do you think to send me away because of last night's little farce with de Claire? If so, you but delay the inevitable. And make me look the fool."

"Don't be more pigheaded than you usually are," the duchess snapped. "I know you and de Claire will settle your quarrel, however little sense it makes to have you both spill your brains over something this trivial. But you will not do it here. And not while Geoffrey needs you." Her voice faltered on the last words.

FitzHugh stopped in midstride. He couldn't remember hearing Constance of Brittany's voice tremble before.

"Tell me quickly this news you have that necessitates my immediate departure."

"A ship just docked with messages from Winchester," Constance said, her eyes shadowed with concern. "Geoffrey writes that he will repudiate the truce."

"What! How could he be so ill-advised? We need this truce as much as does Richard Lionheart, to regroup our forces and garrison the castles on the border with loyal men."

"I know that, and you know that!" Constance all but shouted. "But Geoffrey is all arage at the peace conditions.

He's expected to make reparations to Richard's damned Crusade chest. The king fears to offend the church.''

"So Brittany is to bear the cost of the war, instigated by the king himself to keep Richard Lionheart in check." FitzHugh shook his head.

The duchess nodded glumly. "Geoffrey refuses to accept the conditions. He hates his brother, and swears he'll see that dour-faced sodomite in hell before he'll give him the kiss of peace."

Despite himself, FitzHugh grinned. "Calm yourself, Constance. King Henry demands this truce, and he'll get it. He pulls his sons' strings most skillfully."

"I know, God rot his soul. Henry plays one son off the other for his own ends. Damn the whole Angevin brood, devil's spawn that they are!"

"Do you forget that one sits in your belly?"

FitzHugh watched, amused, as Constance softened both her stance and her furious expression. She placed a protective hand on her stomach and turned troubled violet eyes up to his.

"Nay, I do not forget. That's why I ask you to go to England. Geoffrey needs your steady head, or he'll forswear my child's birthright in this mad game he plays with his brother and father. I would go myself, but I dare not risk my babe in a winter crossing."

"I'd not allow you to take such a journey," FitzHugh told her gently. "You know I'll go."

She came forward and placed a small white hand on FitzHugh's arm.

"Aye, I knew you would. I'm…frightened, Richard. The old king moves his sons about like pawns on a chessboard. He doesn't realize the hatred he stirs. It festers within them all. Of late, Geoffrey carries under his bluff exterior a bitterness so vile it eats at his very soul."

"Aye." FitzHugh nodded slowly and covered the duchess's hand with his own. "I've seen it take hold more, and more."

"You're closest to him, Richard. His only real friend. He

needs you. Go to him and convince him to accept this truce so that Brittany can recover from its wounds.''

Shaking off her uncharacteristic soberness, she essayed a gamine grin. "And then you can take your lady to that moldy old keep you call home and use her riches to bring some civilization to the place."

FitzHugh laughed. He'd first seen Constance as a tiny, indomitable seven-year-old when she arrived in England to meet her boisterous betrothed. She'd made no secret then of her preference for Brittany's windswept shores and majestic forests over England's damp clime. Nor did she now.

With the ease of long friendship, FitzHugh chucked her under her chin. "As you command, my lady."

"Oh, and I have a favor to ask of your wife," Constance added. "I would have her take the Lady Isabeau to England, and chaperone her most closely while I arrange a match for the minx. I'm thinking of Simon de Lacy. His wife died last year, and he needs someone to warm his old bones in bed."

"De Lacy? You'd give that child to a battered old warhorse like him?"

Constance snorted inelegantly. "Child! If she's not bedded soon, she'll melt from the heat between her legs."

She stopped and drew a breath. "'Tis why I thought to send her with you and the Lady Mellisynt. I need to remove her from court before the wench causes a riot. Your isolated holding will serve as well as any I can think of to keep her from mischief."

FitzHugh shrugged. "As you will. I'll leave you now and make the necessary arrangements."

He strode back through the drafty corridors, his face grim. Geoffrey's recklessness worried him far more than he would reveal to Constance. Even before this latest, accursed war, his hot-blooded friend had chafed more and more at his father's heavy hand.

The king was long used to controlling his vast domains in England and France, and to controlling the sons who would someday inherit them. Like a master puppeteer, he made them all dance and jerk on the strings he pulled. FitzHugh knew in his heart, however, that this time the king had gone too far. His decision to curb Richard Lionheart's power by devolving some of his lands on young Prince John had set the brothers at war. The king himself sent Geoffrey forth to battle on behalf of John, yet expected him to pay for the costs of that war. No wonder the duke now rebelled.

FitzHugh threw open the door to his apartments, still deep in troubled thought.

"Shut the door!"

"My lord, look out!"

A wet, hairy body threw itself forward with a hundred and more pounds of determination.

FitzHugh staggered back, his arms instinctively clasping the struggling shape. They went down in a flurry of water and foaming soap.

"Sweet Mother! Ian, help me haul him off. Grab his tail, Bartholomew, and pull."

Mellisynt locked both arms around the dog's huge neck and tugged.

"Stand aside," FitzHugh snarled. Keeping a tight grip on the panting beast, he staggered to his feet. "And shut the damned door before I loose him."

His squire hastened to comply.

"Sit! Be still, you misbegotten spawn of Satan!"

The dog cast FitzHugh a wary look and hunkered down on his one hind leg.

"Well! Of all the ungrateful creatures," Mellisynt gasped, tucking a wet straggle of coppery hair behind her ear. "I've fed him enough to keep a starving family for a year, physicked his hurts, and prepared him a bath, yet the cursed beast ignores *my* every command."

"Mayhap your orders lack a note of authority. As mine obviously did when I told you this hound was to be confined to the stables."

FitzHugh's voice carried soft, silky menace. He felt a stab of savage satisfaction when his wife blinked and wiped wet hands down the sides of her drenched gown. Ian and Bartholomew exchanged nervous glances.

"Well, he did spend the night in the stables...." Mellisynt began, somewhat hesitantly. "But the head groom says he took most violent exception to the presence of stable cats. He broke the rope holding him to chase one tom and, um...upset the horses somewhat."

FitzHugh closed his eyes, imagining the havoc this three-legged monster would wreak running through the stalls of destriers trained to kill and maim with tooth and hoof.

"No one was hurt, my lord," Mellisynt assured him. "At least not very seriously. But the groom sent me a message this morning, most earnestly requesting that I remove him immediately. So I brought him here. Just to feed and bathe him, I swear."

"And then what will you do with him?" FitzHugh inquired carefully.

"Well, I'm not exactly sure. I thought to hire a man to take him back to Trémont. With my own coins, of course."

She gave him a saucy grin that made FitzHugh's dark brows shoot up.

"He needs some care before I can send him on such a journey," Mellisynt continued blithely.

"Surely among the hundreds of servitors who see to the duchess's every need, you can find one to take care of this beast. You need not sully your hands with him yourself."

She took her lower lip between small white teeth and glanced down at the dog, who was dripping water and lather on the tiled floor in majestic unconcern.

"I'm sure I could, my lord. But his eyes have such a sad dignity. I don't mind taking on his care. I...I am used to spending my days attending to infirmity, and feel the lack of any useful occupation."

FitzHugh expelled a long, slow breath. "You'll not have

the time to care for him, nor anyone else. We sail on the morning tide for England.''

''We do?''

''We do. Ian, get you gone and start packing my gear and equipment. And take that imp with you.''

Grabbing Bartholomew's shoulder, the squire hustled out with an air of palpable relief.

FitzHugh waited until the door slammed shut behind them before moving toward the bed. Shedding his soaked surcoat, he rolled up the sleeves of his linen shirt. Mellisynt eyed him warily as he walked across the room.

''Come, let's finish bathing this monster from hell while I tell you what necessitates our departure. Then we'll deal with your rashness in disobeying my orders as it deserves.''

In the dark hours before dawn, Mellisynt snuggled deep in her new fox-lined cloak and settled herself more comfortably in the litter. With the ease of practice, she ignored Isabeau's low-voiced complaints. After her brief taste of court life, the girl was predictably unhappy at being bundled off to what had been described to her as the far end of the earth. Even Isabeau's complaining presence, however, couldn't dim Mellisynt's delicious sense of well-being.

She grinned into the fur brushing against her chin. FitzHugh had been surprisingly gentle with the dog, and satisfyingly less than gentle with her. Her face heated as she recalled the strength of his body pressing into hers, and its hard, driving demand for response. She'd been ready this time, though. This time she'd met him thrust for thrust, and wrapped her legs around his muscled thighs. This time there had been no one-sided dominance, no one-sided effort. Neither she nor Fitz-Hugh expected love in the marriage bed, but what they shared would do very well, very well indeed, she decided.

Bitter cold whipped along the dark streets and snaked through even the thick curtains of the duchess's litter, adding to Isabeau's lists of complaints. Mellisynt had not been best pleased when FitzHugh informed her she was to spend her first winter in her new home chaperoning Isabeau of Bellamy, but in the face of the duchess's explicit request, she could hardly refuse. Not without admitting a most unworthy jealousy, one that she struggled to contain. 'Twas not the girl's fault that men, including her own husband, smiled down at her like besotted oafs.

They arrived at the dock just as the first fingers of dawn began to poke through the dark clouds blanketing the sky. Mellisynt climbed out of the litter eagerly, lifting up her heavy skirts and even heavier cloak to keep them from the garbage-strewn filth lining the wooden piers. Isabeau descended, muttering at the cold. A thin, shivering maid, pressed into service by Constance to see to their needs on the journey, huddled beside them and surveyed the scene with wide eyes. The girl started when FitzHugh's massive figure strode down a wobbling gangplank toward them.

Mellisynt felt a strange thrill clutch her heart at her husband's approach. In the weak, windswept dawn, he looked like a dark warrior descending from the clouds. His huge shoulders all but blocked the sky from her view, and his arms, whose strength she knew well, swept her up in a swirl of skirts.

"You're just in time, lady wife. The horses are stowed, and the shipmaster wishes to leave immediately. Come, I'll get you aboard." He headed for the narrow plank. "I'll be back for you, Lady Isabeau."

A deep, mournful howl, of approximately the same timbre and volume as the great cast-iron cathedral bell that awakened Nantes's citizens each morning, stopped him in his tracks.

FitzHugh's arms tightened to ominous bands of steel.

Mellisynt swallowed and met his disbelieving eyes.

"I tried to leave him behind, my lord, I swear! But he must have sensed my leaving. He wailed most loud and long each time I stepped out the door."

A muscle at the side of FitzHugh's jaw clenched and unclenched rhythmically. Eyeing it with some fascination, Mellisynt hurried on.

"I could not quiet him! He roused half the castle with—" she paused as another deafening howl rolled across the morning mist "—with that. Constance threatened to have him skinned and fed to her pet panthers did I not silence him."

FitzHugh spoke, slowly and deliberately, through gritted teeth. "If that cur comes anywhere near my horses, I'll personally cut out his liver and use it for fish bait."

"Aye, my lord."

The shipmaster greeted the addition of a three-legged beast who added his own deep braying to the din of departure with something less than enthusiasm. Secured by a stout rope to the rail surrounding the raised upper deck, the creature appeared to find his first sea voyage as exciting as did his mistress. Isabeau went below to the warmth of the shipmaster's cabin, but Mellisynt leaned over the upper rail, fascinated by the bustling activity below. Her eyes widened as seamen scrambled to untie the mooring lines and maneuver the three-masted barque out into the river's current. Others climbed like nimble monkeys up into the rigging. Within moments, the swift-flowing Loire, rushing its last few miles to the sea, caught the ship.

As they swept past the docks, rays of early-morning sunlight broke through dark, scudding clouds and painted the city with a patchwork of shadows and gilded spires. Mellisynt stood at the rail, her cheeks stinging with cold. She pulled the fox-lined hood up around her face and watched Nantes's steep-roofed, timbered buildings slip by. Every surge and dip of the ship as it danced with the river's rolling waters thrilled her. This was the way to travel, she decided. Not atop some hard-backed, mean-spirited animal whose every step jolted the very bones in her body.

A dim memory teased at her mind, one of sunlight dancing on a sparkling sea. A man's strong arms tossing her into the air. A woman's lilting laughter as she splashed through the waves. Mellisynt tried to capture the vague, half-formed images that were all she had of her parents. Her father had been a minor knight with holdings along the coast, she knew that much. She knew, as well, that both parents had died of an inflammation of the lungs that had swept away many souls one bleak winter. She'd been taken into a remote castle of her father's overlord, the young duke of Brittany, who later offered her as Henri of Trémont's third wife. Strange how the memory of those long years at Trémont no longer sent a shiver of resentment through her, Mellisynt mused. With the sun and the sea once again tugging at her senses, she felt reborn, as if she'd found the future she'd thought was gone. Clasping the rail, she threw back her head and drank in the life-giving sun.

She was still at the rail when Isabeau came up some time later to take the air. The stuffy cabin made her head ache, she claimed.

"Oh, look, Isabeau! 'Tis the sea."

The wind whipped Mellisynt's hood back as the barque rounded a bend and entered the Loire's wide estuary. Ahead of them, gray-green waves slapped against black rocks on either side of the channel. When the ship caught the tide's ebb, the master shouted an order and men scrambled aloft. Massive sails unfurled, and the ship leapt across the tossing waves.

"How it rolls and swells," Mellisynt exclaimed, holding on to the rail with mittened hands.

"It…it does, indeed," Isabeau agreed weakly.

Tendrils of hair whipped at Mellisynt's cheek and she threw back her head to toss them from her eyes.

"'Tis like riding the wind." She laughed. "Look how those clouds race across the sky, as if the devil himself were chasing them."

A low groan, barely heard above the wind's roar, made her turn. Isabeau slumped back against the sheltering cabin wall, her face as white as the rabbit fur framing it.

Mellisynt crossed the small, sloping space in two quick strides. "Are you ill, child?"

"Dreadfully," she moaned, then added, in a weak, pathetic voice, "I'm not a child."

With one arm around the girl's waist, Mellisynt moved toward the stairs leading to the shipmaster's cabin. Casting a quick, regretful glance back over her shoulder at the foamy sea and scudding clouds, she led Isabeau down the narrow stairs.

The next four days became a blurred confusion of tossing seas and violent illness. Dark clouds piled one on top of another, and fierce rains lashed the ship. They were blown far south and west, into the Atlantic, adding two extra days to the journey as the shipmaster beat back toward the Channel against heavy winds. Isabeau grew more miserable with each passing day. She retched constantly—dry, racking heaves that left her weak and sobbing. FitzHugh came several times to check on them, but found himself routed by the girl's pathetic moans and Mellisynt's snapped order to come in or get himself gone, but in either case shut the door. The little maid sent to see to their needs proved less than useless, succumbing to seasickness within hours of their losing sight of land. Mellisynt found herself in a familiar role, nursing and coaxing and bathing patients' faces with a steady hand.

The ship's cook proved a most welcome companion. A tiny, wizened old man with a gray patch over one eye and three prominent teeth in an otherwise empty mouth, he brought dry ship biscuits, thin soups, and a cold brew steeped from chamomile leaves. Between them, Mellisynt and the little man forced the protesting patients to down what liquids they could.

They sailed into Portsmouth harbor on the last day but one of November. Mellisynt left Isabeau's bedside for the first time in four days and climbed up the narrow stairs. Holding her elegant cloak close to cover her stained, wrinkled gown, she breathed in fresh air in great, welcome gulps.

Ships of all shapes and sizes and numbers of masts filled the quays of England's busiest port. Voices carried across the waters in strange tongues and accents. A steady stream of carriers, bent almost double by the huge casks and bales on their backs, made their way toward the stone warehouses across from the docks. A thin drizzle hung on the air, coating the ships and buildings with a gray sheen.

"How do you fare?"

Mellisynt managed to give her husband a tired smile. In truth, she felt like something rats had gnawed upon. "I'm fine, my lord."

"I've arranged for rooms at a nearby inn, where you and the other women can rest while we finish unloading. We're but a few hours from Winchester. Will you be able to travel this day?"

Mellisynt studied the crease between his thick, dark brows, made deeper than usual by tiredness and the worry she knew he harbored.

"Aye," she replied. "Do you think we are arrived too late? Will the duke have repudiated the truce already?"

"I don't know. The documents are to be signed tomorrow, at the great feast in honor of Saint Andrew. Mayhap there is time yet to reason with Geoffrey."

FitzHugh stared across the docks, his thoughts far away and most uncomfortable, if the troubled look in his blue eyes was any indication. He rubbed his forehead with a tired hand.

"I'll send men to carry Isabeau and the girl above decks. Do what you can to restore them as quickly as possible."

"We'll be ready when you come for us, my lord."

Mellisynt vowed to tie Isabeau and the maid on their horses, if necessary. The brief, worried look that had crossed Fitz-Hugh's face, normally so set and authoritative, had communicated the depth of his concern far more than he realized.

Their bedraggled party arrived late that evening at the great castle of Winchester, once the seat of the Norman kings, to find it a scene of incredible chaos. A distracted household seneschal groaned at their unexpected appearance, claiming there was not a square inch of empty space within the castle. Not only had the king come to wear his crown at the Feast of

Saint Andrew, but he had brought Queen Eleanor from her comfortable captivity to lend support to the reconciliation of their sons. In addition, their daughter Matilda and her husband, Henry the Lion, duke of Saxony, swelled the ranks. The Lion had made war upon his overlord, the Holy Roman Emperor Frederick Barbarossa, and had been exiled from his duchy.

Eventually an exchange of silver pennies won the weary travelers entrance to the castle. Ian, the men-at-arms, and the pages went into town to find a place to bed themselves and the beasts down. The hound's protesting howls echoed across the courtyard as they dragged him away.

Impatient to find Geoffrey, FitzHugh bade the women rest that night. Mellisynt was more than willing to follow her lord's directions. Too weary to take in much of the magnificent castle, she led a still-weak Isabeau and their little maid to the dormer room they would share with six other women. Straw pallets crowded the floor, with trunks and baskets piled high in every corner. 'Twas obvious each of the room's occupants had emptied her wardrobe for the trip to court.

Glancing around at the scattered silks and veils, Mellisynt thought of her brief foray into Nantes's shops. With their sudden departure, she'd had no time to have new gowns made. Her purchases of fine velvet, soft Alexandrine paile and rich purple asterin, all still wrapped in their protective coverings, awaited the seamstress's hands. Sighing, she shed her travel-stained amber robe and joined Isabeau on the pallet they would share.

Chapter Nine

The next afternoon, Mellisynt left Isabeau to the chattering company of the other women and followed a page through Winchester's high, vaulted halls to answer her husband's summons. He awaited her in a deserted garden. Wind whistling over the stone walls lifted bits of leaves and tossed them across brick paths laid out in concentric circles. Black-limbed rosebushes, brutally pruned against the winter cold, thrust their stumps toward a lowering gray sky. Snow hung heavy in the air, and Mellisynt tugged her furred cloak more closely around her.

FitzHugh had discarded his armour and wore only his thick gambeson under his blue surcoat. He waited patiently, one booted foot propped on a stone bench, an arm across his knee, and an austere expression on his face that made the winter garden seem even more bleak. He turned and straightened at the sound of her approach.

"God give you a good day, lady wife."

He bent and brushed a light kiss across her cheek. His lips felt warm against her cold skin, and their rough, velvety touch sent a tingle down Mellisynt's neck.

"And you, my lord."

"I'm sorry to drag you out into such inhospitable surroundings, but I would speak with you in private. The castle is so crowded, there's not a corner where we wouldn't trip over two others' feet."

Mellisynt dismissed the wind biting at her cheeks and nose with a negligent wave. "Have you spoken with the duke? Does he still hold firm to his intent to repudiate the peace?"

"I've spoken with him," FitzHugh responded dryly. "At some length. He was not best pleased that the duchess sent me here."

At Mellisynt's questioning look, his lips lifted in a sardonic half-smile.

"He'd planned on my presence in Brittany to hold his borders and rally his forces if he abjured the truce."

"So your coming has upset his scheme," Mellisynt breathed, trying to suppress a dart of satisfaction at Geoffrey's discomfiture. She'd thought she was beyond her grudge against the duke. "He will have to accept the terms now."

"A rational man would," FitzHugh admitted, "but Geoffrey's heart often overrules his head. 'Tis why I wished to speak with you. If things go as I suspect they might, you may have to make your way to Edgemoor alone. Peter St. Bressé will escort you. You know you can trust him."

Mellisynt nodded slowly. St. Bressé served as FitzHugh's lieutenant, and had traveled with them from Brittany. He was a good man, respectful and polite.

"I've arranged passage on a merchant ship to carry you and your escort from Portsmouth to Edgemoor. My uncle serves as steward during my absences, and will hold you safe. If I do not return, he'll help you manage your inheritance until you are resettled."

His words sent a shock jolting through Mellisynt. The rest of his detailed description of what she might expect on the journey north fell on deaf ears. Her mind reeled at the thought that he might not return. The possibility of losing this man, who had come so recently into her life and was now such a major part of it, overwhelmed her. The idea that she might never again feel his callused hands on her, or his teasing, tantalizing lips, just when she'd come to crave them, rocked her to her core. To think she had wanted marriage to this mighty warrior for his strength and vigor! Of a sudden she wished FitzHugh were every bit as thin and wizened and cowardly as old Henri had been.

She moistened dry lips with the tip of her tongue. "Must you go if it comes to war once more?"

FitzHugh shrugged. "If I can't deter Geoffrey from this course, he'll find himself facing the combined arms of his father and brother. I'm sworn to him, and must follow."

Mellisynt struggled to keep her voice steady. "But if Geoffrey forswears his oaths to his father, to whom he's given homage twice over, for Brittany and for Richmond, why are you bound to follow? Doesn't the fact that he breaks his pledge release you from yours?"

For a moment she feared he might take offense at her probing into these tangled affairs of men. In all her years at Trémont, she'd never dared question Henri so, nor to challenge his dealings. But here, in this windswept, barren garden, with dried leaves rustling at her feet and the sharp, coppery taste of fear on her tongue, she felt the need to know the man behind the fierce, hawk-faced exterior. She wanted to understand his reasons for leaving her, to understand what drove him.

FitzHugh stared down at her, his eyes almost opaque in their silver blueness. He pondered her question, his dark brows drawing together in the characteristic half frown that Mellisynt now recognized so well. A sudden urge swept through her to reach up and stroke away the lines creasing his forehead.

"Some would consider Geoffrey's repudiation of his allegiance to his father sufficient to absolve them of their oaths." FitzHugh spoke slowly, as if testing the sound of his words on his own tongue. "Each man must decide the course of his own honor in such circumstances, as we did in the last war. Should he hold to his sworn lord, or to his lord's overlord? Or to the rightness of the cause? My loyalty to Geoffrey goes beyond any oath of fealty, and I will follow him."

He tilted up her chin with a gentle, gloved fist. "I didn't

mean to frighten you with such dire forebodings, but 'tis best you know how things stand.''

At her troubled look, his somber look lightened. ''You'll be safe at Edgemoor, with my people. Remember, what I have, I hold.''

Mellisynt forced herself to respond to the teasing note in his voice. ''Aye, so you told me. I also seem to recall I fall just below your war-horses on your list of possessions to hold.''

A lopsided grin lifted one corner of his mouth. ''Does that still rankle? Will it help you to know that I'm reconsidering the priorities on my list? I've found that even Voyager, as well trained as he is, can't perform certain necessary services for me. Like this.''

He bent and brushed his mouth across hers. The air had chilled his lips and taken the rough warmth from them. A sharp desire flared within Mellisynt to taste that warmth once more. When he would have drawn back, she wrapped her arms around his neck, holding his mouth on hers. Her fingers tangled in the soft, springy hair of his nape. Opening her lips, she drew him into her.

FitzHugh accepted her invitation most willingly. His tongue met hers in a slow, sweet duel, and his arms tightened around her body until they were two taut bands pinning her against him. Stretched on tiptoe, her arms locked about the massive column of his neck, Mellisynt felt a growing need that half embarrassed, half thrilled her. She moaned deep in her throat and tilted her face to allow him more access.

Widening his stance, FitzHugh settled her weight in the cradle of his thighs. Mellisynt rubbed her hips against him shamelessly, frustrated beyond belief by the thick layers of clothing between them and by the surging lust that fired her blood. They hadn't been alone since their hurried departure from Nantes, and the urge to take him into her, to join with him, arced through her. Angling her lips across his, she deepened the kiss, demanding and taking all he had to give.

FitzHugh tore his mouth from hers. "Damnation, woman," he growled, "if you wish to show me how much more versatile is a wife than a war-horse, I wish you'd chosen another time, another place. There's not a private corner to be found anywhere in this castle."

Mellisynt clung to him, her breath crystallizing on the air in little puffs of vapor. She knew her eyes mirrored the rising need she saw in his, and made no effort to disguise it.

He gave a savage groan, then reached down to catch her under the knees. Striding to a protected corner, where the castle walls formed a V that cut the wind, he stood her upright and thrust her back against the wall. His body cocooned her in a tiny pocket of warmth. Reaching under his surcoat, he fumbled with the ties of his chausses.

"I don't believe we do this," he muttered. "I disremember the last time I had to take a woman against a wall."

"Good," she told him fiercely. "I don't wish you to remember the last time. Only this time."

She pushed his hands aside and burrowed under the layers of his clothing to find his stirring shaft. Enclosing him in both hands and a casing of soft fox fur, she quickly brought him to hardness.

"Jesu," he breathed, reaching for her skirts. "You'd best take my rod while you can. This cold will unman me do we play with it too long."

Mellisynt gave him a wicked grin. "You forget I've been taught well how to bring a husband to his duty."

Sinking to her knees, she took him into the hot wetness of her mouth. FitzHugh swore in startled surprise and braced both hands against the corner walls. When she had him primed to her satisfaction—her most admiring satisfaction—she slid up his length and lifted her skirts.

"Now, husband," she panted.

"Now, wife," he promised, lifting her hips and surging into her wet heat with a force that rocked her back against the stone.

Cushioned by layers of wool and fur, Mellisynt reveled in his fierce assault. She wrapped her arms about his neck once more and struggled to fit her body closer to his, despite the clothing bunched between them. FitzHugh flexed his thigh muscles and thrust upward, withdrew, and thrust again. She buried her face in his neck, breathing in the scent of his skin. Driven by an overpowering, primitive need, she sank her teeth into his taut flesh.

FitzHugh responded with all the force of his powerful body, pinning her against the stone over and over again with fierce, rhythmic movements. Mellisynt tried to clench her thighs against the sensation building in her lower belly, but his torso held her open, exposed, vulnerable. When she closed her eyes and threw her head back against the wall, FitzHugh bent and put his lips to her throat, nipping and sucking at the tender flesh. One of his hands slid from under her thigh and wedged itself between them. Fumbling beneath the folds of cloth, he found her center and began an erotic, maddening massage. The pressure at her core tightened, darkened, then shattered into a thousand blinding splinters of light. A ragged groan tore upward from deep in her throat. Within moments, he echoed her harsh moan, and she felt his hot seed flooding her.

FitzHugh braced his weight on one arm while he held her with the other, waiting for the tide of sensation to ebb. Gradually, reluctantly, he returned to the world around them. Cold singed the rims of his ears. A gust of wind hit his back and ruffled the hair at his neck. He felt himself slide from his wife's wet, slick depths, and forced himself to step back. Mellisynt's skirts fell, and she leaned against the wall with a languid smile.

"You'd best cover yourself before you freeze," she suggested, her eyes on his depleted manhood. "I would not have you permanently crippled."

FitzHugh's bark of laughter echoed in the deserted garden. Grinning, he stuffed himself back inside his clothes.

"You little witch—if I am crippled, you have only yourself to blame."

His voice rumbled with good-humored teasing as he took her arm and led her toward the wooden door to the castle. "Are you so desperate to get the babe you desire that you must make your husband service you on the coldest day of the winter, in a public garden?"

Mellisynt felt a shock of startled surprise. She stumbled beside him, her steps guided by his, her thoughts whirling. She only half heard his smug, satisfied bantering. Dazed, she realized that she hadn't once associated her driving need to couple this day with its possible results. As they entered the hall, heat washed over her, generated as much by the roaring fire in the stone hearth as by her own rushing emotions. By the saints, when had she submerged her desire for a child in her desire for this man? When had she stopped seeing him as the means to give her a babe to love, and begun to see him as someone to love in himself?

Love? What did she know of love, she wondered wildly? What she felt for FitzHugh had none of the sweet, tortured nobility the troubadours sang of. She wanted him in a most basic, primitive way. Was it just desire? Or lust? Was she truly the evil daughter of Eve Father Anselem had so often decried, out only to satisfy the cravings of her flesh? Her head swam with confused thoughts. She ached for a quiet corner, for time to herself to sort through the emotions roiling in her. When FitzHugh stopped at the entrance to the women's quarters, she lifted dazed eyes to his.

"Don't fret, lady wife," he told her gently. "Remember, what I have, I—"

"Yes, yes," she said, interrupting him, anxious to be away from his overwhelming presence. "What you have, you hold."

"I've decided to revise the order of my holdings. You definitely rank above my destriers. With a little more work, you might even replace my prized damascene sword in my affections.''

He kissed her lightly on her nose. ''I'll send someone to escort you and Isabeau to our place at the feast this eve.''

Bemused, Mellisynt made her way to the dormer room and opened the door. Waves of noise and color washed over her. The tiny room was filled to overflowing with chattering ladies and maids, while open baskets and trunks spilled silks and velvets of every shade onto the floor. A cluster of women vied for the thin light by the window, spreading bottles and vials and horn boxes of cosmetics in a dazzling array. Laughter rang across the room as women dug through their finery and called to each other to admire this piece or that. The cloying fragrances of musk and sandalwood and Cyprus oyselet filled the air, accompanied by the tinkling of perforated golden perfume balls.

''Where have you been?'' Isabeau demanded, grabbing Mellisynt's hand and pulling her toward their corner of the room. She didn't wait for a reply, which was just as well, since Mellisynt couldn't for the life of her think of one that would not burn the ears of a young virgin.

''We've but a few hours to prepare for the feast,'' Isabeau complained. ''This ninny the duchess sent to attend us knows naught of applying soot. You must help me.''

Mellisynt blinked and looked at the hapless maid. The girl wrung her hands, tears obviously not far away. Mellisynt dismissed her with a kind nod.

''I don't wish to disappoint you, Isabeau,'' she responded, turning once more to the impatient beauty. ''But I know naught of soot, either. Ah, where do you apply it?''

Isabeau's red, ripe mouth twisted down in a disgusted moue. ''To the brows and lashes, of course.'' She shoved a small round mirror into Mellisynt's hands. ''Here, hold this to the light, and I'll do it myself.''

Mellisynt watched, fascinated, as the girl took a small goathair brush and dipped it into a ceramic pot. With sure strokes, she lengthened and darkened the line of her brow, then dusted her lashes until they gleamed like raven's wings against her alabaster face. That done, Isabeau rummaged through her pots and opened another. The sweet scent of roses drifted above the other, heavier fragrances wafting about the room. Vigorously she rubbed dried petals against her cheeks to augment their natural bloom.

Holding the mirror steady so that Isabeau could complete her toilet, Mellisynt glanced around the room. Her eyes fell upon naked limbs and exposed skin as women bathed and readied themselves. The spicy scent of bay leaves and hyssop, used to subdue the body's odors, filled the air, along with the sharp tang of quicklime as one woman applied it to her upper lip to remove unwanted hair.

"There," Isabeau commented. "That should do it."

Whatever "it" was, it was most certainly done, Mellisynt thought. The girl glowed with color and vibrant life. While Isabeau fiddled with the pots and jars, Mellisynt slowly, unwillingly, turned the mirror in her hands and surveyed the face illuminated there. If the cold and FitzHugh's vigorous attentions had put any color in her face, it had faded well away. Her skin stretched tight across her cheekbones, pale and taut. Her brows and lashes were thick and dark, but lacked the lustrous shine of Isabeau's. And although her lips looked swollen and slightly red from the kisses so recently pressed on them, they did not pout with cherry ripeness. With a small sigh, Mellisynt put the mirror aside. Isabeau's hesitant voice broke into her musings.

"I don't wish to offend you, my lady, but I have some skill with paints and brushes. Do you wish it, I would be happy to add a daub of color to your face."

Mellisynt stared at the girl in surprise.

Isabeau shrugged. "'Tis little enough to repay you for your kindness to me on that accursed ship, when I was so ill. I...I thank you for that, my lady."

Realizing that gratitude sat most uneasily on the beauty's shoulders, Mellisynt smiled. "You're most welcome. And I thank you for the offer, but in truth, there's not much that paint and powders can do for this face."

Isabeau tilted her head, and a determined gleam came into her sea-green eyes. The smile she gave Mellisynt was all woman.

"You underestimate yourself...and me," she chided.

Two hours later, Mellisynt pinned the emerald brooch to her mantle with shaking hands. She'd been stripped, scrubbed, pumiced in places she blushed to recall, sprinkled with more herbs and scented flowers than she could count, and dressed in borrowed linens from the skin out. Having found a cause worthy of her not inconsiderable energy, Isabeau had taken charge of preparing Mellisynt for the banquet as if she were the main course instead of one of the throng of lesser knights' dependents who would fill the lower boards.

"Here, let me help you." Isabeau brushed Mellisynt's hands aside and fastened the emerald securely to the green velvet of her own second-best bliaut, loaned out for the occasion.

"Do you mind that this brooch was your mother's, and would have been yours?" Mellisynt asked, gazing down at the dark head bent before her.

"Of course I mind." Isabeau sniffed, her fingers busy with the clasp. "But I count the emerald well lost if it brings me a wealthy husband in return. One who will shower me with many more jewels than this, and who will be so besotted with my looks he'll be easy as pudding to manage."

Mellisynt took the girl's hands in a loose hold. "Don't count on a husband's wealth alone to bring you joy. I can speak of that from experience."

Isabeau shrugged and drew away to pin her own mantle across her shoulders. "I don't expect joy of a husband, my lady. Only comfort and luxury."

Curious, Mellisynt eyed the younger girl. "And love? Do you not expect love in your life?"

"Of course. But that will come from the knight who wins my favor. Who proves himself worthy to wear red in my honor, showing he's won my regard with his reverence and poetry."

Isabeau's eyes took on a dreamy, faraway look. "When I don a yellow gown and proclaim my acceptance of a lover, it will be for someone strong and handsome and most devoted to me. Not for a mere husband," she finished, straightening.

Mellisynt followed the girl out of the emptying room, confusion wrapping its insidious coils around her once more. In the face of Isabeau's conventional scorn for a husband's regard, Mellisynt hesitated to admit, even to herself, that she had primped and powdered herself for FitzHugh. She recalled the judgments rendered at the duchess's courts of love, which proclaimed it impossible for a man to revere a wife he could have at will. A slow flush added to the tint of roses on her cheeks. If a husband couldn't cherish his wife who came readily to his bed, what must he think of one taken up against a stone wall in broad daylight! Nay, not taken even. One who wrapped her legs around his hips and all but drained the seed from him with her writhing. Shaken, she trailed after Isabeau and the other women, hardly hearing their excited exclamations as they entered the huge, vaulted hall and made their way through the milling masses.

The page FitzHugh sent to guide them to their seats elbowed his way through the crowd, making space enough for the two women to follow him. After a low-voiced argument with another page, punctuated by fierce scowls, scandalous name-calling and a stealthy kick on the shins, he convinced the other to squeeze the occupants of a bench together enough to make room for the ladies. Mellisynt wondered briefly how FitzHugh's solid bulk would fit on the packed seat, then abandoned all thought entirely as a blaze of trumpets signaled the arrival of the high table. She surged to her feet with the rest of the crowd, breath caught in her throat, as the men and women who ruled her world made their entrance.

From her position far down the hall, she could just make out their features. There was no mistaking the king, of course. Even if he hadn't been wearing a gem-encrusted crown, Henry's robust figure and flaming orange-red hair would have identified him. Although he'd passed his fiftieth year, Henry strode forward with the legendary, furious energy that exhausted all those around him. Mellisynt had heard stories of courtiers left to find shelter as best they could under hedge-rows while their demonic king galloped far ahead, often covering a hundred miles and more in a day's travel.

But for all the king's vibrant presence, it was the queen who held everyone's avid gaze. Some eleven years older than Henry, Eleanor still bore traces of the fabled beauty that had elicited the passionate love and implacable fury of two kings. Her gossamer veil drifted as she walked calmly to her seat, showing ebony hair only lightly streaked with gray. Her blue gown fitted tight around waist and hips still slender, despite the birthing of ten healthy children. A wide embroidered belt, studded with gleaming stones, encircled her hips, from which dangled an assortment of precious pendants—silver scissors, an enameled mirror, a pouch of soft leather, and the inevitable vented golden ball filled with aromatic scents. Noticeably absent was the usual dangle of keys, symbol of a woman's power as chatelaine. Eleanor had lost her keys, as well as her freedom, some twelve years earlier, when she'd incited her young sons to an abortive rebellion against their father.

Mellisynt was so struck by this first glimpse of the woman who had won, and lost, kingdoms and who had introduced the world to the concept of courtly love that she didn't hear FitzHugh edge his way through the crowd to her side. She jumped when his hand closed over her elbow, and a deep, husky whisper stirred the hairs by her ear.

"Watch the smile on Geoffrey's face. If it slips, you will know the worst."

She tried to turn, but FitzHugh's grip tightened and held her facing forward. The king raised his hands for quiet and began to speak. Mellisynt strained to hear, but his words were lost over the vast length of the hall and the shifting crowd.

"What does he say?" she whispered furiously over her shoulder.

FitzHugh bent and placed his lips close to her ear. "I pray he says that his sons have agreed to peace. And that he's given them each new honors in recognition of their valor and strength of arms."

"New honors? What new honors?"

A full-throated roar drowned out his reply. It began in the front ranks, among those closest to the high table, and swelled as it rolled down the length of the great hall. The bright banners hanging from the rafters high above fluttered, adding to the sensation of sound and movement that swept over Mellisynt like a tide. While the noise still thundered about the hall, the king turned and motioned two figures forward. Mellisynt recognized Geoffrey instantly. Even over the heads of hundreds of courtiers, the duke's golden-red hair and handsome face stood out. By contrast, Richard Lionheart, duke of Normandy, count of Maine and Anjou, lord regent of Aquitaine and heir to the throne of England, appeared dark and forbidding. Richard had his mother's raven hair and high cheekbones, but none of her smiling charm. He was somber and serious, his square jaw set and eyes steady under dark brows.

The crowd quieted when the two brothers faced each other. FitzHugh's hand tightened on Mellisynt's arm until she thought the bones would break, but she dared not pull away, nor to disturb in any way the ominous stillness that settled gradually over the vast hall. It was as if five hundred people held their breath, waiting, wondering.

And five hundred people, Mellisynt included, let out a relieved sigh as Geoffrey and Richard leaned toward each other, pressed their lips each to the other's cheek, and then returned to their seats. FitzHugh's hand loosened, and he let out a little grunt of satisfaction.

"Why did he change his stance?" Mellisynt whispered as she scooted her hips sideways against the well-padded ones of the matron next to her to make room for her husband.

FitzHugh took a long draft from the two-handed cup set before them. He closed his eyes while the liquid flowed down his throat, as if savoring some exotic elixir instead of a hearty, clove-spiced wine. When he had drained the cup, he turned and related what he knew in a low voice well covered by the din all around them.

"The king offered Geoffrey the chance to lead his men against Toulouse. To recoup the reparations paid to Richard's Crusade chests. I was not sure Geoffrey would take the obvious sop."

Mellisynt's eyes rounded. The house of Toulouse had battled that of Anjou for centuries, but she'd not heard that hostilities had broken out again. "The count of Toulouse has declared war?"

"Nay," FitzHugh said, a wry grin twisting his lips. "But he will as soon as he hears that King Henry claims Montauban, which guards the entrance to the Valley of the Garonne, and the rich Toulouse farmlands. We sail with our armies within the week to besiege the city."

"The lands surrounding Montauban have been part of Toulouse for generations!" she exclaimed. "By what right does the king now claim them?"

"None, in truth, although he cites a distant ancestor who married a sister of the present count's grandfather."

"Why on earth would he try to press such a specious claim?"

"So that Geoffrey might go to war and win back the spoils he had to cede to Richard."

Mellisynt's spoon clattered to the boards. She swiveled in her seat to stare at her husband. He sat there, calmly spearing chunks of roasted boar from the serving platter with his pointed dagger, as if unconcerned that a whole city, if not an entire province, would soon be ravaged as part of a political game. She thought of her probing questions to FitzHugh in the garden earlier, and of her heady belief that she might come to understand him. She knew now that she would never grasp what drove men, particularly the breed of men who called themselves warriors. While her mind churned with visions of bloody battle, and of FitzHugh's inevitable role in it, the object of her concern appeared most satisfied with the situation.

"How can you be pleased that there will be fighting again so soon? I thought you wanted peace for Brittany...time to recover from the last months of war!"

FitzHugh's brows rose at her vehemence. "This *is* peace for Brittany. We take the battle to the Garonne, far from Breton borders, and King Henry will augment our forces with levies of his own. 'Tis an honorable solution to Geoffrey's dilemma. We fight Henry's battles this time, and the king will bear the brunt of the cost."

"But not the brunt of the injuries. Nor the deaths. That will be your charge, yours and that hotheaded idiot you call a friend. He would—"

"Be silent, woman. I'll not have you speak of my overlord in such a voice, nor in such a setting."

The sudden ice in FitzHugh's voice halted Mellisynt's tirade in midsentence. She took her lower lip between her teeth, struggling to overcome the anger that swamped her. Did FitzHugh not see how he was being used? How Henry, and Geoffrey, and all those other highborn rogues at the head table used the assembled knights to their own purposes? They would sally forth, their banners blowing bravely in the wind, their armour shining, to war with another lord as powerful and grasping and hungry as himself. And for what? For hope of booty, for spoils, for lands. For riches.

Mellisynt felt hysteria rising up in her. Was her life ever to be controlled by men who desired riches? First one who sucked coppers from serfs and hoarded his silver in deep cellars. Then one who wed a woman he'd known less than an hour to gain her inheritance and who would spill his blood eagerly to advance his estate. She lifted her cup with shaking hands.

The rest of the long evening passed in a blur. Mellisynt nodded politely when FitzHugh commented on her appearance, expressing his appreciation of Isabeau's efforts. She stood silent while the girl flirted with him after the boards were pushed aside, practicing the smiles and slanted looks that soon had a flock of colorful, hefty young knights surrounding her. Mellisynt refused a halfhearted offer from FitzHugh to join in the dance, sensing his relief in his lighthearted comment that one his size looked much the fool galloping around a room to some damned trumpets.

The press of bodies and noise soon began to close in on her. After the storm of emotions she'd been through this day, she longed for a quiet corner, a place to sort through her troubled thoughts. Yet when FitzHugh drew her into a side alcove on their way back to the dormer hours later, she clung to him, not wanting to think, not wanting to listen to his murmured instructions for the trip north. Not wanting to hear his whispered farewell.

Chapter Ten

Although neither Isabeau nor the little maid succumbed to illness, the journey north proved far more tedious for Mellisynt than the voyage from Nantes. This time they sailed aboard a lumbering merchant ship, stopping at every major port to unload and take on new cargoes. Isabeau delighted in the merchantman's slow, plodding progress, as it gave her a chance to explore the busy markets in the port cities they visited.

Mellisynt accompanied the girl while she wandered through merchant halls more richly decorated than most castles. She waited patiently while Isabeau exclaimed over woolens as soft as clouds from the hinterlands and fingered trinkets and silks coming in from abroad. But she couldn't generate any interest in the luxuries that Isabeau sighed over.

In truth, she was surprised by her lack of enthusiasm. For so many years she'd bemoaned her dull, shapeless robes, and the meanness of Trémont's furnishings. Now she had the splendors of the world at her fingertips, and the means to purchase what she would, yet little tempted her. In the darkness of her curtained bed aboard the merchant ship Mellisynt admitted that much of her ennui had to do with the absence of a certain oversize knight, one whose harsh visage and less-than-gentle manners should not occasion the improper thoughts they did. Her mind returned over and over again to the desolate garden of Winchester Castle, and to the explosion of heat and light FitzHugh's hands and mouth had wrought within her. She tossed and turned in her narrow bed until Isabeau called out crossly that she should take a purge to still her disquiet humors.

Her only relief from the half-formed longings that tormented her was the boisterous company of her younger companions. FitzHugh had commended Bartholomew to her care, along with the sorry hound who seemed to believe he was her second shadow. Hobbling about the deck with surprising agility, the dog attached itself to her by day and howled outside her door by night until she perforce had to grant him entry. Over Isabeau's angry protests, the hound took up residence in the small cabin, sprawling across most of the floor space between the bunks and relegating the maid to a pallet outside the door.

As the ship lumbered north, Mellisynt searched for activities to keep a lively, mischievous youngster occupied. Freed from his duties as page by his lord's absence, Bartholomew harried the shipmaster unmercifully. Once the boy had to be hauled down bodily from the tangle of ropes he'd climbed to, high above the decks. Another time he was fished out of the garbage-strewn waters beside the docks, when his eagerness to help release the ropes sent him tumbling overboard. In desperation, Mellisynt borrowed the captain's ivory-and-malachite chess set, then a set of spillikins carved by one of the seamen. When those diversions failed to hold Bartholomew's attention for long, she cajoled the boy into helping her identify the coastal landmarks they passed. He perched on a stool beside her on the upper deck and shared what sketchy details he knew of the coastal towers and cliffside keeps visible from shipboard.

"Look, my lady," he exclaimed one crisp, sunny morning. "'Tis Orford Castle."

Mellisynt gazed up at massive walls of stone and shell surrounding two circular towers. Rising high above the coastal marshes, the towers commanded a superb overview of the sea-lanes they had been built to protect.

"'Tis the king's own castle," Bartholomew informed her, obviously proud of his smattering of knowledge. "We stopped there when I first journeyed south with my lord. See, the king's standard flies above the walls. Do you see the lion crest, and the golden R on the pennant below?"

Mellisynt turned to stare at the boy. "What is this R? Is it the symbol for King Henry's name?"

"No," Bartholomew told her, scornfully. "It stands for *Rex*. For *King* in Latin," he explained.

"Do you recognize this symbol? This Latin letter?"

"Aye, of course. The pages all spend an hour a day with the priests. 'Tis part of our training." The boy's mouth screwed up in disgust. "I'd much rather be practicing with the lance or bow than translating verses from the psalter."

Mellisynt stared at Bartholomew, not really seeing his wind-tossed golden curls or his dirt-smudged face. Instead, she thought of the rolled parchments buried deep in her traveling baskets, those indecipherable documents that gave her financial independence and made no sense to her at all.

"Do you read them, these verses in the prayer books?"

"Aye, of course." Bartholomew preened like a feathered cock. At her fascinated look, he amended his bold assertion. "Well, I try, most seriously. Father Vincent has worn out any number of switches, beating the lines into my hide."

"If I show you some parchments, can you tell me the words and letters?"

A look of doubt compounded with dread crossed the boy's face, but Mellisynt ignored it. She remembered the night FitzHugh had gone over the betrothal documents with her, explaining sources of rents and incomes. She'd tried to grasp all the details, but within moments her head had begun to spin. He'd finally rolled the parchments up with an exasperated sigh, assuring her that she could rely on the clerics at Edge-moor and his uncle to help her with financial matters. Mellisynt stared across the sluggish waves at the castle slipping slowly past, imprinting the brave *R* from the pennant on her mind. Never again, she swore, would she allow any cleric to hold sway over her. Never again would she be helpless and bound by ignorance in her own keep. Not if she could help it.

Brushing aside Bartholomew's vociferous objections with ruthless determination, she kept him pinned to her side for an hour each day thereafter, poring over the betrothal documents. It was soon obvious the boy had large gaps in his education, but he struggled manfully over each letter, his tongue caught between his teeth and his brow puckered in concentration. Once or twice, when they met an impenetrable word or obscure conjugation, they appealed to Sir Peter for help. St. Bressé's education was not much better than Bartholomew's, and his obvious unease at deciphering words soon won his release from their impromptu classes.

Isabeau laughed scornfully at the sight of a grown woman taking lessons from a reluctant, grubby-faced tutor and declined to join their sessions. She whiled away the slow journey by poring over the treasures purchased at various ports and experimenting with new, exotic cosmetics.

Mellisynt watched uneasily when Isabeau sidled up to Sir Peter, fluttering darkened lashes and laying a white hand on his arm. The serious, unsmiling young knight had but recently wed, she knew, and his wife awaited them at Edgemoor. She didn't interfere, however, since St. Bressé bowed respectfully whenever Isabeau approached and listened most attentively to her pouting comments, but gave no overt sign he was succumbing to the girl's charms.

Finally, on the day the sun entered the sign of Capricorn and the darkest day of winter descended, they sailed up the river Humber's wide estuary and anchored at Kingston upon Hull. Mellisynt huddled on deck in the damp mists, her fur cloak drawn tight around her face, and watched their trunks and baskets being unloaded. They would continue their journey north overland.

With his customary careful attention to his duties, Sir Peter planned the trip in easy stages. He also arranged for a spacious, horse-drawn litter to carry the ladies over the rough roads, which met with Mellisynt's enthusiastic approval. Brushing aside her warm thanks, he explained that Sir Richard had given him most strict instructions not to mount her on any of his valuable horses.

Five days later, Mellisynt's heart thudded with excitement at the first sight of the keep that would be her home for those months spent in England each year. Edgemoor held true to its name. Set atop a high mound of earth not far from the rocky, windswept coast, it looked out over the desolate moors and dales of northern Yorkshire. Here, on the roof of England, Mellisynt sensed that nature was as yet unsubdued. The sky seemed wider and closer, the land harsher. The red sandstone keep appeared starker and more forbidding than the elegant stone castles to the south. This land suited FitzHugh, she decided. It exuded the same raw power, the same untamed ruggedness as her lord. Gazing up at the Edgemoor's high walls, she understood her husband's oft-stated disdain for the luxuries of the royal courts. He belonged here, in this wild land, holding it for the king and the duke against predators from the sea and raiders from the north.

As the massive timber gate swung closed behind her and walls of red stone topped with sharpened timbers surrounded their party, Mellisynt marveled at her excitement. She felt none of the suffocating sense of imprisonment she'd endured within Trémont for so many years. Mayhap it was the sea-laden breeze that lifted the edges of her cloak and blew away the odors of a crowded keep, leaving a tangy scent of salt in her nostrils. Or the cheerful jumble of roving livestock, barking dogs, boar pits, stables, dovecotes and servants' huts that jammed the outer yard, so different from Trémont's austere, shadowed grounds. This keep teemed with life, and with people, she noted, as she climbed out of the litter.

It appeared that every soul in the great hall and from the surrounding farms and villages had gathered to welcome their new lady, or at least to gawk at her. Keeping her cloak gathered close about her, Mellisynt surveyed the assembled crowd with some consternation. While she struggled to find words of greeting, a tall, well-muscled youth detached himself from the group beside the hall's entrance.

"God keep you, Lady Mellisynt. I am William, son to FitzHugh. My father sent word of your coming and bid me travel to Edgemoor to welcome you."

Mellisynt's heart leapt into her throat as she surveyed her son-by-marriage. FitzHugh's voice had roughened with pride when he'd told her of his oldest, William, now two-and-ten years of age and a squire in service to Lord De Burg, justiciar of England. But nothing in her lord's gruff description of the boy had prepared her for blue eyes that sparkled with life in a tanned face surrounded by black curls the exact shade of his sire's. Or for the dimpled smile that William must have inherited from his dam.

"My brother, Geoffrey, is page to Lord Ranulf, earl of Chester, and could not come north to greet you. He would add his most reverent welcome were he here."

From what FitzHugh had told her of young Geoffrey, godson to the duke, Mellisynt doubted his greeting would be reverent. Her lord had described his younger son, not yet nine years of age, as the greatest scamp ever to spring from any man's loins. With a silent prayer that she would breed such sons, Mellisynt smiled and held out her hands.

"I thank you for taking time from your duties to welcome me. Will you stay long?"

"Nay. Lord De Burg leaves soon for Ireland with the king, and I go with him." William puffed a bit at his own importance, then flashed her a boyish grin. "But I have three days' respite, and would show you about Edgemoor. We can cover much ground in three days, with good horses under us.''

Mellisynt stifled a groan. Swallowing, she turned to greet the elderly, white-haired man who came forward.

"Hail, lady. I am Alymer, uncle to Sir Richard and defender of the keep in his absence. He bade us make you comfortable in your new home.''

Mellisynt blinked as the hawk-faced man bent and brushed his lips across her cheeks in the kiss of welcome. Sweet Mother, did all the men in her husband's family have the same massive frame and chiseled countenance? Although Alymer's hair was silvered and his belly slightly rounded with age, he still towered over her.

"Thank you, Sir Alymer.''

"Nay, not Sir.'' He led her forward. "'Tis plain Alymer, late of Swanley, now of Edgemoor. And this is my wife, Hertha.''

The last vestiges of Mellisynt's nervousness faded when Dame Hertha came forward. As round as she was tall, the woman had the friendliest smile and the merriest eyes Mellisynt had ever seen. Hertha bent her head in a quick obeisance, all three chins wobbling vigorously, then detached a huge ring of keys from her wide belt and held them out.

"We're most pleased to welcome our new chatelaine, my lady.''

Feeling slightly overwhelmed by the sudden acquisition of so many new relatives, Mellisynt took the ring from her pudgy hands with a warm smile.

"I accept the keys, but would beg you not to relinquish your place or your duties. I need your help and guidance in learning the ways of Edgemoor.''

The woman beamed, as if she'd been given a great honor, not been asked to continue what must be a crushing burden. Although Edgemoor was considerably smaller than Trémont, with fewer outlying farms and dependents, Mellisynt knew well that the task of ordering its daily living would require all her energy and skill. She truly welcomed the older woman's experience and apparent willingness to continue in her role. Mayhap Hertha's assistance would give her time to master the frustrating parchments.

She turned, beckoning Isabeau forward to introduce her to the others. Leaning gracefully on Sir Peter's strong arm, the girl picked her way over the rough ground. Mellisynt heard a small gasp from the ranks of the women behind Hertha and glanced toward the sound. A slender, plain-faced young woman stared at Sir Peter, jealousy written in every bone of her rigid body. His wife, Mellisynt thought with a sigh. Suddenly the winter months, when they'd all perforce be enclosed within the keep's round walls by snow and frost, loomed long and fraught with unforeseen dangers.

"I don't care what the losses, you will take them forward!"

"For God's sake, Geoffrey, listen to your words," Fitz-Hugh snarled. "You would sacrifice these men to your damned pride."

Rage glittered in the duke's golden eyes. "'Tis not my pride that makes you balk, bastard. 'Tis that you might not win such fat ransoms in open battle as you do by besieging half-defended, petty little keeps."

FitzHugh sucked in his breath. His eyes narrowed on the red face glaring at him from across the wooden camp table. He planted two mailed fists on the table and leaned forward, making no effort to disguise his fury.

"Do you accuse me of cowardice, of shirking battle, my lord duke?" he asked softly, dangerously.

For long, tense moments, friend faced friend. Hostility arced between them. An even deeper red washed over Geoffrey's cheeks. Angevin temper warred with the ties of friendship, and the struggle showed plainly on his expressive face. Outside the tent, normal camp sounds filled the soft spring air, but inside only the harsh, rasping breath of duke and vassal cut the thick stillness. Beads of sweat ran down Geoffrey's temples. With a low growl, he straightened and dashed the stinging salt from his eyes.

"Oh, be damned to you, FitzHugh. You know I would as soon see myself in hell as believe you false to me and your oaths."

Chagrin softened the hard lines of his face, and he gave a rueful smile. This time, however, the calculated charm failed dismally in its aim.

FitzHugh straightened slowly. Rage still spread its icy tentacles in every vein, and he didn't trust himself to speak. In truth, he didn't trust himself not to lean across the small table and knock his friend to the dirt floor. Never before, in all the years of their friendship, had Geoffrey questioned FitzHugh's honor. And never before had FitzHugh allowed anyone to do so and remain among the living.

As if sensing that this time he'd gone too far, Geoffrey unclenched his fist and reached out to grasp FitzHugh's arm. His fingers pressed mail deep into flesh and bone with the iron strength of their hold.

"Richard, 'tis the accursed heat and my own distemper speaking. And this damned game we play with Toulouse. We've spent nigh on four months chasing that slippery old fool around half of France. I've lost what little patience I possess in the process."

FitzHugh stared down at the hand gripping his arm with such painful intensity, thinking that for the first time in many weeks he could agree with Geoffrey. The duke *had* lost his patience, and much of his perspective, in the prosecution of this war. Not satisfied with besieging Montauban, their primary objective, Geoffrey had widened the battle and sent FitzHugh deep into Toulouse.

For months now, they'd fought against overwhelming odds as the crafty count of Toulouse lured the invaders deeper and deeper into his lands. He left burned villages and fouled wells behind so that the invaders had to spread themselves thin to forage for sustenance. Now Geoffrey wanted to divide his forces still further, and send half of them west, to the flat, fertile plain of the river Garonne, where Toulouse was thought to have retreated, while the rest went south to lay siege to the capital. FitzHugh had left his men encamped in a protected vale while he rode furiously back to Geoffrey's camp. He would know what drove this madness before he took even one archer one step farther. He pulled his arm free of the duke's hard grip.

"We achieved our objective in February, Geoffrey. Tell me truthfully why you still push forward, against all odds, against your own knights' best advice. We're private here, just the two of us. What devious scheme have you in your brain now?"

The duke flushed once more. "Why do you think it devious to want to press forward? Why don't you see the advantages of subduing once and for all a wily foe who's long harassed our borders?"

"Because taking Toulouse has no long-term advantages, man! This province is a buffer between the Angevin lands and the French king's domains. Do we take Toulouse, King Philip will be on us with every knight he can call to service or hire out of hand."

FitzHugh paused, and the suspicion that had taken hold in these last bloody weeks hardened into certainty.

"Unless," he continued slowly, watching Geoffrey's eyes, "you have assurances from Philip that he would welcome you as ally. Unless you think to align yourself with him against your father."

Geoffrey's golden eyes slid away. He turned and paced the length of the tent. FitzHugh felt a coldness creep down his spine. Had his friend forsworn himself?

"Nay," Geoffrey finally answered with a troubled frown. "I've made no promises to Philip, although 'tis true he would have me help him throw off my father's dominion on the Continents. He's offered men and supplies to aid us in this campaign, but I've not accepted."

He paused, and for a moment FitzHugh glimpsed the tortured man within the hulking, boisterous shell.

"They have me on a rack, Richard! One pulls this way, one that. I would be my own man, not my father's puppet nor Philip's tool."

"No man is entirely his own," FitzHugh replied deliberately. "All of us have ties, to God, to our liege. You've sworn to your father, you hold Richmond through him and Brittany through Constance. You owe nothing to Philip, nor would you gain by playing his game. He would use you for his own ends."

"I know, I know!" Geoffrey kicked a camp stool angrily. He strode about the spacious tent, agitation robbing his person of its normal fluid grace. "'Tis why I want to take Toulouse, despite my father's urgings to desist. I want to show him and Philip that I can do it! That I need neither of them to jerk my strings. That I'm as fit to rule my own lands as Richard Lionheart does his."

There was a certain twisted logic in his thinking, FitzHugh admitted. Mayhap if Geoffrey showed strength and independence, he would become a force to be reckoned with in his own right. One that could help mold a precarious balance of power on the Continent. If that was truly his goal.

FitzHugh rubbed a weary hand across his eyes. He wanted to believe Geoffrey. He wanted to push aside the remnants of anger from his friend's harsh accusations of moments before, to recapture the trust and boon companionship that had been theirs until Geoffrey's inner devils began to twist and push him into recklessness.

"Lead this foray, Richard, and we have Toulouse. Once he's taken, I will negotiate honorable terms and withdraw, I swear it. I want not the lands—only to show myself capable of taking them."

FitzHugh stared at his friend for a long moment, doubt and suspicion battling with the need to trust. Finally, slowly, he nodded.

* * *

FitzHugh dragged his arm across his eyes to clear the blood and sweat, and tried desperately to get his bearings. Waves of noise rose all around him, battering at him with the force of a blow. The screams of dead and dying, the hoarse shouts of the foot soldiers and the wild shrieks of wounded horses, the sound of steel ringing against steel and arrows twanging into padded leather all beat at his ears. He ducked as a crossbow bolt whistled overhead. The cut on his forehead reopened as it slammed against his helm. A stream of fresh blood poured down, blinding him once more.

With a vicious wrench on the reins, he checked Voyager's plunging advance. He dared not push forward when he couldn't see whether the figures before him were those of his own men or of Toulouse. FitzHugh had led this bold charge at the center of the count's waving line. He knew his foot soldiers had swept forward with him, but at what pace? Were they behind him, or had he penetrated the enemy's line in this last, mad charge and now was surrounded? Swearing, he wiped furiously at his eyes. When his blurred vision cleared, he identified his mud-covered squire just beside him, and a solid phalanx of his own men behind Ian. He let out a ragged, relieved breath and set his spurs to Voyager once more.

"À moi! À Bretagne!"

His hoarse shout barely carried over the roar of battle, but the wave of men followed him forward. The ground was awash with mud churned out of the spring-softened earth by a thousand slashing hooves, and with the gore of half as many trampled bodies. FitzHugh charged at the wavering center line even now folding back against its own flanks. He leaned forward over his mount's shoulder, cutting and slashing as the Voyager surged forward.

Another bolt whistled through the air. With a sickening thud, it drove through the barding covering the destrier's neck. As Voyager screamed and went down, forelegs thrashing, FitzHugh tried to kick his feet free of the stirrups and throw himself sideways. Not quite fast enough, he landed in the mud, one foot trapped under his mount.

The tide of men swept over them both. FitzHugh planted one foot against the saddle and pushed, struggling desperately to free himself from the mortally wounded horse. More fallen knights died from being crushed by their own mounts or trampled by oncoming forces than from battle wounds. He gasped in relief as Ian fought his way through the rush of men to his side. The squire flung himself from his own horse, grabbed his lord's mailed arm, and heaved with all his might. FitzHugh's foot slid out from under the now-still destrier. Without pause, he mounted Ian's horse, leaving the squire to fight his way back to the handlers responsible for the spare mounts. Sword in hand, blood streaming from the cut on his forehead, fire and fear and icy fury coursing through his veins, he charged forward.

Within an hour, it was over. One by one, the count's surviving knights surrendered their standards and their swords. Gradually the roar of battle subsided, until only the screams and sobbing cries of wounded men and beasts carried on the April air. FitzHugh pushed his mailed hood back and surveyed the battlefield wearily. From his position on a small rise, he could see most of the flat plain enclosed by the winding river. The remnants of the count's armies were spread in a thin line along the water's edge, with the bulk of FitzHugh's forces between them. Bodies lay scattered across the devastated plain in grotesque piles alongside fallen horses, abandoned weapons, slaughtered farm animals and burning huts. It was a scene of incredible carnage, one he should be used to but wasn't. Surveying the aftermath of battle with aching eyes, FitzHugh cursed Geoffrey.

"Do we send the captured knights back to Montauban?" A begrimed knight, one of Geoffrey's lesser vassals, slumped wearily in his saddle and awaited instructions.

"Aye. The duke will decide where to incarcerate them until the ransoms are paid. See that the scribes record who was taken, and by whom, so the moneys are distributed fairly when they're received.''

''And the count?''

''I'll meet with him myself and take his pledge. Prepare a tent where he may rest until we restore order and see to the wounded.''

The man nodded and rode away.

FitzHugh rubbed a weary hand across his eyes, inadvertently grinding filth and blood into his wound. Jesu, he was tired. He slumped against the cantle, sheathing his sword for the first time since the bloody battle began. His eyes swept the littered plain, and he wondered again, deep in his soul, if such slaughter was worth the price of Geoffrey's pride.

A small field of clover at the edge of the plain, miraculously unscathed by churning hooves or flaming arrows, caught his attention. Its verdant color was a breath of life amid the stench of death. In the late-afternoon sun, it glowed green and rich, and reminded FitzHugh most forcefully of his lady's luminous eyes. Of how they, too, had glowed with life and passion in a bleak winter garden.

That scene, and others involving a curtain of russet hair and a slender body, had filled FitzHugh's mind more often than he cared to admit these last months. He shifted in his saddle, wondering how one slight, pale woman should have taken hold of his thoughts—and his desires—with so firm a grip. How the image of her awaiting him at Edgemoor had become such a talisman through these months of war and death. It was as if she lured him, drew him home. Never before had he felt such an impatience to be done with the business of battle and seek the softness of a woman's arms.

The realization that he and Geoffrey would return at last to England spurred him to action. As the blazing sun sank into the red-tinted river, clogged with the carcasses of men and horses drowned in their frantic attempts to escape, FitzHugh sent an exhausted courier to summon the senior knights and begin the wearisome process of restoring order after the madness of battle.

Ironically, FitzHugh's very victory became the instrument that delayed his departure for England yet several more months. Geoffrey's successes alarmed his brother Richard Lionheart, who began to mobilize his forces. King Henry himself came to France in late April when the rumor spread that Richard was about to attack Brittany. The king rode across his vast domains at a frenetic pace, bearding first one son and then the other in their respective camps.

In return for his assurance that he would not war with his brother, Geoffrey won full cognizance over the duchy of Brittany and the county of Nantes. He planned a triumphant return to his capital city of Rennes and sent word to all his barons that there would be a great assize the following month.

As holder of the fief of Trémont, FitzHugh was required to attend the great parliament. Sweltering in ceremonial robes under the June sun, he paraded with the rest of Geoffrey's barons through the streets of Rennes. During many a late-night session, he helped the duke forge reforms modeled after those King Henry had implemented in England, designed to curb the barons' independence. Geoffrey's blazing personality and sheer stubbornness forced each measure through the assembled parliament. One by one the fiercely independent Breton lords bent a stiff knee and pledged fealty to the triumphant duke.

By the time the great assize disbanded and the business of implementing the new reforms was done, June had become July, then August. FitzHugh's impatience to be gone grew with every passing day.

"By the saints, 'tis good to be back in the north again!"

Geoffrey slewed sideways in the saddle to face the sea and let the cool breeze ruffle through his sweat-flattened hair. They'd ridden hard since landing two days ago, pushing horses and men, following the coast road north. Just a half hour before, they had splashed across the estuary that marked the beginning of FitzHugh's own holdings.

Below them, waves crashed against the rocks, sending a fine spray up and over the cliffs. Sunlight danced on a dark emerald sea, reminding FitzHugh anew why he clung to these wild lands and the small keep that guarded them. Here, with the rolling moors to the west and the crashing sea to the east, the rest of civilization seemed far away. Here, the burdens of fealty and honor and finding balance in a world of intrigue slipped away. Here, he was home. And here, too, his wife awaited him.

FitzHugh pictured her in the great hall of his keep, her hair demurely veiled and her slim figure clothed in gowns of soft, rich color. He saw her coming forward to greet him with a chatelaine's solemn dignity, to offer him the kiss of welcome. Fingering the pouch at his waist, where a count's ransom in pearls nestled, he visualized how he would drape the ropes of translucent beads around her pale throat in full view of the assembled keep, to show the esteem in which he held his new wife. And how he would remove them slowly, seductively, in the privacy of their room.

"I'm glad I decided to go first to Richmond," Geoffrey said, his booming voice breaking into FitzHugh's musing. "If we had stopped at Winchester before coming north, as my father desired, Constance would have cut off my nose."

"Or your manhood," FitzHugh commented lazily. "She oft swears 'tis the most useless part of your anatomy."

Geoffrey's laughter rang out across the cliffs, and FitzHugh grinned in return. Although both men still carried the scars of their bitter argument in their hearts, FitzHugh's victory, Geoffrey's triumphant assize and the passage of time had helped heal the wounds.

FitzHugh wiped a trickle of sweat from his brow. They'd removed their protective wool surcoats and mailed tunics as they penetrated deep into his lands. Still, the hot August sun beat mercilessly on his sweat-dampened light linen shirt.

"Christ's bones, look at that."

FitzHugh turned in the direction of Geoffrey's wide-eyed stare. Squinting against the sun's dazzle, he searched among the rocks that lined the shore below them.

Geoffrey pointed, "There, where the sand and waters meet."

A figure splashed out of the shallow waves, her white shift lifted high above long, shapely legs. Even from this distance the men could see how the wet cotton clung to her breasts, outlining them in perfect detail. A trill of joyous laughter carried across air as she turned and beckoned to two dark heads just visible in the rolling waters.

"B'God, FitzHugh, if that's one of your villeins, I claim an overlord's rights." Geoffrey's eyes raked the woman's back, lingering on the lush rear clearly delineated by the wet fabric.

One of her companions broke out of the waves and dashed toward shore. FitzHugh's eyes widened in disbelief as he saw the boy's golden curls, unmistakable even from this distance. The second figure emerged and spread three shaggy legs wide to shake the seawater from its massive body. A wave of booming, ear-splitting barks rolled up the cliffside.

Geoffrey flung out an arm and gave FitzHugh a good-natured blow that knocked him sideways in the saddle.

"You've kept this juicy morsel well hidden, you selfish wretch. Send for her this night. I'd like to see her at somewhat closer quarters."

"And so you shall," FitzHugh told him dryly. "You will excuse me, my lord, while I go inform my lady wife that her overlord requests her presence at the keep."

Chapter Eleven

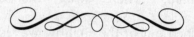

Mellisynt sat atop a sun-washed rock, her knees drawn up and her chin resting on crossed arms. She watched as Bartholomew and the hound raced along the rocky shore. The boy shouted in exuberance at his release from his tutor's stern regimen while the dog jumped and echoed his joy with deafening abandon. She smiled at their lively antics and sturdy figures, thinking how different both child and hound were from when they'd first come into her life. The three of them had grown so close these last months, as winter gave way to spring and spring softened into summer.

With Alymer and Dame Hertha to help in Edgemoor's operation, for the first time in her adult life Mellisynt had had time to enjoy her surroundings. William, her son-by-marriage, had taken her in hand the first week, introducing her to FitzHugh's main tenants and nearby vassals. Although she groaned each time she recalled the long rides with the energetic, boisterous youth, she'd been grateful for his cheerful introductions.

After William left to return to his training, she'd ventured forth with FitzHugh's uncle as guide, tentatively at first and then with growing confidence. She'd visited tenants, brought herbs from the keep's store to ailing serfs, doled out precious seed corn to start the spring plantings. And with each task, she'd explored the wild beauty of her new home. Whether drenched with freezing mist, lashed by spring storms or, as now, bathed in a rare haze of hot sun, the land drew her. After so many years within Trémont's walls, she soaked up the sky and moors like one long-starved.

Her most special time was that spent by the sea. With Dame Hertha's motherly, indulgent cooperation, Mellisynt would slip away from her chatelaine's duties and coax the tutor to release his reluctant pupil. Like a lodestone pointing to the North Star, she and Bartholomew and the hound would head for the rock-strewn coast. They claimed this rough stretch of shore as their own. Out of sight of the keep and the fishing docks to the north, they romped and splashed and grew brown from the sun's rays. Here Bartholomew forgot his page's dignity to become a child once more, and the hound raced the waves as if he had four good legs, not three. And here Mellisynt sat and spun her dreams.

Dreams that centered around the hazy face of her husband. Mellisynt shifted on the hard rock and settled her chin once more. He would come soon, his brief message had said, with the duke. Even the thought of Geoffrey's presence could not dampen the surge of joy she'd felt at the courier's news. She'd gone straight away to lay out her finest robe, fashioned with Isabeau's assistance and trimmed with exquisite embroidery. She would await him on the steps of the keep, she decided, cool and composed, and overwhelm him with her new finery.

A slow smile crept across her face. No doubt she would overwhelm him with her need, as well, once she had him within their curtained bed. Sweet Mother, but these nights had been long. How could one stern, harsh-faced knight have wiped out years of disgust of the marriage bed in just a few short weeks, and then left her, craving his touch? Mellisynt felt a tingling, low in her belly. Soon, she told herself, soon he would be home to satisfy that craving.

She knew she should be back at the keep, overseeing the cleaning and the preparations for their arrival. But ever since that messenger had ridden into the yard yesterday morn and delivered the stained parchment, she'd been unable to concentrate on the tasks at hand. The courier had said he thought the others were but a week behind, and she'd drifted about thereafter in an abstracted way. Even Isabeau, no lover of household chores, had finally exclaimed that she would instruct the cook herself rather than risk salted pudding and sweetened meat from Mellisynt's muddled directions. Isabeau and Dame Hertha had shooed her from the keep with instructions to let the sea breeze blow the hot choler from her body.

So far, at least, the breeze had failed miserably in its task. Even a swim in the cold sea waters had not washed the heat from her loins. Under the damp shift, her breasts tingled and her thighs clenched together in a vain attempt to still the pulsing need between them. Soon, she told herself, soon.

Her lids drooped in languid anticipation, then flew open at a startled shout far down the shore. Scrambling off her perch, Mellisynt searched for the boy amid the scattered rocks. Her heart leapt into her throat when she saw him running frantically toward her, the beast loping beside him. Behind them, far off in the distance, a lone horseman guided his mount down the steep shale path that led to their cove.

Sweet Mother, how had the man slipped past Alymer's guards? They'd had some trouble with bandits a few months past, but FitzHugh's uncle was certain he'd cleaned them out. Her blood pounded now with fear. Had the marauders returned? Had one of the bandits seen them alone and unprotected on the beach? She squinted into the distance, but the rider was too far away for her to make out more than a hazy outline and the faint sheen of the horse's roan coat.

"My lady," Bartholomew panted, "we must hie back to the keep. I don't recognize the horse."

"Come, we'll run along the shore. Mayhap we can round the curve before the tide cuts it off completely."

Abandoning her robes, she grabbed the boy's hand and lifted the skirts of her wet shift. With the hound loping beside them, they raced for the far cusp of the cove, where the cliffs jutted right out into the sea. Already waves dashed against the red sandstone, sending towers of spray up into the blue sky. The waters receded, then swept in once more to cover the narrow strip of sand at the cliff's base. Mellisynt swallowed convulsively as the undertow tugged at her ankles, then staggered when an incoming wave slapped at her thighs. Bartholomew stumbled, thrown off balance by the rush of the sea. Frantic, Mellisynt tugged on his arm with both hands, hauling him bodily out of the sucking sand and water. The hound raced back and forth, woofing in the shallows. Mellisynt cast a quick look over her shoulder and gasped. The rider was bent low over his horse's neck, his face obscured by the flying mane, galloping along the rocky shore, straight at them.

Realizing they could not outrun him, Mellisynt dragged the boy through the swirling water toward the cliffs. Mayhap they could find footholds and climb up, out of the man's reach. Her breath rasped in her throat as she struggled with Bartholomew against the tide's pull. Spray flew in her eyes and coated her tongue, salt vying with the sour taste of fear. She couldn't see through the blur of water stinging her eyes, but pushed forward blindly.

Halfway to the cliffs, they felt the pounding of the horse's hooves behind them and heard a ragged shout from the rider. Mellisynt couldn't make out his words over her own panting breath and the hound's furious barking. She stumbled and cried aloud when her bare toes hit a submerged rock. Bartholomew tugged his hand loose.

"I'll stop him, my lady! You go on!"

"Nay!" she screamed as he darted away from her, right into the path of the oncoming horse. The steed swerved violently and reared, its hooves pawing the air above the boy's head. Mellisynt heard a violent oath, then a splash as the hooves came down again, clear of the small body. The horse leapt forward, straight for her. Before she could turn or run, the rider leaned down and wrapped a hard arm around her waist, jerking her off her feet.

Her breath left with a whoosh as she slammed against the

rock-hard body of her captor. Her nose smashed into his chest, while the sharp bend of his knee dug into her stomach. Unable to move, unable even to breathe, Mellisynt opened her mouth and bit into the flesh under the linen shirt.

''Jesu, woman!'' he roared, jerking the horse to a halt. Ungentle hands yanked her sideways across the saddle.

Mellisynt barely heard the words over the furious pounding of her blood and the hound's frantic growling. She struggled to free herself, twisting and slipping on the wet saddle.

''Be still!'' he thundered, pinning her body against his.

She shook her head to clear the glaze of salt water and soaked strands of hair plastered to her face. Shock swept through her.

''FitzHugh?'' she screeched.

''By all the saints, woman, is this how you greet your—''

His furious shout was cut off as a brown body hurled itself through the air and crashed against them, knocking them both from the saddle. Man, woman and beast landed in three feet of swirling water.

FitzHugh struggled to stand, hauling Mellisynt up by one arm. It took the dog a few seconds longer to regain his precarious balance.

''Hold, you hound of hell!''

FitzHugh's enraged command stopped the animal in its tracks. It quivered with coiled tension, fangs bared and growls emanating from deep in its chest. Bartholomew gave a relieved shout and splashed forward, wrapping his arms about the beast's neck to still the reverberating snarls.

''My lord! 'Tis you!''

''Aye,'' FitzHugh snapped, dragging Mellisynt behind him. He reached for the reins of the nervous, skittering horse. ''I wish to God you'd recognized me earlier and saved us all a dunking.''

Mellisynt couldn't speak. Her throat swelled tight, whether from the residue of fear, or shock or sea water, she knew not.

''We had word you wouldn't leave Winchester for yet a

week," Bartholomew cried, prancing happily alongside as they splashed through the surf toward the rocks. "Everyone is most anxious for your arrival. Word of your victories has spread across the north. All the squires brag and boast of your wins. We can't wait to hear of the battle."

They stumbled the last few feet to shore. FitzHugh's rough hold on his wife's arm loosened, and he swung her around to face him. His eyes traveled from her sodden hair, its dark red tendrils streaked with bits of brown kelp, down the slender column of her throat, to linger on the heaving breasts barely veiled by the wet, clinging linen.

"Did you really cut the count's armies in half, like a sword slicing through soft brains?" Bartholomew's voice was filled with glee at the gory thought. "Did you send them—"

"You'll hear the details in good time," FitzHugh said, interrupting him. "Get you gone, boy."

"But—"

"Now!"

FitzHugh tore his eyes from the rigid tips of his wife's breasts, thrusting against the wet material, to survey the lad's crestfallen face under its cap of wet golden curls.

"I would...speak with my lady wife. Go, and take that murderous cur with you. Ask my uncle to see to Duke Geoffrey's comfort until we return, and I may find something in my baggage of the battle that is yours to keep."

"Truly? What? A sword? A captured banner?" Bartholomew danced on one foot in his excitement.

Obviously confused, but willing to enter into the sport, the hound jumped up and added his booming voice to the child's eager, pelting questions.

The stallion jerked his head up at the din, almost tearing the reins from FitzHugh's grasp. He cursed and turned to soothe the beast.

"Bartholomew, take the hound and go," Mellisynt croaked, finding her voice at last.

The child opened his mouth to protest.

"Now!" Lord and lady spoke in unison.

The boy blinked at their vehemence and wrapped his arm around the dog. He trotted a few paces down the shore, then turned back, a hopeful expression lighting his face.

"A shield, mayhap?"

FitzHugh's low growl sounded remarkably like those the hound had uttered just a few moments earlier.

Mellisynt felt a bubble of laughter rise in her throat. She bit her lip, trying to hold it back.

"You think this amusing, lady wife?"

She glanced up to see FitzHugh's blue eyes glinting down at her. Beads of water sparkled on his dark lashes and trickled down his cheeks. A bit of seaweed dangled from one ear.

"Aye, my lord husband," she gasped unsteadily.

His brows drew together. "You will not find it as humorous when I skewer that damned hound and serve it *en brochette* to the gyrfalcons."

"No, my lord," Mellisynt replied, putting a hand over her mouth to hold back her giggles.

He scowled down at her. "I am not at all used to being unhorsed, and the fact that it was accomplished by a three-legged, lop-eared, sorry excuse for a dog rankles. You will not repeat this event to Geoffrey."

Mellisynt's laughter broke through. Whooping, she bent and wrapped both arms about her waist. When she could catch her breath, she glanced up to see a rueful grin lifting one corner of her husband's chiseled lips. His reluctant smile set her off again. Choking with laughter, she sank to her knees.

FitzHugh followed her down to the sand, a suspicious rumbling sounding deep in his chest.

When her gulping laughter finally slowed to occasional hiccups, Mellisynt wiped her eyes with a sand-encrusted hand. She lay back, propping herself on her elbows. Above, the sky stretched endlessly blue, and white-winged gulls dipped and floated on the breeze. FitzHugh settled himself beside her. For long moments they absorbed the sea and the sun in rare silent companionship.

Feeling wonderfully at ease, she turned and smiled up at him. "'Tis…'tis not at all the greeting I had planned for you."

He reached out and brushed the sand from her cheek, his white teeth gleaming. "'Tis not exactly the welcome I had envisioned, either."

Mellisynt's heart began a slow, steady thumping. Holy Mary, how had she ever thought him stern and hard of face? Water dripping from the dark hair curled on his forehead and ran down his high cheeks and blunt, square chin. She ached to catch the tiny rivulets with her finger, or her tongue, or any other part of her body she could press against his face. And his eyes, sweet Mother, his eyes glinted with a light that rocked her knees, much as the swirling waves had moments before.

He turned at a sound from the still-restive horse. Mellisynt gasped in shock. A red, angry wound, poorly stitched, ran from the corner of his hairline back into his scalp. She lifted one hand to touch the edge, only to draw back when he jerked his head away.

"It burns," he told her with a grimace. "From the salt water."

"Good God, I doubt it not. Come, we must get you home so that I may rinse it and ease the sting."

He caught her before she could scramble to her feet.

"Nay, my lady. I fear there's yet another part of me that burns far worse. One that needs attending immediately."

Her eyes widened in alarm, and she ran them quickly over his body. She saw no other visible wound. She did, however, see his shaft standing rock-hard and rampant against his soaked chausses. Her mouth opened.

"Oh!"

"Oh, yes, or oh, no?" he inquired casually, reaching out one tanned hand to stroke the tip of her breast.

Mellisynt jumped as if seared with a redhot iron. Sitting up straight, she studied the glinting blue light in his eyes. Disbelief and a slow, insidious hope warred in her chest.

"You...you wish to couple here? In...in the sun and open sky?"

"Yes, here."

His voice lowered and washed over her with the slow, rhythmic pull of the waves. "I would have you here, where the emerald sea matches the color of your eyes and the sun heats your flesh to warm silk."

Mellisynt swallowed. "Now?"

"Aye, now. After these long months, I do not care to wait." His hand took possession of her breast once more, kneading gently, rubbing against the puckered tip.

"Nor do I, my lord."

She followed her husky whisper with a sinuous movement that stretched her damp length alongside him. But if Mellisynt had thought this was to be a slow, sweet joining such as she had dreamed of all through the long winter nights and hot summer days, she was soon disabused of the notion. The same hard arm that had lifted her from the surf once more wrapped around her waist. With a quick, fluid movement, FitzHugh rolled over, pressing her into the sand with all the force of his massive body. His head swooped down and captured her mouth in a fierce, consuming kiss.

Responding to his rough urgency, Mellisynt locked both arms around his neck and strained against him. She ground her lips into his, her need rising in hot waves. She reveled in the taste of salt and raw male hunger. Her fingers curled into his neck, feeling the soft, springy hairs and smooth skin under their tips. She opened for him eagerly, taking his tongue into her mouth and exchanging thrust for thrust, taste for taste.

When he tore his lips away to bury his face in her neck, she groaned and tugged at his hair to bring his mouth back to hers. A growl of pure, primitive passion surged up from deep in her chest.

FitzHugh lifted his body from hers enough to insert his hand between them and rip her soggy shift from neck to waist. A warm, calloused hand covered her breast, shaping it to his satisfaction. His eyes feasted on her soft flesh. He bent to partake of the feast, then grunted when a sharp stone cut into his elbow.

Dislodging the stone, he tossed it away. A grin tugged at his lips. "Do you think we shall ever get to couple in our own bed, without rocks or cold winds to distract us?"

"Oh, yes," Mellisynt breathed. "But later. Later."

Impatient, she pulled his head back down to her breast.

Mellisynt rode home wrapped in the warmth of FitzHugh's cloak, cradled against his strong body. As the timbered walls of Edgemoor rose into view, she felt her husband's arm tighten around her waist and shared his sense of homecoming. Her delicious languor dissolved as they neared the great gates and she saw the crowd that spilled out of the hall to greet them. With all her soul, she longed to turn her face into FitzHugh's chest, to pretend she didn't arrive home wrapped in her husband's cloak, her hair straggling down her back, with sand and seaweed decorating all parts of her body. Her face burned, and she sank back into the encircling protection of her husband's arms.

"My lady!" Dame Hertha's shocked voice, and the way in which the rotund little lady completely ignored her nephew, told her she looked even worse than she feared.

"Lady Mellisynt!" Isabeau gasped, her delicate brows arching in disbelief. "You...you've lost your shoes!"

Biting her lip, Mellisynt struggled for an answer. Behind her, her lord's chest rumbled with suppressed laughter. Before she could frame a coherent reply, FitzHugh swung down from the saddle and tumbled her into his arms. With the crowd trailing behind them, he strode up the stairs and through the open door of the great hall. A cluster of men gathered around the central hearth turned at their noisy entrance.

"Well, it appears you found your sea sprite, FitzHugh."

Geoffrey waved an ale tankard in greeting. Alymer turned, his jaw dropping in amazement as his nephew crossed the hall with a shapeless, cringing bundle in his arms. The men surrounding the duke parted, and their amused chuckles added to the heat coursing across Mellisynt's face. She succumbed to the embarrassment washing over her. With a groan, she buried her face in FitzHugh's chest.

"Aye, my lord, I found her. And, as we're both a bit waterlogged, I would beg your indulgence a while longer before we join you at table."

"Go, go," Geoffrey boomed. "We've waited this long while you played in the sand, we can wait a few moments more."

FitzHugh pushed through the milling crowd and crossed to the far end of the great room. A maid scurried to open the door in the wooden screen that divided the lord's quarters from the rest of the hall. Dame Hertha and Isabeau squeezed in with several other women before FitzHugh could kick the door shut.

"Put her down," Hertha commanded, "and get you gone while we attend to her. Your squire and servants await you in our quarters above stairs. You'll find hot water and fresh clothes laid out there."

FitzHugh grinned at the woman as he let his now-squirming burden slide to her feet. "'Tis a sorry welcome you give the lord of the manor, Aunt, casting him from his own chambers the very moment of his return."

"If you behaved more like a lord and less like a rutting dog, you could expect a more gracious welcome." Hertha's twinkling eyes softened the edge of her voice. "Go now, go! Get you bathed and made presentable. We've held dinner until the joints are charred as it is. Do we delay much longer, the men will like to be rolling beneath the boards with the ale they've drunk!"

FitzHugh allowed himself to be pushed from the room. Before the door even slammed shut behind him, the women attacked Mellisynt. Hertha pulled the wet cloak from her shoulders with an exclamation of disgust. Maids reached to strip away the remains of the sodden shift.

"My lady!" Isabeau's luminous aquamarine eyes rounded, then swiftly narrowed. "You do not even wear your gown!"

Mellisynt had not thought her face could heat any further. "I left it on the rocks while I swam with Bartholomew earlier. It, ah, washed away on the tide while I...while we..."

"While you welcomed your lord home," Hertha finished for her, bustling her shivering frame into the tub. She placed a firm hand on Mellisynt's head, grabbed the soap with another, then paused. A knowing woman's grin spread across her dimpled cheeks. "I disremember the last time I saw the boy looking so smug and cocksure. You must have given him quite a ride!"

Mellisynt went under the surface and came up sputtering, as much from the idea of anyone calling FitzHugh "boy" as from the water streaming over her. She tossed her wet hair out of her eyes and grinned back at Hertha.

"Well, I think it's disgusting." Isabeau scowled as she fiddled with the pots and jars she pulled from a small wooden chest. "Such conduct is hardly what one expects from a lady."

St. Bressé's plain-faced young wife glanced across the room, her almond eyes filled with malice. "How would you know the manner in which a lady attends her husband? 'Till you have one of *your own*, you should be less free with your opinions."

Hertha rolled her eyes heavenward, and Mellisynt groaned. Not again! If there had been one twisted thread in the fabric of their lives these last months, it was the unceasing, unremitting enmity between Isabeau and the wife of FitzHugh's lieutenant. Mayhap if the woman had not made such an issue of the knight's attentions to the girl when they first arrived, or if there had been some other man of sufficient rank and address in the keep for Isabeau to practice her charms on, the matter would have died. But the girl had needed no more than one hissed warning from the lady to keep away from her husband to begin a stubborn, determined flirtation. The result was constant, running warfare, which now flared again.

"I'll have a husband soon enough," Isabeau shot back. "I doubt not the duke brings word of a fine alliance. The duchess promised to settle my betrothal as soon as the troubles in France subsided."

"Hah! 'Tis more likely the duchess has forgotten you exist. Or sent you here because she wished to wash her hands of so frivolous and forward a maid. If maid you be," St. Bressé's wife muttered.

"Why, you suet-faced—"

"Enough," Mellisynt ordered through a froth of soap.

Isabeau slammed her pots down and advanced on the other woman, hands on hips.

"You're sour with jealousy, and with good reason. You can't hold your lord's interest, let alone arouse his passion. You have not the beauty nor the wit nor the—"

"Enough, I said!" Mellisynt rose and sluiced the soapy residue from her skin. "Lady Katherine, see that the cooks are ready to serve, if you please. I will be done forthwith."

She waited until the door slammed behind the angry woman, then turned to the girl. "Isabeau, will you work the magic of your pots and jars for me once more, and quickly?"

Still fuming, her cheeks bright with color and her eyes sparkling with brilliant blue fire, Isabeau crossed the room.

When Mellisynt paused just outside the lord's chamber a short time later, her high color came from a mixture of Isabeau's pots, tingling anticipation, and an embarrassed reluctance to join the boisterous group of nobles at the far end of the hall. She smoothed nervous hands down the line of her gown. The shimmering amethyst silk had been her most expensive purchase those long months ago in Nantes, and she'd fashioned it into a deceptively simple robe. Pulled snug against her upper torso by side lacing, it showed off her slender figure admirably. Under the outer robe she wore a soft linen shift, its sleeves and slit neckline embroidered with gold and purple designs. Mellisynt knew the gown's color added much to the warm glow her skin had acquired from these weeks in the sun. She reached up to straighten the thin circlet of beaten gold that held a gauzy veil over her braided hair and took a deep breath, causing her breasts to strain at the tight silk.

This was how she'd wanted to greet her lord, in her fine new robes and sun-deepened color. She chewed on her lower lip, thinking that all her careful planning for his return had gone for naught. Still, she wouldn't have traded one moment in the sand for all the rich robes now nestling in her chest. She looked up and saw FitzHugh coming toward her, his dark head visible above the crowd. He stood out among the throng of guests and household knights by his sheer size and by the richness of his red velvet tunic. Mellisynt felt a queer thrill at seeing him in a robe she'd fashioned with her own hands, as if it marked him somehow as hers. She lifted her gaze from the standard emblazoned on his chest, over the massive shoulders, to the sharp planes of a face that somehow had come to symbolize to her the essence of male beauty.

Their eyes met and held. The cheerful babble filling the room seemed to fade away, the other figures to blur. In that instant Mellisynt felt something flower deep within her, something achingly beautiful and strangely unfamiliar. Something that made her breath catch and her heart thump painfully. Something that lifted her lips in a small, private smile for her husband alone.

FitzHugh stopped before his wife, his stunned gaze moving from the translucent veil over her gleaming russet hair, down the glowing planes of her face, to the soft curves of her breasts, rising and falling delightfully in their casing of violet silk. He thought of all the images he'd carried of her in his mind—of a pale, still bride, a thin, uncertain bedmate, a mud-covered virago rescuing an animal any half-wit would have left to his fate. And he thought, as well, of the golden body stretched beneath his just hours ago on a rock-strewn, sandy shore. None of those vivid images did justice to this vibrant, glowing woman.

A fierce possessiveness, deeper than any he'd ever known, gripped him. He wanted to claim her, to mark her as his own. He fought to subdue this primitive urge, disturbed by its intensity. Jesu, he already owned the woman, and had proclaimed his possession most blatantly this afternoon. Shaking off the strange feeling, he bent over her hand.

"God give you greeting, lady wife."

"And you, my lord. I bid you welcome to your home."

She dipped her head in an elegant little bow, for all the world as if she'd not welcomed him, most energetically, just hours earlier.

FitzHugh restrained his smile, recognizing her need to regain her dignity. He reached into the leather pouch at his waist and drew out a tangled skein of pearls.

"I meant to give you these earlier, but was…somewhat distracted. Now I'm ashamed even to offer them, so pale and lifeless are they beside your lustrous shine."

Mellisynt gasped as he unwound the knotted ropes. He wrapped them once, twice, and then once more, around her neck. Still the heavy rope hung to her waist, gleaming luminescent against the purple of her gown. She ran her fingers over their milky smoothness.

"My lord, 'tis a king's ransom!"

"Well, a count's, at least. I will admit it was a difficult decision. I had to choose between these and another destrier to replace Voyager."

Her eyes flashed up to his in genuine concern. "Did you lose your horse? In battle?"

"Aye," he replied, rubbing a knuckle lightly down her nose. "The loss was most grievous. I sustained it with the knowledge that he no longer topped my list of most valued possessions. You've moved up a notch, lady wife.''

"Harrumph!''

Mellisynt's indelicate snort sounded very much like her equine rival's. FitzHugh laughed and took her arm to lead her to Geoffrey.

Seated at the far end of the boards with the other unmarried maidens, Isabeau felt a mounting sense of irritation as Mellisynt greeted the duke, then took her place at the high table. Jaw clenched, she saw the men bow and kiss the lady's hand, and heard their extravagant compliments on her beauty. When FitzHugh's dark head bent intimately toward his wife's, Isabeau threw her silver eating knife to the boards with an angry clatter.

She'd spent all these months shut up in this miserable keep with only dolts and churls to toy with. Now the duke and Sir Richard were here and she was seated with a bunch of straw-headed, giggling girls. To make matters worse, the men seemed fascinated with the lady of the manor and just ignored *her!*

Isabeau forgot Mellisynt's many kindnesses these last months. She forgot her own growing affection for the woman who had befriended her. All she could think of was how the Lady Mellisynt was garnering the adulation that should come to her. She shot the high table another venomous glance, her teeth grating as even the duke managed to wrest a smile from the lady of the manor. Christ's wounds, were all the men in this hall blind? Could they not see that Mellisynt was *old* under her paint and simpering smile? And skinny as a reed, to boot!

"Is not Duke Geoffrey a man among men?'' the maiden next to Isabeau asked, her dreamy eyes glued to the far table. "I've never seen hair like that on a man. Thick and silky, and halfway between flame and sunlight.''

"He's most handsome,'' another girl agreed, "but Sir Richard is fearsome strong, and not at all hard to look upon. Would that such a one as he asked to wear my colors in a tourney.''

"Bah!" Isabeau muttered, thoroughly put out with these silly girls when men, real men, sat so far away. "You'd be lucky if the swineherd asked to wear your silks.''

"Why, I do believe the Lady Isabeau is upset because the duke brings no betrothal agreements for her,'' the first girl said, tittering. Thoroughly unpopular with the female portion of Edgemoor's occupants, Isabeau was a frequent target for their malice. "Could it be that no man wants you?''

"You know better than that," Isabeau cooed. "Why, your own betrothed assured me just last week that he'd never seen eyes so bright nor skin so fair as mine.'' Her mocking gaze swept the rash of pimples on the other girl's chin.

The maid's sputtering retort was lost as the door at the far end of the hall opened and a band of men entered. Straggling groups had been arriving all evening, coming to meet with the duke as he traveled through the north. Isabeau's eyes brightened at the interruption. Mayhap this latest group would bring a knight more to her interest, one who would appreciate genuine beauty when he saw it. She scanned the men-at-arms and squires, dismissing them immediately as unworthy men. Her gaze fastened on a pair of wide shoulders covered in a jeweled tunic of sapphire blue. Sitting up straighter, Isabeau wet her lips with a quick sweep of her tongue. She tilted her chin over one shoulder, the better to observe the knight and show the thick sweep of her sooty lashes.

Her carefully seductive smile faltered, then disappeared completely as Sir Roger Beauchamp strode past her without the slightest flicker of recognition or interest. He went forward to kneel before the lady of the keep. Isabeau couldn't hear his low greeting or Mellisynt's delighted reply over the fury ringing in her ears.

Chapter Twelve

"Sir Roger!"

Mellisynt greeted him with unaffected pleasure and reached up to give his cheek a kiss of greeting. She drew back, startled, when he turned his head at the last moment and her lips brushed the silky softness of his moustached mouth.

His warm brown eyes danced over her face.

"Now *that* was worth the long ride through some of the most desolate country this side of the Holy Land! If FitzHugh must hide you away up here, those who aspire to your regard should at least be allowed to claim a kiss after such a ride."

Mellisynt blinked in confusion. In the last months she'd forgotten most of the conventions of the game of love played at court. That Sir Roger would suggest he was a contender in the first phase of chivalrous love, in which knights worship their ladies from afar, surprised her.

"You may aspire all you wish, Beauchamp, but if you kiss my wife again, I'll break your head."

Sir Roger laughed and gripped FitzHugh's outstretched arm. "I see your absence hasn't improved either your disposition or your manners. Don't you know 'tis most unfashionable for a husband to discourage his lady's admirers?"

"Hah, Roger, you know FitzHugh never was in fashion, nor will he ever be!" Geoffrey joined them and threw his arms around Beauchamp.

Mellisynt watched, wide-eyed, as they pummeled each

other's backs in that strange greeting ritual men reserved for
their boon companions. The three knights stood in a loose
circle, part of, yet isolated from, the rest of the room, bonded
by experiences only another warrior could understand. She
stood back, forgotten for the moment, and studied them.

They were so alike, all tall and well muscled and tanned
from their days in the saddle. And yet they were each so very
different—Geoffrey boisterous and fiery-haired and quick-
tempered, Beauchamp smooth and polished, with warm brown
eyes and curls any woman would give her right arm for. And
FitzHugh. Ah, there was a man, she thought, so dark of hair
and brow, so lean of face, with eyes that made her melt inside
when they filled with laughter, or passion.

"From where do you come?" FitzHugh asked, leading
them all back to the table. Beauchamp had been with the
duke's forces in the early stages of the campaign against Toulouse, but had left when one of his holdings in England had
been ravaged by a rival baron.

"From Winchester, by way of Richmond," he responded,
attacking a tough ham joint with strong white teeth. "Your
wife sends word, my lord duke, that your balls, and mayhap
your life, are forfeit if you don't show your face immediately
at Richmond."

Geoffrey choked on his wine. "Christ's blood, we landed
but two days ago and rode straight here." He wiped the drops
from his chin and turned to Beauchamp eagerly. "How is
she?"

"Big! Evil-tempered as a bloated sow!" Beauchamp smiled
with wicked glee. "Very pregnant, and most unhappy you're
not there so she can vent her ire on the one who caused such
discomfort. I expect your homecoming will not be quite as
loving as you anticipate."

Geoffrey's face fell. "Hell and damnation! Don't you dare
laugh, FitzHugh! After your frolic with your water sprite this
afternoon, you'll no doubt find yourself in the same predicament nine months hence."

Beauchamp's brows rose as Mellisynt blushed a fiery red. When he opened his mouth as if to comment, she shoved a bowl of sweet plums across the board and all but ordered him to taste them. To her relief, he complied with nothing more than a teasing grin. After a moment, he dug into the pouch at his waist and passed her a small parchment.

"I almost forgot. The duchess charged me to bring you her message, my lady."

Mellisynt's fingers shook with excitement as she broke the seal and spread the square of thin vellum on the table. Taking her lower lip between her teeth, she peered at the script, trying to decipher its whirls and flourishes.

"Shall I read it for you?" FitzHugh asked, his low voice for her ears only.

"Nay," Mellisynt replied. Her finger moved across the inked lines with painstaking slowness. A few more moments passed, and then she looked up, triumph lighting her face.

"Constance sends her greetings. She wishes me to attend her when her time comes. She would have the company of her countrywomen in the birthing of her first babe."

FitzHugh's brows rose, and a glint of respect dawned in his eyes.

"Well done, my lady."

His soft-spoken words suffused Mellisynt with a glow of pride. Dismissing with a mental wave of her hands the many agonizing hours she'd spent with Edgemoor's priest, she basked in her lord's admiration.

"You are a woman of considerable talents, lady wife. What other surprises have you in store for me, I wonder?"

Before she could compose herself to answer, the duke claimed FitzHugh's attention. Mellisynt floated through the rest of the meal and the entertainment that followed on a cloud of joy.

Spurred by the duchess's command, Geoffrey left the next morning for Richmond, taking most of the knights with him.

With the duke's disturbing presence gone, Mellisynt blossomed. Ever afterward, she would remember the weeks that followed as among the happiest of her life.

She preened in her new gowns under her husband's appreciative gaze, and shed them eagerly each night when she joined him in their curtained bed. Shyly she acknowledged the small improvements she'd made to the keep—the tapestries she'd acquired to brighten the walls, the rugs scattered in place of rushes, the dried herbs hung from the rafters to freshen the air.

But her moment of glory came one drizzly morning when she sat with her lord and his uncle, going over the tallies for the year. Confidently she accounted for the portions of grain set aside for malting, for seed corn and for bread-making. She knew precisely the number of bags of flour processed through their mill, the quantity of hides cured, the tuns of ale brewed. And with each accounting, FitzHugh's approving smile warmed her soul.

While Mellisynt glowed, however, Isabeau glowered. The girl waylaid FitzHugh on more than one occasion, desperate for male attention. Although he smiled and teased and flattered her, he seemed preoccupied. Unused to such treatment, she redoubled her efforts. One fine afternoon, Isabeau sought him out in the stable yards and begged him prettily to accompany her on a walk to gather violets for perfume-making.

"Nay, not this day. I promised to take the Lady Mellisynt sailing. She has found an old coracle, and will likely drown herself if I do not show her how it works."

He gave her a gallant bow and strode away.

Isabeau clenched her fists in fury, her eyes on his broad back.

"You'll make no hay with that one," a lazy voice drawled. "He's too besotted with his wife."

She whirled to find Beauchamp leaning against the stable wall, the familiar mocking grin she'd come to hate lifting his lips. Why did this man ever taunt her, and make her feel the clumsy maid?

"That must discommode you." She sniffed, lifting her nose. "Your attentions to the Lady Mellisynt must wait until FitzHugh's attentions wane. She doesn't have the skill to manage more than one lover at a time."

Beauchamp levered himself off the wall and came forward. "Don't impugn the lady with your own impure thoughts."

"Impure!" Isabeau gasped. "You dare say that to me, when you all but drool over her hand!"

"'Tis but a game, child, as well you know."

Isabeau ground her teeth. Goaded, she closed the small space between them and planted herself before him, hands on hips, bosom heaving.

"I...am...not...a...child!"

Beauchamp's laughing eyes slid from her face down to her chest. "Mayhap not," he conceded. "But not yet a woman, either."

"I'm more woman than you know what to do with!" she screeched.

"Ah, Isabeau—" he grinned, sweeping her into his arms "—such silly challenges only prove what a babe you are."

Her foot drew back to kick him soundly on the shins. Beauchamp laughed again and bent her backward, off balance, over his arm. Her foot flailed only air. Burying a fist in her hair, he brought her face up to his and stilled her indignant shrieks with a long, hard kiss.

When he released her her breaths came in gasping pants—whether from fury or sheer surprise, she knew not. She stared up at him, struggling for breath and for the words to wither him on the spot. Before either came, he turned her about and gave her a sound slap on the rear that sent her stumbling toward the keep.

"Go play with the other maids, girl. You're too troublesome to be let loose in the yard."

Red-faced and seething, Isabeau ran from him.

* * *

Still piqued, she joined a group of riders in the outer bailey the next day for a hunt. FitzHugh had arranged it the night before, as much for his guests' entertainment as to provide meat for their table.

"Don't you wish to accompany us?" he asked Mellisynt when she came to see the chattering group of men and women off. "Did you not also add riding to your list of achievements while I was gone?"

"Nay, I chose to learn the sea and swimming. 'Tis much easier on the bones. And so much more...pleasurable."

FitzHugh grinned and stroked the slant of her nose with one curled knuckle. "I see I must show you all the pleasures one can experience in the saddle."

"Stop diddling with your wife, FitzHugh, and let's be gone."

Beauchamp's amused summons rang across the mass of impatient hunters, restless horses and excited, yipping dogs. FitzHugh responded with a good-natured insult, kissed Mellisynt on the nose and moved to the mounting block.

As the throng shifted, preparing to depart, Isabeau's restive horse skittered sideways, bumping into Beauchamp's. His stallion reacted with a fearsome show of yellow teeth and a quick lunge. Cursing, Beauchamp sawed back on the bit and stilled the beast. Reaching down, he took Isabeau's reins in a strong hand.

"If you can't control your mount, you have no business in the hunt."

She glared across her horse's neck. "I'm well able to manage my horse. Loose my reins, sir!"

A mocking light leapt into his eyes. He let his gaze drop slowly from her haughty face, down the long column of her throat, to the ripe bosom displayed to perfection by a figure-molding red silk bliaut.

"Nay," he drawled. "I think mayhap a tight hand on the reins is exactly what you need, girl."

Isabeau's eyes blazed. She shot him a poisonous look and jerked the leather strap free.

How she loathed that man! He seemed to miss no chance to mock her. Even that one kiss, which had kept her awake long into the night, had lacked the reverent admiration she was used to. She didn't understand why Beauchamp should be so resistant to her charms. There wasn't a man in the keep she couldn't twist around her finger if she truly wished to. Nor was there a man she couldn't conquer if she chose to. Her eyes fell on FitzHugh's broad back, just ahead. Desperate for attention and admiration, she urged her horse forward, alongside his.

By the time the riders reached the glade where they would picnic while the huntsmen and their hounds tracked and dislodged the deer, Isabeau had regained a semblance of her composure. FitzHugh's lighthearted gallantry during the ride had restored her self-confidence. When he spread his cloak on the forest floor for her to share, she settled herself beside him with a fluid, languid grace.

"Do you think the limners will raise a stag?" she asked, accepting a horn cup of wine. She really cared little if the silent, sharp-nosed stalking dogs chased down deer or goat. She just wanted to keep this man's attention and exclusive company for a while longer yet.

"They should," FitzHugh answered with a shrug of his massive shoulders. "My uncle says the mild winter didn't thin the herds as usual. With luck, we'll have a good chase and kill. If you come to the Quarry, I'll present you with the heart-bone."

"Oh, I'll most assuredly be there for the kill," Isabeau told him, nodding. Not for a bagful of silver pennies would she have missed the ritualistic quarry ceremony, in which the animal was cut and quartered in a rigidly prescribed order. The lord of the hunt would receive the right forefoot with great ceremony and trumpeting of hunting horns, but the much-prized heart cartilage would go to the fairest lady present.

"I intend to follow the chase," she told FitzHugh. "I rode out often at home, with my father. Many women can't take the rough ride, claiming it bruises their bones. I can't understand such weakness, can you?"

A soft glint came into his silvery eyes, as if some private thought pleasured him. Isabeau preened under the look, expecting praise for her daring.

He smiled down at her and chucked her lightly under the chin with one huge fist. "Don't mistake a lack of skill for weakness, little one."

Isabeau returned his smile with one of her own, reveling in his attention. A movement over his shoulder caught her gaze, and she glanced across the glade to see Beauchamp watching them with narrowed eyes. Deliberately she deepened the curve of her lips into a sultry invitation and lowered her chin until it rested in FitzHugh's hand, as if in a warm caress.

At that moment, the head huntsman rode into the clearing. FitzHugh jumped up and strode over to take the man's report, leaving Isabeau curled on his cloak like a sleek purebred feline. She wet her lips and kept her back to Beauchamp.

The riders left the glade a few minutes later, following the trail of pointed branches the huntsmen had left to mark the way. A second pack of hounds was brought forward and divided into small groups, to be posted in relays along the trail in case the quarry doubled back and outran the hounds chasing him. Within moments, they arrived at the spot where the hart, reportedly full-grown, with a massive rack of antlers, had last been seen. The huntsmen unleashed the dogs, and the riders surged forward.

As her horse thundered alongside the men's, Isabeau grew too excited to mind her graceful carriage. She didn't notice the wind tugging her carefully arranged veil loose from its moorings or the branches tearing at her silk skirts. Leaning forward in the saddle, she felt the thrill of the chase rush through her veins. Shouts of *Cy va! Cy va!* rose all around her as the handlers called to the hounds, and the pure, golden notes of a horn cut across the air to signal the course of their pursuit.

Her breath scraped in her throat and her heart hammered painfully by the time the hounds cornered the stag, forcing it to turn and stand its ground. A single long note on the horn sounded the blowing of the death, and the hunters moved in to make the kill.

When FitzHugh presented her the heartbone some moments later, Isabeau forgot that the primary purpose of the hunt was to feed the keep's residents. She disregarded the fact that warriors and would-be warriors used the exercise to keep their horsemanship skills honed and their vigorous energies channeled. In that moment, she felt as though FitzHugh had arranged this whole expedition for the sole purpose of honoring her. When he bowed and handed her the glistening sliver of bone, Isabeau accepted it with her most stunning, provocative smile.

The hunters returned to Edgemoor just as the sun began to sink below the far horizon. The hart and several hinds filled the carts. Dirty, disheveled, and high-spirited with their success, the noisy party clattered through the gates.

Mellisynt met them in the bailey, duly praising their skill and directing the servants to remove the take to the kitchen sheds for processing. After a day of vigorous exercise and only a light meal in the open to sustain them, she knew they'd be ravenous. She smiled when the group spilled into the hall, chattering and laughing and describing the chase with swooping gestures. Even Isabeau sparkled with more color and animation than she'd shown in a long time.

Mellisynt sighed in relief. Of late the girl's restlessness and irritability had grated on everyone's nerves. In desperation, she'd consulted Dame Hertha, who had pinpointed the source of Isabeau's dissatisfaction with unerring accuracy. She was ripe for bedding, Hertha had snapped. More than ripe. The girl burned with her need.

The two older women had both prayed Geoffrey would bring word that Isabeau's hand was settled. Mayhap when the duke reached Richmond he would remind the duchess to attend to the matter. Mellisynt shrugged and turned her mind to more important concerns. Her eyes swept the table once more to ensure that there were adequate cold meats and bread for the hungry crowd. Seeing empty platters, she frowned and signaled to the senior page.

"Send the boys to bring more platters."

Her brow furrowed as she looked about the room once more. "Why do so few pages serve? Where is Robert, and Bartholomew?"

A look of disgust crossed the older boy's face. "They fell into a sulk because they could not accompany the hunt this morn. Out of mischief, they sneaked away and climbed the apple trees in the orchard. Now they are both in the stables, puking and crying from bellies swollen with green fruit."

Mellisynt worried a corner of her lower lip with her teeth. She glanced over to where Beauchamp and her lord sat side by side, deep in animated conversation. They had full platters before them, at least. Moving to where Hertha sat in comfortable companionship with the other ladies, she begged the older woman to take charge of the table for a few moments.

The warm, musky odor of horses filled her nostrils when she slipped into the stables. She had no difficulty locating the two miscreants. Their moans drew her to the far stall, where an impatient squire and a slatternly house servant attended the boys. The huge, shaggy hound sat on his haunches in the straw beside Bartholomew's head, adding a low, mournful whine to every groan the boys issued.

"How do they fare?" Mellisynt asked, kneeling to place the back of her hand against first Robert's, then Bartholomew's, face.

"Poorly," the squire replied. "They heaved so much they soiled the floor of the keep, so we brought them out here to the straw."

"Ooooh, my lady, it hurts!"

Bartholomew's cry tore at Mellisynt's heart. When he curled into a tight ball and wrapped his arms around his middle, a pain spread through her, as well.

"I know it does," she murmured. "Rest a moment, and I'll go mix a purge to relieve your distress."

"No, don't leave me!" The boy clutched at her hand, tears streaming down his cheek. The dog echoed his pathetic cry with a long, wavering whimper.

"I'll return immediately," she promised, wiping the sweat-drenched curls back from his brow. "I just go to get my herbs."

Bartholomew's tearstained brown eyes filled her vision as she hurried across the bailey and reentered the keep. Distracted, she headed down the hall toward her chamber and the chest of precious herbs kept there.

"What's amiss?"

FitzHugh caught her hand when she would have brushed past him and Isabeau, who stood beside him. His dark brows drew together as he studied her face.

"'Tis naught but a couple of naughty pages who sampled the apples before they ripened," she assured him.

"Bartholomew," he stated with wry certainty.

Mellisynt bit back a smile and nodded. "And another."

Isabeau sniffed. "'Twas Bartholomew who led them both into mischief, I'll warrant. That imp of Satan is ever a pest."

Mellisynt interrupted before Isabeau could warm to her continuing list of grievances against the mischievous page. Their months together had not brought them closer.

"I must brew a concoction to ease their pains. I promised the boy I would return to the stables with it immediately."

"Why not bring them into the keep and tend them here?" FitzHugh asked.

"They've been most violently ill, and are more comfortable in the straw. Besides," she added innocently, "the hound will not leave Bartholomew's side and is most...vocal in his concern for the boy.''

FitzHugh groaned. ''By all means, keep them in the stables.''

''I will. They have a long, unpleasant night ahead. I must change and see to their needs.''

''It'll be lonely without you in our bed,'' FitzHugh murmured, obviously forgetting the presence of the girl beside him.

Mellisynt felt a blush rising and sent him a warning glance. Then, muttering something incoherent, she hurried away.

After their long day, the hunters soon dispersed to their pallets. Tallow torches sputtered low in their holders as the keep prepared for the night. FitzHugh and Beauchamp, more used to long, hard hours on the march, settled themselves in comfortably padded chairs beside the fire, a jug of wine close at hand. Servants moved in the shadows behind them, unrolling pallets, pushing dogs aside with knees and elbows. FitzHugh listened to the sounds with half an ear, his disgruntled thoughts on the stables. He stretched his long legs out toward the fire, wondering at his discomfort. Could he not pass one night without his wife's warm body curled beside him? His mind wandered as he listened to Beauchamp's low-voiced tales of the king's court.

''I think Henry's patience with Geoffrey runs thin at last,'' Beauchamp said quietly, catching FitzHugh's full attention.

''Why?'' FitzHugh asked, pouring himself more wine.

''He suspects Geoffrey is about to throw in with the French king.''

FitzHugh heard a rustle behind him and waited for the stirring to die before he replied, his voice low.

''What cause has the king to think his son would betray him?''

''He has spies at the French court. He knows that Philip corresponds regularly with Geoffrey and teases him with promises of independence if he will but throw off his father's yoke.''

''King Henry has promised the duke full rule in Brittany.''

Beauchamp shrugged. ''And if Henry doesn't keep his fingers out of the duchy? If he interferes again, as he did when he threatened not to ratify the reforms of the grand assize?''

FitzHugh stared down into the ruby depths of his wine. ''That was Geoffrey's grandest moment,'' he mused, remembering those hot, sweltering days at Rennes. ''The stubborn Breton lords fought him every step of the way, but he forced them to accept the same code Henry himself imposed on England.''

''Yet the king was most displeased. He almost stepped in and disbanded the parliament outright.'' Beauchamp shook his head. ''I tell you, FitzHugh, 'tis dangerous the way Henry plays his sons. Even now he won't give Richard Lionheart the Lady Alice, after nigh on two decades of betrothal. The king makes no secret that he enjoys plowing between the lady's soft white thighs. He won't give her up.''

FitzHugh grunted at the sudden image that flashed into his mind, one of another lady's slender white thighs. He muttered a low curse at all rascally pages.

When Beauchamp's brows rose in query, he shook his head with wry self-mockery.

''Let's talk of something other than plowing and planting. I've yet to sow all the seed I stored up while in France, and with my lady in the stables this night, I'm not like to.''

''What! Do you try to cozen me into believing you plant only in one field these days? You? The same man who knocked me senseless to take the woman we both lusted after at Limoges? And that after you had her sister!''

'''Twas not me who knocked you out, you sot. 'Twas the two skins of wine you downed.''

FitzHugh rose and stretched.

''And who supplied the wine? Here, I'll return the favor.'' Beauchamp pushed a leather-covered jug into FitzHugh's hands. "Take it with you to the stables. Even sick pages must sleep sometime."

A wide grin split FitzHugh's face. "Aye, so they must. I'll take the wine, and you may take my bed. 'Tis softer by far than the pallet spread for you."

Beauchamp watched while his friend made his way down the darkened hall, stepping over sleeping bodies en route. A smile tugged at his lips. FitzHugh was more smitten with his lady than Beauchamp had realized. Than the man himself seemed to realize. And, as unlikely as it seemed, the lady appeared as taken with his rough-faced, oft-distempered, over-large friend. Stifling a twinge of envy, Beauchamp rose. He might as well enjoy the comfort of the lord's bed this night, since no one else appeared likely to occupy it.

Not wanting to disturb the sleeping servants, Beauchamp made his way to the far chamber in darkness. He groped for the door latch and let himself quietly into the shadowed room, lit only by the glow of a banked fire. As he turned toward the huge, curtained bed, his shin whacked solidly against the edge of a wooden chest.

"Aagh!"

At his startled exclamation, a dim figure beyond the fireplace jumped up, knocking over a stool in the process. Before Beauchamp could discern much more than its outline, the figure darted toward the door.

His fighting instincts honed by years of battle, Beauchamp reacted without thinking. One hand flew to the dagger sheathed at his belt, and he threw himself across the room. He wrapped a thick forearm around the intruder's throat and pressed the blade to his side.

"Who are you and what do you here, in the lord's room?"

A muffled squawk sounded against his arm.

"Speak," he ordered harshly, forcing the dagger through layers of cloth.

"I—I cannot!"

Fingers clawed his arm, and he loosened it a fraction.

"Do not hurt me!" Sobbing gasps tore from the throat under his bunched muscles.

"Holy Christ!"

Beauchamp sheathed the dagger in a swift, sure movement and spun his terrified prisoner about. Taking her in a brutal grip, he hauled her into the light of the fireplace.

"What do you here, girl?"

Isabeau tried to shake off his hand, still sobbing for breath. He took her other arm and pulled her up on her toes.

"Were you waiting for Sir Richard, you little whore?" A raging fury seized him. "Did you think to follow up on the invitation issued in the glade?"

"N-no!"

"Don't lie to me!" He punctuated each word with a hard shake. "You thought to take advantage of Mellisynt's preoccupation to satisfy the itch between your legs."

Isabeau's mouth fell open. "How dare you speak so to me!" she gasped, between gulping sobs. "No true knight would ever utter such—such crudities to a lady."

"No lady would await a man in the dark, ready to spread herself for him, while his wife labored just a few feet away."

"I didn't! I'm not! I—I—" Isabeau burst into fresh tears.

Beauchamp's fury slowly subsided as he watched huge, crystalline drops pour down her white face and splash against the red silk bliaut. The fact that she was wearing a gown at all sank into his consciousness. Belatedly he realized that if she'd really planned to whore herself, she would have shed her many layers before this. His hands gentled on her arms.

As fresh tears spilled down her cheeks, Beauchamp gave a disgusted grunt and pulled the girl to his chest. Wrapping his arms about her shuddering, sobbing frame, he held her while she cried out her fright.

He felt like the biggest dolt in Christendom. Not only had he come near to skewering a helpless girl, but he'd been all but swamped by a raging tide of jealousy when he'd thought of her in FitzHugh's arms. He stroked her unbound hair with a soothing hand, discovering anew the feel of generous breasts against his chest and the musky scent that was Isabeau's alone.

When her sobs finally subsided, he tipped her chin. His gut clenched at the shimmering wash of aquamarine, surrounded by wet, spiky lashes, that met his gaze. Resisting the urge to sweep her into his arms once more, he addressed her sternly.

"What do you here, Isabeau?"

After several hiccuping attempts, she found her voice. "I...I just wanted to talk. Sir Rich—Sir Richard gave me the stag's heartbone, and made me feel beauteous and...and desirous...and much a woman. I wanted to feel like that again."

Slow tears rolled down her cheeks.

With a crooked smile, Beauchamp caught a silvered drop on one finger. The bead of moisture shimmered on his skin, as lovely and luminescent as the woman who produced it. After a long moment, he flicked the drop aside and stepped back. With unhurried movements, he began to remove his clothes.

Isabeau's eyes widened. "What—what are you doing?"

"'Tis obvious, girl. I'm undressing. When I finish, I'll undress you, as well."

Isabeau stumbled backward. "You're mad," she whispered.

"Nay." He smiled, shucking his braies, then pulling his linen shirt off with a swift tug. "Just willing to make you into the woman you're so eager to become."

As he stalked her, step by step, Isabeau's wide eyes raked his naked body. Her blood began to drum in her veins. She gave a quick look over his shoulder, searching for the door in the dim shadows. Before she could run, Beauchamp reached out and tumbled her into his arms. Her palms flattened against the smooth velvet of his skin, and fiery sensations shot from her fingertips straight to her belly. She opened her mouth, not knowing whether she meant to scream or to suck air into her suddenly breathless body. She did neither, for Beauchamp's lips covered hers in a hard, demanding kiss.

With skilled mastery, he bent her back. She clung to the

roped muscles of his arms to keep from falling to the floor. All the while, his mouth plundered hers and filled her with a heat so intense she thought she would melt. Hardly realizing her own intent, she'd lifted her arms to lock them behind his neck and hold his mouth on hers.

After long, shattering moments, Beauchamp raised his head and struggled for breath.

"Jesu, girl, if you kiss me like that again, you'll find yourself stretched out right here, on the floor."

Isabeau lifted a long, slim finger and traced the line of his lips. "I'm not a girl," she whispered, and pulled his head down once more.

Chapter Thirteen

FitzHugh leaned against the wooden half wall enclosing the stall and watched his wife wipe Bartholomew's face with a soft, damp cloth. Tucking a stray strand of hair behind one ear, she murmured low nothings to the fretful boy as she worked. The other page, Robert, slept soundly in the next stall. The hound rested its massive head on two outthrust forepaws, anxious eyes sweeping from mistress to child and back again. Every few moments, a low, unhappy whine whistled through its lips.

The night lay heavy around them. Far down the stable, horses shuffled in their stalls, blowing softly through their nostrils, as if welcoming the companionship during the long, still hours. Except for the horses and boys—and dog—they were alone in the long building. FitzHugh had sent the other attendants away when he first arrived, thinking to follow through on Beauchamp's suggestion. That notion had been put to rest immediately. 'Twas apparent Mellisynt would have none of him while the child fretted.

FitzHugh watched her gentle hands stroke the boy's face and thought of her desire for a babe. Seeing her with Bartholomew, he understood her need. She'd make a most tender mother. The urge to plant his seed in Mellisynt's womb surged over him, hot and fierce. In that moment he wanted with all his being to see her swell with child, to watch a babe nursing at her breast. He shifted uncomfortably at the sudden ache in his loins.

"He seems to know your hand," FitzHugh commented, as much to distract himself as to share the night with her.

"Aye, I think he does. He's a good lad."

FitzHugh's snort caused the boy to start and the dog to lift its head in warning.

"Shh!" Mellisynt commanded. "He sleeps but lightly."

"Aye. Unfortunately."

Her brows rose at the dry comment, but FitzHugh just shrugged and came around the wall.

"Never mind. What can I do to help?"

As he hunkered down on his heels, his bulk crowded the small stall. The hound lifted one side of its lip in a low growl at the intrusion. FitzHugh growled back, deep in his throat.

"That beast and I will settle affairs one of these days."

"Hush," Mellisynt whispered. "Don't provoke him."

"Me? Provoke him?"

A mischievous grin tilted the corners of her mouth. "You did attack his mistress but short days ago. Now you must hover over his friend like a huge, irritated bear. Get you gone before he feels the need to defend us once again."

"Nay, I would stay and keep you company."

She sat back on her knees, smiling warmly. "I thank you, my lord, most truly. But there's no need for you to stay awake this night, especially after a day's hunt. You need your sleep."

"And what if I have other, more important needs?"

Her glance slid down to his tumescent manhood, clearly outlined against the fabric of his braies. Heaving an exaggerated sigh of regret, she shook her head.

"You must contain your needs, my lord, or find release elsewhere."

"What?"

Mellisynt blinked, confused at his startled exclamation. She swallowed and began again. "I know men can be most irritable when they swell with want and don't achieve release. Henri was wont to use his fist during those times I had my monthly courses.''

"He used his fists? On you?'' FitzHugh hoped the old degenerate was roasting in hell.

"Nay. On himself. Though it rarely brought relief, since he couldn't get his rod to stiffen for any length of— Why do you laugh? Hush, you'll waken the boy!''

FitzHugh stifled the mirth rumbling in his chest and bent to kiss his wife's pert nose. "I'll find some way to ease my discomfort,'' he promised.

He left her then, sending the sleepy squire and stablehands back inside to aid her with the boys. Standing alone in the yard for a few moments, he drank in the richness of the night. Sweet Jesu, it was good to be home again. The air carried a tang of the sea, even above the familiar odors of penned animals and piled manure. Stars shimmered overhead against the black-velvet sky and formed a lustrous canopy above his head. Despite the late hour, FitzHugh felt alive with the night and with the need to couple.

He wondered briefly why he felt no urge to go back to the hall and rouse the kitchen maid who'd serviced him most willingly in recent years. Since his return, the girl had indicated her eagerness to resume their activities. But the thought of burying his face in her warm, generous breasts and breathing in her earthy scent of garlic and sweat didn't draw him as it once would have. Instead, he found himself thinking of a long, slender body with trim hips and pink-tipped breasts that just fit his palms. The ache in his groin thrummed with a steady, pulsing need.

FitzHugh strode across the inner yard, trying to relieve his discomfort with vigorous exercise. Christ's bones, when had his wife become such an obsession that just the image of her naked form would harden him so? He kicked an overturned bucket left by a careless servant out of his path and winced when the clatter broke the night's stillness. Hastily reassuring the guard who called down a challenge at the noise, he smiled to himself in wry derision.

What was it about Mellisynt that drew him so? She wasn't beautiful, as Isabeau was. Her skin had warmed to a golden glow, but her nose was still too short and her chin too determined for the aristocratic standards of the age. And her body, much as he'd come to crave it, lacked the curves and lush earthiness of others who'd shared his bed in the past. Mayhap it was her eyes that drew him, those thick-fringed pools of green that sparkled with laughter and deepened to dusky velvet with passion. Or her smile, hesitant and restrained when first they'd wedded, now more likely to lift at the corners in an impudent grin. Or mayhap her tenderness with boy and beast, displaying so clearly her loving heart.

FitzHugh's long stride faltered. He slowed to a halt a few paces from the stairs leading to the ramparts. Thinking of Mellisynt's tenderness caused a strange ache to rise in a part of his body he'd not hitherto connected with the act of coupling, and certainly never with his previous wife. A queer tightness lodged in his chest, a half-formed longing to have her lay her hands softly on his face and whisper sweet, husky words of...

The solid tread of a guard's footsteps sounded overhead. FitzHugh shook his head, embarrassed to be mooning about in the dark like a lovesick squire, and glad that none had seen him. With a low call to alert the man above to his presence, he climbed the stairs to the wooden ramparts. He made a leisurely circuit of the upper walk, stopping to talk with the guards posted at intervals along the wall.

When he pushed open the gatehouse door, several men scrambled to their feet in surprise, sending stools clattering to the floor. A fire burned in the stone hearth in the center of the floor, illuminating the room with a cheerful glow. Swords, bowls of sand and old rags lay scattered about the floor, indicating that the men were engaged in the age-old pastime of soldiers—polishing their weapons. Shaking off the last of his strange preoccupation with the woman who was his wife, FitzHugh took refuge in the familiar. He settled himself on a stool and accepted an ale horn from one of his men. Leaning forward, elbows on knees, he prepared to pass what was left of the night in the comfortable companionship of other men of war.

Fingers of fog drifted through the bailey when Mellisynt left the stable early the next morning. She paused in the yard, putting both hands to the small of her spine and arcing back to ease the strain. Bartholomew had finally slipped into a sound sleep, after passing the last of the ill-gotten fruit in a series of discharges that mortified him as much as they left him weak and teary-eyed. After cleaning the boy and singing low, silly songs to lull him to rest, Mellisynt had given him back into the care of the squire. She smiled, thinking that after this night Dame Hertha's fruit trees would be safe for the foreseeable future, at least. She lifted her face to the mist, letting it wash into her pores and ease her weariness.

Gradually, awareness of the yard's busy occupants penetrated her tired senses, making her conscious of her stained gown and disheveled hair. More than one maid scurrying to and from the kitchen sheds cast her a curious glance, or a timid smile. Two men carrying thatch to repair the roof of the mews bobbed their heads respectfully, their eyes wide.

Mellisynt returned their greeting and smoothed her hands down the front of her robe. Sweet Mother, she couldn't go into the great hall in such a state, with all the guests most likely still taking ale and bread to break their fast. She hurried around to the back of the main building and climbed narrow stairs to the upper floor. She would cleanse herself in the bower room the maidens shared and send one of them to fetch a fresh robe.

"Well, she all but threw herself at Sir Richard on the hunt. 'Tis little wonder he'd avail himself of the slut."

The malicious, spiteful words drifted out just as Mellisynt reached for the latch to the half-opened door of the bower.

"But to go to his room! Such brazenness! I didn't believe it when a servant told me she'd seen Isabeau slip inside the lord's chamber. With the Lady Mellisynt at the stable, only a few yards away!"

Mellisynt's hand froze on the metal latch. She identified the Lady Katherine, St. Bressé's plain, unhappy wife, as one of the women inside the room. Even as a corner of her mind registered that fact, a slow, insidious hurt began to curl in her belly.

"What did the bitch say when she returned to the bower at dawn? Did you challenge her?"

"Nay, I dare not. She has sharp claws. But I watched her wash the blood from her legs and shift. I would never have believed Isabeau a virgin, but if she was before, she is no longer. Not after a night in the lord's bed." Vicious satisfaction laced the speaker's voice.

"The little whore! Where is she now? Does she dare show her face below?"

"I think she went to the sewing room. I wouldn't have the nerve to face Lady Mellisynt this morn, either, were I her."

The pain in Mellisynt's stomach spread, gathering intensity as it lanced through her chest. She stepped back from the door and leaned against the wall, both arms wrapped tight around her body. No, her mind cried, no! Surely he would not! Not with Isabeau, not here, in what she'd come to consider her own home!

Pushing herself off the wall, she whirled and ran down the dim hallway. She flung open the sewing room door. Three faces turned toward her in wide-eyed surprise.

"I would speak with the Lady Isabeau," Mellisynt told the other two women in a low, furious voice. "Leave us."

The blood drained from Isabeau's face as she scrambled up from her weaving stool. She gripped both hands together and stood, tense and fearful, while the other women left hurriedly.

Mellisynt slammed the door closed behind them. She struggled to contain the rage that coursed through her at the frightened guilt on Isabeau's face. Fury and pain closed her throat, and her first attempts to speak came out as inarticulate gasps. Fists clenched, she moved across the room until only two feet separated her from the white-faced girl.

"So, 'tis true," she managed to croak through stiff lips. "I can see it in your face. You lay with him!"

Isabeau lifted a wobbly chin, as if she would try to brazen her way out of the charge.

"Do not lie to me!" Mellisynt snarled. "Do not dare!"

The girl's false bravado died aborning. Tears filled her eyes, and she backed away.

"I...I did not mean to...I don't know how it..." She broke down, sobbing. "I never thought he would make me feel so...so wanton."

Every gasping word sent another spear of anguish through Mellisynt's heart.

"You whey-faced slut!" Her hand arced out and cracked against the girl's cheek.

Isabeau's cry of pain and wrenching sobs followed her as she turned and stumbled toward the door. Outside, she leaned a shaking hand against the wall and bent over, agony tearing at her gut. Holy Mary, Mother of God, help me, Mellisynt prayed. Help her what? her frantic mind raged. Help her accept that the man she'd come to love couldn't pass one night without plunging his accursed shaft into any available female? That he'd tumble a virgin in their own bed, with his wife but a few feet away?

"My lady, are you all right?"

Mellisynt straightened and tried to focus on the worried face floating before her.

"My lady!"

After a few seconds, the face resolved itself into one of the upper maids.

"I'm...I'm fine," she managed shakily. "I'm but overtired this morn."

"Aye, we heard you spent the night in the stables with the boys," the maid offered with a shy smile. "'Twas most kind of you."

It wasn't kind, Mellisynt wanted to scream, it was most stupid. She'd chosen to care for the boy instead of satisfying her husband's needs, and now faced the result. She dragged in a deep, unsteady breath.

"Would you take word to Dame Hertha to see to our guests this day? I am indeed most tired and would be alone to rest."

Mellisynt waited until the girl nodded and left, then retraced her steps down the back stair to the outer yard. Gathering her soiled skirts, she slipped out of the postern gate and raced into the mist. The beach. She'd go to her private beach. There, among the rocks and gray fog, she'd try to put her shattered soul back together.

"I would speak with you, Richard."

FitzHugh glanced up from the sleek, brown-feathered falcon he held on one gauntlet. A piece of raw meat dangled from his other hand. He gave Beauchamp a welcome grin, glad of the company.

He'd spent the drizzly, fog-swept morning in the mews with his hunting birds, although he would much rather have spent it in his bed with his wife. Hertha had stopped him when he returned from his long vigil with the gate guards, however, and informed him that Mellisynt was overtired from her labors in the stables and would rest. Amused by his aunt's stern, forbidding frown, he'd retreated in good order. But even his prized birds had failed to banish thoughts of his wife, whose feathers he'd much rather be stroking. Glad of Beauchamp's distracting company, he fed the falcon the bit of meat, then passed it to the keeper.

"Speak away, Beauchamp," he said, moving toward the door where his friend waited. Ducking under the low lintel, he stepped into a fine, gray rain.

"Well, Roger?" he asked, when the man beside him hesitated, as if at a loss for words. "What matter brings you out into the rain? Do you seek me out to complain about my bed? Wasn't it soft enough for your brittle bones last night?"

To his surprise, a slow flush crept up the thick column of Beauchamp's neck.

"Aye," the other man muttered. "I found it most soft and accommodating."

FitzHugh's eyes narrowed, then slowly widened. A wicked grin lifted one corner of his mouth.

"Oho! You rogue, did you entice one of the maids to join you between the sheets? Do you fear my lady's anger when she hears you diddled one of the servants in her own bed? And hear she will, you know. There are no secrets in a keep."

"I know." Beauchamp squared his shoulders and looked FitzHugh in the eye. "I did have company last eve. I will tell you that it was most...pleasant. And that I plan to take the girl to wife."

"What? Did the wench suck out your brains, as well as your sap?"

"Cease your crudities, man."

"You pork a serving wench and accuse me of crudities?" FitzHugh gibed.

"'Twas no serving wench," Beauchamp ground out. "'Twas the girl, Isabeau."

The mocking grin on FitzHugh's lips slipped, then disappeared altogether. He stared at the man opposite, anger and disbelief rising in his veins.

"You tell me you despoiled a virgin given to me for keeping?"

"Aye."

"In my own bed?"

"Aye."

FitzHugh's hands curled into fists. "You lecherous whoring knave."

"Save your insults, Richard. You can't call me anything I haven't already named myself. I leave immediately for Richmond to petition Geoffrey for her hand."

"You leave immediately for hell," FitzHugh roared, then slammed his fist into Beauchamp's belly. Sir Roger doubled over. Another fist smashed into his chin with bone-crunching savagery.

Beauchamp's head flew up. He staggered backward, blood streaming from his nose. FitzHugh lunged forward, throwing all the force of his body into a vicious punch that landed just below Beauchamp's breastbone. The wind rushed out of the man's lungs with a whoosh, and he went down.

"Get up, you craven cur."

FitzHugh reached down and grabbed the other's tunic, hauling him to his feet. His arm swung back, then forward. Beauchamp raised a forearm, deflecting the blow. Before FitzHugh could swing once more, he wrested himself loose and staggered back.

"Hold!" he snarled. "Do not raise your hand to me again, or I'll break it off!"

"Not before I take your head from your stinking body!" FitzHugh launched himself forward, propelled by his unleashed fury. The two men crashed to the earth, arms locked around each other, rolling over and over on the hard-packed dirt. Clenched knuckles beat against face and arms, as first FitzHugh and then Beauchamp gained brief mastery.

People poured from mews and stables and granaries and gardens, their shouts filling the air.

"Jesu, what goes on here?"

Alymer, FitzHugh's uncle, pushed his way through the

surging crowd surrounding the combatants, St. Bressé at his heels. The squire, Ian, came running from the armory. They jumped back as the two twisting, pummeling fighters rolled toward them.

"Christ, 'tis Sir Richard! And Sir Roger!"

An agonized grunt rose above the noise as Beauchamp's knee connected with FitzHugh's groin. Taking advantage of his adversary's momentary stunned pain, Beauchamp wrenched himself free and rolled aside. Panting, his eyes murderous, he pushed himself to his feet. FitzHugh dragged himself to his knees and started to rise.

Beauchamp swung his foot back, blood surging through his veins, his every fighting instinct screaming at him to disable his attacker, to smash his ribs and follow up with a boot to the face. His leg muscles bunched, his foot surged forward. At the last second, he twisted, and his boot sliced through the air beside FitzHugh's head. Taking advantage of the movement, his adversary leapt forward, thrusting his shoulder against Beauchamp's thigh. Both men hit the dirt once more, grunting and twisting and struggling for dominance.

FitzHugh's burly uncle watched their furious combat for some moments more, then shook his head. "We'd better separate them before they kill each other."

Sending Ian and St. Bressé to take hold of Beauchamp, he and two others grabbed at FitzHugh.

"Let go!" FitzHugh bellowed, shaking off their hold.

Alymer threw himself at his nephew once more and wrapped both arms around his chest. At his furious shout, the other two took hold of FitzHugh's flailing arms.

"Cease!" Alymer shouted. "This is no way for two knights to settle their differences, whatever they be!"

When FitzHugh tried to break his hold with a quick elbow jab backward, he grunted "Do that again and I'll whack your head with the flat of my sword."

His pained wheeze penetrated the red haze of fury behind

FitzHugh's eyes. While the three men held on for dear life, he fought to bring his rage under control. He sucked air into his lungs in harsh, shuddering gulps. Never taking his eyes from Beauchamp, similarly restrained, he straightened slowly.

"Get out of my keep and off my lands," he growled. "If you dare to show your face here again, I'll slice out your gut and feed it to the dogs."

Beauchamp shook off the other's loosened grip. "I'll return within the week, to claim my bride."

"She'll be a widow before she is a bride, if you set foot on Edgemoor again."

Beauchamp's brown eyes blazed with fury. "I'll return," he promised. Dragging his sleeve across his face, he smeared blood and dirt in equal parts over his cheek. With a last glare at FitzHugh, he turned and crossed to the stables. A furious order sent his squire running for his gear.

FitzHugh spit a stream of blood to the ground and stalked into the keep. Ignoring the maids' frightened gasps and Hertha's openmouthed astonishment, he strode to his chamber and flung open the door.

"Is this how you care for a girl in your household, wife?"

He yanked open the bed curtains, then swore viciously when he saw the empty bed.

"Where is she?" he barked at Hertha, who was peering through the open door, with a crowd of wide-eyed maids at her shoulder.

His aunt's generous chins dropped. She glanced from the unoccupied bed to the man beside it and shut her mouth with a snap.

"Don't shout at me. I swatted your dirty backside more than once in your misspent youth, and I'm not loath to do it again."

She slammed the door on the goggling maids and advanced on her nephew. The sight of this rotund little woman bristling like an angry hedgehog, obviously willing to carry out her absurd threat, lessened some of FitzHugh's fury. He relaxed his iron hold on the bed curtains and wiped a hand over his aching jaw.

"Where is my lady wife, aunt?"

"I thought her here, asleep," Hertha responded, brows puckering. "Mayhap she went back to the stables, to see to the boys. What goes on here, nephew? Why is your face battered and bleeding?"

"I would speak with Mellisynt first. She can explain the matter to you later, if she wishes. Please, send a man to the stables to fetch her. And heat some water so I may bathe my jaw."

Hertha gave him a disgusted look, but turned to do his bidding. FitzHugh saw the door shut behind her with some relief. He had no desire to bring shame down on Isabeau if he could avoid it. He'd send Mellisynt to find the girl and ascertain her state. If she wasn't opposed to Beauchamp, and Geoffrey agreed to the match, mayhap they could bring it off without destroying Isabeau's name. They *would* bring it off, he vowed savagely, forgetting that just moments ago he'd sworn to kill the man he even now determined to see wedded before the next full moon.

The hot water arrived within minutes, carried by his squire. Stripping away his torn and bloody clothes, FitzHugh let Ian bathe his bruises. He was sitting on a stool, clad only in his linen braies, cursing Ian's clumsy hands, when Hertha bustled back into the room. Brushing aside the squire, she picked up the soap and a linen rag and took over the duties of attending to the lord of the manor.

"The Lady Mellisynt is not at the stables," she told her nephew, dabbing at a cut over his eye.

FitzHugh pushed her hand away. "Where is she?"

"I know not." Hertha retorted. She took a fistful of hair and yanked his head back.

"Ouch!"

"Hold still. You've opened the wound on your pate in your little brawl. It'll have to be stitched again." She poked at the half-healed scar on his forehead with ungentle fingers.

"Damn it, aunt," FitzHugh ground out, "forget the wound. Where could Mellisynt be?"

"In any one of two dozen outbuildings, seeing to her duties! You men! You think that just because you come riding back after being gone a half a year and more, your wife can forget the soap-making or cooking or gardening or any other of the chores that demand her attention. I've sent the maids scurrying to find her. She'll be here forthwith."

But Mellisynt did not arrive while Hertha finished tending FitzHugh's wounds, nor even while he pulled on fresh garments with impatient hands. Nor had anyone found a trace of the lady in any of the keep's many outbuildings.

Even Hertha's brow was furrowed in worry by the time the last of the men sent out to search the grounds reported back.

"Has no one seen her this day?" FitzHugh snapped to his aunt and uncle.

Alymer shook his head.

"Mayhap the Lady Isabeau," Hertha suggested tentatively. "I asked among the women earlier. When I queried the girl, she only shook her head and burst into tears."

"Bring her here," FitzHugh ordered. He paced in front of the hearth, a scowl etched across his features, until the two women returned. Isabeau sent him a frightened glance through red-rimmed eyes, but held her chin proudly.

"Leave us. Please, aunt," he requested when Hertha would have protested. Alymer took her arm and drew her away, shooing the servants down the hall, as well.

"Have you seen my lady wife?" FitzHugh began brusquely.

"Aye," Isabeau whispered. "Earlier. This morn."

"Where?"

"She...she came to the sewing room just after we broke our fast."

FitzHugh leaned forward to catch the girl's soft words. "She's not there now. Do you know where she is?"

"Nay."

A gnawing worry curled in FitzHugh's stomach. He turned, thinking to dismiss the girl and mount a search himself, but her tragic face held him. He'd been careless enough of his duty to protect the child; he couldn't leave her in such distress.

"Beauchamp came to me this morn," he told her.

"Aye. He said he would." Isabeau swallowed. "I heard that you beat on each other most fearsomely. Is...is he hurt?"

"Not as much as he should be. Are you all right?"

The gruff kindness, where she'd expected only blows or scorn, nearly undid Isabeau. Tears trembled on her lids, but she blinked them back furiously.

"I am become a watering pot of a sudden," she murmured, shamefaced.

FitzHugh took pity on her. "'Tis not the end of the world. Sir Roger goes to petition Geoffrey for your hand."

"I know. He told me he would do so before he...before he sent me...before I left the..."

"Before you left his bed," FitzHugh finished bluntly. "Did he force you?"

Isabeau's great sea-green eyes widened. After a long moment, she shook her head. "Nay." She sighed, with a hint of her old smile. "I all but forced him."

Despite himself, FitzHugh grinned. "Then 'tis well you're to wed. Don't look so sorry, Isabeau. None but Beauchamp and I know why we fought. You'll be married with your dignity intact, if not your virgin's shield."

"Lady Mellisynt knows," Isabeau confessed, her tentative smile fading. "She slapped my face and called me slut. And I am." Her voice wobbled, tears threatening once more.

FitzHugh frowned, unable to reconcile the Mellisynt he

knew with one who would slap a suffering young woman. Worry ate at his insides. Where was his wife? He patted the girl's arm absently.

"Nay, you're no slut. You're but a pretty little morsel, too sweet for Beauchamp to resist. Rest, child, and all will be well."

"I'm not a child!"

Isabeau's wail fell on deaf ears as FitzHugh turned and hurried out.

Chapter Fourteen

Mellisynt huddled on a flat sweep of rock, her arms locked around her knees. Mist swirled about her, obscuring all but a narrow view of the sea. Below, gray waves crashed against fog-shrouded boulders, while overhead the gulls whirled and swooped, their raucous cries echoing eerily through the thick haze.

Coming here to lick her wounds had been a mistake, she realized. Every so often the mists cleared, as they did now, and gave her a view of the beach below. She stared down at the strip of sand and rock, her heart aching as her eyes sought the spot where she'd fallen headlong into love at the same moment the hound had tumbled both her and FitzHugh into the sea. Where she'd shed the last of her inhibitions as she shed her clothes and welcomed her lord home so shamelessly. Where his rough hands and hungry mouth had taken her beyond physical craving, beyond lust, beyond passion. A drift of soft drizzle obscured the beach once more, shutting off her view. Just as a few malicious words had shut off her dreams short hours ago.

She rested her chin on her knees, letting the dew wash the residue of tears from her cheeks. How could she have been so foolish as to think herself in love? How could she have opened her heart and allowed FitzHugh inside? Just because he was most skilled with his hands and most generously endowed between his well-muscled thighs? Because he seemed to take as much pleasure in their coupling as did she? Because occasionally his eyes gleamed down at her with a soft light she'd mistaken for affection?

Fool, she berated herself, fool! She closed her eyes against a fresh wave of pain. The troubadours were right, she decided when the ache subsided. Love had no place in marriage. 'Twas best to bestow one's affections on some distant knight, to play a measured game, in which a man could not sweep a woman into his arms and break her heart, did she not allow it. She sighed, thinking that this business of love rightly belonged in song and not in real life. It was too painful, too tormenting.

Settling her head more comfortably on her knees, Mellisynt let the muted roar of the sea soak into her soul. Fog blanketed the air, narrowing her world to a gray patch of rock and sea. Once she thought she heard a muffled voice calling, far off in the distance, but the sound drifted away on the thick mist. Exhaustion, both physical and mental, washed over her.

She woke some time later with a stiff neck and cramped legs. She had no idea how long she'd dozed, since the fog had deepened and now hid all but a faint haze of sunlight. Straightening her stiff limbs, she rose slowly, like an aged, tired woman. Her gown was damp clear through, and her hair hung in wet tangles from loosened braids. Pushing the thick strands back with a weary hand, she stepped off the rock ledge and began to trudge up the long, sloping path of the cliff. She would not stay and mope here like a moonstruck lackawit. She was chatelaine, with a house full of guests to see to. And a husband to attend. Mellisynt drew in a ragged breath and curled her nails into her palm.

By the time she'd climbed to the top of the cliffs, she'd buried her hurt deep inside.

Not far from the keep, a muffled thunder sounded somewhere behind her. Mellisynt turned and peered into the gray mist, trying to discern the sound. Suddenly, without warning, a rider broke through the haze, bent low in the saddle, galloping hard and fast straight at her. With a frightened shriek, she threw herself off the path, landing on hands and knees in rough gorse.

The horse was pulled to a dancing, whinnying halt.

"My lady!"

St. Bressé slid from the saddle and scrambled to her side. Urgent hands grabbed her arms and lifted her to her feet.

"Are you hurt?"

"Nay!" Mellisynt gasped, pushing her wet hair out of her eyes.

"Where have you been? Sir Richard has turned out the entire keep to search for you. We've been looking for hours."

"For me? Why?"

St. Bressé blinked at her openmouthed astonishment. "Why? Well, because…because Sir Richard ordered it."

"But I often walk the shore, you know that!"

"Aye, but not when our lord is here, and the keep full of guests."

Mellisynt bit her lip, mortified to be reminded of her discourtesy. With all the turmoil she'd endured last night and this morning, she dreaded having to face the crowded keep.

"Here, mount my horse, and I will lead you in," the knight offered.

"Nay, I'll walk," she muttered, not about to add the discomfort of the saddle to her other, inner hurts.

She trudged beside St. Bressé up the steep path to the gates, then into the courtyard. A chorus of shouts greeted their arrival. Before they'd crossed half the yard, Hertha rolled out of the keep and threw herself at Mellisynt. She staggered back a few paces at the enthusiastic, weighty welcome.

"We've been so worried, girl." Hertha sniffed, wiping a corner of her eye with a long sleeve.

"But why?" Exasperation drew Mellisynt's brows together

in a fine line. "I don't understand all this consternation. You've not fretted when I walked before."

"But then we didn't have your lord pacing about like a snarling bear, worried at your absence."

"He should rather worry at my presence," Mellisynt muttered to herself as Hertha shooed her into the hall. She allowed herself to be hustled down the length of the great room, to the privacy of her chamber. Hertha left her with instructions to strip immediately while she sent maids for hot water and men to find Sir Richard and advise him of her return.

Alone in the bedchamber, Mellisynt stood rooted to the floor. Her eyes fastened on the huge curtained bed that dominated one wall. An image of FitzHugh's long, powerful body crushing Isabeau into the mattress seared her mind. She was still standing, unmoving, when Hertha and a string of maids hastened in with water and a bowl of soft soap. Clucking, the older woman pushed her over to the fire and began to remove her sodden clothing.

Without a word, Mellisynt allowed herself to be stripped, folded into the copper tub and scrubbed. She felt drained, like one whose body had overextended itself and now longed for nothing more than to sink into oblivion. Hertha's scolding chatter fell unheard upon her ears. She bent forward, resting her forehead on her knees, while the maids soaped her tangled hair and rinsed it with fresh water. A lethargy spread through her limbs, only to shatter as the chamber door crashed open.

The maids jumped and squeaked in surprise. A full bucket of water sloshed over Mellisynt's head, streaming into her eyes and open mouth. Gasping, she lifted her head and tried to push aside the curtain of wet hair.

"Leave us!" FitzHugh thundered.

Hertha shook her head and approached the furious man. "Now, nephew, your lady is safe and—"

FitzHugh lifted his aunt by her dimpled elbows and deposited her outside the door. He jerked his head at the openmouthed maids, then slammed the wooden panel behind them and slid the bolt into place. Pushing his glistening, rain-soaked mail hood off his equally drenched head, he approached the copper tub.

Mellisynt gasped. "What happened to your face? And your eye? 'Tis all but swollen shut!"

"Never mind my eye, lady wife," he responded, his voice grim. Leaning over, he grasped both of her bare arms. With one swift tug, he hauled her, naked and shrieking, from the tub.

"Are you mad?"

She tried to wrench her arms loose, desperate to cover herself. Her lethargy fled, and a fury fueled by hurt fired in her blood. "How dare you storm in here and handle me so?"

FitzHugh's hands tightened on her arms. "I'll handle you far worse ere this day is over. How dare *you* disappear like that, with no word to anyone? I've had men out searching for hours."

"Why?" Mellisynt spit. "Why should you look for me?"

FitzHugh stared down at her, dumbfounded. The confounded woman actually glared at him, as if angry that he should care whether she'd been abducted, or slipped off the cliffs and broken her bones on the rocks. Or lost her way in the accursed fog and fallen into one of the bogs that dotted the moors. Thinking of the many horrible fates he'd envisioned in the last hours, and of the cold fear that had lodged in his belly like a stone, his rage surged back.

"I could not believe it when the St. Bressé found me and said you'd *gone walking!*" His voice rose to a furious shout. "Have you no idea of the dangers in this land for a woman alone? Have you no sense at all?"

"I've sense enough to find my way back unassisted and unmolested!" Mellisynt screeched. "Unmolested until you returned, that is!"

FitzHugh's long night of wanting and even longer day of worry came together with the force of two chargers colliding.

A tide of need swept over him, and he began to drag her toward the bed.

"I'll do more than molest you, wife. I'll make sure you don't have the strength left to *go walking* for many a day!"

Mellisynt resisted, twisting in his hold, clawing at the hands clamped like iron bands around her arms.

"Nay!" she screamed. "Nay! I will not be taken in the same bed as your whore. You will not use me so!" She bent, trying to bite his wrists.

Her savagery pierced his pounding desire before her words even registered. Frowning, FitzHugh released her arms. Mellisynt darted across the room and snatched up her damp shift, holding it over her front with shaking hands.

His eyes narrowed as she trembled before him. Folding his arms across his chest, he forced his voice to a semblance of calm. "Explain your words, lady wife."

Her lips twisted in a sneer. "What, were they not clear enough for you? I know not how else to say them! I'll not lie with you in the same bed, on the same sheets, where you fornicated with Isabeau!"

The heat drained from FitzHugh's veins like blood from an open wound, slowly, drop by drop, until he was left with a cold, hard core of disbelief.

"You think *I* sported with the girl last night?"

"I know you did! She herself admitted it!"

"She said she lay with me?"

"She didn't say your name, mayhap, but she didn't need to. She was seen coming to this room last night, and washing the blood from her thighs this morn."

FitzHugh saw the hurt behind the fury in his wife's eyes. He tried to tell himself that circumstances gave credence to her distrust. His rational mind acknowledged that she knew not all the facts. Yet a fierce pride overrode these logical reasonings. In all his years, he'd never compromised his honor. He'd lived by and was known for his word. That his wife, his own wife, would question his integrity was like an iron spike in his belly.

"I would be sure I understand this." His jaw clenched and unclenched with each word. "You think me so lacking in honor that I would deflower a virgin given into my keeping, in the same bed I share with my wife?"

Mellisynt's brows drew together. A faint cloud of doubt edged the anger in her eyes, only to be chased away with a toss of her head. "I misdoubt honor entered into it. More like Isabeau climbed astride your shaft before you could turn her away, had you even wanted to."

His mouth tightened into a grim line. "So now I not only lack principle, I also lack the will to turn aside an untried girl who would steal my virtue."

Mellisynt's frown returned. She gnawed on her lower lip, as if suddenly unsure how to proceed.

"What's the matter, wife, have you no other flaws in my character to bring forth?" FitzHugh uncrossed his arms and moved toward her, one deliberate step at a time. "No other slurs to cast against me, or against the girl whose behavior you were charged to govern?"

"Do not think to turn this on me," Mellisynt cried, goaded. She stepped back, the shift clutched to her breast. "And do not dare to touch me, you bastard!"

A cold, icy rage filled FitzHugh's veins. "I'll do with you as I please. You forget yourself in your accusations, lady wife. Bastard I may be, but you are mine to use, in this bed or any other, no matter how many women I take before you or after you."

FitzHugh saw pain flood her eyes, and almost halted. But hurt pride drove him forward, and something deeper, some last, lingering trace of his confused feelings of the night before. The woman whose touch he'd longed for thought him a lowborn bastard, without honor, without principle. Even when she discovered the truth, he'd know she'd doubted him. An aching sense of loss lanced through him, only to be dismissed contemptuously. If he couldn't have the woman's trust, he'd take what else he pleased.

He halted before her. "Get you into bed."

"Nay," she whispered, her eyes huge, mossy pools.

"To bed, lady wife."

She drew in a harsh, ragged breath. "Nay."

FitzHugh's fists clenched. A lifetime of absolute authority rose within him. His every instinct raged at him to reach out, to take the woman and shake her, to drag her to their bed and subdue her once and for all. No soldier who dared defy him so would live to see the light of day. No mount that refused the command of his spurs or hands would survive in his stables. Nor would any wife of his refuse him.

"If I must force you, I will."

Mellisynt heard the implacability in his voice and felt her heart shatter into a thousand tiny splinters.

"Do not do this, my lord."

Her plea didn't pierce the coldness in his eyes. The last vestiges of her anger drained, and only hurt was left. Swallowing painfully, she moved around his body and crossed to the bed. The wet shift dropped from her numb hands, and she slid between the wool-filled covers.

FitzHugh moved to stand beside the bed frame. For a long moment he stared down at her, his lips pressed together in a grim white line.

Forcing herself to meet his hard look, Mellisynt resisted the urge to pull the covers over her chilled flesh. Shivers racked her, and despite her most determined efforts, a ragged sob escaped her lips.

With a curse, FitzHugh turned and strode out of the chamber.

Not until late in the afternoon could Mellisynt bring herself to stumble out of the bed chamber. Her eyes were red-rimmed with unshed tears, and her throat felt raw.

Isabeau had been waiting, 'twas obvious. The girl caught her as she emerged from the chamber and begged private speech. Mellisynt wanted to scream at her to go away, but couldn't force a sound through her tight throat. Perforce, she listened to Isabeau's stumbling confession. When the girl mumbled Beauchamp's name, Mellisynt's heart seemed to stop in her breast.

"I don't know why I lay with him," Isabeau whispered, her head bowed. "Most times, I don't even like him! He...he belittles me and...and teases me and thinks me yet a half-grown child. But when he kissed me, my lady, I seemed to...to lose all reason."

Mellisynt wouldn't have believed she could hurt more than she already did, but the knowledge that she'd driven her husband to near-violence by her own accusations and jealousy stabbed through her with every breath. Too shattered to deal properly with Isabeau, Mellisynt signaled to Hertha.

"Don't...don't fret, Isabeau," she croaked. "Beauchamp is an honorable man, and will return for you."

She pushed the girl into Hertha's ample arms with a silent plea to the older woman. Hertha led Isabeau away, clucking and murmuring curses on men who couldn't keep their cod-pieces laced.

When FitzHugh returned late that evening, Mellisynt had composed herself and her words of apology. She waited while he stripped and washed and changed into clean, soft robes. He heard her out with a cold courtesy that knifed through her, gave a curt nod, then strode out for the evening meal. Mellisynt trailed after him, miserable and resentful and ashamed.

Thus was set the pattern for their days, and their nights. Ever polite, FitzHugh accorded her the dignity of her position as chatelaine. He included her when reviewing the accounts with Alymer and the cleric who kept their records, and when discussing the strength and weaknesses of the vassals who owed him service. He took her with him when he rode to the villages and farmsteads to meet with tenants. But the smile that had lightened his eyes when he looked at her was gone, as was the warmth from his voice.

While the days were misery for Mellisynt, the nights became sheer torment. Despite his seeming indifference, FitzHugh kept her in his bed. Lying beside him in the darkness, feeling the heat of his body next to hers, hearing the soft rasp of his breathing, Mellisynt grew ever more wretched.

Hesitantly, unused to taking the initiative in their relationship, she tried to bridge the growing gap between them. She took great care with her dress each morn, and went about with a calm, smiling demeanor. Still, he held himself distant.

Finally, taking all her courage in hand, she turned to him in bed one night. To her relief, he accepted her tentative caresses and rolled atop her willingly enough. But while his skilled hands and hard body brought her to pleasure, they did not bring fulfillment. 'Twas as if he held a part of himself back, as if he felt the heat they generated in his body, but not his soul. Mellisynt turned away from him afterward, shamed. She would have slipped from the bed, had he not brought her back down to the mattress with a low, growled reminder of her place.

Though they coupled frequently after that, 'twas without the passion she craved. Each time FitzHugh played upon her body and brought her to peak, then spilled his seed into her with deliberate, paced movements, another corner of her soul curled in despair. She began to hate her treacherous body for its involuntary response, as much as she hated herself from the lack of trust in her husband that had brought them to this pass.

The rest of the residents of the keep were quick to sense the changed atmosphere. Hertha frowned and fussed and queried Mellisynt until the younger woman snapped at her to cease, to leave her be! And then crumpled into an abject heap and wept on Hertha's comfortable shoulder.

Bartholomew, his indomitable spirits fully recovered from his ordeal, took to tagging at Mellisynt's heels whenever he could slip away from his tutors and training. As if sensing her discomfort, the hound would come up at unexpected moments and plop his huge, shaggy head down in her lap. Mellisynt forced herself to laugh with the boy and scratch behind the dog's lopsided ears with a knowing hand, but the joy she found in their company was overshadowed by the ache in her heart.

Isabeau quickly recovered from the fright of losing her virginity and her value as a marriage pawn. Regaining a semblance of her former self, she joined the other maidens in sewing or weaving or singing, with her head held high and the same sultry smile on her lips whenever a man passed near. But Mellisynt knew the smile was forced, and saw that her sea-green eyes held shadows not there before.

When a courier from Richmond arrived, Mellisynt watched FitzHugh read the stiff parchments with mingled dread and relief. She knew the message offered a change from the confused void her life had become.

"Constance sends you greetings and asks that you come to Richmond as soon as you may. Her time is near."

Mellisynt laid aside the woolen shirt she'd been darning. "I can leave in the morning, if that suits you."

FitzHugh shrugged. "As you will."

She bit her lip, then nodded. "Does the duchess say anything of Isabeau, and Sir Roger?"

"Aye," FitzHugh responded, his jaw tightening. "Beauchamp is in the north, carrying messages to King William of Scotland from Geoffrey about the raids across the border."

"In the north! But he was to come here, to claim the girl!"

"I see the duchess's fine hand in this." A hint of acid roughened FitzHugh's voice. "She must ever meddle. I've known her to refuse Geoffrey her bed until she got her way. Most likely she invented this mission for Beauchamp to keep us from spilling more blood.''

Mellisynt lifted her eyes to his, a challenge in them. '''Tis good to hear that some husbands recognize a woman's right to refuse them anything, including their bed.''

"You have many rights, wife,'' FitzHugh told her softly. "That's not one of them.''

For a moment, the air crackled with tension. Mellisynt rejoiced in the first real emotion between them since that disastrous night. She felt a surge of hope, but then the hardness in his eyes defeated her. Swallowing a sigh, she lowered her lashes.

"Isabeau is to travel with you to Richmond and celebrate her betrothal when Beauchamp returns. I'll go and make arrangements for your escort.''

"Do you not accompany us?''

"Birthing is women's business. I'll come for the baptism, or the betrothal, if it should occur first. Until then, there's much yet at Edgemoor that requires my attention.''

She glared at FitzHugh's broad back as he strode down the hall and closed her lips tight against the cry that she needed attention more than the keep! A familiar ache simmering in her breast, she rose to tell Isabeau of her fate.

"You look even worse than I feel!''

Mellisynt slid from the pillion with a weary lack of grace and smiled as the duchess waddled down a flight of shallow steps.

"I have a passing aversion to the saddle, as you might recall, but the roads were too broken to allow a litter.''

She leaned over to embrace the tiny, dark-haired Constance. Both women laughed when a protruding bulge of stomach kept their lips from meeting in the kiss of welcome.

"How does the babe?" Mellisynt asked, trying not to envy the duchess's radiant bloom.

Constance grimaced. "Much better than his dam." She placed a supporting hand under her stomach and walked forward a few more steps to greet Isabeau.

"Welcome, lady. I'm pleased that you've taken the interest of one of the finest of my husband's knights. Do you serve him well, Sir Roger will make you a fine lord."

Isabeau swept her a respectful curtsy, then dimpled. "Does *he* serve *me* well, he'll make me a fine lord."

Mellisynt smiled, glad of the girl's returned spirits. Her lively chatter and excited speculation about the betrothal ceremony had helped pass the three-day journey to Richmond.

Constance laughed and hooked a hand through each woman's arm. "Come inside and rest from your travels. Beauchamp should return within the week. We must plan the betrothal festivities."

She led the way inside the rambling castle, first built by Alan the Red, a Breton follower of William the Conqueror, and added to many times in the generations since. Perched high on a rocky eminence above the river Swale, Richmond Castle was swept by cooling breezes that dispelled the summer heat, but undoubtedly caused much suffering and chilblains in winter.

They passed through Scolland's Hall, famous throughout the north for its arched, oak-beam ceilings, its cavernous fireplaces, and the intricately carved screen disguising the minstrel's gallery. After a brief stop to catch her breath, Constance threw open the door of a suite of rooms with wide windows opening on a view of the river and town below. Scattered ribbons and veils and silver brushes proclaimed the airy bower a lady's sanctuary.

"You'll be comfortable here with the other women, at least until FitzHugh arrives. I'll find private rooms for you then."

Mellisynt merely nodded. For a moment she was tempted

to tell Constance that she would stay in the women's chambers for the length of her visit, that FitzHugh could be housed with the men when he came. She dismissed the thought before it reached her lips. She'd not draw anyone else into the silent war between them.

Both she and Isabeau soon found themselves caught up in the inevitable swirl of gay amusements, lively entertainments and simmering politics that surrounded Constance. Geoffrey was absent most days, seeing to the demands of his holdings, so Mellisynt was spared the strain of his presence except at evening meals.

Isabeau regained her sparkle and her court of admirers as she rode to the hunt, or played at bowls on the grassy west lawn or tried her hand at archery with the other giggling maidens.

Mellisynt fell into her old pattern of sitting quietly, her hands busy embroidering gowns for the duchess's babe and her ears filled with the courtiers' chatter. She listened with amused interest to the cases brought before the court of love. Constance heard all arguments in each case and then issued her ruling with ruthless logic. In one instance, when a knight complained that his mistress would not love him unless he beat her, yet his own chivalry forbade such violent use of the woman he revered, Constance ordered him to obtain a stout birch switch immediately.

Another day, while the ladies and their chevaliers grouped around the reclining duchess in the sunshine of a walled garden, they took up a heated discussion of the thirty-one rules of love. First codified by Queen Eleanor while she was yet the wife of King Louis of France, the law caused much argument. Golden-haired Guy de Claire, who had followed Constance from Nantes, teased her blatantly about the first rule, *Marriage is not a just excuse for not loving.*

Mellisynt plied her sewing and half listened to the courtiers' bantering arguments, enlivened by personal anecdote, sweep-

ing generalities and ribald interpolations. But at the nineteenth
law, when de Claire's smooth voice stated that *If love dimin-*
ishes, it soon ends and rarely revives, her head snapped up.

It wasn't true, she wanted to cry. If it were, why didn't the
pain in her heart lessen? Even if she had made the grievous
error of falling in love with her husband, why did his continued coolness not end her silly infatuation? Why could she not
accept his casual possession of her body and go about her
life?

Mayhap 'twas all he was really capable of. Hadn't he said
himself he'd known nothing of love in his life, that he doubted
its existence? Mayhap she'd only imagined the tenderness in
his blue eyes before her disastrous accusations. Mayhap she'd
just become so enthralled with the sexual pleasures FitzHugh
gave her that she'd fancied herself in love. At the thought of
how he kept her in his bed, yet denied her the closeness she
craved, Mellisynt jabbed the needle into the linen with a vicious stab. The sharp steel pierced her thumb, and a bright red
flower blossomed on the fine fabric. She sighed and lifted the
injured finger to her mouth.

A teasing voice sounded in her ear. "Would that I was
offered such a treat."

"Beauchamp!" she squeaked, dropping the linen and jumping up to clasp his hands. Her eyes widened at her first sight
of his face, considerably rearranged since his visit to Edgemoor. His long, aquiline nose, now flattened at the bridge, was
still slightly swollen. A deep, healing cut slashed through one
eyebrow, giving him an even more rakish appearance than
before. And he sported a yellowish bruise high on his forehead, close to the line of curly brown hair.

"You look remarkably like my husband when last I saw
him," she remarked.

"Nay, don't wound me so," he protested. "Did I think I
resembled that stone-faced monolith, I'd dip my noggin into

a bowl of alchemist's brew and let it eat away the rocky ledges and rough crags.''

Mellisynt laughed and tapped his nose with a light, playful finger. ''It looks to me like one or two of your ledges have already been eaten away.''

A flash of color caught her attention, and she looked over Beauchamp's shoulder to see Isabeau glaring at them. The girl's eyes slitted, and then she turned her back. Mellisynt's hand dropped immediately. She was too intimately familiar with the fruits of jealousy to wish it on another.

''Your betrothed awaits you on the other side of the garden,'' she told Beauchamp with a quiet smile. ''I know you want to greet her. Go, and take with you my best wishes on your marriage.''

Beauchamp glanced across the group of bright-plumaged courtiers. His eyes lingered on Isabeau for a moment, and then he turned back to bow over Mellisynt's hand.

''Thank you for your good wishes, my lady,'' he replied, a roguish smile spreading across his battered face. ''I suspect I'll need them once I take that little vixen to wife.''

''Aye, you will,'' Mellisynt muttered to his retreating back. ''You most assuredly will.''

Chapter Fifteen

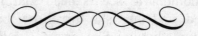

FitzHugh and the duchess's babe appeared at Richmond on the same night, at almost the same hour. Mellisynt was too wrapped up in the drama of birth to take even a few minutes to greet the husband whose arrival she'd both dreaded and desired. With an impatient hand, she brushed aside a page's whispered message that her lord awaited below.

"Tell him I'll attend to him later."

She pushed a strand of sweat-dampened hair out of her eyes and turned back to the woman dragging herself back and forth across the room, leaning on the midwife's arm.

Constance endured the indignities of the birthing process with her usual indomitable spirit. She allowed neither the heat, nor the crowd that invaded her chamber, nor even Geoffrey's well-meant, booming advice on how to pass the babe to distract her from her fierce concentration on the task at hand. She walked, and panted, and stiffened with each pain. As her time neared, she curled on her side in the huge bed while the women took turns rubbing her back and whispering encouragement.

When the perfectly formed infant slid from between her thighs, she closed her eyes against the disappointment of a girl, then opened them immediately and demanded her daughter. Sweaty, white-faced, triumphant, she held the babe, oblivious of the swarm of nurses waiting to clean and swaddle.

Mellisynt lingered long after Geoffrey and the others had left, long after the women had washed Constance and given her herbs to heal her torn flesh.

Under the nurse's jealous eye, she approached the cradle and brushed a bent knuckle down the babe's red, mottled cheek. She looked so small and helpless, with her puckered mouth and wrinkled eyelids. Mellisynt ached to lift the tiny bundle, to hold it to her breast. After a moment, she heaved a quiet sigh and left the royal chambers.

Having no desire to join the revelries in the great hall, nor yet to meet with her husband, she slipped back into the ladies' bower. She picked her way through the litter of scattered trunks and discarded gowns and settled herself on the wide casement window seat. Leaning back against the stone wall, she let the late-summer night wash over her. Far below, torches flickered in the streets of the town crouched against Richmond's massive walls as the citizens celebrated the maid's birth. Above, wispy black clouds scudded across a round silver moon. Crickets chirped in the climbing vines that clung to the outer walls, sounding a light, sweet counterpoint to the singing and laughter from the hall below.

Mellisynt rested her hands over her stomach and stared up at the full moon. She should have flowed with her monthly courses before the silvery orb had waxed half-full. She'd never missed her time before. In her heart she knew that she'd achieved her greatest desire. So why did the knowledge that she at long last carried a babe not fill her with joy? Why did she feel her eyes even now prickle with unshed tears, she who never cried?

With a wrench of pain, Mellisynt realized how misplaced her dreams of just a year ago had been. Immured within Trémont's gray walls, all she'd prayed for was a babe to love and a chance to breathe the open air. Now she had both, and they didn't fill the emptiness inside her. Now she cringed in shame each time the husband she would love took her in casual possession. She hated the way he could manipulate her, stroke her, fire her blood. He'd trained her to his hand as he had his falcons and his steeds.

Mellisynt wondered if she'd ever be forgiven for her lack of trust. If FitzHugh's eyes would ever again fill with the glinting warmth she'd seen the night he wrapped the pearls around her throat. When she'd thought, for one breathless moment, that he might feel the same burgeoning, wondrous love that filled her breast. Mayhap someday, she thought, but could she bear this ache until that distant day?

Wearily Mellisynt slid off the window seat. She was too tired to ponder the problem, or think of any solution. She knew FitzHugh would be up the whole night, celebrating with Geoffrey. This night, at least, she would sleep by herself.

As it happened, she slept several nights by herself. The revelries continued well into the next day, then spilled over into the tourney. Knights who should have been abed nursing sick heads climbed onto war-horses to demonstrate their virility. The tourney carried them far afield, so Geoffrey sent word that they would bed down at one of his vassals' keeps instead of returning immediately.

Both Constance and Mellisynt welcomed their lords' absences. In a rare moment of near privacy, the two sat on the duchess's bed some days later with the gurgling, naked babe between them.

"Do you believe something so delicate and sweet sprang from Geoffrey's loins?" Constance rubbed the baby's tummy with soft, stroking fingers.

Mellisynt smiled. "'Tis a wonder what the sire and the dam pass on. I marveled when I met FitzHugh's son, that he should be so merry."

"The Lord only knows where that comes from," Constance said. "FitzHugh's cheeks crack every time he smiles, and I misdoubt Alicia ever laughed in her life."

"Did you know her well?"

"The Lady Alicia? Aye, I knew her, though I was but a child being raised in Queen Eleanor's household when she and FitzHugh wed. A haughtier bitch never walked the earth! Her father was just a minor knight, but she held herself above her station. She was most unhappy to be given to a bastard. You'd think she conferred the Holy Grail upon FitzHugh every time she spread her legs. 'Tis a wonder she ever bedded with him at all.''

"Mayhap she had no choice in the matter.'' Bitterness laced Mellisynt's soft words. She reached out to play with the babe's waving foot.

"Do you say FitzHugh forces you?'' The sharp disbelief in the duchess's voice brought Mellisynt's head up with a snap.

"Is that so unlikely?''

Constance narrowed her eyes to violet slits. "I've never known him to have to do so. Although he's not the most handsome of knights, his very size usually has the maids in a dither. He has the endowments of a blooded stallion, and knows well how to use them.''

At Mellisynt's shocked look, she added a hasty "Or so Geoffrey tells me!''

She laughed and reached out a finger to push up Mellisynt's sagging jaw. "I swear there are more stories of FitzHugh and Beauchamp and their conquests than were ever sung of Beowulf or King Arthur. Geoffrey thinks that if he keeps me amused with tales of their exploits, I'll not question his. It gives me great satisfaction that both his rutting companions are now bound to women who will keep them on short chains!''

The smug satisfaction in her voice faded at Mellisynt's thin smile. Reaching across the babe, Constance took hold of her hands.

"Tell me true, are you so averse to the marriage bed that FitzHugh must force himself upon you? If so, I can give you herbs to ease your discomfort or simulate a most realistic passion."

Despite herself, Mellisynt grinned. "Nay, I need no aids. My lord is as skilled with his...endowments as Geoffrey told you."

"So what troubles you?"

She bit her lip and studied the gamine face across from her. Never having had any women friends, she was embarrassed to be sharing such intimate details of her life. Yet Constance had known this man who was her husband far longer than she had herself. Mayhap the duchess could help her deal with him.

"I...I lacked trust in my husband, and made a false accusation. I disparaged his honor. He has yet to forgive me."

Constance whistled low and long. "I'm not surprised. FitzHugh wears his honor like a buckler, ever forward. 'Tis all he had in the world for so many years, it's become a damned second skin. So in punishment for slighting his precious honor, he's denied you his attentions?"

Hot waves of red washed up Mellisynt's neck and cheeks. "Nay, he insists I share his bed and uses me most...most thoroughly. 'Tis the using I object to."

Nonplussed, Constance dropped her hands. "You object? Is he rough? Hurtful?"

She shook her head.

"Does he expect you to service him in unnatural ways?"

Not quite sure which of their activities Constance might consider unnatural, Mellisynt shook her head once more.

"Does he fail to bring you to pleasure?"

"Nay," she cried, goaded. "'Tis most pleasurable. But I would have more. I would have his love."

Constance stared across the short distance, her hand automatically reaching to soothe the babe when it gave a fretful cry. As if she were searching for words, her mouth opened, then closed several times. Finally, she sighed.

"I cannot advise you in this, Mellisynt. We each must find

our own way to love. But think on this—FitzHugh would skewer any man who dared question his honor. If he keeps you in his bed and in his arms, despite your lack of trust, 'tis certain he feels something special.''

"Aye," Mellisynt muttered. "He feels the same as when he mounts his prized war-horse!"

Constance laughed and scooped up the babe. "Not quite, I'm sure."

She nestled the child at her breast, and a hovering nurse came forward. Mellisynt slipped off the bed to give the mother and child privacy and returned to the women's dower.

When a clatter of hooves and muffled shouts heralded the return of the men the following evening, Mellisynt was ready to face her lord. He swept into the chamber given over to their use, and her heart thudded painfully in her chest. Huge, begrimed from the ride, his dark hair plastered to his forehead with sweat, he was the most magnificent male she'd ever beheld. She could see the excitement of the tourney still brimming in his eyes and feel it in the way he wrapped his arm around her waist and gave her a kiss that held a promise of the night to come. He lifted his head, only to have the half smile forming on his face twist into a grimace of pain.

"Have you taken an injury?" Worry sharpened her voice and hid the tremor his kiss had caused.

"'Tis naught." FitzHugh set her aside and turned to hand his sword and buckler to his squire.

Mellisynt sent Ian a swift inquiring look.

"A mace struck his shoulder," Ian explained, helping to pull off FitzHugh's stained surcoat. "But my lord held on and trounced Sir Guy. Again!"

FitzHugh's dark head emerged from the folds of material.

Mellisynt gaped at him. "De Claire? You unseated Guy de Claire?"

"Not just unseated," Ian bragged. "My lord took him in

the melee and all but pounded him into the dirt. He won't be spouting his pretty poetry for some time."

Lord and squire exchanged smug masculine grins.

Mellisynt couldn't help feeling a twinge of satisfaction at the thought of de Claire's arrogant nose ground into the dust. Chiding herself for her uncharitable thoughts, she rummaged through the chests for the supply of herbs and medicaments she'd brought with her. When FitzHugh had stripped and seated himself on a stool, she knelt and probed his swollen discolored shoulder. Satisfied that the muscles were bruised, but not torn, she physicked it with what she had at hand and bound it with strips of linen.

"I should send to the stables for your horse poultice," she commented tartly.

FitzHugh shook his head. "Nay, wife. I would not stink up our bed this night. Not when I have been without you and without ease these weeks."

A clutch of pain tightened Mellisynt's heart. She busied herself putting away her salves while FitzHugh rose and rolled his shoulders experimentally once or twice. With a satisfied grunt, he moved to the table holding a pitcher of water and splashed some into an enameled bowl.

Mellisynt watched while he washed himself, knowing she should go to him and do that duty, but reluctant to move. In the fading light, his body showed long and tan and incredibly powerful. Several vicious bruises stained his chest and arms where he must have taken other blows. Wordlessly she handed him thick, rough linens to dry himself with. She stood rooted to the floor as he walked across the room and stretched himself out on the velvet coverlet with a heartfelt sigh.

"Come, wife. Much as I want you, I ache in so many places that you may have to use some of old Henri's tricks this night."

Mellisynt buried her clenched fists in the folds of her skirts and didn't move. After a moment, FitzHugh turned his head on the pillow and surveyed her still form.

"Come."

"Nay." Her whisper barely carried across the wide room.

"I thought we settled this between us, before you left Edgemoor. Did your weeks here with Constance give you the mistaken idea that because she leads Geoffrey around by his rod, you may do so with me?"

Mellisynt gasped. "I have no desire to lead you around by...by anything. But neither do I desire to lie where there is no love."

She stiffened in anticipation. All her years of service as a wife screamed that it was a sin to deny her lord, that she would suffer for it. Her stomach fluttered as she awaited his reaction.

When it came, it totally disconcerted her. Having steeled herself for icy anger or physical domination, she wasn't expecting the amusement that flickered across his face.

"Did we not settle this, as well, months ago, when first we wed? I thought we were agreed such emotion exists only in song." He swung his legs over the side of the bed and started toward her. "Come, no more of this foolishness. I'm too tired to play games. I want you."

She took a hasty step back. "Nay."

The lazy amusement slipped from his face. His jaw firmed ominously.

"Do not try my patience. I'm not in the mood to school you gently this night."

"You will not school me at all," she hissed. "I'm not some dog to be trained, nor horse to be broken. Nor will I lie with you."

For a long moment, they glared at each other, his blue eyes boring into her furious green ones. Mellisynt watched, tension rising in her throat, as the shadows played across his stubble-darkened face. Finally, he gave a curt nod.

"As you will."

He went back to the bed and stretched himself out once more.

She stood in the middle of the room, too stunned to move. Now that she had girded herself emotionally for battle, FitzHugh's capitulation left her floundering. She listened with a disbelieving ear to the rustling of the mattress as he settled himself. Was this a ruse? Did he think to trick her into bed and then attack her?

As soon as the thought entered her mind, she dismissed it. Such was not her husband's way. If he wanted her, he'd take her without resorting to such trickery, overcoming her stiff resistance with his knowing hands and mouth. The memory of just how often he'd done so sent waves of shame through her. Not this night, she swore. Not ever again.

As twilight darkened into dusk, she began to feel foolish standing like a gatepost in the middle of the room. Yet she couldn't move. Her legs felt wooden, and her mind refused to tell her what she should do next.

"Get you in bed," he growled through the descending darkness. "I'll not take you if you do not wish it."

FitzHugh lay on his side, one arm bent beneath his head, and listened to the low sounds behind him as she moved forward and slowly undressed. With every rustle of her clothes, he cursed himself for a fool.

When she'd tilted up her chin and defied him yet again, he'd been tempted to teach her once and for all the foolishness of challenging him thus. But he'd stared down into her white, set face and sensed that this time she would well and truly fight. And at that moment he'd known he could neither hurt her nor try to force her.

In truth, he was tired of wringing a response from his stubborn wife. Although loath to admit it, even to himself, he got only hollow pleasure from their coupling of late. It lacked the wild, sensual explosion of passion he'd tasted with her before.

Before her suspicions and accusations had disgusted him. Before his anger had replaced passion with lust.

Since her departure from Edgemoor, he'd had time aplenty to regret his furious reaction to her lack of faith. She was only a woman, after all. It was foolish to expect her to hold the same standards of trust and respect as men. He'd banished the last, lingering regret for what might have been and hoped the time apart would ease the strain between them, as it had eased his anger. Instead, it appeared to have fueled hers.

His every sense tingling, FitzHugh felt Mellisynt slide into bed behind him. Her distinctive scent, the one that always reminded him of spring and soft blue flowers, drifted across the darkness. His ear picked up the uneven pitch of her breathing, and he smiled grimly. She was as disturbed as he by their confrontation. He wondered if she felt the heat of his nearness, as he did hers. If the fine hairs on her arms stood on end, as his did.

Deliberately he closed his eyes, willing sleep to come. His way of dealing with the strain between them had left him less than satisfied these last weeks. He'd see if her way was any better.

If the lack of physical release bothered Mellisynt in the weeks that followed, she hid it well. FitzHugh himself struggled with a growing frustration and aching need. By night, he called upon reserves of restraint he had never known he possessed to keep from rolling over in the darkness and burying his rigid shaft in his wife's soft body. By day, he spent his pent-up energies in the hunts and tourneys held in celebration of the birth of the Maid of Brittany. He and Beauchamp found themselves paired as partners in list, Roger with the mace and he with the sword. In the furious battle that ensued, the two men lost the last remnants of their enmity in the sweet thrill of victory.

As the day of the babe's baptism drew near, nobles from

across England and the Angevin domains in France converged on Richmond. Just days before the ceremony, Queen Eleanor arrived with all her queenly dignities restored. She'd been released from captivity some months earlier to pacify Aquitaine's hot-blooded lords after Richard Lionheart's stern rule had incited them to rebellion. Her return to power showed clearly in her regal, arrogant manner. She represented the king, who was away battling the stubborn Irish lords to force them to accept Prince John as their titular king. Geoffrey deserted the tourneys to attend his mother, a most singular occurrence for someone as sport-mad as he, one that gravely concerned both FitzHugh and Beauchamp.

They stood at the edge of the great hall together one night, Mellisynt between them and Isabeau in the dance with one of her admirers.

''I like this not,'' Beauchamp murmured, his eyes on Geoffrey's red head, bent over the velvet darkness of his mother's.

As she followed the line of his gaze, Mellisynt's own brows drew together. She'd been at court long enough to understand his meaning. She glanced up at FitzHugh to see him watching the royal pair with a worried frown.

'''Tis said the king's refusal to give up the Lady Alice eats at her soul.'' Beauchamp's low murmur barely rose above the noise of the crowd. '''Tis not just that Henry keeps a mistress, but that she is his son's betrothed, the woman promised to Eleanor's favorite.''

FitzHugh's blue eyes locked with Beauchamp's over Mellisynt's head. ''Lady Alice is Richard Lionheart's concern. Geoffrey would not champion his brother's cause.''

''The lady's become a pawn in this game of kings,'' Beauchamp argued, his voice low. ''Philip of France has sworn to avenge his sister's dishonor, but he knows better than to try to use Richard Lionheart to do it. Richard is too intelligent, too strong-minded, to be used by anyone. Nor does he much care what happens to the lady,'' Beauchamp finished dryly.

The two men exchanged knowing glances. Rumors of the prince's lack of interest in women had floated about for years. Few were surprised that he'd made no move to end the protracted betrothal.

Slowly, reluctantly, FitzHugh nodded. "Of all the sons, Geoffrey is the bravest, and the weakest. He's been hard put to refuse Philip's offers of assistance to throw off his father's heavy hand. With his mother's encouragement, it will be even more difficult for him to resist."

"And the fool will plunge us all into war again."

Both men looked down at Mellisynt in astonishment, as if realizing for the first time that she stood between them.

Whatever FitzHugh would have said in reply to his wife's impetuous remark was lost when Isabeau glided up to claim her betrothed for a dance.

The men's fears sat uneasily within Mellisynt as she bade goodbye to Beauchamp and Isabeau some days later. The couple was returning to Normandy, where Beauchamp's principal holdings lay and their wedding would take place. The duke and duchess planned to leave Richmond, as well, traveling to Brittany as soon as Constance recovered sufficiently. She wanted to be across the Channel before autumn storms swept in to make the crossing unpleasant.

Mellisynt cast a last look over her shoulder at Richmond Castle as she passed through its gates, atop a pillion behind FitzHugh. High above the tallest tower, the duke's pennant fluttered bravely in the late-September breeze. Its golden lion, rampant on a bloodred field, forcibly reminded her of the man himself. Geoffrey was as golden and bold as the lion, and just as bloodthirsty. A shiver racked her, and her arms tightened around FitzHugh.

Mellisynt ran her eyes over her husband's broad back, so close she could lean her cheek against it if she wished to. And the Lord knew she wished to. No more than FitzHugh did she like this unsettled state between them. Surely in the coming winter months, when dark descended early and shut them within Edgemoor's walls, she could bridge the gap between her husband and herself. Surely she could find the means to win back his regard.

These nights beside him in their bed had been torture. The mornings were even worse. She lay abed while he rose and dressed, then left to hunt or joust or ride with the men. Watching him through half-shuttered lids, fighting the sickness that now crept over her each morn, Mellisynt had grown more miserable with each passing day. Somehow she hadn't expected her victory in winning the right to her person to taste so vile.

Just thinking about the bouts of nausea she'd endured made her feel queasy. Of a sudden, the horse's easy gait beneath her legs took on a sinister roll. Mellisynt swallowed and stared resolutely at the roofs of the city buildings as they passed through the narrow streets. Once they left the garbage-strewn streets behind and gained the open road, she'd be fine, she told herself. She only needed to hold on till then.

She did. Barely.

"Stop!" she gasped as their small cavalcade rounded a bend in the road and entered the leafy shade of a thick forest.

FitzHugh twisted in the saddle and frowned down at her. "Why do you wish to stop? Surely you're not sore already?"

Mellisynt swallowed desperately. "I'm beyond sore. Get me down, my lord, and quickly!"

She pushed herself out of his hold as soon as her feet touched the road and dashed for the underbrush. Sinking to her knees behind a stand of willowy ash, she bent over and gave up her breakfast. Finally, trembling and wretched, she leaned back against a tree trunk.

"Here."

To Mellisynt's mortification, FitzHugh hunkered down on his haunches and held out a damp cloth.

"Wipe your face, then take some water to wash your mouth.

He passed her the cloth, then lifted a bulging bladder so that she could hold the spout to her lips. The cool liquid washed away the rank remnants of her meal. She leaned back against the slender trunk and closed her eyes.

"Are you all right?"

Her lashes flew up to see him regarding her with a steady gaze. She nodded, unable to speak. She knew she should tell him about the babe, but couldn't bring herself to the point. Not yet. Not while this tension hung between them and kept them lying awake at night, so close and yet so far apart. He'd know soon enough, in any case, if she couldn't control her stomach better.

"'Tis but a troubled stomach," she said. "I'm still a most reluctant rider."

"Are you sure that's the cause of your distress?" He reached down a hand to help her up.

"Wh-what do you mean?" She scrambled to her feet with a sad lack of dignity.

"I've felt you tossing and turning these nights, my lady wife. You've not enjoyed this enforced celibacy any more than I."

Mellisynt gaped up at him. "You think I pine so for your touch that my stomach is in knots?" she asked indignantly.

"Mine surely is," he said with a grim nod. "Or, if not my stomach, certain other parts of my anatomy."

A slow simmering anger rose in her veins. "I hate to disappoint you, my lord, but I do not crave your rod so much that its very absence curdles my breakfast."

She whirled and would have stomped back to the waiting men if his hand hadn't gripped her arm and held her in place. Mellisynt saw her anger mirrored in his glinting blue eyes.

"How much longer do we play this game? How long do you think to deny me? And yourself?"

"I don't know! Until...until..."

"Until your own need overcomes these silly woman's whims?"

She felt her heart constrict. He truly didn't understand. She wasn't sure she could explain her confused emotions, either to herself or to him. Still, here in this copse of ash, with the leaves fluttering gold above them and the stillness of the forest granting them a cloak of privacy, she felt the need to try.

"There should be more, my lord. More than just need between us."

"There is," he snapped. "There is respect. You have the dignities of your position as lady of Trémont and Edgemoor. You have your own revenues and rents."

She shook her head. FitzHugh's hand tightened on her arm.

"You have my constancy. I don't shame you by taking other women to bed."

"I know," Mellisynt whispered, hating the reminder of her own lack of trust.

"Then what in the names of all the saints do you want from me, lady?"

She stared up at him helplessly. "I want you to look at me as you do Geoffrey, or Beauchamp."

FitzHugh stepped back with a jerk, as if she'd struck him. "What? Do you now call me sodomite? I think I'd prefer you thought me a seducer of young virgins!"

"Nay! Nay! Of course I know you're not like that. I...I just want the bond, the love, the companionship, such as you have with these, your friends."

He gave her a disgusted snort. "If you expect me to share the same relationship with you as I have with my companions-at-arms, you're more addled than I thought. You're fashioned for an entirely different purpose, lady wife. One I'm hard put not to use."

Clearly out of patience, he propelled her toward the waiting men and horses. "You'd best resign yourself to your lot in life, my lady. 'Tis all you're like to get, after all."

He settled Mellisynt on her pillion with a decided plop. She glared at the broad expanse of his back when he swung onto the stallion and kicked it into a slow canter. She could feel the tension coiled in the hard muscles under her fingertips. Despite her high dudgeon, though, she had plenty of opportunity to ponder his words as they continued their journey.

As the miles passed, she felt her anger dissipate and a weary resignation begin to fill her heart. Mayhap she should accept what FitzHugh offered—respect and constancy and the pleasure they took in each other's bodies. That was more, much more, than many women got from their husbands. Mayhap friendship would grow eventually from such feelings, or something close to it. The thought gave her little comfort, and a heaviness settled in her heart. She knew that once they reached Edgemoor, FitzHugh's uncharacteristic restraint would fast dissipate. She wondered how long her own resolve would last before she did what he advised and accepted her lot in life.

As it turned out, she had little occasion to test either FitzHugh's restraint or her own resolve. They were not back at Edgemoor a day before a courier came pounding across the moors. He brought word that the duke had left for the Continent. He went not with the duchess, however, nor did he head for Brittany. Instead, he accompanied his mother, the queen, back to Aquitaine, and bade FitzHugh join him at Poitou as soon as possible.

"'Tis madness." Alymer stomped back and forth in front of the fire. "Do not go, nephew. The duke but seeks to draw you into the web his mother weaves about her sons."

"He is my sworn liege, uncle."

"He's a weak man. His head is turned by the last one who whispers in his ear."

"For that very reason, I must go."

"Nay, nephew."

"Do not, Richard."

He ignored the simultaneous exclamations of his aunt and uncle. Fixing his gaze on Mellisynt, he raised one brow.

"You do not speak, lady wife. What think you?"

Mellisynt took a deep breath. A hundred arguments tumbled through her head and trembled on her lips.

"You will do as your honor decrees."

She met his eyes squarely, then spoiled the effect of her noble words with a disgusted grimace. "Although I think it beyond stupid that one hot-tempered, hardheaded ruffian should drag us all into his intrigues and wars."

FitzHugh laughed and stretched his muscles. "Mayhap I can yet knock some sense into his hard head."

"When do you go?" Alymer asked the question that burned in Mellisynt's mind.

"On the morrow, I suppose. Unless something unforeseen occurs to delay my departure."

FitzHugh's eyes settled thoughtfully on Mellisynt's face.

She met his gaze with a wide, steady one of her own. "I'll go talk to the cook about provisions for the journey, my lord."

Chapter Sixteen

Ever afterward, Mellisynt would rue the stubbornness that made her send her lord off with no sign of her regard other than a cool kiss. She stood beside him in the outer bailey, his men and the keep's occupants crowding around them in the early-morning mists.

"Is that the kind of salute to give a departing husband?"

His low, teasing voice held a trace of its old warmth. Her heart began to thump.

"'Tis the best I can do, my lord. Mayhap I will manage something better when you return."

"You will, wife, you will."

He traced a finger down her cheek and was gone. Mellisynt watched him ride out, the mists dulling the shine of his silver mail and darkening the red of his surcoat to wine. No sooner had his troop disappeared from view than sickness roiled up in her belly and she stumbled to the stews to retch and heave. Dame Hertha fussed and scolded and pushed Mellisynt into a wooden chair before the fire. The hound promptly stuck his muzzle into her lap.

"When is the babe due?"

She laid her head against the chair back. "I'm not sure. May, I think, or June."

"'Tis early days, then." Hertha smiled sympathetically. "I tossed up my breakfast for months with each of my boys."

"Oh, no," Mellisynt groaned.

"And that's the least of all your problems, child. You've much to look forward to. Swollen ankles, an aching back, piles, lack of sleep..."

"Stop! You make me want to curl up in my bed and not come out till spring."

Hertha took her hand and pulled her from the chair. "Nay, you'll do better on your feet. Hard work or a hard man are the only cures I know for breeding ailments. Since you've just lost the one, I'd best get you to the other."

True to her word, Hertha kept Mellisynt so busy through the cold autumn and dark winter months she scarce had time to miss her husband. The harvesting and milling and wine-making took many hours, as did the trenching and ditching around the keep's walls and gardens. Privies and stables were cleaned, their muck spread on the castle garden to prepare it for spring, with a goodly portion being carted to the outlying farms for their use. As the days shortened and the winds grew colder, Mellisynt oversaw the butchering of animals fattened through the fall, ensuring that the haunches and sides were salted or pickled with spices and hung on the great hooks in the vaulted storeroom in the great hall.

Gradually all activity moved indoors, as early snows swept down and blanketed the earth. The women spun and sewed and wove tapestries, while the men repaired horn and leather implements or carved wooden platters and spoons. Reeds and rushes gathered earlier, before the frosts, were plaited into baskets and harnesses and fish creels by the servants.

FitzHugh sent sporadic messages. Fall storms had delayed his departure from Portsmouth for weeks, and he wasted further weeks tracking Geoffrey's erratic movements. The duke had decided to celebrate Hallowmas with Constance in Rennes, FitzHugh wrote, disgust in every line, after having summoned all his knights to Poitou. Now they kicked their heels and waited for their lord to reappear. He was expected back before Christmastide.

Mellisynt's own Christmas, her second at Edgemoor spent without her lord, gained considerable liveliness with the arrival of both FitzHugh's sons. William and Geoffrey came to celebrate the birth of Christ with their father's lady, they told her, eyes sparkling with mischief. And their father had written to threaten them with death, Geoffrey confided, did they not behave most respectfully.

The keep soon rang with shouts of laughter as the boys organized all kinds of entertainments to keep themselves occupied. Mummeries and singing and chess tourneys occupied the nights, while squads of squires and pages and village boys battled with balls of snow and oaken staffs beating upon wooden shields during the day.

Wrapped in a thick woolen mantle, Mellisynt stood at a second-floor window watching them. Her heart leapt into her throat every time William dashed into her field of vision. So tall and muscular and dark of hair. So like his sire. Even his voice, carrying across the crisp winter air, held the same low timbre, although it occasionally still cracked with youth. Sweet Mother, she prayed, give me a son such as this. Or like Geoffrey, whose high-pitched shrieks of laughter she could hear clearly. And give me back their sire, she prayed most fervently. Soon.

In the dark winter nights, alone in her bed, she'd come to the realization that FitzHugh was right. What they had together was more than most husbands and wives found. So it was not the sweet, delicate love the troubadors sang of? So it was compounded of equal parts respect and lust? 'Twould do well enough, she decided. The longer she was without her husband's strong body beside her, the less she was concerned with respect, and the more with lust. The child growing within her kept her awake and restless with strange longings. Her breasts itched and burned and ached for the feel of his hands.

Her womb fluttered with the babe's first movements and sent a tingling awareness of her womanhood through her body.

She tried to write FitzHugh of her feelings, but could find neither the words nor the courage to put them to paper. Instead, she settled for telling him of the babe, and his sons' visit, and the business of the keep. And for begging him to return, whole and sound, as soon as he might.

But FitzHugh didn't return with the coming of spring. As the weeks passed, his messages became less frequent and more terse. The duke had returned to Poitou, he finally wrote in early March, and Eleanor became more strident in her criticisms of the king. She whipped her barons into a froth of hatred, and Geoffrey with her.

After the last terse missive, no word came at all.

"What you plan is treason."

"Be careful, FitzHugh. Even our friendship is not proof against such accusations."

"'Tis no accusation, 'tis simple fact."

The duke pushed himself away from the table. His chair crashed to the tiles as he surged to his feet.

"I will not have you harp at me on this anymore!"

With every fiber of his being, FitzHugh resisted the urge to grab Geoffrey by his velvet surcoat and beat his head against the wall. He glanced around the ring of men crowded into the duke's chamber, but saw no help on any of the faces he surveyed. Some, like Guy de Claire's, held outright hostility. FitzHugh sucked in his breath and tried again.

"Listen to me, Geoffrey. Even now your father prepares to sail from Portsmouth. He's heard of your schemes, and your mother's."

"One wonders where he got his information. And where you get yours, FitzHugh."

At de Claire's sneering drawl, FitzHugh straightened and turned slowly. He knew his prolonged and strenuous opposition to Geoffrey's proposed trip to Paris to align himself with the king of France had begun to grate on these knights. Breton lords all, they saw in the duke's schemes a means to free themselves from King Henry's heavy hand. The muttering and cold looks directed at FitzHugh had become more pointed and more frequent. Of late, he'd heard his name cursed, his power over the volatile duke decried.

"If you have something to say, say it, de Claire. Else take your ugly nose elsewhere. I would speak with my lord without your distracting presence."

A hot tide of red swept up de Claire's face, which bore the visible marks of his last confrontation with FitzHugh, in the tourney just after the birth of Geoffrey's daughter. His nose, which had once been long and aquiline, was now flattened and pushed sideways. His mouth gaped where several teeth were missing. That same mouth now twisted with rage.

"I'll say it, you puling bastard. 'Tis you who fears to lose your lands to King Henry's ire. 'Tis you who sends dispatches to England advising him of what goes on here. 'Tis you who is the traitor to your lord."

FitzHugh's lunge across the crowded room took all but Geoffrey by surprise. The duke threw himself between the two men and held them apart by the sheer force of his bulk.

"Hold!" His bellow rattled the panes of leaded glass. "Hold, I say!"

One massive arm wrapped around FitzHugh's neck in a wrestling hold that he'd used many times before, though never in earnest. His choke-hold tightened when the furious knight tried to wrest himself free. Short of wrestling his liege to the floor, FitzHugh had no choice but to stand, his breath strangling in his throat.

"I have proof," de Claire spit out, his eyes narrowed and feral with hatred. "My men intercepted a courier leaving the city. In his bag was a letter advising the king of your nego-

tiations with Philip. Although unsigned, there were other letters in the pouch, as well, with FitzHugh's seals.''

FitzHugh stiffened, his muscles suddenly rigid as tempered
steel. Geoffrey's arm loosened, then slid away.

''You lie, de Claire.'' The flat, cold denial made the other
knight's red face deepen in hue. ''Produce this courier and let
him say where he got this letter, if it even exists.''

''It exists, bastard.''

Sir Guy turned to Geoffrey, an ugly sneer twisting his features. ''I didn't tell of this sooner, my lord, as I hoped to get
more information from this messenger. Unfortunately, he died
under my men's questioning. I have the documents he had
with him in my quarters.''

''Get them! And the rest of you, get out. Wait outside my
chambers.''

Geoffrey whirled as soon as the door shut behind them. For
long moments, the two men stared at each other, friendship
warring with mistrust in golden and blue eyes alike.

''You can't believe de Claire,'' FitzHugh finally said.

''Damn you, Richard, I don't know what to believe anymore. You've been against me since the day you arrived. Why
will you not support me? Why do you harass me?''

''Because I would save your accursed hide,'' FitzHugh
snarled. ''Listen to me, Geoffrey, this isn't a game. Your father won't slap your hands and send you back to play in the
provinces if you forswear your oaths to him and England.''

''How do you know what the king will do?'' Geoffrey
shouted. ''I don't. His lady wife doesn't. My mother swears
he's mad, that he's been ensorcelled by the bitch he fornicates
with against all the laws of God and man.''

FitzHugh's own voice rose as he gave in to his own rage
and frustration. He'd seen his friend pulled in so many directions in the last months, and waver so many times, he'd lost
every shred of his limited patience. ''Just because your father

lusts after the Lady Alice doesn't mean he can't hold his dominions. He's done so for twenty years and more.''

"He won't hold them much longer," the duke raged. "I will have Anjou and Maine before this month is out."

"You fool! You'll have a cell, next to your mother's."

Incensed, Geoffrey thrust out his arm. The power of that huge limb rocked FitzHugh back on his heels.

"What you do is treason, Geoffrey! It will mean war to the death."

"I've never known you to be so afeard of battle, bastard. Has that little red-haired wench you wed finally turned you against me? Is that why you play the traitor to my cause?"

"Geoffrey, for God's sake, Mellisynt has naught to do with this."

"Has she naught? Ever since you plowed the little widow, you've changed, Richard. Has she drained your manhood, as well as your man root? She looked to be a juicy enough morsel to do so. I may have to try her myself, if she's that good."

"I'll see you in hell first."

Even as he said the words, FitzHugh knew Geoffrey had spoken only out of the accumulated fear and frustration of the last weeks.

Geoffrey straightened and threw back his shoulders. "Aye," he said slowly, each word a painful rasp. "Aye, mayhap you will."

"I tell you, Mellisynt, I cannot help." Constance paced the spacious chamber, her long skirts swirling with each impatient step. "I've argued and cajoled and screamed until I've driven Geoffrey from the palace many times over these past months. He won't listen."

Mellisynt leaned forward in her seat as far as her swollen belly would allow. "I don't understand, my lady. Why does he refuse all offer of ransom? Why will he not at least discuss any terms of release?"

Constance slowed her agitated pacing, then stilled completely. For a moment she stood, a tiny figure clothed in shades of amethyst and lustrous black, shoulders slumped, as if she were too old and far too tired to carry the burdens she did. Finally she turned and crossed the tiles, sinking to the bench beside Mellisynt.

"I fear Geoffrey has lost all power to reason over this. 'Tis as if by losing FitzHugh, he's lost his last tie to a world of order and honor."

"But he hasn't lost him," Mellisynt cried, grasping the duchess's hand in both of her own. "The one message my lord was allowed to send bade me hold true to our allegiances until this matter should be resolved and he is...free."

She stumbled over the last word, still unable to grasp the reality of FitzHugh in a prison cell. To one so strong and so used to roaming the broad fields and plains of Europe, three months and more of confinement had to be unbearable. Her fingers tightened convulsively on the duchess's hand as she recalled the growing frustration and fear of these months. The messages and pleas to Geoffrey, to Constance, to the king himself. The frustrating inability to learn FitzHugh's location, or even the exact reasons for his incarceration. The futile offers of ransom, of bounties, of lands she could cede to the crown in return for her husband's release.

She'd agonized over pledging FitzHugh's lands and fees along with those of Trémont, not knowing if he would praise or curse her for yielding his holdings. She'd been allowed no contact with him, except that one brief message. Yet all her entreaties and promises had been refused. The king, still embroiled in the morass that was Ireland, had replied through one of his ministers that he would attend to the matter when he returned if 'twas not resolved by then. Geoffrey had not replied at all.

Constance tugged her hand free of Mellisynt's painful grip and reached up to stroke her cheek.

"Geoffrey refuses to discuss this matter with me. 'Tis as if he must cut himself off, from FitzHugh, from me, from any that would be his conscience. I think it pains him," she admitted, then gave a low, hollow laugh. "Although my lord duke does not seem to mourn the loss of my bed as much as he does the loss of FitzHugh."

Mellisynt's stomach knotted at the bitterness in the duchess's tone. Her last hope, that Constance could yet use her influence over the duke, died a slow, withering death. She slumped, feeling her body sag with the weight pulling at her middle.

"I'm sorry, my lady," she finally managed.

"I, too," Constance said, with a sigh. "Our union has been turbulent at best, but at least Geoffrey made a pretense of being faithful before. Now he follows his father's lead and flaunts his mistresses in my face. If I did not need a son from his loins to hold Brittany, I would slice off his root with my own hand."

Mellisynt swallowed her instinctive sympathy for the flat misery in the violet eyes that had once sparkled with life and laughter. She knew Constance would little appreciate commiseration. Nor would it help with the more urgent problem at hand.

"Do you know where FitzHugh is held, my lady?"

Constance shook her head. "I heard once 'twas at Bâlfour, but Geoffrey would not confirm it. I think he feared I would order FitzHugh's release, did I know where to send the order."

Mellisynt drew in a shaky breath. Bâlfour was a day's journey south from Rennes, close to the border. Not far from Trémont.

"Will you help me gain an audience with the duke, my lady? He wouldn't answer my letters or petitions."

"'Twill do no good," Constance stated flatly. "He's...he's changed. He's not the man he was."

Mellisynt bit back the retort that she had little enough respect for the man he'd been before. She would deal with him, however he'd changed. Her throat too tight to speak, she sent the duchess a silent plea.

After a moment, Constance sighed. "All right. He's due back late this eve. I'll arrange for you to go to him—if he's not engaged with one of his whores," she added with a touch of acid.

She stood and helped Mellisynt to her feet. Her violet eyes rested on the bulge of Mellisynt's belly, almost indiscernible in the flowing folds of her robes.

"You carry the babe well," she commented with a little smile, as if sharing their women's burden could hold at bay the troubles darkening her world a few moments longer. "You didn't swell up like a bloated pig, as I did."

"Nay, I've gained little in weight. If my stretched skin didn't itch like a dog with ticks and my bladder need emptying but twenty times a day, I would scarce know it's there."

Constance laughed with a trace of her old liveliness. "Well, at least your travails will soon be over."

"I hope so, my lady, I hope so."

Their eyes met in silent determination. Constance nodded and gave her a gentle kiss.

Mellisynt stretched her aching body on the thick velvet coverlet and willed the nagging pain in her lower back to perdition. The journey from England had taken its toll, she admitted to herself, remembering Alymer's protests and Dame Hertha's dire predictions of harm to the babe. But she'd had to try *something,* after months of fruitless, frantic dispatches.

The sea voyage hadn't been difficult. But when she and FitzHugh's lieutenant, St. Bressé, had docked at Dol-de-Bretagne and hired horses for themselves and their escort for the trip to Rennes, the journey had become a nightmare. Even her modest bulk would not allow her to hook her knee around a pommel to ride sidesaddle, nor could she keep her balance on a pillion behind St. Bressé. Teeth clenched, she'd mounted astride a docile mare and ridden the distance to Rennes in acute discomfort. The fact that they had to stop with embarrassing frequency for her to relieve her pressured bladder had only made the long ride worse.

She would have endured the discomfort ten times over, however, if it resulted in FitzHugh's release. Sweet Mother, she ached to see him. Ached to feel his strong arms around her. Ached for the passion she'd thrown aside in her silly quest for love. Although she doubted they could do much to assuage that passion when she did secure his release, not for some weeks yet. She couldn't imagine his desiring to lie with a woman whose breasts had begun to leak and whose legs cramped with increasing frequency. As one was doing even now.

Mellisynt groaned and bent her leg, massaging the aching muscles. Although she'd not swelled to gigantic proportions, as had many other women she'd seen in this state, she'd endured most of the other irritating effects of such dramatic stress on her body. Still, her aches and irritations were minor and easily dismissed. She folded protective hands over her belly, searching for movement under the layers of robe and shift. She was rewarded with a gentle undulation as the taut skin dipped, then bowed, then dipped again under her fingers. A tired smile tugged at her lips. 'Twas indeed FitzHugh's child in there, not the least daunted by the long ride aboard a swaying, jolting mare. Her lord has passed his own endurance to the babe. Mayhap his blue eyes, as well, she mused. And his thick, dark hair. She drifted into a light doze, dreaming of the child and its sire.

"The duchess sent me to fetch you, my lady."

Mellisynt swallowed and nodded to the servant who stood at her door. His flickering torch battled the darkness of the hall beyond, sending eerie shadows against the walls. Pitch hissed and spit, the small sounds loud in the stillness of the night.

Lifting her trailing skirts, Mellisynt followed the man through twisting corridors.

"Lady Constance wished you to know she sent a message to the duke's apartments, requesting a private meeting at this hour on a matter of some urgency."

Mellisynt nodded, sending a silent prayer of thanks to Constance for arranging a private audience. The duke might be more amenable to changing his mind if he did not have to do so in front of an audience of retainers and chamber attendants.

"Through here, my lady." The servant opened an arched door and ushered her into a luxuriously appointed anteroom. She thanked him, drew in a deep breath, and approached the guards posted at the inner door. Tilting her chin, she used her haughtiest tone.

"I am here to see Duke Geoffrey."

The guard flicked a knowing glance over her face, then down the length of her body. His eyes lingered overlong on the swell of her breasts, round and heavy and pushed into high mounds by the square cut of her gown. Of a sudden, Mellisynt wished she hadn't dressed in her finest robe, a rich forest-green velvet embroidered with gold at neck and sleeves. It was meant to give her confidence, but she realized belatedly it also emphasized the lushness of her ripe body.

"Your master is expecting me," she told the guard, her voice dripping ice.

The man flushed and tore his eyes from her neckline. "Aye, my lady." He lifted the iron latch and pulled open the heavy wooden door.

Geoffrey sat in a huge carved chair drawn close to a low fire. He paused in the act of lifting a silver goblet to his lips and glowered at the open door.

"Do you come to plague me yet again, Con—?" His querulous words broke off as he discerned who stood on the threshold. For a moment his face registered surprise, and then settled into an angry scowl.

Mellisynt stepped into the room quickly, before he could order her away. The door swung shut behind her with a thud that she barely heard over the pounding of her heart.

Constance was right, she thought. *He has changed.* The singers had once heralded Geoffrey as the handsomest of the Plantagenets, the possessor of a figure of elegant symmetry, a man of most winning manner. Yet now he slumped heavily in his chair, his body gross with added weight, his face etched with lines of dissatisfaction. Mellisynt felt all her buried resentment for the duke surge up. Stripped of his facade of charm, he looked like a man who would laugh as he gave a child to a withered old lecher to use. Like a man who would incarcerate his best, his only, friend.

"What do you here?" he growled.

Mellisynt buried her clenched fists in the folds of her gown and lifted her chin. "'Tis obvious, is it not? You would not answer my petitions or letters, so I come in person to secure my lord's release."

A slow tide of red crept up his neck at her tone, and Mellisynt knew at once her mistake. She swallowed, and injected a humbler note into her voice.

"My lord duke, I beg you listen to me. I know not why you hold my husband, only that he angered you most grievously. You must know that FitzHugh is your truest vassal. Your truest friend."

Geoffrey stared down into the goblet he held. "He is a traitor, to me and to his oaths."

"What? Never!"

Mellisynt caught herself as his head snapped up and an angry light gleamed from his golden eyes. "Whatever else FitzHugh may have done, he would not betray you," she offered in a low, pleading voice.

Geoffrey stood and slammed his goblet onto the table beside his chair. Red wine splashed onto the fine silk covering the table and spread in a slow, bleeding stain.

"He would, and did, betray my cause. I have evidence, and will hold him to trial."

"You cannot," Mellisynt gasped. "He is a knight, a titled lord. You cannot try him like a common felon."

"He's but a bastard," Geoffrey replied with a sneer. "He earned his knighthood through my graces, and will lose it in the same manner."

Mellisynt fought the panic wrapping its insidious coils around her heart. This man had stood in their hall, his arm wrapped about FitzHugh's shoulders, the glow of friendship in his eyes. Those same eyes now gleamed with a light that sent cold shivers of dread down her spine.

"My lord, let me buy his release. I'll pledge all I have, all I inherited from Henri of Trémont."

"You have naught to pledge," Geoffrey snarled. "The estates of a traitor are forfeit to the crown."

The duke seemed to take great pleasure from her shocked gasp. "That surprises you, you haughty little bitch? Why? Did you think I would allow him, or you, to keep such wealth?"

He sauntered forward and gripped her chin in a hard hand. Mellisynt held herself rigid, unwilling to give him the satisfaction of pulling free.

"Do you think I didn't notice your veiled insults? Your cool reserve whenever you were in my presence? The scorn in your eyes you couldn't quite disguise? Do you think I don't know who turned FitzHugh against me?"

He leaned his face close to hers. The sweet, sickening scent of wine and a heavily perfumed body assaulted Mellisynt's senses.

"Do you think I don't know how you whispered your woman's spite into his ear every time he plowed between your thighs?" His breath thickened and beat against her face in heated waves. "What do you have there, between those slender legs, that would turn a man from his lord, his friend? What milk does he draw from your breasts that would sour him on his oaths?"

His other hand lifted and curved on her breast. His fingers dug cruelly into her swollen flesh.

She didn't flinch, didn't betray by so much as a flicker of an eyelash the disgust roiling in her stomach. His golden eyes narrowed to tawny slits. "How much do you wish your lord restored to you?"

His words sent a spiraling wave of dread down her spine. Mellisynt could feel her muscles tighten, her skin crawl with prickles of revulsion.

"How much do you want the bastard back in your bed?" Geoffrey rasped.

Her hands curled into claws, her nails bit into her palm. Bitter, angry curses welled up in her throat, trembled on her tongue. She bit them back, but could not keep the scathing disgust from her eyes.

He dragged the fabric of her robe down and took the full weight of her breast in his palm. "Do not look so proud and scornful!" he ground out. "You're a whore, for all your fine robes and haughty airs. I saw you romping in the waves those months ago at Edgemoor. I saw your naked skin under that wet shift. And I saw how you were carried into the keep, flushed and reeking with the scent of FitzHugh's spend."

"You vile, lecherous pig! 'Twas my husband I lay with!"

Restraint crumbling, Mellisynt tried to wrench herself away from his groping hands. The rough fingers holding her chin whipped down to circle the back of her neck. He jerked her close, his strength keeping her easily in place.

"Mayhap if you please me mightily, wench, you might lie with him again someday."

The hand crushing her breast released its hold and moved

downward. "Mayhap if you spread your legs and share this—"

His hand batted against the bulge concealed under her flowing robes. He sucked in a sharp breath, his red-gold eyebrows snapping together.

"Aye," Mellisynt told him, her voice low, and vibrating with scorn. "I carry his babe, the child of he who was once your friend above all others. If you try to mount me, I'll not fight you. I'll not risk hurt to my babe. But when you finish, you'd best guard well your person, my lord duke. If I don't skewer you myself, FitzHugh will, someday, somehow."

With a vicious oath, Geoffrey released her and turned away. Mellisynt gulped in a deep, ragged breath.

"Get out of here," the duke snarled. "Get out of here, or I swear you'll join your lord in Bâlfour and whelp your spawn in the dungeon's filthy straw!"

Chapter Seventeen

Mellisynt's small cavalcade crossed the river Vilaine at dusk the following day. In the gathering dimness, the walls of Trémont were barely visible on the high cliff above the river.

She had not dared linger in Rennes to hire a larger escort or allow her men time to rest. If Geoffrey hadn't yet taken her lands in forfeit, he would no doubt try to do so now he knew she was in Brittany once more. She'd slipped out of the city while it was yet dark, covering the bruises on her breast and the despair in her heart. Urging St. Bressé to an ever-faster pace, she'd covered the distance in good time. With every jarring step of her horse's gait, she'd prayed for the safety of her babe and the loyalty of her people.

'Twas strange and most ironic, she thought as the troop began the slow, tortuous climb to Trémont's gates. When she'd left so many months ago, she'd wanted only freedom and a babe. Now she returned, risking both, and praying to find safety and strength in Trémont, where before she'd found only a prison.

"My lady! Holy Father, what do you here?"

Mellisynt slid awkwardly from the mare's back. Her unsteady legs quivered under her, and she would have crumpled to the cobbles had not Sir Bertrand slipped an arm around her waist.

Giving the old knight a grateful smile for his support, she picked her way across the uneven stones.

"I've come to gather the men of Trémont. We ride to rescue our lord."

The old man's eyes blazed in the fading spring light. The remembered taste of battle flavored his voice. "When and where do we go?"

"To Bâlfour."

His step faltered, and the eagerness faded from his face. He shook his head at her questioning look.

"Nay, 'tis not a matter for discussion here, in the darkness of the bailey. Come inside and rest, and we'll discuss how our half-strength garrison is to besiege the duke's strongest, best-manned castle."

Mellisynt fought off waves of hopelessness as she and St. Bressé listened to Sir Bertrand's succinct recital of the few men and sparse weaponry left at Trémont. Most of the able-bodied men-at-arms had been sent in response to the duke's summons weeks ago, taking with them a full complement of stores. They were to serve in the army Geoffrey was amassing, for what purpose Sir Bertrand didn't know, although he had a shrewd guess.

"I'm sorry, my lady. We dared not refuse the duke's summons." Sir Bertrand reached out a gnarled, arthritic fist and patted her hand. "I would gladly lead the men left against Bâlfour, but I fear 'twould be a hopeless cause."

Mellisynt took comfort from the warmth of his grip, even as her mind struggled to accept his words.

"'Tis what you should have expected when you tied yourself to that baseborn knight."

Father Anselem's spiteful voice came out of the dimness at the far end of the hall. He waddled forward, even more portly than before. 'Twas obvious the priest had made even better use of the castle's provisions under FitzHugh's dominion than he had under Henri of Trémont's miserly rule.

Mellisynt surveyed her old nemesis with a dispassionate eye. To think she'd once let this mean-spirited little man have such sway over her. The petty transgressions and verbal battles of her past life seemed so far away, and so unimportant.

"You should have gone to the nunnery, as Henri had planned," the priest continued, his pale eyes filled with malice. "At least you'd have your widow's dower. Now you lose all."

"Nay, Father, not all." Mellisynt rested a hand on her stomach.

"You foolish woman, what good does it do to produce an heir at last if you have naught to leave it?"

Sir Bertrand stiffened and rose from his seat. "Watch your tongue, friar. A priest can as easily lose his living as a knight his estates."

The little man blanched at the steward's bristling approach. He stepped back quickly, stumbling over the hem of his robe. "I but seek to help! I would save Trémont!"

"You would save your own fat hide and comfortable larder."

"Wait, Sir Bertrand." Mellisynt stepped between the two men, her brow furrowed. "How could you save Trémont, Father?"

The priest cast a nervous glance at the old knight and licked his lips. "You could yet have your estates, lady. If you have your marriage to the bastard declared null."

Mellisynt gave a disbelieving laugh. "How could it be null? I carry evidence of its fruitfulness."

"Queen Eleanor had already borne two daughters when her marriage to King Louis of France was annulled because they shared too close a degree of kinship," the priest argued. "Eleanor retained all her honors and inheritances and brought them to the Angevin king, Duke Geoffrey's own father. If you did the same, Geoffrey would have to recognize your claim."

A waft of garlic and nervous sweat assaulted Mellisynt's nostrils. It barely penetrated her consciousness. Her eyes thoughtful, she stared at the priest.

"I have no kinship with FitzHugh," she commented softly. "On what grounds could my marriage be annulled?"

"You and your widow's estate were pledged to the Church. Henri so decreed in his will. The documents were signed, and the entry fees paid, when the FitzHugh came to claim you. Your pledge to Christ comes before any bonds to man."

"You putrid little—"

Mellisynt cut off St. Bressé's angry interruption with a quick wave of her hand.

"How is it done, Father? How would such an annulment be obtained?"

He leaned forward eagerly. "'Tis simple, my lady. You have to appear before an ecclesiastical court, as did Eleanor and Louis, and convince three bishops of the Church's prior claim. Once you are free of the bastard, you could petition the Church to release you, as well. Since you carry a child, they would not force you into a nunnery."

"You've thought this through most carefully."

Her quiet, considering tone encouraged the priest.

"Aye," he said, eagerness running his words together. "When first I heard the FitzHugh was taken and charged with treason to our duke, I—I wrote the bishop of Rennes. He sent a reply that he would hear the case."

"God's bones!" St. Bressé stood, his face flaming with anger. "My lady, you must not listen to this craven's mad schemes. He but seeks to protect his soft living!"

Mellisynt's gaze flicked from FitzHugh's livid lieutenant to the perspiring Father Anselem. Her mind whirled with dazed, half-formed thoughts. Unconscious of the act, she crossed her arms protectively over her belly.

"My lady, you must—"

Mellisynt's trembling voice interrupted St. Bressé's anguished one. "Bring me the bishop's documents, Father. I would see them. And bring me parchment and ink, as well."

Over the heads of the two men, she met Sir Bertrand's

steady gaze. He gave her a long, considering look, then nodded slowly.

"You would go? Just like that? She bids you come, and you go?"

"Isabeau, I must."

Isabeau tossed her sewing onto the table beside her chair and glared at her husband. He crowded the small *solar* given over to her private use. His shoulders blocked the light from the mullioned windows, and his long legs ate up the short distance from wall to wall as he paced impatiently.

"*Why* must you go?" she asked, struggling with a hot surge of jealousy. Not yet wed two months, and her lord would leave her at another woman's summons. "FitzHugh and the duke will resolve their differences. They always do. You need not succumb to Lady Mellisynt's hysterical fears."

Beauchamp stopped pacing, a familiar look of exasperation settling over his handsome features. Isabeau ignored it. She often provoked such looks, and she had her own ways of dealing with them.

"Listen to me, woman, and try to understand. FitzHugh is in prison and stands to lose all his titles and holdings. Geoffrey would bring him to trial like a common felon. Lady Mellisynt asks my aid, and I would give it."

"I know naught of felons and trials," Isabeau answered, shaping her lips into a sulky pout. "I only know that you had ever an eye for the lady."

"Isabeau, for pity's sake, she is wife to my friend."

"And passing fair, is she not?" Her wide eyes lifted to his in an expression both innocent and knowing.

She bit back a smile as Beauchamp's lip lifted in a rueful grin. Her coquette's tactics never failed to amuse him. Or to rouse his interest. He crossed to take her hands in his. Tugging her out of her chair, he wrapped his arms around her waist, his palms shaping the lushness of her bottom.

"The lady is not near as fair as a certain overripe piece of baggage, one who has claimed all my attention of late and drained my energies."

Isabeau snuggled in his arms, fitting her curves to his long, lean torso. A rush of sweet, sudden desire shot through her belly as she felt his rod hardening. By the saints, this man could heat her blood beyond anything she'd ever imagined. These months of marriage had only fired her sexual appetites. Beauchamp was a most skilled and most inventive lover. And most attentive. She knew he craved her body as much as she wanted his. He'd not leave her to go on this fruitless mission, she vowed. The duke and FitzHugh were far away; their problems were Brittany's problems. She was here, and here her husband would stay.

"Have I really drained your energies, my lord?" she murmured into his chest. Her fingers slid down to tease the bulge between his legs. "Have you none left at all?"

"Isabeau," he warned, on a low in-drawn breath.

"Beauchamp," she teased, her voice low and sultry. She raised on tiptoe to kiss the underside of his jaw, her hand still cupping his manhood. "Do not leave me," she whispered. "You're gone enough fighting your own liege's battles. Do not fight everyone else's, as well."

He stiffened and would have drawn away, but Isabeau clung to him with one arm around his neck, one hand at the juncture of his powerful thighs. Her fingers tightened on his codpiece, loosened, then tightened once more. When he failed to respond to her blatant invitation, she lowered her voice and whispered a husky promise in his ear.

"Stay, my lord. Stay here with me, and I will make the staying most pleasurable."

After a long, still moment, Beauchamp eased back to stare down at her. His eyes, usually so filled with laughter or flaring desire, held an inscrutable expression. Piqued at his lack of response, Isabeau redoubled her efforts. She raised both arms and locked them about his neck, drawing his mouth down to hers. Her tongue darted out to trace his lips, then slipped inside to taste the dark honey. Shamelessly, she rubbed her front against his chest, wanting the friction against her breasts.

"Wait." Beauchamp grasped her wrists and pulled them down. "Wait, and let me bolt the door."

She leaned back, her hands on the sewing table behind her, a small, triumphant smile on her lips. When he finished fumbling with the bolt and turned back, she altered the smile to one of sultry desire.

Any thought that she might control the pace of their coupling fled as Beauchamp strode back to her. His brown eyes were no longer unreadable. They flamed with a fierce light that set her blood to racing. His fingers reached for the laces on the front of her bliaut, ripping them apart when they would not give. Cool air kissed her breasts, causing their peaks to harden and stiffen.

Isabeau gasped as he bent her backward, across the table. Strong, hard hands lifted her skirts, loosed her linens, then pulled her thighs apart. A hot blush stole up her neck when he stepped back, surveying her. She lay bared, vulnerable, and aching with need. She could feel moist heat welling between her legs. Her lashes fluttered down, and she quivered in anticipation.

"My lord," she gasped, when yet he waited, prolonging the foretaste. "Enough. Give me what I crave."

"If I come near you, I'll give you more than that which you crave. I'll beat you black-and-blue."

Isabeau's lids flew up. Beauchamp stood before her, his arms crossed and his face set in implacable lines. Confused, mortified, a little alarmed, she tried to scramble up.

"Nay," he said, stepping between her legs and pinning both her wrists to the table. "If you wish to play the whore, you'd best get used to being on display."

"Wh-what?"

He leaned forward, his hips forcing her thighs farther apart. Rough wood scratched at her wrists, the edge of the table cut into the backs of her legs. His chest brushed against her straining nipples, making her flush in mingled want and shame.

Protesting in small, mewling cries, she tried to twist her body sideways. Beauchamp drew her arms up, taking both wrists in one painful hold. His other had gripped her chin. Isabeau flinched at the coldness in his eyes.

"Listen to me, girl, and listen well. Those who use their bodies to gain their ends are whores, whether on the streets or in the marriage bed. I don't want one for a wife. When you are woman enough to understand that, come to me."

Stunned, furious, unable to formulate a single coherent thought, Isabeau watched him walk to the door and slide back the bolt. Giving a little squeal, she scrambled to throw down her skirts and cover herself as he flung open the wooden panel.

Fingers of gold and red streaked the dawn sky when Beauchamp strode from the great hall, pulling on his gauntlets. His squire stood at his mount's head with helmet and shield in hand. He nodded to the squire and took the proffered helmet. He paused before lifting it to his head to cast a quick look up at the tower holding their private apartments.

Isabeau had remained in her little *solar* throughout the night, alternately sobbing and ranting. He'd heard her furious sobs from their bedchamber. A dozen times and more he'd almost given in to his conflicting needs. He wanted to comfort her, to shake her, to bury himself in her honeyed heat again and again. The urge to beat her had quickly passed, to be replaced with a well of self-disgust. 'Twas as much his fault as hers that Isabeau thought she could use her body to win her way. In these last months, he'd indulged her like a child and loved her like a wanton. He gave the narrow *solar* windows one last, regretful glance, thinking that they'd both learned a painful lesson.

"My lord, wait!"

Turning, Beauchamp saw the figure of his wife run out of the keep and across the bailey. He swallowed at the sight of her long, unbound hair flying dark as a raven's wing in the gathering light. Her shift flattened against succulent curves and shadowed valleys. Her bare feet stumbled on the rough stones, and Beauchamp gripped his helmet hard to keep from reaching out for her.

Breathless, she stopped before him. He stiffened, hardening his heart to the appeal in those magnificent aquamarine eyes.

"My lord, I would bid you farewell, and Godspeed." She slipped to her knees in front of him and bent to kiss his hand.

Surprise kept Beauchamp still for long moments. Then a slow amusement filled his eyes as he stared down at this unfamiliar creature. In their months together, he'd seen Isabeau in many guises, from pouting, playful kitten to hungry cat to satiated, purring feline. Never had he seen her with her dark head bowed, kneeling in a penitent's pose.

A tender smile on his lips, he pulled her gently to her feet. "I thank you for your blessing, my lady."

"'Tis...'tis more than a blessing," she whispered, stumbling over the words. "'Tis a wife's prayer. I would be your wife, not your wh—"

He cut off her earnest plea with a light, brushing kiss. She clung to his hand, her fingers pressed against the cold metal gauntlet.

"Beauchamp, I'm sorry. Truly. I didn't mean to— Well, I did, but I won't try again, to—"

He chuckled. "Minx! You'll probably try all sorts of tricks on me before I break you completely to my hand." His eyes softened, and his hand gripped hers. "If ever I do. You are much a woman, Isabeau."

A tremulous smile hovered on her lips. "Thank you, my lord. Come back quickly. God keep you safe, and the lord and lady of Edgemoor, as well."

She stepped back, her toes curling into the stones to keep her balance. That image, of Isabeau's dainty white toes peeping out from under her shift, beguiled Beauchamp for a good portion of the long ride from Normandy. It faded as he crossed the border into Brittany and headed for the small town just north of Castle Bâlfour, where Lady Mellisynt had asked him to meet her. Instead, grim images of the castle's fortifications filled his mind.

FitzHugh grunted, whipping his head sideways to flick the beading sweat from his eyes. His knuckles showed white as his hands strained against the bars. Relaxing his muscles, he took a deep breath and then pushed once again with all his might.

"At it again, m'lord?"

The guard's amused query broke his concentration. Loosening his grip, FitzHugh turned and nodded to the gap-toothed face pressed against the grate in the door.

"Aye, 'tis the only exercise I get in this accursed place." He rolled his shoulders to ease the tension from his hour of pushing and straining. "Unless you can convince Lord Piss-for-Brains to give me access to the exercise grounds."

The guard snorted with laughter, showing the blackened stumps of his few remaining teeth. FitzHugh's arrogant disdain and crude names for the huge, beef-witted knight who governed Bâlfour had provided the entire castle much amusement over the last weeks.

"Nay, I wouldna dare to ask again. The last time you went into the yard, you knocked six soldiers flat on their arses. You were almost through the gates before they brought you down."

FitzHugh kept a careless smile on his face as he fought back a wave of frustration. He'd been so close, so damned close. Another few seconds and the horse he'd grabbed would have broken through the soldiers rushing for the gate. He swore under his breath, hearing for the hundredth time the horse's screams as a hastily thrown oak staff tangled in its legs, bringing it, and FitzHugh, crashing down. At least he'd had the pleasure of feeling his fists smash a few noses and splinter a jawbone or two before they'd fought him to the ground.

When the guard turned away, FitzHugh stretched out on the narrow cot, one leg drawn up, one booted foot hanging well over the edge. Willing his body to stillness and his mind to calm, he traced the patterns of the uneven cracks in the ceiling above. Before his abortive escape attempt, he'd had somewhat finer quarters and much better meals, as befitted a knight of his standing. In truth, he little missed the softer bed or the sauce-drenched meals. One prison was much the same, when there were bars at the windows.

Jesu, how could Geoffrey have left him here these many weeks? His jaw tightened, and anger clutched at his gut. How could Geoffrey believe him a traitor?

Because he wanted to, his inner voice replied with sardonic honesty. Because the duke would rather deny his friend than deny his own twisted ambitions. Once more, FitzHugh cursed the temper that had made him attack Geoffrey, instead of reasoning with him. They'd disagreed before, had come near to blows on more than one occasion, yet always before FitzHugh had been able to exert the discipline he needed to deal with the man's volatile temper.

'Twas his vile comment about Mellisynt that had snapped FitzHugh's own restraint. That, and the sudden lust in Geoffrey's eyes when he'd spoken of her. FitzHugh knew well the duke's carnal appetites, and that flare of hunger had filled him with rage. Even now, the thought of Geoffrey using Mellisynt made his stomach muscles knot.

He fought the fury creeping through him, forcing himself to relax with an iron will. At least he had the satisfaction of knowing Mellisynt was safe at Edgemoor while Geoffrey plotted and schemed here on the Continent. The picture of his wife basking in the sun on the rocks along Edgemoor's shore teased at his mind and at his body. He savored the memory of her long, slender body as a starving man might the remembered taste of a long-past feast. And her eyes, glowing with the new green of a spring day in the light, deepening to emerald in the dark.

A sharp pang of regret lanced through him as he thought of how those same eyes had grown distant and cool in the weeks before he'd left. Of how she'd withheld her body, withheld her love. FitzHugh shifted uncomfortably on the cot, trying to ease the ache thoughts of his wife always brought. It was as much mental as physical, and he'd wrestled with it these many weeks. He thought of all the ways to describe what he felt for the woman he'd wed, and none seemed satisfactory. He only knew he would give much to see a glow in Mellisynt's eyes once again when he...

"I'm to escort you to Lord Piss—Lord Devereaux's chambers immediately, my lord."

FitzHugh turned his head to eye the guard with only mild curiosity. He'd made the trip to the governor's rooms many times before. He had no desire to be harangued once again for a confession, nor to listen to the man's empty threats. When Geoffrey made his move, FitzHugh would act. Until then, he could only bide his time. Still, even Devereaux's thick-headed company was better than none.

Bright light streaming through the great hall's tall windows blinded him momentarily. Narrowing his eyes against the glare, he tried to make out the figures ranged around a table in front of the far fireplace.

"Come in, Sir Richard, come in." Devereaux's guttural voice cut through the stillness of the hall. "You've visitors, with business that will interest you."

The malice in the man's tone alerted FitzHugh even before his mind registered his wife's cold eyes and lifted chin. He slowed his pace for an imperceptible moment, trying to absorb the implications of her presence, then moved across the hall with a steady stride.

Roger Beauchamp stood behind Mellisynt, his protective stance as blatant as the possessive hand held under her arm. FitzHugh's gaze riveted on that hand, then sliced to Roger's eyes. The flat hardness there made him draw in a slow breath. He turned to the fourth figure, a robed and cowled monk. The priest met his piercing stare with a nervous flick of his tongue. Dragging his eyes from the cleric, FitzHugh noted the litter of documents on the table, all covered with gold ribbons and seals.

The red-faced knight who governed Bâlfour rocked back on his heels, thumbs hooked in his belt. A sneer twisted his thick lips. "You will be most interested to learn that your lady has journeyed here to—"

Mellisynt halted him in midspeech. "Please, my Lord Devereaux, I will tell him myself."

His face impassive, FitzHugh folded both arms across his chest and waited while she stepped forward. Beauchamp followed, maintaining his position behind the lady. FitzHugh felt a muscle begin to tick in his cheek.

"I've come to—" She swallowed and began again. "I've come to tell you that I've petitioned the bishop of Rennes to annul our marriage."

Of all the possible reasons for Mellisynt's presence at Bâlfour FitzHugh's whirling mind had formulated, that would never have occurred to him. Stunned, he struggled to make sense of her words. As if from a distance, he heard her continue in a more urgent manner.

"We are to meet the ecclesiastical court within the week to have the matter decided. Lord Devereaux himself examined all the documents. They're in proper order, and..."

She stumbled to a halt as fury flared in his eyes.

"You are mine, wife." He raked her thickened body with a fierce, angry look. "Wedded, bedded, and ripe with the fruit from my seed. You have no grounds to annul our joining, documents or no.''

"I do have grounds," she whispered. "I was pledged to the Church before you. Our vows were invalid.''

Before the surprised guards could stop him, he stepped around the small table and caught her arm in a cruel grip. Jerking her against him, FitzHugh snarled down into her frightened face.

"Vows be damned. You are mine. What I have, I hold!''

She tried to twist away, her free hand splayed across her belly as if to shield it from his rage. Her weight made her clumsy and threw her off-balance. Only FitzHugh's strong grip kept her from falling to the floor.

"Take him, you fools! Take him!''

Devereaux's angry shouts mingled with Beauchamp's low curse. "Release her, bastard.''

FitzHugh shook off the guard's fumbling hold, twisting Mellisynt's arm as he evaded their reach. He faced Beauchamp, fury darkening his face.

"You've tried before to come between me and my *lady* wife," he taunted, his lip curling. "Are you part of this foul scheme, Beauchamp? What do you get in reward? Do you take the next step in your game of chivalrous love and bed the bitch?''

"No!" Mellisynt gasped, clawing at his fingers. "No, I swear!''

Beauchamp lunged forward. With a sweeping chop, he brought his hand down on FitzHugh's arm and broke his punishing grip. Thrusting Mellisynt to safety, he whirled back, ducking just in time. FitzHugh cursed viciously as his blow missed its target.

Moving with lightning speed to take advantage of Fitz-Hugh's lost momentum, Beauchamp pushed up on the balls of his feet. His fist landed with bone-jarring force on the side of the other man's chin. Staggering, FitzHugh fell back.

"Take him, take him!" Lord Devereaux danced on the tips of his pointed shoes in his excitement.

The gap-toothed guard led the charge. FitzHugh went down under the force of half a dozen men-at-arms. He struggled furiously, throwing most of them off, before a vicious kick to the ribs knocked the air from his lungs. The remaining men piled on and pinned him to the floor.

"Stop!" Mellisynt cried. "Order them to stop!"

Devereaux ignored her frantic pleas, his eyes gleaming at the muted grunts and muffled curses as the guards subdued the prisoner. When they staggered to their feet sometime later, a bound, still struggling knight between them, blood flowed from several battered noses. FitzHugh's massive chest heaved with every furious breath, and a red bruise was beginning to darken his chin.

"It will take these many guards and more to protect you, *wife*. That half man you lie with will never keep you safe from me."

Shaking loose Beauchamp's hold, Mellisynt came as close as she dared. "I did not lie with Beauchamp," she sobbed. "I swear! But I had no one else to turn to for help. Sir Roger will provide us escort to Rennes."

"He'll escort us to the grave and beyond before I give up what is mine."

"You have no choice, Sir Richard!"

The robed monk spoke for the first time, his voice throbbing with a zealot's passion. "You must provide witness at the ecclesiastic court or face excommunication."

The threat brought FitzHugh's head up with a snap. As much as any man, he feared for his immortal soul. This same threat had sent King Henry to his knees, to be scourged and made to beg forgiveness for Thomas à Becket's murder. It had held Frederick Barbarossa's hand from the territories he'd conquered when his reach came too near Rome's own vassal states. It made FitzHugh release his breath in a long, slow hiss.

For a timeless moment, no one moved or spoke. Finally, Beauchamp stepped forward, tucking a protective hand under Mellisynt's arm once more.

"We must leave at once if we're to reach Rennes before dark, my lady."

When she stumbled back beside him, he bowed to the governor. "I thank you for your offer of additional escort, Lord Devereaux, but I have sufficient of my own men."

"Are you sure?" The beefy knight cast FitzHugh a dubious glance. "This one's not been easy to handle. He cost me one of my best horses. Let me at least call the armorer to attach a set of shackles."

"Nay," Beauchamp said with a trace of scorn. "He's safe enough, bound as he is. The months without exercise have weakened him. 'Twas not always so easy to send him down."

"Please, can we not leave?" Mellisynt reached out a hand as if to lay it on Beauchamp's sleeve. She caught FitzHugh's furious glare and jerked it back as if scalded. "Please, I would get this business over and done with as quickly as possible. Let us go."

FitzHugh tensed his muscles, testing the strength of the ropes that bound him as he was led from the great hall. The hemp cut into his wrists and gave not an inch. His eyes smoldering, he endured the grunts and heaves of the guard as they shoved him aboard a waiting mount.

Leaning heavily on Beauchamp's arm, Mellisynt was led to her palfrey. Her breath came in shallow little gasps, and she refused to meet FitzHugh's piercing stare.

Even with the aid of a mounting block, she had difficulty gaining the saddle. Her mouth was set in grim, determined lines, and she clung to the pommel with white, straining fingers. Jumping onto the block, Beauchamp placed her foot in the stirrup. His hands cradled her hips and lifted her gently. She settled against the hard leather with a little grunt.

FitzHugh felt his teeth grinding, one against the other. His eyes bored into his wife's back as the other men mounted. At length the cavalcade rode through Bâlfour's gates. Beauchamp's standard-bearer in the lead, and a double column of mounted men-at-arms behind.

With every step of the plodding horses, FitzHugh's skin crawled. He resisted the urge to glance back over his shoulder at the sprawling castle. At any moment he expected a shout, an order to halt and return the prisoner. Even this brief taste of open air made him shudder at the thought of returning to his cell. He swallowed and forced himself to focus on the road ahead.

Beauchamp waited until they'd covered a good five miles before he halted the troop. Riding to the prisoner's side, he sliced the ropes with a quick slash of his dagger.

FitzHugh brought his stiff arms forward with aching slowness, and lifted one hand to rub the bruise on his chin. His mouth twisted in a wry grimace.

"You need not have hit with quite so much force, Beauchamp."

Chapter Eighteen

Beauchamp threw back his head, shouting his laughter to the leafy trees overhead. The sound was rich with relief.

"You're lucky I didn't have the guards knock you unconscious and carry your damned carcass out," he managed finally. "I swear, Richard, I couldn't tell whether you had tumbled to our ploy."

"Do you think you could've landed that blow if I had not?"

The two men grinned, sharing a moment of comradeship that transcended words. FitzHugh leaned forward, and they grasped each other's forearms in a hard grip.

"There's a ship waiting at Dol-de-Bretagne to carry you back to England," Beauchamp told him. "If Lady Mellisynt can stand the pace, we should make the evening tide. Your best—your only—hope is to get to King Henry and plead your case. Geoffrey is beyond listening."

He paused, and his rogue's grin faded. "The time nears when we will all have to chose sides once more. This time, I fear, for good."

FitzHugh nodded, his eyes somber. Releasing Beauchamp's forearm, he greeted Peter St. Bressé, then turned at last to the two figures waiting, still and silent, in the road. His heart pounding, he nudged his horse forward. With each step closer to Mellisynt, FitzHugh felt his chest tighten, but he forced himself to address the man beside her first.

"You make a most convincing friar, Sir Bertrand. You set my knees to knocking with your threat of excommunication."

The old knight nodded, grinning. "I'm much better with a sword in my hand than a Psalter, but I thought that bit was rather a good stroke."

"It was. I thank you, sir."

A slow red suffused Sir Bertrand's face, and he shifted uncomfortably in the saddle.

"Harrumph! 'Tis not me you should thank. 'Tis your lady. She thought the whole scheme out."

"Aye, I thought mayhap she did," FitzHugh said softly, his gaze swinging to the trembling figure of his wife. Throwing his leg over the pommel, he slid out of the saddle. In two strides, he was at her side.

For a long moment, neither moved. FitzHugh stood beside her stirrup, his thirsty mind drinking in the details he'd not let himself dwell on during the tense scene at Bâlfour. She looked pale, with lines of strain etching the corners of her mouth. Her veil was coated with dust of travel, and she once again wore loose, baggy gowns, to accommodate her pregnancy. FitzHugh thought he'd never seen anything more beautiful in his life. He lifted his arms.

Mellisynt gave a little sob and eased from saddle into his strong hold. Her shoulders heaving, she wrapped both arms around his neck and buried her face in his chest. FitzHugh carried her into a copse of trees beside the road and settled on a fallen log, cradling her on his lap. He ached to crush her against him, to taste her mouth and skin, to feel the press of her body against his. Instead, he held her while she sobbed out her fright and accumulated strain. When she shifted and her rounded stomach butted against him, he sucked in a ragged breath.

At length her storm of tears passed. Rubbing her nose against his chest, she sniffled, then raised her face to his. She managed a weak, tremulous smile when he brushed a knuckle against her tear-streaked cheek.

"That's the first time I've ever seen you cry," FitzHugh commented in bemused wonder.

Mellisynt swallowed a hiccup. "I've never had to win my husband free of prison through lies and deception before. 'Twas most unnerving."

"Aye, I expect it was."

"And you frightened me. You were so fierce!"

"Aye, I was."

His calm rejoinders stilled her lingering terror. With the lessening of her fear came the first prickle of indignation. After all she'd endured, the man could at least show a modicum of gratitude. Or give some sign he was pleased to see her! She straightened on his lap.

She sniffed. "You, at least, are most composed, my lord."

"Oh, no, my lady," he murmured. "I'm not the least composed. 'Tis all I can do to restrain my own emotions at this moment."

Mellisynt felt her pulse begin to race at the sudden intensity in his eyes. This was much better.

"Don't restrain them, then," she whispered.

"Nay, this is not the place, nor are you in any condition for me to serve you as I would."

A slow, feline smile curved her lips. This was better by far.

"But when we're back in England, and you've delivered of the babe, you may be sure I intend to beat you soundly."

"What?"

Astounded, she gaped at him. His arm tightened on her shoulders, and he brought her around to face him fully.

"My God, Mellisynt!" he growled. "How could you make such a journey! How could you take such risks!"

"I thought the prize worth the risks," she said, sputtering. She jerked in his hold, incensed. "Obviously I was mistaken! Of all the ungrateful, thankless, churlish louts. Of all the—"

"Be still, before you bounce off my knee."

"I'll bounce off your head, you obnoxious oaf."

FitzHugh caught her fist as it raised in a wide, swinging arc. Despite himself, he grinned. The fear that had begun churning in his belly the first moment he'd seen her in Bâlfour's hall swelled once more, and spilled over into a rush of sensation so intense he all but shook with it.

She looked so indignant, so furious. Her eyes blazed with a green fire that sent a shaft of heat straight to his loins. An aching need swamped his own lingering fear for her and the babe.

With a groan, he wrapped a hand around her neck and brought her lips to his. His kiss possessed, devoured, demanded. Her scent and her sweet, honeyed taste filled his senses and fed his hunger.

After a startled moment, Mellisynt shook her fist loose of his hold and wrapped both arms around his neck. She strained against him, her mouth as fierce and ravenous as his. Her breasts tingled when they rubbed against him, their tips beading and dewing against her shift. Her fingers tangled in the dark hair of his nape. It was longer now, and thicker.

She forgot the constant, piercing ache low in her back. She ignored the bulge of her stomach that bowed her toward him at an awkward angle. Shivery, fluttering waves of sensation undulated through her, and she gave herself up to his kiss.

"Well," she gasped, when at last they separated to draw in harsh, ragged gulps of air. "That's more the response I had hoped for!"

He buried his face in her hair, groaning. "I near died when I saw you in that hall, so white-faced and frightened."

"I *was* frightened," she admitted, burrowing into the warmth of his neck. "And you didn't help, my lord. I was afraid you'd ruin all by getting yourself killed!"

"I was but playing the role you gave me," he muttered into her hair.

"You played it fearsome well! You fooled me!"

"Nay," he protested, lifting his head. "Surely you knew I would guess what you were about."

"How could you guess? The annulment grounds were valid. The documents are real, you know. Lord Devereaux examined them most carefully, and was convinced."

"That one took a crack on his head when he won his spurs that spilled half his brains," FitzHugh snorted, rubbing his chin against her forehead as if he could not allow their contact, once made, to be broken.

"Nay, I knew at once what you were about. Even if I hadn't recognized Sir Bertrand right away, I knew you could never play me false, nor repudiate your vows."

Mellisynt eased her head away from his chin, a slow, painful hope building in her breast. "How could you know that?"

"Your heart is true, my lady."

His breath bathed her cheek, as soft and caressing as the words he spoke. A slow smile lit his eyes.

"You told me so. That day in the forest, when Beauchamp tried to steal you before we wed. You swore then you'd hold to your vows, and you have."

His gaze softened and took on a silvery glow, one that Mellisynt had despaired of ever seeing there again. 'Twas enough, she told herself, enough and more. She needed not the words, the songs, the silly love tokens. She needed only this look, this warm glow. Her hand lifted to stroke the line of his jaw.

FitzHugh felt a queer tightening in his chest. He opened his mouth to speak, then closed it as Mellisynt stiffened, her eyes widening in surprise. Her hand left his jaw to splay across her stomach.

"Holy Mary!" she breathed.

With gathering alarm he watched as her teeth came down hard on her lower lip and a low, hissing grunt issued from her mouth.

"Mellisynt! Sweet Jesu, is it the babe?"

FitzHugh fought an urge to crush her to his chest. After a long, tense moment, she lifted her lids. Thick black lashes framed rueful eyes.

"Aye. At least, I think so. 'Tis either that or a very different set of saddle aches."

"Christ's bones," he swore, "how long have you had the pains?"

"They've come and gone since before Bâlfour."

He gave a disbelieving groan, then stood and stalked toward the road, Mellisynt tight within his arms.

Beauchamp met him halfway, striding through the under-brush with undisguised urgency.

"The advance guard just rode back. There's a troop ahead of us on the road. He thinks they carry the duke's pennant."

Mellisynt clung to the safety of FitzHugh's arms as their band pulled off the road and plunged deep into the woods. The men covered their horses' muzzles with shirts and cloaks to keep them still and held themselves rigid and unmoving in the dappled sunlight. Gradually the thud of pounding hooves and jingle of harness penetrated the stillness of the woods. Mellisynt buried her face in FitzHugh's chest once more and forgot to breathe. Within moments, the troop passed.

"'Tis the duke himself," Beauchamp confirmed in a grim voice. "With a full company of men."

FitzHugh nodded. "They'll be back at full gallop when he hears I'm gone from Bâlfour."

Both men glanced down at Mellisynt.

"I'm all right. Truly. The pains come and go, with long intervals in between. I can ride."

A gleam of laughter lightened the worry in FitzHugh's eyes. "You could not ride when you were whole, wife."

"I got here, didn't I?" she reminded him, a tilt to her chin.

He grinned and shifted her weight in his arms. "Can you

make it to Trémont? 'Tis closest. We'll hold there while you attend to this business of birthing.''

"Nay, not Trémont," Sir Bertrand said urgently. "There's but a skeleton force there. Most of our men were drawn to the duke's levy after you were taken. I expected Duke Geoffrey to garrison the castle with his own men at any time. 'Tis likely they're there now.''

"You must make the ship," Beauchamp urged. "I'll take part of the force and head for Rennes. I can leave enough signs to convince Geoffrey to follow us, and make enough speed that he doesn't catch us. You must take Mellisynt and circle around the city to the coast.''

Mellisynt held her breath at the conflicting emotions chasing across the sharp planes of FitzHugh's face. He glanced down at her once more, his jaw tightening, then back at Beauchamp.

"It galls me greatly to leave you risking capture and fighting my battles for me," he growled. "But I thank you, Roger. I will see my lady safe.''

"There'll be no battle," Beauchamp tossed out with his usual insouciance. "I'll turn east at Rennes and be back across the border before Geoffrey knows who it is he follows. With luck, I'll reach my own keep in time to catch Isabeau before she tumbles out of bed tomorrow morn. God keep you, Richard, and you, my lady.''

He swooped down to plant a hearty kiss on Mellisynt's lips and was gone.

The next hours passed in a blur of clawing, wrenching spasms and heart-stopping fear. Cradled in FitzHugh's hold, cushioned against his thighs, Mellisynt endured the ride with a stoicism that surprised her as much as it did him. He slowed whenever the pains seized her and let her find what ease she could within his arms. When they passed, he gripped the reins again and sent the horse forward. Beads of sweat rolled down his brow and traced lines in the dust coating his lean cheeks.

Resisting the urge to press forward with all haste, FitzHugh stayed off the main roads and kept the pace as slow as he dared. They skirted two smaller towns and gave the walls of Rennes a wide birth. As the sun passed its zenith and Mellisynt's spasms grew more regular, he gritted his teeth. They stopped but once, to water the horses and allow Mellisynt to walk about a small clearing, her face set, her hands clutching FitzHugh's arm.

"Ahhh…" she breathed. "That helps."

She leaned against a sapling and turned her face to the sun. Perspiration rolled down the tendons of her neck and slipped below the line of her shift. With gentle fingers, FitzHugh untied the laces and peeled the linen back above her bodice to give her air.

"Who did this?"

Her eyes flew open at the rasp of cold fury in his voice. She saw his gaze fastened on the ugly bruises marking the swell of her breast.

"Who did this?" he repeated, his jaw clenching.

"It matters not."

"Who marked you, lady wife?"

When she refused to speak, he knew.

"'Twas Geoffrey, was it not?"

His gut knotted at the thought of the man who had been his friend putting his hands on her. Or mayhap more. He started to ask, but took one look at her wide, steady eyes and did not.

"He'll not hurt you again, Mellisynt," he promised.

"Nay, my lord," she replied with a quiet dignity that belied the sweat on her brow and the streaks of dust on her cheeks. "Such a one as he can't hurt me."

She took her lower lip between her teeth, staring up at him with troubled eyes. "His heart—nay, his soul—is twisted in his breast, my lord. He's let the dark side of his being leach the good away, if good there ever was."

FitzHugh dragged a hand down his face, his palm rough against the tightness of his jaw. "There was, once."

He fought the anger that coiled, hard and cold, in his belly. He would settle with Geoffrey at the right time and place.

"Come, if you're ready, we'll press on."

They traveled several more miles before she stiffened in his arms once more and bit down on her lip so hard, droplets of blood ran down her chin. Cursing under his breath, he reined in. His hands covered hers on the swell of her stomach, feeling the roiling, rolling flesh beneath the layers of gown.

"This is madness," he told her when the paroxysm had passed. "We must stop and get you a midwife."

"No!" She gripped his hand with a desperate strength. "No, we won't stop. It's not yet time! Hertha told me I would feel the need to push at the end. It may be hours yet."

"Jesu, woman, it *may* be any minute! Do you want to drop the child in an open field, like a mare?"

She met his angry look with a determined one of her own. "As I recall, you've a steady hand with the horses and are most knowledgeable of treatments and poultices. If the babe should come, I trust you to ease its way. Now go!"

Gritting his teeth, FitzHugh spurred his horse forward once more. Where did this remarkable female spring from, he wondered? The thin, pale little widow, who had trembled in their marriage bed, who couldn't even read her betrothal documents, had blossomed into a woman of incredible strength and indomitable will. His hands still shook at the thought of her crossing the sea, braving Geoffrey's wrath, and brazening her way into Bâlfour to free him. And now she'd put herself and her babe in his hands, trusting him implicitly.

With a silent vow to see her and their child safe, he urged the horse into an easy, loping canter.

FitzHugh would gladly have exchanged a day on the rack for the hours that followed. With each spasm, he could feel the taut flesh of his wife's belly stretch and roll, then tighten under his arm. She never cried out, never asked him to stop. His jaw ached from clenching it so hard, and his arms were leaden from holding her, by the time they crested a hill and saw the sea far off in the distance. The sun hung just above the waves, painting them a deep blood red.

"An hour more, Mellisynt. Can you make it?"

Her lids lifted, and the fearlessness he saw in the depths of her eyes struck at his soul.

"Aye, we can make it. Only...only hurry."

"My lord!"

At St. Bressé's low call, FitzHugh lifted his head. His nostrils flared, like those of a lion that has scented danger. Far down the hill, he saw the patrol. The mounted troop had come around a bend in the road, heading their way. Even from this distance, he could recognize their pennants rippling in the breeze, and knew the golden lions on a bloodred field.

"We must go back!" St. Bressé urged.

"Nay," FitzHugh said, his voice cold as steel. "They've seen us. We can't outrun them." He shifted in the saddle and turned to face the young knight. "Take your lady to the ship."

"FitzHugh, no!" Mellisynt clutched at FitzHugh's arms. "No! Don't let them take you again. Go! Ride away, now. Without me, you can escape them."

"Nay," he told her gently. "Without you, I have no wish to escape. You know in your heart this meeting was meant. Go with Sir Peter, my lady, and take our child home to Edgemoor. God be with you."

He kissed her cheek, drinking in the tang of musky sweat, the taste of dust, and the faint, sweet scent of gillyflowers. Over her protests, he passed her into St. Bressé's strong arms, then kicked his horse into a gallop.

By the time FitzHugh hauled back on the reins and pulled his mount to a pawing, rearing stop, Geoffrey had ridden forward. They measured each other as the swirling dust settled, like two strangers chance-met on the road. The jingle of harness and shuffle of hooves faded from FitzHugh's consciousness. There was only him, and the man he would kill.

"So, Richard!"

"So, Geoffrey."

FitzHugh sat easy in the saddle, one hand holding the reins, the other resting lightly on the hilt of his sword.

"The diversionary force you sent out led us a merry chase," the duke said, his golden eyes gleaming. "I assume 'twas Beauchamp. The dolt at Bâlfour said he escorted your lady on her onerous duty."

FitzHugh shrugged, not revealing his relief that Beauchamp had made good his escape.

Geoffrey's lip twisted in a wry smile. "'Twas a good ploy, that business of the bishops' court. I might've wasted hours riding into Rennes and missed you altogether if I didn't know you—and your lady—better."

"Aye," FitzHugh told him softly, "you do know better. The Lady Mellisynt would not avail herself of a bishop's decree. She holds to her vows, as I do."

Geoffrey flushed at the scorn in his eyes. "Are you so sure, bastard? Did she tell you she came to my rooms? Did she tell you what she offered for your release?"

"She didn't need to. I saw the marks you left. Your manhood must have shriveled apace with your honor, Geoffrey, that you must needs force a gentlewoman."

A slow tide of red washed up the duke's bull-like neck.

"What, have you no answer?" FitzHugh swung his leg over the pommel and slid to the road. "Have these weeks and months of skulking like a gormless knave, swinging from one cause to the other as a rotten carcass swings on the gibbet, totally unmanned you? Have you lost your balls, as well as your integrity?"

A grim smile tightened Geoffrey's mouth, and he dismounted with a semblance of his old grace. His hands were steady as they undid the clasp holding his cloak and flung it aside. Drawing his sword in a slow, unhurried movement, he held it, blade out, hilt to his chest.

"Despite all, it will pain me to kill you, FitzHugh."

"Despite all, I'm glad you will try. 'Tis better to settle this here, and now."

FitzHugh drew his own sword, his eyes never leaving the duke's face. The knights behind them stirred at the sight of drawn weapons, and several pushed forward.

"Hold!" Geoffrey roared over his shoulder. "Hold! This is between me and Sir Richard. Any man who dares interfere will feel my blade in his gut!"

For a brief instant, their eyes met, regret and resignation mingling. This had been long in coming, but now it was here. They both knew full well the love that had once been between them could end only in death.

At the first clash of steel on steel, a shock ran up FitzHugh's arm and a cold, deadly satisfaction sang through his veins. The wild rush that soldiers feel when they charge into battle surged through him. He had a moment's wonder that he should feel no remorse, no hesitation, and then he swung once more.

The blades sliced through the air, to ring against each other with each swing. His world narrowed to a patch of dusty road, a grunting, heaving, flame-haired man, a swish of air with each vicious stroke.

He overreached, and his sword cut air. Geoffrey lunged up on the balls of his feet and thrust. Icy heat seared FitzHugh's side, and the force of metal against bone thrust him back. He smelled blood, saw it dripping from the edge of Geoffrey's blade. His side was afire, but a quick glance down, beneath his arm, showed that the wound had glanced off the rib, slicing flesh but not penetrating.

He felt no pain, only a raw, burning heat that fueled his utter determination. Lifting his sword, he swung and slashed and began the dance of death.

Step by step, he beat Geoffrey back. The horsemen behind the duke pulled on reins, and hooves shuffled in the dirt as they edged out of the way. FitzHugh neither saw nor heard them. His sole focus was the rasping, grunting man before him. Sweat spiraled down, stinging his eyes. Blood soaked his tunic and ran down his leggings.

Pulling on the last of his reserves, FitzHugh threw his shield aside and grasped his hilt with both hands. Swinging the blade with all his strength, he crashed it into the gold-coated embossing on Geoffrey's shield. The protective barrier dropped for a vital instant, and FitzHugh followed with a sideways thrust against the duke's mailed gauntlet that sent his sword flying from a numbed hand. Using his body's forward momentum, FitzHugh slammed his shoulder against Geoffrey's chest. The duke crashed to the ground.

"Do it, damn you! Finish it!" Geoffrey's voice rattled against the hissing, sucking gasp for air. A fearless gleam lit his golden eyes, and a slow, taunting smile curled his lips as Fitzhugh's sword pressed against his throat. Blood welled, flesh yielded.

FitzHugh's knuckles tightened around the hilt. He had but to lean forward a fraction, exert the smallest pressure.

"It's done," he said finally, the tip of his sword lifting. "You're dead to me, as a man, as a friend."

He straightened slowly, painfully. And walked away. The wound in his side made mounting difficult, but he pulled himself into the saddle. He expected at any moment to hear Geoffrey call to his men, to feel hard hands dragging him back down. Silence rang in his ears.

"Is he come yet?"

Mellisynt lifted one hand to push her sweat-slicked hair back from her face. She knelt on all fours, a mound of piled rags beneath her.

"Nay, my lady." St. Bressé's grim face swung from her to the shipmaster at the door of the small cabin.

"We must cast off," the weathered seaman said again, as he had repeatedly the last twenty minutes. "We're losing the tide."

"Go, look again," Mellisynt ordered St. Bressé. "I won't leave yet."

Her head drooped as Sir Peter's feet pounded up the steps. She drew in shallow, panting breaths. A violent spasm wrenched her lower stomach, and she arched, bowing her back against the pull. Her fingers curled into the rags, her nails dug into the bare wood beneath. For long moments she lost herself in the wrenching pressure, forgetting to breathe, conscious only of the need to push. She spread her knees, the bones grinding against the hard floor. Her hair fell forward, blocking the dim light, shutting out all sound. There was only her, and the babe.

The spasm passed, and she sat back on her heels, breath racing into her lungs. Before the mists even cleared from her eyes, another swell began, a wave of sensation that brought her to her knees once more. Head hanging, she clamped her lips down over the rush of air that beat against them and pushed.

"That's it, push down."

She heard his voice as if from a distance, barely discernible through the roaring in her ears. Yet her heart recognized him instantly.

"Push, Mellisynt."

She felt a clean, sharp pain, and a bulge between her legs.

"Sweet Mary, Holy Mother!" she gasped. "It comes!"

The floor seemed to heave under her. FitzHugh took her arms and laid her on her side. She tried to focus on him, to understand the blood that stained his shirt, to ask what had occurred. She couldn't push the words through her constricted throat, and thought they didn't matter, in any case. He was here, his strength flowed around her. She felt him push up her skirts, then bunch the rags under her to ease her hips and cushion the babe.

Mellisynt's eyes widened as she felt the bulk of her child slide forth—first the head, then the protrusion of a shoulder. She looked down, but couldn't see over the robes mounded at her waist. FitzHugh held her leg up in strong, sure hands, his face fierce with concentration.

"'Tis almost done, little one," he crooned. "'Tis almost done."

Mellisynt felt a wild laugh bubble in her throat at the incongruous sight of her husband, his massive frame bent over her, his deep voice singing to the babe between her legs. Swallowing the laugh, she bit down on swollen lips. A last great heave. A slippery, slithering rush. She fell back in triumph.

FitzHugh shouted as the babe slid into his hands.

Mellisynt closed her eyes as a wave of weariness washed over her, sagging her stomach, collapsing her legs. At the first, tentative cry, her lids flew open.

A girl. A tiny, perfect girl, cradled in her husband's huge hands, still anchored to her by the cord of life. Mellisynt reached out, not tired anymore. A need to hold her babe surged through her, sharp and strong. Leaning on one elbow, she nestled her child against her body and used a corner of a rag to wipe the stains of birth from her eyes.

The tiny mouth puckered, and a lusty wail issued forth.

Smiling, Mellisynt looked up. "Thank you, my lord."

Chapter Nineteen

"How can you sit there so calmly?"

Mellisynt stopped her furious pacing to glare at her lord. He sprawled in a huge, carved chair, his long legs crossed at the ankles. He looked completely at ease, for all the world like a farmer sitting before a comfortable fire instead of a knight about to meet his king.

"Our fate was decided weeks ago, when we left Brittany. We'll find out what it is soon enough."

"I cannot stand this uncertainty! King Henry could've given some indication of how he'll rule on our petitions. Instead he sent just that one short summons!"

"Most like he's been awaiting word from Geoffrey, to see whether he will come forward."

"That puling catiff," Mellisynt sniffed. "I wish you'd skewered him when you had the chance."

FitzHugh shook his head, a rueful smile tugging at his lips. "I thought motherhood was supposed to make women soft and gentle. You've grown more fierce with each passing week."

She stopped beside his chair, slicing through the air with an angry hand. "Why did you let him live? When you had him down, your sword at his throat?"

"I told you, lady wife, many times over. Must we argue this yet again?"

FitzHugh sighed as she turned away and resumed her pacing. She couldn't accept that he'd spared Geoffrey's life. In truth, at times he found it hard to accept himself. His rational mind told him he'd live to rue the moment when he'd wiped the sweat and blood from his face and stared down at the duke, sprawled defenseless in the dirt.

"We shouldn't have surrendered so tamely to the king's men when they came." Mellisynt picked up the thread of the argument. Her skirts brushed against the stone flooring as she measured the length of the chamber, then back again.

FitzHugh studied the Flemish tapestry above the cold hearth, refusing to be drawn into another area of contention. His wife had wanted to close Edgemoor's gates when the king's summons came, and hold the keep against all comers. As if he could hold out against the king's forces.

By all the saints, he'd never understand women, at least not this particular one. This last month, she'd been so unlike herself, full of irritation and despondency. Instead of rejoicing over their escape and the birth of the babe, Mellisynt had seemed to fall into a black humor.

She passed his chair, her stride agitated. FitzHugh's gaze followed her, sliding down the slender frame outlined in emerald silk. The tight bodice lacing emphasized her swollen breasts, ripe and full for the babe. The thought of those white breasts, threaded with a fine tracery of blue veins and tipped with nipples wet and slick from little Meridyth's suckling, sent a shaft of heat lancing through him.

Christ's blood, he wanted her. Had wanted her for weeks. His aunt's stern admonition that his lady needed time to repair her body humors after birth, and Mellisynt's own uncertain temper, had stayed his hand, if not stilled his wants.

Many women went through swings in their temperament, Dame Hertha had confided to him after one long, frustrating night. His wife had seemed healed and willing that day, yet turned from him that night with a snapped comment that she was not ready. FitzHugh had gritted his teeth, taken as much of her in his arms as she would allow, and waited.

Only the babe seemed to bring them together, the tiny scrap of gurgling, smiling humanity that even now slept in a cradle beside the bed. FitzHugh found himself drawn to the laughing infant, dawdling beside her cradle at odd moments in the day. Many times Mellisynt joined him, cooing and murmuring in the manner of all parents, and for a few moments, at least, they were at peace.

When the king's summons had come, Mellisynt would not leave the babe behind, nor would she allow him to come alone to Kenilworth, where the king would wear his crown at the Feast of Saint John and hear petitions. FitzHugh had resigned himself to the commodious, slow-moving horse-drawn litter that carried mother, babe and tiring nurse, but protested vehemently the three-legged mongrel that loped beside the wagon, fangs bared whenever anyone dared approach. Luckily, the little page Bartholomew had been away on a visit to his parents, or FitzHugh doubted not that Mellisynt would've brought him, as well.

Perforce the journey south had been slow and wearisome, as had the waiting once they arrived at Kenilworth. They'd been two days now awaiting the king's summons.

"Do you think Henry will allow you to keep Edgemoor?"

FitzHugh schooled his patience and answered, as he had many times in the last days, "I don't. Although Edgemoor isn't part of the honor of Richmond, and thus not Geoffrey's to dispose of, I pledged to him when I first won the keep. The king may see it as his son's rightful fief and want to install a knight loyal to Geoffrey to hold it."

Mellisynt whirled and faced her lord, a hand on either hip. "How could he support Geoffrey, even now? How much evidence does he need of his son's treachery? The queen herself admitted their plotting and scheming when she was brought back from Aquitaine!"

Heaving himself out of his chair, FitzHugh moved to stand beside his wife. Her clear eyes glowed with indignation and frustration.

"I know 'tis difficult for one such as you, who holds true to her oaths, to understand these Angevins."

"I know only that they would use you, and I like it not!"

"Mellisynt, there's naught to like or dislike. King Henry has ruled these lands for thirty years and more. He's curbed his sons' power before, and thinks to do so yet again. But they're his blood, his line. Where he can, he'll support them."

"Bah!" Mellisynt threw up her hands. "Damn all these Angevins! You should've skewered Geoffrey when you had the chance! You've lost all because of him."

"Does the thought of losing Edgemoor distress you that much?" FitzHugh asked, folding his arms across his chest and watching her with thoughtful eyes.

"'Tis our home, your sons' patrimony. 'Tis all you have, now that Trémont is lost."

"Nay, I have you, and strong, healthy children. And my sword arm. I earned my way before with the strength of my arm, and can do so yet again."

A troubled frown marred her brow, and she stepped forward, laying her hand on his. Whatever she would have said was lost as a sharp rap sounded on the chamber door.

From where it rested on the floor beside the cradle, the hound lifted its massive head and growled low in its throat.

Mellisynt stood stock-still, the hairs on the back of her neck lifting. It had come, the moment she'd dreaded since their ship touched the shores of England. Her frantic glance darted from the door to her lord's face.

He covered her hand where it rested on his. "Don't worry so, my lady. Trust me to care for what is mine."

The knock sounded once again. The hound's growl deepened in pitch to a rumbling, reverberating snarl. The baby began to fret, making the little mewling, sucking sounds that preceded her full awakening.

"My lord, listen to me. I have yet the documents from Trémont. You could use them."

"What documents?"

"The petitions of annulment. You could put me aside and take another wife, one with lands in the king's holding." Both her hands gripped his arms now, the fingers digging into his hard flesh. She ignored the frown that settled like dark thunder on his brow.

"I've thought much on this since we returned. I know you wed me for Trémont, and now 'tis gone. The castle's garrisoned by the duke's men, the revenues reverted to Brittany's treasury. You've lost all you gained by our joining."

FitzHugh's eyes gleamed silvery blue as he stared down at her. "For God's sake, woman, is this what's been troubling you these weeks?"

She swallowed, forcing the words through her dry throat. "You fulfilled your part of our bargain. I have Meridyth. If I can't give you Trémont in return, I would give you the chance to—"

"My lord, the king awaits!"

The herald's voice called through the wooden door, accompanied by another, louder rap on the panel. Responding to the threat, the hound surged up, its feet spread protectively. A deep, ear-splitting bark rolled across the room and bounced off the walls, accompanied by the lusty wails of the babe.

"Jesu, woman! I disbelieve you wait until this moment to throw such arrant foolishness at me."

He pried her fingers loose and took both wrists in a hard grip. "We'll discuss this later, when I return."

Mellisynt watched him stride from the room, then responded instinctively to the baby's lusty cries. Settling herself in the chair FitzHugh had so recently vacated, she unlaced her bodice and put the child to her breast. The hound hunkered down beside the chair and rested his muzzle on her foot.

Her heart aching, Mellisynt curled her hand around her daughter's dark head. The familiar tug and pull as the child suckled drew at her very soul. Ever since the babe's birth, she'd felt a heaviness of spirit she could not throw off. Dame Hertha had clucked and scolded and prepared cool, moist foods to soothe her choler. But even such delicacies as veal soaked in vinegar and cucumber hadn't lightened her bleak humor.

FitzHugh had been first confused, then concerned, over her moods. He alternated between a gentleness that made her want to weep and an imperfectly disguised impatience to resume the activities of their marriage bed. But as much as she ached to take his body into hers, to feel the thrust of man to woman, husband to wife, once more, Mellisynt couldn't seem to cast off the dark melancholy that held her back.

When the summons had come for FitzHugh to meet with the king, she'd plummeted into a deep despondency. He would lose Edgemoor, she knew, as he had lost Trémont. That was when she'd dug out the creased and weathered annulment documents. She'd used them once to free him from bondage, and would use them again. She'd release FitzHugh from the marriage bargain that had gained her all and him naught.

The babe gurgled and kneaded her fists against Mellisynt's tender breast. She shifted the child to her other nipple, wiping the dribble of thin milk from the tiny rosebud mouth with a loving finger. While the babe suckled contentedly, Mellisynt leaned back and made her plans.

FitzHugh strode through the high-ceilinged halls with a heavy tread. Of all the addlepated, idiotic, vaporish, *female* notions! To think he would set her aside to take another heiress! To imagine he would care more for lands and rents than for his wife and child!

"Wait here, my lord. I'll advise the king of your presence."

He threw the herald a look of such irritation that the man blinked in surprise. Several courtiers lounging in the anteroom started forward, smiles of greeting on their lips, only to fall back at his fierce scowl.

All these weeks! All these weeks he'd handled her so gently, trying to help her through this uncharacteristic melancholy. Gentleness be damned, he fumed. When this audience with the king was through, he might not have a holding to call his own, but he would have his wife.

"The king will see you now, my lord."

With a start, FitzHugh recalled himself to the business at hand. Forcing down his irritation, he followed the man into the king's private audience chamber.

At fifty-three, Henry was in the full vigor of his middle age. He'd lost none of his legendary frenetic energy to advancing years. His hair was yet more red than white, and he traveled like the wind. To his courtiers' dismay, he still crammed twenty hours or more of hunting and work into every day, and rarely sat down. As FitzHugh knelt on one knee before him, Henry waved an impatient hand and strode about the chamber.

"Get up, man, and tell me in your own words what this insanity is with you and Geoffrey."

FitzHugh rose and quickly surveyed the three men in the room. The king's chancellor, the lord of the exchequer, and the most powerful baron in England, Lord Ranulf, earl of Chester, stood around a table scattered with parchments and maps. They could not sit while the king paced. Ranulf, who had taken FitzHugh's youngest son into his household for training, nodded in greeting.

Taking a deep breath, FitzHugh responded to the king's question. "I have abjured my vows of vassalage to your son, the duke."

"Abjured! Christ's blood, man, I heard you all but sliced

off his head. And this after he kept you imprisoned. What happened between you?''

Familiar as he was with the king's constant motion, FitzHugh nevertheless found it disconcerting to be addressing his shrewd face one moment, his back the next, as he circled and paced. Henry stopped to sign a document on the wooden table with a quick flourish. Throwing the quill pen down, he whirled and faced FitzHugh once more.

''Well? What caused two men who've fought and wenched and spilled blood together for twenty years and more to fall out so?''

Looking into the king's golden eyes, eyes that were so like Geoffrey's, FitzHugh tried to shape the words that would tell him that his son sought to betray him. A sour taste filled his mouth.

''The king knows of Geoffrey's discourse with Philip,'' Lord Ranulf put in, easing the way.

FitzHugh nodded and faced the king. ''Then you probably know, as well, Geoffrey thought I had betrayed his schemes.''

''But you did not.''

''The duke thought he had evidence to the contrary.''

Henry turned, his motion stilled for once.

''Would you? Would you have come to me with word of what my son plots?''

FitzHugh drew in a deep breath. ''Nay, my lord. Not while I was pledged to him.''

The men at the table stiffened, but the king didn't move, nor speak. FitzHugh met his look squarely.

''I tried to dissuade him, my lord king, with all the power of our friendship. But I would not betray him while yet I owed him homage.''

He paused, and a silence descended, broken only by the light trilling of a small bird on the window ledge. The earl of Chester stepped forward, his shaggy brows drawn together over an angled face that reflected his years and his heavy responsibilities. Many feared this man, who was advisor and confidant to the king. He held dominion over vast lands in England and on the Continent, and wielded a heavy sword hand. FitzHugh had fought with him more than once, and found him honest, if harsh. His youngest son could have no better man to foster with.

The earl's deep bass rumbled across the stillness. "I will take Sir Richard's homage, my lord king. I will have any man who stood true to his oaths until they were honorably dissolved."

The king's eyes narrowed on FitzHugh. "I've spawned rash, hot-tempered sons. But for all their bullheadedness, they dance yet to my tune. I'll bring Geoffrey within bounds, right enough. He'll need you then, Richard. He'll need your friendship and counsel, as he has before. Hold to him, and let me ease these troubles between you. I'll restore your holdings in Brittany, and give you new honors, as well."

For a long moment, FitzHugh stared at his king. The thought occurred to him that each man, king or peasant, knight or priest, had some fatal weakness. Some blindness that obscured his vision. For all Henry's wisdom in ruling his domains, for all his military daring and natural shrewdness, he couldn't see his weakness in handling his own sons. Geoffrey would not come back, nor would he dance any longer to the king's tune.

FitzHugh wondered briefly what his own blindness was, then thought he knew. It awaited him even now in the chamber they shared. His jaw firming, he shook his head.

"Nay, my lord king. I cannot serve as Geoffrey's vassal."

Henry measured him for interminable seconds. "So be it!"

"And he shall pledge his knight's duties to me?" the earl prodded.

The king waved a weary hand. "Aye. I've not enough honest men in this realm to scorn one who holds true. Put your sword and Edgemoor's men in service to Chester. I'll have the articles of enfeoffment drawn up and subscribed."

Already Henry's mind had moved to another matter. He strode back to the table and took up a document. Lord Ranulf nodded once more to FitzHugh and turned to join the ensuing discussion.

Bowing to the king's back, FitzHugh turned and left the chamber. The crowd of courtiers waiting outside had swelled in number, drawn by hopes of conducting their business at this wearing of the crown. Squeezing through the mass of bodies, he was hailed by more than one acquaintance. FitzHugh returned their courteous greetings, but precluded any lengthy discussions by the simple expedient of pressing forward at a determined pace.

At length he reached the far doors to Kenilworth's great main hall and escaped into the dim corridors. He strode forward, his step lengthening, feeling as if a great burden had rolled off his shoulders. He was free of Geoffrey and all oaths to him at last. He had but one problem left to resolve, one irritating, stubborn, achingly desirable problem.

"Mellisynt!"

The door to their chamber crashed open before he remembered the sleeping babe. He winced as the wooden panel banged against stone and swung back to jar against the frame.

No wails greeted him, no deafening bark, no instant demand for quiet. Frowning, FitzHugh moved into the room. A quick glance told him they were gone, and the child's nurse, as well, if the empty adjoining room was any indication. His eyes fell on the rolled parchments left neatly in the center of the table. Knowing well what they contained, he disdained even to open them.

Within the space of twenty minutes, he'd summoned his bewildered squire, assembled his troop, and ascertained through liberal distribution of silver pennies Mellisynt's direction. Grim-faced, armed only with his sword, he led his men south, clattering over the uneven cobbles of the great road leading from Coventry to London.

They made uneven progress against the tide of travelers streaming into the city for the festivities to be held this eve. Freedmen driving livestock and carts piled high with farm goods to sell at fairs thronged toward the city. Penitents and pilgrims on their way to the holy observances brushed shoulders with traveling jugglers and itinerant tinkers. The Church celebrated the Feast of Saint John with much pomp. After the solemn church services, the citizens would continue the festivities with much more abandoned midsummer's eve rituals.

Cursing the crowds and slow progress, FitzHugh reined in. The way was blocked by a shouting, gesticulating, immovable crowd. The remains of an accident, an overturned farm cart, spilled over the roadway into the ditches on either side. Cabbages lay strewn across the cobbles, providing fodder for the animals caught in the milling mass and convenient balls for the small boys who kicked them back and forth, shouting and laughing.

"Stand aside!"

His squire's shout was lost in the din.

Exasperation tore at the last shreds of FitzHugh's temper. Somewhere beyond this heaving mass of humanity, farm animals and spilled vegetables was his lady wife. Turning his mount's head, he set his spurs to its flanks. The great warhorse cleared the ditch in a flying leap, then pounded across the open field. Ian and the rest of his men scrambled to follow.

He cut back toward the roadway when he'd passed the bulk of the crowd. Ignoring the gawking travelers, he spurred his horse forward. His eyes and attention were concentrated on the road ahead when a reverberating, rolling barking penetrated his consciousness. Sawing on the reins, he hauled his mount to a dancing, skittering stop. Stunned, he saw Mellisynt standing beside a litter, babe in one arm, hound baying at her side. His mind barely registered the fact that the wagon was headed north, back toward Kenilworth and Coventry, as he pounded across the short distance separating them.

"By all that's holy," he bellowed when his horse thudded to a stop beside her, "how dare you leave me so!"

Heedless of the milling troops or gawking crowd, Mellisynt laughed up at his thunderous face. "I thought 'twas right and honorable to leave. I'd gone but a few miles when I decided 'twas neither, only stupid."

"Those are the first sensible words out of your mouth these last weeks and more," FitzHugh growled, clearly not appeased. His black brows were drawn together in a scowl so familiar Mellisynt's heart ached with a mix of crazy joy and relief. He'd come. He'd come for her, even as she was heading back to him. He'd come for her, disdaining lands and the chance to remarry.

"You will ride with me, lady wife. Give our daughter into Dame Ellen's care."

With a happy smile, Mellisynt passed her babe to the wide-eyed nurse.

FitzHugh turned to his squire. "Lead the escort for Dame Ellen and my daughter back to Kenilworth. We will join you at the castle."

"Aye, Sir Richard."

Mellisynt held her breath as FitzHugh nudged his horse forward until it, and the man astride it, filled her vision.

"Take my hand."

She stared at the fist held down to her, seeing the strength in the curled fingers, the tracery of scars among the dark hairs. With a tiny, breathless sob of happiness, unheard by any except her and the man above her, she took his hand with both of her own and was swung up onto the saddle before him.

The hound whined and padded to stand before the horse. FitzHugh's destrier shuffled uneasily, rolling its eyes at the shaggy beast blocking the way.

"Take care of your lady, and I will take care of mine," FitzHugh commanded softly.

Great, liquid brown eyes surveyed them both for the space of several heartbeats. Finally the hound returned to the litter and plopped its muzzle onto the cushions beside the babe.

An iron arm banded Mellisynt's waist, and the powerful stallion whirled and headed for the open fields. The wind whipped away her veil. She threw back her head against the solid wall of shoulder behind.

A wild exhilaration filled her, and her blood began to pound in rhythm with the horse's hooves. The darkness of the last month faded. The gripping hurt that had dogged her short journey from Kenilworth, had set her weeping, and at last had made her order the men to halt and turn around, fled. As much as she wanted this man, he wanted her.

They left the open fields behind and entered the leafy darkness of the forest. The horse shuddered to a halt, its great withers twitching and quivering beneath her legs. Rough hands took her waist and turned her on the saddle. She floundered against FitzHugh's broad chest, struggling to draw her leg over his thighs and regain her balance. A hard hand on her rear helped her settle, and brought her into direct and intimate contact with his body.

Mellisynt's eyes widened as she felt the rigid hardness beneath her bunched skirts. Her gaze flew up, and her breath stopped at the blue flame in his eyes. With a savage groan, FitzHugh covered her mouth with his.

Her nerves screamed with need. Her need flamed into aching want. And as his mouth gentled on hers, drawing out her taste with tongue and teeth, her want melted into love.

He dragged his head up and framed her face with two huge hands.

"Listen to me, wife. You are mine. Now and always. There is no document, nor man, nor priest, who can take you from me."

"Aye," she whispered.

"Nor will you escape me. If you try to leave, I'll track you down, wherever you may think to go."

"Aye."

"What I have, I—"

He stopped and drew a slow, ragged breath.

"I know not the pretty words sung by troubadours, Mellisynt. I can only tell you that what I have, I hold. And I hold you in my heart."

A soft smile curved her lips.

"And I you, my lord."

She leaned forward and touched her mouth to his, drinking in his warmth, giving of her own. He claimed to have no poet's skills, but Mellisynt knew she'd heard the sweetest song of love ever sung.

His left arm wrapped around her waist once more and brought her up against his body. Beneath her legs, FitzHugh's thigh muscles bunched as he kicked the stallion into a slow, rolling walk.

Mellisynt looked with regret at the cushion of green beneath the trees.

"Do we not stop here, my lord?" she murmured against his mouth. "For even just a little while?"

"Nay," he replied, his voice husky. "But I remember promising to show you all the pleasures one can experience in the saddle. 'Tis time you learned to ride, lady wife."

* * * * *

Author's Note

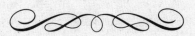

Have you ever had the perfect vacation? I have—several in fact! But one that stands out above all others was when my husband and I took a badly needed break from our military duties and jumped on a plane headed for Europe. We had no reservations, no itinerary and only a vague intention of exploring parts of France we'd never seen before.

What we discovered was Brittany. Wonderful, stormy, sea-washed Brittany. Cities marked by narrow, twisting medieval lanes. Ancient castles perched high atop inaccessible crags. Thick, creamy fish stew sopped up with crusts of mouth-watering bread. And a proud, fiercely independent people with a rich history. It was while reading about the Bretons that I became fascinated by the story of their duchess, Constance, and her rogue of a husband. I had no idea then that I'd some-day write a novel that featured this extraordinary woman as one of the characters!

You may be interested to know that Duke Geoffrey finally did rebel against his father's iron hold. In 1186, a year after the conclusion of *Sweet Song of Love*, Geoffrey forswore his oaths, fled to Paris and allied himself with his father's arch enemy, Philip of France. While the two kings girded for war, the incorrigible duke died from a wound taken in a jousting tournament. Constance subsequently gave birth to his post-humous son, Prince Arthur, and was later forced by King

Henry to wed the dark, brooding Ranulf, Count of Chester. She agreed to speak the marriage vows, but in their wedding night...

Well, that's another story!

Tyler Brides

It happened one weekend...

Quinn and Molly Spencer are delighted to accept three bookings for their newly opened B&B, Breakfast Inn Bed, located in America's favorite hometown, Tyler, Wisconsin.

But Gina Santori is anything but thrilled to discover her best friend has tricked her into sharing a room with the man who broke her heart eight years ago....

And Delia Mayhew can hardly believe that she's gotten herself locked in the Breakfast Inn Bed basement with the sexiest man in America.

Then there's Rebecca Salter. She's turned up at the Inn in her wedding gown. Minus her groom.

Come home to Tyler for three delightful novellas by three of your favorite authors: Kristine Rolofson, Heather MacAllister and Jacqueline Diamond.

HARLEQUIN®
Makes any time special ™

Visit us at www.eHarlequin.com   PHTB_T

To my husband

I am the pretty one!

#1 *New York Times* bestselling author

NORA ROBERTS

brings you more of the loyal and loving,
tempestuous and tantalizing Stanislaski family.

The Stanislaski Sisters

Natasha and Rachel

Coming in February 2001

Though raised in the Old World traditions of their
family, fiery Natasha Stanislaski and cool, classy
Rachel Stanislaski are ready for a *new* world of love....

*And also available in February 2001 from
Silhouette Special Edition, the newest book in the
heartwarming Stanislaski saga*

CONSIDERING KATE

Natasha and Spencer Kimball's daughter Kate turns her
back on old dreams and returns to her hometown, where
she finds the *man* of her dreams.

Available at your favorite retail outlet.

CELEBRATE VALENTINE'S DAY WITH HARLEQUIN®'S LATEST TITLE—

Stolen Memories

Available in trade-size format, this collector's edition contains three full-length novels by *New York Times* bestselling authors Jayne Ann Krentz and Tess Gerritsen, along with national bestselling author Stella Cameron.

TEST OF TIME by **Jayne Ann Krentz**—
He married for the best reason.... She married for the only reason.... Did they stand a chance at making the only reason the real reason to share a lifetime?

THIEF OF HEARTS by **Tess Gerritsen**—
Their distrust of each other was only as strong as their desire. And Jordan began to fear that Diana was more than just a thief of hearts.

MOONTIDE by **Stella Cameron**—
For Andrew, Greer's return is a miracle. It had broken his heart to let her go. Now fate has brought them back together. And he won't lose her again...

Make this Valentine's Day one to remember!

Look for this exciting collector's edition on sale January 2001 at your favorite retail outlet.

HARLEQUIN®
Makes any time special ™

Coming in January 2001 from Silhouette Books...

ChildFinders, Inc.:
An Uncommon Hero

by

MARIE FERRARELLA

**the latest installment of
this bestselling author's popular miniseries.**

The assignment seemed straightforward: track down the woman who
had stolen a boy and return him to his father. But ChildFinders, Inc.
had been duped, and Ben Underwood soon discovered that nothing
about the case was as it seemed. Gina Wassel, the supposed kidnapper,
was everything Ben had dreamed of in a woman, and suddenly he had
to untangle the truth from the lies—before it was too late.

Available at your favorite retail outlet.

Silhouette®
Where love comes alive™

Visit Silhouette at www.eHarlequin.com   PSCHILD_T

From bestselling
Harlequin American Romance author

CATHY GILLEN THACKER

comes

TEXAS VOWS

A McCABE FAMILY SAGA

Sam McCabe had vowed to always
do right by his five boys—but after
the loss of his wife, he needed the small-town security
of his hometown, Laramie, Texas, to live up to that
commitment. Except, coming home would bring him
back to a woman he'd sworn to stay away from.
It will be one vow that Sam can't keep....

On sale March 2001
Available at your favorite retail outlet.

HARLEQUIN®
Makes any time special ™

Visit us at www.eHarlequin.com   PHTV_T

LINDSAY McKENNA

continues her most popular series with a
brand-new, longer-length book.

And it's the story you've been waiting for....

Morgan's Mercenaries:
Heart of Stone

They had met before. Battled before. And
Captain Maya Stevenson had never again
wanted to lay eyes on Major Dane York—
the man who once tried to destroy
her military career! But on their latest
mission together, Maya discovered that beneath
the fury in Dane's eyes lay a raging passion. Now she
struggled against dangerous desire, as Dane's command
over her seemed greater still. For this time, he laid claim
to her heart....

Only from Lindsay McKenna and Silhouette Books!

"When it comes to action and romance,
nobody does it better than Ms. McKenna."
—*Romantic Times Magazine*

Available in March at your favorite retail outlet.

Silhouette®
Where love comes alive™